The Gates Of Walpurgis

A novel by

Richard Webster

This novel is dedicated to

the memory of

Dennis Wheatley

1897 – 1977

CONTENTS

PART THREE – JULIAN FARADAY

PROLOGUE

The house stood some way back from the road. It lay behind a screen of fir trees on a steep bank, so that only its roof, eaves and upper windows were visible, and only from the most oblique of angles as I sped past; a brief glimpse of dark grey tiles and white painted timber floating on top of a sea of greenery. And then it was gone. But I knew it had to be the place.

"It's so well hidden, you'll probably drive right past it, the first time you go there," Alan had told me, and he had been right. It was the only house around here, the only human dwelling in an empty, desolate landscape of rolling uplands and high escarpments. Only a few patches of woodland and the occasional barn broke the starkness of the view, so that one might have thought the location of the house would have been more easily apparent, even to the untrained eye. And yet it was so well concealed by the folds and fissures of the terrain that it might not have existed at all. Only the stand of mighty Scots pines, with their distinctive high canopy, marked the location. It was a less bucolic, more forbidding sort of a place than I had anticipated, and I felt an odd, momentary sense of dread as I turned the car around in the entrance to a field and made my way back to it.

I approached more slowly this time, trying to get a proper sense of my newfound isolation. Not for the first time in the past few days I wondered about the wisdom of my having so readily agreed to come here; at the uncharacteristic impetuousness of my decision, and whether I was truly suited to exist by myself in such an environment, so far removed from the urban hustle and bustle, and the noisy rhythms of humanity to which I was used. And yet, here I was, and I knew that there was no going back, even if there was something unsettling about the sheer emptiness of the landscape. This was now my home, at least for the next few months.

I had been late getting away from London, and it was long into the afternoon by the time I reached the west-country market town of Marlborough, with no time to explore the wide main street flanked by elegant buildings, a place I had skipped breezily through on Google Street View, a couple of nights previously. I had envisaged a rather more leisurely entry into my new domain, drawing out the moment of my arrival at the house, with much of the day left to get established and acquaint myself with the immediate area. But instead, aware of the light seeping away, I had passed through the town without stopping, picking up a minor road on the other side and heading west for a few more miles to my destination. A sign by the side of the road announced the imminence of the World Heritage Site of Avebury, with its millennia-old henges and standing stones. It was a place I had never visited, in spite of its relative proximity to my erstwhile home in London. I would have plenty of opportunities now.

The light was fading by then. It was the last week in February, late winter on the cusp of early spring, but the days were still short, and by the time I found the house, the sun was dropping fast through a pale blue sky, the dying embers of its light pushing weakly across the barren landscape.

And that was how I first encountered Badcombe Hollow, on a late afternoon, at the end of winter, very much alone and with mixed feelings of anticipation and trepidation.

It was well named; at least the hollow part was. As I turned onto the single-track road that led to the entrance, I saw that this quite substantial house sat within a natural dip enclosure. It was screened not just from the front, by the stand of Scots pines by the roadside, but from the back as well, by a tall retaining bank that was higher than the steeply gabled roof. This was a property that appeared to have been literally hollowed out of the landscape.

Only to the sides was the terrain more open, where the grounds of the house were bordered by gently sloping fields of bare earth that would doubtless be covered in crops, later in the year, but for now looked like a pale brown corrugated mat, stretching to the horizon.

I passed through a gateway without a gate and down a gravel drive that opened out to a hammerhead by the front door to the house, and where I brought the car to a halt. For a long moment, I waited there, the engine idling, as if I expected the door to be flung open and some person or persons to come out and greet me, even though I knew the house was empty.

It felt an imposing sort of place as I sat there, staring at it through the car window. I lived in a small, first floor flat that would have occupied only a fraction of the space before me. This grey stone building, on its substantial footprint, had two main floors, and a dormer windowed attic floor above. The roof was tiled in dark slates and there was a porticoed entrance. There was a certain grandeur to the property, which for some reason made it feel as if I didn't really belong there.

I got out of the car and looked around. At one time, so I understood, the people who lived here had also owned the surrounding fields, but these had been sold long ago, leaving only the house and the garden, and a small paddock to one side. There was a cool breeze ripping across the downs and into the hollow, and I felt its chill after the warm fug of the car.

I stared up at the austere grey stone of the house and its leaded windows in thick timber frames, and thought how utterly closed up it felt, as if it had been unoccupied for a long time, although I knew that somebody had been living here until just a few days ago.

I reached in my pocket for the keys Alan had given me, and the code to the alarm system that was written on a scrap of paper, and it was then that I saw it for the first time, out of the corner of my eye.

At the edge of the garden stood a long grass mound. It was about the same length as the house, and was perhaps ten or twelve feet high along its top. It formed a natural boundary to one side of the property, and I had been told there was a footpath in the adjacent field, linking a trackway along the crest of the downs to the road below.

Although I was a first-time visitor to these parts, I like to think that I had enough of a grasp of pre-history to have known what it was, even if Alan hadn't told me about it, the same night he offered to lend me his house.

It was a burial mound.

PART ONE

ALAN MACKAY

CHAPTER ONE

The Reunion

Monday 16th February 2015

He had changed far less than I would have expected. It had been nearly twenty years since I had last seen him in the flesh, and the best part of ten since I had come across him on television or seen his picture in the newspaper. There were a few flecks of grey around the temples in the long mane of dark hair, and a few more lines to his face, but otherwise the person sat across from me in the sitting room of my flat was the same Alan Mackay that I had known so well, all those years previously.

His telephone call earlier that afternoon had come completely out of the blue, and to say that I had been surprised to hear his voice would be something of an understatement. I almost dropped the phone.

He had got my number from a mutual acquaintance, someone I had also not encountered for many years. It was ironic, really, because I had been meaning to have my landline disconnected for months, since I barely used it these days, and it only tended to ring when people were trying to sell me something. But I was bad at getting around to things, and so the old phone on its cord had remained, silently gathering dust, housework being something else that I rarely got around to. But if I had got rid of the phone, as I had intended, then Alan might never have found me, and I would never have heard of Badcombe Hollow, and none of what followed would have happened.

We had been close once, Alan and I, constantly in each other's company, and the best of friends. Except we can't really have been all that close, to have fallen out of touch for so long. But there had been a time when it felt as if we were as thick as thieves.

We met at university, back in the early nineties. It was only a redbrick. And not even one of the good ones. It was more one of those low to middling, fifth choice on the UCAS form sort of establishments; the fallback option, which catered mainly for the just intelligent enough children of the middle classes. It was situated in a dull, provincial town, made only marginally less dull by its large, and mostly despised student demographic. This was back in the days when higher education was free, and the preserve of the theoretically privileged few, whilst the rest of the world went about its business, often regarding those of us who opted for the alternative of a three-year holiday from reality with a certain degree of contempt. At least they did in our particular university town. It was a manifestation of that whole town versus gown thing, I suppose, except that all makes it sound much grander than it was, and our place certainly wasn't grand, and nobody wore gowns, except at graduation, and I didn't even go to my graduation. They may well have been justified in their low regard of us, my fellow townsfolk, but I still had a good enough time while I was there. I did very little work, scraped my finals, got my piece of paper, and in the process enjoyed a sufficient number of the usual, formative university experiences to make the whole thing reasonably worthwhile. To me, at any rate, if not to the wider society who paid for me to do it. But it was fun at the time. And it was where I met Alan.

We were doing different courses, and had largely different interests, so it was only the coincidence of our having been allocated adjacent rooms in the same accommodation block that caused our paths to cross. In fact, we might still have failed to become friends, had it not been for one particular incident, early in our first term.

I had returned to my room late in the evening, having been out on an organised pub crawl around the town; one of those drearily predictable Freshers Week events that I had reluctantly signed up for, at the behest of the gaggle of fellow students I had found myself thrust together with at Registration, and with whom I had formed that uneasy but inevitable bond that comes from being in an unfamiliar place surrounded by people one doesn't know who happen to be in the same situation. I think it was Evelyn Waugh who said that one's second year at university is spent divesting oneself of the acquaintances one makes in the first. I think it equally applies that one spends one's second week as an undergraduate distancing oneself from those whom one had latched onto in the first week, and who one would then come across periodically over the next three years, and feel obliged to offer wary nods of recognition. People one might have known, but chose not to.

It had been a particularly gruesome evening, even before people began succumbing to the effects of the alcohol. I think I had realised by then that I didn't much care for my new acquaintances, and several long hours of shouted half-conversations about nothing of interest had done little to change my mind. So, when the cry of "last orders" eventually came, in whatever sticky-floored, smoke-filled pub we had pitched up at by then, I had felt an almost overwhelming urge to escape. There had been ominous talk, earlier in the evening, of going back to someone's room after closing time, to continue the festivities, and when this was mooted again, on leaving the pub, I had been quick to make my excuses. I detected little in the way of genuine disappointment on the part of my fellow drinkers. Most of them I barely spoke to again after that evening. They were the people that I chose not to know.

So, I couldn't have met Alan at a better time, although the circumstances were rather unusual.

"Where the hell is he?" said the girl I found sitting outside my door when I got back to my hall of residence that night.

She was quite a sight, with hair dyed bright blue, and an impressive number of hoops and studs in her ears, nose and lips and, for all I knew, the rest of her anatomy as well. It looked as if she had been crying. I wondered how long she had been sitting there.

"I said," she hissed up at me, "Where … is … he?"

She enunciated each word with an angry exactitude, as if attempting to communicate with an idiot, or someone with only a rudimentary understanding of English.

"Where is who?" I said, feeling perplexed and realising that I was moderately intoxicated.

"Alan. That's who," she said, getting to her feet. "I know he's in there. Let me in so I can speak to him."

"I'm sorry," I said. "This is my room. And I don't even know who you mean."

This was clearly not the answer she wanted, and with a look of pure hatred she pushed past me, and stormed off down the hallway, slamming the door shut behind her.

At that moment the door to the room opposite mine opened a crack and a worried looking face peered out.

"Has she gone?" it said.

"You must be Alan," I said.

I recognised him, although we had not spoken before, and I hadn't even known that he was my neighbour. But I had seen him around the campus a few times, where he stood out somewhat, in a way that he probably wouldn't have done in a big city institution – always dressed from head to toe in black, and with a large hooped ring in one ear, and a cigarette permanently dangling from his mouth. Rock and roll chic, I had thought, even if he seemed to be trying a bit too hard. The last time I had seen him had been the day before, when he had been stood at the bus stop, holding an electric guitar loosely by his side, in a pose I had thought at the time might have made quite a good album cover.

"I am," he said, "Although not if she's asking."

"I'm Richard," I said, and we shook hands with an affected, theatrical formality.

"Lucky escape," he said, glancing down the now empty corridor. "I met her at that awful Freshers Disco thing. She was so up for it, it wasn't true. Knew it was a mistake at the time, but you know how it is."

I didn't, really, back then, but I nodded sagely, as if this was an all too common occurrence in my own life.

"It was a heat of the moment thing," he went on. "I think I was just desperate for an excuse to get out of the Freshers Disco. She hasn't stopped pestering me ever since. We spent the night at hers, so I didn't think she knew where I lived, but she must have found out somehow. Lucky for me, whoever it was told her, gave her the wrong room number. I didn't even know she was out here until I heard her voice just now. I've been listening to music in my room since about eight, so goodness knows how long she was sitting outside your door."

He fished a pack of cigarettes out of his shirt pocket and offered me one.

"No thanks, I don't smoke," I said.

"Hope you don't mind if I do, now I know we're neighbours."

"Not in the slightest."

Both of my parents were smokers, so I had grown up permanently wreathed in a cloud of second-hand tobacco. Whatever damage it might have done to me, I had become completely inured to its smell.

"Apparently there's talk of banning it in halls," he said. "Hopefully it's just talk, otherwise I'll have to move out."

He lit the cigarette, inhaled deeply, and blew out a long stream of smoke.

"So," he said, "What's your story, then?"

"I just went on the Freshers Pub Crawl," I said, as if this was some sort of explanation.

"Yeah, I heard about it. Not really my scene. Tell me, did any of the pubs look like they did live music? I mean, not tonight, but were there any, you know, posters about gigs, open-mic nights, that sort of thing?"

"Not that I noticed," I said.

"Just what I thought," he said, ruefully. "Not much of a music town, by the looks of things. I went to a rehearsal yesterday with some blokes on the other campus, but they were shit, really. Well, they weren't shit, so much as their music was. Not my sort of thing at all.

"Synthesisers," he said with a grimace. "Very 1980s."

"So, what are you into?" I asked.

He motioned behind him, through the open door of his room, to a large poster of someone I recognised as the guitarist, Ritchie Blackmore.

"That," he said, simply. 'I'm 1970s all the way. As in, proper rock. Not that I'll ever play like the great man over there –

nobody ever will – but that's the sound I'm aiming for, if I can ever find any fellow musicians in this back of beyond town. You don't play an instrument, do you?"

"I'm afraid not."

"Oh well, always worth asking. Anyway, that's my musical niche, so to speak. Anachronistic as fuck, I know, but there's always room for a bit of niche, don't you think? Something for the aficionados to enjoy, while everyone else gets on whatever the latest craze is."

"Not a fan of the Brit Pop, then," I said.

"Oh, I wouldn't say that. Some of it's pretty bloody good. I mean, those guys from Manchester, well, best pub band ever, I reckon, but I'll stick with my heavy metal, and I'm more than fine with playing in front of a load of old rockers. And, needless to say, I'm obviously looking forward to all the hedonism and excess; smashing up the odd hotel room, that sort of thing. But that's all to come. I'm still at the song writing stage."

"Always good to have goals," I said.

"I like to think so. How was the pub crawl, by the way?"

"Pretty grim."

"Thought as much. Fancy a real drink, and some decent music?"

"Sounds good."

"Excellent. I hope you like Deep Purple."

And that was the start of it. We became firm friends from that point onwards; inseparable really, in the way that close friendships can be at that age. For all the ostensible differences between us, there was a common sensibility, and a cheerful cynicism about the way we looked at the world, which bonded us together.

After we moved out of halls at the end of our first year, we shared a house in the town for the remainder of our time at university, together with Magdala, Alan's girlfriend, who later became his wife, and two other members of the band he had assembled by then, and with whom he would go on to have such success.

And he deserved it, because he was seriously good at what he did, even back then, perhaps particularly back then, before it all got grown up and serious. He was much more of a free spirit in those early days, happy to live in the moment and surrender to his passions. And yet he had an inner core of strength and confidence, which could sometimes manifest as arrogance, and he was always the unquestioned leader of any band he ever played in, as well as its creative driving force.

He was a star in the making, and he knew it, but he wore the mantle lightly, as if he didn't. But I think he always believed he was going to make it big, one day, even if he didn't seem to care very much about it. It wasn't so much a sense of entitlement. It was more a relaxed, almost insouciant self-belief, propelling him constantly forwards. Don't get me wrong. He was a superb musician who could coax magic from a set of guitar strings, and a fine songwriter, but he was also a born leader. He had that knack of making people want to follow him, and in those days, I probably would have followed him anywhere.

I had nothing to offer on the musical front, but I became the band's unofficial manager and Alan's occasional muse, dealing with the business side of things, such as there was one, back then, booking venues, dealing with the finances and generally making myself useful. I even drove the bus. Or, at least, the minibus. It was odd in a way that I should have become part of Alan's circle at all, but I think he liked having a friend who wasn't part of the band. So, he could complain about them, perhaps. Which he did frequently, because for all his laid-back style, Alan was something of a perfectionist.

But they were happy days, with considerable fringe benefits, in the form of the myriad young women who would attach themselves to the band and, I was gratified to discover, those like me who were merely associated with it. Alan told me never to refer to them as groupies, and I don't think I ever did, but I enjoyed myself enormously, nevertheless, and these camp followers became ever more numerous as the band became more and more successful. It probably helped that Alan's band purveyed a sort of muscular, hedonistic, aggressively heterosexual hard rock that was definitely not with the times, and was really a throwback to another era entirely. Not that I cared. I was having the time of my life.

It was also during this period that I learned to write. It started with an article about the band that I did for the local newspaper, which was followed by a tour diary I wrote during the summer after we graduated, when we embarked upon a predictably debauched tour of the provinces, and which was subsequently published in one of the music papers of the time. It was then that I decided to become a journalist, since I think I knew that managing a band wasn't really for me, however much fun it was. Besides, the band was becoming seriously successful by that stage, and as a result, ever more professional.

They got their first big break just a year after university, and it was a very big break indeed, supporting a globally successful mega-band on the European leg of a world tour, and their first album, which was a modest success, followed soon after. I was a cub reporter for a large circulation regional newspaper by then, but whilst no longer in day-to-day contact with Alan and his group, we remained in close touch, and I went to as many of their gigs as I could. I even had a walk-on and highly forgettable role in the first music video they did.

Their success grew considerably from then on. A second album was recorded, which sold over a million copies, followed by a European tour, and then a third album and then a world tour. But by this time Alan and I had lost touch. I liked to think that this was the inevitable growing apart that occurs as people get older and their interests diverge, for I was fairly successful in my own field by then, but I knew in my heart of hearts that it was most likely because of a particular newspaper article I had written.

It was certainly something I regretted in retrospect, although it was beneficial to me at the time. I had been attempting to move up from the regional to the national press and was vying for a spot on a daily tabloid. In doing so, I rather shamelessly traded on my erstwhile association with Alan, and his by now very successful band, and offered to write, on spec, a piece detailing the more lurid aspects of life on the road with Britain's latest, up and coming hard rock combo. Although highly complimentary about the band and the music, I was rather less discreet than I should have been, in my eagerness to produce the sort of sex, drugs and rock and roll account that the newspaper wanted. The piece was duly published and I got my job with the paper, but I lost a friendship as a result, thanks to allowing myself to be blinded by ambition. There have been far worse crimes of betrayal in the chequered history of the tabloid press, for sure, but that was my particular one, and for a time I hated myself for it, whilst still enjoying the material benefits it had brought me.

Alan had been furious about the whole thing, and we fell out severely as a result. We sort of patched things up, but it was never the same between us after that, and over the course of the next year or so, we came to see far less of each other, and I stopped getting free tickets to their concerts. And then we quite simply drifted apart, although I continued to take an interest in the fortunes of the band.

They eventually split up in the early 2000s. But whilst the other members had gone on, with varying degrees of success and failure, to solo careers, or to perform in other groups, Alan himself had chosen to stop working, and had retired from the business. He must have been fairly wealthy by then – apart from being the band's leader, he had also been its principle songwriter, and thus the beneficiary of most of its royalties – but it had still seemed a shame to me that such a gifted musician should cease to practice something that he was so good at.

His name had cropped up now and again over the years. His divorce from his second wife, a model of some repute, had made the newspapers, as had the dalliance with hard drugs, and a spell in rehab. I recalled one of those whatever-happened-to-so-and-so pieces in one of the Sunday newspapers from a few years back, and also seeing him appear once on a late-night TV show, where he was one of various talking heads reminiscing about the music of the 1990s, but since that, nothing. He had simply faded from public view, to a rural retreat in the west country, it was said, and I had thought about him less and less as the years had passed. Up until that February afternoon I had more or less assumed that our paths would never cross again.

And yet here he was, Alan Mackay, retired rock and roll star, sitting just a few feet away from me, as we talked about old times.

"You know, I've been meaning to get in touch for ages," he said. "I just never seemed to get around to it."

"Likewise," I said, not entirely truthfully.

"Plus, I hardly ever get up to London these days."

"Nor me to the west-country. Where exactly was it that you ended up living?"

"Middle of nowhere, basically, believe it or not. North Wiltshire. I like the quiet life in the country these days. It's funny. I was always determined never to do that whole rock star gerontocracy, faux country squire thing – I used to despise those sort of people, thought they'd sold out – and yet, that's exactly what ended up happening. Anyway, it's not literally in the middle of nowhere – it's roughly midway between Avebury and Marlborough – but it's out on its own, with no other houses around."

"Avebury, as in the stone circle?" I said.

"Yeah, that and all the rest of it. I got really into all of that, actually. You know, pre-history, standing stones, burial mounds, the whole thing. The place where I live is literally covered in it. I've even got a Neolithic burial mound at the end of my garden. Big, too, and quite famous in its way. It gets a few visitors, and unfortunately there's a footpath right the other side, so people think it's public property and climb up it, but it's actually on my land."

"Didn't we used to say that property was theft, or some such nonsense, back in the day? I remember you writing a song about it."

He grinned at the memory.

"Yeah, well, I don't believe any of that crap now, any more than you do, I'd imagine. Didn't really believe it back then. These days, I definitely hold to the view that an Englishman's home is his castle."

"So, what's it like?" I asked. "The castle, that is?"

"Well, it's more of a posh farmhouse."

"Old?"

"Not particularly. Late nineteenth century. All the fields got sold off back in the 1940s, so it's not a working farm any more, but it's a big house, with a huge garden and a paddock. And the burial mound. And the countryside around there is stunning – rolling downland, big escarpments, masses of open space."

"It sounds nice," I said, trying and failing to picture my once close friend in such a rural setting.

"It used to belong to Dorian Slake," he said.

"Dorian who?" I said.

"Slake. Ever hear of him?"

I shook my head.

"Well, no reason why you should have done. He's fairly obscure, these days. I imagine you've heard of Aleister Crowley?"

"Yes, vaguely," I said. "He's on the *Sergeant Pepper* cover, isn't he?"

I knew this was one of Alan's favourite albums.

"That's the one. Famous occultist in the first half of the last century. Once dubbed the most evil man in Britain. Well, Slake was one of his disciples. He was part of a group that Crowley assembled around him, who used to get together to howl at the moon and summon up Satan, or whatever the hell they did.

"Anyway, when Crowley died in 1947, Slake tried to carry on his work, and bought Badcombe Hollow – that's the name of my house – so he could set up a sort of commune, devoted to the pursuit of witchcraft. But he didn't have a lot of success. He wasn't able to recruit many followers and he became a bit of a laughing stock amongst his fellow occultists. But he got up to all kinds of weird shit in that house, apparently."

"Such as?"

"Oh, you know, the usual. Spells, séances, incantations, trying to raise the dead, that sort of thing. He was a full-on disciple of Satan. Very heavy stuff indeed. But he obviously didn't have the charisma of his former mentor, and he ended up rattling about on his own in there. Kind of pathetic, really. He went mad in the 1960s and hung himself."

"Not in your house, I hope."

"Thankfully no. Not quite, anyway. He did it in some woods nearby. You can see them from the house. According to local legend, he used to conduct witches sabbats up there, back when he still had a few adherents to his cause.

"Anyway, do you remember the cover of the third album that we did; our last one, as it turned out?"

"Of course. It's on one of the shelves behind you. It's got a giant, burning pentagram on the front."

"Yeah, well, that's all a bit embarrassing now. But we got into that stuff for a while; me and the band. But we were never properly into it, in the sense of actually believing it. It was just a bit of fun, as far as we were concerned, not that it stopped some of your colleagues in the tabloid press from making a big deal out of it, and making us out to be even more depraved than they already thought we were."

"Now that you mention it, I do remember something about that," I said, wincing inwardly at his reference to the sort of newspapers I used to write for.

"It was all bullshit. We just liked the iconography. It was more of a cultural reference to the 1970s and '80s, and the sort of heavy metal music we had grown up listening to, and which had been such a big influence on us. You know, all that talk there was at the time about back masking – playing records backwards and getting a satanic message out of it. Stuff like that. It was all a complete load of bollocks, but some people seemed to think we were taking it seriously.

"We weren't," he said, emphatically.

"But I got reasonably interested in the whole thing," he went on. "You know, from an intellectual point of view. That was how I got to learn about Slake, and on a chance visit down to Wiltshire one day for something else, I decided to kill some time by going to have a look at his house.

"And that was how I found Badcombe Hollow. And guess what? There was a For Sale sign outside. It had changed hands a couple of times since Slake died, and the day I saw it, it had apparently been empty for the best part of a year.

"So, I bought it," he said. "Not, I hasten to add, because of any morbid obsession with Dorian Slake. I just liked the place. It was the right time for me. I'd been out of the band for a while, got over some pretty bad drug problems, got divorced again and just wanted to get away from it all; escape the rat race and move to the country."

"Not haunted, or anything, is it?" I said with a wry smile.

"It is according to some of the locals, but I would think only because Slake used to live there. I've never encountered anything unusual there at all, and nor has anyone who's stayed with me. It's just a pleasant place, in a pleasant location, but with a bit of an unfortunate reputation.

"You'll have to come down for a visit, one day," he said.

"I'd like that," I said, wondering if this would ever happen.

"It won't be for a while though. You see, I'm going away next week to California. I won't be back for the best part of a year."

I raised my eyebrows enquiringly.

"I'm getting back in the business," he said.

"You mean the band's getting back together?"

"God, no. I really don't want to get into that whole scene again. Way too old for it now. And I don't need the money, so I don't have to do one of those pension tour things that all the old rockers seem to be doing these days.

"But I miss the creative side of it, working with other musicians. So, I'm going to go back to the studio, do some session work, and some producing."

"In California?"

"Yes. Los Angeles. I leave next week, and I won't be back until Christmas. It's the reason I'm up in London today. I had a meeting at the Savoy this morning, with the outfit I'm going to produce an album for. They're on their way back to the States from a tour. I was about to get the train and head back home, and then I had the sudden, crazy idea of looking you up."

"I'm glad you did," I said. "It's been too long."

"It certainly has," he said.

There was a long silence, and I wondered if I should say something about the article that had caused such a rift between us, but was worried about spoiling the atmosphere, since it really had been good to see this person again who had once been such an integral part of my life.

But it transpired that he was thinking the same thing.

"Look, about that whole business with the newspaper article," he said, "I shouldn't have made so much out of it."

"I shouldn't have written it," I said.

"Well, maybe. But I completed over-reacted. I'm sorry about that. I've been meaning to say that for a long time, actually. I mean, it's not like it festered with me, or anything. We just lost touch."

"That was just as much my fault," I said.

"Well, water under the bridge now, even if it's been a bloody long bridge. But I have kept up with what you've been up to, you know? I always read your articles, whenever I come across one."

16

"Really?" I said, surprised.

"Yes. Once you stopped writing for that awful rag, at any rate."

"Touché."

"The thing is," he said, "I think you're a damn good writer. I really admire your work."

"And I think you're a damn fine musician," I said. "I'm glad you're getting back into it."

We grinned at each other across the small room. It felt good to have gotten the subject out in the open. It no longer lingered over our conversation.

"Anyway," said Alan, "Now we're back in contact, we'll have to make sure it stays that way. When I get back from America, that is. Open invitation to come and stay in my allegedly haunted house, whenever you like."

"It's a date," I said. "So what's going to happen to the place while you're gone?"

"I'm letting a friend stay there, rent free. I'm way too attached to the place to sell it, and I don't need the money from renting it out. I'd rather have someone I know living there, looking after it properly."

He glanced at his watch.

"Look," he said, "I know it's still early, but I've got to be on a train back to Wiltshire, later this evening. I've still got loads to sort out, before I ship stateside. How about we go out for dinner? My shout."

"Sounds like a very good idea," I said. "What did you have in mind?"

"You know what? I really fancy a curry. It's the only thing wrong with the countryside. Not enough good curry places. Know anywhere decent?"

"I know just the place," I said.

CHAPTER TWO

The Offer

We went to a Bangladeshi restaurant in Brick Lane I had frequented many times over the years, to carry out interviews or ply sources for information, and where they knew me well enough to find me a table at short notice.

"So," Alan said, as our drinks were brought to the table. "Tell me a bit more about you. It's mainly been all me, up to now."

"There's not really much to tell," I said. "Just a lot of words read once and turned into pulp, although that's a bad analogy these days, since everything went online. Makes it even more transient, I suppose."

"Or permanent, depending on how you look at it. When something's in cyberspace, it's buzzing around up there forever, I presume. Whereas your pulped articles or whatnot get turned into whatever pulp gets turned into. What does pulp get turned into?"

"Paper, I think. That's an interesting way of looking at it."

"I'm digressing. You sound a bit jaded about the whole thing."

"I suppose so. Bored of it, certainly."

"Didn't you sail a bit close to the wind with the law, a few years back? That can't have been boring."

I winced at this reference to my former career in tabloid journalism, but we had been bound to get there eventually.

"Yeah, guess you heard about that," I said.

"Hard to miss," said Alan. "Took me aback a little, you might say, seeing my old mucker up before the beak, getting grilled on that whole phone hacking thing. Unreliable witness, economical with the truth, possible perjury charges; all sounded pretty heavy. Lucky to get out the other side of it, by all accounts. Any truth to any of it?"

"Most of it, and I was bloody lucky to get away with it. In my defence, a lot of it was about me protecting a source, which is somewhat sacrosanct in our profession or, at least, it should be, and I had to put that ahead of any possible legal jeopardy. And I refused to incriminate someone I'd used to do surveillance for me, and who had employed less than legal means in doing so."

"As in hacking phones, I assume," said Alan.

"I really couldn't say. I mean, I will literally never say. And I know a lot of that – most of that – was inexcusable. It was the wild west back then; people were getting away with all sorts, and that definitely had to be addressed. I wouldn't deny that for a moment. And I crossed the line, too. But I was trying to take down a corrupt politician, with some very dubious overseas connections. This wasn't some celebrity shagging thing. But I took it too far, and it blew up in my face and more or less ended my career in investigative journalism with it."

"What happened to the politician?"

"Tipped for the cabinet, apparently."

"Figures. Anyway, as a former celebrity who's done a fair amount of shagging, I'm not in favour of any of it, just so you know – big fan of privacy, ever since I retired – but I'll give you the benefit of the doubt on the pursuit of the crooked pol, and say that zeal merely got the better of you."

"That's a kindly way to put it," I said. "Anyway, every cloud, and all that. I ended up going to France."

"I know. I used to read that article you did – French Living, or something?"

"Yes, they were good days. Mostly. I spent three years there, living in Paris and travelling around. I'd been doing tabloid investigative stuff for over ten years, and I didn't want to do it anymore, so I jumped at the chance to be a feature writer. I mean, it was just lifestyle pap, really, not exactly stretching. But it was a good gig. I got to live in Paris, and I saw a lot of France. I even got married out there."

Alan raised his eyebrows.

"I missed that," he said.

He made a show of looking around the restaurant.

"So, where the hell is she, mate?"

"Marianne? Still in Paris. Living with an architect. We got divorced about a year ago."

"Sorry to hear it. What was she like?"

"She was quite something. Pretty. Smart as a whip. Sexy as hell. Wonderful cook. On your case from dawn to dusk and a fearsome temper. Mainly remember the temper. But yeah, she was really something. Too much for me, though."

"Sounds like a long day at the office," said Alan.

"She was definitely that," I said, "And a very sharp operator."

"How so?"

"She really screwed me on the divorce. I had to cash in everything, so I could keep the flat we were just in."

"Ouch. I've been through a couple of those myself, but fortunately managed to stay solvent each time. The benefits of a good lawyer and cast iron pre-nups."

"I was never very good with the small print side of things," I said, with some bitterness, the good mood of the evening suddenly punctured.

"Shit. That's not good. Got anyone on the go now?"

"Nothing at all. Out of the game. You?"

"Bit of a thing with a local girl. Down in Wiltshire. We met through a shared interest in Avebury and its history. At a lecture. Organised by the National Trust. Which I belong to, by the way. I know, what is the world coming to? How very fucking rock gerontocracy of me, but I'm as happy as Larry, so who gives a shit? But it's not the sort of way I used to meet women, I'll grant you that. Bright girl, though. Sexy and clever. A bit like your Marianne, by the sounds of things. But I've kind of let it lapse. I want to go to America with a clean slate; keep my options open."

That last statement was a very Alan thing to say, I thought. He hadn't changed that much.

"Well, as for me," I said, "I think I need to find a rich widow, and pretty sharpish."

"Things can't be all that bad, surely. Journalists do okay, don't they, even in the internet age?"

"Well, actually, I'm not a journalist, any more. Not a practising one, at any rate. I quit, you see. Six months ago. To write a novel, as clichéd as that might sound."

"No kidding. Seriously?"

"Yep. I'm a proper penniless writer these days, and that tiny little flat is my garret."

"Well, good for you, mate. I always thought you had a creative side. How's it going?"

"I've written about half of it. And I have a publisher semi-interested. It's more fun than journalism, that's for sure. It just doesn't pay anything. Not yet, anyway."

"I want to hear all about it," Alan said, as our food arrived.

****

During the course of our meal, I told him about the book and its inspiration – living in Paris, my travels around France, and my tempestuous and ultimately disastrous relationship with Marianne. I didn't let on quite how parlous my financial situation had become, but I imagine he got the drift. It was embarrassing, in a way, with him having been so successful, particularly as I had always been "the sensible one", back in college. But I had made some bad choices in my life, Marianne being only one of them, and when I had been doing well, I had never bothered to save for a rainy day. So, I was where I was. It was nobody's fault but my own.

He seemed genuinely interested in the book I was writing and asked several surprisingly pertinent questions about the plot and the characters, which I was more than pleased to answer. In truth, it was good to talk to someone about it. Writing can be a lonely occupation.

"Anyway," I said, as our plates were being cleared away, "I'm probably going to downsize. Well, not downsize; that would be impossible. But re-locate somewhere cheaper, so I can finish the book. That flat may not look like much, but I own it outright, and it's in a good location, so I could sell it, or I could get a decent rent for it. I've got a colleague at my last paper gagging to rent it off me. So I might do that. Then find something small and cheap to rent in a less well-heeled part of London. That's the vague plan, anyway."

"Sounds like a pretty good idea to me," said Alan.

He suddenly frowned and reached into his pocket, pulling out a cell phone. He glanced at the screen.

"Bugger," he said. "I need to make a quick call. Time for a cigarette break, anyway. Back in five."

He seemed distracted when he came back.

"Something up?" I asked.

"My house sitter just bailed on me," he said. "Remember Degsy, the session guy we used on the first album?"

"I think so," I said. I dimly recalled Alan recruiting someone of that name to play rhythm guitar on a couple of tracks, back when the band was just a four-piece ensemble. "Tall guy with a Jesus beard?"

"That's the one. We've kept in touch a bit, over the years. He lives in Bath, which is just down the road from me. So, I offered him the use of the house while I'm away. But he just got a gig playing for some band I've never even heard of, so now he can't do it. Bugger. I really thought that was all sorted out. I'll have to go to Marlborough tomorrow and get an agent to rent it out. Oh, well, my own fault. Serves me right for putting my faith in a flaky musician."

We left the restaurant shortly afterwards. At Alan's suggestion, I accompanied him on the cab ride back to Paddington Station, so that we could have a farewell drink.

The concourse was still busy, even at that time of the evening, and I waited while Alan went over to the giant board to check on his train.

"Next train to Pewsey's not for another half-an-hour," he said when he came back. "Time enough for a large one, don't you think?"

I was already feeling mildly drunk from all the beer we had consumed in the curry house, not to mention the pub we had gone to on the way, so a large dollop of spirits was the last thing I needed. I had forgotten what a night out with Alan could be like, even a relatively low key one such as this, and I was seriously out of practice. But I was in a good mood, pleased about the reunion with my old friend, and didn't want to disappoint him.

"Great idea," I said.

We went into one of the station bars, where I bought two large scotches which we carried over to a table in the corner.

"This has been really good," he said, as we sat down. "We'll do this again, when I get back."

"For sure," I said.

We fell silent for a moment and drank our drinks. The scotch hit the back of my throat with a fiery blast, and then went straight on to my head.

"I've just had an idea," said Alan, at last.

"This isn't going to be like your idea about taking down the university flag, is it?" I said, remembering the first time we got properly drunk together, shortly after we first met.

"God, no. That was a hell of a night though, wasn't it?"

"I'm surprised you can remember it."

"I remember everything," he said. "Everything about those days. Looking back now, I think they were some of the happiest of my life, actually."

There was a trace of sadness in his voice as he said this, and he looked down at his drink for a long moment, before shaking himself out of his temporary reverie. I thought little of it as we sat there in the bar that night, but I look back now and wonder at his state of mind when he spoke those words, and whether or not it was at that precise moment that he decided to put his plan irrevocably into motion. Because with the next sentence he spoke, my life changed forever. I just didn't know it at the time.

"How about you live in my house, while I'm gone?" he said.

"What?"

"Why don't you live there?"

"Live in your house?" I said dumbly.

"I'm serious," he said. "It's going to be empty for nine months. I don't want some stranger living there, and I don't need the money from renting it out. You just said yourself that you're looking to move out of your place. What could be more ideal? You live in my house for nothing, rent yours out, and live on the proceeds. It's not like you need a lot of money down there, anyway, because there's fuck all to do. And just think, you'll have all that solitude to finish your book. What could be more perfect? Ex-tabloid journalist and aspirant novelist moves to the country. And then you could write a book about that. And it's a chance to get out of the big city for a while. Breathe some clean air. Enjoy some peace and quiet. Did me the world of good."

"I'm not exactly a countryman," I said, playing for time, my mind in something of a spin at this most unexpected development.

"Neither was I until I moved down there," said Alan. "Now, I wouldn't live anywhere else. You'll really like it."

"But this is absurd," I said. "I mean, we only just met again, after nearly twenty years. You can't just let me go and live in your house. It's crazy."

"What's crazy about it? You need a place, I need a house sitter. It's all fate, man. It's meant to be. Totally meant to be."

"Yes, but ..."

"No buts about it. Look, I realise this is all very spur of the moment, so have a think about it. But I'm going to have to know by this time tomorrow, otherwise I'll have to make alternative arrangements. So, think about it, and then just say yes."

"Okay, yes," I said.

"Yes, you'll think about it, or yes, you'll do it?"

"Yes, I'll do it."

We grinned at each other.

"Brilliant," said Alan. "Thanks, mate."

"Not at all," I said. "Thank you. I can't really believe this just happened. I'm going to go and live in Wiltshire. Bloody hell."

"They're going to love you down there. Like I said, this was all fated, somehow, like perfect timing, or serendipity, or something."

"Where the hell is it, again?" I said, shaking my head with disbelief.

"A few miles outside Marlborough. Look, my train's going to be leaving soon, but I've got to come up to town again at the end of the week. I need to see my management company and my accountant before I fly out. So, I'll be back here on Friday."

He took a pen out of his jacket pocket and wrote a number on a napkin.

"Give me a ring at this number tomorrow, and we'll fix up a time to meet," he said. "I'll bring a set of keys up, directions, code to the alarm system, anything else I can think of."

"Okay, fine," I said. "I'm really going to take care of the place. You know that, right?"

"Of course. And there's not really a lot of taking care to do. Everything's in good shape, and the bank pays all the bills. Just lock up when you go out, give the garden the occasional once-over, and clean up after yourself if you have a wild party and trash the place. My train's about to go. Walk with me to the platform."

We left the bar with my head reeling, and not merely because of the alcohol. This day had started just like any other, and then it had ended like this. It all felt rather mad.

As we reached the platform Alan showed his ticket and then turned around and, to my great surprise, since he had never really been a physically demonstrative person, grabbed me in a bear hug.

"It's been great seeing you again, Richard," he said. "And thanks so much for doing this for me."

"Thank you for letting me do it," I said, releasing myself. I felt almost speechless at the rapid developments of the past ten minutes.

I waited as he set off down the platform. Just before he got onto the train he turned and raised his arm to me in farewell.

I raised mine in return, and then he stepped up onto the train and disappeared from view.

For a long moment I just stood there, oblivious to the people passing around me, and trying to take it all in. My mind was already trying to process the sheer number of things I needed to do over the next few days.

It was all so hard to believe, I thought, as the train pulled away. That Alan should suddenly re-appear in my life, and then change it so much, in the course of one afternoon and evening. Perfect timing and serendipity, he had called it. Standing there on the platform that night, it all seemed too good to be true.

Needless to say, it was.

CHAPTER THREE

Preparations

The next few days passed in a blur of activity, as I closed down my life in London, and prepared to move to the west country.

The morning after seeing Alan I woke up with a hangover, accompanied by an acute sense of panic at the life-changing decision of the night before. Thankfully, I had so much to sort out, in such a short time, that doubts and second thoughts were luxuries I couldn't afford.

The most pressing priority was to rent out the flat, since this was to be my sole source of income for the next nine months.

Fortunately, my former colleague was still interested in taking it and, anxious to seal the deal, I arranged to meet him for lunch in Covent Garden that same day.

Mike Turner wasn't exactly a close friend, but we had always got on fairly well, back when we were working together, and it was good to see him again for what turned out to be my second alcohol sodden meal in twenty-four hours. I could feel it beginning to take its toll, as much needed coffee was brought to the table.

"It doesn't really sound like your kind of thing," said Mike, as he stirred his coffee. "You know, Wiltshire. Always had you down as more of a Chianti-shire type – vineyards and olive groves; not muddy fields and constant rain."

"I'm sure it doesn't rain every day," I said. "But you're right. It's not exactly my scene, but I'm actually feeling quite excited about it. I'm looking at it as a chance to acquaint myself with my own country, for a change, instead of dashing off abroad all the time. And I'll be able to finish the book. In fact, I'm quite looking forward to leading a hermit-like existence for a bit."

"Alan Mackay, eh?" said Mike. "God, there's a name from the past. Haven't heard anything about him for years. I didn't realise you two were close."

"We were, a long time ago," I said. "We lost touch."

"Well, I must say, this works out well for both of us. My fiancé is going to love living in Chelsea. I'm going to earn a lot of credit for this. So how much rent do you want?"

We haggled gently for a while, but by the time the bill came, we had an agreement. It was a bit less than I had hoped for, but it would still be more than enough to live on while I stayed rent free at Alan's.

Mike agreed to take the flat until Christmas, with an option for a further six months after that. Quite what I would do about having somewhere to live when Alan came back from America in December, I wasn't too sure, but I'd cross that bridge when I came to it. We shook hands on the deal and I returned to my flat that afternoon with a huge weight off my mind.

The following day involved numerous phone calls and emails, but by the end of it, I had essentially tied up the financial and administrative side of my move. It was remarkable what one could accomplish in a short time, when one really put one's mind to it, I thought.

I did, however, in the midst of all this frenetic activity, find the time to go and buy a map of the Marlborough Downs. They looked big, empty and rather desolate. I saw that Alan's house was marked on the map, as was the burial mound, just off a side road that didn't lead anywhere, and at the bottom of what appeared to be a steep escarpment. I noticed the woods, at the top, the ones in which the house's erstwhile owner, Dorian Slake, had killed himself.

I also looked up Slake. Although a figure of considerable obscurity, he had a reasonably extensive entry on Wikipedia, much of it devoted to his association with the notorious Aleister Crowley. His biography included a black and white photograph of an utterly normal looking person of late middle age, dressed in a dark suit.

There was no specific mention of Alan's house, although it was noted that Slake had moved to the countryside near Avebury in 1947, where little more was heard of him until his death by his own hand in 1965. There then followed a fairly lengthy summation of his occult interests, and the various groups and organisations of this type to which he had belonged. As I had little interest in the subject, and because I tended to find such people and their beliefs risible as well as pathetic, I didn't bother to read any more.

With my affairs more or less sorted out, I could now devote my attention to the activity I had been dreading the most. Packing.

My furniture was staying in-situ, but I still had to clear the flat of most of its contents, which proved to be a daunting task, and which I was still busy with when Alan returned at the end of the week.

"Jesus," he said, as he stood in the doorway surveying the chaos of packing cases. "I wouldn't have thought you could fit so much into this place."

"Nor me," I said, slumping wearily into an armchair.

"Surely you're not taking all this down to Wiltshire," he said. "I did say stay in the house, not have it," he added.

"God, no. Most of it's going into storage. I'm only going to be taking a box of books and a couple of suitcases."

"What's happening to the furniture?"

"Staying here for the tenants, thank goodness."

He noticed me looking at the two large bags and guitar case he was carrying.

"I decided to move my flight forward and fly out tonight," he explained. "In fact, I was hoping I could cadge a lift to the airport later on."

"That's the least I can do," I said.

"Thanks. So, when are you moving down there?" he asked, as he picked a pile of books off the sofa and sat down.

"On Tuesday," I said. "I should be just about sorted out by then."

"Tuesday? Oh, well, that should be okay," he said. I couldn't help but detect a trace of disappointment in his voice. "I don't like leaving the place unattended for too long," he said. "But that's fine. Tuesday. That's fine."

He seemed to brush aside his concern and started flicking through some CDs stacked on a packing case.

"I'm certainly keen to get down there," I said.

"And I see you've got yourself a map," said Alan, nodding at the open map of the Marlborough Downs on the table. "You needn't have bothered. There's one in the house."

"I was curious," I said. "I wanted to get a feel for the place, before I move down there. Your house is on it."

"I guess it would be," he said. "It's practically the only thing in that valley.

"It certainly looks remote," I said.

"It's bloody remote, all right," he said, lighting a cigarette. "Put some coffee on, and I'll tell you all about it."

****

For the next couple of hours, he talked about the house, and the area in which it was located, for which he quite clearly had a great deal of empathy. When he spoke of Avebury and its hinterland, of the grass burial mounds and standing stones, and the vastness of the empty downland landscape, there was a real gleam in his eyes, which reminded me of how he had been back in university, during the early days of the band.

He showed me some photographs of the house and it did indeed look impressive. As did the Neolithic burial mound in the garden.

"Try and keep any passing tourists off it, if you can," he said. "I can't stop them using the footpath on the other side, but sometimes they hop over the fence so they can clamber up it."

"I'll do my best," I said, although it was hard to see what harm could come to a grass mound, thousands of years old, from such occasional incursions by the curious.

He gave me a set of keys to the house, and the code for the alarm. He explained in some detail how to find the place, and how well concealed it was, on account of a stand of fir trees to the front, and by virtue of the natural depression in the ground in which it sat.

Getting my map, he spread it out before us, and embarked upon a long discourse on the prehistoric and natural attractions of the immediate area – Avebury, Silbury Hill, West Kennet Long Barrow, the Ridgeway – places which were little more than names to me at that stage, but which I found I was already looking forward to visiting. Watching Alan point these places out on a map made me feel as if I was embarking on a holiday, and I had to remind myself that I was primarily going there to work.

He then turned to more practical considerations – where to buy petrol, the best local pubs, and the relative merits of the nearby towns of Marlborough, Pewsey and Devizes.

"Oh, one fairly crucial thing," he said, towards the end of his peroration, "You don't own a dog, or any other pets, do you? I mean, you haven't got one here, so I'm assuming not. It's just that I can't abide them in the house, because of my allergies. They'd drop hair all over the place, and I'd suffer for it when I got back."

"I don't remember you having those sorts of allergies," I said.

"Late developer. Anyway, it's a moot point, I assume. You don't have a dog, do you?"

"No. No pets."

"Good."

By the time he had finished it was long past lunchtime, and so I ordered in a pizza, and fetched a couple of beers from the fridge.

"You know, I'm going to miss that place so much," he said at one point, while we were eating.

"In fact, I can't even begin to describe how I'm going to miss it," he repeated, suddenly sounding quite maudlin.

His tone of voice seemed to suggest that he was never going to see his house again, but when I suggested as much, he brushed this off in slightly irritated fashion.

"Just musing," he said. "I'll be back the week before Christmas, exactly like I said. Probably just a case of cold feet before the flight. But I'm going to miss being there a lot," he finished, shaking his head sadly.

Looking around at my semi-packed up flat, I fervently hoped that he wasn't having last minute second thoughts. But a moment later he seemed like his old self again, and before long, we were heading off to the airport.

I waited with him until his flight was called, and then walked with him to the departure lounge.

"I guess this is where we say goodbye," he said as we reached the security checkpoint.

"It's all hellos and goodbyes with us at the moment, isn't it?" I said. "Good luck out there, and thanks so much again for letting me live in the house."

He looked at me in an odd way, and for some reason I thought he was going to hug me again, as he had a few days previously at the railway station, but instead he offered me his hand, which I shook.

"Good luck to you too. Take care of yourself down there," he said.

"It's Wiltshire," I said. "I'm sure I'll be fine."

"Just be careful," he said. "Place like that, you never know."

It seemed like a strange thing to say, but before I could ask him what he meant, he turned and walked off. This time, unlike when getting on the train a few nights previously, he didn't look back.

I stood there for a moment and wondered at the oddness of life.

Then I went back to the flat to carry on packing.

****

It was after the weekend that followed that things started to become just a little curious.

By late Monday morning, I finally had everything done. The packing cases containing all my worldly goods had gone off to a nearby storage warehouse, and I was left with just the small collection of bags and boxes that were going to accompany me down to Wiltshire the next day.

The flat felt bare and empty without its familiar clutter, depressingly so, and I decided to head off to my local pub for lunch.

Just as I was about to walk out of the door, the telephone rang. It was the old landline that hardly ever rang any longer, and which I realised with dismay I still hadn't gotten around to having disconnected.

One final job to do before tomorrow, I said to myself as I lifted the receiver.

It was Helen Moore, the editor of a small circulation magazine I had once submitted an article to. They mostly specialised in esoteric subjects which I had little interest in, but Helen and I went back a way, and I had written a piece for them a year ago, on the labyrinth of subterranean tunnels beneath Paris, and had offered to do more for them in the future, should a suitable opportunity arise. Although I was mainly focused on the book these days, I was still keen to keep my hand in with the odd bit of journalism, and even though the magazine didn't pay a lot, every little helped since I had quit full-time employment.

"Actually, I'm glad you rang," I said, after we had exchanged the customary pleasantries. "I'm about to move down to the country for a while, so I won't be contactable at this number any longer. In fact, I'm about to get it disconnected."

I gave her my cell number.

"Where are you going?" she asked.

"Somewhere in Wiltshire, near Avebury. I'm actually going to be looking after the house of a friend of mine – Alan Mackay. He used to be big around the turn of the century."

"Funny you should mention that," she said. "Oh God, Richard. I'm so sorry, but I rang because I've got a bit of a confession to make."

I sighed inwardly. I liked Helen, but she was a terrible gossip, and notoriously indiscreet.

"You see, he telephoned me," she went on when I didn't say anything. "Alan Mackay telephoned me. About a month ago. He said you two were old friends and he wanted to get in touch with you. But we have a strict policy here about not giving out that sort of contact information, so I didn't give him your number, but I probably gabbled on a bit more than I should have done."

"About what, exactly?" I asked.

"Well, nothing earth shattering. But he'd read that piece you wrote for us, about Paris, and he was interested in what else you might be up to. He said he was thinking of doing an autobiography, and wanted someone to ghost write it, and that you two were friends – which I had no idea about until then, by the way – and so he was wondering if you might want the job."

"I see," I said, as my mind attempted to process this unexpected news.

"Yes, but that's not the bad part," she said. "I kind of prattled on as I sometimes do – well, I was a bit thrown, I suppose, suddenly finding myself on the phone with a bona fide rock star, even a retired one – and I'm afraid I told him about your book."

"What about it?"

"Only as much as I know, which isn't much. But I kind of implied that because you were busy writing your own book, you might not have time to do his, but … Oh God, I'm so sorry …"

"Yes?"

"Well, I mentioned that you had left the newspaper you used to work for, and that you might, you know, need the money. I'm really sorry, Richard. I shouldn't have talked about you like that. And then, to make it worse, I didn't even tell you about it before now. But he did sort of swear me to secrecy."

"Really? How come?"

"He said he'd just remembered another way of getting hold of you, and he wanted it to be a surprise, because you hadn't seen each other for such a long time. I feel terrible about it all now."

"Don't worry about it. It doesn't matter at all," I lied, since I was more anxious at that moment to get Helen off the phone so I could think, than I was about admonishing her.

"Thanks for being such a sweetie about it," she said. "So, are you going to do it?"

"Am I going to do what?"

"Ghost write Alan Mackay's autobiography?"

"I'm not sure. We're still discussing the details."

"Well, thanks for giving me your number. Have a lovely time. And if I need an article any time, I'll be sure to let you know."

"Thanks, I'd like that. Bye, Helen. We'll speak soon."

Fat chance of that, I thought, as I put the phone down.

So, Alan's impromptu phone call of a week previously hadn't been the spur of the moment impulse he had said it was. He had obviously been planning it for some time. But why? Was it guilt at having allowed our friendship to lapse, but not wanting to let on about this, in order to make our sudden reunion seem as casual as possible? It wasn't a wholly improbable or dishonourable explanation for having been economical with the truth; likewise, the whole ruse to Helen about ghost writing a book.

But it was him knowing about me quitting the paper, and writing my own book, and by implication being strapped for cash, that I found more troubling. If he had known all that, why act so surprised when I had told him about it? Was it just a case of covering the tracks of his enquiry to Helen? Or might it merely have been politeness, and not wanting to steal my thunder and let me tell him about it myself? These were both potentially plausible explanations, but they didn't quite seem to ring true.

I was about to put it out of my mind, and go to the pub, but it was nagging at me, so I decided to call someone else.

Hunting through my address book, I located the number of the person Alan had said he got my number from, back when he supposedly had the impetuous idea of calling me the week before.

Dan Nichols was a freelance writer for the music press who I had first met at university, when he came up to interview Alan just before we graduated, and when the band was beginning to get noticed. We had kept in vague touch during the intervening years, somewhat reluctantly in my case. He was a chippy individual, who always seemed to display considerable bitterness to anyone more successful than him, which invariably meant the musicians he wrote about. In truth, I couldn't stand the man.

"Dan. It's Richard. Great to speak to you again," I said, when he picked up the phone.

"Richard, well I never," he said. "It has been a very long time, hasn't it? Are you still in the pay of the awful Murdoch press?"

"No, these days I'm a penniless author," I said.

This news seemed to cheer him, and we chatted for as brief a time as I thought I could get away with before I got to the point of my call.

"Remember Alan Mackay?" I said.

"Of course. My first ever interview, which you set up, as I recall. Great musician, in his day, but a total sell-out now, like most of them when they get to that age. I heard he reinvented himself as a country gent and lives in some bloody great pile down in Somerset, or somewhere. No offence, mind. I know you two used to be close."

"None taken. Anyway, the reason for my call was to thank you, basically. For putting him in touch with me. We met up a few days ago and it was really good to see him again."

"Oh, that," he said. "No problem. I was fairly surprised to hear from him myself. He's totally dropped off the radar, these days."

"I know, it was like a bolt from the blue."

"Guess it must have been."

"So, it must have been about this time last week, when he phoned you," I said, trying to sound as casual as possible. "Lucky you were there."

"No, it was about a month ago," said Dan. "Or three weeks, maybe."

"Right. Well, my mistake. But thanks all the same. He might not have been able to track me down, without you giving him my number."

"No worries. How was he, anyway? He's not thinking about getting back into the business, is he? There's a lot of that going on now. Old rockers cashing in."

"No, not that I know of. But if I hear anything, I'll be sure to let you know."

"Thanks, I'd appreciate that. It's been a long time since I had a genuine scoop. We should get together for a drink some time."

"I'd like that. I've got a fair bit on at the moment. Maybe give you a ring in a couple of weeks?"

Less chance of that than my writing another article for Helen, I thought, as I put the phone down.

The information from Dan essentially confirmed what Helen had told me. Alan had been trying to track me down for some time, and had known rather more about my current situation than he had let on.

I wondered what else he hadn't told me.

I recalled him saying that on the day I took him to the airport he had appointments here in town, with his accountant and his management company. I had no idea who his accountant was, and they wouldn't have told me anything anyway, but the management company, who I did recall the identity of, was a different matter. Their brief was to represent his commercial interests, so they would be able, up to a point, to answer a few questions.

I flipped open my laptop and googled them, and then dialled their number. A receptionist put me through to the relevant department.

"Hello," I said. "I'm a journalist hoping to interview Alan Mackay, and I understand you represent him."

"Hi, I'm Trish," said a woman's voice. "I'm not sure that we do, actually. Hold on a moment, I'll check."

I heard the tapping of computer keys on the other end of the line.

"No, sorry. He's no longer on our books. We used to represent him, but it says he ceased using our services in 2007."

Alan was full of surprises today, I thought.

"Oh, right," I said. "I must have got the name of the wrong company. Do you know who he's with now?"

"I can find out," she said.

I knew from past experience that these agencies had access to a register of who was managed by whom, and that this was freely available information.

"It doesn't look like he's represented by anyone," said the woman a moment later. "Isn't he retired, these days?"

"Yes, I believe he is. I was hoping to do a retrospective interview."

"Maybe he's got a website," she suggested.

"Yes, probably. I'll try that. Thanks for your help."

I put down the phone and went back to my laptop. Googling Alan Mackay generated a predictably long list of hits, but he didn't appear to have a website.

I typed in the name of the band he had said he was going to work with in America, and who he claimed to have been meeting a week previously, when we first met up again.

It didn't take long to confirm that they had indeed been in London recently, on the way home from a European tour. So, Alan may have been telling the truth about that part. Or he may just have done some research for his cover story.

But why? Why would he do such a thing? And if he was getting back into the business, as he had said, why didn't he have representation? Alan may have been flaky in many ways, but he had always been remarkably shrewd about the commercial side of the music industry, even early on. It was part of the reason he had become so wealthy, in spite of having had a relatively short career.

I was on the verge of phoning him, but it would still have been the middle of the night on the west coast of America.

Instead, I decided to see if a long lunch in the pub might alleviate the doubts that were now starting to nag at me.

****

It was late in the afternoon by the time I got home, and several pints of beer had done nothing to ease my anxiety about having been lied to.

I decided to phone Alan. It would be morning by now in California.

I dialled the number he had given me.

"This number is not in service," said an electronic voice in reply.

Thinking I had misdialled, I tried again. Same answer.

More and more peculiar, I thought. What was I supposed to do if there was a problem at the house, and I had to call him in an emergency?

I thought of the musician he had told me about, the one who was originally going to be looking after the house, and who by dropping out had supposedly opened the way for me to do so instead. Maybe he might be able to shed some light on the situation.

I called Dan Nichols again.

"Well, well," he said when he answered the phone. "Nothing for years, and then two phone calls in one day. What can I do for you this time?"

"Do you remember Degsy Miller; session guitarist on Alan Mackay's first album?"

"Of course. Bloody good musician. What about him?"

"I was hoping to get in touch with him, and wondered if you might know how to find him?"

"You'll need a medium," said Dan.

"I beg your pardon?"

"He's dead. Died about ten years ago. Heroin overdose."

"God, I'm sorry to hear that," I said, my mind now going into a complete spin.

"Yes, a terrible waste, as always. What did you want him for?"

"Oh, just a piece I was thinking of writing. About the early days of the band. Well, sorry to have bothered you."

I went and sat down to try and gather my thoughts. Something was very wrong.

Firstly, my reunion with Alan a week previously had not been an impromptu event at all. He had been planning it for some time.

Secondly, Alan had been making enquiries about me for at least a month, and had known, prior to my seeing him, that I was no longer a working journalist, was writing a book, and was in some financial difficulty. Goodness knows what else he might have found out. I wondered for a moment if he had spoken to Marianne in Paris, but nothing on God's earth would have compelled me to telephone her to find out.

Thirdly, Alan had, at the very least, lied about meeting his management company who, it transpired, didn't even represent him any longer. It was also possible, perhaps even probable, that his story about working in a studio with a band in California was a fabrication. All I knew with any certainty, because I had been there at the time, was that he had departed a few days ago on a flight to Los Angeles.

Fourthly, his story about Degsy Miller having agreed to look after his house, and then subsequently having reneged on this, was a complete fiction, since Degsy Miller had been dead for ten years.

And fifthly, Alan had given me a telephone contact number that was no longer in use. He had, therefore, to all intents and purposes, disappeared.

And yet, there on the coffee table in front of me were the keys to his house.

Somehow, for some reason, Alan wanted me to live in his house, which was, to put it mildly, rather mind-boggling. Did he have some other reason for going to live in California, which he didn't want to tell me about? Another spell in re-hab, that he hadn't wanted to admit to? Was this some sort of elaborate favour to me, the struggling writer who had been his best friend, but who he had ignored for the past twenty years? Was this some bizarre act of altruism? Or was there some other, more sinister or malevolent motive at work? I needed an explanation, and yet there seemed to be no way of obtaining one. I wondered whether I really wanted to move into his house, having been so misled about the whole situation.

I stared at my packed bags in the corner of the room.

The flat was rented, I told myself, and I certainly needed the money, as well as needing somewhere to finish my book. Perhaps this was a gift horse I shouldn't be looking in the mouth. And however dishonest Alan had been with me, and for whatever reason, I had given him a solemn undertaking that I would look after his house.

He hadn't allowed me time for second thoughts. Perhaps that had been intentional.

I walked over to the window and stared down at the street below. One way or the other, I needed to make a decision, and I needed to make it now.

A few moments later, I had.

CHAPTER FOUR

Arrival

I stared at the burial mound at the end of the garden. It was an innocuous sight, really. A mere hump of grass, with a small stand of trees to one side, and ploughed fields beyond. A blip in the wider landscape. A steeply sided mound of earth, perhaps twelve feet high, perhaps a bit less, with clumps of daffodils at its base which were about to start flowering. To the casual observer, it was nothing more than a grass embankment, that could have been formed at any time. And yet, it was thousands of years old, and concealed a mass grave. It was this knowledge that gave the mound such presence in a garden which otherwise seemed entirely predictable for a country property of this scale.

A stone wall encircled gently undulating grounds, which rose up at the front to the group of three Scots pines on their rise overlooking the road and screening the property from those going past. Beside the house, neat flower beds filled with bare rose bushes formed a border to the gravel driveway, on the other side of which was a great swathe of lawn, with an island shrub bed in the middle, and at the end opposite the burial mound, a gigantic beech, stripped of its leaves, and showing its intricate network of branches.

A single storey brick outbuilding with wide timber doors, presumably a garage, was situated at the end of the driveway. I walked over to it as I delayed the moment of my entry into the house, so that I could properly take everything in. Having spent the past few years living in a small flat in London, and before that a top floor apartment in Paris, it was a welcome novelty to find myself in possession of a domain such as this. I thought of being out here in the summer, lying beneath a canopy of pale green beech leaves and dappled light, screened off from the outside world by my protective stand of Scots Pines.

I looked into the small paddock which Alan had told me was part of the property. It was separated from the main garden by a timber post and rail fence, and accessed via a weathered five bar gate. The field itself contained a couple of large, specimen trees amidst clumps of hassock grass, and was separated from the road by a tall hedgerow.

Next to the house's main façade, and continuing its line, was a yew hedge with an archway cut into its centre. As it was almost beckoning me to pass through it, I dutifully stepped through the aperture in the dense greenery and entered a vegetable garden. It looked a well- ordered patch, if currently devoid of vegetables; its bare earth divided by timber walkways in neat parallel lines. There was a shed with a corrugated metal roof at the far end, above which rose the huge retaining bank that ran along the back of the house. The shed was mounted on concrete blocks, with a gap underneath, which Alan had told me contained spare keys to the front door, just in case I should ever lock myself out. Beside the door, so he had said, and so I crouched down and reached beneath the weathered timber structure, and sure enough I felt my hand close around a metal tin, which rattled when I shook it. I retrieved the tin and opened it, saw the two keys inside, and then closed it again and returned it to its hiding place.

Useful to know, I thought. I had a habit of locking myself out of places.

I followed a path through the plots of bare, turned earth, and past a mass of skeletal fruit bushes until I was standing beneath the steep overhang at the back of the hollow. This high natural wall should have made the rear garden dark, but because the sides to the property were so open, the setting sun in the west was casting its light across it, and suffusing the kitchen garden with a bright glow, which seemed somehow incongruous on such a chill day.

The path continued on around the back of the house, as did I, glancing through the windows at a large kitchen, and some sort of utility room, with a door to the outside.

I knew the door would be locked, but I tried it anyway, and then reached into my pocket for the bunch of keys Alan had given me in London. I tried a few until I found the right one, and felt the lock click open as I turned it. Then I locked it again, as I still wasn't ready to enter. I wanted to see the rest of the garden first.

I carried on to the west side, and across a terrace set beneath a timber pergola until I was back at the front again. I decided to walk over to the long barrow. It loomed ever larger as I drew closer to it, and when I reached its base, some impulse made me want to climb to the top.

The grass was wet and slippery, almost causing me to lose my footing as I scrambled up the steep bank. I walked along the short summit, staring out across the vast, empty landscape. It was a magnificent view. The stone circles of Avebury, I thought, must be close by but out of sight, somewhere to the west, hidden by the folds of the plain. In the far distance there was a blur of grassed escarpments, and before them a patchwork of rolling fields, dotted with small woods. There was a larger wood closer to the house, just a few hundred yards away, to the west, clinging to the upper edges of a steeply sloping field. The woods looked dense, impenetrable, and almost mysterious in the grey half-light.

I felt my foot brush against something on the ground, causing me to look down.

It was a small bird, some kind of thrush, and it was dead.

I stared down at it for a moment, and then crouched beside it to inspect it more closely. The bird didn't appear to have been injured in any way. In fact, there wasn't a mark on it, so I was curious as to why it should suddenly have expired on this grassy mound. I decided to deal with it later and turned my attention back to the house.

It had an imposing presence, its grey stone walls supporting the tiled roof with its pointed dormer windows. Seeing the house close up, in the midst of these surroundings, made me understand why Alan was so attached to it. There was an unmistakeable grandeur about it; something about the smoothness of the stone, and the angular precision of its structure and detailing.

And now it's mine, I thought. At least, it is for the immediate future.

It was time to go inside.

I retrieved the bunch of keys and, after some trial and error, undid both locks, opened the front door and stepped inside. I was immediately greeted by the bleep of an alarm system.

The control panel was just inside the hallway, and I tapped in the four-digit number that Alan had given me, and everything was quiet again. I stepped further into the hall, my footsteps loud on the timber floor. Everything seemed so large, compared to the tiny accommodation I was used to, an effect accentuated by the plain white walls and high ceilings. I recalled Alan telling me that he had completely remodelled the interior of the house when he had first bought it, and it had a modern feel, in contrast to the more predictably antique exterior. Only a softly ticking grandfather clock of dark, burnished wood at the foot of the stairs seemed vaguely out of place.

Various rooms led off the large hall and I went into all of them. The kitchen was as large and well equipped as it had appeared from my glimpse through the window. There was a range for cooking, as well as a conventional oven, and a tall fridge-freezer that was the largest of its kind I had ever seen. The middle of the room was dominated by an island unit topped in thick, gleaming black marble. There were high stools with padded seats set around it, and a ceiling mounted rack above, from which hung pots, pans and ladles. I pushed it gently and there was a soft clang of stainless steel and copperware.

The kitchen floor was covered in rivened tiles, dark grey to complement the black marble, and there was a walk-in larder, and an impressive array of gadgets on the long runs of worktop. Everything about the kitchen looked well made, state of the art, expensive. For the first time since living in France, I was looking forward to cooking again.

I glanced into the small utility room that led off the kitchen, and from where one could get into the back garden, and was gratified to see several coats hanging from hooks by the door, as well as wellington boots, walking sticks and two umbrellas. Other than the coat I had brought with me, I had little of this sort of thing myself, so it was good to see that I was thoroughly equipped for a long stay in the country, without needing to go out and buy anything.

Another door from the kitchen led into the dining room where there was a long rectangular table of dark wood, topped with glass, around which were eight high backed chairs. Like the kitchen, this was at the rear of the house, up against the high retaining bank, but just as the kitchen was naturally lit by large windows to the east, so this room got its light from a set of glazed doors to the west that led onto the terrace with the pergola. I imagined sitting out there on balmy summer evenings, watching the sun go down over the woods on the other side of the field, or eating supper in the darkness beneath a string of lanterns.

I returned to the front of the house via a second internal door from the dining room, and past a study that I glanced into briefly. It looked neat and well ordered, with a computer, printer and scanner. A row of Alan's platinum selling discs, as well as a great many framed album covers filled one of the walls. Beneath them were propped no less than eight of his guitars, including a twin-stemmed 12-string that I remembered going with him to buy in a mood of great celebration, the day the band first got signed to its record label.

There were two sitting rooms, both at the front of the house, and set to each side of the staircase. To the east was the sort of traditional reception room that one would typically have associated with a house such as this, with a large fireplace, and a formal arrangement before it of two high-backed, winged armchairs on either side of a long sofa. The un-fenestrated sections of wall were clad from floor to ceiling with densely filled bookshelves, the books of a mostly antiquarian appearance. Alan had never been much of a reader, I thought to myself, but he had become something of a book collector, at the very least, in the years since I had known him.

The other sitting room, on the west side of the house, although one window's length longer than its companion room to the east, was more of a cosy snug, in spite of its greater size, and the place where I imagined spending most of my time, as I presumed Alan did. Rugs lay upon a timber floor, and there was a large and luxuriant looking sofa, facing an enormous television screen. There was a wood-burning stove, and yet more books lining the walls, except in this room they were of a more contemporary vintage. As I perused some of the spines I noticed several histories of the local area, many with Avebury in the title, and others about the prehistoric era more generally. At the far end of the room, facing west, was a large picture window that framed a view of the burial mound at the edge of the property. Another place to watch the sun go down, I thought.

I returned to the hallway and noticed another door. I opened it and saw that it led down to a cellar. Flicking on the light I went halfway down the steps and saw a quarry tiled floor, with various alcoves leading off it, so that it appeared as if the cellar extended beneath the entire house. I decided I would explore it on another occasion, as I was more keen right then to see the upstairs.

I went back up to the hall and ascended the wide staircase. Matching the footprint of the two reception rooms on the ground floor were two large bedrooms. The larger one on the west side I assumed was Alan's, since it was clearly the master bedroom, and because another three of his guitars were mounted on one of the walls. A glazed door led onto a small balcony. I opened it and stepped out. From here I was looking across the top of the burial mound to the woods on the other side of the field. There was a single wrought iron chair on the balcony, and on the floor, a heavy glass ashtray, filled with rainwater. I imagined Alan sitting up here on sunny evenings, smoking, and plucking at one of the guitars.

We had agreed that I would sleep in the main guest bedroom on the other side, which faced east as well as north, and which would thus get the morning sun. It was a pleasant room, sparsely furnished, with a large, metal framed bed, and an oak dressing table, flanked by a pair of occasional chairs. The walls were a pale cream colour and looked freshly painted. Doors set into an alcove revealed a large storage closet within, that I would just about be able to fill a quarter of. A watercolour painting of nearby Silbury Hill, green and verdant beneath a blue sky, hung above the bed. Looking at it made me think of summer again.

The remainder of the floor contained two further bedrooms, both much smaller, although still of reasonable size. One had a bed in it, whilst the other contained Alan's prodigious record and CD collection, something I was looking forward to browsing through. There were also two bathrooms. One was an en-suite, accessed from Alan's room; the other was the bathroom I would use, which felt enormous compared to the one in my flat.

Back on the landing, another staircase led to the top floor, accessed via a narrow door, which was ajar. I climbed the steep stairs into a dark corridor, where I switched on the light, to reveal the closed doors of four rooms. Two of the rooms were bedrooms, each of which had a dormer window, and from where there were long views across the plain. I opened the door to the third room, on the other side of the corridor. It was a small bathroom, with no window, just a roof light. I wondered if I would ever even bother to come up to this floor, so generous were the accommodations beneath me. It wasn't as if I was expecting visitors.

The door to the fourth room was locked, secured by a hasp and staple, and a heavy-duty padlock. Mildly intrigued, I tried each of the keys in the set that Alan had given me, but none of them fitted the padlock. I guessed he was using the room to store some of his more personal or private possessions.

I went back into one of the two attic bedrooms, and sat down on the bed.

It really was quite a place. I felt glad that I had decided to come and live here, even if the various curiosities and deceptions behind Alan's offer were still nagging at me and had occupied my thoughts for much of the drive down.

I decided to go and collect my bags from the car and set about sorting myself out.

It was while I was going back down the stairs that I noticed the picture, which I had been oblivious to when going up. It was on the wall at the bottom of the staircase, next to the grandfather clock. It was a portrait and it depicted a man of about my age, wearing a suit, and sitting before a sideboard of such dark mahogany that it was almost lost in the background, and upon which, in a somewhat incongruous pairing, were a human skull and a vase of white flowers. The man was staring intently at the viewer. Something looked oddly familiar about him, and then on closer inspection I realised who it was.

I was looking at a picture of Dorian Slake. I recognised him from the photograph I had come across when researching him a few days previously. The erstwhile owner of this house; the occultist who had been a disciple of Aleister Crowley; the man who had apparently gone mad here and hung himself in the woods. The woods on the other side of the field by the house. And here he was, at the foot of the stairs.

There was an inscription in the bottom right-hand corner of the painting. It read, "DS, 1964".

DS – Dorian Slake. A self-portrait, painted shortly before the man chose to take his life.

I looked closely at his face for any sign of the interior madness, perhaps even the reputed evil that lay within, but he looked entirely normal. He may have been the inspiration behind Alan buying this house, I thought, but there was nothing very interesting about him, as far as I was concerned.

I went outside to fetch my bags.

CHAPTER FIVE

First Night

Although Alan had left me a well-stocked freezer, and there were enough tins and dried goods in his larder to feed a small army, I hadn't had time to pick up any fresh food or other staples on my way down, and so I decided to go out and eat on my first night, and then go shopping the following day. Besides, having unpacked my things and got established, I felt restless for some reason, and felt the urge to go somewhere.

It had long been dark by then, but the garden, I had discovered, was equipped with several outside lights, controlled from a panel next to the burglar alarm, and I switched them all on. There were lights on the front and back of the house, illuminating part of the driveway and the rear garden, another one washing the walls of the little brick garage, one in the large island shrub bed, and another shining on the long barrow from the foot of the clump of trees beside it. It made for an alluring, almost enchanting sight, I thought, as I looked out across the garden from the bedroom while I got ready.

I had made this discovery in the kitchen, where Alan had taped a sheaf of instructions to the fridge – everything from where to buy milk to where the fuse box was, plus various useful telephone numbers of utility providers, local tradesmen and suchlike. It was an impressively comprehensive list, immaculately typed, and not at all reminiscent of the rather disorganised person I had once known. It even recommended a couple of places to eat, including an Italian restaurant in Marlborough which was part of one of the better chains, and where I had decided to go for dinner that evening.

I set the alarm and killed the lights, both inside and out, and double locked the front door behind me. There was something satisfying about the ostentatious crunch of gravel beneath my feet as I walked to the car. It felt good to be here, I thought, however unusual and unexpected the circumstances, and to be heading out on such a fine, crisp night.

I set off down the road in the direction of Marlborough, with the spectral tangles of the hedgerows flashing past me. The night was so clear that I would periodically be afforded glimpses of the wider landscape of the plain, so empty and desolate that it seemed almost lunar in appearance. Already, I was coming to feel an appreciation for this terrain, perhaps because it was so vast and open, compared to the cramped city streets to which I was used.

Before too long, I was back in Marlborough's wide main street, which I had first passed through a few hours previously. The centre of the street comprised a double row of parking bays and I had no difficulty in finding a space at that time of the evening.

I got out of the car and looked around at the grand illuminated buildings that lined both sides of the street in this historic market town. It would have been an exaggeration to describe the scene as busy, but there was a reasonable hustle and bustle about the place, given that this was a rural town on a midweek evening in late winter.

Wrapping myself in the warm folds of my coat, I decided to walk around for a bit before going to the restaurant.

It felt somehow liberating to be in an unfamiliar place, where nobody knew me, like being a tourist on holiday. I walked the length of each side of the street, peering into the lit windows of the various shops and establishments, and then went into a cosy looking pub for a pre-prandial drink, which I took to a tiny table by the fire, where I listened to the crackle of the flames and the background hum of masculine west country accents.

By the time I came out I was ravenously hungry and realised that I hadn't eaten since breakfast. I made my way over to the restaurant, which was only about a third full, looking forward to a hearty meal.

As I ate I reflected upon the strange turn of events of the past week. I still felt uneasy about the whole situation, but I decided to stop fretting about it, and to put aside the inconsistencies in what Alan had told me, and about where he in fact was at this precise moment in time. I had been trying his phone periodically since the previous day, but to no avail. I decided to stop trying.

He would get in touch in due course, I told myself, and I would eventually get the answers I was seeking in respect of the various whys and wherefores of everything. Or else, I wouldn't. In the meantime, I would simply stop thinking about it, enjoy the house and the unfamiliar milieu, and finish my book. What would be with Alan would be, and that was all there was to it.

I was in good spirits as I ate my meal. Too good, as it turned out. As pudding was brought to the table, I suddenly realised that I had consumed the best part of a bottle of wine, in addition to a large gin and tonic in the pub. Because I was so used to living in town, and getting the tube or cabs everywhere, or simply just walking, I had completely forgotten that I had driven here, and would have to drive home.

Cursing myself for having made such a stupid mistake, I wondered what I was going to do. I have a reasonably high tolerance for alcohol, and felt that I was perfectly capable of driving home with care along a few country lanes, but I was unquestionably over the drink-drive limit, and losing my licence would be a very bad move indeed, now that I was a country dweller. I would have to get a taxi and come back the next day to get my car. Thus, resigned to this course of action, I polished off the bottle of wine.

I had coffee and left the restaurant. It was still a fine night, if bitterly cold. I recalled a taxi rank near to where I had parked and walked over to it. I was relieved to find a cab waiting with its "For Hire" light on.

The driver, a man of about sixty but with a rockabilly quiff to his silver-white hair, looked up from the paperback novel he was reading as I approached the cab.

"Where to?" he asked as I climbed into the back seat.

"Place called Badcombe Hollow," I said, and explained roughly where it was.

"I know it," he said. "Little bit of a trek, this time of night. I'll have to charge you something for the return journey."

"No problem," I said, and we set off. So much for saving money by moving to the country, I thought.

"That's where that musician fellow used to live," the man said as we started to leave the lights of Marlborough behind us and head into the countryside. "I didn't know the house had changed hands."

"It hasn't," I said. "The owner is out of the country for a few months. I'm just looking after the place."

"Well, it's a lovely spot out there," said the cabbie. "In spite of its reputation," he added after a beat.

"What reputation would that be?" I asked, playing innocent, and knowing full well what he was referring to.

"Supposedly haunted, so people say. Apparently, the place has some sort of curse on it, if you believe in that sort of thing. And then there's the reputation of the previous owner."

"You mean Dorian Slake?" I said. I didn't believe in haunted houses or curses, but I was moderately interested in Slake's ownership of the property.

"That would be him," said the cabbie. "Thoroughly nasty piece of work, by all accounts. Into all sorts of strange stuff. You know, dabbling with dark forces, and summoning the devil, like something out of a horror film."

"Did you ever meet him?"

"No. I'm not that old, you know. But I lived here then. I'm Marlborough born and bred. But I was only a boy when he was at Badcombe Hollow. He was long gone by the time I ever heard of him.

"I'm Keith, by the way," he said. He reached into the glove compartment and took out a card, which he passed to me.

"You ever need a taxi, let me know," he said.

"Thanks," I said, and introduced myself.

"So, what about the people who've lived there since?" I asked, suddenly finding my inner journalist. "Did you meet any of them?"

"Only the gentleman who lives there now," he said. "I've taken people there a few times, or collected them, and driven them to the train station in Pewsey. He's had a few parties out there, over the years."

"Any good stories?"

"I probably shouldn't say, what with you being a friend of the owner and all."

He didn't say anything for a moment, so I waited. From experience, I knew that when people wanted to tell you something they generally did, and it was best not to try and prompt them. I had also ridden in a lot of taxis over the years. Keith struck me as the sort of cabbie who liked to chat.

"Well, there was this one time," he said, as we turned off the main road, and onto the narrow lanes that led to Alan's house.

"It was about three years ago. He was having a big party up there. Round about the middle of the evening, I was doing a drop-off in Pewsey, and got a call to go and pick someone up at the station and take them to Badcombe Hollow. It was a woman. She was middle aged, I suppose, well dressed, looked very well to do. You know, moneyed type. Anyway, she seemed a bit stressed. I got the impression she was late for whatever it was she was going to.

"So, we arrive at the house, and the outside was all lit up. There's burning torches all along the driveway, and around the bottom of that big, pre-historic burial mound he's got in the garden. It was quite a sight.

"Anyway, I'm getting her stuff out of the boot and she goes up and rings the bell to the house, and your friend the musician comes out. In a very peculiar get-up, shall we say? Some sort of black robe with a hood on the back."

"Fancy dress party?" I said.

"Could have been. Except a moment later another couple of people come out, and they were wearing the exact same thing. A man and a woman. Black robes with hoods. So, what kind of fancy dress party is it where everyone's got the same costume on?

"But that wasn't the end of it. You see, your friend, I don't think he realised I was there at first. He must have thought she'd driven herself over there, because he starts having a real go at her for being late, and then he suddenly notices me standing there with her suitcase. He was furious, and screamed at the woman for having brought me there. Then he sent me off with a right flea in my ear, which I didn't appreciate, I can tell you."

"That does all seem a bit odd," I said. We had arrived at the house.

"The funny thing is, he came in to see me a couple of days later," said Keith, as he brought the car to a halt. "Came into the taxi office at lunchtime and asked to see me. This time, he was as nice as pie. Very contrite, he was; apologised for having been short with me the other night; said it had been a costume party for his birthday and he was annoyed about the woman getting there late. Then he gave me a hundred quid. A tip, he said, for the trouble. Way over the top, but I took it anyway. Would have been rude not to."

"Do you remember the date?" I asked. "Or the time of year?"

"I do remember the date, as it happens. It was the 30th of April. I remember because it was just after our wedding anniversary, and the wife and I had been down to the coast for a couple of days. That night I drove over to his house was my first day back at work."

I absorbed this information without saying anything. Alan's birthday was in November.

"So, what do you think they were up to?" I said, as I reached into my wallet for the fare.

He was silent for a moment.

"Not my place to say," he said.

Except you're going to anyway, I thought.

"Well," he said, after another beat. "There was a rumour that he was holding séances here, and some talk about ceremonies around a fire in the woods on the other side of the field. Black magic type stuff, if you can believe that. Apparently where that Slake bloke killed himself, all those years ago. But it was just rumours. I never took them too seriously. You get a lot of that around here. You know, rumours. Especially about outsiders.

"Don't worry about the return journey," he said. "Just the fare to here will be fine."

"Thanks," I said. "In that case, do you think I could book you for tomorrow morning? I need someone to pick me up here and take me back into Marlborough, so I can collect my car."

"No problem at all. What sort of time?"

"Ten o'clock okay?"

"I can do that."

I thanked him again and paid the fare, plus a generous tip, if not quite of Alan Mackay proportions.

"Tell me," he said, as I was getting out of the car, "If you don't mind me asking, what brings you all the way out here? You're more than just a caretaker, I assume?"

"I'm here to finish writing a book," I said.

"Horror novel?" he said with a chuckle.

"No. That's not really my kind of thing. It's a sort of semi-autobiographical story set in France. I used to live in France, you see."

"Oh, right," said Keith, slowly, as if this revelation made him faintly uneasy.

"I like thrillers, myself," he went on. "Something with a good story. Robert Ludlum's my favourite. Second time I've read this one," he added, nodding at a thick paperback with a luridly embossed cover on the seat beside him.

"Yeah, that's a good one," I said.

I hadn't read it, but I had seen the film.

"Anyway, you've picked a good spot for it," said Keith. "You'll get plenty of peace and quiet out here, that's for sure. I wouldn't concern yourself too much about any stories you may here about this place. All a lot of mumbo jumbo, if you ask me."

"I couldn't agree more," I said. "It doesn't concern me at all. Goodnight, Keith. See you in the morning."

"Ten o'clock sharp."

I watched him drive away.

It seemed that Alan wasn't quite as disinterested in the sort of escapades indulged in by Dorian Slake as he had made out, I thought. Something else he had been less than honest about. And his story about celebrating his birthday on 30th April had obviously been a fabrication.

Rather than go straight into the house, I walked over to the long barrow, and climbed carefully up it, hoping that I wouldn't stand on the dead bird that I remembered I still hadn't disposed of. A job for the morning, I resolved.

I looked out across the dark plain. There were no other lights visible, and I felt like the last man on earth standing up there, listening to the wind rip through the stand of Scots Pines by the roadside.

My gaze turned to the woods on the other side of the field, and I found myself imagining Alan and a gaggle of occultists dancing around a fire in there; and Dorian Slake killing himself.

Each to their own, I thought. It didn't particularly bother me, and I certainly wasn't worried about the house's reputation for being haunted. That was just fanciful nonsense. It was interesting to me only in so much as it revealed a little bit more about Alan, and just what it was that he had been getting up to, these past twenty years. At the very least, it suggested that the band's flirtation with occult themes on their third album wasn't quite the casual bit of fun and commercialism that Alan had implied that it was. But none of that had anything to do with me, or with me being here. It was part of Alan's story, not mine.

I was about to go into the house when I noticed a light. It was coming from the woods.

It disappeared for a moment, and then I saw it again, a short distance away from where it had previously been.

It was someone with a torch, I realised. Someone was moving around in there, close to the edge of the field. What on earth they were doing up there at that time of night, I couldn't imagine. I followed the path of the light as it moved through the woods, and then it either went out, or moved out of view.

I continued to watch the woods, but it didn't reappear. After a while, I went inside.

CHAPTER SIX

Marlborough

I awoke the next morning unsure where I was, and a long time seemed to pass before I realised that I was in the guest bedroom at Alan's house. My first full day. It was a good feeling, like the first day of the school holidays. There was a spring in my step as I made my way downstairs.

I was more than a little dismayed, therefore, to find that the portrait of Dorian Slake at the foot of the stairs had somehow detached itself from its hook during the night and lay broken on the floor.

Great, I thought, as the notorious occultist stared at me through the distorted lens of cracked glass. My first breakage.

I would obviously have to get it fixed, but as there was no real urgency to do so, I gathered up the damaged portrait and the larger pieces of broken glass and carried them through to the study and laid it all on the desk. I'd find a framing shop in Marlborough and get it mended at a later date, I decided.

I found a dustpan and brush under the kitchen sink and swept up the remaining shards of glass. This done, I examined the hook on the wall, expecting to find it loose, but it was perfectly secure.

Wondering how the picture had managed to fall to the floor and break, and not exactly thrilled at the prospect of having to pay to repair something I had neither broken nor had any desire to look at, I nevertheless determined that I would not allow this minor annoyance spoil the start of the day.

I went back into the kitchen to make coffee. While I was waiting for it to brew, I compiled a shopping list for my trip to Marlborough.

Once the coffee was made, because it was such a fine morning, I put on my coat and took it out into the garden.

I found a bench at the east end of the garden that was catching the morning sun. From there I could see across Alan's meadow, down the gentle slope of the valley towards the road, unseen behind the hedgerows. It may have felt isolated but I liked being here. It was all such a contrast to my normal morning routine in London, and I felt relieved that I hadn't allowed my very legitimate doubts about Alan to cause me to miss this moment. For the first time in a long time, perhaps since bidding a final farewell to Marianne in Paris, I felt a sense of calm contentment. Country living was going to be good for me, I thought.

As the arrival of Keith and the taxi drew closer, I went back into the house to get ready and then, having locked up and set the alarm, I returned to the garden to deal with the unfortunate dead bird on the burial mound.

Somewhat to my surprise, and relief, the small bird was still intact, and its corpse hadn't been savaged by some wild animal in the night. I picked it up by its feet and was about to carry it down to the dustbin by the gate – collections on Thursdays, according to Alan's long list of notes and instructions – when I realised that another bird was lying by my feet. This time it was a blackbird, and just as dead as the thrush in my hand, and also completely unmarked.

How very odd, I thought. I wondered if it had been here the night before, when I had stood on top of the barrow and seen the light in the woods, or if it had expired that morning.

Having deposited both birds in the dustbin I waited at the end of the driveway for the taxi to arrive, which it duly did, one minute before the appointed time.

"Lovely morning," said Keith cheerily, as I got in.

We chatted away about this and that on the drive to Marlborough and as we approached the outskirts to the town, I decided to tell him about the light in the woods the night before, and what might have caused someone to be up there after dark.

"It does sound a bit unusual," he agreed. "Could have been someone out poaching. But that's very unlikely, these days. It might have been a burglar, casing the joint."

"That's reassuring," I said.

"There's quite a lot of that around here," said Keith. "Big houses, out on their own, with no neighbours around. Rich pickings for criminals."

"There's an intruder alarm in the house," I said, "And locks on all the doors and windows."

"Well, you should be alright, then. Plus, with someone living in the house, much less chance of that sort of thing. Probably the reason why your friend wanted someone in there while he was away."

"Yes, I guess so," I said. "I suppose it just made me wonder a bit, because of what you were telling me about people using those woods for certain extracurricular activities. You know; dancing around bonfires in robes and suchlike."

"Well, you never know," said Keith. "Those woods have certainly been known for that, over the years. According to the rumours, anyway. But I reckon it was most likely a prospective burglar. Now he knows you're living there, he'll probably give up, and move on elsewhere."

We had arrived in Marlborough, and I asked Keith to drop me at the taxi rank in the high street.

"By the way," he said as I got out, "That Dorian Slake fellow, who used to live at Badcombe Hollow. Are you still interested in finding out some more about him?"

"Yes, reasonably interested," I said.

In truth, I was less interested in Slake than I was in about why Alan was seemingly so interested in him, but it sort of amounted to the same thing. I also hadn't quite managed to shake off the pull of my old profession, and the journalist that still just about survived in me told me that there might be a good story in it, somewhere down the line.

"There's a bloke who drinks in our pub," said Keith. "The one over there, by the Minster. Old fellow. He used to work in the fields by your house, back when Slake lived there. Got a few stories to tell, you might say. I could arrange for the two of you to meet up one day, if you like."

"Thanks, that's very kind of you," I said. "I'd like to do that some time."

"Maybe next week then," said Keith. "I won't be around for a few days. I'm taking the wife to Bristol to see her sister. But I'm around next week. I usually have a pint in there most lunchtimes, so it's no trouble. Give me a ring and we'll fix it up. Or just drop in between one and two any weekday. Odds on that I'll be there."

I thanked him again and said goodbye, and then I went to fetch my car. There was a parking ticket on the windscreen.

Perfect, I thought. So far, moving to the country was proving to be rather expensive, what with taxi journeys, broken pictures and now this.

I pulled the sticker off the window and saw that the charge was only a fraction of what it would have been in London.

I suppose that's some consolation, I thought, as I stuffed the ticket into my coat pocket. I went and bought a permit from a machine to cover the next few hours, and then headed off to explore the town.

It was an agreeable sort of place, particularly on such a crisp, bright morning. I bought a bun from a bakery which I ate on a wooden bench, and then I pottered aimlessly about for the best part of an hour, taking in the mix of ancient stone, and half-timbered buildings, as well as the grand brick structures of the Georgian and Victorian eras. It was all a little bit twee, compared to the vibrancy and modernity of my own city, but I kind of liked it for all that. It certainly seemed a prosperous place, with its boutique shops and smart looking town houses, and absent the boarded-up frontages, takeaways and fly-by-night charity shops that had become such a feature of the urban landscape. It was a pleasure to walk around and, as on the previous night, I felt as if I was on holiday.

I found a picture framing shop, which I noted for future reference, and also, to my pleasure, a shop selling antique books and prints. I had a lifelong love of bookshops and had frequented many over the years when living in London and Paris.

I stepped inside to the pleasing accompaniment of a tinkling bell, and perused the heavily laden shelves. There were a great many books on local topography, and the nearby megalithic sites around Avebury, and in one corner there was a cabinet full of first editions, which I had to restrain myself from looking at too closely, such was my weakness for old books. I reminded myself to make a careful examination of Alan's own rather impressive library.

I finally managed to escape having made only one purchase, a 1930s gazetteer of the Marlborough Downs, filled with old sepia photographs.

"I'm sure I'll be back again," I said to the elderly proprietor as I left with the book tucked under my arm.

It was almost midday by then, so I decided to have an early lunch in town before I went food shopping. I went back to the pub I had gone to the night before and bought a beer and ordered a sandwich. When it arrived, I took it over to the same table by the fireplace where I had sat previously.

As I ate, I leafed through the book I had bought. One could tell straight away that it was from another era, and not just because of the black and white photography. There were pictures of farmers wearing flat caps and holding the reins of shire horses, crop fields being threshed by hand, and milk being delivered in metal urns, carried on horse drawn carts. There were also pictures of Silbury Hill, and the famous chambered long barrow at West Kennet, and of the stones at Avebury, as timeless as the other photographs were dated.

It was when I was about halfway through the book that I came across a picture of Alan's house. It was identified by a caption beneath it as "The Farm at Badcombe Hollow", but I would have recognised it anyway by then.

The house itself looked to have changed little in the intervening years and I was about to continue turning the pages when I was struck by something odd about the photograph. For a moment it was hard to figure out quite what it was, and then I realised.

The steep retaining bank at the back of the house was several feet lower than it was now. I could tell this because the top of the back of the hollow that I had encountered the day before reached just above the roofline of the house. But in the photograph the bank appeared only as high as the top of the first floor, just beneath the dormer windowed attic floor.

I wondered if it was just a perspective thing, but I was fairly sure that it wasn't. The top of the bank was definitely lower in the picture.

I turned to the front of the book to check the date of publication. 1935. Alan had told me that Dorian Slake bought the house in 1947, immediately after the death of his mentor, Aleister Crowley. This meant that the level of the retaining bank had most likely been built up subsequent to Slake's purchase of the house.

So, was Slake responsible for building up the bank, or one of the subsequent owners? Had Alan done it? And what could possibly be the reason for it?

There was no logical explanation, I thought, as I sipped my beer. Such a large quantity of earth could only have been spoil from some excavation elsewhere on the property. But what could have been excavated? It was possible that the brick garage in the garden could have been built after 1947 – its location was out of shot in the picture in the book – but even if it had been, digging out the footings for it would have produced nothing like the volume of earth that had been deposited at the top of that bank. So, what could have been dug out, and where?

Yet another little oddity, I thought, as I left the pub, even if it didn't seem a matter of great importance. I put it out of my mind and went off to do my shopping.

Having located the various places I needed to visit during my walk around the town that morning, I methodically set about getting in what I needed, visiting the supermarket, the green grocers and finally the butchers, where I bought two steaks and a pound of sausages. I then took this all back to the car and drove to a wine warehouse I had come across during my walk, and bought a mixed case of French wine, a crate of beer, plus scotch, gin and some cans of tonic water. Although Alan had left a certain amount of alcohol in the house, I didn't feel right about dipping into it, and preferred to have my own stock that I could work my way through with impunity.

I arrived back at the house and after confirming to myself that I had indeed been right about the change in the height of the bank, went inside to unpack my shopping. Once this was done, I made some coffee, wrote a cheque to pay my parking fine and put it in an envelope, and checked my e-mails on my laptop. They included a long and effusive one from Helen Moore, apologising again for having been so indiscreet when talking about me to Alan, and promising to let me know if she needed an article from me.

Maybe I should write one about Dorian Slake, I thought.

Switching off the laptop, I decided to go for a walk.

I remembered that Alan and I were the same shoe size, and I was able to fit comfortably into the pair of wellington boots in the utility room, as I was into the waterproof shooting jacket hanging from one of the hooks by the door. Feeling like the slightly bogus country gentleman that I in fact was – I even availed myself of a walking stick – I headed off.

On leaving the house and going down to the road, I took the footpath beside the burial mound that led across the field and from there through the woods to the top of the escarpment. From studying the map I had bought, I knew there was another path along a ridgeway there.

When I got to the top I looked back down at the house. Because of the high bank of the hollow, I could only see the grey tiles of the roof, and the tops of the trees along the road. It was a reminder of how screened off the house was, and from up there it was almost as if it had fallen into the folds of the earth.

The sun was lower in the sky by then, but it was still a fine day. I had a clear view to the north, and an unimpeded one of the large mound of Silbury Hill, somewhere else I planned to visit that week, before I started in earnest on the book again. I experienced the almost exhilarating feeling of suddenly having much before me. It was back to the first day of the school holidays vibe of the morning.

As I walked along the high ridge, it was the sky that made the most impression on me, more so than all the undulating greenery beneath it. Simply the sheer size of it. It seemed so vast; the biggest sky I had ever seen, stretching like a giant sheet across the landscape of the plain. I felt dwarfed by it, like a tiny speck beneath the huge protective canopy.

I followed the path for about an hour, not seeing a single soul, and with no objective in mind, other than to enjoy the fresh air, the solitude and the chance to think my own thoughts. Then as the sun started to slip down through the enormous sky, I turned to walk back the same way, figuring that this would get me home just before sunset, in the gloaming, at a good sort of moment to re-enter my new domain, and settle in for the night. Images of curtains being drawn, and fires being lit, flashed pleasingly through my mind.

As I reached the woods near the house, I noticed another path branching off to the west from the main one, and decided I'd follow it for a short way and see if it led anywhere. I recalled from the map that there was a lane somewhere on the other side of these woods, and thought this was likely the way to reach it

It was a dense thicket of a wood, and it felt dark in there, now that the daylight was fading. The trees were mostly deciduous, but although bare for the winter, they grew so close together that there was a hemmed in, oppressive feel about the place, and the pathway seemed to get ever more narrow, the further I went along it.

I was about to turn around and head back when I noticed a clearing a little way in front of me, so I decided to continue on until I reached it, and then turn back.

The small clearing must have been the oldest part of the wood, because it was encircled by larger, mature trees. It would be a nice spot for a picnic, I thought. Then I noticed the ash and charred timbers at my feet. I was standing beside the remains of a fire.

I recalled the stories about witches' sabbats in these woods, and couldn't help but wonder if this was evidence of some such gathering in the recent past. I also remembered that these were the woods in which Dorian Slake had hung himself. I looked around at the high, mature trees and presumed that it had been from one of their branches that he had done the deed. It was a chilling thought.

It was then that I saw the pentagram. It was about the size of an old seven-inch record, and had been burned, by the looks of it, into one of the trees, at about chest height. A five-pointed star with a circle around it. Someone must have done that with a branding iron, I thought.

This didn't seem quite such a bucolic spot any longer. I decided I didn't want to have a picnic there any time soon.

As I turned to go back to the path there was a loud crack from somewhere in the undergrowth. Startled, I wheeled around to see where the noise might have come from. The dense screen of trees stared impassively back at me.

Then I heard it again, but not so loud this time, as if the source of the noise was getting further away. I realised that someone must be walking away from the clearing.

Could they have been spying on me, I wondered.

Although not one to spook easily, I was in no mood to try and follow whoever it might have been, and with the woods becoming ever darker, I decided it was definitely time to get back home.

I walked back to the main trackway and from there out of the dark thicket and into the fields. When I reached the house, I mounted the long barrow and looked back towards the woods.

The sun had almost gone now. Its dying embers were being filtered through the trees towards me, and the early evening sky was streaked with red.

But then something else caught my attention.

At the edge of the woods, just inside the field, was the figure of a man. He was standing quite still, seemingly looking towards me. He was too far away for me to make out his features, and because he was stood in line with the setting sun, he appeared almost as a silhouette.

I surmised that he was the same person I had heard in the woods and wondered why he was watching the house. I also couldn't help but speculate about this being whoever it was I'd seen up there with a torch the night before.

For some reason I imagined that he was going to walk down towards me, and perhaps explain himself, but he remained completely still, seemingly unconcerned at my having seen him.

I decided to go into the house, to see if I could get a better view of him from the balcony outside Alan's room.

In some haste, I let myself in, switched off the burglar alarm, and made my way upstairs.

But by the time I stepped out onto the balcony, the man had gone.

CHAPTER SEVEN

Second Night

The odd appearance of the man in the field aside, I was in a good mood that evening. Feeling settled into the house and fully provisioned, I was looking forward to the night ahead in my grand new surroundings.

I fixed myself a large gin and tonic, which I took upstairs to sip whilst luxuriating in a hot bath, and when I came back downstairs, I opened one of the bottles of wine I had bought, and set about making supper. I put potatoes on to boil, made a salad and a French dressing, and then put one of the steaks into a griddle pan I had found in Alan's predictably well-equipped kitchen. In between times I went into the main sitting room and lit the fire that had been left made up, and drew all the curtains in the house. Having lived for so long in small apartments it felt good to have so much space to roam about in.

I had thought about laying the table in the dining room, but I would have felt faintly ridiculous eating in there by myself, and so I ate my supper perched at the island unit in the kitchen. The local, organically raised steak was delicious, and was perfectly complemented by the Rhone Valley red I had selected from my case. After I had finished eating and washed up, I made coffee, which I carried through to the sitting room where the fire was roaring away nicely.

My intention that evening had been to do nothing more strenuous than picking a film from Alan's huge stock of DVDs, and then probably falling asleep on the sofa. But reinvigorated by the coffee, I found myself wanting to do something, and so I decided to explore the house a bit more.

I started in the other sitting room, which was really more of a library, and where I had a good look through Alan's antiquarian books and modern first editions. It was an impressive, valuable collection and so enjoyable was it to browse through that I was only moderately disappointed to discover that it included the book on the surrounding downland in times gone by, that I had purchased that morning in Marlborough.

The small box room on the first floor, which was full of records and CDs, was just as much of a delight. Alan had always been possessed of pleasingly eclectic tastes when it came to music, and this was reflected in his collection, which also included a complete set of his own music, with various editions of his albums from different countries, in a bewildering variety of sleeves, all of his singles, and a bootleg CD of one of the band's last ever concerts. And there was much else besides. Alan had clearly developed a penchant for collecting things. I started to create a shortlist of things I wanted to listen to while I was staying in the house, putting the selected items into a pile on a chest in the corner.

It was while I was doing this that I came across the photograph album on the floor, propped against one of the boxes of records. It was the sort of thick, heavy, leather-bound album one used to see all the time, but which had become ever less ubiquitous in recent years, thanks to the advent of digital photography and social media.

I started flicking through it from the beginning and saw that it included several pictures of our time at university, and the early days of the band. There was even a picture of me in there, standing next to Alan in the front room of the house we had shared for the best part of two years.

But it was the later photographs in the album which I found of most interest, because they had been taken after Alan had moved here. There was one of him leaning nonchalantly against a standing stone, presumably at Avebury, wearing dark glasses and smoking a cigarette, and then various shots of Badcombe Hollow, including several in the snow, with the escarpment and woods above the house looking positively alpine. There was also a picture of Alan and a woman I didn't recognise, sitting on the side of the burial mound, which must have been taken in the spring, because the daffodils at the foot of the barrow were in full bloom. The woman was of a startlingly gothic appearance, dressed from head to toe in black, and heavily made up. She looked distinctly out of place in such a rustic setting.

There were some other pictures of the house and garden, one of which had obviously been taken when Alan bought the place, as he was brandishing a For Sale sign and grinning broadly as he stood in the driveway. I noticed that the level of the bank behind the house was the same as it was now, at roughly the same height as the dormer windows on the attic floor and deduced from this that it must have been Dorian Slake or a subsequent owner, and not Alan, who had raised it, for whatever reason.

One photograph towards the back of the album gave me pause for thought. It showed Alan standing in front of the house next to another man. He was aged in his late fifties or early sixties, with silvery-grey hair, and was wearing a dark suit with a matching waistcoat. His formal dress and distinguished, almost haughty bearing made him appear as incongruous a companion to Alan as I could possibly imagine. I wondered who he was.

I closed the album and put it back in the box and then returned downstairs. The fire was down to its last glowing embers and as it was getting late by then, I decided to let it go out, rather than stoke it up any further. I made a mental note to make it up again the following morning, ready for the next night, for it was chilly up on those downs in the evenings, I had discovered. I recalled seeing a log store at the back of the house.

In two minds as to whether to settle myself into the sofa with a book for the remainder of the evening, or continue my exploration of the house, I plumped for the latter option, and went to have a look around the cellar.

I flicked the light switch on the narrow stairwell and made my way down into the bowels of the house. It was a large cellar, which extended beneath the building's entire footprint. It seemed well maintained, and looked to have been recently painted, and was not at all the sort of dark and dusty basement one might have expected to find.

A central area with a quarry tiled floor and brick walls that had been painted white led off to various rooms, and I went into all of them. A couple were mere repositories for assorted items of junk and old furniture, and there was also a boiler room, and a narrow cloakroom containing an old-fashioned toilet with a high-level cistern. One room had been set up as a workshop, with tools hanging neatly from racks on the walls. In another room I found a small but impressive collection of wine, the bottles lying on their sides in bays cut into the walls that would have been designed for just such a purpose. I looked at some of the labels and mentally gave Alan top marks for taste, since they included some very good bottles indeed. Although I would continue to procure my own supplies, I might just have to avail myself of one or two of these bottles during the course of my stay, I thought.

The last room I went into was the largest, and about the same size as the bigger of the two sitting rooms on the ground floor, which it lay directly beneath. I switched on the light and somewhat to my surprise found that I was standing in a room that was completely empty, save for a large and rather threadbare rug covering most of the floor. The room was in as good a condition as the remainder of the cellar, with its clean white walls, and without a trace of dust, but it seemed curious that there was nothing at all in it, aside from a shabby rug.

On closer inspection, however, I noticed that there were hooks on the walls of the kind one would use to hang pictures. But where were the pictures? I recalled the locked room on the top floor of the house and wondered if Alan might have moved them in there for some reason, in advance of my arrival. There had been no sign of a collection of unhung paintings anywhere else. But if he had put them away somewhere, then why? And who hung pictures in a cellar, anyway? Were they perhaps lewd murals that he didn't want me to see?

Unsure why such a thought should have occurred to me, I was about to leave the room and go back up into the house, but some instinct made me lift a corner of the large rug with my foot.

It was enough to reveal two black painted lines forming a point and meeting a curved line. I pushed the rug back another few inches and saw a peculiar symbol painted between the lines. Intrigued, I rolled back the rug to expose the entire floor.

To say that I was taken aback by what I found would be a considerable understatement. I was both shocked and somewhat repelled.

A giant pentagram had been painted onto the tiled floor in neat black lines. It was the same five-pointed star set within a circle that I had seen on the tree in the woods, earlier that day, but on a much larger scale, and with a variety of strange symbols painted into the various sections of the geometric design. Some of them I recognised as shapes – there was an Alpha and an Omega, for example – even if I had no clue as to their purpose, whereas the others were a complete mystery to me.

I nevertheless realised, and not without a strong measure of distaste, that my once close friend was, at least on some level, involved in the occult, and it had been no coincidence at all that he had chosen to purchase this house that had once belonged to a notorious satanist. The precise extent of Alan's interest was unclear, and I had no way of knowing if this was all just some exotic parlour game to him, or if he took it much more seriously, but he was involved in something, of that there was no doubt. This discovery, together with the story that Keith had told me the night before, about the people wearing cloaks in the garden, proved that Alan had been far from honest when he had brushed off any suggestion of an active interest in such things. I wondered again about the missing pictures from the walls, and just what it was that they might depict.

Although I considered occult beliefs to be utterly stupid, I knew that they attracted some disturbed and even dangerous people. I hoped to goodness that Alan hadn't gotten himself involved with anyone like that, and that this was just an idiotic hobby.

Rather wishing that I had limited my explorations that night to the main part of the house, I manoeuvred the large rug back over the pentagram.

Just as I was about to leave the room, I heard a noise from outside. There were two small openings at the top of one wall that would have been designed to take ventilation and, during the day, a limited amount of natural light into the cellar, via gullies set into the flowerbeds. I had no doubt that it was from outside that the noise had come.

A moment later, I heard it again, the unmistakeable sound of footsteps on gravel. Somebody was walking across the driveway, and by the sounds of it, they were going towards the house rather than away from it.

I rushed out of the cellar and up to the hallway. Taking a deep breath, I flung open the front door.

There was nobody there. The driveway was empty, and the only sound was the wind rushing through the trees.

I closed the door again and locked it. My ears hadn't deceived me, I thought. There had been someone outside, and it was quite possible they were still somewhere in the grounds. I couldn't help but wonder if it was the same person I had seen spying on the house.

I decided to confront whoever it was, assuming they were still somewhere on the property. I went through to the kitchen, remembering that I had seen a torch in the drawer by the sink.

I pulled the drawer open and rummaged through it until I found the torch. It was small, little more than a penlight, but it would have to do. Then, as I closed the drawer and looked up again, I saw something that made me scream.

Standing outside the window, so close that his face was almost pressed to the glass, was a man. He was wearing a hooded top, so I couldn't make out his features, but he was definitely male. Suffice to say, he seemed rather less surprised to see me than I was to see him.

My equilibrium recovered, and now more angry than alarmed, I made as if to go out to the back garden via the door in the utility room so that I could confront him. But the man seemed to anticipate this, and moved off in the other direction, towards the west side of the house.

I turned and ran through into the dining room and unlocked the doors that led onto the terrace, catching a glimpse of the man running across it as I did so. By the time I got out there, he had reached the burial mound, which he ran up, and then after pausing to look back at me, he leapt from the top, over the fence that ran along the other side, and into the field. As I reached the top of the mound, rather less athletically than he had, I could just about make him out, running across the field, away from the house and towards the woods.

I watched him run away until he was swallowed up by the darkness.

CHAPTER EIGHT

Ernst von Draken

I slept poorly that night. The intruder in the grounds had been disturbing enough, but it was the pentagram painted onto the floor of the cellar that weighed more heavily on my mind. As did the possibility that the two things might in some way be connected, although I didn't see how they could be. I could only presume that the man in the garden had been a prospective burglar, although that didn't seem to tally with him being the same person who had been watching the house from the woods, since that person, having seen me in the garden the previous day, must have known that the house was occupied. So why would he be inclined to prowl around the garden at night? And because of the reputation of the woods for occult activity, and that wretched pentagram in the cellar, I couldn't help but wonder if there was some connection after all.

These thoughts swirled round and round in my head until, shortly before dawn, I fell into an uneasy sleep.

I was still thinking about it when I ate breakfast the following morning, perched at the island unit in the kitchen, although by that stage the man in the garden seemed like a more pressing problem than Alan's peculiar extra-curricular activities. I debated whether or not to contact the police – the man had been trespassing, after all – but I wasn't sure what good that would do, as he was long gone by now, and thanks to the hooded top he had been wearing, I wouldn't have been able to give them much of a description. I had looked over at the woods from the balcony outside Alan's room immediately upon getting up that morning, but there had been no sign of anyone, not that I really expected my intruder to have spent the night up there.

Since I have a well-honed ability to rationalise uncomfortable possibilities, by the time I had finished coffee I had just about managed to persuade myself that the intrusion of the night before had been nothing more sinister than an attempted burglary, which was unlikely to re-occur, now that I had made my presence in the house abundantly clear. I further persuaded myself that Alan's strange little habits were none of my business.

I decided to put it out of my mind and go to Avebury.

It was a grey, misty sort of day and the downs looked bleak and rather miserable as I drove the few short miles to the famous stone circle.

Unsurprisingly, since it was a weekday in late winter, there were only a handful of vehicles in the car park, and I stopped next to a ticket machine, from which I bought a day's parking permit. I then followed a path into the village and from there entered the vast megalithic site.

It was much bigger and more spread out than I had anticipated. In my ignorance, I had expected something much more compact, like Stonehenge, but the stones at Avebury were ranged over several fields, intersected at various points by a road, and with a long line of stones, which I subsequently learned was West Kennet Avenue, stretching off into the distance.

I wandered slowly around the complex, enjoying the peace and quiet, thanks to the sparse number of other visitors, and then walked to the end of the Avenue and back again. The stones, giant sarsens which had been dug up from the surrounding downland, moved here, carved into shapes and then buried upright in the ground, appeared almost impossibly large, and one could scarcely imagine how this place had come to be built, during such supposedly primitive and unsophisticated times, and the stupendous effort it must have taken. Somewhat to my surprise, I found it an awe-inspiring place, an effect accentuated by the dramatic scenery encircling it, particularly the long, high ridge overlooking it a couple of miles away, which I had learned from the book I had bought the day before was called the Ridgeway and was quite possibly the oldest known trackway in the world.

Perhaps it was the age of the settlement, or perhaps it was the mystery of why it had been built, but I was much taken with it all, far more than I had expected I would be, and I determined to learn more about it during my extended stay at Alan's house.

I made a modest start in this regard by looking around the museum in the village, after which I visited the bookshop where

I purchased two books, one on Avebury specifically, and another on the Neolithic and Bronze Age periods more generally.

It was lunchtime by then, but I was in no great rush to return to the house, so I ate a bowl of soup in a deserted National Trust café and then, having dropped my books off in the car, headed off down another track to Silbury Hill.

There was a light drizzle falling but this seemed to make the huge man-made mound of earth, sometimes referred to as England's pyramid, appear even more dramatic as it loomed up out of the murk. One wasn't permitted to climb up it, but one could get quite close to its base, and I took several photographs of the huge grass edifice. As with the stones, it was the scale of the endeavour that impressed as much as anything.

Then, with the skies clearing, I continued the short distance to West Kennet Long Barrow, a chambered burial mound that was even older than the standing stones of Avebury, and which made the barrow in Alan's garden look small by comparison. One could even go into it a short way, and I went into the dark space via its sarsen clad entrance and wondered if the tomb I was standing in resembled in any way the one that lay beneath the grass mound I now happened to live beside.

It was mid-afternoon by the time I returned to the house, planning to light the fire in the sitting room and curl up on the sofa with my new books, and possibly doze off for a while to compensate for my lack of sleep the night before.

However, as I turned into the driveway, I saw a car parked there. It was a sleek black Jaguar, the owner of which was stood with his back to me, looking at the burial mound.

As I got out of the car he turned around, and I immediately recognised him from the photograph I had seen the night before, of the man in the dark suit standing beside Alan in front of the house. He was older now, with hair that was completely white, but just as formally dressed as the man in the photo, wearing a camelhair coat over a grey pinstripe suit. It was unquestionably the same person.

"Hello," I said. "Can I help you?"

"I was looking for the owner of the house," he said, as he walked towards me.

"If you mean Alan Mackay, then I'm afraid he's not here," I said.

"I see," said the man. "When I heard the car just now, I thought it might be him. Do you know where he might be?"

"He's away at the moment," I said. "I'm looking after the house for him while he's gone," I added by way of explanation.

The man gave an audible intake of breath and raised his eyebrows at what was evidently unexpected news.

"In that case," he said, recovering his equilibrium, "You must forgive me for calling by unannounced. Alan is an old friend, you see, and I've not been able to contact him, these past few days. I happen to have an engagement near here this evening, and so I thought I'd drop in and make sure there was nothing wrong."

"That's perfectly alright," I said. "I haven't been able to get hold of him myself, as it happens. I think there must be something wrong with his phone."

"Yes, that must be it. I am Ernst von Draken," he added, rather portentously.

I shook his proffered hand and introduced myself. He had the most piercing blue eyes I had ever seen, and there was something haughty and overbearing in his manner, in addition to the theatrically antiquated way in which he spoke. I took an instant dislike to him.

"So, Alan has left you in charge," he said. "May I enquire where he has gone?"

"To America," I said. "He's in California. I understand he's producing a record over there."

"Really?" said von Draken, clearly taken aback by this revelation. "He said nothing to me about this."

"Well, that's where he is," I said. "He was kind enough to offer me the use of the house while he's away."

"That was very kind of him. And when will he be returning, may I ask?"

"Some time in December, so he told me."

Von Draken made no attempt to conceal his surprise.

"But that's quite impossible," he said. "He knows he has to be here for …"

He stopped himself, and continued: "What I mean is, I simply can't believe that he would absent himself from his beloved house for such a long period."

"Well, it would appear that he's done just that," I said.

"Alan always was full of surprises," said a tight lipped von Draken. "Forgive what might appear to be excessive curiosity on my part, but Alan is like a son to me, you see, and it's most unlike him to be uncontactable. I can only hope that he is fully well."

"I'm sure he'll be in touch soon," I said. "You've obviously visited here before, I take it?"

"Yes, a great many times. Alan is the most marvellous host. In fact, it was I who recommended that he purchase this house. You see, I was acquainted with the previous owner."

I processed the fact that Alan had told me yet another untruth, having claimed that he had come to live here by pure chance, following an impromptu visit to see the house once lived in by Dorian Slake. I assumed that this was the previous owner to whom von Draken was referring.

"You mean Dorian Slake?" I said.

"I do. I say, may I trouble you for a glass of water before I resume my journey?"

I figured that this was probably an excuse to have a nose around the house, and I had already had quite enough of Ernst von Draken for one day, but I didn't really see how I could refuse. He had also piqued my curiosity somewhat.

"Of course," I said. "Do come in. I can make you a cup of tea, if you prefer."

"Just water, thank you."

"No problem."

I unlocked the front door and disabled the alarm, and then beckoned him to follow me inside. But as I reached the kitchen I looked around and saw that he was still standing in the hallway, looking at the blank space on the wall where the painting of Slake had hung.

"Where is the portrait that hangs on this wall?" he asked sharply.

"It broke," I said.

"That is a very valuable painting," he said. "I would have expected someone put in charge of this house to have taken greater care with it."

"In that case," I said evenly, "You should address your complaint to the person who hung it there. It fell off its hook in the night, breaking the glass and the frame."

"I see," he said, appearing somewhat mollified by this. "You must forgive my displeasure. It's just that it's a painting that means a great deal to me. And to Alan. May I see it?"

"It's in Marlborough, being reframed," I lied.

"I can only hope that the framers attend to it with suitable care."

"I'm sure they will. Come into the kitchen and I'll get you that glass of water."

I noticed him looking around intently as we walked through the house, as if checking to see if anything else might be out of place. The way his eyes moved reminded me of a snake. For some reason, I couldn't help but feel uncomfortable in his presence.

He stood by the island unit, his eyes seeming to bore into my back as I poured a glass of water from the tap.

"So, you knew Dorian Slake?" I said, as I passed him the glass. "He sounds like quite a character."

"He most certainly was," said von Draken. "You have read up on him, I take it."

"Only a little."

"Well, I wouldn't put too much store in what you might read. It is the misfortune of a true visionary such as Dorian Slake to be misunderstood in his own time. I was lucky enough to know him for a short period, when I was a young man, and he made a very strong impression upon me."

There was a trace of reverence in his voice, as he spoke the words. I had deduced by then that von Draken likely had the same interest in the occult as Alan evidently did. I considered mentioning the pentagram in the cellar but chose not to. If von Draken didn't know about it, I didn't want to embarrass Alan by telling him; and if he did, I preferred to keep my own knowledge of it up my sleeve for the time being.

"I really wouldn't know," I said. "I know barely anything about the man, and have no interest whatsoever in his activities."

"I see. And yet here you are in his house."

"Here I am in Alan's house," I corrected him.

"Quite so. And possession is, as they say, nine tenths of the law. I shall leave you to enjoy the remainder of your stewardship."

He drained the glass, his eyes never leaving mine as he did so, and then he put it down on the counter with great precision.

"Well, as I said, I must be getting on my way. Thank you for your time. I don't suppose we shall have the pleasure of meeting again."

Hopefully not, I thought.

"As and when Alan gets in touch, I'll be sure to let him know that you'd like to speak to him," I said, as I opened the front door for him.

"Thank you, but that won't be necessary," said von Draken. "I can assure you, I shan't have any difficulty at all in locating him. Good day to you."

And with that, he strode briskly to his car, got in without bothering to take off his coat and drove away, affording me a curt wave as he did so.

As I watched him go, a thought occurred to me. Could von Draken somehow be responsible for the person who seemed to be keeping watch on the house, and who I had chased off the property the previous evening? Was today's visit some sort of follow-up to this, having established that someone other than Alan was in residence here?

As I went back inside, I felt a pang of concern about the sort of people Alan had got himself mixed up with.

What the hell are you into, Alan? I thought, as I walked into the kitchen, before something rather distracted me from these thoughts.

There on the counter, the glass that von Draken had set down with such exactitude, only moments previously, lay broken in a mess of small pieces.

CHAPTER NINE

More Visitors

Following the various incidents and discoveries of my first two days spent living at Badcombe Hollow, things settled down for a while after that. There was no further sign of the man in the woods, I didn't hear again from Ernst von Draken and Alan himself remained incommunicado. I was still intrigued, and not a little concerned about it all, but there was nothing I could really do, other than fret about it, and so I chose instead to put it out of my mind and enjoy my new life in the country.

In the two weeks following von Draken's visit, I established a routine that was usually the same every day. Each morning, after breakfast, I would sit at the island unit in the kitchen and work on the manuscript for three to four hours, typically writing somewhere between a thousand and fifteen hundred words. At this rate of progress, I would have the first draft completed by the summer, with several months still left ahead of me to revise it, before Alan's return.

After a light lunch, I would head off for a long walk in the surrounding countryside, sometimes going from the house, sometimes taking the car somewhere. Thanks to the mostly dry weather during this period – there was only one day when heavy rain kept me marooned in the house – I was able to cover some considerable distances; never less than five miles at a time, more often closer to ten.

These long, solitary walks were a source of great pleasure, as I became ever more familiar with the landscape of the Marlborough Downs, and the Vale of Pewsey to the south.

In those happy, early days, before things took a decided turn for the worse, I had a fine time wandering on the great plain, surrounded by so many vestiges of pre-history. I walked on the Ridgeway, going north to the ancient camp of Barbary Castle, and south to the intersection with the Wansdyke, another old trackway on yet another great escarpment. I visited Windmill

Hill, another part of the wider Avebury complex, the causewayed enclosure of which was older even than the great henge itself. I went to Oldbury hill fort, with its giant eighteenth-century white horse, cut into the chalk slopes above the village of Cherhill. And I spent a couple of afternoons merely wandering the narrow lanes that led from the house, bordered by hedgerows that were starting to come into leaf.

Typically returning home in the late afternoon, I would spend an hour or so revising my writing of that morning, and then after bathing I would cook myself a meal, after which I would retire to the sitting room with a book or a film, before taking myself off to bed at around midnight, and then getting up the next morning and doing the same thing all over again. I was as focused on my work as I could remember being for a very long time. I didn't even get around to reading up on Avebury, and the thick paperback novel I had gone out and purchased on the morning of my departure to Wiltshire, remained unopened beside my bed. All of my mental energy went into my work, and all of my physical energy went into my exploring my surroundings.

It was a solitary time, but I was more or less content. The strange events of my initial encounter with Badcombe Hollow started to recede from my memory, and I didn't bother to take up Keith the taxi driver's offer of an introduction to someone who had once worked in the fields around the house, back when Dorian Slake had lived there. I decided that I could care less about the peculiar occultist and whatever it was he had got up to within the walls of the house and beyond, sometimes in the company of Ernst von Draken, who I cared about even less. I didn't go down to the cellar again, and the pentagram on the floor lay undisturbed beneath its rug.

So, by the Monday following my second weekend in the house, I was well and truly established, and had only broken with my routine that morning in order to attend to some much-needed housework.

At around ten o'clock the front doorbell rang. I put aside the attachment I had been trying without success to fix to the vacuum cleaner and went to answer it.

An elderly man with a thick, bushy beard, and with a knapsack on his back and a large camera hanging around his neck greeted me.

"I'm very sorry to trouble you," he said, "But I wondered if I might take a closer look at your long barrow."

"My … long barrow?" I replied, in a bemused tone.

It felt like such an unusual question.

"Yes, if you wouldn't mind. You see, I'm doing a study of all the burial mounds in this area, and this is one of the last ones on my list, and there's a much better view of it from here than there is from the footpath."

"Oh, right, the barrow," I said. "Yes, of course. No problem at all."

The man seemed oddly delighted by my answer.

"Thank you very much," he said effusively. "I'd been led to understand that the previous owner wasn't too keen on people coming over to this side to look at it."

"Actually," I said, "The previous owner is still the present owner. But he's away at the moment, and I'm looking after the place for him. It's perfectly okay with me. Besides, what he doesn't know about won't hurt him, will it?"

"I'm very grateful," said the man. "You see, at this time of day, from the other side, not only is the fence in the way, but the sun is in my eyes as well. But from this angle, the light is absolutely perfect for a photograph."

"Yes, it's a beautiful morning," I agreed.

And the long barrow did look rather pleasing in the sunshine that day, I thought, as I glanced over at the mound of lush, green grass, with the clump of daffodils at its base now fully in bloom.

"I was just about to make some coffee," I said. "Why don't I bring one out to you?"

"That's most kind. I've been walking since before nine o'clock this morning. I'm staying at the pub near Avebury and head off in a different direction every day. A cup of coffee would go down very nicely indeed."

I left him to photograph the barrow while I went inside to make the coffee, which in truth I hadn't been planning to do, having only finished breakfast an hour previously. But I had experienced such little human contact over the past couple of weeks that I felt pleased to have some company.

By the time I returned outside the man was scrolling with evident satisfaction through the shots he had taken. We took our coffees onto the terrace and sat on the wrought iron chairs that were set around a timber picnic table. It was the first time I had sat out here since moving into the house.

"Do you mind?" said the man, taking a pipe from the folds of his coat.

"Not at all."

He introduced himself as Robert Cameron and told me that he was a retired history teacher from Southampton, with a passion for pre-history, who aspired to walk to every single burial mound in Wiltshire. I explained that I was an old friend of the owner of the house, which I was looking after while I finished writing a novel.

"Well, you seem to have picked a good spot to do that," he said.

"I certainly don't want for peace and quiet," I said, "But it sounds like a fascinating project that you've undertaken. Is that the sort of thing that you used to teach?"

"Oh, heavens no," said Robert, puffing on his pipe. "Pre-history is very little taught in schools, I'm sorry to say. Modern history was my particular area, delivered to a lot of bored sixth formers, most of the time. 1815 to 1945, to be precise. The Congress of Vienna to the end of the Second World War. Not that we'd ever get that far. Lucky to get them to the Russian Revolution, by the time the exams came around. Anyway, following a mercifully early retirement, I developed a curiosity for the more ancient past. And so here I am."

As he said this, he stretched his arms out, indicating the high plains around us.

"Of course," he went on, "Part of the reason it's so little taught in schools is because we know hardly anything about it. Nothing was written down in those days, so it's traditionally been the preserve of archaeologists more than historians."

"I'm only just starting to learn about it myself," I said. "But I've found it very interesting."

"Well, you couldn't be in a better place to start," said Robert. "There's more evidence of pre-history in this area than anywhere else in Britain. Or the world, probably," he added.

"What can you tell me about this particular piece of evidence?" I asked, nodding over at the burial mound.

"Badcombe Long Barrow? Not too much, I'm afraid. According to the archaeological record, it's either late Neolithic or early Bronze Age. So, it's about four thousand years old, and constructed around two thousand BC. It's the only barrow in this particular vicinity, so would probably have served a fairly small settlement, most likely in these fields somewhere, perhaps beneath the relative shelter of the escarpment.

"The people of those times were quite religious," he went on. "Even if not in ways that we would recognise today. But death and burial, and a desire to worship their ancestors, was very important to them. And of course, they were far more advanced than we tend to give them credit for. Just look at their constructions in this particular area – the great earth mound of Silbury Hill, for example, not to mention the effort they went to in extracting those enormous sarsen stones from the ground and erecting them at the henge at Avebury. They were incredible people, and yet we know only the tiniest amount about them."

"So, who would have been buried in this particular mound?" I asked. "I mean, in as much as we might have any idea about it?"

"We have some idea, but not much. We know from grave goods, recovered from other such burial sites, that it would probably have been the most prominent members of the community that were laid to rest in such a way. So, the barrow could contain a chieftain and his family. But it's never been excavated, so we simply don't know. But we only know the slightest amount about that whole period generally. It's largely a mystery to us. And what we think we might know is mostly educated guesswork."

"I'm kind of ashamed that I didn't know a bit more about it myself until a few days ago," I admitted. "This must be one of the greatest historic sites on earth, it's in my own country, and I've only just found it. It's lucky that it's been so well preserved."

"That wasn't always the case," said Robert. "In fact, a lot more of the site is visible now than it would have been only a hundred years ago. We have Alexander Keillor to thank for that."

"The man the museum at Avebury is named after?" I said.

"Yes. He lived at the manor, next to the church. Heir to a marmalade fortune, of all things, and one of life's great philanthropists. He used to own Windmill Hill, until he gave it to the nation. Did a lot of excavating around Avebury in the early twentieth century. Dug up a lot of the stones and put them back up again."

"Dug them up again? Why were they buried?"

"In times gone by," said Robert, "People weren't as conservation minded as they are now. Or as interested in history," he added. "You see, these fields around us might have been teeming with life once, a major crossroads and meeting point of the Neolithic world. I mean that literally, because this is where the Ridgeway crosses the Wansdyke. But by the time the Romans got here, its heyday had long since passed. Nobody knows why. The Romans built a camp up on the hill above Cherhill, where the old Iron Age hill fort was, and the rest of the area just went back to nature. The Romans weren't interested in it, and barely made any reference to it, or to Stonehenge, either; it was nothing more than a minor curiosity to them, all these carved stones poking up out of the ground. It was just some ancient, quirky foible of these primitive Britons whose country they had come to colonise.

"Then, later on, there was more and more agriculture in the area, and the stones were often in the way. Made it too difficult to plough the fields and neutralised some good farmland. So, a lot of the stones got buried."

"How on earth did they manage that?" I asked.

"Not as difficult as you might think," said Robert. "A lot easier than getting them put up in the first place, that's for sure. What they used to do is create a pit, next to the stone, and then they'd dig out the foundation, knock the stone over into the pit, and then cover it all up again. Keillor retrieved quite a few that had been concealed beneath the ground like that. But you need to know where to look, of course, and he did.

"Actually, in many ways, the people who buried the stones were unwittingly doing this place a huge favour. Being buried protected the stones; preserved them for future generations, like us. A lot of stones were smashed up and lost forever."

"You mean they were deliberately destroyed? Why?"

"Sometimes for religious reasons. Some of your more zealous Christian types in these parts didn't much care for pagan monuments in their midst. Or else, the stones got broken up and plundered for building materials.

"Anyway, what you see now at Avebury, impressive though it may be, is only a flavour of what would have been here before, and people are still trying to piece all the details together. Part of what makes it all so fascinating."

We chatted for a while longer, and then he bade me farewell and headed off on his way. As I watched him traverse the path across the field, I thought of what he had told me about the barrow, and imagined some high-born figure being laid to rest in there, thousands of years previously, and of a whole tribe of people living in what was now Badcombe Hollow.

That afternoon I had a second visitor.

Having decided after lunch that this was going to be a day for chores, I had chosen to do some work in the garden, rather than going for my normal afternoon walk.

The little brick garage at the end of the drive contained various items of gardening equipment, as well as Alan's car, wrapped in a tarpaulin. There was also a petrol lawnmower in there that I managed after some effort to coax into life, and I gave a light cut to all the lawns, presumably their first of the year, depositing the cuttings in a timber bay in the back garden, up against the high bank of the hollow. I then swept the paths and washed down the furniture on the terrace, which I had noticed was covered in bird droppings and other detritus when I had drunk coffee with Robert out there.

Just as I was finishing up and feeling quite virtuous after my day of housework and gardening, a small hatchback car entered the driveway. A woman got out and walked over to me.

"Hello," she said. "I was looking for Alan."

She was an attractive woman who I guessed was aged in her late twenties or early thirties, with long dark hair tied in a ponytail, and a face that glowed with a healthy sheen. Even in jeans and a thick sweater, I thought she looked pretty great, although I detected a trace of anxiety in her voice.

When I told her that Alan was away for an extended period and that I was looking after the house for him, she appeared visibly more relaxed.

"I'm Megan," she said.

"Richard," I replied.

"So how do you like living down here?"

"I love it. It's a great house, and a beautiful area."

"It is a wonderful area," she said, with obvious enthusiasm. "How do you spend your time here, when not tending the grounds, that is?"

"I'm writing a book. I'm about half-way through it."

"Oh, right. Fiction or non-fiction?"

"Fiction. It's a novel. But with some real stuff in it, so it's sort of semi-autobiographical. It's set in Paris, where I used to live. I was a journalist."

"But now you've mended your ways?"

"Something like that," I said with a grin, thinking that she had a nice way of speaking.

"And Alan's definitely away for a long period, right?"

"Yes, until Christmas. I hope you don't mind me saying so, but you sound kind of relieved that he's not here."

"It's that obvious, is it? Yes, I am really. Sorry, I probably shouldn't say any more, what with you being his friend and everything."

"Actually, I barely seem to know him, these days."

I explained how we had been close friends at university, but had then drifted apart, until our surprise reunion, three weeks previously, and how he had come to offer me the use of his house while he went to America.

"I see," she said. "Okay, well in that case, I might as well tell you, not that it matters now. We were involved for a little while. You know, we had a thing. Me and Alan. But it didn't really go very well, and when I went away to France, just after Christmas, we sort of left things hanging. I only got back the day before yesterday. I've been plucking up the courage to come over here and draw a line under everything.

"I hate loose ends," she added. "I mean, it was only a very short-lived thing, and we weren't really compatible, as it turned out. I kind of regret the whole thing, actually. He didn't mention me, did he, when you two met up?"

"You're not an archaeologist, by any chance?"

"Oh God, he did mention me. What did he say about me?"

"Hardly anything. He barely said anything about you. I think I asked him if he was involved with anyone, and he said something about seeing someone who was an archaeologist round here, and that it had sort of petered out, which was just as well, what with him moving to the States, etcetera. And that was really it. Seriously. No indiscretions at all."

"Okay, well, that's good."

Yes, I thought. It was good. It was good because I was guessing that Megan wasn't involved in Alan's more outlandish hobbies. And it was good because I thought Megan was one of the prettiest people I had ever met.

"Sorry to gabble on about it all, in that case," she said. "Mild case of euphoria."

"No worries. Would you like some tea?" I asked, willing her to say yes.

"Thanks, but I should really get going and leave you to get on."

"Nothing left to do," I said, letting the rake I had been holding drop to my feet.

We sat on the terrace, which was in full sun at that time of the afternoon, and which I was pleased I had spent some time cleaning up, prior to Megan's arrival.

She told me that she was a post-graduate archaeology student at Bath University, and that she was working part-time at the National Trust shop in Avebury while she finished her thesis, the subject of which was the ancient settlement on Windmill Hill.

"I'm so attached to this area," she said. "Everything about it is so fascinating. I'm from here, you see. I grew up in Devizes. My parents still live there. I got taken to see the stones at Avebury when I was a little girl, and I've been hooked ever since. I don't think I could ever get tired of this landscape. I think writing about it is just my way of getting to spend even more time here."

"Is that how you met Alan?" I asked. "Through a shared passion for the megalithic?"

"Yes, very much so. I can't imagine that our paths would have crossed otherwise. He had a very genuine interest in it all, and quite a lot of knowledge, as well. We met at a lecture at the visitor centre at Avebury, and it sort of went from there. Or didn't, as things turned out. I hope this isn't a reflection on me, but whenever we were together, he only really seemed to come alive when we were talking about archaeology. He's a bit of a strange one, that's for sure."

"So, what have you been doing in France?" I asked, keen to change the subject.

"I was at Carnac, on the west coast of Brittany. Biggest megalithic site in the world. It's a long way from Windmill Hill, different period even, but I got the chance to go and join a dig for six weeks, and I decided to take it. Good timing, really, because of the whole Alan thing. But it was fun, despite some pretty basic conditions. We stayed in huts, like a barracks, and it was freezing at night. But I enjoyed it."

"I've been to Windmill Hill," I said. "I went last week. Nice place. Had a job finding it, though. You barely know it's a hill, from the Avebury side."

"I know. It's very deceptive, isn't it? The gentlest of slopes up there, from this side, and then a big, steep scarp on the other. I love it there. And it's so important; the forerunner, in so many ways, of everything else around here. The first settlement. That we know of, anyway. So where else have you been?"

I told her a little of my excursions up to that point, and she seemed impressed at the range of my wanderings.

"Now you've got the overview, I'd try to focus in on one area," she said. "You know, really get to know it well. That's what I'd do."

"Anywhere in mind?"

"The east side of the Ridgeway is good," she said. "North of Overton. And there's a great swathe of country on the north side of Marlborough. The sarsen fields there are so beautiful, and very few people go that way, so it's lovely and peaceful. You could even walk there from here, if you went via West Lockeridge."

"That sounds good," I said. "Maybe you could show you around sometime," I added, a little clumsily.

She hesitated a moment.

"I think I should be up front and say that I'm really not looking to get involved with anyone at the moment," she said. "Sorry for being so direct about it."

"It was the last thing on my mind," I lied, back-tracking, and inwardly cursing myself for having over-reached with such a transparent conversational segue. "But I really do want to get to know this area better, so maybe I could pop in at where you work sometime, if I had any questions."

"Of course. Sorry. Didn't mean to sound over-sensitive."

"No problem."

"And I'd be happy to help," she added.

She looked at her watch.

"In fact," she said, "There is something rather special I could show you now, to get you started over in that vicinity."

"Oh, really?" I said, far more enthusiastic at the prospect of seeing some more of her, than anything she might have had in mind to show me.

"Sure, why not? Look, I've got to be in Marlborough for six, but what are you doing for the next couple of hours?"

"Absolutely nothing at all," I said.

CHAPTER TEN

The Devil's Dolmen

It was, as Megan had promised, a remarkable sight. From a distance it had looked like a mere jumble of stones, but as we had drawn closer it started to take on shape and form, and now, standing beside it, one was confronted by an immense piece of megalithic architecture.

A giant boulder lay as a capstone upon a cluster of upright stones, held there purely by its own weight, in a manner that looked impossible to achieve, like a great stone table, the top of which appeared as fragile and prone to collapse as could be, but which had nevertheless stood here for thousands of years. I thought it was one of the most incredible things I had ever seen, and yet here it was, in an otherwise unremarkable field, absent any other monuments of pre-history, innocuously residing beside a little used trackway. It was both understated and awe inspiring.

Although not a high structure, for one could reach up and touch the capstone, it impressed as much as anything because of its sheer bulk, and its presumed great weight, and the way in which the huge stone at the top seemed to balance so precariously on the tops of its supports. One could look through it, via a triangular gap between the stones in the middle, and as I walked around it, I noticed that it had a strikingly different appearance from each angle, one of which made the capstone look like a reptilian head, mounted upon lichen covered shoulders of stone.

"What is it?" I asked Megan.

"It's called the Devil's Dolmen," she said.

"What's a dolmen?"

"It comes from a Breton word – *taol maen*. It means stone table. It's when you get a large, flat or flattish stone, supported by upright stones."

"But obviously not built as a table for giants," I said.

"No. It's a tomb. Or rather, the entrance to a tomb. They call these portal tombs, portal meaning doorway. That's the doorway."

"What do you mean?"

"See the gap through the stones, from this angle. Roughly triangular shaped? That's the doorway."

"Doorway to what?"

"To the afterlife. For people to pass through on the way to the afterlife. The people who were buried here."

"But if that's the entrance," I said, "Where's the tomb?"

"We're standing on it. There was a huge barrow here once, but it got ploughed out, long ago. Now, all that's left is the dolmen, but it's quite something, isn't it? The only dolmen in the whole Avebury area, and hardly anyone even knows it's here. And yet it may well be the most impressive megalithic monument in this part of Wiltshire. I thought you'd like it."

"I most certainly do," I said. "Thank you for bringing me here."

We had left the house in two cars, with me following her along the maze of country lanes, watching the bob of her ponytail as she led the way. After joining the Marlborough Road, we had turned off again after a short distance, following a long access road that led steadily upwards, and then went past some stables before terminating in a car park on a high ridge, with some grand views to the west. Avebury would have been just a few miles away in that direction, but out of sight, on the other side of the Ridgeway.

We had set off along the pathway, heading north, and with Megan playfully refusing to let me know what it was that we had come to see.

"It's about a mile or so's walk," she said, "Down in that valley beneath us. A place called Clatford Bottom. There's something very special down there. But I'm not going to tell you anything about it yet. I want you to see it for yourself first. I hope you don't mind."

I didn't mind at all. Megan, I had discovered, in the very short time that I had known her, was rather a delight to spend time with.

We followed the hard track for a while, and then turned off onto a barely defined, grass path that led down into a valley, and from there into the field with the dolmen in it, where we were now standing. We were surrounded by downland, containing not a trace of civilisation, save for an old brick barn a few hundred yards away. It was a beautifully remote spot that I would have been much taken with in any event, even if I hadn't been so distracted by the person who I was sharing it with.

"And from here," she said, pointing towards the desolate plain that lay to the north, "There are endless possibilities, in terms of places to go and explore. Just a few fields from here, there's a wonderful, rocky sarsen valley that sits in the lee of the Ridgeway, where they dug up the stones to build Avebury. Or just keep heading north. There's loads to see up there. Alternatively, follow that path by the hedgerows over there, and you cross the road, and eventually end up back at your place."

"I'll do that sometime," I said. "I'll certainly come back here again."

There was something infectious and appealing about her unabashed enthusiasm.

"So how long has it been here?" I asked.

"These sort of tomb entrances are typically early Neolithic," said Megan. "Say, 4,000 to 3,000 BC, so five to six thousand years old."

"It would have been an amazing feat of construction, to get that massive stone perched up there," I observed.

"I'll say. According to local folklore there have been several attempts to tear it down over the centuries – a considerably easier task, one would have thought – but nobody ever managed it."

"Why would anyone want to dismantle it?" I said.

"Various reasons. Utility – these things were massively in the way for farmers who needed to plough these fields. And superstition, of course – the desire to destroy something people in times gone by would have seen as un-godly and un-Christian. That went on a lot around here. Many of the standing stones you see today at Avebury got tipped over, and buried under the ground, and it was only in the early twentieth century that that they got stood up again. At least, those ones that hadn't been broken up and carted off to use as building materials."

Her words were an echo of what I had been told by Robert that morning, but I didn't want to interrupt her in full flow; not when it was such a pleasure to listen to her.

"People actually did that?" I said, trying to sound incredulous. "That seems like such an act of vandalism."

"You're looking at it from a twenty-first century point of view," she said. "But in the Middle Ages, and beyond, people would have had a very different opinion about places like this. They had their churches to worship in. They didn't need standing stones."

"How do you break up stones like this anyway?" I asked. "I mean, way back then?"

"You basically dig out the foundations, and create a big pit next to the stone, and then you just tip it over. Once it's lying in its pit you set fires around it, to heat the stone, and then pour cold water over it. When you do this, it makes the stone crack, which means it can be broken up into smaller pieces.

"Fortunately," she went on, "Most of the stones were just buried, rather than broken. So, the medieval period farmer who buried a stone on his land to make way for crops, was inadvertently preserving these monuments for future generations."

"You know, a walker I met this morning said the very same thing to me," I said. "About seeing things with twenty-first century eyes, and about how people at one time wouldn't have cared very much at all about any of this.

"Until Keillor came along," I added.

I'm trying to impress her now, I thought. Possibly not the best idea with a post-grad archaeology student.

"Well, Keillor was important, certainly," she said, soberly, very much the academic now. "Although if he hadn't come along when he did, I'm sure someone else would have, eventually. But he wasn't the first pioneer, by any means. John Aubrey was researching this area back in the seventeenth century. He even got Charles the Second interested. And then William Stukeley came along a bit later and carried on the good work. You should check out all the drawings he did. You can find them all on-line, and we sell a lot of them as prints, in the shop. They're very stylised; there's a lot of artistic licence, but they're still great artefacts. So there have been a few enlightened people associated with this place, over the years, but you're generally right; properly looking after sites like this, respecting them, is a relatively recent thing."

"And this place is called the Devil's Dolmen" I said, nodding towards the giant rocks.

"Yes," she said. "Or sometimes," she added, pointing at the rough triangular gap beneath the capstone, "The Devil's Doorway. You see, some people believe that whilst the souls of humans used to pass through that door after death to the afterlife, so the Devil himself would use it as a way of entering our world.

"But that's just local folklore," she continued. "There's masses of that around here, particularly in relation to this site. According to legend, the Devil sometimes shows up here at night with eight oxen and tries to pull the dolmen down, and all the while a white rabbit, with burning coals for eyes, sits on the capstone, directing operations."

"Why would the Devil want to destroy his own doorway?" I said.

"Good question. Folkloric tales aren't always very consistent. And God knows where the rabbit fits into it. Climb up and look at the top of the capstone."

"Why?"

"You'll see. Just do it."

I was happy to oblige. I would have stood in that field for the rest of the day if she had asked me to.

I scrambled up the base and peered across the top of the capstone.

"What do you see?" she said.

"Lots of little hollows in the surface," I replied.

"Well, according to one of the legends about this place, if you pour water into any of those holes at night, and then come back in the morning, it will have been drained dry. By a demon. I always meant to try it."

"Nice little story," I said as I hopped back down onto the grass beside her. "Got any others to tell me?"

"There's supposed to be a black dog that guards it at night, protecting his long dead master. But that's not an uncommon story about burial mounds, or other sacred spots in the landscape. They're often said to have dog protectors. Maybe the mound in your garden has one."

"I've not encountered it yet," I said, as I made another slow perambulation around the dolmen.

"This is certainly an inspirational place," I said. "It makes me want to write about it."

"Actually, that reminds me. Thomas Hardy wrote a short story about these stones in 1881. It's called 'What the Shepherd Saw'. Another ghost story."

"I'll look it up," I said. "I can see why you find this place so appealing."

"Oh, I'm not all that interested in the folklore, really," she said. "I mean, it's part of the story, and it's fun to tell you about, but I don't believe in things like that. These sorts of tales are interesting, because they teach us about what people believed in the past. But there's more than enough real history here for me. Such as who used to live here. You see, someone dowsed this site, back in the 1950s, and found masses of water under the ground. There could have been a whole settlement in this area that we don't even know about yet.

"My next project, after I finish with Windmill Hill," she said.

"Well, thank you for bringing me here," I said. "I shall come again."

The light was starting to fade by then, and so we walked back. I had enjoyed my time with Megan and was sorry it was coming to an end. By the time we reached the cars I had persuaded her to swap telephone numbers, ostensibly for the purpose of enabling me to ask her questions about the area and its history.

We'll see about that, I thought to myself. I kind of thought she might have been thinking the same thing. And I was more than okay with that.

We said goodbye, and I watched her drive off down the narrow lane. Then I returned to the house in a better mood than I had been in for a very long time.

CHAPTER ELEVEN

The Portrait

Two days after Megan's visit, I was about to set off for Marlborough to buy groceries when I remembered the broken Slake picture. Although I had no great desire to see the portrait hanging up again, I knew that I would have to get it fixed sooner or later and decided that I might just as well do it now.

I went into the study to fetch it but as I picked up the badly damaged frame the whole thing collapsed in a mess of broken wood and glass. Cursing loudly and wishing that I had left the wretched thing where it was, I went to fetch a dustpan and brush to clear it all up.

What was left of the frame was in such a parlous state that I decided to dismantle the whole thing. I carefully removed the last pieces of jagged glass and eased the picture out. It was an oil painting applied directly onto a board and there was a mark around the perimeter showing the outline of the frame that the repairer would be able to follow.

I slipped a small piece of the frame into my pocket in order that it could be matched and went to find something to put the picture in, returning from the kitchen with a large plastic carrier bag.

As I was about to slide the gloomy portrait of the occultist into the bag, I noticed some writing on the back. Mildly intrigued I carried it into the kitchen, cleared a space on the island unit and lay the picture face down.

Set in a neat block of dense black script, applied in a felt tip pen, was a bewildering series of numbers.

There was nothing else marked on the back of the painting to indicate what they might mean, and at first sight no obvious pattern or sequence to the numbers. It appeared as nothing more than a set of random, meaningless figures.

I was about to put the picture into its bag and think no more about it, when some old journalistic instinct made me decide to copy the numbers for future reference. I opened my pad and wrote down the numbers exactly as they appeared on the back of the painting.

100685149763103699086715103677116668
189693112634099699152696118649047693
066647156656118681125708225668196629

Looking at the numbers again, I was still unable to deduce anything from them. There were the same number of digits on each line, I noticed. Thirty-six digits on each of three lines; one hundred and eight in total. But they could have meant anything.

Yet another little curiosity, I thought as I put the picture in the bag and left the house.

When I arrived in Marlborough, I went first to the framing shop.

"Yes, we can do that," said the elderly proprietor, holding the picture out in front of him.

He had a goatee beard, and a pair of horn-rimmed glasses dangled from a chain around his neck.

"Are you sure you want to use that type of frame, though? A thicker frame might look better around a dark oil painting like that."

I explained that the picture wasn't mine, and how it had come to break whilst in my care, and hence the need to restore it to its original condition.

"In that case," said the man, "We'll use an identical frame, and your friend will never be any the wiser about what happened to it.

He worked out a price for the re-framing that made me wince a little, but as I didn't really have a lot of choice in the matter, I agreed to it, and arranged to collect the repaired painting in a few days' time.

With this chore out of the way, I headed off into the town. Since I was in no great rush – oddly, or not, ever since meeting Megan, I had found it difficult to concentrate on the manuscript – I bought a newspaper and went into a café to read it over a cup of coffee.

Afterwards, on the way to the butchers, and in keeping with what had become by then a very leisurely morning, I passed by a charity book and record shop, and decided to pop in.

A young woman with very pale skin, and wearing a vivid tie-dyed shirt, and with her head stuck in a book, looked up at me briefly, and then went back to her book. I was the only customer in the shop.

I browsed around for a while and picked up a couple of paperbacks and a CD. It was while I was paying at the counter, the woman having temporarily set aside her book with a marked lack of enthusiasm, that I noticed the flyer behind her head.

It was an advertisement for a concert in Bath, not much more than thirty miles away, by someone whose name was very familiar to me.

Pete Taverner had been the bass player in Alan's band, and aside from Alan, the band member I had got on with the best. He had been the least wild, most even natured and grounded of them all. I knew that he had pursued a solo career since the band split up, but whilst our paths had crossed a few times since losing touch with Alan, I still hadn't seen him in years.

The concert was taking place that night. I decided to go. If I could get to speak to Pete afterwards, it might be a chance to find out a bit more about Alan and his mysterious behaviour.

There was a number for the venue at the bottom of the flyer which I tapped into my phone and, gathering up my purchases, I went outside to make the call.

I got through almost immediately and was pleased to discover that there were still tickets available. I bought one on my credit card, and then had a sudden idea, and asked for two tickets instead.

This accomplished, I dialled the number that Megan had given me.

"Hi," I said when she picked up. "I hope I haven't called at a bad time, or anything?"

"No, it's fine. I'm outside the shop on a break. What can I do for you?"

Whilst imagining her soft features and glossy ponytail in the courtyard outside the Avebury visitor centre, I explained about the concert that night, and then asked as casually as possible if she might like to come with me.

There was an agonising moment's hesitation at the other end of the line.

"It's a bit short notice," she said, as if playing for time while she decided.

"I know. Sorry about that. Did you have plans this evening?"

"I rarely have plans. It's just that I did say the other day that I wasn't really interested in going on any dates at the moment."

"This is definitely not a date," I said, even though, as far as I was concerned, it most definitely was.

"No?"

"No. Emphatically not."

After a little more cajoling, I persuaded her to go with me.

CHAPTER TWELVE

An Evening in Bath

It was about an hour's drive to Bath along the back roads. I picked Megan up in Marlborough, outside a grand old building where she rented a room. I had been looking forward to seeing the bob of her ponytail again, but she was wearing her hair long that evening. She still looked pretty damn good, though.

"Looks like a nice sort of place," I said as we drove away from the ivy clad mansion set behind its high brick and flint wall.

"Isn't it, just?" she said. "Real touch of the gothic. It used to be a rectory. I got put onto it by one of the girls in the shop. It's a great big rambling old house, and the owner's away a lot, so I often get the run of the whole place. It's a bit pricey, but I don't mind paying a bit more for character. I love old places. I mean, I could go and live with my parents in Devizes for free, but I much prefer being here on the plain, surrounded by everything."

"You really love it up here, don't you?" I said, looking over at her as the countryside flashed past us.

"Yes, I really do," she said. "I love the vastness and the wildness of the plain. And I love the feeling of walking in the footsteps of our ancestors from thousands of years ago. I don't think I'd ever want to be anywhere else. Not for long, anyway."

"I walked to the dolmen from the house, yesterday," I said, hoping to impress her.

"Good for you. How was it?"

"It was good. It took a while, to walk there and back from the house, but it's a nice walk."

"Try going north next," she suggested. "Drive to the place we went, and then just head north along the main path until you feel like coming back. There's some lovely, empty country up that way."

"I'll do that," I said. "Look, about tonight; I'm quite keen to speak to this guy, after the gig, if possible. And if that's okay with you," I added.

"Of course. No problem. You've probably got a lot to catch up on."

"Actually, it's less that, and more about wanting to find out a bit more about Alan."

I told her something of the peculiarities that had led to me coming to live at Badcombe Hollow; about how the timing of Alan's offer had seemed so contrived, and almost too good to be true; how I had found out about him checking up on me, weeks before our supposedly impromptu reunion; how nobody seemed to know anything about his studio project in California; and how he had lied about having someone else lined up to look after the house who had dropped out at the last moment, but who, it transpired, had actually died ten years previously. I didn't tell her about the pentagram in the cellar, or the watcher in the woods, or my suspicion that Alan may have developed an unhealthy curiosity in the occult, and in his house's erstwhile owner. But I did tell her about the visit of Ernst von Draken.

"He sounds like an unlikely sort of person to be friends with Alan," she said.

"I know," I said. "The way he told it, his relationship with Alan is more of a father and son kind of thing, or mentor and pupil, or something. He certainly didn't seem very pleased to find me living in Alan's house. And very surprised, too, that Alan wasn't there."

"It almost sounds as if Alan's disappeared deliberately," said Megan.

"Feel free to tell me it's none of my business, but I don't suppose you picked up on any unusual behaviour when you were with him, did you?"

"No, not at all. At least, not that I can think of. I mean, we didn't know each other for all that long, and all I really discovered during that period was that he seemed to be more interested in local history than he was in me. He seemed to be picking my brains, a lot of the time."

"About Windmill Hill?"

"No, not so much. He was more interested in the place I took you – the Devil's Dolmen. He was particularly keen to find out more about the folklore surrounding it, not that he really needed me to tell him about that; he could have looked it all up."

How fitting, I thought but didn't say, that Alan should have expressed an interest in that particular site, with its demonic connections.

"What about the barrow in the garden?" I asked. "Was he interested in that?"

"Not especially. Not that I noticed in conversation with me, at any rate. Mind you, there's very little known about that particular barrow. It's one of those that's always rather perplexed the archaeologists. So, there's not much I could have told him about it, even if he had asked me."

"And he never said anything about getting back in the music business?"

"No. That definitely never came up. But I will say one thing, though."

She waited a beat.

"Now you mention it, he was a bit preoccupied about something," she said at last. "Yes, I did get a sense of that. Like he had something of great importance weighing on his mind. But that was just my intuition. He never said anything to me about it. If you're going to ask your friend about him though, after the concert, can you do me a favour?"

"Of course."

"Can you not say anything about me and Alan having been an item? It was such a short-lived thing, and I'm kind of embarrassed about it now."

"I won't mention it. We may not even get to speak to Pete, anyway."

We arrived in Bath just as it was getting dark. We had plenty of time to spare so rather than try and find somewhere to leave the car in the centre of town, I went instead to the large park by the Royal Crescent, and we walked to the venue from there.

Bath was a place I knew reasonably well and liked very much, and it turned out that Megan felt the same way about it, and so we enjoyed our walk down into the town, chatting happily to each other as we passed through the grandiose settings of the illuminated parkland, and then the tall stone edifices of the Georgian streets.

The concert was in a subterranean nightclub beneath a high, raised pavement, right in the heart of the city. I had been here before, although not for many years, but it didn't seem like it had changed much in the interim.

Nor had Pete, I thought, when he walked onto the stage, carrying his guitar loosely by his side, and leading his troupe of fellow performers. He still possessed the kind of lean and hungry looks that had briefly, and rather to his disdain, made him such a pin-up, back when Alan's band had been so successful.

As the lights dimmed, Megan flashed me a smile, and I detected a frisson of girlish excitement which I found immensely appealing. Right then, finding out more about Alan seemed supremely unimportant, and I was just glad to be there.

The band played for over an hour and they were very good. Pete had been the bass player in Alan's band, but he had subsequently switched to lead guitar, at which he had always been proficient, even back then. He had been the most accomplished musician in the band, even if Alan had been its creative inspiration, and I was pleased to discover that he had lost none of his instinctive talent in the intervening years. He even let rip with a couple of excoriating solo pieces. The ovation at the end of their set was loud and heartfelt.

As people started to drift off, I motioned for Megan to follow me through to the backstage area, where we were confronted by a powerfully built bouncer, although he had a friendly demeanour.

"Sorry, no visitors backstage," he said, all smiles and beefy forearms.

I explained that I was an old friend of Pete's and asked if he would pass on the message that I was keen to speak to him.

"Wait here," said the man, disappearing behind a curtain.

He returned with a bemused looking Pete in tow, but then when he saw me, he smiled broadly.

"They told me it was you, but I couldn't quite believe it," he said. "Richard. Bloody hell, it has been a long time."

"Too long," I said as we shook hands.

"This is my friend Megan," I said.

"Pleased to meet you, Megan."

"Hi. Great concert. I really enjoyed it."

"Well, thank you very much. So, what brings you all the way down from London?" he said to me. "You didn't come all this way just to see me, surely."

"Actually, I'm living down here now," I said. "Temporarily, at any rate. Near Marlborough. The last I heard, you'd moved to Devon."

"Still there. My enchanted little valley by the sea. You'd never get me out of there, now. Apart from the odd excursion like this. We're on a tour. Well, small tour. Just a couple of weeks in the West Country, but that's as much as I can take, these days, before I have an overwhelming desire to get back home."

"I enjoyed your album," I said, referring to the solo work he had done after Alan's band split up.

"Thanks. I should probably do another one, but I don't really want to do all the stuff that comes with it. You know, all the bullshit. I just like playing, these days, having fun and earning a bit of pocket money. Then I bugger off back to Devon. You know Alan lives down in these parts, don't you?"

"I know. It's actually where I'm living at the moment. I'm looking after Alan's house while he's in America."

Pete seemed rather taken aback by this.

"You're at Alan's?" he said incredulously. "I mean … well, I haven't seen Alan in years. I knew he lived out this way, but we haven't been in touch for a long time. I tell you, coming out here and seeing you standing there, I got a real *déja vue*. It was weird. Like old times. I almost expected to see Alan standing next to you."

"Have you got time for a drink?" I asked.

"Most definitely. There's a pub up on the pavement above us. Meet there in about ten minutes?"

A short time later we were ensconced at a corner table in the crowded pub. I had forgotten what an engaging companion Pete could be, and after catching up for a while, he brought Megan into things by asking her lots of questions about Avebury.

"We've played there," he said. "Couple of years ago. Festival of the Stones. We're going back this summer. You guys should come along."

"That sounds like fun," said Megan, glancing briefly at me, and making my heart give a little flutter as I contemplated the prospect of Megan and I going there together. In the summer. Months hence. As an item.

I made a silent wish.

After some further talk about Pete's musical career in the time since I'd last seen him, and my attempt to cease being a journalist, and to become a novelist instead, the conversation turned to the subject of Alan.

"So, he's gone back into the business, has he?" said Pete. "I've got to say, that surprises me. I would never have thought that. I really thought he'd left all that behind for good."

"When did you last see him?" I asked.

"Best part of ten years ago, I should think. It was after he moved down here, but we met up in London, with the rest of the band. It was a business meeting. The record company wanted to do a greatest hits album. Actually, they wanted us to re-form and do a tour, but there was absolutely no chance of that happening. Alan didn't need the money, and the rest of us didn't need the grief. We let them put out the album, but there was no way we were re-forming; absolutely no way."

"How come?"

Pete stared down at his drink for a moment before replying.

"How much do you know about the band splitting up?" he asked.

"Not much. It was after Alan and I fell out and lost touch, so I only know whatever was on TV or in the newspapers. It was played as a relatively amicable split, with people going off to pursue their own creative interests. I take it the reality was somewhat different?"

"Very different. It was all down to Alan, basically. But look, I probably shouldn't be saying any of this, what with you and him being friends again, and you living in his house."

"Funny you should mention that," I said.

I told Pete what I had related to Megan on the journey over; about my unexpected reunion with Alan, and the other revelations that had flowed from it, although I left out the part about Ernst von Draken.

"So, you're definitely not speaking out of turn," I said. "In fact, I'm quite keen to find out a bit more about it."

"Fair enough. Well, it all kicked off around the time of the third album. You remember the theme of that album? And the cover?"

"Yes. A deliberate echo of the occult themes in heavy metal in the 1970s, and just in case anyone should be in any doubt, the album cover had a giant burning pentagram on it. It came up briefly in conversation with Alan when I met him recently."

"And I presume he told you it was all bullshit, a gimmick and a marketing ploy by the record company, etcetera."

"Something along those lines."

"Well, it wasn't. I mean, for the rest of the band, it was nothing more than a bit of fun. A joke, you could say. Not a very funny one, in hindsight, but definitely not something to be taken seriously. Except for Alan, it was."

An image of the pentagram in the cellar flashed through my mind but I kept the thought to myself.

"You see, for the rest of us, it was just wearing a costume; we were play acting," said Pete. "And I think it probably was for Alan too, at first. But then he started to take it all much more seriously, and before long, it was like the occult was all he was interested in. Do you know, he actually wanted us to take part in a séance? Seriously. We were all supposed to go to some house in Bayswater and sit in a circle and hold hands, or something. I mean, you remember what we were like. Can you really imagine the rest of us doing something like that? We just pissed ourselves laughing when he asked us to do it, because we thought it was a joke, but he was deadly serious. Looking back, I think that moment was the beginning of the end. It was when he realised that this was something he was going to have to get into on his own, without us."

He paused, and took a sip of his beer.

"It was also around that time that he got really into astrology. Well, fair enough, I've got nothing against it. But it got to the stage where he was consulting these weird astrological charts before he made decisions about stuff. He even wanted to arrange the band's schedule around it. God, we ripped the shit out of him over that. But he was very serious about it. And all sorts of other occult stuff, as well. I even heard he got some goat symbol tattooed on his back, but I never saw it. Anyway, by that time, we were pretty close to splitting up. We'd just had enough of it all by then. And don't forget that we had much more incentive to keep the band going than he did. He owned most of the royalties, so he was set up for life. The rest of us made most of our money from touring. But we didn't want to work with him anymore. And then the old man was the last straw."

"The old man?"

"Well, I say old. Back then, he might have been in his middle fifties, and that's not really very old these days, is it? But he seemed old to us, plus he had this silver-white hair, and he dressed very formally. He was always wearing a suit, camel hair coats, that sort of thing. Not your average heavy metal band hanger on."

Ernst von Draken, I thought.

"He was into the occult in a very big way," said Pete. "He became a sort of mentor to Alan. He was living in Greenwich then; nice place by the river, and this guy was living there with him. Used to come and go as he pleased, and he treated Alan like a servant, not that he seemed to mind. It was like he was in awe of the guy. He had a real hold over Alan.

"They were always going off to places together. Or we'd be rehearsing over at Alan's house, and this guy would waltz in carrying an old book under his arm. He was a rare book dealer, apparently. That's how Alan met him. Anyway, they'd have to go off right that minute and look at it together. It was like the rest of us didn't exist. But then he totally looked down on us all. I'm sure that he turned Alan against us, as well. Things weren't very good by then anyway, but he was definitely the catalyst that tipped it all over the edge.

"He was called Ernst something, believe it or not. I can't remember his second name. It was something similarly foreign sounding. But he was certainly English, and he had a very upper crust sort of accent. I think his family were refugees from Hungary or somewhere, after the war. I remember Alan telling me something about that. I can't remember his name, though. I think it was von Bulow, or something."

"Von Draken?" I said.

"Yes, that was it. Von Draken. You don't know him, do you?"

"He turned up at the house, the other day. Looking for Alan."

"No shit. Those two are still close then."

"They are the way he told it. Except Alan obviously failed to mention that he was going to America, so maybe they're not. He didn't seem very pleased when I told him he'd be away till Christmas."

"Poor old Ernst. He must have been a bit miffed to hear about his protégé jumping ship like that and striking out on his own."

"It does all seem rather peculiar," I said. "And you haven't been in touch with Alan at all, these past few years?"

"Barely. Not face to face, at any rate. I gave him a call a couple of years ago, when we were coming to play that gig at Avebury. I thought he might like to come and watch us, what with him being just down the road, but he said flat out he had no intention of coming and wasn't even interested in music any more. I was a bit put out, to be honest. Anyway, that was the last time we spoke."

We talked about other things after that, until it was time to leave. When Megan excused herself to go to the bathroom, Pete took me to one side.

"Look, I didn't want to say anything before," he said, "But if I seemed a bit surprised when you told me about living in Alan's house, it was just because of that whole feud between you, after that article about the band came out. I didn't realise he had it in him to bury the hatchet like that."

"He made out that it hadn't been such a big deal," I said. "That we'd just fallen out of touch."

"That's not what it seemed like, back then. I mean, the rest of us couldn't have cared less. We actually liked it. It made us out to be much more dangerous and exciting than we really were. But it became a real thing with Alan. That man seems to have an infinite capacity to bear a grudge."

"In that case, why the sudden rapprochement, and why the generosity in lending me his house? Which is a pretty bloody nice house, as you can probably imagine. It doesn't make any sense."

"I know," said Pete. "A lot of what you've told me about him doesn't make sense, including him going off to America to produce an album. I'm going to make some enquiries about that. If I find anything out, I'll let you know."

"Thanks," I said, and we exchanged telephone numbers.

"It's been good to catch up again after all these years," I said. "I'll definitely come and see you play at Avebury in the summer. Come and stay at Alan's, if you want."

"I don't know," said Pete. "It might not go down too well with the rest of the band. We're usually in pubs or B&Bs. They might think I was getting fancy on them."

"Then bring the band, too."

"What would Alan think about that?"

"What do we care?" I said, and we both laughed.

Later, on the journey home, Megan and I discussed the conversation with Pete, and I raised the subject of Alan's seeming interest in the occult, whilst leaving out some of the more lurid details, like the pentagram in the cellar.

"An interest in the occult doesn't necessarily need to be sinister or malevolent," said Megan. "I mean, it might seem a bit nutty to those of us who aren't into it, but it doesn't have to be evil with a capital E. You get white magic. You know, wiccans and modern pagans and all that kind of thing. We get a lot of those sorts around Avebury, especially during crop circle season. They always seem a bit out there, but essentially harmless."

"I suppose so," I said. "It may be that Alan's into something like that. I just hope he hasn't got himself into anything more serious."

"Not much you can really do about it if he has," she said.

"True enough. I guess I'll just forget about it until he comes back, and then have a long chat to him about it. Or not."

"By the way," she said, "He never gave me any clue that he was into anything like that. In case you were wondering," she added.

"I wasn't," I said. "I've come to the conclusion that Alan plays his cards pretty close to his chest."

"Mind you," she said, "Pete was right about that goat symbol on his back."

"Really? How do you … oh, right."

"It didn't do anything for me," she said. "I can't stand tattoos."

"I don't have any."

"I'm pleased to hear it."

We smiled at each other in the darkness of the car. I decided that I didn't want to think about Alan when it so pleasant to be thinking about Megan. I felt in a good mood as we drove the remainder of the journey in companionable silence, surrounded by the desolate plain, and I felt even better when, as I dropped her off in Marlborough, she agreed to come to the house for supper that Friday.

So, it was only marginally deflating when, on getting home and walking across the driveway, I looked over at the woods and saw there was a light up there again.

Evidently, whoever it was who liked to lurk about up there was back.

CHAPTER THIRTEEN

Pursuit in the Woods

The day after the concert in Bath, I decided I should get back to work. I sat down at the island unit in the kitchen immediately after breakfast and applied myself for over four hours, producing a more than acceptable two thousand words. I went for a short walk from the house after lunch, as it was a beautifully sunny spring day, and I needed to get the fug out of my head, but as soon as I returned home, I got straight back into it, and wrote another thousand words. By the end of the afternoon, as the shadows were lengthening, I was going over the day's output and feeling pretty virtuous when my phone rang.

It was Pete.

"Great to see you again last night," he said.

"Likewise," I said. "I really enjoyed it. So did Megan."

"Cool. Look, I rang about Alan. You know, following on from our conversation last night. I've found something out."

"Oh, really?"

I had barely given Alan a second thought that day but now he came charging back into my consciousness.

"Yeah. It was the thing about producing another band's album. That just didn't ring true to me, given his complete lack of interest in the whole profession these days. Also, producing? Really not Alan's forte, believe me. I mean, don't get me wrong, he was a good songwriter, but he's no producer. It's a very different sort of skill, and he definitely doesn't have it.

"Anyway, I still have a few contacts in the business, so I called my old agent, and got him to call the agent of the band he told you he was going to produce for, and guess what?"

"What?"

"He'd never even heard of Alan Mackay."

"Shit. That was a complete lie then."

"And not the only one he told you, by the sounds of things. But it's very strange. What do you think he's up to?"

"God knows. I don't even know where he is. He hasn't answered his phone since I saw him off at the airport."

"And that was a flight to America, I presume?"

"Yes, to Los Angeles. I saw him go through security, so he couldn't have faked that. But all we know from that is that he went to LA."

"From where he could have gone anywhere in the world," said Pete. "Maybe he's on some kind of retreat, or detoxing or something."

"It's possible, I guess. I did wonder about that. It wouldn't be the first time."

"What are you going to do?"

"I don't know. Nothing, I suppose. Not look gift horses in mouths. The book's going great, the house is free, and I've discovered that I like living in the country. Also, this time tomorrow, I'll be preparing dinner for the lovely Megan."

"Worth staying put then, I'd say. But take care of yourself, and if we don't speak before, I'll see you when we come down in the summer."

I went out to the garden to think.

Alan's whereabouts and motives were now a complete mystery. Almost everything he had told me, from our reunion onwards, had been a lie. His reasons for asking me, someone against whom he had apparently held a decades' long grudge, to live in his house, were utterly inexplicable. It was almost as if he had set me up in some way, and I had walked straight into it.

And yet, here I was, and everything I had said to Pete about how I enjoyed living here, about the book going well, and my pleasure at meeting Megan had been true. I was in no mood to leave, and with the flat in London rented out, and my finances in the parlous state they were, I had nowhere to go anyway. Alan had enticed me here, and in a sense, had made me his prisoner, albeit in a very gilded cage. But why?

I trudged around the garden for the best part of an hour, playing the whole thing over in my head, and trying to make some sense of it all. I got nowhere.

Before going inside, I mounted the long barrow. It was almost dusk by then, and the sun was like a red ball, hanging low in the sky above the woods.

I heard a soft thud on the grass beside me and looked down. A dead bird was lying on the mound. Another one. It was a small wood pigeon, and it must have expired only moments before, falling from the sky and missing me by a matter of inches.

Instinctively, pointlessly, I looked up. The skies were clear, and I knew that there were no overhead power cables anywhere in the immediate vicinity. So why should three birds, in less than three weeks, happen to fall dead upon this particular spot? It simply didn't make any sense, and it forced me to contemplate something far more disturbing than the myriad peculiarities about Alan.

Was it possible that Badcombe Hollow, and the area around it, was in some way cursed? Were the rumours true? Could that be what was causing dead birds to fall from the sky? Had Dorian Slake put a curse on this place? Or had Alan?

I told myself that such thoughts were ridiculous. There were no such things as curses. Just people stupid enough to think that there were.

I was about to pick the bird up to dispose of it when something on the near horizon caught my eye. Standing at the edge of the woods was the figure of a man, looking towards the house.

My watcher was back.

Suddenly angry, I made a snap decision. Alan's machinations might be a mystery to me, and there was nothing I could do about dead birds falling all over the lawn, but someone obsessively watching the house, day and night, was within my power to deal with, or at least to confront.

Stepping off the mound, I went down to the road and from there onto the footpath that led across the field to the woods. Feeling the sort of intense irritation that I hadn't known since being married to Marianne, I was determined to have it out with this person, whoever he was.

As I started along the path, I had every expectation that the man would melt away into the woods, but he remained standing there until I was at least halfway across the field. On account of the hooded coat he was wearing, I was unable to make out his features.

As I drew nearer, he turned and stepped into the woods. I quickened my pace to a trot in the hope of closing the distance between us, and not lose him in the dense thicket. By the time I reached the perimeter of the wood, I was breathing heavily.

It was dark in the woods. The sun had almost set by then, and everything was in thick shadow, the small copse suffused by an all-pervading gloom. There was no sign of the man.

I stood still and strained to hear where he might be. Almost immediately I heard the rustle of undergrowth a short distance away and set off at a run in the direction of the sound. Weaving through the trees, I moved as fast as I could until I reached the top of a small rise, where I stopped to catch my breath and look for the man. I couldn't see him; nor could I hear him.

Cursing to myself at the thought that I had lost him, I continued on through the wood, and before long I stumbled across the narrow path that led to the clearing. For want of a better option, I set off in that direction, hoping that the man was doing the same thing, and this was the reason I could no longer hear him crashing through the foliage. The thought also occurred to me that the man could have hidden himself along here, and was waiting for me to pass, before either doubling back towards the house, or pouncing out at me.

In other circumstances this might have made me pause, but anger and adrenaline kept me moving.

I reached the clearing where Slake had killed himself and continued along the path on the other side. It was then that I finally caught sight of the man, walking ahead of me. I fell into step behind him and then he passed around a bend in the path and I lost sight of him again.

Quickening my pace, I rounded the bend and saw the man in the near distance. I thought I had closed the gap on him a bit, although he was still moving briskly along the path. It was a small wood, and I knew that at this pace we would soon reach the other side.

Then the man suddenly stopped and turned around, and I instinctively stopped as well. For a moment the two of us just stood there, staring at each other through the gloom. The man's face was mostly obscured by the hood of his coat, but I instinctively believed this was the same person I'd seen up here at night with a torch, and the same person I had caught snooping around the garden.

Feeling unnerved by the way in which he was just standing there, seemingly waiting for me to approach him, and now acutely aware that I was alone with a strange person in a dark wood, I steeled myself and started to walk slowly towards him.

I got to within about ten feet, so close that I could hear him breathing heavily through the hood of his coat, when he turned and bolted off through the undergrowth.

Emboldened by his flight, I set off in pursuit, the two of us crashing noisily through the dense thicket of trees. But he was faster than I was, and I could sense him pulling away from me again.

I felt the woods become lighter, and realised we must be reaching the far perimeter, where I knew there was a farm track that led back to the road. As he dipped out of sight down a slope, I wondered if he had a car parked there, and moments later, just as I reached the edge of the wood, I heard an engine cough into life.

I emerged from the trees a few feet from the car, just as he drove away. The spin of his wheels sent a cloud of dust and gravel into my face.

I stood and watched him drive off at pace down the track. I had been only seconds from catching up with him, and now he had got away.

But I had managed to read the car's number plate.

CHAPTER FOURTEEN

Haunted House

I dreamt about the woods that night. I was running through the undergrowth, just as I had the previous evening, but in an inversion of my pursuit of the man who had been watching the house, this time it was me who was being chased. After what seemed like ages, I found myself in the clearing where Dorian Slake had killed himself, beside the tree with the pentagram burnt into it. Rivulets of blood were running down the trunk, and when I put my hand on the pentagram, it came away bloody. And then I was back at Badcombe Hollow, and it was dusk, and I was staring at the burial mound, where someone was standing, looking out across the field towards the woods. It was a woman, but I couldn't see her face, because she had her back to me. She had long dark hair and was wearing some kind of animal skin. I approached her across a lawn that was soaked with dew and littered with the corpses of dead birds. I ascended the side of the mound, expecting her to turn around, but she kept her back to me, and was seemingly fixated by something in the woods. As I drew within a few inches of her I saw that her hair was wet, and I could smell the damp fur of her cloak. I reached out towards her, and just as my hand made contact with her shoulder, I woke up.

I lay there in the semi-darkness of the dawn, feeling an odd mixture of relief that it had only been a dream, and regret that I hadn't seen the woman's face. Then, deciding that I was unlikely to get back to sleep, I got up and went downstairs.

As I drew the curtains in the sitting room I saw that there was a heavy mist outside, so thick that I could barely see beyond the boundary of the garden. I looked over at the burial mound, recalling the woman in the dream who had stood there. I rarely remembered dreams, but this one had been different. It had been vivid, real, frightening, and I still felt unsettled by it.

Maybe this place is starting to get to me, I thought.

Remembering that Megan was coming for dinner that evening, and with much to do, I decided to capitalise on my early start.

Two hours later, with the sun streaming in pale shafts across the garden as it burned off the mist, I was eating breakfast after a sustained bout of housework, and feeling like I'd got a massive head start on the day. I decided to go and do what I needed to do in Marlborough before it got too busy, but I knew that I had a telephone call to make first.

Darren Summers was a private investigator from London who I had employed a fair bit over the years, back when I had been a tabloid journalist. He operated in that grey area between what was strictly legal and what wasn't, which made him an excellent source of information. He also owed me a fairly large favour, thanks to my not helping the police with their enquiries, so to speak, a few years back; something that had almost got me into quite a lot of trouble myself.

It was still relatively early, and I guessed he was at home, because I could hear the sound of children's voices and a television in the background.

"Richard," he said, "Long time no speak. What are you up to these days?"

I told him a little about my current circumstances, and the book I was trying to finish.

"Must feel a bit quiet down there, after Paris and London," he said.

"It is," I said. "But I like it. I think I could even get used to it. How's business?"

"What business? Nowhere near enough of it, basically. It doesn't help that your old profession's walking on eggshells at the moment, after all the recent misdemeanours. It's unfortunate that my working life is coinciding with one of this country's periodic fits of morality. Not good for business at all. I'm even doing the school run these days, that's how much time I have on my hands."

"Sorry to hear it."

"Things will pick up eventually," he said. I heard him light a cigarette. "People have short memories. They'll get over it. So,

what can I do for you today? You're not going to offer me work
are you, by any chance?"

"Sorry. Just a small favour, if you were able."

"Oh well, at least it's nice to feel wanted. What do you need?"

"I need you to trace a car, if possible. Dark blue Ford Fiesta.
Just to see if there's anything on the owner."

I gave him the registration number I had memorised the night
before, and then repeated to myself like a mantra all the way
home, so as not to forget it.

"Should be straightforward enough," said Darren.

"Well, if you have a moment, can you look up someone called
Ernst von Draken? About seventy or a bit older, rare book dealer,
probably lives in London."

"Ernst von Draken. Sounds like a villain in a Bond film.
What's his story?"

"I'm not sure yet. Maybe nothing. I just need the basics.
Where he lives, if possible, and whether he's got a record."

"Consider it done."

"Thanks. Much appreciated."

"If you hear of any real work, let me know. The way things
are going, I might have to get a proper job."

"Heaven forbid," I said, before hanging up.

I headed off to Marlborough. It had turned into a fine day by
then, and I was in a good mood as I drove along the pretty country
lanes.

In town I went first to the picture framing shop, to collect the
Slake portrait in its new frame.

The proprietor lifted it onto the counter, and I immediately
recalled how much I disliked this moody self-portrait of an
occultist. The framer had done a good job, and I paid the bill
while it was wrapped up in corrugated cardboard and brown
paper.

Depositing the portrait in the back of the car, I went off to buy
things for my dinner with Megan. Even the thought of shopping
for the meal caused me a frisson of excitement and anticipation.
I hadn't felt this way for a very long time, and I was determined
to make a success of the evening. With that in mind, I didn't
exactly stint on the provisions, even if I had just spent what felt
like a small fortune getting that wretched picture fixed. I bought

smoked salmon, a brace of partridges, and the fixings for an apricot stuffing that Marianne had taught me to make. I also bought the two most expensive bottles of wine I could find, even though I was still well stocked back at the house – a white Chateauneuf du Pape, and a Pomerol.

Might as well go the whole hog, I thought.

Once I'd got home and put things away, I carried on with the housework. By the early part of the afternoon, satisfied that the house was as spotlessly clean as it was ever going to be, I set about preparing the dinner. Finally, by the time of Megan's arrival shortly after six, the partridges were ready to go in the oven, I had bathed, lit the fire in the sitting room and the wood burner in the snug, and set the table. I don't think that I had ever before put so much effort into a dinner date.

Megan arrived carrying a book.

"Avebury Beyond the Myth," I said, reading the title as she passed it to me. "Thank you. But you really shouldn't have."

"I wanted to say thank you for taking me to the concert the other evening," she said, shrugging herself out of her coat. "And for tonight, of course. It's excellent. I've read it a couple of times. It's a very good overview of the whole place, without going into too much complicated detail."

"Should be perfect for me then," I said.

"Plus, it has pictures," she added.

"That always helps," I said. "Anyway, thank you. And welcome. I'm glad you could come."

"Me too," she said, holding my eye for a moment.

I felt a delicious flutter in my stomach. The evening ahead was looking very promising indeed.

****

Dinner went as well as I could have hoped, and Megan seemed suitably impressed. The white Chateauneuf perfectly complemented the smoked salmon, as did the Pomerol with the stuffed partridges.

Megan was a delightful companion; bright, charming and amusing. Plus, she looked heavenly in the candlelight. If I thought I had been moderately attracted to her before, I was on the verge of being completely smitten with her by then.

"You are a little treasure," she said as I brought pudding to the table; a compote of raspberries and blueberries on a meringue base. "Someone should snap you up."

"They should," I agreed. "But really, it was a pleasure to cook a meal like that for a change. It's been a while."

"Where did you learn to cook like that? In France?"

"Yes, mostly. From my ex-wife. She went to some fancy cookery school in Paris when she was a teenager. She never took it up as a career, but she was very much at home in a kitchen."

"Do you miss her?" Megan asked.

"God, no. She was a nightmare to live with. Or I was. Maybe we both were. Anyway, I think it was just one of those things that wasn't meant to be. Not very much to tell, really."

I had no wish to relate to Megan the details of the end of my marriage, not when the person sat across from me was so much more interesting, and especially when that person was leaning towards me over the table in such a way that I could see the cleavage of her breasts, and which was making the candlelight dance across the gold chain around her neck.

After dinner I tried to persuade her to go and relax by the fire while I made coffee, but she insisted on helping to clear away the dinner things, and then we found ourselves in the kitchen, loading the dishwasher and chatting like a domesticated couple.

"Have you been buying art?" Megan said as she noticed the Slake portrait, still in its protective wrapping, propped against the wall in the corner of the room. Unpacking and re-hanging it had been the one thing I hadn't gotten around to doing that afternoon.

"No, it's Alan's," I said. "I broke it, so I had to get it fixed. Except I didn't break it. It broke itself. It fell off its hook on my first night here and the glass and frame broke. So, I had to get it mended. I picked it up this morning."

"Did you use the framing shop in Marlborough?"

"Yes, the one in the high street."

"They're good. A bit expensive though."

"Tell me about it. It's a portrait of Dorian Slake," I added.

"Dorian who?"

"Slake. You know, the famous occultist who used to live in this house."

She looked at me blankly.

"You mean, you've never heard of him?" I said.

She shrugged.

"Should I have done?"

"No, I suppose not. I mean, I hadn't heard of him until Alan told me about him. He didn't mention him to you?"

"Not that I remember."

"Well, famous might be overstating it a bit, but I thought he'd be fairly well known about in this locality."

"He may be, but not by me. I'm Neolithic girl, remember? If something didn't happen at least four thousand years ago, I'm unlikely to have registered it. So, Alan bought the house of some occultist. I suppose I shouldn't be surprised, after what we were talking about the other night. No wonder he wanted to live here."

"Yes, although that's not the way he explained it to me. According to him, he heard about this place because of Slake, but it wasn't what drew him to buy it. Now, I'm not so sure."

"The plot thickens," said Megan. "Shall we hang him up again?"

It was the last thing I wanted to do, as I was much keener to get Megan beside the fire in the sitting room, but she seemed intrigued by the picture, and I was happy to humour her, and so I hefted the heavy package onto the island unit.

"Not the most cheerful looking person," she said as I removed the paper and cardboard to reveal the face of the occultist. "I do vaguely remember this painting, as it happens, but Alan never said anything about it, the couple of times I came here. I thought it was some ancestor, or something. What did you say he was called?"

"Dorian Slake."

"Right. What do you know about him?"

"Not much. Apparently, he was a disciple of Aleister Crowley."

"I've heard of him," said Megan. "Devil worshipping guy, right?"

"Yes. Well, anyway, he bought this house after Crowley died in the late 1940s and tried to set up some sort of commune for occultists. To continue his late master's work, I suppose. But I don't think he was very successful. Going by what Alan told me, he lost his mind and hung himself in the woods on the other side of the field. In 1965, not long after he painted himself.

"It's a self-portrait," I added.

"Oh, yes," said Megan. "DS. 1964. How very creepy. Have you been over there?"

"Over where?"

"To the woods. The place where he killed himself."

"Yes, a couple of times. There's a big old beech tree in a clearing there, with a pentagram burned onto the trunk. I think it's probably the tree he hung himself from."

"Yuck. That's even creepier. I think I'd find it just a little bit unsettling, living in his house. But it probably explains a bit about Alan."

"Yes," I said. "Though not in a very good way."

"No, not in a good way, I agree. So, are we going to hang him back up, or not? Sorry, bad choice of words."

"We can do. I left the hook in the wall."

Accompanied by Megan, I carried the painting out into the hallway, and hung it in the vacant patch of wall by the stairs.

"Level?" I asked Megan over my shoulder.

"Down a little bit on the right."

"How's that?"

"Perfect."

I stepped back so that I was standing beside her, and we looked at the painting in silence for a moment.

"Maybe he'll feel a bit happier, now that he's at home," Megan quipped.

"I'm just glad it's somewhere I don't have to look at it very often," I said as we walked back into the kitchen.

Just as I was putting the coffee on there came the sound of a loud thud from the hallway.

"I don't believe this," I said, as I went out there.

The picture had come off its hook again, even if I didn't see how it could have done. It was lying on its side on the floor, thankfully not broken.

"Nice work on that hook," Megan said from the doorway to the kitchen. "I'm guessing you're not so adept at DIY as you are at cookery."

"Alan's handiwork, not mine," I said. "Although I am rubbish at DIY, as it happens, and more than comfortable with my inadequacy. It must have slipped off, somehow. At least it didn't break this time."

I went over to the hook in the wall and tried to jiggle it in my hand, but it appeared just as solidly fixed as it had before. With great care, I hung the picture back on it.

"There you go, Dorian," I said under my breath. "Try not to fall down again."

I finished making the coffee, which we carried through into the sitting room. There was a pleasing crackle to the fire, and everything felt beautifully warm and snug. Megan sat down next to me on the sofa, so close that our shoulders were touching, but neither of us made any move to sit further apart.

"How about some music?" she said.

"Sure. What do you feel like listening to?"

"I know Alan's got a great collection."

"Like a record shop. He's got very varied tastes, as well. Highly eclectic."

"The last time I was here, he showed me all these records and CDs he had in a little room upstairs. I guess they're still there?"

"They are. I've been working my way through them."

"Well then," she said, setting down her coffee cup, "Why don't I go and see if I can pick something suitable for the occasion?"

She put her hand on my knee as she pushed herself up from the sofa, and I felt a tremor of excitement.

I heard her go up the stairs and sank luxuriantly back into the soft cushions. Right then, and despite all my well-rehearsed misgivings about coming to live here, life seemed pretty damned good; as good as it had felt for a very long time.

But as these thoughts were drifting pleasantly through my mind, there came a crashing sound from the hallway, so loud that I half-jumped out of the sofa.

I dashed out there to find the Slake portrait, not lying on the floor beneath its hook again, as I had supposed, but beside the opposite wall, which it had seemingly struck with sufficient force to smash the glass and break the frame. It was as if someone had flung it across the room.

"What was that noise?" I heard Megan call out from upstairs.

I was momentarily too dumbstruck to speak.

This, I said to myself, is simply not possible. How did that happen? It couldn't happen. It just wasn't possible. Pictures didn't fly off walls.

I might have stood there, perplexed by these thoughts, for a very long time, if it hadn't been for what occurred next.

From upstairs came the loudest, most piercing scream I had ever heard in my life. Followed by another, and then another, in rapid succession.

It was Megan.

Just as I was about to rush up there, she appeared at the top of the stairs, which she then ran down, so fast that she lost her balance at the bottom and fell into my arms.

"What is it?" I said.

She was as white as a sheet and there were tears streaking her face. Her whole body was trembling violently.

"There's someone in the house!" she shouted at me.

"What?"

"There's someone upstairs. Some woman. There's some crazy woman in the house!"

CHAPTER FIFTEEN

Decisions

"What?" I shouted.

"There's a crazy woman up there," Megan shouted back at me.

"What do you mean? There can't be. What are you talking about?" I said.

Megan was gripping me so hard that her knuckles were white. She tried to say something but could only manage a strangled moan. She was clearly terrified.

With some difficulty I manoeuvred her shaking body to a chair by the front door and sat her down in it.

"Tell me what happened," I said, kneeling beside her.

She made a visible effort to get control of her emotions, and then looked directly at me. There were fresh tears in her eyes.

"There's someone in the house," she said.

"There can't be. That's impossible."

"There is. She must have been upstairs the whole time we were having supper. She attacked me."

As she said this, she cast a fearful glance over my shoulder and up the stairs.

"But that's not possible," I said, even though I couldn't help looking around.

"I know what I saw," she snapped at me, with anger blazing in her eyes. "I'm not making this up. There's someone up there. They must have broken in while we were having supper, or something. Jesus Christ, I can't believe there's someone in your house. We've got to call someone."

"Hey, take it easy," I said.

I tried to pull her into my arms to comfort her, but she pushed me away.

"How can I?" she shouted. "There's some mad old woman in your house, and the fucking bitch attacked me. What are you going to do? We should call the police. Where's the phone?

You've got an intruder in the house. We have to call the police. Right now. You have to call someone. She's probably some psycho. She looked crazy. She might have escaped from somewhere."

"Wait a second," I said. "Look, if there's anyone up there …"

"What do you mean, if? I told you what I saw. How can you not believe me?"

"I do … I mean …" I stammered, not knowing what to say.

"She's up there," said Megan fiercely, almost spitting the words. "Go and see for yourself."

"I will. I'm going up there now to check it out," I said, trying to sound much calmer about the whole thing than I actually felt. "What I was about to say was, the person upstairs doesn't have any way out of here, other than down those stairs. So, whoever is up there … well, they're contained; they're not going anywhere."

"What the hell do you want her contained for?" she snapped.

It seemed like she was angrier with me now than she was frightened about whatever it was she had seen upstairs, but I figured that was probably a positive development, because she seemed calmer, less hysterical.

"I mean, she can't get away," I said. "Before I go up there, tell me exactly what happened."

"Okay," she said, drying her eyes with the back of her hand. "But then you have to call the police. Okay, so I went upstairs; I was going to the little trunk room with the CDs in it. And it was really dark up there, and I couldn't remember where the light switch was, so I'm reaching around for it …"

"Wait," I said. "Do you mean you were in the trunk room, or were you out on the landing?"

"Out on the landing. I never got into the room. I was out on the landing, and I was reaching around for the light switch, and then something grabbed my wrist."

She shuddered at the memory before continuing.

"Somebody's hand grabbed my wrist. And I screamed, and then it pulled me towards them, and I saw its face. It was a woman, with a horrible face, and dark straggly hair, like an old hag; and her face was just a few inches from me, and she sort of snarled at me."

"Snarled at you? What do you mean?"

"I mean she growled like an animal. Who the hell is she, Richard? What are you going to do?"

"I'm going to go up there."

"No! Don't be stupid. Just call someone."

"I have to go and look for myself."

"Why?"

"I just do."

"I don't want to sit down here by myself."

"It'll be okay. I can't not go up there. You'll be fine. To get down here to you, she'd have to go through me, and that's not going to happen."

In fact, I was seriously spooked by then, and much less confident about going upstairs than I was trying to sound. I think what I found most unsettling was not so much the thought of confronting some deranged old woman but wondering how long she had been up there. Had she really broken into the house that night, or was it possible that she could have been there ever since I arrived, hidden away on the top floor somewhere, and maybe wandering around the house during the night, while I slept?

"It'll be okay," I said again.

Megan looked as unconvinced as I felt.

I went and stood at the foot of stairs and stared into the darkness at the top.

"Hey," said Megan from behind me. "What happened to the picture? Was that the noise I heard when I was up there?"

"Yes," I said, still looking up the stairs. "It broke again. I don't know how it happened."

"That doesn't make any sense," she said.

"No," I said. "It doesn't."

None of this makes any sense, I thought, as I started to walk up the stairs. I felt truly afraid. If Megan hadn't been there, I'm sure I would have fled from the house. I might have even driven back to London.

Once at the top of the first flight of stairs, I reached for the light switch, half-expecting a hand to emerge from the darkness and grab me. But this didn't happen, and I flicked on the light.

There was nobody there.

Feeling more frightened than at any time since childhood I made my way tentatively into each room. As I did so, I switched on the lights, and then left them on. I went first into my room, and then Alan's, then the other two bedrooms, and then the two bathrooms, all of which were empty.

I looked anxiously at the door to the staircase that led up to the second floor.

It was closed, and I thought that I had left it open, but I couldn't be sure. I knew that I was going to have to go up there, but for some reason I was finding it hard to make my feet move.

"What's happening?" I heard Megan call out from downstairs. "Is everything okay?"

"I'm fine," I shouted down to her. "There's nothing here. I'm going up to the top floor."

Taking a deep breath I turned the handle to the door, which opened with a gentle creak. I looked up at the pool of blackness above me and remembered there was a light switch by the door, which I groped around for, not taking my eyes off the stairs in front of me. The click of the switch sounded unnaturally loud in the silent house, but I was relieved that it illuminated an empty flight of stairs.

Now for the hard part, I thought, as I stepped onto the first tread of the staircase.

It took a real physical effort to get me up there, and my legs felt heavy, and my heart was pounding in my chest as I slowly mounted the steps.

After what can only have been a matter of seconds, but which felt much longer, I reached the top and looked down the brightly lit corridor. I pushed open the door to the first bedroom, a room I hadn't been into since I first arrived at Badcombe Hollow and found it to be just as empty as it had been on that day. The second bedroom was likewise devoid of any presence, other than my own, as was the bathroom.

Finally, I came to the door to the locked room, the interior of which was starting to interest me rather more than it had when I first saw it, but it was still padlocked shut.

Breathing a little easier, I went back down to the first floor and did a more thorough search, looking under the beds and in the wardrobes. I checked the little balcony outside Alan's room. I then went back up to the attic floor and searched it again, although there were fewer potential hiding places up there. I also checked the windows on each floor, all of which were closed, and locked from the inside.

I returned downstairs. Megan was sitting in the chair where I had left her. She was still visibly upset.

"Nothing," I said. "I looked everywhere, but there's nobody up there."

"But that's not possible," she said. "I know what I saw. I know what grabbed my hand up there. I saw her face."

"I know," I said, sitting down on the bottom step of the staircase. "It isn't possible, I agree."

"I didn't make it up you know," she said, with anger in her voice again.

"I believe you. But there's nobody up there, so I can only assume that you … well, that you …"

"That I what?"

"That you saw a ghost," I finished.

There was a long silence.

"I don't believe in ghosts," said Megan.

"Neither do I. Or at least, I didn't until about ten minutes ago."

"And now you do?"

I shrugged.

"How can I not?" I said. "I mean, something happened to you up there, and it obviously can't have been human. Look, I can hardly believe that I'm saying this, but there must be some sort of paranormal explanation; for what happened to you, and for that picture flying off the wall and smashing."

"You think the two things are related?"

"I think they must be. The picture smashed a few moments before you saw whatever it was that you saw. So maybe the person, thing or whatever it is broke the picture and then went up and confronted you. Jesus, I can't believe I even said that. It's just so bizarre. But I can't think what else it could be."

"But if she broke the picture, how did she get upstairs and into that room before me? I was already upstairs when the picture broke."

"Good point," I said. "So, in that case, maybe the two things aren't connected. Except it feels like they must be."

I sighed deeply, and shook my head in bewilderment at everything that had happened in the house that night.

"We know that Alan is heavily into the occult," said Megan. "Do you think this could be something he conjured up, either deliberately or inadvertently? I also can't believe that I just said that, but do you think that might be possible?"

"It could be," I said. "It could be something Alan did, or Dorian Slake, back when he lived here. You see, it's not the only weird thing that's happened since I came here."

"What else has happened?"

I told her about the dead birds I had found on top of the burial mound, and how a glass in the kitchen had smashed, seemingly of its own accord, immediately after the visit of Ernst von Draken.

"None of that makes any sense either," she said.

"Nope," I agreed, staring down at the floor. I could barely believe I was having such a conversation. It was bizarre, surreal, laughable even, and yet in that moment, frighteningly real.

"Also," I said, "I'm fairly sure that someone has been watching the house. Although in this case, we're definitely talking about something human."

I told her about the person who had been prowling around up in the woods at night, and the intruder in the garden, and the man watching the house from the edge of the field, all likely the same person, and about my chase through the woods of the previous evening.

And then I told her about the pentagram painted onto the floor of the cellar.

"Jesus Christ," said Megan. "Anything else you're not telling me?"

"No. That's everything."

"I don't know how you sleep at night. I don't know how you can even stay here."

"I don't really have a lot of choice," I said. "This is where I live at the moment. But I think I might be leaving all the lights on tonight."

It was a depressing thought. And despite my shock at recent events, and the feeling of utter confusion that I was experiencing, not to mention suddenly having to come to terms with a newfound belief in the supernatural, I was still more than a little crestfallen that my chances of a night of romance with Megan appeared to have nosedived. In fact, Megan seemed pretty pissed off with me right then, for having invited her into my haunted house of horrors.

Not surprisingly, she left soon afterwards. I tried to persuade her not to, suggested that she was in too much shock to drive, that she should at least stay and have some coffee, but to no avail. She was genuinely shaken up and I could tell that she wanted nothing more than to get out of there.

She was sweet about it all, of course, her anger with me having eased somewhat, and as we walked to her car, she thanked me profusely for supper, and promised to be in touch soon. But I knew that the increasingly intimate mood that had been growing between us had essentially evaporated, snuffed out by some crazy spectral bint that Alan had seemingly invited into his house.

I was feeling somewhat deflated by it all, to put it mildly, although it was at least keeping my mind off the fear.

I watched her drive away, and then continued to stand there, tracking her progress across the vast moonlit plain, until the lights of her car eventually disappeared from view.

I turned and looked over at the lit windows of the house, not relishing the night that lay ahead, so different to the one I had planned.

But in that moment, I made a resolution.

I was going to get to the bottom of this. If it was the last thing I did, I was going to get to the bottom of this.

Because I knew that on some level Alan had played me by getting me to come and live here. And whilst I might have had no idea about why he had done this, I was absolutely determined that I was going to find out. I might have been stupidly lured into this little web of his with my eyes wide open, but now I needed to take the initiative. I had once been a journalist, after all. Investigating things was something that I could do. And I was going to find out what was happening here; with Alan, with the house, and with all the other strange things that seemed to be associated with this place.

And in order to do this, I was going to have to go right back to the beginning, to the catalyst for all of this, and the reason why Alan had moved here.

I was going to have to start with Dorian Slake.

PART TWO

DORIAN SLAKE

CHAPTER SIXTEEN

The Life of an Occultist

Dorian Slake was born on 15th January 1920, in the coastal town of Torquay in Devon. His father was a minor industrialist who had started out with next to nothing and then became very wealthy in the years leading up to the First World War. His mother, by contrast, was the daughter of a baronet, and from one of those families that was far less well off in 1918 than it had been a generation previously. Her union with Slake Senior was therefore a mutually beneficial arrangement, providing status for one and financial security for the other.

Dorian was their only child, and he enjoyed a privileged life, growing up in a large house in the Devon countryside, and attending the best prep and boarding schools, where he evidently excelled, and in the autumn of 1938, he took up a place at Merton College, Oxford, reading History.

For reasons that were unclear, but which may, according to the rumours, have had something to do with an act of financial impropriety – it was said that Slake had used his position as the secretary of a college society to obtain money by dishonest means – Slake left Oxford in early 1940 and returned to the family home on the outskirts of Torquay.

Just a few weeks later, both of his parents died when the motor launch they were navigating along the River Dart mysteriously caught fire and exploded. There was nothing in the official record to suggest foul play, but Dorian Slake was questioned at length by the police, who were understandably suspicious as to why he hadn't accompanied his parents on their boat that day, having apparently cried off going on the excursion just before it cast off from Dartmouth. By the time that I read about this, there was a strong presumption that Slake had indeed murdered his parents, but back in 1940, in a society more pre-occupied with a potentially imminent invasion by Nazi Germany, the police enquiries led nowhere, and Dorian Slake became the sole inheritor of his parents' estate.

By this time, Britain was entering its second year of war with the Axis powers and so given Slake's age, and the existential nature of the threat, one might have expected him to have been conscripted into the armed forces, but this did not occur. Slake had suffered from asthma since childhood, and it would appear that this was sufficient to provide him with an exemption from military service.

And it was also this medical condition that brought him into the orbit of the man who would become his mentor – the notorious occultist, Aleister Crowley.

There was, I soon realised, vastly more information on Crowley than there was on Slake. In fact, in occult terms, Crowley was something of a superstar.

Born into a devoutly Christian family in 1875, Crowley had attended Cambridge University in the last years of the nineteenth century, where he developed an unhealthy interest in all things occult and esoteric, getting himself inducted into the Hermetic Order of the Golden Dawn in 1898.

A sexual libertine and a drug addict, who struggled with heroin and cocaine addiction for much of his adult life, he spent the following years doubling down on his occult pursuits, becoming ever more expert at the practice of magic, often in tandem with sexual licentiousness and ritualised drug use. Some of these magical ceremonies were reputed to involve the raising of spirits and demons, and it was said that more than one of the participants to them went insane as a consequence.

As to Crowley's precise state of mind during this period, then this was harder to gauge, for he was undeniably intelligent and articulate, educated and well-travelled, and with the independent means to indulge his myriad obsessions, although he became ever more financially distressed as he became older, and would go on to die in a state of penury. But he unquestionably sought to commune with some very dark forces indeed.

As his life and associations became ever more depraved, and as his acknowledged taste for orgies and sadomasochism descended into still more perverted realms, amidst rumours of pederasty and bestiality, so did Crowley become ever more notorious, coming to be dubbed "The wickedest man in the world". There would be several other contenders for that particular title during the first half of the twentieth century, I thought, but I still considered him to be a vile and disgusting individual, as I sat there, reading through the details of his life. Quite why he should have been posthumously converted into a counter-cultural icon, and exemplified by some for his exhortation to "Do what thou wilt", and to indulge one's interior passions regardless of cost or consequence, was completely beyond me. I imagined that it had as much to do with the moral vacuity of the generation seeking to rehabilitate him, as it did with any serious examination of Crowley's philosophy and motivations, which seemed to have no redeeming features whatsoever.

But in his own time, at least, he had been a person of very bad repute indeed, and subsequent to the First World War he found himself drifting around Europe and North Africa, with a rag-tag following of fellow mystics, sexual partners and various other hangers-on, rarely welcomed in any one place for very long. He was even deported from Italy by the government of Mussolini, where he had set up a commune of occultists called the Abbey of Thelema on the island of Sicily. After sojourns in places as disparate as Tunis and Berlin, Crowley returned to England in the early 1930s.

He was in poor health by then, and also in considerable financial distress, a state of affairs caused, in part, and with no small measure of irony, by his propensity for suing, usually unsuccessfully, those who had accused him in print of being a sadist and a pervert, and a worshipper of the devil. In 1935 he was declared bankrupt.

And in 1940, he met Dorian Slake for the first time. This was in World War Two, and it was the time of the blitz, and Crowley had left London to go and live in the relative calm and safety of the seaside resort of Torquay. Whilst there, he fell ill with the asthma which had plagued him all his life, and it was while he was in hospital that he met and became acquainted with a young man in the same ward, being treated for the same condition. That man was Dorian Slake, and he and Crowley became close associates from that moment onwards.

Quite why this should have been the case was hard to divine, since Slake had not been known for possessing any sort of esoteric curiosity in the years up to that point. There may well have been a financial motive, as far as Crowley was concerned, given that Slake was the inheritor of a modest but not inconsiderable fortune. As for Slake, and what he saw in Crowley, nobody really knew. Perhaps, in this older man, with his much storied past and his exotic proclivities, Slake saw something that he was searching for in his own life, some emptiness which might somehow be addressed by surrendering himself to his darkest and most sordid impulses. Whatever it was, Slake became a devoted adherent to his new mentor.

In 1944, Crowley moved back to London, and Slake went with him, and then shortly afterwards they set up in Hastings, on the Sussex coast, another seaside resort like Torquay, where they took adjacent rooms in the same boarding house. By this time Slake was in the curious position of serving as both secretary and general factotum to Crowley, whilst at the same time being his principal financial benefactor. But more than anything else, it was a master-pupil relationship, because it was during this period that Crowley educated Slake in the mysteries of the occult. According to one account, Dorian Slake was formally anointed as Aleister Crowley's successor at a satanic ceremony held in London in the autumn of 1947. It was to be the last time that Crowley ever ventured away from the seclusion of his Hastings boarding house, but it was a significant event, and the torch had been passed on.

Crowley died in December of that year, and Dorian Slake was one of twelve mourners who attended his funeral at Brighton Crematorium. And then, a year or so later, he went to live in

Wiltshire, at Badcombe Hollow, as I now knew, although this wasn't mentioned in any of the biographical detail that I dug up that morning.

Details on his life in the west country were scant, and it soon became clear that Slake was a subject of public interest only in as much as his life intersected with that of Crowley. It was said that he had tried to form a commune here, much along the same lines as the Abbey of Thelema that Crowley had presided over on Sicily, but nothing had ever come of it, and instead he slipped into obscurity, living a lonely and reclusive existence until whatever demons he had conjured in his mind eventually drove him to take his own life in 1965, at the age of just forty-five.

That was the basic biographical information on Dorian Slake, and there really wasn't very much of it. To find out anything more, I was going to have to cast the net more widely, and dig a little deeper.

Following Megan's departure, the previous evening, the remainder of the night had passed quietly. There had been no further occurrences of peculiar phenomena, and I had not, to my immense relief, encountered the spectral old woman who had confronted Megan on the landing.

Not that I slept particularly well. I had passed a fitful night in a locked bedroom, with the bedside light on, and alert to every creak in the house. When not worrying about who or what might be lurking outside the door, my mind flitted between trying to find some rationalisation for what was going on in Alan's house and wondering how I was going to get my budding romance with Megan back on track.

Ridding this house of whatever spirit or demon was haunting it seemed like the best way forward, I thought, as I lay there watching it get light outside. It was still almost impossible to believe that I was even thinking such thoughts, and yet I was. It was the new reality of living at Badcombe Hollow.

When I eventually got up, feeling predictably tired and out of sorts, I decided that doing some research into Dorian Slake was still the best way to start, as I had determined to do after Megan's departure the night before. In all honesty, I couldn't really think of what else to do.

After a breakfast for which I had little appetite, I flipped open my laptop and connected to the internet, and typed Slake's name into Google, just as I had several weeks previously before moving down here, but back when I had far less reason to be interested in a dead occultist.

From there, I was directed to another couple of sites containing much the same information. As far as the official record was concerned, Dorian Slake was a very minor figure in British occult history, little more than an aspirant sorcerer who, had it not been for his association with the much more famous Aleister Crowley, would likely have slipped into complete obscurity. It didn't tell me much, but it told me the basics.

Now was the time to broaden my search.

Having practised journalism in the age of the internet, I was reasonably adept at navigating my way around the mass of information, most of it superfluous, and much of it inaccurate, that attached itself to any given topic, and because of the lurid nature of Slake's life, these details had multiplied at an exponential rate. And yet I knew that amidst all the fevered speculation and conspiracy theories there would be some genuine nuggets to be found. It was a case of knowing how to strip away the obvious rubbish, and cross-check that which seemed more promising, until such a point where it could be deemed to be broadly reliable. The information age, I had discovered, was a double-edged sword; one could drown in a torrent of data before clutching upon something useful. This needed to be an exercise in patience and calm deliberation, if I was going to gain a fuller understanding of my subject.

But try as I might, I was unable to penetrate the veil of dense inconspicuousness covering Dorian Slake's life, and two further hours of diligently surfing got me nowhere, other than giving me a dull ache behind my eyes, and a pain in my lower back from sitting hunched at a screen.

I walked over to the window and stretched. The plain had been covered in thick cloud all day, and now there was a light rain falling. It was a gloomy scene, in keeping with my mood.

I decided to call Megan again. I had telephoned her earlier that morning to check if she was okay, but there had been no reply, so I had left a message, and asked her to call me. This time she picked up.

"I got your message; I was about to call you back," she said, not wholly convincingly.

"How are you doing?" I asked.

"Well, considering that last night was the most terrifying experience of my entire life, I guess I'm not doing too badly. How about you? How was the rest of your night?"

"Quiet, thank goodness. Not very relaxing, though."

"No, I can imagine."

"I was about to pop into Marlborough," I said, even though I had no such plans. "We could meet up, if you like."

"I'm not there," she said. "I'm at my parents' house in Devizes. I'll probably be staying here for the weekend."

"Right. Well maybe next week, then."

"Yes, maybe. Let's see how it goes. I've got a lot of university work to do next week."

We talked for a while longer, but I could tell that her heart wasn't really in it. I was being brushed off, albeit tactfully. It seemed that whatever chance I might have had with Megan had all but evaporated following her paranormal encounter in the house. It was hard to blame her. Instead, I chose to blame Alan, and his idiotic meddling with dark forces.

Feeling too restless to resume my research, I went for a walk in the rain. I donned Alan's waterproof shooting jacket and spent an hour tramping the lanes that led from the house. It didn't do anything to improve my temper, but I probably benefited from the fresh air.

As I walked beside the dank, wet hedgerows, I tried to gather my thoughts.

I was convinced that Dorian Slake was the key to whatever it was that had compelled Alan to buy Badcombe Hollow, and also to the thing that seemed to be haunting it, rather than any specific interest in the occult and devil worship that Alan himself may have acquired in the years since I had known him. I needed to find out more about Slake, beyond the routine and readily accessible material I had uncovered thus far.

As I got back to the house, I had an idea.

Helen Moore may only have been the editor of a small circulation magazine, but its primary focus was the occult and the paranormal, a subject that I knew she was reasonably conversant in. She also owed me a favour, thanks to having been so indiscreet when talking to Alan about me.

Once inside I deposited my coat and boots and went straight through into the kitchen, put the kettle on and opened up my laptop. I then scrolled through my phone until I found Helen's number.

She picked up on the first ring.

"Helen? It's Richard."

"Hey, you. How's it going down there in deepest Wiltshire?"

"Could be better, could be worse. On the plus side, it's a truly lovely spot, and I'm starting to enjoy the whole country living thing. But there's a downside, unfortunately. I seem to have aroused the interest of a coven of satanists."

"Oh, my God! How very dramatic. That must be rather exciting for you."

"Well, that's one way of putting it. Anyway, once a journalist, always a journalist, so I'm doing some research, and I seem to remember this is a subject your magazine has taken an interest in from time to time. So I was hoping I might tap you for a bit of information.

"There may be an article in it," I added.

"I like the sound of that," she said. "What do you need to know?"

"Well, for starters, what do you know about a satanist called Dorian Slake?"

"The Aleister Crowley disciple? Not much. I know he's been dead for years. Why do you ask?"

"Because I'm living in his house."

"Really?" she exclaimed.

I definitely had her interest now, I thought.

"Yep. Slake lived here between the late 1940s and his death in 1965. He hung himself in some woods just beyond the property. I've seen the place where he probably did it."

"So, Alan Mackay bought Dorian Slake's house. Well, how about that? Wasn't his band into that whole scene for a while? You know, like Kiss, or something."

"Kiss?"

"American glam rock band. It stands for Kids in Satan's Service. Well, so some claim. The band always denied it."

"Oh, yeah, I remember them. Yes, like that, I suppose. But according to Alan, they never took it seriously. It was more of a cultural reference to the hard rock scene of the 1970s and the 1980s. You know, all the occult imagery, and the heavy black eyeliner, and the back masking that was supposed to have gone on, so that if you played a record backwards you could hear incantations to the devil."

"That's mostly an urban myth," said Helen.

"Sure. But the point I'm making is that Alan claimed it was very much a style over substance thing with him. He said it was all about image. But now, I'm not so sure."

"Well, he was obviously serious enough about it to buy the house of a notorious devil worshipper, if only a minor league one. Sounds like he did a Jimmy Page."

"Jimmy Page? Sorry, I'm not following you."

"He bought Aleister Crowley's house in Scotland. A place called Boleskin House, on Loch Ness. He doesn't own it anymore."

"Right. I didn't know that. Jimmy Page always sounds very, you know … pleasantly normal."

"I'm sure he is. Having an interest in the occult isn't necessarily the same thing as practising it. Often, people get into it because it piques their intellectual curiosity. Anyway, it'll be a nice piece of symmetry if you write an article for me, what with Crowley being Slake's mentor. Mind you, Crowley's semi-respectable these days; more counter cultural icon than prince of darkness."

"I know. The Sergeant Pepper cover. Still sounds like a nasty piece of work, to me."

"And to me. But we live in non-judgemental times. You can't condemn people for anything, these days. But he's always sounded thoroughly unpleasant. And I'm sure Slake was, too, but he's very insignificant, compared to Crowley, although I can see why his house might be a magnet for today's generation of devil worshipper. So, what are they doing? Planting upside down, burning crosses on your front lawn? Killing your cat and hanging it from a tree?”

“Nothing so dramatic And I don’t own a cat. But I heard a story about occult ceremonies being held here. There are rumours about it, locally. There’s also some weirdo hanging around the woods, keeping watch on the house. And I’m more convinced than ever that Alan Mackay was seriously into all of this.”

“They do things like that?” I added, incredulously.

“Do things like what?”

“What you were saying before. About killing cats and displaying the body.”

“That, and much worse. These are some very sick and depraved people, Richard.”

“So, what do you know about it all?”

“About what? Dorian Slake, or the practice of satanism more generally?”

“Either. Both.”

“Well, as far as Slake is concerned, I don’t know very much about him at all. No more, probably, than you’ve already found out for yourself on Wikipedia. I know a couple of obscure websites I can give you the details of. They would have a bit more information, but there’s not really much to be had. Nobody knows very much about Dorian Slake, and what little they do know mostly relates to his association with Crowley.

“I did try to research him once, myself,” she said.

“How did you get on?”

“I didn’t get much further with it than you, by the sounds of things. Although it wasn’t for lack of trying. There is one quite interesting sounding rumour from the 1960s on one of the websites I’m going to give you the details of, but that was it.”

“Tell me more.”

“Hold on. I’ll e-mail you the links to those sites while I think of it.”

I heard the tap of a keyboard on the other end of the line and, a moment later, there was a soft ping from my laptop to tell me that I had mail.

“Okay, that’s done,” she said. “Anyway, I didn’t get anywhere with this, wasted quite a bit of time on it, actually, but it sounded quite interesting, not to mention disturbing.

Apparently, in 1964, so about a year before he killed himself, Slake kidnapped a child to use as a human sacrifice in a black mass.”

“Jesus. What happened?”

“It’s all very tenuous, but the story is that he was thwarted by some expert on the occult who tracked down Slake’s coven and snatched the child back.”

“How come Slake wasn’t arrested and charged?”

“I really couldn’t say. Lack of evidence, maybe. That’s as much as I know, apart from the name of the person who supposedly rescued the child. He was called Julian Faraday. An academic from Oxford. I mean, I don’t know if that’s what he was when he came across Dorian Slake, because he would have been fairly young back then, but that’s what he was by the time I heard about him. He taught in one of the colleges, but according to the rumours, he spent most of his time investigating satanic cults.”

“And you didn’t try and track him down, and ask him about it?”

“Hey, what am I, some dilettante? Of course, I tried. That’s what I was alluding to when I said about having wasted a load of time on it. Yes, I definitely tried. I actually spoke to the guy. I confronted him outside one of his lectures, a public one, and asked him straight out about it. But he completely brushed me off and wouldn’t tell me anything. But I persisted with it. I even door-stepped him outside his office. You’d have been proud of me, darling, what with you being an old red-top man and all that. Anyway, after that he threatened me with legal action for harassment, so I backed off.”

“Maybe I’ll try and speak to him,” I said.

“Well, good luck if you do. He’d be pretty old by now, assuming he’s even still alive. This run-in he had with Slake, assuming it happened, took place fifty years ago.”

“Okay,” I said. “So much for Slake. What can you tell me about satanism in the UK more generally?”

“Nothing that you won’t be able to find out for yourself online, or in a good library. Just remember that it’s a very broad church, no pun intended. There are probably a few thousand adherents in this country, maybe ten thousand at most, but there are masses of different groups and sects, and their beliefs and practices vary enormously. And always bear in mind the ninety-nine percent rule."

"What's that?"

"It's a saying. Basically, ninety-nine percent of those describing themselves as satanists are nothing but sad little fantasists who get their jollies by dancing naked around graveyards and participating in the occasional orgy. I mean, a hell of a lot of this is just an excuse to dress up and have casual sex with strangers. But then you have the one percent who take it a lot more seriously – the ones who really, truly believe – and they're a lot more dangerous. And then there's a tiny proportion of that group – the one percent of the one percent, if you like – who will literally go to any lengths in the name of their beliefs, however depraved, perverted or even murderous."

"And which of these categories would Dorian Slake have fitted into?"

"He was in the one percent of the one percent. No doubt about it."

I rang off a short time later, having promised Helen that in the event I did decide to write about Badcombe Hollow, she could have first refusal on whatever I produced.

Feeling tired, but knowing that I should get back into it, I clicked open one of the links that she had e-mailed to me.

It took me to a site detailing the history of satanism and other forms of occult worship, in which Dorian Slake was mentioned, but once again, only in relation to his association with Aleister Crowley, and I learned nothing new about the man whose house I was living in. It was interesting, however, inasmuch as it provided me with more information about what one might refer to as mainstream satanism, as opposed to the more violent, even murderous version, allegedly practised by Slake.

I discovered that there was an actual Church of Satan, founded by an American called Anton LaVey in 1966, and which even had its own reverend ministers. The more I read about it, the more idiotic it sounded, even though its adherents were at pains to distance themselves as far as possible from the sort of shenanigans typically associated with their faith in the public imagination, such as dancing naked around fires in deserted churchyards, trying to raise spirits and suchlike. As far as they were concerned, they were merely exercising their right to free expression, and their faith was more about an exploration of the self, allowing one to satisfy one's own individual desires (or perversions, I thought) absent any moral censure. Indeed, much of what I read was couched in the language of libertarianism and anarcho-capitalism – sort of, H L Mencken or Ayn Rand, but with pentagrams and upside-down crosses, if you will – and which I deemed to be pseudo-intellectualism of the shallowest kind.

"Do what thou wilt shall be the whole of the law," as Crowley had said, but it didn't really wash with me. Aside from anything else, there was a selfishness about this so-called old religion which very much contrasted with what I knew of other mainstream faiths, with their emphasis on community, charity and compassion. I may not have been devout in my own faith, but I could at least appreciate the societal benefits that flowed from it, even if some of its proponents often failed to live up to their high ideals. But at least they had ideals, I thought. There was nothing remotely high-minded about any of the satanic creeds I was reading through that morning. At best, they represented a self-justifying manifesto for freaks and narcissists, and try as they might to demystify and mainstream their faith, there was still a deeply unpleasant undertone to much of what I read.

The so-called Eleven Rules of Satanism were a case in point.

"If a guest in your lair annoys you, treat them cruelly and without mercy," read one of the rules, whilst another read, "If someone bothers you, ask him to stop. If he does not stop, destroy him."

Charming, I thought, and what sort of person describes their home as a lair, anyway?

"Do not harm little children," read another of the rules, which seemed so completely self-evident, one wondered why it had to be explicitly spelt out.

By the time I got to the end of the various articles I had decided that whilst most of these mainstream adherents to the practice of satanism may have been a danger only to themselves, they were still some of the stupidest people on the planet.

The other link from Helen took me to a much more salacious sort of website, full of unsourced information and breathless speculation. What I discovered there didn't add greatly to the sum total of my knowledge of Dorian Slake, but it filled in the bare bones of his biography with some truly unpleasant details, even if much of it was highly speculative.

There was a little more information on Crowley anointing Slake as his successor, by someone who had supposedly witnessed the ceremony in London where this took place, and then written down the detail in a journal, which was then discovered amongst this person's private papers on their death, and eventually purchased by a devil worshipping sect in California in the late 1970s.

The journal entries had been transcribed on the website, and although it was the very definition of unreliable, unsourced information, I read it anyway. It described a highly complex ceremony involving ritualised sex and drug use, and the killing of a goat, the blood and entrails of which were smeared over Slake's naked body. An orgy was then described, in all its explicit, pornographic detail, and in a passage of writing so lurid I concluded that it had almost certainly been made up.

The most interesting thing about the piece was the implication that Slake's elevation by his mentor was not wholly welcomed by much of Crowley's coven, who regarded the callow young man as something of an interloper, as well as having a very unstable personality. Slake was not well liked, it seemed, even among his fellow devil worshippers.

Scrolling on through the website I found a couple of references to Badcombe Hollow. One described Slake's unsuccessful attempt to recreate Crowley's Sicilian Abbey of Thelema there, by assembling a commune around him, and how he was never able to gather together more than two or three people at a time, and how these people would go on to drop out after only a few days in the house. It all sounded a bit pathetic, but whilst it may have reflected nothing more than Slake's disagreeable nature, there was also a hint that some of these house guests had been disturbed by something they had experienced in the house, and I couldn't help but wonder if this was the same thing as the apparition witnessed by Megan. The other reference to Badcombe Hollow merely related the fact that Slake had lived here from 1949, and speculated that the pagan mythos associated with Avebury may have been what had drawn him to this area.

Finally, I found a single reference to the incident Helen had referred to, about the abduction and subsequent rescue of a child who had been kidnapped by Slake in order to be killed as a human sacrifice in one of his ceremonies, and which had occurred in 1964, shortly before Slake took his own life. There was little detail on the event itself, merely a brief description of the large London mansion where the ceremony took place, and its possible connection to a former coven that had assembled there under the tutelage of Aleister Crowley. In fact, it was very likely the same place where the anointing of Dorian Slake had occurred, back in 1947. But I was interested to note that Slake had been so enraged by the failure of his repulsive and abominable plan to sacrifice a child to Satan that he never recovered from it. It was said that he returned to Wiltshire a broken man, and was never heard of again, until he committed suicide by hanging himself from a tree in the woods next to the house. His last words, according to an un-named satanist who claimed to have spoken to him the day before he took his life, had been a series of curses and damnations upon the person who had foiled his diabolical scheme.

One Professor Julian Faraday, I thought.

I switched off the computer. It was dark in the house now, and completely silent, save for the ticking of the clock in the hall.

So that was the life of Dorian Slake, I thought. The one percent of the one percent.

CHAPTER SEVENTEEN

The Old Man

The following day was Sunday, and it passed without incident, or work. I neither carried out any further research nor experienced anything out of the ordinary. I read, went for a long walk, cooked a meal, and tried to relax and not think about ghosts or satanists. I succeeded better than I thought I would, and might almost have persuaded myself that things were settling back down to something like normal again. But that night I experienced something that left me in no doubt that Badcombe Hollow was afflicted by paranormal phenomenon, and that removed entirely any faint, lingering suspicions I may have harboured that Megan's encounter with some kind of demonic entity, not much more than twenty-four hours previously, had somehow been a product of her imagination.

It started with a dream. It was similar to the one I had experienced two nights before, in that it began with me in the woods, by the tree with the pentagram burned into its trunk. I seemed to be waiting for something, but I had no recollection of what this might have been. Then I found myself back in the garden, as I had before, except this time I was standing alone on the top of the burial mound, staring across the field. A figure in the distance was walking towards me, from the direction of the woods. As it drew closer, I realised it was the woman who had stood on this mound in the previous dream. She was shouting something at me, but I was unable to hear her.

I woke up. It was still the middle of the night. The clock on the bedside table read ten past three. I lay there in the darkness listening to it rain outside.

It was just as I was drifting off to sleep again that I heard it. A faint noise from above my head, barely discernible, but enough to bring me out in a cold sweat of sudden panic.

I raised my eyes to the ceiling, hardly daring to breathe as I listened. For a while there was nothing, and then I heard it again.

A creak above my head. And then the creaking sound moved across the ceiling, and I realised what it was.

It was the sound of footsteps. Somebody was walking around on the top floor.

Too frightened to move, I lay there listening to whoever or whatever it was walk across the floor above me.

It was already the ghastliest experience of my life, but it was about to get much worse.

The sound suddenly faded, only to return again, moments later, louder this time, and from a different direction.

Then it faded again, and then I heard it distinctly. The sound was now coming from directly outside my room. I could hear footsteps on the landing.

They approached the door to my room and stopped. I was more afraid than I had ever been. My heart was pounding and I could only breathe in shallow gasps. But I was too terrified to move as much as a muscle. A small part of me was still just about rational enough to believe that I should jump out of bed, switch on the light, and then unlock and fling open the door, confronting whatever it was that was standing out there.

But such actions were completely beyond me. I was simply too afraid. More than afraid. Petrified beyond my wits' end would be a better way of describing it. So, I just lay there, staring at the door through the gloom, and waiting for the person on the other side to make the first move.

For what seemed like a very long time there was complete silence in the house. I wondered if whatever it was could have gone.

There was a knock on the door.

Three soft taps.

I wanted to scream but I couldn't make my voice work. My heart was now beating at such a rate that I thought it was going to explode in my chest. All the time I kept my eyes on the door, not even daring to blink.

And then I saw the handle move; watched the lever angle downwards to its fullest extent, and when this failed to open the locked door, something started to push against it.

I had never, in my entire existence, felt more helpless as I did, lying there, watching the door rattle in its frame.

And then it just stopped, and a few moments later I heard footsteps moving away from the door. I then became aware of another sound. At first, I couldn't tell what it was, and then I realised. It was a sob. It was the sound of someone crying.

As disconcerting as this was, it was nothing compared to what followed. The sobs quickly turned to snarls of anger, and barked shouts in a guttural language I did not recognise, and which were more animal than human. It was horrible, a sound born of despair, anguish and above all, rage.

I continued to lie there. What else could I do? I was digging my fingers so tightly into the sheets by then that they ached, and it felt like they were going to burst through the mattress.

Then the sound faded, and then it stopped, and then there was nothing. My breathing slowly returned to normal as I realised that whatever had been out there was now gone.

I felt exhausted by the whole experience, like every drop of energy had drained from my body. I dearly wanted to flee from the house, jump in the car, and get as far away from Badcombe Hollow as I possibly could, but I was too afraid to move from the relative sanctuary of my room. Needless to say, I never got back to sleep again.

I got up a few hours later, feeling truly wretched, but thankful for the daylight, and no longer having to resist the urge to simply bolt from the house. I was, however, considering checking into a hotel in Marlborough that night, just to be able to sleep properly, but I knew that would be a negative and cowardly way to confront this problem, which would still exist as soon as I returned to the house. So, feeling a little braver in the light of day, I determined that I was not going to let this defeat me, although I didn't go up to the second floor to draw the curtains that day, not relishing a possible meeting with whatever it was that dwelt up there.

All that I could practically do was continue with my research into Dorian Slake, and see where this led me. And continue to keep my bedroom door locked at night.

It was all nuts, of course, but it was also the new reality of my life. Somehow, I had to find a way of coping with it.

Having the day before recalled the offer by Keith, the taxi driver, to introduce me to someone who had worked at a neighbouring farm during the period of Slake's residence at Badcombe Hollow, I had made arrangements to meet them in Marlborough that lunchtime. After several desultory hours mooching about the house, nominally undertaking some chores, but in reality, accomplishing little, I headed off for my appointment.

It was another wet and miserable day, which did little to improve my mood as I drove through the now familiar network of lanes that led into town. I parked in the high street, and made my way over to the pub where I had arranged to meet Keith.

He got there just after me, accompanied by a much older man.

Keith introduced him as Alfred Jackson. He looked to be in his late eighties, or even early nineties but although he was clearly frail, with rheumy eyes and a slight tremor to his hands, there was a sheen of good health about him, which spoke of a lifetime of working outdoors. I subsequently learned that he had not retired from the farm where he had worked since boyhood until he was seventy-five years old, and that he kept active by tending to his allotment on the edge of town, where he was an almost daily fixture, and where he enjoyed some repute as the grower of prize-winning vegetables.

After the introductions were made I bought a round of drinks, and we settled down at a table by the fire.

"So, you'd be the gentleman who's living up at the old Slake house," Alfred said to me. He spoke slowly, with the soft burr of a west county accent.

"Yes, for the best part of a month now," I said.

"And how do you like it over there?"

"I like it very much," I said. "It's certainly a nice change. I live in London normally."

"Oh, I see," said Alfred. "Londoner, are we? Never been to London."

"Really?"

"No. Never wanted to, either."

"Um, right. Well, like I said, it's very different to London, and a very pleasant place to live."

"Aye, that it is."

"I'm enjoying the peace and quiet," I said. I wasn't planning to tell them about the strange events of the past few days. It all seemed too fantastical to talk about with a couple of near strangers, and I didn't want our meeting to be distracted by this, when my intention was to find out as much as I could about Dorian Slake.

"Anyway, much as I like being there, I understand that the house has something of a reputation, so I was interested in finding out a bit more about it."

"Well, I can remember when that place was still a working farm," said Alfred. "The Livesey family owned it, but it was the grandfather who built the house, back in the eighteen hundreds, so there were three generations of the family who lived there. They owned all the land around there, on both sides of the road. It was one of the biggest arable farms in these parts."

"And you worked for them?" I said.

"No, I worked for the Russells. They had the other big farm round here. I started working for them in 1940, when I was just a teenager. I worked there my whole life until I retired, apart from a couple of years in the army at the end of the war.

"It was around the time I came back that old man Livesey sold the place. He lost his only son in the war, you see. He was a nice lad, all set to follow in his father's footsteps. He died on D-Day. He got shot as he came off the landing craft. Killed outright. He didn't even make it onto the beach. His father never got over it. He was a broken man afterwards. His heart just wasn't in the farm anymore, what with nobody to leave it to. So, he sold up and moved away. I don't know what became of him. He went to live with relatives, for a while, and there was talk that he emigrated to Canada, but I don't know about that."

"But the house was sold separately from the rest of the farm?" I said.

"No. The Russells, who I worked for, they bought the whole thing. But they lived over in East Kennet, and they didn't need two houses, so they sold the house on separately, a year or so later."

"To Dorian Slake."

"Yes. That would have been around 1947 or 1948. Nobody knew a thing about him when he moved in there. Didn't know too much afterwards, either. He kept to himself, you see. Bit of a recluse, you might say. All we knew was that some outsider lived there. I don't think I even set eyes on the man until a few years after he came here. But by then, there were plenty of rumours about the place."

"Rumours?"

"About strange goings on up there. At night. Ceremonies and suchlike in those woods across the field. There was even talk of devil worship."

He took a sip of beer before continuing.

"There was this old boy I used to know. He was a little bit of a bad penny, you might say, but he used to help us out on the farm sometimes, when we were busy and needed the extra help, like during the harvest. Well, he was a poacher, you see. Not that I hold with that, but they were hard times just after the war, and there were a lot of poor folk around here. I mean, where's the harm in taking the odd rabbit? Or helping yourself to a pheasant from one of the pens? I'm not saying I agree with it, but for some people it was a way of life. Take a little, but don't get greedy. Where's the harm?"

I felt like we were getting away from the point, but I sat there quietly and let him talk.

"So, my mate, he used to go poaching in those woods near your house. Always been good for rabbits up there. So, one night, he was up on the edge of the woods, looking back down towards your place, and he sees a group of people coming across the field from the house. Wearing dark cloaks and carrying burning torches, if you can believe that. So, he hides there in the undergrowth and waits for them to go past, and then he follows them. There's a clearing up there, with some old trees around it …"

"I know it," I cut in. "I've been there. It's where Slake eventually killed himself, isn't it?"

Alfred appeared mildly displeased by the interruption.

"It was," he said. "But we'll get to that part in due course. We don't want to get ahead of ourselves, do we?"

"No, of course not," I said. "I'm sorry. Do please carry on."

"I'll have to remember where I was, now," said Alfred, looking down at his beer. Keith gave a slight eye roll and grinned at me across the table.

"Yes, that was it," said Alfred, "My mate follows them to the clearing, and then hides himself a little way away, and he watches them, while they have this sort of ceremony. Apparently, they lit a fire in the clearing and stood round it. There were thirteen of them, so he claimed, all in a circle, and that Slake bloke was the leader of it all, like a high priest or something. Said it was the weirdest thing he'd ever seen, not that he understood what was going on. He said there was a lot of chanting in a foreign language, like they were praying to something. And then they killed two chickens."

"Bloody hell," said Keith. "Where did they come from then?"

"They took them up there with them. A black one and a white one, apparently, according to my mate. At the end of this ceremony, or pagan meeting, or whatever it was, your man Slake pulls these birds out of a box, holds them up above the fire and cuts their throats. Then they all smeared themselves in the blood. Then afterwards, well, that's when the funny business started."

"Funny business?" I said, not quite sure what covering oneself in chicken's blood whilst chanting in a strange language constituted, if not very funny business indeed.

"Yes, of a sexual nature," said Alfred, with evident distaste.

"How do you mean?" said Keith, leaning forward keenly in his chair.

"Like they were all at it with each other. You know, doing it. And all together, as well. Blokes with other blokes; all sorts."

"Like an orgy?" said Keith.

"I wouldn't know the terminology for it like you do, Keith, but yes, I suppose that's what it was."

"You still get a lot of that going on," said Keith. "You know, orgies and whatnot in the woods. You hear a lot about things like that in my line of work. Happens all the time, apparently, over at Savernake Forest. People turn up in the middle of the night, pull up off the road, and then they get their kit off, and have at it with complete strangers. It's called dogging."

"What's it got to do with dogs?" said Alfred.

Once again, I felt like we were drifting from the point, so I steered Alfred back to the night in question.

"So, getting back to that night in the woods?" I said. "What happened after that?"

"Nothing. That was it. They put their cloaks back on, put the fire out, and went back to the house. And they never knew they'd been watched the whole time. Mind you, my mate was pretty shaken up by it. And he never poached in those woods again. Never. Not as long as he lived."

"Didn't he report it?" I asked.

"Report it to who? The bloke's hardly going to admit that he was out poaching. Besides, we tend to mind our own business in these parts. I wasn't going to say anything. What folk get up to in their own time is no concern of mine. But people knew there was some odd business going on up there. There was even talk that Slake put some sort of curse on the house, to stop people snooping around. Not that I believe in things like curses, mind. But it all helped to give the house a reputation for being evil and unholy, and not somewhere to venture after dark. It kept people away from it. It was like there was an atmosphere about the place, and some people could pick up on it, and some couldn't. People said that animals could sense it, and never went near there. You couldn't even walk a dog along the lane outside the house, without it shaking and howling. I know that because my late brother-in-law had dogs, and he told me he couldn't get them anywhere near the place."

I recalled Alan's instruction that I should bring no pets onto the property. Now I understood why.

"Did you ever meet him, or speak to him?" I asked.

"Who, Slake? No. He wouldn't have talked to the likes of me. But I don't think he spoke to anyone much, or even left the property very often, apart from going to Marlborough for his shopping. There was talk that he used to go up on the plain and look at the barrows and the standing stones, but I never came across him when I was up there, and I used to go walking there a lot when I was a younger man.

"I only ever saw him at Badcombe Hollow, when I was working in the fields there. You used to see him sometimes, standing on that burial mound and looking over at the woods. He always wore a dark suit. Sometimes he'd stand there and watch you, while we were in the fields. The man used to give me the creeps.

"As far as I'm aware, there was only one person from around here who he was acquainted with, and let's just say that it was someone no normal person would want for a friend."

"Why? Who was he?"

"It was a she. A woman called Doreen Smithers. She lived over at Stokeley. It's a little village up by the Ridgeway, about ten miles north of here. Very remote place. Middle of nowhere. Just a farm and a few houses. Well off the beaten track, even today. The sort of place that doesn't lead anywhere; and where they don't take kindly to strangers. She was from there. She lived in a cottage on the edge of the village. Somewhere else normal folk used to keep a wide berth of."

"How come?"

"Because Doreen Smithers was a practising witch. She used to read people's fortunes at the country fairs. They said she could look at a glass of water, and tell you your future. Load of nonsense, if you ask me, but back then there were folk in these parts who still held with that sort of thing, particularly up on the Ridgeway. Some of them probably still do. Old beliefs die hard, up there. So, she had a fair few believers to work on, did Doreen Smithers. There were rumours she used to sell curses for money, and apparently that was how Slake came to have the curse put on his place, as a way of protecting it. She and Slake were pretty thick, by all accounts."

"What happened to her?" I asked. "Is she still alive?"

"No. Long gone. Died a couple of years after Slake. She had a daughter. Slake's child, according to the rumours, but I wouldn't know about that. I never even saw her. I suppose she'd be in her fifties or sixties by now. I don't know what became of her."

I noted down the name of the village next to that of Doreen Smithers. It might be worth checking out at some point, I thought.

"Do you remember anything about Slake dying up in the woods?" I asked.

"Remember it very well, as it happens. We were working in the next field. Harvest time. I saw his body get carried out of there. Apparently, some bloke was walking his dog and found him swinging from a beech tree in the same clearing where he used to hold his ceremonies. The police came and cut him down, and then they carried him back to the house through the field, covered in a sheet. Saw him go by me as close as I'm sitting next to you now."

"What happened then?" I asked. "I mean, where was he buried?"

It was an item of information I hadn't been able to find out, despite all my incessant googling the day before.

"I wouldn't know. I heard some people came and had the body taken away, once the coroner had finished with it. Friends of his from London, apparently. I suppose they had him buried up there, somewhere."

"What happened to the house? Did he leave it to anyone?"

"All I know about that is hearsay."

"Hearsay is fine," I said. "It all helps to paint a picture. How about another drink?"

"Wouldn't say no to another half in there," he said, handing me his glass.

"Keith?" I asked.

"I'm alright, thanks," he said. "I've got to drive the taxi this afternoon."

I went and bought two halves; one for Alfred and one for me.

"So, what about this hearsay then?" I said as I returned to the table.

"It was just talk," said Alfred. "I heard it from old man Russell, the farmer I worked for. He was on the parish council, and he was one of those who always had his ear to the ground. He told me there was some sort of dispute about the place; that Slake was massively in debt, and so his creditors ended up taking it.

"Then it stood empty for a couple of years before anyone lived there again. A retired colonel bought it, but he didn't stay there long. Then a family moved in. They were there for a few years, and then they moved out. It's changed hands a few times since, but nobody has ever stayed for very long. Until that musician bloke bought it. He's been there longer than anyone since Slake.

"You see, the place is supposed to be haunted, and they say that's what drove Slake mad, and made him kill himself. Anyone who stays there too long gets to the point where they can't take it anymore.

"Have you experienced anything like that, since you've been in the house?" he asked, looking me straight in the eye.

"No," I said, after a beat. "Nothing like that. Not so far."

"So, what's your interest in all this, if you don't mind me asking?" said Alfred. "Keith tells me you used to be a journalist. Are you going to write about Slake?"

"Maybe," I said. "He certainly sounds like an interesting and unusual character. So yes, I may do. You've been very helpful, in fleshing out some of the details. Thank you."

"Don't thank me yet. You haven't heard the best bit."

I raised my eyebrows enquiringly.

"It's just speculation, mind you," he went on. "Some rumours that went around after Slake died. I probably shouldn't say."

But you're going to, anyway, I thought.

Alfred drained his glass and set it down on the table.

"There's something about that hollow your house sits in," he said. "The steep bank behind your house. About the way it is now, compared to the way it was when Slake bought the place."

"I know." I said. "It's bigger."

Alfred seemed rather taken aback, and not a little disappointed at my knowing this.

"Oh, well, good for you, then."

"Sorry to steal your thunder. I don't have any idea why that bank is so much higher, only that it is."

I explained about the book of old photographs, and how this had shown that the retaining bank at the back of the house had once only been as high as the first floor, whereas now it extended well above the roofline.

"What would he go and do that for, then?" Keith interjected.

"Because I'm guessing he was building something there, isn't that right, Alfred?" I said. "Because all that earth at the back got excavated from somewhere. And there lies the mystery. Slake didn't build anything during his time there, apart from the garage at the end of the driveway, but nothing that would require that sort of excavation."

"That's because, whatever it was that he built, he built underground," said Alfred. "So, the rumour goes, anyway."

"What, you mean under the house?" said Keith.

"Maybe, maybe not. I reckon he started under the house and ended up somewhere else."

"But hold on a moment," I said. "Slake lived there alone. How could he ever have managed something like that?"

"Because he had people do it for him," said Alfred. "And that part's no rumour."

Keith and I waited for him to continue, but it seemed like he wanted to draw this out, pleased to have regained the initiative following his surprise at my having known about the extended height of the retaining bank.

"Go on then, Alfred," Keith said, at last. "Out with it."

"It was a few years after Slake moved in," said Alfred. "Around the time of the coronation. So, about 1953. That's when I first became aware of it, from ploughing the fields on the west side of the house. It may have started a bit before that. And it went on for about a year afterwards."

"What do you mean?" said Keith. "What was going on?"

"People working over at the house. A whole gang of them. At least six men. They used to get driven over there in a couple of cars, every morning, and then get taken away again in the evening. After a while, I picked up the pattern of it, and it was regular as clockwork."

"Where did they come from?" I asked.

"From up near Swindon, apparently, so I heard. They lived in some sort of camp over there. An old army base, I think. I heard they were foreign. From somewhere like Germany, except it wasn't Germany."

"Hungary?" I ventured, recalling that this was where Ernst von Darken supposedly originated from.

"Could have been. Really couldn't say. Anyway, the whole point of them being foreign, according to the rumour I heard, was that they didn't speak any English. So, nobody could ask them about what they were doing, and the whole thing could be kept secret."

"Did you ever see them working?" I said.

"Hardly at all. That place is pretty well screened off, with the hollow at the back, and the trees at the front. But occasionally, if I happened to be at the very top of the field, you'd see people carrying earth to the top of the hollow.

"But no evidence of anything they built?"

"No. That's why it had to be underground."

"Any idea about what it might have been?"

"According to one rumour I heard, it was some kind of temple."

A satanic temple, I thought. How fitting, if true.

"But you don't think it's under the house?" I said.

"I wouldn't say so, no. I mean, why dig out a brand new chamber underground, when you can excavate an existing one?"

"How do you mean?" I said, before it dawned on me.

"Of course," I said. "He built it under the burial mound."

CHAPTER EIGHTEEN

The Hidden Temple

As soon as I got back to the house I went and stood on the long barrow.

Could it be possible that Dorian Slake had constructed a satanic temple in there, hollowing out the existing Neolithic burial chamber to create a large underground cavern? And had Alan known about this? Had he learned about it from Ernst von Draken, who had been acquainted with this place since Slake's time and who, by his own attestation, had persuaded his wealthy friend from the music business to buy it? Had this all been a deliberate plan to return the property and the secret it concealed into the hands of those sympathetic with the aims of the temple's creator? Was this the reason why von Draken appeared to have such a proprietorial interest in Badcombe Hollow? Had Alan somehow reneged on whatever understanding he had with von Draken by going off and leaving the temple unguarded? And where did I fit in to all of this?

My mind spun with these myriad questions, as well as one further, rather more pertinent one.

If there was an underground temple somewhere beneath my feet, how the hell did one get into it?

Slake had clearly not been able to get his hired hands to dig down into it from the area of the mound itself, since this would have exposed his activities to the outside world. Even in a place as relatively remote as Badcombe Hollow, such an excavation of a protected historic monument would have been noticed. And it would have been stopped, even if the burial mound did happen to sit on private land. He had to have tunnelled in from somewhere else, and come up into the burial chamber from underneath. Hence the large amounts of earth which had to be moved, and which ended up on top of the retaining bank.

But where did he start from? And even if the entry point had subsequently been covered up again, how did one get into the temple now? There was no point in going to all the trouble of building something like that, if you couldn't then get into it and use it.

I knew that the cellar had a solid floor, a mixture of quarry tiles in some areas and bare concrete in others, but I went down there and checked again anyway. This confirmed that there was nowhere that could have led further underground, unless Slake had completely sealed up the passageway after building it, which simply didn't make sense.

I went back out into the garden and checked inside the little brick garage at the end of the driveway. This might have been a likely place from which to access a tunnel leading to the burial mound, and what better way of concealing an excavation like that from prying eyes than by building it within an enclosure like the garage? But this building also had a solid floor; a hard-wearing vinyl, which had been laid on what felt like a concrete base. I even lay on the floor and reached underneath Alan's car, to confirm that this was the same type of floor surface. It felt as if it was, although I would have to move the car to be absolutely sure, something that I was unable to do, since I had previously tried, and failed to locate the keys.

Most peculiar, I thought, as I emerged into the light of the garden. Could Alfred have been mistaken about all of this? Could the gang of workers he had seen been here for another purpose? Were the rumours about the underground temple just rumours? But then there was still the evidence of the earth piled onto the back of the hollow.

As I was pondering on this, my telephone rang.

It was Darren Summers, my private investigator friend.

"I've got a result for you on that car," he said. "It belongs to one Billy Matthews. Age thirty-seven. Lives in Devizes. That's in your new neck of the woods, I think. Here's the address."

"Hold on a second," I said. "I'm in the garden. Let me go into the house so I can write this down."

I went inside and grabbed my pad from the table in the hall, and went through into the kitchen.

"Go ahead," I said, and I transcribed the address he gave me.

"Anything else on this guy?" I said.

"Yes. He's got a criminal record."

"That sounds promising. What did he do?"

"He was done under the Cruelty to Animals Act. Five years ago. He got pulled over on some minor traffic violation and the police found something rather unusual in the back of his car."

"What did they find?"

"Two live chickens in a box. A black cock and a white hen, to be more precise."

I recalled Alfred Jackson's story about the strange ceremony in the woods, back in Dorian Slake's day, also involving two chickens, one black and one white.

"Much used in witchcraft, apparently," Darren was saying, as if reading my thoughts. "So, the police suspected ritual animal slaughter, and got a warrant for his place in Devizes. He was keeping goats and chickens in his front room, believe it or not. Waiting to be killed in some ceremony, presumably. And he had a load of other exotic pets in there. You know, snakes, spiders, lizards, that sort of thing. Who would want to keep things like that?

"Anyway, they charged him. Seems like he's heavily into the occult, because he tried to claim his human rights were being infringed by the prosecution, owing to his belief in all things ungodly, but the judge wasn't having it. Gave him an eighteen-month suspended sentence, and banned him from keeping animals for the next ten years. He got off lightly, if you ask me. Sounds like a real sick bastard."

"He certainly does," I agreed.

"So have you got a bunch of satanists living next door, down at Cold Comfort Farm?"

"Something like that, by the looks of things," I said. "How about the other guy I mentioned – Ernst von Draken. Did you find anything out about him?"

"Only in the sense that there was hardly anything to find out. He's one of those people who doesn't reveal much with a quick search, which may be significant."

"How do you mean?"

"I mean, some people are easy to find out about, especially in the electronic era. They leave little signatures everywhere they go, which makes it easy to get a line on them. For people like me, that is, who vaguely know what they're doing, and know how to access computerised records. Like with chicken-man in Devizes. He was easy. But this von Draken character; he's a whole different kettle of fish. He's obviously very good at covering his tracks. Based on my experience, I'd say he's gone to a lot of trouble to make it very hard for people like me to find out anything about him. I could find out more, but it would take some time."

And money, I thought. Something I didn't have. Renting out my flat and living at Alan's for free had done a lot to alleviate my financial situation, but I certainly didn't have the resources to hire a private investigator.

"You were right about him being a book dealer," said Darren. "It was one of the few bits of information that I did get, and I only got that because it was from something that was in an on-line trade journal. Something about a sale of rare alchemical books, from a few years back. But apart from that, I got nothing. Not even an address."

"Well, thanks for trying, anyway," I said.

"There was one thing, though," said Darren. "A direct connection to Billy Matthews. You see, when Matthews got arrested and charged, it was von Draken who bailed him out. His name appears in the court records. So, the two of them are definitely connected, but I figure you already knew that."

"I was getting there," I said. "But thanks for confirming it."

"No worries. Look, if you ever want someone to have a proper dig into this guy, let me know, will you? I'd like to have a crack at finding out some more about him. Just for the challenge of it."

"I will do," I said, although in the absence of a sudden change in my personal circumstances, I couldn't see how this would ever be possible.

I thanked him again and hung up, and then reflected upon the little I had learned.

Billy Matthews, the person I had followed in the woods, and almost certainly the person I had caught prowling around the garden at night, was both a satanist, and connected to Ernst von Draken, who I deduced had told Matthews to keep watch on the house, albeit for reasons that remained a mystery. Also, the fact that Matthews lived in nearby Devizes made me wonder if he and von Draken might be members of some coven local to this particular area, and to which Alan had also belonged.

It was more food for thought, even if it appeared to be generating more questions than answers.

I went back outside to continue my search for an entrance into Dorian Slake's underground temple, but I got nowhere, despite combing every part of the grounds. I even got a fork from the shed and dug down into the compost heap in the vegetable garden, disturbing a hibernating slow worm, but it was all to no avail. As tantalising a clue as Alfred had handed me in the pub, it seemed like another dead end.

It was late afternoon by then, and I decided to go into the house to make a pot of tea.

Just as I was approaching the front door, my eyes happened to flick over to the adjacent window, which looked out from the hallway.

Through the window, I saw a face, watching me.

It was only the briefest of glimpses, but it was enough to make me cry out in shock and almost fall over into a flowerbed.

It had been a woman's face; the same woman I had seen in my dream and, I was guessing, the same woman Megan and I had encountered at different times in the house.

Feeling emboldened for some reason, I flung open the front door. There was nobody in the hallway, but I could hear footsteps above me. She was going up the stairs between the first and second floors.

Suddenly fortified by anger, and determined to confront whatever this thing was, I ran up the stairs to the first floor, and from there to the staircase to the attic floor above. Just as I started to go up the second flight of stairs I caught sight of her, albeit very briefly, in the form of the cloak she was wearing pass out of my line of sight as she moved along the second floor landing. I got up there just in time to see her go into one of the two small attic bedrooms. The door closed firmly behind her.

I walked up to the closed door, by now feeling considerably less brave, and caught between two impulses – to open the door and see who was there; or merely to stand outside the door, immobilised by fear.

Finally, with my nerves screaming, I reached for the door handle, and with a hand that was clammy with sweat, depressed the lever.

I could barely breathe as the door swung open with a gentle creak.

The room was empty.

CHAPTER NINETEEN

Windmill Hill

My latest encounter with the apparition notwithstanding, the next couple of days at Badcombe Hollow passed quietly. I experienced no further sightings of the apparition, and by the second night, even managed something approximating a decent night's sleep, albeit with the bedroom door locked, and with most of the lights in the house left on.

My research into Dorian Slake had been reasonably productive, but nevertheless seemed to have hit something of a dead end. However, there was still the issue of Doreen Smithers who, according to Alfred, was a local witch Slake had been close to, and with whom he had quite possibly sired a child. I was considering paying a visit to Stokeley, the village on the Ridgeway where she had lived, but the weather had taken a decided turn for the worse that week, and I didn't see much point in trekking over there in the pouring rain. The story about the temple underneath the burial mound was another lead that wasn't going anywhere, even though I spent a fruitless morning down in the cellar, probing every inch of the floor for some clue as to how one might get in there. Needless to say, I didn't find one.

That just left Billy Matthews, the satanist from Devizes, who I suspected had been keeping Badcombe Hollow under surveillance, on the instructions of Ernst von Draken. I considered confronting Matthews at the address Darren Summers had given me, but I wasn't sure what that would really achieve, in practical terms, and so decided it would be better to keep that piece of information to myself for the time being.

I did, however, do some further research into the practice of satanism.

Switching on my laptop, I went to one of the occult-themed websites that Helen had pointed me in the direction of and flicked through some of the more recent articles. There was one about suspected ritual child abuse at an approved school in the north of

England, which was predictably ghastly, and another in a similar vein concerning a satanic cult in London that preyed on the homeless, in particular young runaways. Neither article referred to any sort of supernatural activity. They were all about the evil and depravity of humankind, with the occultist angle seemingly nothing more than an excuse to indulge in various obscene and disgusting acts; a bit of ritualistic window dressing for all too earthly perversities. I quickly moved on to another article about a police raid on a black mass in a derelict church in Manchester, and from there to voodoo in modern day Haiti, suspicious livestock deaths in the West Highlands, an eyewitness account of a séance and an interview with a self-confessed witch.

After a couple of hours of reading this I decided that I'd had enough and switched off the computer. As complex and nuanced as the subject might be, with some satanic cults clearly more dangerous and malevolent than others, the whole thing was thoroughly distasteful to my mind. I felt a degree of contempt towards Alan for having ever gotten involved in it.

I did, however, decide to see if I could pursue things any further with regard to the person called Julian Faraday, the occult expert and one-time adversary of Dorian Slake, who Helen had told me about.

"Hi, me again," I said, when she picked up the phone.

"Country life really must be boring after all, for you to keep phoning me up," she said. "Or have you rung to say you've finished it?"

"Finished what?"

"You know, the article you said you were going to write for me."

"Oh, that. Still a work in progress. In fact, I've been gathering so much material down here, it's starting to feel more like the subject of a book."

"That sounds super. But I don't publish books, darling, I publish a magazine. Three thousand words maximum. That's the rule. Fifteen hundred would be even better. I think that's about the limit of our readers' attention spans."

"They speak very highly of you, too. Look, seriously, if this did turn out as a book, how about working with me on it. Not now, but when it's done. And helping me tout it around. I don't have any contacts in that field. We'll split the commission. How about it?"

"Can't tell you how much I'd prefer an article for April, round about now, but that's just tantalising enough to keep me sweet. So, what do you need?"

"Hardly anything. Just some contact details, if you have them. You remember that academic you were telling me about? Julian Faraday? The professor with a penchant for the paranormal, who investigates hauntings, covens and cults, and may once have had a run-in with Dorian Slake? I want to try and contact him."

"Good luck with that. I told you, I didn't get anywhere with him, just the brush-off of all time. Brusque would be an understatement."

"Maybe he didn't appreciate getting door-stepped at one of his own lectures," I suggested.

"Probably not. But I was a go-ahead sort of gal in those days. Little Miss Pushy. Veritable force of nature, and all that. But he was a complete dead end. He'd be long retired now, anyway, if he's even still alive."

"Give me the name of the college he taught at, all the same. I might as well give it a shot."

"I can do better than that. I can give you their number. Hold on a second."

I heard the sound of a filing cabinet opening and closing, and the rustle of papers, and then she came back on the line, and read out the number to me.

"You know, if he speaks to you, when he wouldn't speak to me, I'm going to be a bit miffed, to say the least."

"I know. But I'm sure nothing will come of it. Thanks all the same, though. I'll speak to you soon."

"Just remember – fifteen hundred to three thousand words, preferably with pictures, and I absolutely promise I'll print it."

"If it happens, you'll be the first to know. Thanks, Helen."

I dialled the number she had given me, which turned out to be that of the faculty office in Faraday's college.

I spoke to a girl with a lilting Welsh accent who it transpired was a student working there during the Easter vacation, and who was happy enough to chat. She confirmed that Professor Julian Faraday was indeed associated with the college, but was essentially retired, although he maintained some sort of emeritus status, because he still kept an office there. He gave one or two lectures a year, generally on the subject of paganism and Christianity in the early Dark Ages, something about which he was evidently highly expert.

"I went to one of his lectures at the end of my first year," the girl said. "It was very interesting, even though it's not my period, at all. I'm late Medieval. Wars of the Roses. But he was a very good speaker. He told us all about pagan rites and rituals, sacrifices, that sort of thing. Quite gruesome, but it made for an interesting lecture. Apparently, he's a serious expert on witchcraft."

"Is he, indeed?" I said. "I don't suppose he's at the college now, by any chance?"

"No. It's the holidays. And he's hardly ever here, anyway. Just for the lectures. I think it's the only time I've ever seen him."

"You wouldn't know where he lives, I suppose?"

"No. Sorry."

"Do you have a contact number for him?"

"Just this one."

I thanked her and hung up. It didn't seem as if this particular lead was going anywhere, and it had been tenuous enough to start with.

It had stopped raining, and a watery sun was pushing at the clouds. I decided to go for a walk, and so there was a pleasing serendipity when, just moments later, Megan happened to telephone, suggesting the same thing. I felt my mood improve considerably at the sound of her voice.

"I've been cooped up in my room working for the past three days," she said. "I'm going a little bit stir crazy. And it's the first time the sun's been out in ages. Plus, it would be good to see you," she added, after a beat.

"It would be good to see you, too," I said.

After a short, pleasing silence we arranged for her to pick me up outside the house in as short a time as it would take her to drive over from Marlborough, so keen was she to take advantage of the sudden break in the bad weather.

I couldn't help but notice the way in which she emphasised the part about picking me up *outside* the house. It seemed that she was still in no mood to return to the interior of Badcombe Hollow after her last experience there and, self-servingly, I debated in my mind whether or not to tell her of the apparition's most recent manifestations.

I was still pondering this as I stood in the driveway waiting for her to arrive. It was a beautiful day by then, with an almost sheet blue sky, in complete contrast to the grey and dank conditions of late, and the soaking wet lawns of the garden were glistening in the sunshine. As I heard her turn off the main road and into the lane, and then saw the little hatchback come into view, and Megan's face smiling at me from behind the windshield, I put all such thoughts of ghastly apparitions out of my mind, so pleased was I to see her.

I thought she looked lovelier than ever as I got into the car beside her. She was wearing a white Arran sweater that reached almost to the knees of her jeans, and she had her sleek hair tied into the familiar ponytail that suited her so well.

"Isn't this weather just fabulous?" she said, as we drove away from the house. "And it's been so foul, the past few days. I simply had to get out. I hope you weren't in the middle of anything frightfully important."

"I couldn't have been more pleased to hear from you," I said, honestly. Her good mood was infectious.

"So where do you want to go?" I asked.

"I thought we could go to Windmill Hill; the place I've been writing about incessantly since I last saw you. It'll look lovely up there today in this sunshine. But I want to show you a different way of getting there; from Cherhill."

"Fine by me," I said, settling back into the passenger seat, and more than happy to be led by her. I was already enjoying the temporary respite from the worries of living at Badcombe Hollow.

As we approached the village of Cherhill from the east, Megan suddenly slowed the car and turned off onto a narrow access road that led to a parking area next to some gallops.

"This is a good place to know about," she said as we got out of the car. "You can go in all sorts of directions from here, and there's always parking."

She led me through a small copse of beech trees and onto a grass path on top of an embankment, which she told me would once have been the old road to Bath. After only a short time heading west along this path in the direction of the great escarpment above Cherhill, we turned off and walked across a field to the road below, which we crossed, heading north now towards Windmill Hill, and with the long line of the Ridgeway beyond forming the distant horizon.

"You'd hardly know it's there," said Megan, pointing across the patchwork pattern of fields and hedgerows towards the gentle mound of the hill.

"It's so well hidden," she went on. "It's only from the west side that you really notice it. And yet in historic terms, it's the most important place in the whole landscape; the oldest settlement; more significant in its way than Avebury, Silbury or West Kennett.

"I love it here," she added. "As you can probably tell."

It wasn't hard to see why, on such a beautiful day, and with the undulating and seemingly endless plain all around us bathed in sunshine.

We made our way along a bridle path that was bordered on either side by screens of hawthorn, which were starting to show their white flowers, and when we reached the small wood on the steep, western side of the hill, I stopped and took some photographs of the view. We ascended through the trees to the top of the hill, and then wandered slowly around the barrows and embankments that marked out the ancient settlement. There were long views across the plain in every direction, and Megan pointed out several landmarks, before launching into a long peroration on the difference between a round barrow and a bell barrow. I didn't register a lot of the detail, but I loved her enthusiasm, and I loved the way in which the strong breeze that was blasting across the grassy summit was making little wisps of hair fall over her face, which she would periodically brush away.

I asked if I could take her photograph, beside one of the barrows, and she was reticent at first, but she soon relented, and I took a picture of her sun kissed face.

The grass was soaking wet after all the rain, but we found a tree trunk to sit on at the edge of the wood. We sat there for a time in companionable silence, listening to the wind riffling through the trees, and enjoying the understated prettiness of the Neolithic settlement, and our exclusive ownership of it on that fine day; enjoying being with each other too, something we both seemed to be increasingly sensing. It was a good feeling.

Inevitably, however, we eventually discussed the elephant in the room that was Badcombe Hollow.

I realised by then that I had to be completely honest with her, and so I told her everything. I told her about my research into Dorian Slake and the practice of satanism, and about the pentagram I had found painted on the floor of the cellar. And then I told her about my terrifying experience in the house a few nights earlier, when something had tried to get into my room, and then my further sighting of the apparition a day later, when I had followed it up to the attic floor.

"God, how awful," said Megan. "It must have been the same thing that I saw."

"I think I've been seeing her in my dreams, as well," I said.

"Maybe she lived in the house once."

"I'm not sure. In one of the dreams, I got quite close to her. I didn't really see her face. She had her back to me. But he was wearing a kind of cloak that looked like it was made from animal skins. So, I was wondering; maybe she's from your period."

"My period?"

"You know, from Neolithic times."

"Oh, right, the long barrow," said Megan.

"Yes, that too. I mean, I am basically living next door to a Neolithic graveyard. So, I'm thinking it's maybe the place itself that's haunted, the hollow rather than the house. In other words, something much older than the house."

"That would make sense, I guess," said Megan.

We looked at each other for a moment and then we both burst out laughing. Clearly, nothing about any of this made sense. If someone had told me a week previously that I would have been having a rational conversation about an apparition, with a PhD student, no less, and with me being a cynical ex-journalist, I would have thought them insane, and I dare say that Megan would have done, too. But a lot had changed in a week, for both of us.

"Do you think Alan knew about it?" she said.

"Not according to him," I said. "I asked him if the house was haunted when he first told me about it, and the connection it had with Dorian Slake – you know, in a light-hearted sort of way – and he said that it wasn't. He told me he'd never experienced anything like that. But then we know that he wasn't exactly honest with me about a lot of things, so who knows?"

"Do you think it's what drove him away?"

"I've thought about that. But then why go to the elaborate lengths of getting me to live there? Or why not just sell the house, if it was bothering him? The place must be worth a small fortune. Why not just sell up?

"So, I'm actually wondering if he put it there," I said. "You know, conjured it up?"

"But why on earth would he do that?" said Megan. "Even assuming that he could."

"I don't know. To protect the house, maybe? To freak me out, for some reason. Look, I know this all sounds crazy, but we know that Alan was heavily into the whole occult scene. Maybe that long barrow's been haunted for thousands of years, since way before the house was even built, and Alan found out about it somehow, and he found some way of re-animating whatever was in there and getting it to manifest itself."

"You're making out like he's some kind of sorcerer."

"Maybe not him, then. Maybe it was this other guy, von Draken; the one who came to the house, looking for Alan, and who Pete told us about the other night. The person who got Alan interested in the occult in the first place. I've done some digging into him too, as it happens?"

"Oh, really?" said Megan. "What did you find out?"

I told her about the call to my private investigator friend, ostensibly to discover the identity of the person who had been watching the house, and how this had led to a connection with von Draken.

"I think Alan was part of an occult group," I said. "I think he was part of a coven; something that Dorian Slake started back when he lived in the house, and that Alan and his mentor von Draken have been continuing. And I reckon there's something about the house, or the hollow it was built in, or the old burial mound, or something around there, that's important to this group. Maybe there's some ancient evil there that attracts them to it. Maybe that's what made Slake want to go and live there in the first place. We know that von Draken knew Slake. He told me himself. I think he and Slake started this thing off, back in the fifties or sixties, and then Slake died and the coven lost control of the house. And then it changes hands a few times, until von Draken can persuade his friend and fellow occultist, who just happens to be a wealthy, retired rock and roll star, to buy it back for them. It's like Alan's the guardian of the place, or something. And then for some reason he jumps ship, and seemingly disappears off the face of the planet.

"And contrives to put me there in his place," I finished.

"That's a pretty wild and elaborate theory," said Megan.

"I've had a few sleepless nights to put it all together," I said.

"I suppose there's a certain logic to what you're saying. I mean, I see what you're getting at. But it does all sound a bit crazy; you must admit."

"You haven't heard the best part," I said.

I told her about my meeting with Alfred, the elderly farm hand who had worked in the fields next to the house while Slake had lived there, and who had seen his body carried out of the woods after he had killed himself.

"He claims there's a temple underneath the burial mound," I said.

"Not possible," said Megan, shaking her head vigorously. "Definitely not. Neolithic people dug underground to bury their dead, but they didn't worship down there.

"They worshipped up here," she said, pointing out across the plain, "Where they could see the sun and the stars. They worshipped in the stone circles they spent so much time and effort constructing. Trust me on that one. You've got to go much later into history to find people building stuff below ground like that. That would be late Roman era; Mithraic and early Christian periods. People who were persecuted, and so had to worship in secret. It's not a Neolithic thing at all, especially in a place where they buried their dead."

"But I don't mean a Neolithic temple," I said. "I mean something much later. Something Slake built. Something this guy Alfred saw him build. Under the burial mound. A temple. A satanic temple."

"Jesus. Seriously?"

I shrugged and rolled my eyes.

"Welcome to my new world of what's serious and what isn't," I said. "Yes, I suppose I am serious. This guy was very plausible. Says he saw him building it; but on the sly, digging into it from somewhere under the house. Slake even went to the lengths of hiring in foreign workers to do the work. People who didn't speak any English, and so couldn't be quizzed about it by the locals. And that explains why the level of the bank behind the house is higher now than it was before Slake bought the place. You see, I found this book. It was full of old photos of Avebury and the Marlborough Downs, and there was one in there of Badcombe Hollow. Back then, the bank only reached to the first floor. Now it goes as high as the roof. Slake built something there; something that took a huge amount of excavation. It's not above ground, so it must be below ground."

"In that case," said Megan, "How do you get into it?"

"You don't," I said. "That's what I can't figure out. I've searched every inch of the place, and I can't find a way in. So, I can only assume that after Slake built his temple, he sealed it up again. Or someone else did. Alan, maybe."

"But what's the point of having a temple, satanic or otherwise, that you can't use?"

"My thoughts exactly. It doesn't make sense. Unless Slake or Alan or whoever was so desperate to stop anyone from getting in there that they poured concrete into the entrance."

"Maybe they were desperate to stop something from getting out," said Megan.

"Yes, I had considered that possibility too," I said.

"Not a pleasant thought," she said. "Anyway, assuming that you're not going to be breaking up the floor and digging holes all over Alan's cellar, where do you go next with this?"

"I'm not sure that there is a next. I mean, I don't know where I go from here, other than waiting for Alan to get back, so I can have it out with him. Or maybe get someone in to, you know, cleanse the house, or something. Cleanse it spiritually. Maybe get that foul apparition he conjured up to go away, at least. Do you know any spiritualist types?"

"Not personally, but the wider Avebury area isn't exactly short of that sort of person."

"There's the witch," I said. "I could look into that."

"The witch?"

"Another little snippet I got from Alfred. According to him, Slake was more or less a recluse. But the one association he did have was with an old witch who lived around here. A woman called Doreen Smithers. Presumably she was part of Slake's coven. Apparently, she lived in a little village called Stokeley, somewhere up on the Ridgeway. Do you know it?"

Megan shook her head.

"I think I've seen it on a map," she said. "Does this witch still live there?"

"Long dead, apparently. But it might be worth checking out."

"Sounds like a bit of a long shot. I'll help you if I can, though.

"If you want me to, that is," she added.

"I would," I said. "Thank you. I'd appreciate all the help I can get."

"I won't pretend I wasn't very badly shaken by seeing that thing the other night. But I suppose I'm pretty intrigued about it all, as well. Maybe we'll figure it out, somehow; two heads being better than one, and all that. But if you don't mind me saying, I think you need to start a bit closer to home."

"How do you mean?"

"I mean, most of what you've found out so far is from decades ago, mostly concerning people who are no longer alive. But your best lead in this is Alan, isn't it? You know him. You're his friend. You're living in his house. It must be full of clues. Surely the best way to get to the bottom of all of this is find Alan, or at least find out where he's gone, and what he's up to."

I knew that what she was saying made considerable sense.

"You're right," I said. "I need to look at it more from the Alan angle. It's the freshest trail."

"Basically," she said, "You need to search his house."

"I know. That's just what I was thinking. Want to help?"

CHAPTER TWENTY

The Locked Room

Megan wasn't exactly thrilled at the prospect of entering the house again, but by the time we had walked back to the car I had managed to persuade her. It had been her idea to search it for clues, after all.

"It doesn't seem quite so menacing on a bright, sunny day," she conceded, as we drew up in front of the house.

It was long past lunchtime, and since neither of us had eaten since breakfast, I made us each a sandwich, which we ate at the island unit in the kitchen before commencing our search of the house.

"So, what exactly are we looking for?" I asked, semi-rhetorically, as I carried our empty plates over to the sink.

"I guess we'll know when we find it," said Megan. "Anything out of the ordinary, I suppose; any sort of clue as to where Alan might be. That must be the key to all this. What's he been up to, and where has he gone?"

"Okay. Let's get to it."

We started in the larger of the two sitting rooms.

"If this was a book or a film," I said, "This would be the part where I'd say, 'Let's split up', to get it done quicker."

"I suppose it would," said Megan. "But, just to be clear, we're not splitting up. At any point. Even if I have to tie myself to you."

"Fair enough. I did search the cellar by myself, the other morning."

"What was that like?"

"Like being in my own private horror film. I kept expecting that thing to jump out of the shadows at any second."

"I can imagine. Did you find anything?"

"Not a thing."

"Well, at least we don't have to look down there," she said.

"Don't you want to see the pentagram on the floor?"

"Thanks, but I think I can live without it. You know, once you've seen one pentagram, etcetera. Actually, I'm not sure if I ever have seen a pentagram, at least not like the thing you described, but I certainly don't need to this afternoon."

It didn't take long to go through both of the sitting rooms, in spite of the temptation to get distracted by Alan's prodigious book collection, and a search of the kitchen proved similarly fruitless, aside from a small business card I found in a drawer.

Bethany Weyland
Medium and Spiritualist

There was a Bath address and a telephone number printed on the underside of the card.

"Did Alan ever mention going to see this person?" I asked Megan, showing her the card.

"No," she said. "Not to me."

I put it aside for future reference. It might be worth following up at some point, I thought.

The study took longer to search, since it contained a great many files, detailing everything from Alan's finances to the household accounts, but this room also yielded little useful information. I was, however, interested to note that Alan was far wealthier than I had imagined. The most cursory examination of the file marked 'Finances' revealed that he had cash, stocks and other assets with a combined value of almost ten million pounds. Alan had done well out of the music business, I reflected, but he hadn't done that well. He had clearly made some judicious investments in the years since he retired. I couldn't help but wonder if he had somehow used occult means towards such ends, having discovered during my research into the practice of satanism that personal gain and worldly riches could be a strong motivating factor for those who chose to follow such a path. Albeit in exchange for one's immortal soul, I recalled. If one believed in such things, of course. I was starting to think that I might.

We moved upstairs. I sensed a certain degree of tension in Megan as we stood on the first-floor landing where she had encountered the apparition.

I was feeling it too. I had realised by then that there was just something about this house that simply got to one. I wondered again if it had got to Alan, for all his evident enthusiasm for playing with dark forces, and if this was what had compelled him to leave.

We started in Alan's room. Just as when looking through his files in the study, I didn't feel at all comfortable about going through his personal things. But I reminded myself that Alan had employed a considerable amount of deception to get me to come and live here, and that this more than justified my snooping.

It didn't take long. Alan seemed to have become almost fanatically tidy in middle age and Megan, I had discovered by then, was highly efficient and methodical, perhaps reflecting her academic training and disciplined mind. In any event, we found nothing in there of any interest, and a search of the other bedrooms also failed to uncover anything out of the ordinary; likewise, the little box room where Alan kept his records and CDs, and where I had already had a good root around.

As we climbed the stairs to the second floor there was a violent gust of wind outside, and moments later we heard the clatter of rain on the roof. The light had dropped perceptibly.

"A storm. How very apposite," said Megan, as we stood in the gloom of the attic landing.

"Is this where you saw her?" she said.

"Yes, and that's the room she went into," I said, pointing towards the door to one of the two bedrooms.

"Might as well start in there, then," she said.

There was a loud creak as I pushed the door open, and I felt myself tense as we stepped across the threshold.

The room was just as empty as it been the last time I had come in here, in pursuit of the apparition. It was also devoid of anything of interest, as was the bedroom next door. As much as I enjoyed any excuse to be in Megan's company, I realised that our bright idea atop the summit of Windmill Hill was all turning into a bit of a bust. But she seemed just as determined to carry on as I was.

"So, what's with the locked door?" Megan said as we emerged from the second bedroom, motioning towards the room at the end of the corridor.

"I've been kind of curious about that, myself," I said.

Megan walked over to the door and gently tugged at the padlock.

"We have to open it," she said.

"I saw a set of bolt croppers in the cellar," I said.

We looked at each other.

"Let's do it," she said. "We have to know what's in there."

"I don't know," I said. "It would technically be breaking and entering. I mean, he obviously put that lock on the door for a reason."

"Which is precisely why we need to see what's on the other side."

"I know. I'd just feel bad about it, I suppose. It would be crossing a line, somehow, in spite of the circumstances.

"You just read Alan's bank statements, and then you looked through his underwear drawer. I'd say that the line has been well and truly crossed."

"Yes, but he'll never find out about those things," I ventured. "He'll know if I break into that room."

"No, he won't," said Megan, peering down at the padlock. "It's a suited lock. You can replace it with one with the same serial number. Alan's key will still work, and he'll never be any the wiser."

"Okay, you've persuaded me," I said. "But I'm not going back down to the cellar by myself. You have to come with me."

"No problem. I'm not staying up here by myself. Plus, we said no splitting up, right?"

The trip down to the cellar was thankfully uneventful, and a few minutes later we were back outside the locked room, and I was manoeuvring the blades of the cutters over the padlock.

"Here goes," I said, as I prepared to cut through it, suddenly feeling anxious at the prospect of opening the door.

The heavy croppers were more than a match for the padlock, and I cut through the metal hoop with a simple snip. We stood there for a long moment, staring at the door.

"In we go, then," I said softly, as I lifted off the broken padlock and reached for the door handle.

I depressed the lever and the door swung open. As it did, Megan gripped my arm with both hands. I think we were both feeling somewhat unnerved by then.

It was gloomy in the room, but not dark, as it was lit by a small dormer window, through which I could see grey sky, and against which I could hear the patter of the rain. There was a light switch by the door, which I flicked on, illuminating the room in harsh yellow.

The interior looked as innocuous as the other rooms on that floor. I felt deflated at the realisation that the forcing open of the door was unlikely to be the afternoon's Eureka moment. And I was now going to have to buy what would probably be a very expensive padlock.

It was a tiny space, the smallest room in the whole house, not much more than a walk-in cupboard, and it contained only two things; a mobile hanging rail, loaded with clothes, against one wall, and a long wooden chest against another.

Feeling an odd mixture of relief and disappointment, I stepped into the room, with Megan close behind me. Outside, the rain suddenly increased in intensity and hammered down onto the roof above us. A gust of wind made the room's tiny window rattle in its frame.

"Not exactly what I was expecting," I said, as I stood beside the heavily laden hanging rail.

"What were you expecting?" said Megan.

"Good question. I'm not really sure."

We took an end each and started to work our way through the clothes on the rail, enjoying a certain amount of light relief as we uncovered some of Alan's old show costumes.

"Well, I know where to come if I ever want to borrow a sequinned jacket," said Megan, as she came across one particularly lurid garment.

"I can't believe he'd want to keep that," I said. "I can't believe he even wore it."

"Or that he'd feel the need to keep it locked up. I'm thinking, if there's anything interesting up here, it's going to be in that box."

"It looks like a linen chest," I said.

"It is a linen chest," Megan said, as she crouched down beside it and lifted the lid, revealing a stack of neatly folded, cream coloured bed linen.

"But what lies beneath?" she went on. "Come on. Help me empty it."

I knelt down beside to her, and we lifted out the pile of sheets and pillowcases until the chest was empty.

"I don't get it," said Megan. "Why would he lock up his bed linen?"

"Wait a minute," I said. "We're not looking at the whole trunk. This thing has a false bottom."

Taking out the linen had revealed a chipboard base to the chest that was clearly some way above the level of the floor. There was nothing holding it in place, and there was a hand-hole cut into the middle, which meant that we would be able to lift it out.

"Goodness, you're right," said Megan. "It must be hiding something."

When we pulled out the board, the first thing we saw was a pile of folded black fabric.

"Black sheets?" said Megan. "Who has black sheets on their bed?"

"They're not sheets," I said, as I took one of the pieces of fabric from the box and unfolded it. "This is a cloak."

I held the cloak out in front of me. It was completely black in colour, and seemed to be made from an expensive, silk-like fabric. It had a hood at the back, and a belt around the middle. There were three of them in the chest.

"Satanic robes, I assume," said Megan. "For wearing when attending black masses and other such ceremonies."

"You wouldn't go walking down Marlborough High Street in it, that's for sure," I said. "Except on Halloween, perhaps. Let's see what else is in here."

The remainder of the chest contained several packs of black candles, which I knew from my research were a typical accoutrement at most satanic rituals. There was also some sort of mixing bowl, some small bottles of ointment, and two heavy, silver-plated chalices.

If there had been the slightest doubt before that Alan worshipped the devil, there could be none now. The pictures in the trunk further confirmed this.

Lying beneath the cloaks were five small paintings, narrow enough to fit in the trunk, thanks to their letterbox shape. They had been painted in acrylic, straight onto thin board, and they appeared to be part of the same series, depicting the various stages of a witches' sabbat. The scene was a ruined chapel, set in a steep, rocky valley. The rocks reminded me of the sarsen stones that were strewn across parts of the Marlborough Downs.

The first painting depicted a group of people wearing black cloaks. The same sort of black cloak that we had found in the chest. The group had formed a circle around a fire, and it was clear that the picture was depicting the meeting of a coven. I counted the figures and there were thirteen of them.

In the second painting, some sort of high priest was officiating over their ceremony, his arms outstretched, whilst the remainder of the coven looked on in rapt attention.

In the third painting, the priest was draining the blood from a chicken or cockerel into a chalice, whilst before him, a naked woman lay on a stone slab that looked like an altar.

The fourth painting depicted an orgy, with the coven having divested themselves of their robes, and fallen upon each other with unrestrained abandon. The high priest had mounted the woman on the altar and appeared to be screaming up at the sky. It was like a grotesque parody of a painting by Hieronymus Bosch.

In the final painting in the series the group of satanists were lying, sated and exhausted amongst the rocks, whilst above them hovered a horned creature that was part-man, part-goat, with a pentagram on its forehead, and who I recognised as Baphomet – the devil himself.

All the paintings bore the same set of initials in the bottom right-hand corner. DS. Dorian Slake.

I figured they must have been the paintings missing from the walls in the room down in the cellar. The room with the pentagram on the floor.

"Well, we definitely know what Alan's into now," I said to Megan as we knelt beside each other in the tiny room, looking at this unedifying tableau.

"But we still don't know where he's gone," she said.

"No. On that subject, we're no closer at all."

We put everything back into the box and returned downstairs. It was early in the evening by then, and we both felt like a drink. I made gin and tonics, which we carried through into the sitting room. Outside, the heavy rain that had resumed during our search of the house had now escalated into a full-blown storm. It was so dreary I had to put the lights on.

"I'm sorry that didn't yield anything more concrete," I said, as we sat down. "But thank you for your help, all the same."

"That's okay," said Megan. "It was worth a try. At least we found his dressing up box. And those awful pictures," she added. "We know for certain that he's into some sort of devil worship."

"But his whereabouts remain as elusive as ever. I thought we might have found something."

"I know. I'm kind of sorry I suggested it now."

"No, it was well worth doing. Anyway, maybe I'll just forget about it all. Until he gets back, at any rate. Or gets in contact with me."

"Yes, but in the meantime, you still have a haunted house to live in. That's no nearer to being resolved. If you had managed to find out where Alan is, he might at least have known something about that."

"He may know something about it," I said, "But that doesn't mean he would have told me. You see, there's something I haven't told you about Alan and me."

I told her how Alan and I had fallen out, after we left university, and how that had led to us being effectively estranged for most of the next two decades, until he had suddenly showed up at my flat; the same day he offered me the use of this house.

"I think I might have been a bit of a mug," I said.

"You mean, you think this might all be some elaborate revenge plot?" said Megan. "That Alan was getting back at you by putting you in this house, and conjuring up some demonic entity to torment you? It sounds a bit far-fetched. How did he even know you'd agree to come and live here?"

"He knew I was on the ropes, financially, because he'd checked up on me. And because I more or less told him. But I agree. It does all sound a little fanciful."

"I think it's more likely that he conjured that thing up for his own purposes, couldn't control it, and ended up running away from it. And maybe at that point, decided to pass the problem on to you."

"Yes, it could be that" I said. "Or it could be that it was here before he bought the house, and he wanted to get away from it. Or he raised it, and then couldn't control it. Or something else altogether."

I got up and walked over to the window. The rain had reached a torrential pitch and was falling so hard onto the roof of Megan's car in the driveway that the drops were ricocheting off it like bullets. I felt depressed. All my research of the past few days seemed to have led nowhere.

"How about staying for supper?" I said, turning back to face Megan.

I had been planning on asking her this for most of the afternoon, and now seemed like as good a time as any.

"I'm sorry," she said. "I'd love to, but I have something this evening."

Perhaps sensing my disappointment, she went on: "Maybe in a few days? There's a place in Marlborough I could take you."

"Okay," I said. "I'd like that. Call me about it?"

"Will do," she said, smiling emphatically.

There was still something hanging in the air between us. I sensed it, and she sensed it, but it wasn't going anywhere for the moment.

We sipped our drinks and talked of other things until it was time for her to go.

"Bloody hell," she said, as she opened the front door and saw the sheets of rain falling outside. "I didn't bring a coat, because it was so gorgeous earlier, and I've got an errand to run on the way back to Marlborough. There isn't an old coat of Alan's that I could borrow, is there?"

I went through to the utility room and came back with a long, fawn coloured overcoat.

"I'm afraid it's not very glamorous," I said.

"Better that than one of those black cloaks upstairs," said Megan. "Thanks. I'll bring it back next time."

"Sure. Whenever. It's not like Alan's going to miss it."

I held the coat open for her and she turned her back to me and slipped her arms through the sleeves. I felt a tremor of excitement at the faint touch of her body against mine, and then she turned around so that her face was only inches away, and we looked at each other for a long moment. Then I drew her towards me and kissed her.

"I think that's been a long time coming," she said, when we finally released each other.

"Feels that way," I agreed.

"I'll see you soon," she said, as she pulled gently away.

Feeling as contented with life as I had felt disappointed, only moments earlier, I watched her dash through the rain to her car and drive away.

CHAPTER TWENTY-ONE

The Witch's House

It rained incessantly for the next two days. According to the proprietor of the off license in Marlborough, where I went during a brief excursion into the deluge, it was the wettest spring he had ever known, in the best part of sixty years living there.

"Gets you down, weather like this," he said, and it was hard to disagree. The sodden landscape made for a dismal scene, and I became a virtual prisoner in the house, which felt as if it was under siege by the elements. I even considered going away for a couple of days, and perhaps travelling up to town for a break from it all. It was only the proximity of Megan, and the anticipation of seeing her, that kept me at Badcombe Hollow during those dank, miserable days.

By the end of the week, however, the weather appeared to be on the turn, with the rain reduced to a persistent drizzle, and the prospect of fine conditions in the days to come. I was returning home after my first proper walk since going to Windmill Hill when Megan telephoned, and suggested meeting up in Marlborough for supper. I felt a pleasant skip in my heart when I heard her voice and knew that I was well on the way to becoming smitten.

We went to an Indian restaurant at the end of the high street. Megan arrived, moments after me, and we greeted each other with a kiss, as if this was the most natural thing in the world, and there was an easy familiarity about us as we chatted of inconsequential matters whilst ordering.

"How's the research into Slake and your haunted house going?" she asked as our starters arrived.

"It isn't, really," I said. "I had another look through Alan's files, but there's nothing out of the ordinary in there, and certainly nothing to suggest where he might have gone."

"What about the you-know-what, that's been stalking the house? Any more appearances?"

"Thankfully not. I did have one thought, though."

"About what?"

"About those ghastly pictures, Alan had hidden in the trunk. And about the portrait of Dorian Slake. The one that keeps falling off the wall."

"Where is that, by the way?"

"I put it down in the cellar. It's in the room with the pentagram, appropriately enough. Anyway, you remember we assumed those paintings were by Slake; because of the initials – DS? Well, I think they might stand for something else."

Megan looked at me enquiringly.

"Doreen Smithers," I said. "The witch that Slake consorted with when he lived here. She's DS as well. They could be her initials."

"That's certainly possible, I suppose. But where does that get you?"

"Nowhere, really. I'm still thinking of taking a trip out there, though."

"Out where?"

"To the place where Doreen Smithers lived. Up on the Ridgeway."

"What for? You said she's been dead for about fifty years."

"I don't know. Background, mood music. I've been thinking about writing a book about all of this. So, I thought I'd go up there tomorrow. It's supposed to be good weather. Why don't you come along?"

"I'm away this weekend. Sorry. I'm staying with my parents in Devizes again. My father's been in hospital for an operation, so I've been helping out."

I hid my disappointment at this news. Regardless of whether or not Megan had been free for an excursion on the Ridgeway, I had been hoping to see her at some point over the weekend, in order to continue where we had left off with our kiss in the hallway of Badcombe Hollow.

"Are you sure it's really worth it?" she was saying. "I mean, if it's such a long time since she lived there. What's there going to be left to see?"

It was a perfectly good question, to which I obviously didn't have an answer. Maybe I would be better off trying to revive my novel, and forgetting about this whole thing, I thought, as the conversation moved onto other subjects.

By the time we finished dinner I had more or less persuaded myself to try and put it all behind me. I had a book to finish, one that I had already started, and in which a publisher had expressed an interest. The last thing I needed was the distraction of another writing project. Anyway, courting Megan over the coming months was going to be a lot more fun than investigating a bunch of devil worshippers.

After dinner, I walked Megan back to her digs. She didn't ask me in. I had wondered if she might but didn't mind that she hadn't. Megan was going to be a long project, I told myself, but she was definitely worth it. We shared a long kiss as we said goodbye and agreed to meet up the following week. Driving back to Badcombe Hollow that night I experienced a feeling I hadn't known since the early days of Marianne and realised that I was falling in love. All of a sudden, the dead end I had reached in my research into Alan, and Slake, and Doreen Smithers, and all the rest of it, seemed like a blessing. It felt as if a new page was being turned.

After another mercifully quiet night, I got up on the Saturday morning with every intention of resuming work on the manuscript. I had breakfast and then set myself up at the island unit in the kitchen, just as I had done during those early days in the house, and I flexed my fingers above the keyboard that morning with a genuine sense of purpose. But after less than a paragraph I realised that my heart wasn't in it. Maybe it was a sense of unfinished business about the witch up on the Ridgeway, or wanting to daydream about Megan, or merely the sight of a blue sky after so many days of rain, but I felt restless and wanted to go out. I deleted what I had just written and decided to go and look for the witch's house. Maybe I'd write about all of this after all, I thought. Not a book, since that would require too much research and hard work on a subject that I found distasteful, but perhaps I could do an article on it for Helen's esoteric magazine and earn a little cash for my trouble.

Ten minutes later, I was tooling along the back roads, with an Ordnance Survey map, my camera and a notebook on the front seat beside me, feeling pleased about my decision.

It was a lovely day, sunny and blustery, with scudding clouds, and fierce pools of light, tracking across the patchwork of fields. The plain almost had a glow about it. It felt liberating to be heading out, and away from Badcombe Hollow, after the dreary entrapment caused by the days of continuous rain.

The tiny village of Stokeley was easy enough to find on the map, since there was nothing much else in its vicinity, and it appeared as an isolated dot in the eastern lee of the Ridgeway, next to a wood and surrounded by steep escarpments. It was accessed by a minor road which passed by some woods on the other side of the village, and which then eventually made its way back to the main road. It was a place in the middle of nowhere, and on the way to nowhere. The only other notation in the whole of the grid square was the word 'ruins' in italics, at the far edge of the green block of woodland, about a mile or so from the village.

I drove around the outskirts of Marlborough and headed north, running parallel to the line of the Ridgeway, in the direction of Stokeley, on roads that became narrower and ever more devoid of other traffic. It was pretty, remote country, populated with the occasional farmstead, and hamlets so small that they didn't have names. As I travelled north the landscape became more rugged, the cultivated fields giving way to high grazing pastures, woods and hills, and with even fewer signs of human settlement.

Anxious that I hadn't yet reached the turn-off to the village I pulled over to the side of the road and checked my map, but I seemed to be going the right way. A cool breeze gusted through the open window, and on the escarpment above me I noticed two buzzards circling. I might have been the only person for miles around.

I continued along the narrow, half-broken road, alert for any sign of the turning east to Stokeley, which for mile after mile stubbornly refused to appear, almost causing me to stop again, and turn around in case I had somehow missed it.

And then I saw it; a weathered sign bearing the name of the village, half-obscured by the thick foliage that clung to the sides of the road. I braked sharply and turned on to what was little more than a track, feeling a spray of gravel under the wheels of the car.

I knew that I must only be a mile or so from my destination. I felt excited. It was good to be on the trail of something again, heading into the unknown in search of a story, not entirely sure what I was going to find. My old journalistic instincts, long suppressed, had come back to life, and I was experiencing a real sense of anticipation as I drew nearer to the village, notwithstanding the fact that I was merely going to look for the house of someone long dead.

Dorian Slake would have driven these roads, I told myself, and possibly Alan as well. I was following in their footsteps, by entering the domain of this erstwhile witch of the Ridgeway.

The village itself was tiny, and consisted of a mere handful of houses, the largest of which was part of a working farm, albeit devoid of human activity on that particular morning, since there was not another person to be seen as I slowly cruised through the remote settlement. I passed by a few cottages, joined together in a terrace, but nothing else of note. There was no church, or shop, or village hall, not even a green or other such communal space. And then, only moments after entering the village I found myself on the other side of it. So much anticipation for such little reward, I thought to myself, although I wasn't sure what I had really been expecting.

Nevertheless determined to explore, I parked the car on a grass verge by the entrance to a field and slipping my camera into the pocket of my coat, walked back into the village.

There was still no obvious sign of humanity. No smoke rose from any of the chimneys, no dog barked on my approach. The place appeared deserted. But as I walked past the line of terraced cottages, I detected the flicker of a curtain.

I suddenly didn't feel alone anymore and wondered if I was being watched. I reminded myself that I was a stranger in a remote community, and therefore it was only natural that I should be the object of some curiosity. I also recalled Alfred referring to the insularity of the people who lived in this village, and how they didn't like outsiders. It was an unsettling recollection.

I reached the farm and stood by the entrance to its yard, ostensibly regarding the view over to the high escarpment of the Ridgeway, so it didn't look like I was snooping around. The place appeared neglected and run down and was bordered by a series of derelict barns. The metal gate to the adjacent field was rusty and hanging askew of its post.

For some reason I felt distinctly uneasy in this quiet, deserted place, as if some sixth sense was making the hairs on the back of my neck stand up. I told myself this was irrational, and a symptom of my having lived too long at Badcombe Hollow, and yet the feeling persisted. I felt a strong desire to leave, and strike off into the surrounding countryside, which looked a much more appealing prospect on that sunny morning than the bleak little settlement in which I was standing.

But I still hadn't identified the house where Doreen Smithers had lived. I presumed it must have been one of the terraced cottages, but there was no way to find out. The early excitement of my excursion had all but evaporated, and I realised that this had been something of a fool's errand. I decided to go for a walk in the woods on the edge of the village, and perhaps find the ruins I had seen marked on the map.

I turned and walked back through the village, as deathly silent as before, absent even the sound of birdsong. When I reached the car, I made to follow a track on the other side of the road, which was signposted as a footpath, and which led up a steep rise and into the woods, but then I noticed another, barely defined path beside it, its entrance so overgrown that one might easily have missed it. Peering through the dense foliage I saw that it ran back towards the village, almost parallel to the road, but obscured from it by the tall hedgerow along its edge.

Wondering where the path led, I decided to follow it. I pushed my way through the splays of hawthorn blocking the entrance and stepped onto what had once been a cobbled pathway and was now covered in moss and weeds. After only a few metres the path turned sharply away from the road and opened out into a small orchard of gnarled, withered fruit trees that appeared long untended, set in tall meadow grass that came up as high as my knees, and which made my shoes and the bottoms of my trousers wet as I walked through it. At the far end of the orchard was a high screen of conifers. For some reason I knew that I was going to find something on the other side.

I found a house, broken and long abandoned. It would have been a small cottage once, built of stone, with a tiled roof, and a tall chimney, from which one imagined smoke rising. But not today. The approach to the house was so overgrown that its lower elevations were in danger of being swallowed up by the encroaching vegetation, and its immediate curtilage was littered with smashed tiles and moss-covered timber. One of the gables was in a state of partial collapse, and there was a large hole in the roof. None of the windows had glass in them, and appeared as dark, blank apertures, cut into stonework that was charred as well as weathered.

The house had obviously been gutted by fire, and long ago. Kicking aside a clump of stinging nettles, I looked through a ground floor window into what might have been the parlour, and where through the gloom I could just make out the grating of a fireplace, and the vague red hue of a quarry tiled floor amidst all the surface debris.

I think I would have known it was the witch's house even without the rather obvious clue that had been marked on the smooth stone lintel to the window. It was another pentagram, set in a circle, just like the one carved into the tree trunk in the woods above Badcombe Hollow. Someone, at some time, whether years previously or the day before yesterday, and whether out of jest, mockery, respect or devotion, had left this mark upon the house. This was the erstwhile dwelling place of Doreen Smithers. I felt a chill pass through me as my mind conjured an image of some snaggle-toothed old hag performing spells in this house and worshipping the devil on this very spot.

I took some photographs, including a close-up of the pentagram, whilst speculating as to whether the house had been destroyed by fire whilst the witch had lived here, or at some point subsequent to her departure.

Not particularly wanting to hang around but feeling that I should make as thorough an examination as possible of the ruined house, I slipped my camera back into my pocket, hauled myself up onto the ledge of the window and jumped down onto the floor of broken tiles.

I picked my way carefully through the mess of charred timbers and other detritus, my eyes peeled for any further clues that I was in the former dwelling place of a witch.

The old house had a sour, musty smell about it, and it felt cool in the shadow of the broken walls. At the end of the building, the encroaching vegetation had almost completely taken hold. Brambles poured through the windows and a large clump of stinging nettles covered the lower half of the far wall.

I was about to turn around and leave when I thought I saw something written on the wall. It was mostly obscured by the dense foliage, so only the tops of what looked like letters were visible above the mass of nettles. But it looked as if some words had been painted onto the stained, flaking render, some time back before nature took over.

I pushed my way through the nettles towards the wall and then trampled them down with my feet to a sufficient extent that I could step back and see what was written there.

The short line of black painted text left me in no doubt that I had found the house of Doreen Smithers, the black magician of the Ridgeway, and the former consort of Dorian Slake.

BURN IN HELL – WITCH

CHAPTER TWENTY-TWO

The Ruined Chapel

It was a relief to be outside again, and to walk away from that foul house. When I got to the edge of the garden I turned back and took a final series of photos of the cottage exterior, a bleak ruin with a dark history. I didn't plan on returning there. For all the ostensible prettiness of the surroundings, there was something pervasively sinister about it.

Suddenly, from somewhere behind me, a distinct noise broke the silence, causing me to wheel around. It had sounded like a twig snapping. I scanned the trees and hedgerows but saw nothing. And yet I had definitely heard something. Not for the first time since arriving at the village, I wondered if I was being watched.

I wanted to get away from this horrid place, made dark by the shadow of the tall screen of fir trees. I felt a sudden yearning to get back into the more open countryside where I had left the car. I wanted to be somewhere that wasn't so hemmed in, and from where I could see a reasonable distance around me. Just being close to Doreen Smithers' house was making me feel spooked.

I walked briskly back to the road, all the time alert for any sign of the person who may or may not have been watching me from somewhere, but I saw nothing out of the ordinary.

I was breathing a little easier by the time I reached the road, and the sight of my car on the grass verge where I had left it was a reassuring one. But rather than drive away, I chose instead to follow the other path that led off this part of the road, and which went across a field towards some woods. I recalled from my map that there were ruins marked on the other side of these woods, and I decided to see if I could find them. It seemed like a much more pleasant prospect that exploring the charred remains of the witch's house.

The route across the field was steeper than it appeared from the road. When I reached the edge of the woods I turned back and looked down at the tiny hamlet of Stokeley that was now beneath me, and seemingly just as devoid of activity as it had been when I had walked through it earlier that morning.

I peered into the woods and at the vestiges of a faintly defined path. Shrugging off a frisson of unease at the prospect of getting lost in there, I set off along it.

It was a beautiful old wood, full of ancient beech that was yet to come into leaf, but which on a summer's day must have made for a luscious green canopy above the path. The woods were more open here than they were in the dense thicket above Alan's house, making everything much lighter, and I could feel the warmth of the sun on my face. The mildly disturbing experience of visiting the witch's house faded to a memory, the further away I got from the village, and before long I felt as if I was on any other hike, on any other day. It was simply beautiful countryside, completely unspoiled.

I followed the undulating path through the trees, occasionally catching glimpses of the sun splashed fields that lay beside the wood. I knew from the map that the woods were about a mile across, at which point the landscape opened out into a high valley, and it was here that I expected to find the ruins.

On two occasions during my walk, I thought I heard something moving about in the undergrowth. Both times I stopped and looked around, but saw nothing. And yet that same sixth sense from back in the village had kicked in again, and I had the strong suspicion that I was being watched. I nevertheless tried to put it out of my mind and pressed on.

I eventually reached the end of the wood, from where there was an arresting view over a vast expanse of upland pasture, strewn with rocks that I recognised as sarsen stones, and dotted with grazing sheep, some of whom looked up as I emerged from the trees.

As I stepped into the field, I realised that it was divided across the middle by a steep cleft in the landscape concealing an upland valley, or combe, so narrow in width and steeply sided that one might have missed the fact that it was there. It was a deceptive sight, almost like a trick of the eye; a hidden valley, obscured from view by the natural fissures of the rolling, green terrain.

As I drew closer, it became more obvious and soon I was standing above a deep canyon, steeply terraced on both sides in a series of long, horizontal strips lined with thick hassocks of grass, and by a more gentle rise at one end, which was the head of the valley. In the other direction, the flat, narrow bottom snaked off on a meandering route towards some farm buildings in the distance, gradually losing its definition as the landscape became less steep and more open.

But my attention was immediately drawn to the area right beneath me. Down at the bottom of the combe there was a small, ruined structure of broken stone. It was bordered on one side by several large boulders that looked as if they might have been placed there, as an entrance to the site, and on the other by a stand of three fir trees, one of which was mostly dead, and which had its top sheared off, as if by a bolt of lightning. Even at this distance, I could tell that the building had once been a small church or chapel.

I carefully made my way down the slope, causing a group of sheep in my path to trot away to either side of me. I paused in my descent beside a clump of small, gnarled, thorn-covered trees grouped around some sarsen stones. A lone sheep peered out at me from within the little enclosure with a slightly annoyed look on its face at my having intruded upon its natural refuge on the hillside. It pushed itself to its feet and stalked off to join up with the rest of the flock.

The trees had been stunted by countless winds and grew precariously at an angle off the steep slope. I had to stoop down low beneath their prickly, sinewy canopy to get myself into the sheltered cluster of rocks. I sat on a slab of smooth sarsen, jutting out of the ground like a carved seat. It afforded a view through the bare but densely entangled foliage down to the ruined chapel, a hundred or so yards away.

Just one side of the nave remained more or less intact, identifiable as such by the gaping, arched apertures set into the ancient stonework that would once have been a row of windows, the glass within them long since gone. None of the roof remained, and the gable at one end had been reduced to a tall and unruly pile of stones, whilst that at the entrance was no longer in existence at all. The interior of the nave, completely open from the direction in which I was looking at it, was a mess of loose stones and slabs, and what looked to be the remains of a buttress, lying on its side across the rubble. For some reason, Shelley's *Ozymandias* came to mind. I felt as if I was looking upon a once proud and mighty monument, now broken beyond repair, gradually crumbling away to nothing in this remote valley.

I left my perch and continued down the hillside. The closer I got to the old chapel, the more I felt that there was something oddly familiar about it, but it wasn't until I was standing amidst the broken vestiges of the nave that I realised what it was.

I was sure this was the place that had featured in the series of paintings that Megan and I had found hidden in Alan's house; the place being used as the setting for a witches' sabbat, as depicted, most likely, by Doreen Smithers, the acolyte of Dorian Slake. I felt a chill within me as I stood there, recalling the lurid images of the coven in this very spot, imagining Slake himself officiating over some twisted, evil ceremony.

There were charred timbers by my feet, the remains of a fire, of uncertain vintage. I couldn't help but wonder if this was still the site of satanic activity; if a coven still gathered here to worship the devil, before ravishing each other amongst the stones, and perhaps performing even worse acts. It was an unsettling thought.

I looked around for any sign of the satanic altar upon which a nude woman had been lying in one of the paintings, as a prelude, presumably, to being ritually murdered by the high priest of the ceremony, in front of his cowed, hooded minions. I found a large, flattish stone slab that might have been it. My suspicions increased when I noticed a rough, narrow channel, seemingly cut into its surface, leading to a small, bowl-like depression at one end. I recalled from my research that such channels were used for gathering blood spilt upon the stone and directing it into a chalice.

This had to be the same place as that in the paintings, I thought. It was simply too much of a coincidence for it not to be. And what a well-chosen site for occultists to go about their ghastly business this was; in a remote and hard to reach location, concealed from even a short distance away by the steep folds of the landscape. My revulsion at its function aside, I felt a real sense of triumph at having discovered it.

I walked slowly around the ruin, taking masses of photographs, including several of the pagan altar, and of the open windows to the surviving section of nave, simply because it looked so dramatic, set against the blue sky.

But it was at the end of the chapel, where the chancel and the altar would once have been, and now a huge pile of broken stones, that I made a truly grisly discovery, starkly reminding me that this was no mere romantic ruin, for all its outward, bucolic charm.

On a smooth slab amidst the cluster of rocks, an object had been placed. It was a head. The decaying, decomposed head of a goat.

Most of the outer skin had gone, save for a fur covered flap between the creature's horns. What was left of the skin around its mouth was pulled back, revealing its bared teeth in a ghastly, rictus grin. One of its eyes was missing, presumably plucked out by the crows that wheeled high in the sky, above this ruin. The other dead eye stared dolefully back at me.

Sickened by this act of cruel depravity, and suddenly feeling as uncomfortable as I had in the burned-out witch's house, I felt the strong urge to be on my way.

After one final look around, I started to climb back up the steep slope of the valley, stopping at about the same level as the little clump of trees where I had rested on the way down, and where I took a series of pictures of the small, ruined building.

But when I got to the top of the slope, I saw something that stopped me in my tracks, just as abruptly as the goat's head in the chapel had.

Standing a short distance away, at the edge of the woods, was the figure of a man. He was watching me. It was a scene reminiscent of the watcher in the woods at Badcombe Hollow, and for a time the two of us stood there in our respective positions, staring at each other.

This person must have followed me through the woods, I thought, and he may well have been observing me at the witch's house, as well. I suddenly felt very exposed, being in such an isolated place, far from civilisation, save for a village where they didn't welcome strangers.

Determined not to be intimidated, I started to walk towards the man, who remained immobile. More shades of the incident at Badcombe Hollow, I thought to myself, although something about the man's build told me that it was a different person. As I got closer, I saw that he was a man of about my own age, wearing a long coat and carrying a stick that looked like a shepherd's staff. For some reason, I didn't think he was a shepherd.

When the distance between us was reduced to a few yards, I steeled myself for a confrontation. But then the man turned his back on me, and headed off into the woods, the trees seeming to swallow him up. As I entered the woods myself, I soon saw him again, not bothering to conceal himself as he watched me from beside a deadfall at the top of a short rise in the ground. Just as brazenly, he walked down and fell into step behind me as I passed him. I made a conscious effort to ignore him, although I was feeling increasingly tense.

By the time I got to the other side of the woods, he was still following me, although he had dropped back a short distance, so that he was no longer right behind me. I made my way through the field towards the road, and the reassuring sight of my car parked on the verge. When I reached the gate at the bottom of the field, I looked back, and saw that the man had got closer again, and was now only fifty yards or so behind me.

Torn between waiting for him to get to me, and having it out with him, or getting away from there as swiftly as possible, I decided that discretion was the better part of valour and got hastily into the car, tossing my camera onto the passenger seat, where it landed with a dull thud.

The man emerged onto the road just as I drove away, and through the rear-view mirror I saw him standing there, watching me, until I passed around a corner and lost sight of him.

Perhaps they really don't like people they don't know around here, I thought as I drove away from the village. It felt as if I had been escorted off the premises. But this moderately unsettling aspect to my visit to Stokeley aside, I was pleased with what I had accomplished. I had found the witch's house, and I had found the ruined chapel depicted in her paintings, somewhere that looked as if it was still the scene of occultist activity. I may have been no further on with regard to ascertaining the whereabouts of Alan, but my putative article on the twenty-first century practice of witchcraft in rural Wiltshire was definitely starting to take shape.

I arrived back at the house in the early afternoon, following a provisioning stop in Marlborough. Feeling an acute need to see Megan and figuring that the morning's discoveries afforded me the perfect excuse for an impromptu telephone call, I took my phone from my pocket as I stood beside the burial mound and rehearsed what I was going to say to her.

Just keep it nice and casual, I said to myself, and then somehow segue things into an offer to drive over to Devizes and take her out that evening.

The screen of my phone showed a missed call and a message. Whoever it was must have tried to phone me while I was in the high valley containing the ruined chapel, where there was unlikely to have been a signal.

The short message was from Pete Taverner, the musician in Alan's old band who Megan and I had met up with in Bath. He wanted me to phone him. As soon as possible.

"Hi Pete," I said when he picked up. "It's Richard. You left me a message. What's up?"

"I'm afraid I've got some very bad news," said the voice at the other end of the line. "It's about Alan."

"Alan? What about him?"

"He's dead."

CHAPTER TWENTY-THREE

Aftermath of a Death

"Alan's dead," Pete said again. "I can't believe it, but it's true. He's gone."

I felt the blood drain from my face, and I almost dropped the phone.

"How?" I said. "When? I mean, what happened?"

My mind was in turmoil as I tried to process what I had been told. I felt that this had to be some sort of mistake, and that this simply couldn't have happened.

"A couple of days ago," Pete was saying. "In Lima, Peru, if you can believe that."

"In Peru? What the hell was he doing in Peru?"

"God knows. At least we know where he went, now."

I slumped down by the side of the burial mound.

"How did you hear about this?" I said.

"From someone I know at his record company, who got it from a journalist down there. It'll hit the news here soon; it maybe already has. I think they're still notifying family members. I don't know if his mother's still alive, do you?"

"I must admit, I never even bothered to ask him, when we met up recently. I never actually met any of his family. He had two sisters, I think."

"Yes, one older, one younger. I remember his younger sister came backstage after one of our gigs, once. I think she was called Debra. I really don't know much about them. Alan was always a bit of a closed book, as far as his family were concerned, and not close to them at all, as far as I could tell. They weren't even at his first wedding."

A memory flashed through my mind, of Pete and I sitting with Alan in a pub in Luton, on the morning of his wedding, wearing ill-fitting suits, and downing double vodkas in a haze of cigarette smoke while we waited to go to the registry office. Happy times. A lifetime ago.

My thoughts shot back to the present with a sickening lurch.

"So, what do you know?" I said to Pete.

"I know a bit," he said. "The record company gave me the contact details for the journo in Peru who broke the story, so I called him. He told me as much as he could, in return for a couple of quotes.

"Turns out he had been there for about a fortnight," Pete went on. "He was staying in some real fleapit of a place, and hardly ever came out of his room. It sounds … I don't know, it sounds like he had some kind of breakdown. Anyway, according to this guy in Lima, there was a big commotion up there one night, and when the proprietor went up to check out what was going on, he found him dead up there."

"You mean he'd been murdered?" I said.

"No. There was no sign of foul play, and he didn't kill himself, either. According to the coroner, he just died. They're calling it sudden death syndrome. His whole system just shut down, and he died from a massive stroke or heart attack, or something. I don't think the guy I spoke to was quite clear about it himself. It's all a complete bloody mystery."

"Drugs overdose?" I ventured.

"I wondered about that. But apparently not. At least, not according to the toxicology report. He just … died. I mean, I know that it does happen, and God knows, he abused his body enough over the years, but I still can't believe it."

"Why did you say you thought he'd had a nervous breakdown?" I said.

"Well," said Pete, "This is where the whole thing gets even more bloody weird. You see, when they found him, he was on the floor of this shit-bag hotel with all the furniture pushed to the sides of the room, and he was lying in the middle of a huge pentagram he'd painted on the floor."

"Oh my God," I said.

"Yeah, well, we know he was into stuff like that. Never thought it would kill him, though."

"So, what are you saying? That he died performing some kind of satanic ritual?"

"Not according to the guy who I spoke to. You see, he was clutching a crucifix when they found him and … God, this is even more bizarre, but apparently all the walls of the room, the windows, everything, were plastered with pages from a book. Turns out they were pages from the Bible."

"Alan wasn't religious," I said, after a beat.

"No, he wasn't. Sounds like he's spent the past couple of decades batting for the other side."

"Looks like something changed his mind," I said.

"Seems that way. According to the guy I spoke to, the theory down there is that he was trying to protect himself from something evil or unholy; you know, like some demon or something. As crazy as that bloody sounds."

Unfortunately, given all that I had learned about Alan in recent times, and given what I had witnessed myself, it didn't sound all that crazy at all.

He died of fright, I thought. Something literally scared him to death.

"Maybe less crazy an idea in a place like Peru than it would be here," I said.

"Yeah, I guess so."

"So, what happens now?" I said. "To Alan, I mean. They'll fly the body back here, I presume."

"I suppose so. As soon as I hear anything about the funeral, I'll let you know."

"Thanks. God, this is a terrible thing to have happened."

"I know. I'm still trying to process it all."

We reminisced for a while and then after I hung up, I pushed myself to my feet and went into the house.

I started to make coffee, then decided I didn't want any, and in something of a daze, my mind assailed by myriad conflicting thoughts, I went back out into the garden, where I wandered aimlessly around.

Inevitably, it seemed, I found myself back at the burial mound. I could still see the slight depression in the grass where I had sat on the ground whilst speaking to Pete. I felt, for some reason, as if my whole life had changed over the course of the past hour. I simply couldn't believe that I would never see Alan again, which was making me feel incredibly upset, even though I saw the irony in this, given that we had fallen out of touch for so long. But before all of that, we had been so close. He had been my best friend.

You poor, stupid bastard, I thought to myself as I stood upon the long barrow. What infernal idiocy took you from here to some anonymous hotel room in a foreign capital, to die in such gruesome circumstances, scared to death by the demons in your mind?

Or by something more tangible, perhaps. I thought about the apparition that both Megan and I had seen in this house, something real and undeniable, and couldn't help but wonder if had been something similar which had brought about Alan's death. I recalled the heart stopping fright I had experienced on the night when something had tried to get into my room.

I had speculated that the entity haunting Badcombe Hollow was something conjured by Alan himself, either to protect the house, or else to torment me. But perhaps it hadn't been like that at all. Perhaps this apparition, this demon, or whatever it was, had not been something that Alan had invited into his house, but something that had driven him from it, as it had almost driven me from it, a few nights previously. There was still so much that I didn't understand.

But on one thing I was absolutely clear. There was something very, very bad here; in the house, in the garden, in the surrounding fields and woods. And in the ground right beneath my feet, under this burial mound, in the temple to Satan that Dorian Slake had built, decades previously, and which had drawn Alan to come and live here. It was something terrible; something evil. It was also, as Alan himself had discovered, something deadly as well.

I looked down at my feet, my mind's eye peering through the grass and earth to the temple chamber beneath, the entrance to which remained as elusive to me as ever, and which I would probably now never find.

No longer wanting to stand above whatever monstrosity lay beneath, I stepped off the mound, and made my way over to the stand of Scots Pines on the boundary of the property. The sun was starting to dip in the sky by then, and I realised it must be well into the afternoon. I hadn't eaten since breakfast, but I wasn't hungry. I leaned against the sun-drenched bark of one of the trees and looked out across the beautiful, desolate plain, at a complete loss as to what to do next, but feeling like I should be doing something.

I decided to phone Megan.

I should tell her about Alan, I thought. I also felt the need to hear another human voice, particularly hers.

She was predictably shocked by the news, and even more so about the little detail I was able to add. Her happy tone on answering the phone was instantly replaced by one of horror and bewilderment.

"It's just too pitiful," she said. "To end up dying in a place like that, all alone and thousands of miles from home."

"I know," I said. "Although I suspect the cause of his death was a lot closer to home than Lima, Peru. This must be connected to this stupid occult crap that he was into. I know this sounds crazy, but I feel sure that there was something demonic involved. My best theory is that he had some kind of falling out with his coven, or whatever it is that he's in – I mean, maybe that's why he left this place and disappeared in the first place – and then they somehow conjured up a demon to scare him to death."

I recalled the words of Ernst von Draken; his last words to me on the day that he had come to this house, about how he would have no difficulty in locating Alan's whereabouts. Had the mentor turned upon his former pupil, in some sickeningly murderous way?

"A few weeks ago, I would have said that was totally insane," Megan was saying. "But now, after what I saw at the house that night, after what you've seen, and what with everything we've found out about Alan recently, it all sounds horribly believable."

"I know," I said. "Who would have thought that such a lovely place could conceal something so unspeakably foul?"

"Speaking of horrible things in lovely places, how did it go over at Stokeley?" Megan said. "Did you go there? Did you find the witch's house?"

"Yes. I found the village, such as it is, and I found the witch's house, long abandoned. And then I went to this old, ruined chapel, a mile or so away, on the other side of some woods. I think it's the same place that's in the pictures we found in the trunk room."

Not much more than an hour previously, I had been so excited at the prospect of telling Megan this, but not any longer. Given what I now knew had happened to Alan, the very thought of the place made me feel sick to my stomach.

"I guess it's not all that relevant now," she said. "Look, Richard, I know we haven't known each other for very long, and I really hope that's going to change, actually …"

"Me too," I cut in.

"Well, I'm glad to hear that," she said. "Anyway, it's not my place to give you advice, obviously, but I'm going to, okay?"

"Okay."

"You need to get out of that house. I'm serious. There's something very wrong about that place. It was bad enough before, but given what's happened to Alan, it's just not safe to stay there. You said yourself that the house is harbouring something unspeakably foul, you used those exact words, and whatever that something is, it probably got Alan killed."

"I hear what you're saying," I said. "But, you know, there's a part of me that feels that I should stay. Despite everything. I sort of feel that I should see this through, somehow, and find out what the hell's been going on here. I feel like I need to find out why this happened to Alan. It's like I owe it to him to do that."

"You don't owe him anything. How can you even think that, after the way he deceived you; after all the lies he told to get you to come and live down here. It's like he deliberately put you in danger, maliciously so. Please, Richard. Don't stay there.

"I don't want to lose you," she said, her voice softening. "I only just found you."

"Nice of you to say that," I said.

Neither of us said anything for a long moment.

"It's probably all moot, anyway," I said at last. "Staying here or not isn't exactly my choice."

"How do you mean?"

"I mean, this isn't my house. And it isn't Alan's house, either. Not anymore. It belongs to his family now; his mother, his sisters, whoever he's left it to in his will. Whoever it is, I don't imagine they're going to want me living here. If they've got any sense, they'll put the place on the market and get shot of it."

"I guess so," said Megan. "I didn't think about it like that. But in any case, why hang around, even for a few more days? Just get out of there."

"Maybe," I said. "I'm going to track down Alan's family, see what they want me to do; see if I can, you know, be helpful in any way. But tomorrow. I can't face it today. And they probably only just found out about all this, anyway."

"It'll be on the news, I suppose," said Megan.

"I guess so. The story may have even broken already. Pete got what he told me from some journalist down there, so it's only a matter of time."

"How ghastly for his family," said Megan. "As if what happened to Alan wasn't bad enough in itself, but I bet the press will have a field day, particularly with some of the more lurid details."

"As an ex-member of the press, then I'm sorry to say you're probably right," I said.

I wondered how long it would be before someone from my erstwhile profession turned up on the doorstep of Badcombe Hollow. By early the next morning at the latest, I figured.

"Just be careful, okay?" said Megan.

"I will. I promise."

We spoke for a short while longer and agreed to meet up as soon as she got back from visiting her parents.

I continued to stand by the Scots Pines, looking across the plain, thinking not about Alan now, or this house, or what I was going to do about finding somewhere to live, but about Megan's affectionate words to me, and how good they had made me feel, in spite of the terrible news I was processing.

Whatever else happened, I thought, the prospect of a relationship with Megan was not something I was going to walk away from. I'd rent a cheap room in Marlborough for a few months, if I had to. For all the mystery, and horror and unhappiness that had so far accompanied my stay here in Wiltshire, Megan was the one undeniably good thing that had come out of it all, and I was determined not to let anything get in the way of our relationship.

I was about to go back inside when my telephone rang. I retrieved it from the pocket of my coat and saw the words

"Unknown Number" on the screen. I wondered if it was a journalist, calling to speak about Alan, and realised that I had no idea what I was going to say if it was.

"Hello?" I said cautiously.

"Good afternoon. May I ask, am I speaking to a Mr Richard Weaver?" The voice was male, well spoken, authoritative.

I confirmed that he was correct, thinking that this person, whoever he was, sounded far too polite and well-mannered to be a journalist.

"Forgive me for calling like this, and without a formal introduction," he said, "But it's rather important that I speak to you."

Definitely not a journalist.

"That's perfectly okay," I said. "How can I help you?"

"My name is David Samson," he said. "I'm a lawyer with the firm Chambers, Cathcart and Lockhart. We represented Alan Mackay. I'm not sure if you've heard the very tragic news?"

"I have," I said. "I just heard about it a short time ago. It's terrible. I can hardly believe it."

"Yes, it's really the most dreadful news, and I'm sorry to have to contact you so soon after the event. But, you see, Alan left certain instructions, in the event of his death, concerning you and his house, Badcombe Hollow. I take it that's where you are now?"

"Yes. I presume you're telephoning to ask me when I'm going to be moving out."

"No, that's not the reason at all. Very far from it, as a matter of fact. But I do need to speak with you."

"Fire away," I said, perplexed at this latest development.

"If you don't mind, I need to speak to you in person. I'm calling from London and hoped I might be able to drive down and see you tomorrow. I can be there for nine o'clock, if that's okay with you."

"I guess so. I mean, yes, of course, that's fine. I'll be here. Can I ask what this is all about?"

"I'd much prefer to wait until we meet, before going into this any further. I'm sorry to sound so elliptical about it all, but Alan was quite specific in his instruction that I speak to you in person, when I met with him, three weeks ago."

"You saw Alan three weeks ago?"

"Yes. In Rio de Janeiro."

"Where?" I said, struggling to process this information. "I mean, I thought he was in Peru. You know, when he died."

"Yes, he was," said Samson. "I understand he moved on there, shortly after our meeting. Look, I know this must all sound a bit confusing, but hopefully things will become clearer when we meet. You see, I'm sorry to say that Alan feared that something like this might happen and asked me to come and see you in the event that it did. He also gave me something to give to you."

"What did he give you?" I asked.

"A letter," he said. "Alan wrote you a letter."

CHAPTER TWENTY-FOUR

The Lawyer

David Samson was a man of about my own age, smartly dressed in a grey pinstripe suit, and with the sort of permanent tan that attested to long periods spent in warmer climes.

This made a certain amount of sense, I thought, as I looked across at him, standing beside the island unit in the kitchen, while I made coffee. I had done a Google search on Chambers, Cathcart and Lockhart the night before, and whilst they might have had offices in London, they were registered in Bermuda and were, by all accounts, the sort of firm who operated only at the very highest end of the market, catering for the rich and famous, as well as the rich and famously disreputable.

Alan certainly hadn't stinted in retaining the best possible legal counsel, I thought, and must have expended considerable funds in doing so.

Samson had arrived at Badcombe Hollow, as promised, at nine o'clock sharp, sweeping into the driveway in a black Mercedes, and I greeted him on the steps to the front door. He shook my hand with a rather grave expression on his face, in keeping, I presumed, with the sad circumstances that had initiated this visit, and then politely asked me to provide proof of my identity. I went up to my room to get the passport I had brought down here with various other papers and documents I hadn't wanted to leave in the flat, and presented it to him.

"Yes, that all appears to be perfectly in order," he said. "Thank you. I'm sorry to have to ask, but it was essential that I clarified that you are who you are."

"I am who I am," I said.

He became more personable and less lawyerly as we chatted over coffee, even though we were discussing a bleak subject.

"I see that it's made the papers now," he said, pouring milk into his cup.

"Yes, and it was on last night's news," I said. "But there wasn't much in the way of any further detail about what actually happened. It was mostly a re-cap of Alan's career."

"Yes, well, we've been able to exert a certain amount of influence there," said Samson. "At least, in terms of keeping some of the more salacious details under wraps."

Wondering how on earth they might have managed this, in an age of 24-hour news from multiple on-line sources, I figured that this firm of lawyers carried a fair amount of influence. After watching various news reports into Alan's death, the previous evening, and despite much speculation, I had gone to bed none the wiser as to why this meeting had been scheduled. Most intriguing to me of all was the letter from Alan, that Samson had referred to when we had spoken on the telephone, and which I assumed was in the black attaché case by his feet.

"Let's go through to the sitting room," I suggested, and I led him through to the more formal of the two ground floor reception rooms. It was somewhere I had spent hardly any time since taking up residence in Alan's house. As I motioned Samson to one of the armchairs and sat down in the one opposite, I reflected that it was the first time I'd been in there to do anything other than draw the curtains, since the evening I'd had a drink in here with Megan. After we searched the house, and before I kissed her for the first time.

Once we were settled, the lawyer got straight down to business.

"I realise this must all seem a little unusual, even irregular," he said, "And in a way, I suppose that it is. You see, we'll be handling the probate matters, following Alan's untimely death, and executing his last will and testament, and my coming here to see you today takes us rather ahead of that process. But your friend retained our services some time ago, and we regarded him as a most valued client. He left some very specific instructions in respect of you, and your tenure of this house, when I met him in Brazil three weeks ago."

"What was Alan even doing in Brazil?" I said. "I mean, it was my understanding that he was in Los Angeles, and now I learn that he was in Rio, and then Lima. I'm more than a little confused, to say the least."

"As to Alan's precise reasons for being where he was, I really couldn't say," said Samson. "Not, I hasten to add, for any particular reasons of confidentiality, but because I simply don't know. Where he chose to spend his time – his last days, as things sadly transpired – was entirely his business. We merely served his interests to the best of our abilities, as we will continue to do, until all outstanding matters have been satisfactorily discharged."

Samson was now very much back in lawyer mode, I thought, and I was more curious than ever as to the reason for his visit.

"However," he went on, "As you were his friend, and as Alan specifically instructed me to be as candid with you as I could, I will say that he was in a very nervous state when I met with him, and he gave me the strong impression that he was on the run from something, or at least in hiding from someone. I have no idea who that person or persons may be, although I can confirm that it was not a legal problem of any kind, and that at the time of his death he wasn't wanted for any crime, in any jurisdiction. I know that because our firm is obliged to check these things, and I'm telling you that because, as I said, Alan asked me to be as candid as possible. However, I have absolutely no idea who the person or persons he was hiding from may have been; only that he was most keen to conceal his whereabouts, and that he stated to me his intention never to return to the United Kingdom."

Ernst von Draken, I thought, but didn't say. That was the person he was in hiding from, even though I had no clue as to why.

"So, what was the purpose of your meeting with him?" I asked.

"A couple of days before we met, Alan contacted our offices in Bermuda. That's where I'm based, as it happens, and so I was despatched down to Rio de Janeiro to meet him. It was our first meeting. He had taken my firm on as his legal representatives some time ago but had made relatively little use of our services in recent years, but as we considered him such an important client, we naturally acceded to his request for a meeting in Brazil. But it was the first and, as it turned out, only time I ever met him.

"The purpose of the meeting was essentially to put his legal and financial affairs in order, and to make some changes to his will. We don't have offices in that part of the world, but we do maintain a reciprocal relationship with another firm in Rio, and they kindly permitted us to use their premises for the meeting.

"Alan didn't tell me the reasons for making the changes, and it naturally wasn't my place to ask. I did wonder if he might have been suffering from some kind of terminal illness, but I rather doubt that was the case and, as I said, I was left with the undeniable impression that he was in hiding from someone, as he was most keen that I should not reveal his whereabouts.

"Not that I would have done, under any circumstances whatsoever, as I was at pains to assure him," he added. "But as things turned out, it would appear that even the assurances of his lawyer were not sufficient, as he evidently left Rio and moved on to Peru, shortly after our business was concluded.

"But now I'm speculating," he said. "And it's really not my place to do that. Alan's business is, or rather was, Alan's business, and what I'm here to do today is to address the subject of you, and specifically, you being in this house."

I thought I knew what was coming next.

"Look," I said, "Alan very kindly lent me his house while he was away, but I fully understand that, following his death, this arrangement no longer stands. Obviously, the house now belongs to his family, and I'll need to move out. I can assure you that I shall arrange to do so very shortly."

"Actually, Mr Weaver," said Samson, "That won't be necessary at all. You see, Alan asked me to come and see you in person, in the event of his death, in order to both give you a letter, which I shall do before I leave, and to convey to you a very specific item of information regarding this house?"

I looked blankly at him.

"He's given it to you," said Samson.

"Alan's given me this house?" I said slowly.

"Yes," said the lawyer. "Alan requested various changes to his will when we met, most of which is obviously confidential, until such a time as the will is read, but one of the changes was to make you one of the beneficiaries, and to bequest to you this property, and all contents therein."

"So, this is now my house?" I said, sounding rather stupid, and with my mind in something of a spin.

"Well, legally speaking, no, it isn't, not yet at any rate. It all has to go through probate, in the normal way, but once it has done, then yes, this will all be yours. And in the meantime, Alan asked me to convey to you, and to his family, his wish that you should be able to continue to live here, if you so wish.

"Now," he went on, "I have to advise you that it isn't necessarily quite as simple as that, and Alan's family would be within their rights to challenge your current occupation of the house, just as they would be within their rights to challenge the will, although as far as that's concerned, I can assure you that it is, from a legal perspective, absolutely watertight. But I think it's very unlikely that they would pursue either course of action. You see, Alan has written to his family, making clear his wishes in this respect. They will, in any event, be very generously provisioned for in the will, since Alan was quite wealthy, and his other assets greatly exceed the value of this house, many times over.

"He authorised me to tell you that," Samson added, and I felt a pang of guilt, given that I already knew this, having been through Alan's financial records on the day that Megan and I searched the house.

"I see," I said, still trying to take make sense of it all. "I have to say, I'm a little taken aback by all of this, to say the least."

"Of course," said Samson. "That's perfectly understandable. Hence, I think this was the sort of news better conveyed in person, although Alan specifically instructed that I should do so anyway. I realise this is all coming out of the blue, as it were, but the matter is quite clear. This is now your house. Or rather, it soon will be."

"You know, I feel kind of bad about it," I said. "It's like I've profited from Alan's death."

"I'm afraid that's the nature of bequests," said Samson, a kindly tone to his voice replacing the all-business approach of our conversation up to then. "It was Alan's wish that you should own this house, and so perhaps it's better to think of it that way."

"So, what happens now?" I said.

"The process of probate will take its course, and then when the will comes to be read, probably in a few weeks' time, once various other matters pertaining to Alan's death have been resolved, and assuming nobody challenges the will, your ownership of the house will become formalised, and we'll forward to you all necessary papers, deeds and suchlike. You'll then be free to retain or dispose of the property as you wish."

"I see," I said quietly, trying to take it all in.

"I'm duty bound to ask if you've understood everything that I've said to you," said Samson.

"Yes," I said. "I mean, I don't understand why Alan should have made me this very generous bequest, but you've been totally clear about things."

"Good. Well then, that just leaves the letter that Alan wrote to you."

He clicked open the attaché case, from which he retrieved a small, letter-sized envelope with my name on it, marked 'Care of Badcombe Hollow'.

"Alan asked that I should deliver this to you personally," said Samson. "He also recommended that you read it in private, so if you have no further questions at this stage, I'll take my leave of you and get back to London. I have a flight home to Bermuda later this afternoon, although I'll be back here for the reading of the will, whenever that may be. I'll also leave you this card, with contact details for the firm's offices in London, in case you need to get in touch with us for any reason."

He stood up and handed me the card and the envelope, and then I walked him to the front door, where we shook hands.

Just as he was about to get into his car, he looked back at me.

"Just out of curiosity," he said, "Do you think you'll stay here?"

"I really don't know," I said. "I obviously have a lot to think about."

"It's a very fine house," he said.

"In its own way," I said.

I watched him drive away and returned to the sitting room, where the letter from Alan was sitting on the occasional table next to the sofa where I had left it.

Slipping the lawyer's card into my pocket, I opened the envelope.

The letter was dated three weeks previously, presumably just prior to the time when Samson had met with Alan in Brazil, and it was hand-written, in a slanting scrawl I recognised as Alan's handwriting.

Dear Richard

In the event that you receive this letter, then it will mean that I'm dead and, sadly, I believe you will receive it, and probably not long from now. It will be given to you by a lawyer called David Samson, from a firm called Chambers, Cathcart & Lockhart. I will be meeting him tomorrow and will be giving him this letter to give to you, in the event of my death.

So, I suppose, when you read this at Badcombe Hollow, you will be hearing from a voice beyond the grave, which sounds a bit ghoulish. However, I can assure you that I am completely sound of mind as I write this.

It's a hard letter to write, and I can't help but think that as I sit here with my pen in my hand, you would do far better at this, what with you being the wordsmith and everything, but I'm going to do my best, so here goes.

I'm sorry. In a nutshell, that is the point of this letter. To say that I'm sorry.

I've told you a whole pack of lies, you see, although you're probably aware of some of them by now. But there never was a producing job in California, and apart from changing planes in Los Angeles, the day after you saw me off at the airport, I haven't even been to California. I'm writing this from Brazil, which is where I flew to from LA, and after I've met with the lawyer tomorrow, I'll be moving on again. After that, if there is an after that, I really don't know.

Most of what I told you after we met up again that first time, and subsequently, was untrue. Even our supposedly impromptu reunion was a deception, because I'd been researching your whereabouts, and your current circumstances, for quite some time. And I also lied about having someone lined up to look after Badcombe Hollow, who then dropped out at the last moment. There never was any such person. It was always my plan to get you to go and live there, and fortunately for me, you fell for it.

About twenty years ago, back when the band was still going, I got mixed up with some very bad people. They were sorcerers. They showed me things that I could hardly believe. They had real power, you see, and they could conjure things; things not of this world. And they said they could help me. They said they could make me powerful beyond my dreams. And then I made the worst decision of my life. I'm not going to go into any more details because it's probably better that you don't know any more than you have to, for your safety, and for your peace of mind. But in essence, I made a pact, and it was the reason I bought Badcombe Hollow. The funny thing is, I never even liked the place all that much, despite what I said to you the other day, but the people I'd got involved with said that I had to buy it, and so I did.

You see, there's something underneath the house that's very important to them, and the whole reason for me being there was to guard it, and to make sure that nobody got into the thing they wanted to protect, even though they never even told me about this until recently. But it was my job to be the guardian of it, and I'm sorry to say, Richard, it was part of the reason why I wanted you to go and live there, so it would look like the place was still occupied and being protected, and to buy me some time so that I could get away. But I was kidding myself, really. You can't hide from these people. I thought I could. At the time we met up, I truly thought I could get away with it, and start a new life over here, but I was wrong. I know in my heart of hearts that they're going to track me down, because they have ways of doing this that you wouldn't believe if I told you. Sooner or later, they'll find me.

The other reason for getting you to go and live there was pure malice, I'm sorry to say. It was to do with that article you wrote about me and the band, all those years ago. I never quite got over it, I'm afraid. There are some very odd and disturbing things that happen, in and around my house, some of which you may have experienced already. So, I decided to expose you to that. Out of pure spite. And I'm very sorry about that, because I realise now that there are a lot worse things in the world than newspaper articles. So, it was a very bad thing to do, but I'm going to try and make it up to you.

I'm giving you the house. Once I'm gone, it's yours. That's part of the reason for meeting up with my lawyer; so that I can change my will. The house and everything in it will be left to you. And if, by some miracle, I am able to escape the terrible fate likely awaiting me, and am still alive a year from now, then I have arranged through the lawyers for it to be gifted to you. But I believe that it will all happen much sooner than that. Anyway, you're welcome to it. It's the least I can do. But there's a condition. Or more of a request, or a plea, since I'm not in any position to make demands.

Get rid of it. Seriously. As soon as the will goes through, and it's legally yours, put it on the market, and get shot of it as soon as you can. It will be someone else's problem then, and you'll get a good price for it. Which will set you up for a long time and enable you to finish your book. Or do whatever you want to do with the rest of your life.

So, sell it as soon as you can. But in the meantime, move out, because it's not safe there. And whatever you do, don't be there on the night of 30th April. Trust me on this, Richard; you really don't want to be there on that night. 30th April 2015. Remember that date, and make sure that you are far away from the house when it comes around.

And one more thing. The people I was mixed up with will probably contact you at some point. They may already have done so. They have their own reasons for wanting you out of the house. Be very careful of these people, because they are truly dangerous. One of them, the leader of the group, is called Ernst von Draken, and he and I go back a long way. He may come and see you, looking for me, maybe he already has. Be very careful around him. There's a woman, too, who's often with him. Her name is Catherine Falaise. She's a witch, and she possesses some very dark power. Keep well away from her.

Anyway, that's it. I'm sorry to have put you through all this, but I hope the gift of the house in some way makes up for it. I know you must have loads of questions but trust me when I say that they're mostly things that I either couldn't answer, or that you wouldn't want answered. I know that I'm going to have a lot to answer for myself, when I pass into the next world, and all I can hope for is forgiveness.

When I arrived here in Brazil, we flew in over the rainforest, and I looked down, and I remembered how, back when we were at university, we used to talk about doing a trip somewhere like this someday, but we never did, and now we never will. And thinking about that made me sad.

Sorry for everything, Richard. You were a good mate, better than I deserved. Good luck to you in the future, and if you can find it in your heart to forgive me, then wish me luck too.
And please, please, get out of that house before 30th April.
Yours truly,
Alan

CHAPTER TWENTY-FIVE

The Funeral

Alan's funeral took place two weeks later, on the outskirts of west London, close to his family home.

I travelled up with Megan, picking her up outside her lodgings in Marlborough. She had wanted to come, despite having known Alan only briefly, and I was pleased to have the company, although we would be travelling back to Wiltshire separately, as I planned to spend an extra day in London.

Needless to say, the circumstances of Alan's death, his letter and his bequest to me of the house, dominated our conversation on the drive.

I had shown Megan the letter a few days previously, when we had met for dinner in Marlborough.

She read the letter slowly and then handed it back to me.

"How did you feel about it, when you first read it?" she said.

"Pretty cut up, to be honest," I said. "In spite of what he's done, and in spite of whatever twisted occult shit he was into, in spite of everything, I feel incredibly sorry for him. I wish he'd asked me for my help, instead of tricking me into living in his house, while he went off on the run to South America."

"Realistically, what could you have done to help him?"

"Not much, I suppose," I said with a shrug. "It's just, he was my best friend once, and as perverse as it might sound, I feel like I've let him down in some way."

"It is perverse," said Megan, with a hard edge to her voice. "You haven't let anyone down. He let you down. And whatever it was that he was into, he got himself into. And it got him killed. There's nothing you could have done about it."

"I guess so," I said quietly. I had hoped for a more sympathetic reaction.

"I'm sorry," she said, her tone softening. "I don't mean to sound callous, and I know he was your friend, but it's just the way I see it."

"Well, you're probably right," I said. "And you were certainly right about it being unsafe to be in the house. Alan said so himself."

"But what is it about 30th April that's so significant?" she said. "Why did he say you had to be away from the house on that date in particular?"

"Well, according to my very cursory research into the practice of satanism, it's the most important date in their calendar. It's the eve of Mayday; also known as Walpurgis Night. It's like Christmas, or something."

"And these satanists that Alan was involved with have something special planned for that night?"

"Looks that way."

"You know when he says he made a pact; do you think he meant a pact with the devil?"

"I think it's more likely that he meant a pact with Ernst von Draken, who would be more of an emissary to the devil, I suppose, but something along those lines."

"Can't believe we're even having this conversation," she said.

"Nor me," I agreed, as our food was brought to the table.

"Anyway," she said, once the waiter was out of earshot, "On the plus side, at least he left you the house. You'll sell it, I assume."

"As soon as the will goes through probate, and I've got the deeds in my hand, it's going on the market," I said.

"And then I suppose you'll move back to London?"

There was just the faintest note of dejection in her voice as she said this.

"Actually, no," I said. "I'm thinking of looking for a place down here, maybe even in Marlborough."

"I'm rather pleased to hear you say that," she said.

"I was hoping you would be. Of course, whatever I buy won't be anywhere near as grand as Badcombe Hollow. I'll be looking to get a good chunk of change out of the sale, but I plan to carry on renting out the house in London, which will give me some income, so I don't have to dip into the capital from the sale of Alan's house too much."

"And in the meantime? You'll move out of there, right?"

"Probably. Not this side of the funeral, but yes, I'll probably move out."

I was being less than honest with Megan on this point, but I hadn't wanted to spoil the atmosphere of our reunion dinner by getting into it with her. I knew that she didn't want me in the house, but whilst I was touched by her concern for my welfare, a part of me was resisting the urge to move out, as I couldn't help but see this as running away from the problem. Added to which, Badcombe Hollow was now my house, after all. I didn't see why I should be evicted from my own home.

But I did decide to be more forthcoming on the drive to London, and then immediately wished that I hadn't. Megan was less than impressed by my reasoning.

"So what if it's your house now," she said angrily, twisting in her seat to face me. "It doesn't make it any less dangerous. Alan told you so himself in his letter. And you've experienced that thing or whatever it is in there twice, not counting the time when it attacked me. For Christ's sake, what more do you need to convince you?"

"Well, as it happens," I countered, "I haven't seen that apparition thing again, plus no more dead birds on the burial mound, so I'm wondering if it's maybe just gone away."

"Just gone away?" she repeated. "You really think that? Or do you think it's more likely just waiting to pounce out at you, the next time you go upstairs in the dark?"

"I was actually wondering if it might have something to do with Alan's death," I said. "Nothing out of the usual has happened there at all, ever since I got the news. That could be significant."

"I doubt it," said Megan, turning her attention back to the road in front of us.

The remainder of the journey passed in a strained silence and I regretted having raised the subject.

The funeral took place in a pretty medieval church, in what appeared to be a very well-heeled suburb on the west side of London. There was a smattering of press outside, a couple of whom I recognised, and to whom I offered nods of recognition, and the church itself was almost completely full.

Alan's coffin was already next to the altar, looking unfeasibly small, I thought. It was made from some dark, gleaming mahogany, and had been garlanded with white flowers. A group of people, who I assumed to be Alan's immediate family, were already seated at the front of the church.

As we took our seats, I saw Pete Taverner sitting next to a blond woman I assumed was his wife, and Jack Charles, who had been the band's drummer.

Recognising Megan and I, Pete raised a hand in greeting, and gave a wry smile. I didn't recognise anyone else; that is, until right before the service started.

Ernst von Draken entered the church wearing the same dark pinstriped suit that he had been wearing on the day he showed up at Badcombe Hollow. The heels of his patent leather shoes clicked noisily on the tiled floor of the church as he walked down the aisle. As he went past me, looking for a seat, I exchanged a brief, raised eyebrow glance with Pete, who was sitting in the adjacent pew.

He was accompanied by a woman of indeterminate age, dressed all in black, and with her dark hair tied into the severest of buns. She was heavily made-up, and I recognised her from the photograph I had found in Alan's house, of the woman beside the burial mound in the garden, and from Alan's letter. Catherine Falaise, I thought, von Draken's witch.

I watched them take their seats and wondered why two practising satanists would bother to attend a church service, even if it was for the burial of one of their own.

The proceedings were relatively short, and predictable enough in their format. We sang two hymns, there were bible readings by each of Alan's two sisters, and a cousin who I thought I might have met once, delivered an econominium on Alan's life. And there were prayers, naturally, during which I couldn't help but steal a glance across the pews to observe von Draken and his female companion. Both remained seated upright, staring straight ahead of them.

When the service was over, Alan's coffin was carried down the aisle, with both Pete and Jack amongst the pallbearers. We followed it outside, where a light drizzle was falling, and watched as it was lowered into the grave. Von Draken and his companion had positioned themselves slightly apart from the rest of the group, and I as I looked over at them, he caught my eye, and offered me a brief nod of recognition.

The wake was held at Alan's mother's house, a short distance from the church. I guessed this must have been the place where Alan had grown up. He had always been pointedly vague about such details when we had known each other at university, remarkably so, given how close we had been. He'd told me that he was from somewhere around London, which I supposed was technically true, although I had never pictured him coming from such a prosperous, leafy suburb. His mother's house turned out to be a large Georgian mansion, set in extensive grounds, which made Badcombe Hollow look modest by comparison.

"Bit of a turn up, isn't it?" said Pete, echoing my thoughts as he stood next to us in the driveway as we waited to go in.

"Certainly is," I agreed. "This doesn't fit with Alan's back-story at all. But then he hardly ever mentioned his parents, the whole time I knew him."

"He was a bit of a closed book, that's for sure," said Pete.

"I truly had no idea," I said. "We always stayed at mine, whenever we came up to London."

Pete introduced us to his wife, Andrea, and then I shook hands with Jack.

"Good to see you again," he said. "In spite of the horrible circumstances, that is."

"Likewise," I said. "It's a shame Billy and Chris couldn't make it."

I was referring to the two other members of the quintet who had made up Alan's band.

"They're in Japan," Pete said. "Touring with their new band. They sent flowers, I think. I spoke to Billy a few days ago, and he said he was going to write to Alan's mother."

Just then there was a crunch of gravel behind us, and I looked around to see Ernst von Draken approaching, accompanied by his gothic companion.

"Hello, Ernst," said Pete. "Long time, no see."

"Good afternoon, *Mr* Taverner," said von Draken, emphasising the 'mister' as if to show his displeasure at being addressed by his first name.

"And Mr Charles too, I see," he said, nodding at Jack. "Weren't there a couple more of you, I seem to recall?"

"Billy Carter and Chris Parry," said Pete. "They couldn't make it. They're in Japan."

"Yes, quite so," said von Draken. "And Mr Weaver is here as well, I see. Are you still in residence at Alan's house in Wiltshire, or have you had to move on?"

"I'm still there for the moment," I said evenly. I had no wish to furnish von Draken with any further details as to my living arrangements, let alone my prospective ownership of Badcombe Hollow.

"So, Ernst, old chap," said Jack. "What are you up to these days? Still playing with the old Ouija boards?"

I winced inwardly as he said this, fearing that von Draken might be provoked into an ugly verbal confrontation, and recalling that Jack had always possessed a combative streak, happy to goad all and sundry, if the mood happened to take him, including one memorable occasion when he had squared up to a group of skinheads after a gig in a rough pub in Manchester. I remember being scared out of my wits at the prospect of getting dragged into a brawl, and then being immensely relieved when two bouncers stepped in to break it all up. But Jack had not shown a trace of concern for his own safety. He was endearingly reckless that way, and there had always been something a little bit crazy about him. But then, he had been the band's drummer, so a little bit of crazy was almost expected.

Von Draken looked at him with obvious distaste but refused to rise to the bait.

"If you'll excuse me," he said, after a long moment. "I must go and offer my condolences to Alan's mother."

He stalked off towards the house, with the heavily made-up woman in tow.

"Twat," said Jack, as he walked away.

"Seconded," I said.

"Thirded," said Pete. "That's when it all started to go wrong for Alan, I reckon; when he met that fucking tosser."

"Pete!" his wife admonished him. "We're at a funeral."

"Sorry, love," said Pete. "Long story. I'll tell you about it later."

The wake was held in two adjoining ground floor reception rooms, and in the black and white tiled entrance to the house, from where a sweeping stone staircase led to the upper floors. I couldn't help but chuckle to myself at the memory of Alan coming to stay at my house a couple of times while we were students, not so very far from where we were now, and camping on the floor of my bedroom, when we could have been staying in luxury in this vast house. I recalled his uncharacteristic politeness when meeting my parents, and how he had charmed my mother, who took a lot of charming. I had always assumed that he came from relatively humble circumstances, and yet that was very clearly not the case. It made me think that however close we had once been, he had always been something of a mystery, even before he retired to the Wiltshire countryside to pursue his interest in the occult.

Jack, Pete, Andrea, Megan and I settled ourselves at a table in the far corner of one of the rooms and spent an hour or so speaking of inconsequential things, none of us wanting to address the horribly morbid subject that was Alan's death. I looked around at one point to see if I could spot von Draken, but there was no sign of him, and I wondered if he had taken his leave of the proceedings as soon as he had spoken with Alan's mother.

But returning from the toilet and walking across the grand entrance hall, I saw him standing by the front door with his back to me, in conversation with his gothic companion.

"I'll go and bring the car around," I heard him say, before stepping outside.

I continued to make my way back to the wake, as surreptitiously as possible, so as not to alert the woman to my presence, since I had no wish to speak to her. But the sound of my footsteps on the tiled floor caused her to look around sharply and feeling that it would appear rude to simply breeze on past, I walked over to her with the most disarming smile I could muster.

"Hello, I'm Richard," I said as I approached her. "We met earlier. On the way in."

"Catherine Falaise," she said, after looking at me curiously for a moment. There was the trace of a foreign accent to her voice.

Well, that confirms it, I thought. I was face to face with an actual witch.

There was an awkward silence as I wondered what to say to her.

"Did you know Alan well?" I asked.

"Yes, you could say that I knew him quite well."

"Oh, really?"

"Yes. We had several shared interests."

She said this with the flicker of a smile in the corner of her mouth, as if challenging me to ask what these so-called shared interests might have been, even though we both knew.

"So, you would have visited Alan's house in Wiltshire?" I said.

"Of course," she replied. "Ernst and I visited Alan there on several occasions."

"I'm staying there at the moment," I said. "Alan asked me to look after it for him while he was … you know … away."

I let the sentence trail off. The woman was looking straight into my eyes in a way that I found quite disconcerting. There was a hardness about her heavily made-up face which suggested a distinct lack of human empathy; something cruel and pitiless in her features. Whether I was projecting onto her what I suspected about her penchant for the occult, or whether she possessed a seriously bad aura, I really couldn't say, but there was something ineffably dark and off-putting about her, which made me want to take a step back. I had only been in her presence for a few moments, and yet for some reason, she was making my skin crawl.

"So, how do you find being at Badcombe Hollow?" she asked me.

Again, there was the hint of a challenge in the way she phrased the question.

"I like it well enough, for the most part," I said evenly. "The location is certainly very beautiful."

"There is a lot more to that area than mere beauty," she said, before dropping her eyes, in a way that was studiedly and transparently enigmatic.

"Much, much more," she said.

"I'm not sure I know what you mean," I said, deciding to play along.

"I mean that one is privileged to be in such a sacred place; a focal point of such power."

"And what power would that be?"

She smiled and said nothing.

"Well, I've not felt it," I said. "Tell me, were you acquainted with the previous owner?"

"The previous owner?"

"Dorian Slake."

"No. I was not so fortunate. It was before my time."

She said this with another faux demure drop of her eyes, as if in reverence for the deceased occultist.

"I heard that he was a devil worshipper," I said. "Got up to all sorts of mischief in that house, apparently."

"I really couldn't say."

"And quite mad, too, by the sounds of things. Well, I suppose one would have to be, to believe the things he did. It clearly disturbed him enough for him to take his own life. I saw the place where he did it. A dismal way to end it all, up in those woods. Pathetic, really."

I had hoped to provoke a reaction from her, but she gave no outward sign of having been offended by my remarks. She merely smiled slightly, as if to herself, and then cocked her head in the direction of the driveway.

"That must be Ernst with the car," she said. "It's been most interesting to make your acquaintance, despite the very sad circumstances."

The words were spoken without a trace of sincerity. It was as if we both knew a game of sorts was being played out, but that this was a mere skirmish; a prelude to some greater battle yet to come. For some reason, I knew this wasn't going to be our last meeting.

I watched her click down the steps in her heels to the waiting car, where von Draken was standing beside the open passenger door, in a gallant sort of pose. He watched attentively as she somewhat decorously got into her seat and then, with a curt nod in my direction, stalked back to his side of the car, got in, and drove away in a roar of gravel.

I went back to the wake, and the table where Megan and I had set up camp with the band.

"Where did you get to?" said Pete, as I sat down.

"Got talking to the Morticia Adams character who came here with von Draken," I said.

"Satanic arm candy," said Pete. "What's she like?"

"As weird as him, but with even less human warmth. You ever see her before?"

"What, back in the day? I don't think so. It was usually just von Draken and Alan. It was all very master and pupil; closeted away with their old books and astrological charts. But we didn't really get much of a look in, back then. Goodness knows who Alan was mixing with. Did she say that she knew him?"

"Yes. She's been to the house. She was just telling me about it."

"Makes you wonder what the hell he'd gotten himself into," said Pete.

"All the time," I said softly. "Have you spoken to Alan's mother yet?"

"Just now."

"What was it like?"

"As you'd expect. Pretty difficult. But she's nice. Remembered me from when she came backstage at a gig once. First time we played at Wembley Arena."

"Oh, yes, I remember that," I said. It was the last time I ever saw the band perform live, but I hadn't been on good enough terms with Alan by then to go backstage that night.

I took a gulp of the glass of white wine I had collected when we first came in, and which was now warm.

"Guess I'd better go and speak to her," I said, dreading the prospect of the conversation to come.

Alan's mother was a small, frail woman who looked to be in her late seventies or early eighties, and the shock of Alan's death had clearly hit her hard.

I introduced myself and told her how sorry I was.

She had a kindly way about her, as if she was acutely aware of how uncomfortable people must have felt, approaching her on such a terrible day, wrestling inwardly with the presumed obligation to say something, anything, but not knowing what. But she did her best to put me at my ease, as she doubtless had with countless others that day. We spoke with gentle amiability for a short while before we returned to the subject of Alan.

"I just can't believe it's all happened," she said. "And to die so far from home. I can't even think why he was in such a place, and how it all came about. Nobody can tell us anything. Do you have any idea?"

"No, I don't," I said, looking down at my feet.

I had some idea, of course, but I wasn't going to add to this grief-stricken woman's distress any further by recounting some of the bizarre things I had learned about Alan in the preceding weeks.

"You must be the person he's given his house to," she said.

I wasn't sure whether to feel embarrassed at my good fortune, or relieved that we were no longer discussing the circumstances of Alan's death.

"Yes, I am," I said. "It was very generous of Alan, and quite unexpected as well."

"The lawyer told us all about it," she said. "He said it was Alan's wish that you should have it, and that you should be allowed to stay there while we wait for the will to be read. I just want you to know that's perfectly alright by me.

"In case you were worried about that," she added.

"Thank you," I said. "I'm very grateful."

"It was what Alan wanted," she said. "Will you live there now? I've heard it's in a nice place. I never saw it myself. For some reason, Alan was never very keen on us visiting. But he showed me some photographs once. The countryside there looks very pretty."

"It certainly is," I said.

"So, you'll live there now, I hope," she said.

"Yes," I lied. "I'll live there now. And I'll never forget that it was Alan's house, and that he gave it to me."

I could see that there were people behind me, waiting to pay their respects, compelling this sweet old woman to endure once again what she had just endured with me. I was about to turn to go, when she suddenly gripped my hand in hers. Her skin was mottled with age and had the texture of paper.

"I must ask this," she said. "The lawyer we met; he told us that Alan was trying to hide from some people; that he had become involved with some people and then had tried to get away from them. Is that true?"

"Yes, that's what he told me, too," I said.

"Do you know who they are?" she said.

"No, I don't."

Another blatant lie. There are few feelings more wretched, I thought, than that induced by lying to someone's grieving mother, but because the truth was so dreadful, I thought it the better option.

"Do you think you could find out?" she said. "I understand that you used to be a journalist, so I thought you'd probably be good at finding things out. Do you think you could find out about this?"

"I could try," I said, not able to think of another answer.

"Please try," she said. "As you probably know, being Alan's friend, he and I were not very close. I only ever went to one of his concerts, and I never visited with him at any of the places where he lived. He just wasn't very close to his family, not once he'd grown up. But I loved him very much, and I was very proud of him. But I think he got in with some bad people. And I think that these people, whoever they are, drove my son to his death. And if that's true, they should be brought to justice. Will you at least try to find out. Just say you'll try. That's all I need to hear."

There were tears in her eyes. Looking into the face of this elderly woman whose life had been so horribly changed forever, who was condemned to outlive her own child, and who just wanted some kind of answer as to why this had happened, affected me greatly. Just as I was about to fob her off with yet another untruth, I suddenly experienced, if not quite an epiphany, then at least a brief moment of clarity.

"Mrs Mackay," I said to her. "I will try and find out what happened. And I will do everything I can to ensure that the people who are responsible are held to account for this. I promise you that I will do this. For you, and for Alan. You have my solemn word."

This time, I hadn't lied. The fog of the past two weeks following Alan's death had suddenly cleared, and I now realised what I had to do. I just didn't know how I was going to do it.

CHAPTER TWENTY-SIX

The Package

As I planned to stay up in London for another day, I drove Megan to Paddington Station, from where she would take a train back to Wiltshire. I chose not to relate to her the detail of my conversation with Alan's mother, or the undertaking I had made to her.

I shall save that doubtless difficult discussion for another day, I thought.

She seemed in a better mood with me as we drove into London, perhaps relieved that the funeral was over, and we shared a long and passionate kiss in the car before she went to catch her train.

"Call me when you get back tomorrow," she said. "Maybe we can meet up in Marlborough and have supper or something."

I had arranged to stay with my parents that night, who I hadn't seen since shortly before moving to Badcombe Hollow.

They were still living in the same house in Chiswick where I had grown up, and aside from the pleasure at seeing them, there was a certain comfortable familiarity about going back there, and the prospect of spending the night in my old room.

I took them out for a supper to an Italian restaurant I knew they liked, and we spent the evening catching up on our respective news.

They had been shocked and saddened to learn about Alan's death, as they remembered him from when he had come to stay during our university days.

"No age at all," said my mother, with a shake of her head. "It must have been terrible for his family. Was it drugs, do you think?"

"Apparently not," I said. "They don't know what it was. He just died."

"And what with you living in his house, and everything," she said. "I expect you've had lots of press round, asking questions."

"Actually no," I said. "Alan pretty much dropped off the radar, once he packed up the music business. I haven't had anyone round, thankfully. I don't think anyone outside his immediate circle even knew that he lived there."

"It just said Wiltshire, in the obituary in the *Telegraph*," my father said. "So, what's the place like? Nice part of the world down there, I should think."

So, I told them all about Badcombe Hollow, and the prehistoric monuments in the locality, whilst omitting all details of dead occultists and witches, underground temples and satanic covens, not to mention the apparition that haunted the house.

But as I did so, I realised that, somewhat to my surprise, I missed being there, missed the peace and quiet, the pleasing views, the solitude.

I didn't tell them about Megan – far too early days to get those sorts of hopes up – but I did tell them about Alan giving me the house, about which they were as taken aback as I had been when the lawyer had first told me about it.

"Goodness," said my mother. "Now why would he go and do a thing like that? I mean, it's not like you're family."

I agreed that it had all been very unexpected, and that it had been very generous on Alan's part.

"Must be worth a fair bit, I'd have thought," said my father. "Big place like that, down in the country. You'll sell it, I assume."

"Yes," I said. "I plan to put it on the market as soon as the formalities are out of the way. It looks like I'll get quite a bit for it. It's far too big a place for me to live in by myself, anyway."

Plus, it's haunted, I thought but didn't say.

For the remainder of the evening, I detected a subtle but unmistakeable sense of relief on the part of my parents, at hearing about my good fortune, and realising that my previously parlous financial situation, ever since my divorce, something which had been intimated to them by me, if never fully spelt out, would soon be a thing of the past.

If only it were that simple, I thought.

The following day, after saying my farewells, I went into town, where I had some errands to run, and where I planned to go and see Darren Summers, my private investigator friend.

I had decided that if I was going to get to the bottom of this whole business, I was going to need some help, and there were things that Darren could find out that I never could. Early that morning I had been to the bank and cleaned out most of my account, such as it was, and then drawn more cash with my credit cards, borrowing against my imminent windfall when I came to sell Badcombe Hollow. I could live frugally in the meantime, I told myself, and I still had more rent to come from the flat.

I couldn't reach Darren on his mobile, and when I phoned the house, his wife told me that he was going to be out for most of the day, but that I should call round at about six o'clock, when she expected him back.

With much of the day to kill, I headed into London, where I did a bit of shopping, had lunch at the same Indian restaurant where I had gone with Alan, went for a walk around Hyde Park, and then went to see a film at the cinema. I also called Megan and said I would be late back that night, so wouldn't be able to see her that evening, although I didn't tell her the reason why.

I got to the private investigator's house in Southfields a few minutes after six o'clock, parking just off the busy Merton Road and then walking the short distance to his tall, terraced house. I had been here several times before, back when I was a working journalist, and had routinely been stretching the boundaries of what was strictly legal in the pursuit of stories, with the assistance of the cheerfully amoral ex-policeman. Darren was very, very good at what he did, and I knew that if there was any dirt to be dug on Ernst von Draken, or merely just interesting information obscured from the public domain, then he was the man to get it for me.

His wife, Jeanette, let me into the house, and I found him in the basement kitchen, cooking supper for his two young girls.

He seemed genuinely pleased to see me, as I was him, and after getting me a beer from the fridge, he handed his culinary duties over to Jeanette, and led me upstairs to his study, a veritable nerve centre of computers and other electronic equipment that I remembered well from days of old.

"I've got some work to put your way, if you're interested," I said, as I settled down into an over-stuffed armchair in the corner of the room, while Darren perched himself behind his desk, and plucked a cigarette from a large metal box.

"Paid work this time," I added. "And thank you again, by the way, for that free favour from a few weeks back. Much appreciated."

"No problem," he said, lighting up. "What did you have in mind?"

"Looking into one of those guys from last time. The older one. Ernst von Draken."

"Oh yeah, him. The Hungarian guy who bailed out your prowler. The rare book dealer."

"That's the one. I remember you saying he was hard to investigate, covered his tracks well, something like that?"

"On a cursory examination, yes, but with more time, I'm sure I could find out more."

"That's exactly what I'd like you to do," I said. "I can pay you for three days, maybe four tops, if it looks like it might be worth it. I'd like you to do some digging."

"I can do that. What are you specifically trying to find out?"

"Where he lives, for one thing. Sources of income, any run-ins with the law, or other peccadillos. You know, the usual."

"I'll see what I can find. Book trade may be a way in. And I can find out if the law have ever been interested in him. Any other pointers?"

"Try and see if you can find any connection between von Draken, and someone called Dorian Slake, now deceased. Died in 1965. Also, a woman called Doreen Smithers, likewise deceased, but I don't know when. She lived in a village near Marlborough, and she may have had a daughter, who would probably be in her fifties or sixties now. The name of the village is Stokeley, and there may be a connection to von Draken there as well."

Darren wrote down the names I had given him.

"So, what's this all about?" he said.

"I'm not sure yet. But it has something to do with the occult. All the names I've given you are connected to that, including the village of Stokeley. There's a ruined chapel there, by the way. That may help with any search."

"Occult as in devil worshippers?" said Darren, making a note on a yellow legal pad. "That's what the Matthews kid was into, wasn't it? The one who was snooping around your house. Sounds a bit out of your field."

"It is. And I don't know yet, as to whether they're actual devil worshippers or not, or if it's something else. Something criminal, maybe. I'm hoping you can find out some things that I can follow up on, get me started."

"I'll certainly do what I can," he said. "I'll have to fit it in with a couple of other things I've got going on, but I should be able to get back to you in a week or so."

We settled on a fee, which I paid him in advance, in cash, from the money I had drawn out on my credit cards that morning. He gave me a pretty good discount, for old times' sake. Then, having declined his offer of a second beer, I went to do battle with the early evening traffic.

It was gone nine o'clock by the time I got back to Badcombe Hollow. The traffic had been slow, coming out of London, but as soon as I cleared the outskirts of the city and got onto the motorway the way home seemed to open up before me, and it felt almost liberating to be heading back into the countryside.

It was a fine night. As I got out of the car and stepped onto the gravel driveway, I detected less of a chill in the air than of late, a sign, perhaps, that spring was finally on the way.

I looked up at the dark house and reflected that, notwithstanding the potential menaces that lurked within, it felt good to be home again. For this was now my home, to all intents and purposes, even if I planned to sell it as soon as the various legalities were completed. In spite of the circumstances which had brought this about, it was both gratifying and reassuring to know that, for the first time in my life, I was moderately wealthy, or soon would be.

I went into the house and, as was my custom, ever since the night Megan first saw the apparition upstairs, turned on all the lights, feeling a slight tension as I passed from room to room. But everything was as it should be, and the interior of the house was exactly as I had left it, and almost eerily quiet, save for the ticking of the grandfather clock in the hallway.

When I got up to the first floor I went into my room and tossed my overnight bag onto the bed, and I was about to go and run a bath when I heard the faint crunch of gravel amidst the enveloping silence. Somebody was outside. Before I could process this thought any further, there was a loud knock on the front door.

Puzzled at why someone should be calling at this hour and wondering, hopefully, if it might be Megan, I quickly made my way downstairs. Flicking on the outside light, I opened the door.

There was nobody there. With the sense of pleasant anticipation that I had experienced only moments earlier replaced by one of mild unease, I stared out into the gloom. Whoever had knocked on the door had clearly vanished, although they couldn't have gone far in the short time it had taken me to get downstairs, and I couldn't help but speculate if they were hiding somewhere in the garden, watching me.

Then I noticed the box on the driveway. It had been left about ten yards from the porch. A timber box, with the same approximate dimensions as a case of wine. Somehow, I doubted there was wine inside.

Feeling oddly unwilling to walk over to it, I continued to stand in the doorway. I scanned the grounds again, but there was still no sign of anyone, and the only sound was the wind riffling through the Scots Pines on their rise at the edge of the property.

I recalled that there was an outside light illuminating this part of the driveway and went back inside to switch it on. When I returned to the open front door a large swathe of gravel before me was lit by a soft yellow glow, with the box almost centred within it.

With a considerable feeling of trepidation, I walked over to it, all the time keeping my eyes peeled for any movement around me. Although I appeared to be quite alone out there, I couldn't shake the feeling that someone might be watching me from the shadows.

The box was made of timber matchboard, and as I stooped down to inspect it, I saw that my name had been written on it in black marker pen, using large block capital letters. Beneath this were the words 'c/o Badcombe Hollow'.

A small catch secured the top of the box and, somewhat against my better judgement, I released it and slowly lifted the lid.

I'm not entirely sure what I expected to find in there, and so there was a certain sense of anti-climax, blended with relief, when I saw nothing more sinister inside than a pile of black fabric, on top of which was an unmarked envelope, which I lifted out. It was unsealed, and contained a single sheet of paper, folded. I put the envelope down and reached into the box and started to pull the silk-like fabric out, until I realised that there was nothing beneath it, and that this, and the envelope appeared to be the sole contents of the box.

I pushed it back inside, thinking as I did so that it looked exactly like one of the satanic cloaks that Megan and I had discovered in the locked room on the top floor of the house.

Why is somebody sending me devil worshippers' garments, I thought to myself?

I decided to unfurl the thing properly, and read the letter that had come with it, when I was safely back inside the house. I felt exposed out there, knowing that the person who had delivered this odd package must still be close by, and was quite possibly watching me now from some hiding place in the garden.

I tossed the envelope back into the box and closed the lid. Then I picked it up and carried it into the house, locking the front door behind me, and killing the outside lights.

I took the box into the kitchen and set it down on the island unit. Flipping open the lid again, I reached in to take out the envelope.

As I did so, I felt a sharp stabbing pain in my hand, which I pulled out of the box with a startled yelp. It felt as if I had been pricked by a needle.

What I saw when I looked in the box made me recoil with horror.

Lying coiled on top of the cloak, and partially concealed by its folds, was a snake. It was pale grey in colour, and covered in black zig-zag markings, and with an arrow-shaped head. I recognised it immediately as an adder.

Barely able to believe what had just happened, and momentarily rooted to the spot by the dawning realisation that I had been bitten by a venomous snake, I continued to stare into the box. The snake's eyes were fixed on me as intently as mine were on its, and then it drew itself back into an S-shape, and struck at me, affording me a terrifying glimpse of its open mouth and fangs as its head lunged towards me. I jumped back, avoiding a bite to my face by the narrowest of margins, but managing to lose my balance and fall over at the same time, pushing over a stool as I did so, which fell to the floor with a loud clatter.

In something of a frenzy, I tried to push myself to my feet, but so frantic were my movements that I got one of my legs tangled in the stool and fell over again.

From my prone position, I cast a fearful look back to the box on the counter, which the snake was now sliding out of, unfurling a long body that was almost a metre in length.

I kicked the stool away and got up, not knowing whether to run from the room or try and encourage the snake to stay in its box, so I could close the lid again. But by then the whole body of the snake save for a wisp of tail was on top of the counter, and seeing me, it drew its head back and struck at me again, although this time I was far enough away to be able to stand my ground. I made to grab the cloak to throw over it, but it seemed to anticipate my intentions and lunged at me yet again, this time opening its jaws so wide that I could see the pink inside of its mouth, and the pair of needle-sharp white fangs within.

Surely this couldn't be normal behaviour, I thought. I knew that adders were venomous, and potentially dangerous, but they weren't supposed to be aggressive, and it had always been my understanding that they were fearful of humans and would only bite if trodden on or cornered. But this was a seriously angry snake, and it continued to watch me intently, its body coiled and ready to strike.

Aware now of a throbbing pain on the back of my hand, where I had been bitten, I looked down and saw two spots of blood next to each other, marking the puncture wounds where the snake's fangs had penetrated the skin.

Although I was fairly sure that bites from this type of snake were hardly ever deadly, I realised that this was still a dangerous situation. I was going to have to seek medical attention, urgently.

Clutching my bitten hand, I hurried out of the kitchen and kicked the door shut behind me. I knew that the adjoining door into the dining room was closed, as was that to the utility room, so at least the snake was contained in one room, until someone could come and deal with it. Right then, my immediate priority was to call an ambulance.

As I reached into my pocket with my good hand to get my phone, I realised that the hand that had been bitten was still clutching the envelope I had taken from the top of the box.

For some reason, and in spite of more urgent considerations, I decided that I needed to see the letter that was inside. I opened the crumpled envelope and drew out the single sheet of folded paper.

It comprised just one line of script, in neat block capital letters.

STAY AWAY FROM OUR VILLAGE. STAY AWAY FROM OUR CHAPEL.

CHAPTER TWENTY-SEVEN

Targeted

The ambulance arrived first, followed shortly afterwards by a police car and then, sometime later, a herpetologist from Bristol Zoo, who came to deal with the snake. By midnight, I had quite a houseful at Badcombe Hollow.

There was talk about taking me to hospital, but I wasn't keen, and as I'd shown little reaction to the bite by then, other than a slight swelling to my hand, and with the pain having subsided to a dull throb, and no other ill effects, it was decided that I could stay at home. The paramedic who had arrived with the ambulance cleaned the wound, dosed me up with antihistamines for the snake venom, and antibiotics for any secondary infection from the bite, whilst monitoring my various vital signs for any indication of a more serious reaction. He was a large, burly man called Barry, with a thick beard and a cheery manner, and he spoke in a broad Wiltshire accent.

"Can't say we get many of these," he said as he knelt beside me in the sitting room, checking my blood pressure.

"I can't believe you get any," I said. "You mean, you've done this before?"

"Actually, you're my fifth in about seven years," he said. "You get a lot of adders over in the Savernake Forest, and people do get bitten occasionally, but there's rarely any serious harm done, other than the shock of it, of course. If you're relatively young, and healthy, and the bite isn't too bad, then there's not too much to worry about."

"But it's a venomous snake, right?"

"Oh, they're venomous, all right, but it's a very mild venom, compared to most vipers, and they often don't inject much of it when they bite defensively like that, as opposed to when they're killing prey. They're ambush predators, you see. They use their camouflage to hide in the undergrowth and then pounce out at things like mice, lizards and small birds, and they use the venom to kill them. It's too precious to waste on a human being like you. It looks like that's been the case here. If he'd injected a lot, there'd be a lot more swelling to your hand, and puckering to your skin, but looking at it, you'd barely know you'd been bitten. Still no nausea or dizziness?"

I shook my head.

"Tingling sensations, numbness to the lips, anything like that?"

"Nope."

"Then I think you're going to be fine."

"If you're trying to make me feel better, you're succeeding," I said. "It sounds like you know a fair bit about this. What were the odds of that?"

"I know. I'm very interested in snakes, as it happens. So, it was a lucky night for both of us, in a strange kind of way."

"I suppose it was. Do people get seriously ill from adder bites? In this country, I mean?"

"A few. But usually only if they're very old, or very young, or have some other accompanying health problem. And in case you were wondering, nobody has died from one of these things since 1975, and there were only about a dozen deaths in the hundred or so years before that. And they're not an aggressive snake. They're quite timid really, and much more scared of us than we are of them."

"This one didn't seem very timid to me," I said. "It was actually pretty fierce, the way it kept striking at me."

"That is odd, I agree," said Barry. "But then the whole thing is odd anyway, isn't it, what with him being here in the first place."

"Sent to me in a wooden box, you mean?" I said.

"Well, that too, obviously. I'm sure the police out there are going to want to ask you some questions about that," he said, nodding towards the two police officers, who were waiting in the hallway while he treated me, and casting the odd anxious look towards the closed door to the kitchen.

"No, what I meant is," he went on, "Whoever put that in there, where did he find it at this time of year? It's still early, barely spring. These snakes are only just coming out of hibernation."

"Maybe he got lucky, whoever he was," I said.

"Could be. Or he could be someone who keeps snakes, you know, indoors, in a heated tank."

"Interesting theory," I said.

I was thinking of Billy Matthews, the person I had caught snooping around the garden, and who had been watching the house from the woods, back when I had first moved in. He was known to keep exotic pets.

"There you go," said Barry, as I swallowed the antibiotic he gave me. "Should be all fine. But we'll hang on for a while, just in case any other symptoms develop."

"I'm sure there's no need," I said. "I mean, I wouldn't want you to have to hang around for no reason."

"Well, I've got a bit of an ulterior motive, as it happens," he said. "I'd quite like to wait for the snake man from Bristol Zoo to arrive and get a look at this adder of yours. If that's okay?"

"Knock yourself out," I said.

"I think the police would like a word now," he said, and as he moved away the two policemen came into the sitting room. They were both constables, one called Andrews, and the other called Jessop. Andrews was the older of the two, and took the lead, while his colleague made notes in a small black book. They seemed slightly bemused by it all, as well they might have been, I reflected, whilst at the same time, not a little gratified at having been called out to deal with something so unusual. I supposed it made a welcome change from their usual routine of dealing with drunks in Marlborough High Street at kicking out time.

I went through the events of the evening with them, from coming home, to hearing someone outside, to finding the box, and then getting bitten by the snake.

"And that's all there was in the box?" said PC Andrews. "Apart from the snake, that is. Just some sort of black cloak?"

"That was it," I said.

"So, there was no note that came with it? Nothing like that?"

"No, nothing like that," I lied. "Just the box, the cloak and the snake."

I had debated long and hard, before the policemen had even arrived, as to whether or not to tell them about the note. Although I hadn't personally called them out – they had been alerted to the situation by the 999 call handler, after I had blurted out that the snake that had bitten me had been sent to me in a box – I realised that not only was I being dishonest, but I was potentially hampering an investigation too, by not giving them the full facts. But still I decided to hold back on the detail of the note. To do otherwise, I judged, would be to open up a whole can of worms regarding my investigation into a local coven of satanists, Dorian Slake, Alan and all the rest of it, and I really didn't want to go there with them. If they could find anything out from fingerprints on the box, or fibres on the cloak – which I rather doubted on both counts – then that was one thing, but I felt that this was my case, and not theirs, and I didn't want them in the way. Now, more than ever, having been subjected to this bizarre attack, I was determined that it was going to be me who got to the bottom of this. A police investigation into the inhabitants of the village of Stokeley, for example, the place I had just been warned in no uncertain terms never to go to again, might only serve to drive my prey deeper into the shadows.

It was, in so many ways, a wholly wrong and irresponsible approach to take, I could see that, and yet it was the one that I had determined to follow. Perhaps there was still something of the old red-top journalist in me, after all.

The police also referred to my press background, and I supposed that they had run some sort of check on me on the way over.

"Must have ruffled quite a few feathers over the years, I would have thought," Andrews was saying. "Have you ever upset anyone badly enough for them to want to do something like this?"

"No," I said, honestly, this time. "I really can't imagine that I have. And I haven't been a practising journalist for well over a year."

"Any other enemies?" he enquired.

And so it went on until, a short time later, the herpetologist from Bristol arrived.

He was a young man, probably still in his twenties, with very pale blond hair, and sporting a thin goatee beard. He was called David, and seemed genuinely enthused about the whole situation, in spite of the long, late-night drive to get there. He came into the house carrying a set of aluminium tongs, which I presumed he was going to use to catch the snake, and a clear plastic container with ventilation slits and a carrying handle, which I guessed he was going to put the snake into once he had caught it.

I gave him a description of the snake, where I had last seen it, and how it had acted.

"Awesome," he said as he headed off towards the kitchen, with an animated Barry in tow. The policemen ceased their questioning then and went out to watch developments from the safety of the hallway, while I remained slumped on the sofa. It was almost a party atmosphere by then. I would have offered everyone coffee, if it hadn't been in the kitchen with the adder.

"Still on the counter," I heard the herpetologist call out from the kitchen.

"Mind if I come and watch?"

Barry's voice.

"No problem. But stay well back. This one looks a bit feisty."

Through the doorway to the sitting room, I could see the backs of the two yellow-jacketed policemen, hovering at the entrance to the kitchen, and craning their necks to look in.

"Shit," one of them said, taking a sudden step back into the hall and then giving a mock shudder.

A few moments later, the snake had been caught, and was in its secure plastic container, still looking angry, as it watched us through the pale Perspex, for I had by then joined the gathering in the hall. David the snake catcher may have seemed a bit goofy, but he certainly knew his subject.

"Definitely an adder," he said. "Vipera Berus, to be precise. Britain's only venomous snake. Male; fully grown. Actually, pretty large, for an adder. They don't normally get that long."

"How can you tell?" I said. "That it's male, I mean."

"From the colour," said David. "Adders are sexually dimorphic. Which is to say, they're different colours, depending on which sex they are. Males are pale grey with black markings. Females are pale brown with dark brown markings. Hence, this chap is a male."

"Why was it so aggressive?" I said. "I mean, I can understand it biting me when I stuck my hand in the box, but why did it keep on striking at me?"

"Well, this is where the whole thing starts to look a bit nasty," he said. "For the snake, that is, as well as for you. I need to take a closer look, but my impression is that this snake has been very badly mistreated. It's got some marks on it that don't look like normal wear and tear, more like it's been consistently beaten with something. Given that, by the sounds of it, this was sent to you for some malicious reason, I suspect this was done to make the snake react violently to any form of human contact, because normally these guys just get out of the way. They don't want to be around people at all, and only stand their ground if they're cornered. Biting is very much a last resort for them. This one had been beaten, and probably starved as well, to make it as mean as possible. That's my theory, anyway.

"You'd have to be a really sick bastard to want to do that to a creature," he added.

Oh, they're sick bastards all right, I thought but didn't say. You should see the other things they get up to.

"Anyway," said David, "The one consolation, from your point of view, is that it must have so depleted its venom resources that by the time it bit you, it didn't have much left, hence you haven't had much of a reaction to that bite. Otherwise, it could have made you very ill indeed."

I knelt down and looked the snake coiled in its plastic box, and felt rather sorry for it, in spite of the grief and panic it had caused me.

"What will happen to him now?" I said.

"We'll look after him," said David. "Back at the zoo. Hopefully coax him back to full health, and then release him into the wild, somewhere sufficiently far away from human habitation. And hopefully these guys" – he nodded over to the two policemen – "Will catch the bastard who put him in that box."

I experienced a momentary pang of guilt for not having offered them Billy Matthews' name, but I had decided on my course of action, and there was no going back now. Besides, if I had given them Matthews' name, I would have had to explain how it was that I knew his identity, which would have further complicated matters.

David left soon after with his snake, followed by Barry, and after a few more questions it was time for the police to go too. They took the box and the cloak with them as evidence.

"Quite a night," said PC Andrews as we stepped out into the driveway. "Makes a change from normal, that's for sure."

"For me, too," I said.

"Well, if you think of anything else or if something like this happens again, let us know. My contact details are on this card."

"And if you do come to have any idea about who might want to target you like this, I trust you'll tell us," he added.

"I will do," I said, taking the card and putting it in my pocket. Something in his tone suggested that he didn't think I was being wholly honest with him about this, but realised he wasn't going to get anything more out of me that night. I wondered again if I was being foolish by not saying anything, and if this was something I would later come to regret, but I tried to put the thought out of my mind.

I watched them drive away, and then I was alone at Badcombe Hollow again.

I went inside and locked the door. I hadn't eaten since lunchtime, but I wasn't hungry. I felt totally exhausted.

I went upstairs, and without even bothering to undress, fell onto my bed, and within minutes was asleep.

CHAPTER TWENTY-EIGHT

Von Draken's Offer

In spite of my fatigue, I slept poorly that night, plagued by feverish dreams, and with a dull ache in my hand where the snake had bitten me, which I felt every time I woke up.

I also saw the apparition, for the first time since Alan's death.

I awoke from a dream about walking through a field of adders, immediately conscious that there was someone else in the room. It was the old woman, and she was standing at the end of my bed. I gave a strangled cry and shut my eyes tightly, trying to will the vision away, but she was still there when I opened them again.

Too terrified to move, I lay there staring at her, gripping the sheets by my side so hard that I thought they might rip, and with my heart hammering in my chest.

For about a minute we watched each other. She didn't move at all, and I even started to feel a little calmer, once I realised that she wasn't about to leap onto the bed. Which is to say, I was still absolutely petrified, but to a marginally lesser degree than I had been when I first woke up. Everything's relative, I suppose. Perhaps, having been bitten by a venomous snake only a few hours previously, a mere apparition didn't seem quite as menacing as it had before.

And yet there was more to it than that. I was reasonably sure by then that I wasn't dreaming, and just about rational enough to think clearly about it, and it struck me that, the incident with Megan aside, there had been nothing malevolent about this spirit manifesting in the house. It was bizarre, unexplainable and quite obviously frightening, and yet I didn't any longer feel threatened by it. I was almost starting to get used to the apparition's occasional appearances, not that I wouldn't have given almost anything to get rid of it.

In spite of my groggy state, this thought started to develop in my mind in quite an interesting way, but before I could go any further with it, the apparition suddenly faded away, as if swallowed up by an invisible mist, and before long I had fallen back into a feverish sleep.

It was gone nine o'clock by the time I woke up, and the sun was streaming through the windows, as I hadn't bothered to draw the curtains the night before.

Barry, the paramedic, had told me that I was very unlikely to suffer any further ill effects from the adder bite, but had nevertheless alerted me to various unpleasant symptoms that could conceivably occur, and advised that if any of them did, I was to phone for medical assistance immediately. Thankfully, I wasn't experiencing any of them. Even the ache in my hand had gone away, as had the slight swelling. I wondered how the snake was getting on, over at Bristol Zoo.

But even if I wasn't suffering from the effects of snakebite, I was still feeling decidedly out of sorts, thanks to the whole trauma of the event, lack of sleep, and not having eaten for the best part of twenty-four hours, not to mention the middle-of-the-night visitor to my bedroom.

I decided that today was going to be a quiet day, so having bathed and dressed I was making my way downstairs and trying to remember what food I might have left in the fridge when, to my annoyance, there was a knock at the front door.

I wondered if it was the police with some follow-up questions from the night before, or perhaps, God forbid, another unwanted delivery, but it was neither of these things, although it was certainly unwanted. It was Ernst von Draken.

I found him standing on the porch with his back to me, looking out over the garden. As I opened the door he turned around sharply and greeted me with an odd sort of half-nod, half-bow.

"Good morning," he said. "You must forgive me for calling unannounced, but I wondered if I might talk to you about a rather important matter."

As much as I might have disliked the man, and held him at least indirectly responsible for Alan's death, and also wondered if he was responsible for the adder in the post, I was hardly going to say no. Von Draken was at the very heart of my investigation into what had happened to Alan, and whatever it was that was going on in his erstwhile home. Anything he might have to say was therefore of interest, however distasteful I found his company.

"Please come in," I said, and stood aside to let him enter.

He walked past me into the hall, where he stood and looked around with a vaguely proprietorial air. He was dressed in his trademark pinstripe suit and was holding a slim black attaché case loosely by his side, causing my mind to flash back to the lawyer's visit, the day after I heard the news about Alan's death.

"I see that the portrait of Dorian Slake is still missing," he said, casting his eyes over to the blank spot on the wall.

"Yes, it's still at the framers," I lied.

"It seems to have been there for a very long time," he said, with obvious displeasure in is voice.

"Let's go into the kitchen," I said. "I'll put on some coffee."

"Nothing for me, thank you," said von Draken.

"Well, I'll make one for myself, if you don't mind," I said. "I've not been up long. There was an incident here last night, so I didn't get to bed until very late."

"An incident?" he said enquiringly, as we went into the kitchen. "What sort of incident?"

"Someone, I've yet to discover who, decided that it would be terribly amusing to send me a live adder in the post. I'm sorry to say that it bit me."

"Goodness, what a very unpleasant experience that must have been. Who on earth would wish to do such a thing?"

"I can't possibly imagine," I said, looking him straight in the eye.

He looked directly back at me.

"But you're quite recovered, I assume?" he said, with the flicker of a smile.

"Yes. No permanent harm done. I didn't even need to go to hospital."

"I'm so pleased to hear it," he said.

I turned away and started to make the coffee. I wasn't sure if von Draken himself had been responsible for sending me the snake, or if it had been a case of one of his more zealous followers taking matters into their own hands. For some reason, I thought it was more likely the latter, but I still decided to prod my visitor a little further.

"Obviously, the police have been informed," I said. "I understand they have a number of leads which they will be following up."

If this further untruth disturbed him in any way, he gave no sign of it.

"That's good to hear," he said. "Let's hope for a speedy resolution of the case."

While I finished making the coffee he went and stood by the window with his back to me.

"Such a beautiful garden," he said at last. "And so hidden away from the rest of the world, down here in this natural hollow."

"I understand that it's not the only thing that might be hidden from view around here," I said.

"I'm sure I don't know what you're referring to," he said.

"Just local gossip," I said, as I poured my coffee.

"Shall we?" I said, nodding towards the hallway.

He followed me into the more formal of the two sitting rooms, which I had last used when talking to Alan's lawyer, and I motioned for him to sit down on the sofa. I took one of the winged armchairs by the fire which, being a bit higher off the ground, I felt for some reason gave me a slight advantage over him.

He settled his large frame into the sofa, placing the attaché case by his feet. He crossed his legs, a polished black wingtip bobbing in my direction as he did so. His eyes moved quickly and methodically around the room, as if deliberately registering its every detail.

"So?" I said. "To what do I owe the pleasure of this visit?"

Von Draken said nothing for a moment.

"Mr Weaver," he said at last, "I'm most grateful for your hospitality in allowing me to speak with you this morning, but I think we both know that there is nothing in the slightest bit pleasurable for either of us in this meeting. That being the case, do please allow me to come directly to the point."

"Very well."

"I understand from Alan's family that you are now the owner of Badcombe Hollow."

"Yes, I am," I said. "Or, at least, I will be. It has to go through probate. But yes, Alan bequeathed the property and its contents to me."

"That was, if I may say, exceedingly generous of him."

"Yes. And it was also most unexpected."

"Indeed. Forgive the presumptuousness of my question, but may I ask what your intentions are, regarding this house?"

"You may. I intend to sell it. You see, on the face of things, it's a very nice house, but I find some of the uses to which it has been put over the years rather sordid and unpleasant. Consequently, I don't plan on putting down any roots here."

"I see," he said, with a thin smile. "In that case, it would appear that our interests might coincide in a way that is mutually beneficial."

"And how would that be?" I said.

"I'd like to purchase it from you."

"You want to buy this house?"

"Yes."

I said nothing for a moment, and we watched each other across the room.

"Well, it'll go on the market in due course," I said. "You're quite welcome to make an offer for it when it does."

"Actually, I'd much prefer not to wait."

"Why would that be, may I ask?"

"I have my reasons. So, you see, I am proposing a private sale, without the house going on the open market."

"A private sale?"

"Yes. That way, you could settle this all much quicker than you might otherwise have done, thereby enabling your early departure from a place you claim to find distasteful. And without incurring any agent's fees, I might add."

I set down my coffee cup and got up and walked over to the fireplace.

"Mr von Draken," I said, "Even if I were minded to sell the house to you in such a way, it's not presently mine to sell. It still has to go through the normal legal processes. Alan's will could be contested. There are a great many things that could hold it up, or even thwart it altogether. Anyway, as things stand at the moment, it's simply not mine to sell."

"I appreciate that," he said. "Therefore, I'm proposing that you sign a legally notarised undertaking that you will sell me the house for an agreed sum, in the event that you come to inherit it, as expected.

"Now," he went on, without giving me a chance to respond to this rather extraordinary offer, "I have made some enquiries, locally, and I understand that in today's reasonably buoyant housing market, taking into account the size of the house and the rather substantial grounds, and its location, one might expect to raise something in the region of one and a half million pounds from its sale. I'm sure that you've made preliminary enquiries of your own, so I'd be interested to learn if that accords with your own expectations."

I had made enquires, as it happened. I had been to see an estate agent in Marlborough a few days before for an informal chat to gauge the market, taking with me some photographs of Badcombe Hollow, and the agent had advised that, although he'd need to come and do a survey to be certain, I'd probably be able to ask about one point six, or one point seven million for it.

"It does more or less accord with them, as it happens," I said.

"I'm pleased to hear it," said von Draken. "In that case, you may be gratified to learn that I am prepared to offer you the sum of two million pounds for the purchase of this house."

Momentarily taken aback, I wasn't sure what to say.

"I should add," he went on, "That the money would be paid to you in full, as a lump sum, denominated to you in any way you wish, wherever you wish, in return for your written undertaking to make the house over to me, in the event that you eventually obtain ownership of it."

"And if I don't, for some reason, get ownership of it?" I asked.

"That's very unlikely. I understand that Alan's will is considered to be watertight, from a legal perspective. But say, for sake of argument, that it isn't, or that one of Alan's siblings were able to successfully contest the will – also a highly improbable outcome – then I would have lost a considerable sum of money. But that is entirely my concern. Your own personal windfall would be quite unaffected."

"And all I have to do is agree to sell the place to you, in the event that I come to own it," I said.

"And to move out of here within one week," he added. "From today. One week from today. That would also form part of our agreement and is also, I should add, entirely non-negotiable."

"I see," I said, turning away and staring at the fireplace, as if contemplating his offer, whereas in reality I was wondering why he should be making it.

"I have a draft document here with me, if you would like to see it," he said, motioning towards the attaché case at his feet. "If you are agreeable to its terms, we can get everything signed in the presence of my solicitor, and yours, if you wish, in the next couple of days. What could be simpler? You will be a wealthy man, in exchange for agreeing not to live in a house for which you evidently have little affection. This is, you might say, a once in a lifetime opportunity."

"Yes, it certainly seems that way," I said quietly, sitting down again opposite von Draken.

"So, you agree?" he said.

I could almost see the gleam in his eyes as he spoke the words, and I deliberately waited before speaking.

"It's about the time factor, isn't it?" I said at last.

"I'm sorry. I'm not following you."

"You offering to buy the house like this, in cash, and for more than its market value. It must be to do with the time factor."

"I'm afraid you'll have to explain what you mean," he said, with a trace of irritation creeping into his voice.

"I mean, this can't just be about you wanting the house. It has to be about you wanting the house now. Otherwise, why not wait until it goes on the market? That's probably only a few months away. Maybe less. So why not wait? But for some reason, you can't wait. It has to be now. So why is that? What is it that's so important about this house that you have to have it right now?"

He stared at me without saying anything for a long moment.

"I have made you an offer, Mr Weaver," he said finally. "A most generous offer, if I may say so. My reasons for doing so are entirely my own."

"In that case," I said, "Let me see if I can guess."

"Is this really necessary?"

"Indulge me," I said tartly. "While I weigh up your most generous offer."

With a slight roll of the eyes, he waved his hand, motioning me to continue.

"Well, reading between the lines of a letter I received from Alan – oh, by the way, you may not have known that, but he wrote to me, shortly before his death, and what he said was rather interesting – anyway, according to this letter, I'm given to understand that you're frightfully keen to be in this house on the night of 30th April, which is less than two weeks away. A little light research that I've done into the matter tells me that this date is sometimes known as Walpurgis Night, or the Eve of May Day, the most important festival of the year for devil worshippers. Like Christmas, I suppose, but without the good cheer. And I'm inclined to believe, Mr von Draken, that you are such a devil worshipper yourself, as indeed Alan was, and Dorian Slake, one of the previous owners of this house, and an acquaintance of yours, if I recall a previous conversation between us correctly. How am I doing so far?"

"Rather too well, as it happens" he said. "It appears that Alan has been somewhat indiscreet, which is most regrettable."

"Actually, he didn't tell me all that much," I said. "A lot of it I've worked out for myself. But there's more. May I go on?"

"Please do. I simply can't wait to hear what you have to say."

"Dorian Slake used to hold sabbats up in the woods above the house, along with a dozen other members of his group. Or coven, I think you'd call it. Maybe you went to some of them. I'd imagine that you did. The scene of all sorts of shenanigans, according to someone I spoke to; ritual animal slaughter, orgies, people dancing around in cloaks. Sounds most distasteful to me, but possibly not to you. Anyway, I think Slake also used a place up on the Ridgeway for the same purposes, near a little village called Stokeley. There's an old chapel there, a sort of romantic ruin, very picturesque. He used to go there with a woman called Doreen Smithers, a practising witch. She was quite the artist, as well. I reckon she did that portrait of Slake that usually hangs in the hallway, as well as some satanic tableaus of the chapel at Stokeley that I found in a locked room upstairs. But that's not the best part."

"And the best part is?"

"They had a third venue, Slake and his group of devil worshippers, and then subsequently, you and Alan and whoever else make up your particular coven. And it's right here, at Badcombe Hollow, under the ground somewhere, probably underneath the Neolithic burial mound. A subterranean satanic temple, purpose-built in the 1950s. You see, I spoke to someone who saw it being built, back when Dorian Slake lived here. Apparently, he hired a gang of foreign workers, maybe Hungarians, I'm thinking, because that's in your neck of the woods, isn't it? Smart move. You hire workers who don't speak any English, so people don't get to find out what they're doing. No awkward questions down at the pub in the evening.

"I haven't found the way into it yet, but I will, believe me. And when I do, I'm going to demolish it. I do own it, after all.

"So that's roughly where I'd got to, up until today. And then you show up, and offer to buy this house off me and, what's more, you're so keen to get your hands on it, you can't even wait to buy it on the open market. So instead, you make me this inflated cash offer, just to get me out of here in a week.

"And that, Mr von Draken, is how I know that this morning's visit is all about having me out of here in time for Walpurgis Night on 30th April. You must have something very special planned."

"That is my business, as I intimated previously," he said.

His voice was barely above a whisper, and there was hatred in his eyes as he looked at me.

"So where is it?" I said.

"Where is what?"

"The underground temple? Or rather, the entrance to it. The temple, one assumes, is underneath the long barrow. But how do you get into it? I'm going to find out eventually, so you might as well tell me."

"So that you can do what, exactly?" said von Draken. "Demolish it, as you threaten? Destroy something that's offensive to your Christian sense of piety? Obliterate something built by one of the greatest visionaries of our age, for reasons someone such as you could never comprehend? Why should I do that? Do please tell me."

"Thanks for admitting it's actually there," I said. "Anyway, maybe I won't destroy it. Once I inevitably find it. I might turn it into a party room, put a pool table in there, or build myself a granny annex. Who knows?

"Or maybe," I said, looking him straight in the eye as I did so, "Maybe I'll just write a very revealing story about it all. Featuring your good self, naturally."

"That would be most unwise," he said, returning my stare. "And if this is some sort of negotiating ploy, on your part, to get me to raise my offer, then it won't work. My offer is final."

"So is my decision," I said. "I'm not selling the house. Not to you, at any rate. Not for two million pounds; not for three million pounds."

He looked at me for a long moment before he spoke again.

"You know, I might have expected a rather different reaction, from one such as yourself," he said.

"What do you mean?"

"Do what thou wilt, shall be the whole of the law," he said. "You have encountered this particular phrase during your recent research into the left-hand path, I am sure."

"Aleister Crowley, the Book of Thelema," I said. "What about it?"

"A man should follow his true path in life."

"Still don't understand what you mean."

"You shouldn't imagine that you are the only person capable of doing a little light research, Mr Weaver. I've been looking into you, as well. Former tabloid journalist. A rising star of the Murdoch press, back in its heyday, before certain public enquiries took place. And a real trooper for the cause, by the sounds of things. Suspicion of phone hacking, and various other kinds of sharp practice; failure to assist the police with their enquiries; accusations of perjury. You seem to have had a rather chequered career, Mr Weaver."

"Maybe I did, maybe I didn't. What about it? What's it got to do with any of this?"

"Surely, it's obvious. I would have expected someone with your background to be rather more selfishly driven; to have an eye for the main chance, if you will, and not give a damn about anyone else. In fact, in different circumstances, I might have considered you a worthy recruit to the cause."

"Are you offering?"

"To recruit you? No, we're well past that. But I am offering you a large amount of cash to walk away from here, no questions asked, and notwithstanding your professed defiance of a moment ago, my reading of your character suggests that the greater part of you rather wishes he could do just that. So, I would advise you not to fight that impulse, Mr Weaver. I would advise you to act according to your true nature and sell me this house."

"Your reading of my character, as you put it, couldn't be more wrong," I said, even though he was actually about half-right.

"We'll see."

"No, we won't. And I'm going to repeat what I said before, because it didn't seem to penetrate, last time. I am not selling you this house. Ever. Not for all the money in the world. And now I'd like you to leave."

"You are a most foolish and headstrong young man. I can assure you that you'll come to regret this decision. There are other measures that I can take, you know. Things I can do that would make it most uncomfortable for you to remain in this house."

"More snakes in the post?"

He gave a humourless chuckle.

"Sometimes," he said, "The more ardent of my followers allow their emotions to get the better of them and take matters into their own hands. I myself would never have done something so crude as sending you a venomous snake in a box. No, I meant that there are things I can do, events that I can set in motion, that you would find most unpleasant, not to say dangerous. Things not of this world."

"If you mean that old hag, or whatever it is, that you've got haunting the house, then that's not going to get me out of here either," I said.

He looked at me curiously for a moment.

"I have no idea what you're talking about. But you might reflect upon what happened to the last person who crossed me."

"You mean Alan?" I said.

He nodded.

"You sick bastard."

He merely grinned at this insult and got to his feet, picking up the attaché case.

"Just think about it," he said.

"So, you're admitting that you were involved in Alan's death," I said, getting up to face him.

"I admit nothing. But you might care to consider that Alan was my very dear friend, almost like a son to me, and his passing saddens me greatly. Imagine, therefore, how little I would care about the fate of someone who means nothing whatsoever to me."

"That sounds like a threat."

"You may interpret it however you wish. But do think very carefully about what happened to Alan. Think about what might happen to you. Think also about the potential fate of that delightful little friend of yours, the pretty archaeologist from Marlborough who has been helping you with your amateur sleuthing. Her name is Megan, I believe. You might wish to consider her welfare, if not your own."

I took a step towards him, my fists clenched.

"If anything happens to her …" I began, but I was stopped dead in my tracks. For some reason, I suddenly couldn't move. It was as if there was an invisible barrier between me and the satanist. All the time he kept his eyes fixed on mine, with an effect that was hypnotic. I noticed that the room had become cold, and my breath was growing shorter, as if someone was pressing on my chest. As von Draken watched me struggle, there was the glimmer of a smile from the corner of his mouth.

"What are you …?" I gasped.

And then he simply released me from whatever hold it was that he had put on me, turned smartly on his heel and strode towards the front door, while I continued to stand there, breathless and shaken by what had just occurred.

He looked back at me from the hallway as he opened the door, plucking a card from the top pocket of his jacket and placing it on a windowsill.

"My number is on that card," he said. "You have three days to accept my offer. Should you choose not to, then I can assure you that the consequences will be more terrible than you can possibly imagine."

And with that, he was gone.

261

CHAPTER TWENTY-NINE

Alliance of Two

"He did what?" Megan exclaimed over the telephone.

"He put some kind of hold on me," I said. "It was like being hypnotised, except it wasn't, really, because I was completely aware of what was going on, but I couldn't move. It was like I'd been nailed to the floor."

"Oh, my God. How long did it last?"

"Only a few seconds. It stopped as soon as he left the house. Before that, even. From when he got into the hallway. He obviously has some kind of dark power, as bizarre as that might sound, but maybe only when he's in close proximity. Or something like that. God, I don't know."

"What did he want, anyway? Why did he come round in the first place?"

"Long story."

It was the morning after von Draken's visit. The previous day felt like a bit of a blur. Whatever the satanist had done to me, it had left me feeling exhausted, and with a fearful headache, although I had been at a fairly low ebb anyway, so it may have been a cumulative thing. I had done little for the remainder of the day, and it wasn't until the following morning that I had even felt like speaking to anyone, although the sound of Megan's voice at the other end of the line had done much to lift my spirits. It transpired that she was over at Devizes for the day, with her parents, but would be back in Marlborough that evening, and I arranged to collect her from her lodgings and take her out for supper. There would be plenty of time then to recount my various tall tales about adders and absurd offers to buy the house.

Feeling considerably better about life, and with a new sense of resolve in my determination to defy von Draken, and not sell him the house, I called Darren, to see how his investigations were going.

"Ah, it's Van Helsing of the west country," he said, as he picked up the telephone. "Hold on a minute, I'll go somewhere quiet."

I could hear a cacophony of children's voices in the background.

"Easter holidays," he explained a moment later. "It's doing my head in a bit."

I heard the sound of a door closing and then the snap of a cigarette lighter.

"You've rung for news, I take it," he said.

"Yes. Is there any?"

"Little bit, but this von Draken character is proving to be a very tricky subject."

"How so?"

"It's like I said after I took a quick look into him before. This is someone who has gone to great lengths to put a cloak of obscurity around himself, and that's quite hard to do these days. There's not supposed to be any such thing as privacy any more, what with us leaving our digital imprints all over the place. Except he doesn't seem to leave any. Or else he's very good at covering his tracks. And that in itself, of course, makes one think that he's got something to hide. But I'm buggered if I can find it.

"He doesn't have a criminal record, and he's not known to the police in any way at all. I spoke to one of my few remaining contacts at the Met; one of the ones who hasn't been scared shitless by Celebrities Against Hacking, or whatever they are, and they'd never even heard of the guy. And they have a section that deals with the sort of stuff you say he's into. You know, devil worshippers, cults, that sort of thing. He's not on any of their lists.

"He has tax records, though. Nobody hides from the bloody taxman. And he pays a fair bit of it, all on investment and trust income, so he's obviously worth some money. But that was it, as far as the official record is concerned. He's not even registered to vote. I have an address, though, from his tax records. Very well-heeled part of Chelsea. Sounds like an apartment block. I thought I might check it out later, speak to a few neighbours, maybe."

"If you do, be careful," I said. I told him about von Draken's visit to Badcombe Hollow, and the adder in a box that I suspected he or one of his acolytes was responsible for.

"Jesus Christ," he said with a low whistle. "This all sounds a bit more serious than people dancing around a fire, bollock naked."

"Yeah," I agreed. "I think it might be."

"Well, I'll certainly be careful," he said. "Anyway, I have got a couple more things for you. Firstly, regarding von Draken. We know that he's involved in the rare book trade, so I followed up on that angle. I like old books myself, so I phoned around a few of the antiquarian places up here in town, and got lucky. Spoke to a guy in Bloomsbury who used to know him a bit, although he hadn't come across him in years. But he'd sold books to him in the past and done well out of him. Very serious collector, by all accounts, big into old occult volumes, rare alchemical texts, grimoires, demonologies, all that sort of stuff. Supposed to have one of the best collections in the country."

This tied in with what Pete Taverner had told me of what he had known about von Draken, back when he had been acquainted with the band, but it didn't really get me anywhere.

"And the other thing," Darren was saying. "Doreen Smithers. I had a quick look into her. She did have a criminal record. Animal cruelty, same as that other geezer I checked out for you. Charged with keeping animals for ritual slaughter, back in the early seventies. Got off with a suspended sentence. Anyway, as you thought, she's long gone. Died in 1978. One daughter. Abigail Smithers. Father unknown. Born in Marlborough General Hospital in 1955, so she'd be about sixty now. I haven't managed to track her down yet."

"Don't bother," I said. "Leave her for now. Focus on von Draken."

"Will do, boss. Although short of staking out the place he lives, I'm not too sure where else to go with him. Probably keep working the property angle, but that's time consuming and I know that funds are limited.

"And doesn't necessarily lead anywhere," he added.

"Any chance of loaning me a bit more time on tick, just in case it does?" I said. "I'm going to be loaded, once I sell this place."

"Sure, no worries. Gets me out of going to *The Lion King* again with the wife and kids. God, I hate the school holidays."

"Thanks, I really appreciate it. Anyway, there was another reason I rang. I've got something on von Draken for you, which might speed things up a bit, and avoid you having to stand around on street corners, trying to look incognito."

"Cool. What have you got?"

"His telephone number."

"Shit. You don't even need me. How did you get that?"

"He gave it to me."

"Oh, well, that would help, I suppose. So, are you saying …?"

"Yes, I think I am."

"Are you sure?" he said.

I thought for a moment, von Draken's recent damning words about my journalistic past suddenly crowding my mind. But this time was different. This time I was on the side of the angels. Right? I took a deep breath.

"Yes," I said. "Look, I know it's asking a lot, and I hate to even ask, but …"

"No, it's fine," he cut in. "I'll do it. Ends justify the means, right?"

"This is a seriously bad guy, so yes, this time, I think they really do."

I gave him the number, and a short time later hung up the phone.

This whole thing had now escalated to another level, I thought.

I had just asked Darren to hack von Draken's voicemail.

****

As it was a fine day, I spent most of it out in the garden, mowing the lawns, sweeping the paths and generally tidying the place up. By mid-afternoon, as I stood back to admire my handiwork, I realised that I had a proprietorial feeling about Badcombe Hollow now, and so picturesque did the grounds look that I wondered if I really did want to sell the house after all. But then I remembered the satanic entity stalking the house, and the diabolical temple somewhere beneath my feet, and I realised that I did. Just not to Ernst von Draken.

I went inside, took a long bath and got ready for the evening. Shortly after six o'clock I headed out to go and meet Megan.

The days were getting longer by then and the tall channels of hedgerow that flanked the lanes, now in full leaf, were bathed in golden, early evening sunshine. I felt suddenly flushed with optimism at the prospect of the summer to come. As I drove into town, I allowed myself to daydream about finding some small house, somewhere in these valleys, to while away days such as this. In the company of Megan, naturally.

I found her sitting in the garden of the house she lodged in, curled into a wrought iron chair on the terrace in her own little patch of sunshine, her head buried in a thick hardback book.

She looked up with a smile, as I approached.

"If I stay in direct sunlight, it's just warm enough to sit outside," she said.

I stooped down to kiss her lightly on the forehead. Her hair smelt faintly of apricots.

"I'd ask you in for a drink," she said, "But the owners are here. Not that that's a reason not to come in, but they're all full of the cruise they just went on, and we'd probably get stuck with them for ages. This weather is glorious, isn't it? It's making me think of summer."

"I was thinking the same thing, on the way over," I said.

"This place is heaven on a warm day," said Megan, nodding towards the garden.

It wasn't difficult to see why. Although not a large garden, it was enclosed by a high stone wall, lined with specimen trees. There was a formal interior of straight paths criss-crossing square and rectangular flower beds, bordered with parterres of clipped box. From somewhere came the soft gurgle of water from a fountain.

I glanced down at the book in her lap.

"*Imprints of a Forgotten Past*," I said, reading the title. "Good?"

"If you like pre-history," she said dreamily. "It actually made me want to be up on the downs, experiencing it instead of reading about it."

"Maybe we could do a long trek up there, later in the week," I suggested. "We could take a picnic. I've still got so much exploring to do."

"I'd like that," she said, taking my hand in hers and squeezing it gently.

I looked into her eyes and thought that she had never looked prettier. Inwardly, I cursed the fact that my meeting Megan had coincided with all the other stuff I was having to deal with – my haunted home, Alan's death, von Draken – and for a moment I contemplated selling the house to the satanist after all and whisking Megan away for a long holiday on the proceeds.

It was still an option, I told myself. There was still the best part of two days until the expiry of his offer. It would only take one telephone call to set the ball rolling. But I knew in my heart of hearts that this was something I couldn't seriously contemplate. I was determined to see this business through now. And I also felt the need to prove to von Draken, to prove to myself, maybe, that these days I was more than a greedy, selfish, devil-may-care journalist. So, I knew that I had to do this. I just wasn't looking forward to breaking the news to Megan.

We drove west out of Marlborough, heading towards the large orange sun that was dipping towards the horizon, saying little and enjoying the drive. We were comfortable in each other's company by then, and no longer felt the need to fill every silence with aimless conversation.

I took her to a country pub just outside Avebury that I had been to by myself a couple of times. It wasn't the grandest of places, and the food was adequate rather than good, but it was a big, rambling building, full of nooks and crannies where we could ensconce ourselves, away from prying ears, and where I would be able to recount to her the various events of the past couple of days.

We bought drinks and ordered our food at the bar, and then settled ourselves at a table in the corner by the fireplace.

Over the course of the next hour, I brought her up to speed on everything that had happened since I dropped her at the station after Alan's funeral. I told her about the time I had spent in London, the package containing the adder that had greeted my return and the various excitements of that night, and then von Draken's visit, and the strange spell he had seemed to put on me. The only thing about which I was economical with the truth was hiring Darren to investigate von Draken and Doreen Smithers, let alone the proposed hacking of von Draken's phone, although I alluded to the hiring of some "outside help", as I put it, to look into one or two elements of the case. This wasn't because I didn't trust Megan, but because I had a strict confidentiality agreement with Darren, forged over many years of periodically hiring him for legal and not so legal snooping.

I had wondered if Megan might have probed me further about this, which would have been awkward, but in the event a venomous snake in a box on my front door step kind of trumped everything else I told her that evening, even von Draken offering me a huge sum of money to sell him the house and clear out by the end of the week.

"I would have died of shock," she said. "I'm absolutely petrified of snakes. I can't even watch them on television."

"I don't like them much, myself," I said. "I like them even less, after the other night."

"You really think this von Draken person would do something like that?"

"More likely an over-zealous follower. Maybe it was one of those, 'who will rid me of this troublesome priest' type affairs. But I'm certainly holding von Draken responsible."

"You should have told the police."

"Told them what? I don't have any proof."

"You've got circumstantial evidence. Not to mention him being in some sort of cult. You've got enough for them to investigate him, at least. Frighten him off, maybe."

She wasn't wrong, but I didn't want to admit that the real, underlying reason why I had been less than forthcoming with the police was because I regarded this as my story, my scoop, my investigation, and nobody was going to stop me from pursuing it.

Instead, I steered the conversation in another direction.

"I need to find out why he wants to be in my house so badly on 30th April," I said. "That's the key to this. Being in the house on Walpurgis Night. That's what this is all about, I'm sure. This isn't about von Draken, per se, or me, or Alan or Dorian Slake, or any of that. It's about the house. Slake bought that house for a reason, and von Draken persuaded Alan to buy it for the same reason, and now von Draken wants it for himself. I need to work out what it is about that house that's so damned special to him."

"The underground temple under the long barrow, surely," said Megan.

"The alleged underground temple. I'm still no closer to finding a way into it. I'm starting to wonder if it's really down there."

"Let's assume for sake of argument that it is. In which case, given the black magic scene we know that von Draken's into, it's highly probable that he wants to hold some sort of ceremony there on Walpurgis Night, presumably a sabbat with his coven."

"Sure, but why there, specifically? Why not the ruined chapel I went to, or the clearing in the woods where Slake killed himself, or any other place that these groups would normally use for their gatherings? Why does it have to be at Badcombe Hollow?"

"Because I suppose it's special to them in some way. The site, I mean. Not the house as such."

"What do you mean, the site?"

"I mean, there's a late Neolithic, early bronze age burial mound there. This is an ancient site. It's been considered sacred since long before someone decided to build a farmhouse there, and long before Slake would have built his temple. The place itself is special, significant."

"But why?" I said. "What would make people think that of a place?"

"Various reasons. There might be an underground spring there. Most of these ancient tribes had shamans, holy men; people with an aptitude for detecting these sorts of things, like dowsers looking for earth currents or telluric energies, beneath the ground. They might have believed there were certain earth energies contained within that valley."

"Earth energies? You believe in that kind of thing?"

"Not really. Not at all, actually. But this isn't about what I believe, or what you believe. It's about what people believed thousands of years ago, and what people like Ernst von Draken may still believe now. And it's not really all that outlandish, and there's nothing inherently evil about it. Most churches you've ever been into have been built on sites like that, places that were considered sacred in pre-Christian times, and which the new religion appropriated. The existence of the long barrow at Badcombe Hollow more or less demonstrates that there's something about that particular part of the landscape that people in the distant past would have considered very special indeed. That said, being just down the road from Avebury, that's hardly unique to the area."

"Exactly. So why there, and not some other place in the landscape?"

Megan shrugged.

"Maybe because it's discreet and out of the way. You're not going to have a black mass on Silbury Hill, or West Kennet, or down the Avenue, or any of the other well-known places, are you? You'd get caught."

"Then use the old chapel at Stokeley, or the clearing in the woods," I said.

"There could be other things about the place where your house is, that give it some kind of occult or magical significance. Some alignment with other points in the landscape, maybe, or with the heavens above. The ancients were great sky watchers, real pioneers of astronomy. Or it could be on a ley line. If there are such things. There could be all sorts of reasons."

"Alignments in the landscape," I said, as I digested what she had been saying.

"Precisely."

"And lining up with Badcombe Hollow."

"Maybe. But, anyway, regardless of the why, and assuming the when is 30th April, don't you need to focus on the how?"

"I'm not following you."

"I mean, regardless of why these devil worshippers want to be at your house on 30th April, they're clearly determined to be there, determined enough to offer you two million pounds for the place, so I think you need to be worrying about how they plan on accomplishing this if you don't go along with them."

"I have thought about it," I said. "And I don't see how they can, if I simply refuse to co-operate. If they try to get in there by force, I'll just call the police, and have them all arrested for trespass, or breaking and entering. They can't physically drive me out of there. I'll just wait them out until the end of the month, and there's absolutely nothing they can do about it? Is there?"

She looked at me archly.

"I think you know the answer to your question. It's not going to be that simple. There are other things that von Draken can do. Supernatural things, dark forces, whatever the hell you want to call it. Think about that thing that's been creeping around in there.

"Think about what happened to Alan," she added.

"We don't really know what happened to Alan," I said. "But I'm not saying that you're wrong, and I shouldn't be concerned. I am. I'm scared shitless about it half the time. Look, it's hard to explain, but I just feel like I owe it to Alan to carry on with this. I think that whatever it was that he was into with von Draken, he was trying to get himself out of it, and that's what got him killed. And I can't just let that go. So, I can't walk away. I need to stay with this. At least until I know more; until I know enough to maybe get something on von Draken, and close down whatever sick operation he's running. Regardless of whether it's all bollocks or not. I mean, it's about what people believe, right? Isn't that what you said a moment ago? So, however erroneous his belief about the significance of Badcombe Hollow, he believes it, and he plans to act on it. And I plan to stop him."

I looked down at my drink.

"Sorry to rant," I said.

"That's okay. It's quite endearing, in a way. I just wish it was about something else. This really scares me."

"It scares me, too."

"But you've made your mind up."

"Sorry, but yes, I think I have."

We looked at each other for a moment without saying anything, and I was suddenly aware of the noise and bustle of the pub around us.

"Okay," she said at last.

"Okay, what?"

"Okay. I'm in. I want to help."

I said nothing and stared down at the table.

"Not quite the effusive reaction I was hoping for," she said, after a moment.

"No, sorry," I said. "It's not that it doesn't mean a lot, you offering to come on board like that, and it's not as if I don't need all the help I can get. It's just that there's something else. Something I haven't told you, about von Draken's visit to the house."

"What is it? What haven't you told me?"

"He threatened you. He threatened me, and he also threatened you. He knows about you, somehow, and he suggested that you might get hurt, were I to continue my poking around in his affairs. Sorry. I should have told you."

"Yes, you should have done," said Megan. "You really should have done. It sounds like I might be in danger whether I help you or not."

"I know," I said, feeling my face flush with embarrassment. "I suppose I imagined it was an empty threat, on his part, and I didn't want to worry you unnecessarily. I thought that if I could keep you out of it …"

I let the sentence die away, unfinished.

"Sorry," I said again. "I feel like I've been very selfish; or at least very one-eyed about it all, because I'm determined to make von Draken pay for Alan's death. But the last thing I'd ever want would be to put you in danger."

Megan reached out across the table and laid her hand on mine.

"No, it's okay," she said. "If you'd done otherwise, it would have been like giving in to blackmail, and that's never the right thing to do. Look, I still want in on this, okay? I want to help you. I don't want you to face this on your own."

"Are you sure?"

"Yes. I'm sure. But next time, tell me about stuff like that, okay? If we're going to be a team, then we need to be honest with each other."

"It's a deal," I said. "And thank you. And the minute they try anything serious, I'll call in the police, I promise. And I am going to sell the house, as soon as this is all over."

"That's the best news I've heard all evening."

We grinned at each other across the table.

"So," she said. "What's next? Look for the entrance to the temple?"

"We could do. But I was actually thinking about contacting the spiritualist whose details Alan had in the house. Bethany Weyland. She lives in Bath. I'm wondering if Alan went to her for help, to try and cleanse the house, perhaps, or for some kind of protection from the demons that were haunting him. Either way, if he was in contact with her, she may know something."

"That sounds like a plan. We could call her and maybe go over there tomorrow, if you want?"

"It's a date."

"There's something else we need to do first, though," she said.

"There is?"

She nodded.

CHAPTER THIRTY

A Violent Assault

As soon as we got back to the house, we fell upon each other. We had barely spoken on the drive from the pub, and the air had been thick with tension and anticipation. Once through the front door and into the hallway, we could no longer restrain ourselves.

As I kicked the door shut, I pulled Megan towards me and she responded in kind. We pressed our bodies tightly together, kissing each other with a fierce urgency. We half-stumbled up the stairs, meeting in another passionate embrace as we reached the first-floor landing and fumbling with each other's clothes. I had never felt so completely overcome with longing for another person, never felt such intense desire as in those moments when we manoeuvred each other towards my bedroom.

Outside the door I pulled her towards me again, pushing my body into hers whilst kissing her mouth, face and neck. She made a moaning sound, and I felt her nails dig into my back.

And then, out of the corner of my eye, I saw it. Over her shoulder, in the pool of darkness behind, the face of the old hag suddenly appeared out of the gloom, just inches away.

I wanted to scream, but I couldn't, because Megan's mouth was clamped upon mine, but she must have sensed something in that split second, and I saw the surprise in her eyes just in the moment that the old woman's hands slipped around her neck from behind, brushing past mine as they did so, and then suddenly she was yanked violently away from me into the darkness.

I screamed then, a strangled, delayed reaction, at the same time falling backwards, such was the force with which Megan had been pulled away from me. She was screaming too, and through the gloom I saw her being dragged violently by the neck.

I scrambled to my feet and rushed towards her, but by then the old hag had pulled her struggling body into the bathroom, and just as I reached the door it slammed shut in my face, so hard that it rattled the frame. I frantically tried to open the door, but it seemed to be stuck, as if it was locked. I could hear the sound of a violent struggle on the other side, interspersed with screams from Megan, followed by the most awful choking sound, as if she was being strangled.

I threw the whole weight of my body against the door, but it wouldn't budge. Again, I rammed my shoulder against it and this time it gave, and I almost fell into the room.

It was virtually pitch black in there, but I could make out the shape of the hag as she crouched over the bathtub, in which Megan was lying at an angle, literally fighting for her life as the old woman strangled her.

I tried to pull her off, grabbing at the rough folds of the cloak she was wearing, and as I did so the dark shadow of her face turned towards me, and let out a snarl that was more animal than human, and then she took one hand off Megan and struck out at me, catching me a glancing blow on the side of my head, and causing me to lurch away from her.

Remembering the light switch that hung from a cord by the door I slapped my hand against the wall looking for it, hitting the door jamb so hard with my knuckles that I gave a shriek of pain. In the same instant Megan, who was still being pinned to the bathtub by the old woman, made a gurgling, choking sound, as if the very life was being squeezed out of her.

I managed to grip the light cord and yanked on it, suddenly flooding the room with a harsh, white light.

The old woman vanished in that very instant. Megan lay in the bathtub, her body at a contorted angle, with her head flat against the bottom of the bath, and her legs dangling over its sides. I rushed over to her, and pulled her out and into my arms, and as I did so, she started to scream uncontrollably, her body going into convulsions of shock.

I was more scared than I had ever been in my entire life. The whole incident had lasted only a few seconds, but it had felt like much longer. It had knocked the life out of me. I felt my hands shake as I held Megan in my arms, willing her to stop screaming.

As we lay there on the bathroom floor, clutching each other, and with Megan's screams replaced by loud sobs, I realised something very clearly.

The demonic entity that was haunting this house had just tried to kill someone.

****

I'm not quite sure how long we remained there on the floor. I doubt that I was even capable of movement, such was my state of shock, upset and disbelief. It felt as if I was glued to the cold tiles.

Megan was even more traumatised. She pressed her face tightly into my shoulder and hooked a trembling arm around my head. I could hear the thud of her heart against my chest.

Sometime later, perhaps minutes, perhaps longer, she stirred beside me, and slowly pushed herself to her feet. I could see the beginnings of an ugly bruise on her neck where the old hag had tried to strangle her.

She looked at me with fierce anger in her eyes.

"Get me out of this fucking house, now," she said.

I looked up at her pathetically.

"Megan, I'm sorry …" I began.

"Get me out of this fucking house," she shouted.

I got up and tried to embrace her, but she pushed me roughly away.

"Take me home. Now."

I led her out of the house in a mood of utter despondency. As she got into the car I looked back at the house, cursing it, wishing I'd never set eyes on it, and in that moment wanting only to be rid of it.

And I realised something else as I drove away. I was now truly scared of Badcombe Hollow and the evil that resided there.

Megan refused to speak for the whole drive to Marlborough. A couple of times I tried to say things, but she stared resolutely ahead at the dark windscreen, and the sentences died away, unfinished.

When we pulled up outside the large townhouse I looked up and saw lights coming from the upper floors and imagined Megan potentially having to explain her tear-streaked face and the bruises on her neck when she went inside, but being unable to explain the unexplainable. I wondered if the people she lived with might have thought that I had done this to her. The thought horrified me. And yet, in a sense, I had done this to her, with my pig-headed determination to continue living in that house, and my willingness to take her back there that evening, in spite of what I had known might happen.

I switched off the engine and turned in my seat to look across at her. Everything suddenly felt very quiet. I wondered if she might talk to me now, in this moment of relative calmness; if we might somehow comfort each other, even try and make some sense of what had just happened. Mostly, I just wanted to continue being with her. I wanted to persuade her to give me another chance, away from here, if necessary, or at least away from Badcombe Hollow. I would have sat in that dimly lit street with her for the rest of the night, if I could have done.

In the event, all I could manage to do was stammer a half-sentence about how sorry I was, and how I'd do anything to make it up to her, while she sat there, saying nothing, inscrutable in the darkness.

She turned to face me, and for a moment I thought she was about to engage with me, but then she evidently thought better of it, and unbuckled her seatbelt with an angry tug.

"Don't ever contact me again," she said, as she got out of the car.

CHAPTER THIRTY-ONE

The Spiritualist

Bethany Weyland lived in the middle of a long three-storey terrace in a street leading off Bath's Royal Crescent. It was a much grander looking residence than I would have expected the home of a spiritualist and medium to be. Perhaps I had anticipated something more exotic; certainly, less well heeled; but judging by the elegant townhouse I was standing outside, either the spiritualist industry was more lucrative than I had thought, or Ms Weyland had private means.

There was no sign on the door, but I knew it was the right place. I had telephoned that morning to make an appointment, and not only had she encouraged me repeat the address back to her, but she had described the street, and even advised where I might leave my car in nearby Victoria Park. There was a clipped efficiency about her that also didn't quite seem to gel with my vision of a typical spiritualist.

I hadn't been back to Badcombe Hollow since I had left with Megan the night before. Following her final angry words to me – the last words she would ever speak to me, if she was to be believed – I had continued to sit in the car for some time, rather pathetically wondering what to do next. I was simply too afraid to go back to the house, and the thought of confronting again the thing that was there made me feel physically ill. And so, eventually, with one last, doleful look at the lit upper floor window that I assumed was Megan's room, I had sheepishly booked into a hotel in Marlborough for the night. I then passed several long, miserable and largely sleepless hours considering how truly parlous and horrible my situation had become.

But as dawn broke, I found that I had recovered some of my resolve, and I was so angry by then about the attack on Megan, and how this had scuppered our relationship, that I determined that I was going to continue with my investigation, and somehow get to the bottom of this whole business. Perhaps too, I thought to myself, albeit more in hope than expectation, if I could somehow remove the demon, or whatever it was from the house, I might still have a chance with Megan.

Fortunately, I had put Bethany Weyland's card in my wallet before going to meet Megan the day before, and so I had no need to return to the house to fetch it. I would, of course, have to go back at some point, but the longer I could delay this the better, as far as I was concerned.

After toying with breakfast in the hotel's cavernous but mostly empty dining room, I telephoned her, and set up an appointment for eleven o'clock that morning. She sounded pleasant enough on the phone, and thankfully had not asked my reason for seeking her services, merely giving me the rather precise directions to her house.

I got to Bath with plenty of time to spare and went for a walk around the park to try and get things clear in my head. Potential developments with Bethany Weyland notwithstanding, and pending any further information on von Draken, I needed to find some other line of enquiry to pursue, to keep open as many lines of attack as possible, and somehow try and take the initiative.

Some expert help would be welcome too, I reflected.

Pausing by an ornamental pond where an old man was feeding some noisy ducks, I recalled my attempt a few weeks previously to contact Julian Faraday, the elderly academic who had reputedly tangled with satanic cults in the past.

On an impulse, I took my phone from my pocket and dialled Darren's number.

"Nothing so far," he said, on answering. It sounded as if he was driving, and I assumed he was referring to Ernst von Draken.

"Actually, I didn't ring for that," I said. "I need you to get someone's number for me. I'm almost certain it's going to be ex-directory."

"Shouldn't be a problem. Who is it?"

"He's an academic from an Oxford college. Or at least, he was. He's retired now, but still lectures there occasionally. Name of Julian Faraday. Professor Julian Faraday. Probably lives in or around Oxford, or else somewhere in that general part of the country. Do you reckon that would be possible?"

"Piece of piss. I'll call you back when I've got it."

Feeling that I now at least had a couple of irons in the fire, I headed off for my appointment with Bethany Weyland in a slightly more positive frame of mind, and easily found the house, just as she had described it.

I pressed the bell, which made no sound, but a few seconds later I heard the click of steps on a tiled floor, and the door opened to reveal a striking looking woman of early middle age, with long raven black hair, smartly dressed in a red silk shirt and grey tailored slacks. She had the sort of high cheekbones and finely sculpted features that might have attested to a Nordic or eastern European background, but when she spoke, her accent was pure English Home Counties.

"Mr Weaver," she said, extending her hand. "You obviously found me without any difficulty, and on time, too. Do please come in."

Her hand was cool to the touch, and she had long fingers, like a pianist.

"Thank you for seeing me at such short notice," I said, as I stepped into the hallway.

"Actually, I don't see very many people, these days," she said, closing the door behind me. "I no longer advertise my services, and as you can see, there's no sign on the door, so I don't get passing trade. Much to the relief of my neighbours, I'm sure. How did you come to hear of me, may I ask?"

"From a friend," I said. "He had one of your cards."

"Oh, those. I haven't given those to anyone in a very long time. It's clearly serendipitous that you found me, in that case. Come on through. We'll go in the sitting room."

I followed her down a black and white tiled hallway and into a large, sun-filled drawing room that faced the street.

She motioned me to sit on a long sofa beneath the window, while she opted for an armchair with a high back by the unlit fire.

Just as I had done a couple of days previously with von Draken at Badcombe Hollow, I thought as I sat down.

She folded her elegant frame into the chair, crossed her legs and looked at me curiously.

"This isn't what you expected, is it?"

"How do you mean?" I said.

"I mean this house and, I suppose me, as well. I take it this doesn't fit with your stereotypical image of a spiritualist."

"Well, now that you mention it," I said, "I don't suppose it does, really."

She smiled.

"What did you expect?" she said. "A gingerbread cottage hidden away in the woods? A tent in some fairground? A covered wagon in a gypsy encampment?"

"I suppose so," I said, smiling sheepishly back at her. "Maybe I'm not sure what I really expected."

"We're not all Mystic Megs," she said. "In fact, very few of us are. Spiritualism is actually something of a family business for me. My great-grandfather was one, although he was much more than that. He was one of the great educationalists of his time, and founded a boarding school in his name; one that was very much a beacon of free thinking and progressive values, during what were less enlightened times. My grandfather and then my father continued the tradition, and then when the school closed in the 1970s, we moved here. I took on his practice, so to speak, after his death. He taught me, you see. My father taught me everything I know, and I've done my very best to uphold his high standards.

"What I'm really trying to say, Mr Weaver, is that there is no quackery here. Many people may mock what we do – communicating with the departed; trying to interface with the spirit world – but we take it very seriously. I hope you do as well, and this isn't all about you trying to uncover some salacious story for the edification of your readers."

"I'm sorry," I said, genuinely confused. "I really don't know what you're getting at."

"Well, you are a journalist, are you not?"

"How did you know that?"

"It wasn't very difficult. I merely typed your name into Google. I must confess, however, that I've never read any of your work. But I understand that you wrote for a tabloid newspaper for many years, during the course of which you uncovered, so to speak, a number of scoops. I'm also aware that you were cited in two separate phone hacking trials."

The words were spoken in the same even and pleasant tone with which she had greeted me at the door, but there was a certain hardness to her expression now.

"Well, I can assure you, Ms Weyland …"

"Please, call me Bethany," she cut in.

"Of course, and please call me Richard," I said. "I can assure you, Bethany, I'm not here to write a story about you. I don't even write stories for the papers, any longer. I'm here because I need your help."

"In that case, please forgive my presumption about your motives for coming here."

The earlier warmth returned to her features.

"That's perfectly alright," I said. "I know that my former profession hasn't exactly covered itself in glory in recent times. And I have to take my share of the blame for that. I was very much part of it all. But my reasons for being here are quite genuine."

"In that case, please go ahead and tell me about them."

"Thank you. But before I start, we should probably discuss your fee."

"Let's talk first. I don't charge for a consultation. Once I know the reason for your visit, I'll be able to tell you whether I can help you or not."

This news came as a considerable relief. What with hiring Darren to investigate Ernst von Draken and moving out of the house and into a hotel, my already meagre funds were becoming seriously depleted.

"So?" she said, looking at me expectantly.

"Well," I said slowly, "I suppose this is really all about my friend. The one who had your card.

"His name was Alan Mackay," I said.

I detected a slight intake of breath, and for the first time during our encounter the highly poised Ms Weyland appeared to lose her equilibrium somewhat.

"I take it that name means something to you," I said.

"Yes, it does. I know Alan Mackay. How is he getting on these days?"

"Getting on?" I said. "He's dead. He died a few weeks ago."

"He's what?" she said, with a detectable note of anguish in her voice.

"I'm sorry, I assumed you would have known," I said. "I mean, it was on the news."

"I don't watch the news. I had no idea. Oh, my goodness. That's terrible."

"I'm sorry that you had to hear about it like that."

"It's not your fault. I had to hear about it sometime. And it's not as if we were close, although I did know him. But I'm just so sorry about it. Did he die … at his house?"

"No. He died in Peru, of all places."

"How did he die?"

"They're not really sure. It's officially unexplained. But something like a massive stroke. Reading between the lines, it sounds as if something frightened him to death."

"Oh, my goodness," she said. "How dreadful."

"I was staying in his house at the time," I said. "I've been looking after it for him. I'm still there. In fact, it's my house now."

"I take it we're talking about Badcombe Hollow," she said.

"Yes."

"Then in that case, I'm sorry to say that there's nothing I can do to help you."

I stared at her for a moment.

"You've been to the house," I said.

"Yes. Once. With Alan. I didn't stay very long. I'm afraid it had a rather bad effect on me."

"I know what you mean."

"So, you've seen it?" she said.

"It?"

"The thing that's taken up residence there."

"Oh, yes. I've seen it alright. Last night it tried to kill someone very close to me. Have you seen it?"

"No. But your friend described it to me."

"I see. I'm sorry, I thought from what you said … I mean, about the house having an effect on you …"

I let the sentence hang.

"It did," she said. "In fact, I never made it beyond the driveway. The place is absolutely drenched in dark energy. I would think that the apparition haunting the house is just one manifestation of this, and I certainly never witnessed that part of it. But Alan told me about it. He thought it had been put there by someone. Some people he was involved with."

"I think he was right," I said.

There was an awkward silence. It was as if both of us had information to convey to the other but wasn't sure who should go first.

In the event, I did. I told her pretty much everything. I started with my surprise reunion with Alan and his offering to lend me the house; his story about going to America, and how this had started to fall apart, even before I got to Badcombe Hollow; my early experiences in the house, and the watcher in the woods; what I had been told about Dorian Slake and Doreen Smithers and their satanic cult; about Alan's mysterious death and his giving me the house; about Ernst von Draken and his offer to buy the house; and about the ruined chapel at Stokeley and the adder that had been sent to me following my visit there. I told her about the underground temple that was rumoured to lie beneath the house, but which I had been unable to locate. And I told her more about the demonic woman haunting Badcombe Hollow, describing in particularly graphic detail the attack that Megan had been subjected to the night before.

It took the best part of an hour to explain everything to her. She listened quietly throughout, interjecting only occasionally with questions on some of the finer points of detail.

"Your friend seems to have presented you with something of a poisoned chalice, by gifting you Badcombe Hollow," she said, when I had finished.

"It came with his most fervent recommendation that I cash in my prize and sell the place as soon as possible," I said.

"And yet you say you turned down flat just such an offer."

"From the satanist who's most probably responsible for Alan's death? Damned right I turned him down."

"I'm quite sure I understand your sentiments. Indeed, I applaud them. But if you don't mind me asking, what do you actually hope to achieve? In practical terms, I mean."

"What do I hope to achieve? Well, I suppose it's about getting evidence against von Draken. I want to prove that he's been running a satanic coven on the Marlborough Downs, all these years. That, and solve the mystery of Badcombe Hollow, and why it's haunted."

"The mystery of your house, as you put it, is a much deeper question, but with regard to this man, von Draken, why do you think that gathering evidence against him will accomplish anything? It's not against the law in this country to worship the Devil. Or to participate in orgies, for that matter."

"Satanists do other things as well," I said. "Some of them. The real hard-core believers. They do horrible things to animals in their sacrifices. And even to humans, occasionally. And there have been documented cases of child abduction. And child abuse. And even, in the worst cases, the ritual killing of children."

"But you don't know that the coven you've encountered is involved in anything like that, however depraved their beliefs might be. You may find it difficult to uncover the sort of evidence that could lead to criminal charges being brought."

She spoke the words kindly, patiently, with the ghost of a smile, as if gently lecturing a child.

"Then I'll try them in the court of public opinion," I said. "I was a journalist. I can write about this; expose them, whoever they are. Some of them could be prominent figures. Revelations about these sorts of activities could be extremely embarrassing to them. It might open a whole can of worms, other people could come forward. Who knows what could come of it?"

We stared at each other in silence for a moment.

"You're clearly very determined," she said at last.

"I am," I said.

"So why are you here? I mean, where do I fit into all of this? How can I help?"

"I hope you can help with the deeper question you alluded to a few moments ago. I hope you can help me understand what it is about Badcombe Hollow that makes it how it is. I hope you may know something about what its secret is, why it's haunted, why things happen there that defy rational explanation, and why it's so special to a satanic cult.

"And then I'm hoping you might tell me how I can defeat it," I added.

"In that case," she said, "I'm afraid you're going to be very disappointed. On both counts. Diagnosis as well as cure. And I couldn't be sorrier about that, because I would dearly like to help you. But I can tell you about what little I know; about how Alan came to see me, and how I did try to help him, and was unable to."

"Anything at all that you can tell me would be helpful," I said. "And I certainly appreciate it."

"You know, in so many ways, this goes against my ethics," she said.

"How so?"

"In the sense that your friend was my client, for want of a better term. I made a vow of confidentiality to him and pledged never to reveal what he told me."

"Doesn't his death, and the manner of it, change that somewhat?"

"Not really. A promise is a promise, and in any case, we likely have a different concept of the finality of death. But the reason I'm going to be open with you is because I know beyond all doubt that you were a true friend to Alan, that you cared about him, and that your intentions, as well as your motivations are, shall we say, pure and honourable."

"How exactly do you know that, if you don't mind me asking?"

"I can just tell. I am a medium, after all."

Another flicker of a smile.

"Right," I said, grinning back at her. "Although you weren't too sure about me, when I first got here."

"Exposure to you has convinced me otherwise," she said.

"That's good to know. It's usually the other way around."

Another brief smile as she crossed her legs, and self-consciously brushed an imaginary piece of fluff from her trousers.

"So, what can you tell me?" I said. "How did you come to know Alan?"

She paused for a moment, as if preparing in her mind what she was about to say.

"I first met Alan a little over six months ago," she said. "When my course started."

"Your course?"

"I ran a series of seminars last year, on ancient occult practices that involved communing with the dead. Spiritualism before the word spiritualism was invented, if you like. Alan signed up for it. Six weekly, ninety-minute sessions. Numbers were limited, of course, because I did it from here. But that was okay with me. I prefer small groups.

"Alan came to every session. You get a lot of dropouts, with these sorts of things. People mistakenly think they're going to learn how to practice magic, however much you tell them otherwise at the outset. Or else they have reasons of their own for coming; questions specific to their own lives, to which I simply don't have the answer, and when they realise this, they leave. I thought your friend might have been one of those, when I first met him.

"But he wasn't. He never missed a class. He asked intelligent questions and contributed to the discussions. You might say he was a model pupil."

I chuckled inwardly as I recalled Alan's hatred of the classroom during our time at university.

"I had no idea who he was, at the time," she said. "I mean, about him having been a famous musician, and all of that. He didn't offer anything about himself to the group. But I could tell he was troubled. On the inside. It's very easy for me to pick up on things like that. But he never said anything. And outwardly, one would never have known that he was troubled in any way at all.

"But he sought me out, after the last seminar had finished, and asked to speak to me about something he described as being of a private and disturbing nature. I wasn't wholly surprised. For some reason, by then, I suspected that he may have had an ulterior motive for being there.

"So, I asked him to tell me about it, but I now know that he only told me part of the truth. Much of what you told me today was news to me. But he told me a little of his background, and about his house, but not about the person who used to live there.

"He said that he had gotten involved with an occult group, many years previously, and that he now very much regretted this. He described them as magicians. He never said anything about satanism, although I had my suspicions. These sorts of people tread a very fine line – between white magic and black magic; between the right-hand path and the left-hand path; between good and evil."

"Why do you think he kept that from you?" I interjected. "The satanic part of it, I mean."

"Perhaps he thought that if I knew that, I would have been so horrified and disgusted that I wouldn't have tried to help him," she said. "And he may have been right. Black magic is something I find utterly loathsome. Anyway, he only told me that the people he was mixed up with were serious and dedicated practitioners of magic, and I chose not to press him on the matter. I must confess, I was very curious about it all by then, and I wanted him to tell me more.

"He said that the house he lived in was very special to them. That there was some sort of ancient, supernatural power there. And that it was his job to protect the house; to act as its guardian. He actually described himself as that. As the guardian. He said that he had taken a solemn oath to do this, and there would be terrible consequences if he reneged on the deal.

"But he said that there were other things protecting the house; supernatural forces he couldn't control, and which put a sort of aura over the place. He said he wasn't able to sense this himself, but any trained medium could, and he also said that animals were terrified of the house and wouldn't go anywhere near it."

"One of the first things he asked me, when he offered to lend me the house, was whether I had a dog, or any other pets," I said. "He claimed it was to do with his allergies."

"Animals are incredibly sensitive to other-worldly forces," said Bethany. "In a larger animal, such as a dog or a cat, it would merely inspire great fear, but for a smaller creature, the shock could literally kill them. It probably explains why you've had birds dropping dead from the sky. Badcombe Hollow is a fulcrum of dark energy, and Alan's circle of magicians, as he described them, found a way of tapping into that.

"He also told me about the temple under the ground, but not that it had been built by a satanist. But he did say that it was connected to the burial mound in his garden, so I assumed it was quite ancient; certainly pre-Christian. I never imagined it to be as modern a creation as I now know that it is. Alan said that it was incredibly important to his group, but that they never actually used it. What's more, he said that he had never even seen it or been into it. Apparently, it has some special significance on a particular night in a particular year, which sounded quite bizarre."

"Walpurgis Night," I said softly, half-whispering the words.

"I'm sorry?"

"That's the night of special significance," I said. "30th April, this year. Walpurgis Night. But not any Walpurgis Night. *This* Walpurgis Night. At the end of next week. That's what they've been waiting for, all these years."

"The eve of Mayday," said Bethany. "The Devil's night. But why this one in particular?"

"Beats me," I said. "But it explains why von Draken is so desperate to get me out of the house. I said as much to him myself, when he offered to buy it, and he didn't exactly deny it. It seems that Alan giving me his house has put something of a dent in their plans.

"So, when you spoke to him, he didn't give any clue as to exactly where the temple might be? Or not so much where it is, because it's probably under the burial mound, but rather how one might get into it? Where the access is?"

"No," she said. "I'm sure he didn't know. In fact, I did wonder if that was part of his motivation for confiding in me; if he was drawn less by a sense of remorse at the things he might have done, or more by feeling put out that the people who had entrusted him with the guardianship of their temple had nevertheless chosen to keep him in the dark as to this particular detail. I got the feeling he was angry about that."

"What else did he tell you?" I asked.

"On that particular occasion, nothing. It was getting late by then, and I had another appointment, so we arranged to meet again a few days later. I could sense there was something else that he very much wanted to tell me, and I was right.

"At this meeting, it was a very different Alan sat across from me, just where you are now."

"How so?"

"He was in a highly distressed and agitated state. He said that he was being plagued by terrible nightmares, and they always involved the long barrow on his property. But that wasn't the main cause of his anxiety."

"What was?"

"He believed the house was haunted; that there was something evil there, over and above the spells that were being used to protect it. Something from within the house itself."

"The old hag," I said.

"Yes. The entity or whatever it is that he told me about was exactly as you described it earlier. He said that it was appearing before him frequently, and becoming ever more menacing, even violent."

"So, what do you think it is?" I said.

"I really have no idea. Alan thought it had been put there by the occult group he was involved with. He thought they were becoming suspicious of him, wondering about his commitment to the cause. And so he believed they had conjured up this demonic being to keep him in line, but without telling him. I thought it was a bit of a wild theory, to be honest, but he'd convinced himself of it. Anyway, the whole situation with the frequent visitations by this entity was driving him crazy with fear."

"I know the feeling."

"Yes, as does your friend who was assaulted last night. Has it ever tried to attack you?"

"Not yet. Just scared me half to death. You said before that the house had a bad effect on you. What happened?"

"Alan wanted me to see the house for myself, so that I could experience the phenomena and see if there was anything I could do about it. I wasn't at all keen. I'm not a psychic investigator, let alone an exorcist, and given what I know now, Alan would have been better off contacting a priest, rather than a spiritualist. But he can be very persuading, as I'm sure you know, and I can't pretend that I wasn't intrigued by what he had told me. So, I agreed. He wanted me to go with him right then, but I wasn't able to, and so he came and collected me the following day and took me there. It was a very brief visit, as it turned out, not to mention extremely embarrassing to me.

"The aura of the place hit me as soon as we drove through the gates, before then, even. I started to feel it as we turned off the main road and got onto the lanes that lead to the house. And when I stepped out of the car, I knew that I wasn't going to be able to go in there. I mean, I've spent my whole life attuning my psyche to pick up on things like that, so I knew that it was going to have an effect on me, but I've never experienced anything like that before. It was like I was standing in front of an invisible force field that was pushing me away from the house.

"Although I knew it was futile, I tried my best to walk up to the door, and that's when I embarrassed myself rather dreadfully, by being violently sick into a flower bed.

"Alan was sweet about it all, of course. But I could tell he was disappointed. I really think he'd come to invest a lot of hope in me, by then, albeit badly misplaced, and he truly thought I could help solve his problem. As it turned out, I couldn't even confront it."

"Anyway, he drove me home, apologised for having put me in that situation, and thanked me for trying to help him. And that was the last time I ever saw him."

"And then he ran away," I said. "That was his fall-back plan, when he couldn't crack the problem of the house. He ran away, but they caught up with him anyway."

"I'd be tempted to speculate that his plan involved more than just running away," said Bethany.

"What do you mean?"

"I mean, it involved you. Getting you to live in the house, and whatever elaborate ruse he had to put together to make that happen. He did that for a reason."

"I've thought about that," I said. "I think he did that to throw the satanists off the trail, particularly if he thought they might have been keeping watch on the house. Having me there made the place look occupied. He probably did it to buy himself some time."

"That may have been part of it. But I think Alan chose to make you the guardian of the temple that's concealed beneath his house. It's like he handed the responsibility to you, and whether you like it or not, you are now responsible. You see, in ancient cultures, the guardianship of a temple was considered a sacred duty. I would guess that Alan couldn't simply walk away from something like that, for reasons that go beyond any practical considerations about deceiving the coven as to his whereabouts. I think there was a symbolic side to it, as well. If he was going to leave the thing that he had sworn to protect, he had to nominate a successor, in order to mollify, or so he hoped, whatever unearthly power he swore the oath to."

"And so, he nominated me," I finished for her.

"He may have done. I'm only speculating. Anyway, that's as much as I know. I'm sorry it was so little.

"And for having brought you fear, not hope," she added.

"Please don't be sorry about anything," I said, getting to my feet. "You've been very helpful, and also very honest and candid, for which I'm most grateful."

"What will you do now?" she said, standing up to face me.

I realised that I was at a complete loss as to what to say and cast my eyes around the well-ordered drawing room as if in search of inspiration. I suddenly felt very tired.

"What am I going to do?" I repeated. "Honestly, Bethany, I really don't know."

"I'm sorry that I can't help you," she said. "But I truly can't. Not with this. It could literally kill me. You do understand, don't you?"

"Yes. I do understand. And this is something that I have to do myself. Somehow."

She walked me to the front door, and as I made to step outside, she gently took me by the arm.

"I'll pray for your friend," she said. "For his soul."

"You pray?" I said. "Forgive me for saying so, but I'm just a little bit surprised to hear that."

"As would my father be," she said. "If he were still alive to hear me say it. He was a devout atheist, and he brought me up to be one as well. But that was then. These days, I find that I pray quite a lot. And so, I'll pray for your friend. And I'll pray for you, as well."

CHAPTER THIRTY-TWO

Seeking Professor Faraday

As I stepped out onto the pavement, I switched my phone back on. By the time I got to the end of the street it had bleeped at me twice in quick succession.

I looked at the screen and saw a missed call and a text message, both from Darren. The message merely read, "Call Me".

"I've got that number you wanted," he said. "Didn't want to text it."

"Hold on," I said, fishing my notebook and pen from my coat pocket whilst clamping the phone between my ear and my shoulder.

"Thanks," I said, as I wrote down the number. "I don't know how you do it."

"You don't want to know."

"I guess not. Nothing on von Draken yet, I take it?"

"Quiet as a mouse, but it's early days. As soon as I have anything on that, I'll let you know."

I had re-entered the park, so I walked over to a bench and sat down. I looked at the number for Julian Faraday that Darren had given me. It was for a landline, and I recognised the code as the one for Oxford.

Taking a deep breath, and not entirely sure what I was going to say, I dialled the number.

There was no reply. After several rings it went to answer phone, and I hung up without leaving a message.

Frustrated, I made my way back to the car, whilst trying to compose in my head a relatively succinct and coherent message to leave for this person I had never met or spoken to before. By the time I had settled in the driver's seat, and opened the windows to allow in the cool, fresh spring air, I had more or less succeeded,

This time, however, the telephone was answered.

"Am I speaking to Professor Faraday?" I asked.

"You are. Who is this, please?"

The voice was deep, rich, imbued with authority.

"My name is Richard Weaver. I'm investigating a satanic coven in …"

"How did you get this number?"

"Um, from a friend. You see, I …"

"And who might that have been?"

"Well, I can't really say, but I …"

"I'm afraid I very much doubt what you're telling me, Mr Weaver. You see, I make it a point only to give this number to my most trusted confidantes, and I find it most difficult to believe that any of them would have passed it on to you."

"Professor Faraday, if I could just have two minutes of your time, I'm sure you'll understand the reason for my call."

There was a long silence on the other end of the line.

"Very well," he said finally. "You have two minutes. What is the reason for your call?"

"I'm calling from Wiltshire. Well, from Bath, actually, but I live in Wiltshire. And I've come across an occult group down here. They're satanists, and I think they're planning something big for 30th April, you know, for Walpurgis Night, and I understand that you're something of an expert in these matters, and so I thought that might be of some interest to you."

"Walpurgis Night is the most important date in the satanic calendar. To learn that a particular coven may be planning something for that night is hardly news. Every satanic group on the planet is likely making such plans. What makes yours so special?"

The tone of his voice was polite but impatient, as if he was speaking to a not terribly bright child.

"I think this is a pretty serious group," I said. "They've been pestering me for some time, now; like staking out my house, keeping watch on it from some woods, stuff like that. Also, one of them recently sent me an adder in the post.

"It bit me," I added, a little plaintively, and in an attempt to elicit some sympathy.

"How very unfortunate," Faraday said. "And what, may I ask, did you do to upset them, to invite such an unpleasant prank?"

"Nothing. Well, maybe something. I found a ruined chapel in the countryside that I think they use for their ceremonies, but I don't think that's what this is really about. They want my house, basically. That's what this is all about. I mean, it's only just become my house. You see, it was a surprise bequest from the previous owner. I don't even like the place. I'm planning to sell it, but I've been there for a couple of months, and there's definitely something not quite right about it."

That's putting it mildly, I thought.

"And it's not just me who thinks that," I added. "I just met with a spiritualist who knew the previous owner; the one who left the house to me. She couldn't get anywhere near the place. She says it has an aura around it, as if it contains some sort of evil spirit."

There was silence at the other end of the line, and so I ploughed on.

"Anyway, it seems to be special to them in some way. You know, to this group of satanists. Not the house so much, as the grounds around the house. I've done some research, and I think there's some sort of subterranean temple there. I haven't found a way into it yet, but I'm sure that's what's behind all this. They can't get to it while I'm there, so they want to get rid of me."

"I see," Faraday said at last. "And they've told you this?"

"Not in so many words. But they've made various threats and inducements, to encourage me to leave, and I know that it's very time critical to them, and it's all about me being out of there by Walpurgis Night. They seem to think there's something special about the one coming up next week. Apparently, they've been waiting years for this; decades in fact. Ever since the temple was built in the 1950s."

"Who exactly communicated this to you?"

"Their leader. He's a man called Ernst von Draken. Does that name mean anything to you?"

"No. It's the first time I've heard it."

"I think he's quite powerful, and he's definitely a satanist. The last time he was here, he put some kind of spell on me, like he'd hypnotised me."

"One doesn't have to be a satanist to hypnotise someone," said Faraday. "I'm quite skilled in the practice myself, as it happens."

I detected a certain weariness in his voice, as if he was becoming tired of our conversation.

"He's put a curse on the house," I gabbled on, desperate to try and keep his attention.

"Really?" Faraday sounded sceptical. "What sort of curse?"

"I don't know. But there's something haunting the house. Something over and above the evil that already resides there. Something more recent, perhaps, that's been put there. An old woman, like a hag or a witch. Possibly some sort of abhuman," I added, recalling something I had read about demonic, humanoid entities. "I'm pretty sure it's something that von Draken conjured, and he used it to try and control the previous owner, and now he's using it to frighten me out of the house. Last night, it attacked a friend of mine. It tried to choke her."

"That sounds most unpleasant. Is she alright?"

"Yes, she's okay. She doesn't want to go back to the house again."

"I'm not surprised."

"Yes, but I'm not going to be intimidated by it. Or by them."

"That's most admirable."

"Maybe, but I need your help?"

"My help? I'm not sure why you think I might be able to help you."

"Because I know that you've got involved in this sort of thing before," I said. "That's what I've heard, anyway. And given the potential significance of what's coming up, I want to stop whatever it is they're planning. Or at least expose it to the glare of publicity."

Faraday waited a beat before saying anything.

"Mr Weaver, on Walpurgis Night, satanist and other occult groups all around the world will be holding sabbats. There's nothing at all unusual in this. It's been going on for centuries."

"And that's okay with you?"

"No. It is most certainly not okay with me, as you put it. I find such activities as will be enacted on that night to be both foolish and obscene, and occasionally dangerous, as well. But if you've researched this matter at all, and it sounds as if you have, then you'll know that for all their idiocy, most of these so-called satanic sects are essentially harmless. I've no reason to suppose that the group you've come across is any different. If you happen to believe otherwise, then you should contact the police."

"Yes, but they're desperate to get into my house. When they're not sending me snakes and demons, they're even offering me money for it. This von Draken person offered me two million pounds, far more than the house is worth, to be out by the end of the month."

"Well, in that case, I'd take it, if I were you," said Faraday.

"You're not serious?"

"Of course, I'm serious. You've already said that you've only been in the house for a few weeks, and you're planning to sell it, so you can't be all that attached to it. Get rid of the place. Take the money and run. Let them have at it."

"So, you really don't care that a group of devil worshippers have something planned for 30th April? Something that might possibly be of huge significance?"

"I very much doubt that it's of any significance at all, other than in their addled minds. But whether I care about it or not is simply irrelevant. There's no more that I can do about it than you can. I'm merely making the point that if this group doesn't have their sabbat at your house …"

"Not in my house," I cut in. "In the temple that's supposed to be underneath it."

"The one to which you have not thus far found the entrance."

"Yes, but …"

"But nothing. The same point still stands. If they don't hold the ceremony there, then they'll simply hold it somewhere else. And I'm sorry to say that there's absolutely nothing that you, or I, can do about it. Now, if that's quite all, I have things to do, so …"

"The house used to belong to Dorian Slake."

I half-shouted the words, causing a woman walking past the car with a pushchair to look at me curiously.

"It was Dorian Slake's house," I repeated. "He lived there from the late 1940s until 1965. He killed himself nearby. He's the one who built the temple under the burial mound, in the

1950s. I even spoke to someone who saw him building it. You knew Slake, didn't you? I heard that you had a run-in with him, shortly before he committed suicide. Some rumour about you rescuing someone he'd kidnapped for a human sacrifice."

"That was a very long time ago, Faraday said quietly. "And it's merely a rumour. I have nothing at all to say on the matter."

"But you know about Dorian Slake," I said.

"Yes. I know about him. He was a thoroughly bad man. You might even go so far as to say that he was evil. But he's long dead, and he can do no harm now. That the house so sought after by the coven you speak of should happen to have once been his is moderately interesting, I grant you, but it really doesn't alter the fundamentals. It merely helps to explain why a group of modern day satanists should be so drawn to it. As I said, my best advice would be to dispose of the house, to have no further contact with this group, and if you feel that your life, or that of anyone else is under threat, to alert the authorities."

"That's it? That's the sum total of your advice?"

"It is. This conversation is over, Mr Weaver. You have had more than your two minutes. I applaud your good intentions in wishing to confront and expose this group of occultists, but would counsel you not to do so, and to leave well alone. And one more thing. I would ask that you never call this number again. It is a private, unlisted number, and if you do call it again, I will take appropriate legal steps. Is that clear?"

"Yes, that's perfectly clear," I said, my voice betraying the deflation I felt.

"Goodbye, Mr Weaver."

The line went dead.

I continued to sit there, at a complete loss as to what to next, and then my phone rang.

I wondered if it was Faraday, calling me back because he'd had a change of heart about helping me, but as soon as I looked at the screen, I recognised Darren's number.

"Hi, what's up?" I said, my tone disinterested, still thinking about my rebuff from Faraday.

"I got a hit on von Draken's voicemail," he said. "Right after I spoke to you."

That made me sit up in my seat.

"Anything good?"

"Might be. It was about a meeting that's taking place this evening. At somewhere called Black Thorn Farm."

The name vaguely rang a bell with me, but I couldn't place it.

"And there was also something about a chapel," Darren finished.

This immediately got my attention.

"Can you play it back to me?" I said.

"Sure. Hold on a second."

Moments later I heard a woman's voice. Not old, not young, and with a faint foreign accent. I was fairly sure it was Catherine Falaise, the woman who had accompanied von Draken to Alan's funeral.

"Ernst, darling," said the voice. "I'm still in Bristol, and it's taking ages, so I'm going to go straight to Black Thorn Farm when I'm done, and I'll meet you there. Nine o'clock at the latest, so there'll be plenty of time to get to the chapel for the ceremony. See you later. Bye."

"Thanks, Darren," I said, as the message ended. "It does mean something to me, as it happens."

I hung up and contemplated this turn of events. Assuming that the chapel being referred to was the one at Stokeley, then I'd have to check the map again to be certain, but I was fairly sure that Black Thorn Farm was the collection of buildings I had seen in the far distance on the day I'd been over there. I therefore surmised that von Draken's group were going to rendezvous there that night, prior to a ceremony at the ruined chapel.

Excited at having something tangible to report, but having nobody to report it to, I decided to call Faraday. He wasn't exactly overjoyed to hear my voice again.

"Look," he said, with obvious irritation in his voice, "I can't say that I don't admire your persistence, but I thought I told you explicitly never to contact me again."

"I know," I said, "And I'm sorry. But some information came in just after I spoke to you, which I thought you should know about."

I waited for him to say something, but there was silence at the other end of the line.

"Well?" he said, at last. "I'm waiting. What is it? What is this critical piece of information, that you felt so compelled to telephone me about?"

"It concerns Ernst von Draken," I said. "The leader of the coven. Someone just called him about a meeting they're having tonight."

"How on earth were you able to ascertain such a thing?"

I thought for a moment before continuing and decided that the situation warranted my coming clean with Faraday.

"Because I got someone to hack into his voicemail," I said.

"How very enterprising of you. Isn't that highly illegal?"

"Yes, it is, but it's a chance I had to take."

"Is it indeed? And I assume that this telecommunications expert who did this for you, is the same person who obtained my unlisted number."

"Yes, it was."

"Such experts must be hard to come by. How is it that you happen to know such a person?"

"I used to be a journalist."

"Ah, and so the pieces fall into place."

There was evident distaste in his voice.

"Sure, whatever. Look, I know it's not something I should have done, and with regard to finding out your number, I'm truly sorry about that. But I'm kind of fighting this battle by myself at the moment, and I need all the help I can get. Anyway, concerning this message, I'm almost certain it involves the ruined chapel I told you about. I think von Draken's group is going to have a sabbat there tonight. The chapel was referred to, and the person also mentioned having a ceremony there.

"Well, in that case, Mr Weaver, you can relax, because this coven that you've locked horns with is a particularly amateurish one."

"What do you mean?"

"I mean, nobody holds a sabbat at this point in April, with Walpurgis Night only a few days away. It simply doesn't happen. Sabbats are held on very specific nights of the year, connected to the passing of the seasons. Tonight, is emphatically not one of them. I therefore infer from this piece of illegal phone hacking that you have chosen to implicate me in that this coven is far from serious. In fact, I'd stop worrying about them altogether."

"Please, Professor, I didn't just get into this today. I think I've learned enough about this coven to be very worried indeed."

"That is entirely your prerogative. Goodbye, again, Mr Weaver. I trust this is the last time that I hear from you."

Pompous old sod, I thought, as he hung up the phone.

I got out of the car and started to pace about the park, trying to evaluate my options, and decide what I was going to do with this information that Darren had unearthed for me, and wishing that I could discuss it with Megan.

Before too long, however, I had made a decision.

I dialled Faraday's number yet again.

This time, I got his answering machine, so I left a message. I imagined him standing angrily over his phone, listening to my voice.

"It's me again," I said. "Sorry. I know this is extremely irritating for you. And I assure you that this is the last time that I'll ever telephone you but go ahead and report me if you really have to. I'm past caring, anyway. I just wanted you to know that I've come to a decision. I don't know what von Draken is planning to do in this chapel this evening, but I'm going to find out. I'm going to it, you see. I'm going to go to the ceremony. There's a place nearby where I can watch them from, and that's exactly what I'm going to do.

"So, I just kind of wanted someone to know that. You know, in case something happens to me. Maybe then you'll start to take this seriously. The chapel is marked on the map. As a ruin. It's about ten miles north of Marlborough, just off the Ridgeway, near a village called Stokeley. It's on the other side of some woods.

"So do with that whatever you want. And like I said, I'm not going to call you again. But now you know. There's going to be a black mass in Wiltshire tonight. And I'm going to be there."

CHAPTER THIRTY-THREE

On the Trail of the Satanists

I drove back to Wiltshire in a state of some excitement. Regardless of what Faraday had said, I was determined to follow up on this tangible piece of intelligence from Darren. After all, I reasoned to myself, what was the point in breaking the law if I didn't do anything with the information that I gleaned from doing so? This was a chance to see von Draken's coven in action, from the concealed vantage point that I had already identified on the slope above the ruined chapel. I was going to take it.

Exactly what I was going to do afterwards, I wasn't quite sure, but I would at least have evidence that the chapel at Stokeley was being used as the meeting point for a satanic coven, and I might yet find some way of using this against von Draken. Perhaps by shining the light of unwelcome publicity upon his operation, I might help to thwart it in some way. As I drove along the country roads, I decided that I'd deploy the best weapon I could against him and his devilish crew, just as I had intimated to Bethany that I would. I would write about them. I'd write a full-on exposé about the coven, based upon my own experiences of living at Badcombe Hollow, and with my report of the sabbat that night as the crowning piece of evidence. And I'd name names when I did so. And then I'd get one of my contacts in the newspaper industry to publish it, and if they wouldn't, then I'd publish it myself on-line, and if Ernst von Draken wanted to sue me over it, then so be it. Finally, I felt like I had a plan.

My renewed sense of optimism and purpose did suffer something of a dent, however, as soon as I turned into the driveway of Badcombe Hollow. I knew I had to go in there, because there were things in there that I needed, but I certainly didn't relish the prospect of re-entering that house after the harrowing events of the night before. And yet all was quiet and peaceful as I stepped out of the car and looked up at the now familiar stone edifice. Bathed in pale sunlight, and set beneath a clear blue sky, it was hard to believe that so many terrors lurked within it.

Taking a deep breath, I unlocked the front door and allowed it to swing open but felt decidedly unwilling to step over the threshold. Instead, I had to suppress the urge to simply turn tail and bolt from the property.

Get a grip, I told myself. You're going to have to try and sell this house to someone at some point soon. You won't do that if you're hiding in the garden.

I entered the house, and then proceeded to walk slowly into every room, all the time expecting the thing that had attacked Megan to jump out at me. By the time I reached the top floor my nerves felt shredded, but I had at least confirmed that the house was empty. For now, at any rate.

Breathing a little easier I returned downstairs and retrieved my map of the Ridgeway from the sitting room. I took it through to the kitchen and spread it out on the island unit.

Finding Stokeley, I traced a line with my fingers through the adjacent woods and to the ruined chapel, and from there, about a mile over to the west, I saw Black Thorn Farm marked.

I had been right. This farm was the one that I had seen from the chapel ruins, and I now knew that it was where von Draken's coven was going to assemble that evening, before going to the chapel for their ceremony, presumably by way of the path that led through the valley. I had already identified a suitably concealed position above the chapel from where to observe this, but now I needed to find a way of getting to it, since I knew that it would be most unwise to park on the outskirts of Stokeley, as I had on my previous visit, as this was only likely to draw attention to my being there.

I saw that the road from the village went past Black Thorn Farm, before eventually re-joining the main road. The farm and its immediate environs were clearly out of the question. I needed to find somewhere in between the two places where I could discreetly tuck the car out of the way. It also needed to be somewhere from where I could relatively easily get to the chapel in the dark, and find my way back again.

Roughly midway between the village and the farm, and at the top of an escarpment that led directly to the fields above the chapel, a bridle path was marked. Even more promisingly, there was a building of some kind shown there, perhaps a barn, and this meant that the path should be wide enough to take a vehicle. I reckoned that if I turned in there, I'd not only be sufficiently hidden away from the prying eyes of any curious villagers, but also at a good place from which to walk to the chapel, without having to blunder through the woods in the darkness. I recalled that the moon had been virtually full the night before, and the weather conditions were clear, so negotiating a bridle path and some fields shouldn't be too much of a problem.

Feeling satisfied that I had a good plan, and with several hours to kill before I needed to make my way over there, I set about fixing myself something to eat, as I had a long night ahead of me.

I put several rashers of bacon into a pan and cut slices from a rather stale loaf of bread to toast. I chopped some tomatoes to cook with the bacon, and got two eggs out of the fridge, which I scrambled. I then poured orange juice into a jug and started to brew a pot of coffee. It felt strange to be occupying myself in such a mundane task as preparing a simple meal, given everything that was going on.

I ate in the dining room, which I realised I had hardly used at all throughout my stay at Badcombe Hollow, looking out through the pergola at the long barrow and the fields beyond.

After I had eaten, I took a long bath, shaved and put on a fresh set of clothes. Then I took a small knapsack of Alan's that I had found in a cupboard and put into it the map, my camera, a torch, a warm sweater and a bottle of water. I was as ready as I was ever going to be for my covert mission to the ruined chapel at Stokeley.

I left the house feeling tense and apprehensive, but imbued with a real sense of purpose, and I was in oddly good spirits as I motored along the country lanes in the direction of the Ridgeway.

Shortly after turning north, I decided to stop at a country pub I had been to once before and liked, since I realised that there was still a little time to go until sundown, and I wanted to trek over to my hiding place under cover of darkness. I also didn't want to have to endure an inordinately long wait, once I was there. The message to von Draken had referred to being at the farm by nine o'clock, and thus leaving plenty of time to get from there to the ruined chapel. This obviously implied a departure from the farm at some time after nine o'clock. I figured that if I aimed to arrive at Stokeley by half-past eight, this would get me to my concealed vantage point by about nine, in plenty of time to watch the coven make its way over there from the farm.

I bought a large whiskey and took it over to the fireplace, where I settled into an overstuffed armchair, and spent a pleasant enough half-hour, sipping my drink and thinking about what I might do with the money from the eventual sale of Alan's house. The abrupt termination of things with Megan notwithstanding, I was still of a mind to find somewhere to live in this vicinity, with change left over from the sale of the house to put away for a rainy day, and the rental on my flat in London to give me some income. I decided to start house hunting, as well as getting Badcombe Hollow onto the market, once the current business with von Draken came to an end, as it presumably would, one way or the other, after Walpurgis Night.

Soon it was time to be on my way, and I walked back out into the car park to see that the sun had now slipped low in the sky. It continued to get darker as I drove along the narrow, twisting lanes, and by the time I reached the turn-off to Stokeley the sun had set, and dusk had settled over the rugged, empty landscape.

After I passed the grass verge near Doreen Smithers' house where I had parked on my previous visit, I was soon climbing up the steep hill, and as I reached the top, I slowed down to a crawl, so as not to miss the bridle path I had spotted on the map.

I found it easily enough and was pleased to see that there was no gate across the entrance and that the beginning of the path was both wide enough to accommodate my car, and had a gravel surface, which made it easy to negotiate. Ahead of me, through the fading light, I could see the outline of the building I had noticed on the map, and as I drew up to it, I realised that it was not a barn, as I had supposed, but an electricity sub-station in a small compound, surrounded by weld-mesh fencing.

I brought the car slowly to a halt and killed the lights and the engine. It was eerily silent all around me, and for a moment I debated the wisdom of coming up here.

At least it's better than sitting at home by yourself in your haunted house, I thought, as I forced myself with some effort to get out of the car.

The bridle path was easy to follow as it was bordered with tall hedges to either side, and I walked along it for what must have been about half a mile without incident. It was a still night, with barely a breath of wind, and almost ethereally quiet in the enveloping darkness of the steep, thick, tangled hedgerows.

Some way along the path, I noticed the woods I had walked through on my previous visit appear on my right-hand side. I figured that if I kept going, I would come to the field I had accessed from these woods previously, and from there it would be only a short distance to the chapel.

Although not typically afraid of the dark, I found myself getting more and more spooked, the closer I got to my destination. But I was committed by then and determined to go through with my plan.

Before too long, I reached the field, and then walked through the familiar litter of sarsen stones until I got to the top of the steep valley.

It was fully dark by then, but I could see the ruins of the chapel, and I felt a tremor of excitement. I was here. I had arrived.

Using the position of the chapel as a guide, I was able to locate the clump of small trees and rocks about half-way down the slope, which I had noticed on my last visit, and from where I planned to spy on the coven.

In the distance, I could see the lights of the farm, and I imagined von Draken and the other satanists gathering in there and preparing to walk over to the chapel. But aside from this one glimmer of civilisation in the far distance, everything else around me was in darkness, lit only by the moon and the stars. I was quite alone up there, standing above the steeply sided valley, with its desolate, broken chapel. Even the sheep that had been in the field on the previous occasion were nowhere to be seen. I wondered if they belonged to whoever owned the farmhouse and had been moved to another field to get them out of the way for the ceremony.

I carefully made my way down the slope. The grass was soaked in dew, and I stumbled a couple of times, but I managed to stay on my feet. When I reached the trees, I sat down heavily on one of the outer rocks and looked down at the chapel, little more than a hundred yards beneath me. The moonlight was washing the broken walls and piles of stones in a pale white light. It seemed a particularly appropriate setting for the witches' sabbat that was about to take place and thinking of this made me feel both excited and frightened at the same time. Whether through fear, or the chill of the night, I felt a shiver go through me, and this prompted me to take the sweater I had packed out of my knapsack. I took off my coat, pulled the sweater over my head, and then put the coat back on, and slipped the camera I had brought with me into one of its deep pockets. I was ready.

I stepped back behind the trees and settled down to wait.

CHAPTER THIRTY-FOUR

The Black Mass

I saw them as soon as they left the farm; a line of burning torches, bobbing across the landscape like tiny orbs of light, as the satanists approached the chapel along the floor of the valley. They walked in single file, as if in a procession. There were thirteen of them.

As I watched from my hiding place amongst the trees, I felt vindicated. I had been right. I had been right to have von Draken's communications hacked, and I had been right when I had told Faraday that there was going to be a ceremony at the ruined chapel that night. And I was here to witness it. After weeks where it had felt as if I had only been able to see glimpses of the truth, things were about to get very real indeed.

It took them about twenty minutes to cover the distance to the chapel. When they got close enough to be almost beneath me, I hunkered down in my hiding place, confident that I was sufficiently concealed from view, but still able to observe whatever it was that was about to happen.

As to what this might be, I was almost entirely ignorant. I had done a certain amount of reading on the subject of sabbats and black masses, but there was no set format, as far as I could tell; no order of service which the group would automatically follow, as if by rote. For all I knew, I could have been about to witness ritual animal slaughter, a series of chanted invocations to the devil, or a mass orgy. Or quite possibly all three.

As the coven picked their way through the broken slabs of stone into the main body of what would once have been the nave of the chapel, I focused my attention on the person walking at the front of the line, who I assumed was the leader. And who I further assumed was Ernst von Draken. Thanks to the burning torch that each member of the group was carrying, and the clear night sky, the scene was well illuminated, but the coven were all wearing black cloaks with hoods, and I couldn't see any of their faces.

But the figure at the front looked to have the build of von Draken, and when he turned to face his followers and then called out to them, I was certain that I recognised his voice.

"Prepare yourselves," he shouted to them. "Our company is assembled. Prepare the scene for the ritual to our lord and master."

The group dispersed itself around the chapel ruins, each of them planting their torch in the ground to form a circle of flames, with von Draken remaining in the centre. I noticed that two of them had been carrying a large wicker chest between them, as well as their torches, and this was set down beside the slab of stone I assumed was used as a satanic altar. Von Draken remained completely still throughout, while his minions created the circle around him.

Once the torches were in place, two members of the coven broke the circle and approached the stone slab, where they dropped to their knees, as if in supplication, at the feet of von Draken, high priest and master of ceremonies, officiating over proceedings from beside his makeshift altar.

The two satanists then got up and each drew a large candle from within the folds of their dark cloaks, which they placed at either end of the altar and lit.

A third person came out to join them. He or she was carrying something, which they put onto the altar, as a centrepiece to the two candles, although this person did not kneel in supplication before von Draken, as the others had. I thought I recognised the object as a chalice.

Leaving von Draken standing alone by the altar, the three members of his flock withdrew back to their positions in the circle. The whole scene was played out in total silence. The only sound was the crackling flames of the torches and the slightest breath of wind.

Von Draken stepped over to the box on the ground by the altar slab, opened it, and peered inside. He then reached down with both hands and pulled out the struggling figure of a young lamb. Clearly terrified, it started to bleat loudly, the sound of its cries unnaturally loud in the calm of the night. It became even more distressed as von Draken lifted its wriggling body above his head as if holding a trophy.

He shouted something at the night sky in a foreign language that I didn't recognise, and then he passed the lamb to one of the coven, who had stepped forward out of the circle and knelt down before him.

"Tether the sacrifice," I heard him say, and the lamb was carried over to the only remaining section of chapel wall, where it appeared to be fastened to something with a piece of rope. It had stopped crying by then, but I had a horrible feeling there was worse to come, as far as this poor, defenceless creature was concerned.

"It is time," von Draken shouted, drawing my attention back to the group, all of whom, I noticed, were now kneeling beside their torches.

Von Draken made his way slowly around the perimeter of the circle, stopping beside each satanist and touching them lightly on the head, before stooping down and saying something I couldn't hear.

Once he had replicated this action with the entire coven he returned to the centre of the circle, raised his arms and called out to the heavens.

"Hear us, master. Hear us, your loyal and obedient servants. Hear us and accept our sacrifice to your eternal glory. Hail Satan!"

"Hail Satan," shouted the coven in unison.

"We exist to serve you, master. You are the true lord of our world. We serve you until our last breath. We serve you until our last drop of blood. Hail Satan."

"Hail Satan."

"You are the one and only true God. You are the outcast, the desolate one, the pitiless nail of Megiddo, the ruler who shall recover his lost realm. Hail Satan."

"Hail Satan."

"We swear violence and fury to your adversaries, revered lord and master. We spit on your enemy, the Nazarene, and all those who preach his word. Hail Satan."

"Hail Satan."

"We beseech you, master, to hear the invocation that we shall make to you in this place, so that we may transform your night of celebration into your greatest triumph. The time has come. The elements are in place. We are ready to open the gates of Walpurgis. Hear our entreaty, master. Grant us your wisdom. Hail Satan."

"Hail Satan."

Von Draken lowered his arms, and the coven rose to their feet. He then stepped over to the altar and reached into the wicker box in which the lamb had been brought to the ceremony and pulled something out of it.

It was a wooden crucifix, about two feet high and one foot across. Thanks to the light from the torches, I could just discern a figure, presumably that of Christ, affixed to the cross section.

Von Draken held the cross out in front of him and seemed to contemplate it for a moment. Then he threw it violently to the ground, and a collective growl of anger sounded from the coven.

Each of them then took it in turns to step into the circle and approach the cross lying on the ground. They all spat on it, and a few of them stamped on it as well. One member of the coven, a female who had opened her cloak to expose her nude body beneath, picked up the cross and thrust it between her legs, as if feigning the act of masturbation.

When they had all had their turn at desecrating the cross, von Draken picked it up again and carried it over to the pile of rocks at the chapel's ruined gable, and propped it upright amongst the pieces of stone, but upside down, in a deliberate inversion of its Christian symbolism.

The circle having re-formed, von Draken picked up the chalice on the altar, and held it briefly over his head with both hands before setting it down again. He then reached into his cloak and withdrew a handful of what looked like small, white discs. As he started to break them in his hands and toss the pieces into the chalice, I realised that they were communion wafers.

The chalice was passed anti-clockwise around the circle, and each member of the coven spat into it. This was clearly a very calculated desecration of the Christian act of communion, although it was about to get far worse. When the chalice was returned to von Draken, he put it down by his feet, lifted his cloak, and urinated noisily into it. As he returned the chalice to the altar there was a murmur of approval from the rest of the group, which he lifted his arm sharply to silence, as if annoyed at this apparent breach in protocol.

He then delved into his cloak again, and this time took out a rolled-up scroll of papers, which he unfurled as he resumed his position at the centre of his circle of acolytes.

"Kneel," he shouted. "It is time for the invocation. So, kneel. Kneel as the wretches that you are before our master."

The coven did as it was told, and von Draken started to read from the sheets of paper. Although he did so in a loud, clear voice, in a way that seemed like he was carefully and deliberately enunciating each syllable of each word, I had no idea what he was saying. The words were in a foreign tongue, and spoken in a strange, guttural, discordant dialect that was like no language I had ever heard before. Realising that this was likely the most critical part of the ceremony, I wished that I had brought some sort of recording equipment with me, so that I could have captured this mysterious dialogue, and perhaps get someone to translate it for me. Meanwhile, the ugly dirge continued on and on, as the coven remained silent and seemingly enraptured, hanging on every word of their diabolical priest.

After what felt like a long time, but which was probably not more than a few minutes, von Draken came to the end of his unintelligible peroration. He rolled up his script and put it back into the folds of his cloak. He then pointed at one of the coven, who immediately scurried off, before returning moments later with the tethered lamb. The satanist handed the animal over to von Draken, and then resumed its kneeling position in the circle.

I was pretty sure I knew what was coming next, but that didn't make it any less foul or upsetting when it did.

Von Draken drew a long knife from his cloak. Its blade glinted in the flame of the torches. Holding the lamb by its ears, so that it screamed with pain as well as fear, he plunged the knife into the poor creature's neck, before swiftly drawing the blade across its throat. A spray of blood gushed from the lamb, whose legs were still kicking, and I noticed von Draken wipe some down the front of his cloak, before touching his bloody hand to his forehead.

Appalled at this act of wanton, disgusting savagery, but nevertheless thankful that the suffering of the lamb was at an end, nothing could have prepared me for the depravity of what happened next.

Von Draken held up the now inert body of the lamb, as if offering it to the assembled company. Its partially severed head was hanging in the most gruesome way from the rest of its body, held only by a thin strip of skin and fur. He tossed the lamb into the centre of the circle and shouted some sort of command, at which point the coven sprang to their feet and threw themselves upon the body. Then, in a frenzy, they quite literally started to tear it apart, howling with excitement as they did so.

I simply couldn't look any longer, and I closed my eyes at the horror of it all, and offered a silent prayer to the lamb, whose corpse was being so hideously defiled, as well as a further one that this grotesque scene should end as soon as possible.

Eventually, silence descended upon the valley once again. I opened my eyes and saw the various members of the coven withdrawing back to their positions in the circle.

Still shaken, but relieved that the revolting scene I had just witnessed was over, I wondered what was going to happen next.

From the centre of the circle, von Draken lifted his arms to the sky, as he had done before, and shouted something that the coven shouted back as onc. I had no idea what had been said.

The circle then broke up, and the satanists came together within the perimeter of torches, where they formed a tightly bunched semi-circle in front of von Draken. It was as if they were waiting for him to give some sort of command.

Saying nothing, he slowly lifted his arm and pointed at one of the coven, who stepped forward and walked over to him. Von Draken knocked the hood from the person's head, revealing the face of an elderly woman. He then said something indistinct, upon which she unfastened her cloak and let it fall to the ground, revealing her naked body. Von Draken took a step towards her and grabbed her sagging breasts with both hands and kissed her full on the mouth. There was a murmur of excitement from the rest of the group.

He then took hold of her hair and pushed her roughly to the ground so that she was knelt before him with her head inclined upwards to look into his face. At this point, another member of the coven stepped forward and crouched down behind her, and then reached around and cupped her breasts in his or her hands. Someone in the semi-circle made a loud, animal-like cry of apparent ecstasy and started to remove their own robe.

I was fairly sure that I was about to watch an orgy, which was a pretty ghastly thought, although still preferable to seeing a young sheep stabbed to death and then torn apart, limb from limb. But in spite of the unpleasantness of what I presumed I was about to bear witness to, I knew that there was an upside to this. If the satanists were going to divest themselves of their hooded cloaks, then I would have a much better chance of identifying them later.

Slowly and carefully, so as not to make a sound, I reached into my coat pocket for the camera I had brought with me. Although a small model, I knew from experience that it took excellent night shots, and the zoom would easily cope with the short distance between me and the chapel. Here was the chance to collect some actual hard evidence against von Draken and his group, I thought.

It had been some time since I had used the camera on its night setting, and without any light to work with, I struggled to find the correct position on the control dial, cursing myself for not having done this earlier, in daylight. I could hear the coven stirring with excitement as von Draken and his fellow satanist continued to grapple with the old woman's naked body, while she moaned with apparent pleasure.

Having got the camera set up as I thought it should be, I pointed at the scene through the viewfinder, and to my pleasure saw that von Draken had removed the hood of his cloak, to reveal his distinctive mane of silvery white hair.

Although I'd had little doubt before, I now knew beyond question that it had been him leading the ceremony, and with any luck, I was about to capture an image of him in the most compromising of positions.

While I had been getting the camera ready another member of the coven had stepped forward and disrobed. It was another female, who I recognised as Catherine Falaise, von Draken's witch. She was squatting on a stone slab, rubbing one hand over her breasts while the other was thrust between her legs. She was almost perfectly backlit by one of the burning torches behind her and I zoomed in on her with the camera.

My finger hovered momentarily over the shutter button as I struggled to keep the camera steady and then, with the obscene gyrations of the woman masturbating directly in the middle of the frame, I pressed lightly.

I've done a number of stupid things in my life but taking a camera to a stakeout of a black mass and not checking beforehand to ensure that the flash was switched off would probably have to rank as the most boneheaded and idiotic thing I have ever done.

To my absolute horror, the flash exploded as I took the picture, illuminating the area in front of me like lightning.

For a moment, time seemed to stand still, as the satanists stared, bewildered at the source of the light and I stared back at them. I knew they couldn't see me, but they would have known that someone was in the clump of trees, just a matter of yards away from them, and it was almost as if they couldn't quite believe it.

And then, predictably enough, all hell broke loose.

CHAPTER THIRTY-FIVE

Hunted

The coven swarmed out of the chapel ruins and started to run up the slope towards me. They were screaming at the tops of their voices; a collective snarl of murderous fury, directed straight at me.

"Kill him," I heard von Draken shout, as he pointed towards my hiding place. "Find him and kill him."

I grabbed my bag and scrambled out of the clump of trees and tried to run up the slope, but it was so steep and slippery that I fell to the ground almost immediately. Powered by the adrenaline of sheer terror I pushed myself to my feet and made my way as quickly as I could towards the top of the embankment, at times using my hands to grip the hassocks of grass and propel myself upwards. When I reached the top, I looked back down in the direction of the chapel.

The coven was about halfway up the slope, moving together in a pack. Some of them were carrying their torches. I didn't like to think what the others might be carrying, but I knew from the sacrifice I had witnessed that at least one of them had a knife.

In a complete state of panic, but thankful at least that they didn't appear to have got any closer than when they had first seen me, I started to run along the top of the embankment towards the bridle path I had followed earlier in the evening. I figured that the car was about half a mile away, and I was planning to run every yard of it.

As I approached the entrance to the path I stopped and looked around again, seriously out of breath now, but too scared to be fatigued. The coven had reached the top of the slope and were now stretched out in a rough line as they ran towards me. There was a small knot of burning torches at the front, which seemed to be moving faster than the remainder of the column, and which were presumably being carried by the younger, fitter members of the group. To my dismay, I saw that they had closed the gap between us, and that gave me a real dilemma, because at the rate at which they were gaining on me, they were going to catch up with me long before I reached the car. I wasn't going to make it. I was going to have to try and lose them in the woods.

Sprinting off again, I veered off towards the treeline. The woods loomed up before me like a dark edifice set against the night sky. I plunged into their shadow and then clambered over the barbed wire fence that separated them from the field.

Don't get caught on the barbed wire, I shouted silently to myself, but I didn't, and with the fence safely negotiated I found myself in the darkness of the woods.

I looked back into the field, in the vain hope that the pursuing coven might have missed my sudden manoeuvre by the bridle path and chased off down it, but inevitably they hadn't. They had all tacked off towards the woods and were now coming towards me in a long line, like beaters on a pheasant shoot. They were less than fifty yards away now and closing in on my position.

I had entered the wood at the foot of a small rise, and I crashed through the trees to the top of it, in the hope that I might from there get some sense of the lay of the land. In as much as I was focusing on anything right then, aside from minute-to-minute survival, I had the vague notion that my best chance of getting away from there was to lose the coven in the woods, and then somehow double back towards the path I had come from, and then follow it to the car.

I could see nothing from the top of the rise other than a great, dense mass of trees all around me, and so I pushed on as quickly as I could.

They'll be in the woods by now, I realised and, sure enough, I almost immediately heard the trampling of undergrowth behind me. None of us are going to be moving through these woods quietly, I thought to myself, and that had both advantages and disadvantages, as far as my situation was concerned. As long as they kept moving, I'd be able to hear where they were, but they would be able to hear me too, and could gauge my direction of travel accordingly. I also had to contend with the distinct possibility that some of my pursuers would know these woods a lot better than I did and would be much better able to negotiate them in darkness.

I continued to press noisily on through the dense carpet of ferns, twigs and leaves beneath the trees, continually stumbling on things and careering off course. The coven had got much closer to me now. I realised that I was going to have to hide, and do so very soon, before they were right on top of me. An image of the lamb in the chapel being torn apart passed fleetingly through my mind and seemed to inject a momentary burst of speed into my legs.

I saw a large deadfall with a pit in the ground next to its upturned roots, and I was about to duck down into it before I realised that it was far too obvious a hiding place. I staggered on, losing all sense of direction as I got ever deeper into the woods, my sense of where I was defined purely by the sounds of those chasing me.

I reached the edge of a small clearing ringed with mature trees, and suddenly had an idea. These trees were substantially thicker in girth that the tall, slender pines that filled most of the wood. I could hide behind one of them, wait for whoever was behind me to go on past, and then double back towards the valley.

With only seconds to spare, I decided that it was the best option I had, although it took quite an effort of will to make myself stop running away from the various furies in pursuit. But I was just about thinking rationally enough to understand that continuing to run through the wood simply wasn't an option any longer.

I stooped down behind a massive beech tree and almost folded myself into the grooves of its trunk, trying desperately to regulate my breathing, so as not to give my location away through a series of noisy gasps when one of the satanists inevitably reached the clearing, something that could only be moments away.

But they must have sensed that I had stopped running because the sound of their pursuit suddenly ceased too. Out of sight, but from somewhere alarmingly close by, there came the crackle of a burning torch.

"Spread out," I heard a voice call.

Squeezing myself ever more tightly into the clefts of the tree, I continued to crouch there, with my heart pounding in my chest, knowing that I had to remain completely still if I was going to evade detection.

Moments later, I heard someone enter the clearing. I tried not to breathe as they drew closer, wishing that I had possessed the presence of mind to find a branch or a rock, or anything else that I might have used as a crude weapon. Instead, my plan was entirely contingent upon not being discovered. There was no fall-back scenario. With my chest feeling as if it might explode with the tension, I slowly turned my head to one side.

A member of the coven stood just feet away from me, but looking straight ahead, at the dark screen of trees on the other side of the clearing. He was wearing a cloak, but he had pushed back the hood so I could see his face, illuminated by the torch he was carrying. He was a large, burly man of late middle age with a thick beard, and he was breathing heavily from the exertion of the chase. To my horror, I saw that in his other hand he was holding a knife with a long, serrated blade. I had little doubt that if he discovered my hiding place, he would use it.

After several agonising seconds he made his way out of the clearing. I watched him as he entered the trees and then he was swallowed up by the darkness, save for the burning glow of his torch, which seemed to be floating through the woods, away from me.

In case it was a trick, or lest he should hear me as he walked away, I continued to hide by the tree, still scared out of my wits, but feeling a certain amount of relief as well. It looked as if my plan had worked. Assuming that the members of the coven were roughly keeping pace with each other as they swept through the woods, they should be getting further away from me all the time. All I had to do now was get back to the valley by the way I had come, locate the bridle path, and follow it back to the car.

I slowly rose out of my crouch and stood up, careful to make as little noise as possible. A cloud must have passed over the moon while I had been hiding, because everything seemed suddenly darker. Keeping my eyes fixed on the area of woods into which the satanist had now completely disappeared, so that even his torch was no longer visible, I edged backwards out of the clearing.

Suddenly, something grabbed me from behind. A black-clad arm curled around my chest whilst a hand clamped itself across my mouth, stifling my scream.

Pure terror coursed through my veins. They had caught me. One of them must have stayed behind while the others continued on, just in case I managed to slip through them. Any second now, this person would alert the rest of the coven and they would all be upon me. I simply had to get away if I wasn't to be murdered in these woods.

I tried with all my might to shake the person off me, but they were simply too strong, and then I was spun around and pushed backwards into the trunk of the same tree that I had just been hiding behind.

I was now face to face with my captor, who was holding onto the collar of my coat with one hand, whilst the other remained pressed against my mouth, and that was when I noticed that there was something different about this satanist, compared to the others in the coven. Although dressed from head to foot in black, it was wearing not a cloak with a hood, but a black windbreaker and trousers, and had a balaclava pulled down over its face.

"Keep quiet," a voice hissed from behind the woollen mask.

The voice sounded female.

I struggled both to get free and to cry out but managed neither.

"Quiet," the voice said again. "I'm not with them, and I'm not going to hurt you, but I need you absolutely silent, otherwise you're going to lead them right to us. Do you understand?"

Utterly confused, but thankful at least that I hadn't been captured by the coven, I nodded at her. She then slowly removed one hand from my mouth, whilst releasing my collar with her other hand. For a long moment we simply stared at each other in the darkness, and then she pulled the balaclava from her head.

She was a young woman with fair hair that was tied back behind her head, and skin that looked very pale against the blackness of the night, and her dark clothing. She was wearing a small pack on her back, with a torch poking through one of the side pockets. She looked tough, determined and, judging from the way in which she had pinned me to the tree, she was clearly not someone to be trifled with. What on earth she was doing in those woods I had absolutely no clue, but as she now looked like my best chance of salvation, I couldn't have been more pleased that she was there.

"Who are you?" I said, excitedly. "What are you doing here?"

"There's no time for that now," she said. "I'm the person who's going to get you out of here alive. That's all you need to know. Okay?"

"Fine by me."

From deep in the woods, I could hear the sounds of the coven moving through the dense undergrowth as they continued to look for me.

"There's a bridle path that goes from the top of the valley to the road," I whispered. "That's where my car is."

"I know," she said. "We need to get over there, but we need to be very quiet while we do it."

I wondered how it was that she knew where I had left my car, but as this was one of only several unexplained developments in the past couple of minutes, I figured that this question could wait until we were safely away from the coven.

"Don't worry, I'll be as quiet as I can," I said. "But I think they've gone. We should be behind them now."

"No, we're not. They tricked you. They're forming a circle and then they'll come towards each other and tighten it until they find us. So, we're going to have to sneak through them."

"How do you …?" I began, but she cut me off.

"No questions. Just follow me, and don't make a sound."

Not inclined to argue, I followed the woman through the woods. Every so often she would halt in her tracks and hold her hand up to get me to do the same. I could hear the satanists all around us by then, and periodically caught a glimpse of one of their burning torches through the trees. They seemed to be everywhere, forming a noose around us, just as she had said they were going to. I felt my fear from earlier, temporarily alleviated by my encounter with this mysterious saviour, return in a rush, as I wondered how we were going to get out of the woods without being spotted.

As we stepped as quietly as possible through the bracken she suddenly stopped and motioned for me to get down on the ground. She crouched down beside me and whispered in my ear.

"There's one of them up ahead, guarding the way back to the valley. There's no way to get past him on this path."

"Can we go around?" I asked.

"No time," she said, craning her neck to look behind us. "The others are starting to come this way."

As she said this, I became aware of voices somewhere in the gloom from the direction we had just come from. They didn't sound very far away.

"What are we going to do?" I said in a strangled whisper, betraying how frightened I was.

"I'm going to deal with him," she said. "Stay right behind me and do what I tell you."

I followed her crouched form down the track towards the cloaked figure I could now see standing with his back to us, looking in the direction of the valley.

Suddenly, the woman's pace quickened to a run, at which point the satanist must have heard something, because he suddenly wheeled around to face us. But he was too late, because the woman was right on top of his position by then, and she suddenly leapt at him, bringing him to the ground. I heard the loud slap of flesh on flesh as she punched him in the face, and then she straddled his chest, putting one hand over his mouth, as she had done with me, to stop him from crying out, although he was struggling violently.

"Get over here," she hissed back at me. As she spoke, she picked the large knife the satanist had dropped when she ambushed him, and threw it off to the side, where I heard it land in the bracken.

"Get on top of his legs," she said.

"What …?"

"Just do it. I need to tie his hands and feet, and he's bloody strong, so for Christ's sake just sit on his legs."

I did as I was told, doing my best to hold the kicking legs of the satanist on the ground while she continued to hold his head down.

"Reach into my pack," she said.

"What am I looking for?" I said as I opened the top flap of the backpack.

"A roll of duct tape. Take it out and tear off three strips."

With the satanist's body bucking wildly beneath me I located the roll of tape and started to tear off a strip.

"Pass me one piece at a time," she said, looking back at me. "And hurry up. The rest of them are going to be here any minute."

I started to hand her the strips of tape. She put one over the man's mouth, then wrapped the next one tightly around his wrists, dextrously performing both actions one-handed, while her other hand remained pressed on the man's throat. Once this was done, she took her hand off his throat and punched him hard in the face for the second time, and then rolled off his chest and scurried round behind me.

"Give me the other bit of tape," she hissed urgently.

I thrust it into her hand as I watched the dazed figure on the ground struggle to raise his head, and she then wrapped the tape around his ankles. I doubted that these bonds would hold for long, but they were enough in that moment to keep him on the ground and prevent him from calling out and giving away our position.

"What are we going to do with him?" I said, as we rolled off his body onto the forest floor.

"Nothing," she said, stamping on the satanist's torch to extinguish it. "We're going to leave him here. The others will find him eventually. Now, come on. We need to get the hell out of these woods."

I needed no encouragement whatsoever on this count and with her leading the way, the two of us started to jog along the path.

We reached the edge of the woods at roughly the same spot where I had entered them and climbed over the fence into the field. I was about to dash off in the direction of the bridle path, but she held up her hand to stop me.

"Wait," she said. "I need to know if they're following."

We looked back into the woods, and few seconds later saw a cluster of torches converge together in the middle distance and then move in our direction.

"Shit," she said. "They've found him already. Okay. We need to keep moving."

We made our way through the field and then started to run along the bridle path. My legs felt like lead by then and I was gasping for breath, but I knew that I had to keep moving. My strange new companion must have been much fitter than me, because every so often she would stop so that I could catch up with her, and as I did so, motion for me to keep going while she watched our rear, and then shortly afterwards she would catch up with me again. After a few minutes, and when I judged that we were about half-way to the car, I looked back as well, and saw that the coven were now on the path behind us, their torches appearing like fireflies against the night sky, although they were thankfully still some distance away.

As we got ever closer to the road, I started to believe that we were going to get away from them after all. As I ran, I reached into my coat pocket for my car keys, wishing that I had had the foresight to turn the car around so that it was facing the road, thus facilitating a quicker getaway.

Suddenly a figure burst out of the hedgerow just ahead of us, causing me to stop in my tracks and scream out.

"Wait," said the woman, grabbing me by the arm. "It's okay. He's with us. Come on. Keep going."

As we drew level with the figure, I saw that it was a young man, also dressed in black.

"What happened back there?" he said as we reached him. I detected the hint of an Irish accent in his voice.

"Very pissed off witches' coven," said the woman. "And definitely tooled up for violence. I bought us a little bit of time but they're on this path, right behind us. They're about a minute away. How far are we from the cars?"

"Not far. Just around this bend. Is that him?" he added, nodding in my direction.

"Yes, it's him," she said. "Did you get the equipment back to the car?"

"Only thing that stopped me following you into the woods, you bloody lunatic. Yes, it's safe. Reckon I caught the whole ceremony. At least, until our friend here decided to do some flash photography."

"Yeah, look, I'm really sorry about that," I said. "And thank you . . ."

"Thank us later," the woman snapped. "Come on. Let's go."

We moved off down the path at a brisk jog, and moments later I saw my car in the near distance. There was another one parked next to it, a black four-wheel drive vehicle that looked like a Range Rover. As we approached it, I could just make out the figure of someone sitting in the back.

"Get in," said the woman, putting her hand on my shoulder, and pushing me towards the vehicle with the mysterious occupant in the back.

"But what about my car?" I said.

"Just get in," she shouted. With such vehemence that it made me flinch.

“We’re okay, I think,” said the man, who had stopped a little way behind us, and was looking down the path. “They’ve fallen back a bit. But they’re still coming this way.”

“Hold on,” I said to the woman. “I need to get in my car, and you need to get in yours, and …”

“No, you don’t” she cut in, albeit in a calmer, kinder tone of voice than she had adopted before.

“You really don’t,” she repeated. “You need to get into this one.”

She opened the back door of the Range Rover and motioned me inside. After a moment’s pause, I did as she had asked and climbed into the back seat.

The person sitting there looked across at me as I got in. He was an elderly man, but with an imposing physique and with handsome, leonine features. He had a grey beard, which was neatly trimmed, and was wearing a dark coat with the collars turned up. Even before he spoke, I was fairly sure that I knew who he was, and as soon as I heard his deep, rich baritone, there was no doubt at all.

“You must be Mr Weaver,” he said. “My name is Julian Faraday. I think you might need my help.”

PART THREE

JULIAN FARADAY

CHAPTER THIRTY-SIX

Faraday and his Group

"You obviously got my message," I said. "Thank God you did, because …"

"We'll get to that later," the man called Faraday said, briskly. "Right now, we need to put some distance between us and this coven you seem to have got so worked up. Give me your car keys."

"What?"

"Just give them to me. I doubt you're in a condition to drive, and I need to talk to you."

I handed him the keys, and he slid down the window and gave them to the woman, who was staring intently down the bridle path.

"About a hundred yards and closing," she said. "Cutting things a bit fine, Julian."

"They don't have vehicles up here, so they can't follow us," he said. "But they may alert someone down in the village who can, so be careful. Use standard evasion techniques, split off from us after the village and go north onto the motorway. Then double back to Marlborough. We'll meet in the high street and then go from there to the house. And Kate, be very careful."

"Got it," said the woman as she moved towards my parked car.

"We're coming to stay with you for a few days," said Faraday, turning around in his seat to face me. "I apologise for the lack of notice, or indeed an invitation, but I trust you have no objection?"

"Um, no, I mean ..."

"Excellent. Let's go, Michael," he said, addressing the man we had met on the path and who was now sat in the driver's seat of the Range Rover.

I heard shouts from behind us and looked over my shoulder through the rear window. I could see the flames of a burning torch heading towards the car. The engine roared into life, and we lurched forward, to the accompaniment of a loud spray of gravel. Looking back again, I saw my own car reversing at speed behind us, and as we turned onto the road and started to go down the hill, the woman span my car around with a screech of brakes and then followed us.

I sank back into my seat and breathed a long sigh of relief.

The village of Stokeley was completely dark as we drove through it, with not a single light shining from any of the windows. It looked closed up, uninhabited, almost deathly. And yet I wondered if unseen eyes were watching out for us from the darkness, having been alerted to our presence by the coven, as Faraday had intimated that they might. Thankfully, no sudden blaze of headlights appeared before us as we made our way through the village to the junction on the other side. I fervently hoped this meant that the immediate danger was over.

After we turned left at the junction, the woman driving my car went right and I turned and watched her drive away until the tail lights disappeared from view. We had split up, as Faraday had instructed, and suddenly all was pitch black around us as we accelerated swiftly down the country lane.

"Do you think she'll be alright?" I asked Faraday, anxiously.

"She'll be fine," he said. "I'm probably being over-cautious, but we can't afford to take any chances, and splitting up makes it a lot harder for them to follow us. That said, I don't believe they are. We're fortunate that their cars will be back at the farm where they assembled earlier this evening. I must say, I had no idea it was such a violent group, to actually pursue you through the woods like that. Kate was rather foolhardy, rushing off in there after you."

"If she hadn't, I'd probably be dead by now," I said.

"I fear you may be right about that. This is a more serious situation than I anticipated. We were ill prepared on this occasion, but we appear to have gotten away with it. I suppose you could say it was a bit of a rushed operation on our part, subsequent to our speaking on the telephone this afternoon. And on yours' too, I gather. Michael told me about your sudden illumination of proceedings, shall we say."

"It was a stupid mistake," I said. "I should have checked the camera before I even got there. I feel like a bloody fool."

"Everyone makes mistakes," said Faraday. "But against these people, a mistake like that can get you killed. And tonight, it very nearly did. Just be grateful that Kate is as headstrong as she is capable."

"Who are you people?" I said.

"All in good time," said Faraday. "Here, have some water."

He passed me a bottle from a pouch in the seat in front of him, and I drank greedily from it. The adrenaline of the chase and the danger I had been in had ebbed away now, and I felt completely shattered, almost as if I wanted to go to sleep.

Faraday seemed to sense that I needed some time to recover my equilibrium, and the next few minutes passed in silence. The softly illuminated cocoon of the car felt safe and comforting after the terror that I had just endured. I let my head fall back against the soft leather seat and watched the dark hedgerows flash past us.

"How did you find me?" I said at last.

"It wasn't very difficult," he said. "Your telephone message gave fairly specific instructions as to where tonight's ceremony was to take place. We then consulted a map, and presumably came to the same conclusion you did, regarding how best to get to the valley."

"I wasn't sure if you'd take my message seriously."

"Nor was I. As you could probably tell from our earlier conversation, I wasn't inclined to take you very seriously at all, particularly since the satanist you referred to – this Ernst von Draken character – is someone I've never even heard of. And as I said on the telephone, nobody holds a black mass one week before Walpurgis Night. It simply isn't done. But the connection with Dorian Slake was nagging at me, even while we were speaking. Then I listened to your message. It left me in little doubt that you were determined to go through with this. So, I decided to take the chance and come down here, along with my two colleagues. I'd imagine that we got here shortly after you did.

"Kate and Michael monitored the whole ceremony from a little further back along the valley."

"How did they do that?" I said. "You can't see the chapel from up there."

"No. But with the help of some very state of the art and rather expensive equipment, they were able to hear it, and it's all been recorded. We do that, you see, when we can. It's safer for us. And it helps separate the wheat from the chaff. I must say, I'm rather intrigued to listen to it. They were on their way back just after the sacrifice when they saw the flash from your camera, and then you suddenly came tearing up the hill and ran off into the woods, pursued by thirteen angry devil worshippers. Kate went after you entirely at her own initiative, leaving Michael to guard the rear. I wasn't at all happy to hear about it when he radioed to tell me, although he at least had the presence of mind to get the recording back here. Please don't think that I wasn't concerned for your welfare, but we were heavily outnumbered this evening. I was actually on the verge of contacting the police when you got back to the cars. Thankfully, it didn't prove necessary to involve them. But you're lucky to be alive. Both of you are."

"So are you some kind of … I don't know, anti-satanist group, or something?"

"Something like that. But we'll get to that. For now, I want to talk about you."

"About me?"

"Yes. I want to know everything you know. I want to know how it is that you're living in Dorian Slake's house. I want to know about this coven. I want to know about all of it. From the very beginning."

And so, I told him everything. For the second time that day, I told my story. Faraday listened quietly throughout, only occasionally interrupting to clarify something or other, just as Bethany Weyland had, some hours earlier.

I started with Alan turning up at my flat and his seemingly out of the blue offer to lend me his house while he went to America to produce an album, and how this story had started to fall apart, even before I got to Badcombe Hollow. Then I recounted the stories I had subsequently heard about strange goings on at the house, possibly related to devil worship. I told him about the person who had been watching the house from the woods, who I had managed to identify as one Billy Matthews, a reputed satanist. I told him about the old man I had met, and his stories of black masses being held in the woods, and how Dorian Slake had built something in the grounds beneath Badcombe Hollow. I told him about Ernst von Draken and his two visits to the house, the first to enquire after Alan's whereabouts, and then subsequently to both cajole and threaten me to leave, and how I surmised that this had something to do with him needing to be there on Walpurgis Night.

"Why do you suppose that?" Faraday asked, in a rare interjection.

"Because of Alan's letter," I said. "The one he sent me before he died. It suggested that something of great significance is going to happen at Badcombe Hollow on the night of 30th April. He also warned me not to be around, and I'm sure it's part of the reason why he fled the country in the first place."

"But they found him anyway."

"Yes. They found him, and they killed him. I think they summoned up some sort of demon who frightened him to death."

"Tell me more about that."

I told him what I knew about the bizarre circumstances of Alan's death, and then the visit by the lawyer, and the bequest of Badcombe Hollow, and how I wanted nothing more than to sell the house and get the hell away from there, but how I was determined not to sell it to Ernst von Draken, the man I held responsible for my friend's death.

I told him about how I had come to discover Stokeley, and the burnt-out house of the witch, Doreen Smithers, and how from there I had found the old chapel where an hour previously I had witnessed a black mass in its ruins.

I told him about the adder that had been sent to me, along with a warning never to set foot in Stokeley again, and the dead birds on the long barrow, and the pentagram in the cellar, and the portrait of Dorian Slake with the strange numbers on the back of it, and how the spiritualist I had spoken to earlier that day had told me that the house was so suffused with evil that she couldn't get anywhere near it, and anything else I could think of.

And, finally, I told him about the demonic old woman who was haunting the house, and how it had attacked Megan, and my belief that this entity had been conjured by von Draken or one of his acolytes, first to intimidate Alan, and then as a way of driving me out of there.

By the time I had finished, we were on the outskirts of Marlborough. I figured that we must have travelled there by the most roundabout, elongated of routes, since the journey had taken far longer than it normally would. I presumed this was to ensure that we hadn't been followed.

We entered the town and drove into the wide high street, where I saw my parked car, with Kate standing next to it, smoking a cigarette. As we pulled up alongside her, Faraday slid down his window and she tossed away the cigarette and stooped down to look into the car.

"Any problems?" Faraday asked her.

She shook her head.

"Nope. All good. I definitely wasn't followed."

"Nor were we. We're going to go to the house now. Provided I can stand it, we'll set up base there."

"Okay. I'll follow you. How are you doing?" she added, nodding in my direction.

"I'm okay," I said. "Thanks to you."

"Don't mention it," she said, a little curtly.

"See you over there, then," she said to Faraday, and then she turned away and I watched her get into my car. I felt as if I was more than just a literal passenger at this point. It was like I was now in the charge of these people, and they had temporarily taken control of my destiny. And yet I felt curiously resigned to this state of affairs; almost relieved. I felt like a child who had gotten into something over my head, thinking that I could cope with it, and then when I realised that I couldn't, was secretly glad that the grown-ups had arrived on the scene.

"What did you mean, back there?" I said to Faraday as we drove out of town again, heading in the familiar direction of Badcombe Hollow.

"About what?" he said.

"When you said that we were going to the house, but only if you could stand it. What did you mean by that?"

"Well, you told me that you spoke to a medium, earlier today, and that she was able to detect such a mammoth amount of satanic energy coming from your house, that she was physically unable to enter it."

"Yes. Apparently, it has the same effect on animals. I remember Alan telling me that I couldn't take a dog there. Because of his allergies, he said at the time, but now I know differently."

"Yes, animals have an extraordinarily high degree of extra-sensory perception when it comes to that sort of thing. As do a small number of humans including, it would seem, the spiritualist you spoke to. As it happens, I also have some very limited abilities of that kind. So, if the house really has been put under a satanic protection spell, I might find it difficult to enter it myself."

"What happens then?" I asked.

"We'll cross that bridge if we come to it. It's an old curse, by the sounds of things, likely somewhat diminished since Slake put it there. I certainly expect to pick something up, given the considerable impact it had on your spiritualist friend. But I don't expect to be overpowered by it."

"I asked the spiritualist why I couldn't detect it," I said, "And she told me that most of us simply aren't attuned that way. She used an analogy about tuning a radio and getting onto the right wavelength."

"That's actually quite a good way of explaining it," said Faraday.

"Yes, but the thing is, what's the point of it, if most people are oblivious to it?"

"Because those who might have an adversarial relationship with a coven likely would detect it, or at least have someone in their ranks – such as myself, for example – who could do so. It would make it very difficult for anyone but the most gifted of adepts to cleanse the house spiritually. And it's more than just a mere barrier to those such as me. It would also considerably augment anyone attempting a satanic incantation or spirit raising in there."

"There's so much I don't understand about all this," I said.

"Don't be so sure," he said, in a kindly tone. "I'd say that you've been learning about this subject at a highly accelerated rate. Almost a crash course."

"We're at the house, Julian," said Michael. They were almost the first words he had spoken since we had escaped from the coven.

We pulled into the driveway to the familiar crunch of gravel and parked in front of the house. My car swept in moments later and stopped next to us.

"Right then," said Faraday, opening the car door. "Let's see what we've got here."

"Nice looking place," said Michael approvingly, looking around the darkened garden. There was a brisk wind blowing through the Scots Pines, making it sound as if the branches were moaning. The house reared up in front of us, a silent edifice of stone.

"Yeah, doesn't always feel like it, though," I said.

I walked up to the front door with Faraday beside me, and Kate and Michael following behind. I unlocked the door and let it swing open, and then reached inside and flicked on the light and disabled the burglar alarm.

"After you," I said to Faraday, with a wry grin.

He nodded and stepped past me into the house, and the three of us followed him in.

Faraday walked slowly into the centre of the hall and looked around him.

"Wait here," he said, as he started to ascend the staircase.

We watched him walk up the stairs until he disappeared from view and then waited rather awkwardly as we listened to him move around on the upper floors.

It was my first chance to look at Kate in the light. She was an attractive woman who looked to be in her middle to late thirties. Her fair hair was still tied tightly back behind her head as it had been when accommodating the balaclava on top of it, and I thought she had a finely sculpted face, which had a sheen of health about it, as if she spent a lot of time outdoors. There was a hardness there too, I thought. She looked like she would be a bad person to cross, as she had demonstrated when overpowering the coven member in the woods earlier that night.

Michael appeared somewhat younger, not quite out of his twenties. He had a pleasant face with a mop of unruly ginger hair and was wearing the same sort of dark coloured clothing as his companion. Whilst Faraday had a certain mystique about him, these two, in their paramilitary attire, were anything but esoteric.

"So, can I get you anything?" I said, for something to say, as much as anything.

"Let's wait for Julian," said Kate.

Moments later Faraday came back downstairs, with a look on his face that seemed to convey both puzzlement and distaste.

"Well," he said. "The specialist you consulted was not exaggerating. There is some very dark energy in this house. Much evil has been done here. Done, reflected upon and contemplated. It's seeped into the very bones of the place."

"Can you stay here, Julian?" said Kate.

"Oh, yes," said Faraday, almost absent-mindedly, stepping away from us, and thrusting his hands into his pockets as he looked around the hall.

"I can stay here," he said. "I can feel it, but it's not affecting me. Not physically, at any rate. I can stay here long enough to defeat whatever it is that covets this place."

"Can the house be cleansed?" I asked him. "You know …spiritually … or whatever?"

"It can," said Faraday. "It will take an extremely powerful adept to do so, but yes, what has been put here can be driven from here. But now isn't the time for that. As much as anything, it would likely alert this von Draken person and his coven that they're up against a certain degree of expertise on our part. I would rather keep that up our sleeves for now.

"Actually, it's the demonic entity they appear to be conjuring that concerns me more. Von Draken must have a very skilled adept in his ranks to be able to do such a thing, even if he can only make it appear for limited periods of time. That worries me."

"You and me, both," I said, half to myself, as I recalled the horrifying attack on Megan, only twenty-four hours previously.

Faraday turned to face me.

"Mr Weaver," he said, "I must apologise for the way in which I rather summarily dismissed you, earlier today. It would appear that you have indeed run up against an occult group of some power, and in doing so, involved yourself in the most dangerous game known to mankind. A good deal of this affair including, I must say, quite why it is that this coven should be so anxious to get their hands on your house on Walpurgis Night, remains a complete mystery to me. But with your permission, I would like to stay here with my colleagues for the next few days to try and find out.

"And I dare say we could use your assistance as well," he added.

"My assistance?" I said. "How on earth can I assist with any of this?"

I knew there was a strongly self-serving impulse behind my question. Being back in the house at night, even with three other people, had spooked me badly, and I was feeling an almost overwhelming urge to leave.

"You can assist us in a great many ways," said Faraday. "You've been living with all of this for some time now, and you were once closely acquainted with the owner of this house. I would imagine that there's quite a lot we can learn from you. And, as you can see" – he motioned towards Kate and Michael – "Our numbers are somewhat limited. And we are up against a group of adversaries who number at least thirteen."

"But I don't have any experience of this," I said.

"Nor did any of us, at one time," Faraday said. "Of course, you have had some rather hair-raising experiences in this house, not to mention what happened to you this evening. So, I would quite understand, were you to choose to absent yourself from the scene; to depart the field, as it were, and hole up in some hotel, while we stay here and wait for Walpurgis Night …"

"You might not have to wait that long," I cut in. "Von Draken gave me an ultimatum, the last time I met him. He gave me three days to accept his offer for the house and said something about terrible consequences if I didn't. The three days are up tomorrow."

"All the more reason to beat a hasty retreat," said Faraday. "And I'm certainly not going to judge you, should you decide to do that. And yet you, of all of us, have perhaps the strongest motive of all to stay, given the terrible fate that befell your friend. In your position, I believe I would fervently wish to confront this head on and overcome it."

There was more than a hint of a challenge in his words, and we both knew it, but they had nevertheless served to fortify me, and I knew in that moment that I was going to stay and see this through; and that these three strangers standing in my hallway were now my comrades in arms, at least until daybreak on the day after Walpurgis Night.

"I rang you, Professor Faraday," I said. "I asked for your help, and you came. You all did. And I'm very grateful. You're welcome to stay here for as long as you need to. And I'm staying too."

Faraday nodded at me, and then stepped forward and shook me by the hand.

"Let's get to work," he said.

CHAPTER THIRTY-SEVEN

Faraday Tells His Story

In spite of all the excitement, the next hour or so was taken up with various mundane housekeeping matters as Faraday and his team moved into the house, and I played host. It was an unfamiliar role to me, ever since the end of my marriage to Marianne.

I made up the bed in the other spare room on the first floor for Faraday, and then did the same for Kate and Michael in the two small bedrooms on the attic floor.

"So, this is one of the places where you see the spectral old hag, is it?" Michael said as he hefted a large black tote bag onto the bed, where it landed with a creak. "Good to know."

"I've seen her on the first floor, as well," I said. "And downstairs. All over. This is the room that I followed her into once. But once I got in here, she'd vanished."

"The adept controlling it was probably knackered by then," Michael said, as he started taking things out of his case. I noticed a bible and a crucifix in amongst his clothes.

"What do you mean?" I said.

"What he means," said Kate, as she walked into the room, "Is that controlling a demonic entity like that requires a huge amount of energy, even for someone skilled at raising spirits. They'd only be able to make something like that manifest for very limited periods of time. Thank goodness. Otherwise, she'd be rattling around in here all day long."

"Have you ever come across anything like that before?" I asked her.

"God, no. Neither of us has. This is all way out there, even for us. But not for Julian. He's witnessed stuff like this. He's told us about it."

"And you believed him?"

"Of course."

She seemed surprised by the question.

"Actually, she took a bit of convincing, the way Julian tells it" Michael said. He sat down heavily on the bed and started to take off his shoes.

"Kate is one of life's sceptics," he said. "Me, I'm a lot more persuadable. But then, I'm conditioned that way."

I looked at them enquiringly.

"Michael is in training to be a priest," said Kate.

I thought of the bible and the crucifix. Not just props, then.

"Sounds like I'm in good hands," I said. "Are you here in an official capacity, may I ask?"

"Well, not here, specifically," he said. "But my church is aware of what Julian does, and we work together from time to time. Combining our forces in the face of a common enemy, you might say. I've sort of been seconded over to him, for the past few months."

"And what does he do?" I said to him. "I mean, all of you. What do you do? Who are you?"

"Just a group of people determined to fight evil, I suppose. Or at the very least, to put some bad folk out of business, and disrupt their various shenanigans."

"Most of what we do is on a much more down to earth level," Kate said. "Our focus tends to be on groups that practice satanism in such a way as to cause harm to others, and the vast majority of such people have no occult power whatsoever. But that doesn't mean that they aren't capable of some pretty awful things, over and above whatever they get up to in their twisted ceremonies."

"Such as?" I asked.

"Such as blackmail, for a start."

"Blackmail?"

"Of course. It's pretty compromising, wouldn't you say, being exposed as a devil worshipping fruitcake who gets their jollies out of attending orgies in graveyards? Often, people get lured into these groups, just so they can be blackmailed. Or intimidated in some other way. Plus, they do terrible things to animals, they desecrate churches, and they brainwash people into joining their cults. And then some of them are paedophiles and other kinds of pervert. Those ones are our number one target. The ones who abduct children and other vulnerable people, either to abuse them sexually in their ceremonies, or in the most extreme cases to kill them in sacrifices."

"That really goes on?"

"More than you'd think," said Michael. "It's what we've just been dealing with for the past few weeks. We've been keeping tabs on a coven up in Yorkshire who we're pretty sure tried to kidnap a child to use in a sacrifice. Fortunately, they didn't succeed, and we've been able to give quite a bit of useful information to the police. It's in their hands, now. We'd only been back a day when you contacted us, so it was lucky timing. Mind you, this all seems a bit different to the usual group of freaks and perverts. This feels like the real deal."

"The one per cent of the one per cent," I said softly, recalling what my friend Helen had told me, during the early stages of my research into satanism.

"What's that?"

"Just something someone said once," I said. "So, are we dealing with true evil here? I mean, I guess I'm asking you as a priest. Is that what you think we're up against?"

"Well, I'm not actually a priest yet," said Michael. "But I'd have to say, it's starting to look that way."

"That's the reason you joined up, isn't it?" Kate said quietly from the other side of the room, where she was leaning against a chest of drawers. "To confront true evil. To fight the good fight. And now we're well and truly in it."

"I suppose you could say that it was," said Michael. "And, yes, we're in it now."

"And how about you?" I said, turning to Kate. "Why did you join up?"

"I have my reasons," she said, and then rather abruptly left the room.

I went back downstairs, where I found Faraday in the kitchen, perusing the broken portrait of Dorian Slake that he had earlier asked me to fetch for him.

"A good likeness?" I asked.

"Yes," said Faraday, looking up. "At least, as far as I can recall. In fact, much as I dislike saying it, it's really rather a good painting, technically speaking."

"So, you knew him, then."

"By reputation. I was certainly never acquainted with him. You could barely say that I ever met him. But I encountered him once, very briefly. It was a long time ago, nearly fifty years ago, and I was a very young man at the time. But I know as much about him as anyone would care to. At least, I thought I did before tonight. But I know that he was a thoroughly evil person. More so than most people realise. I'm afraid I have no idea what the numbers on the back of the painting mean, but they might warrant some further investigation at some point.

"We must form a plan of action," he said, changing the subject. "Where are the others?"

"Upstairs, unpacking. Getting settled in."

"We're not here on holiday," said Faraday, with a trace of irritation in his voice. "It's already late, and we have much to discuss."

Just then, Michael and Kate appeared in the doorway to the kitchen. Michael was still wearing his black garb from earlier in the evening, but Kate had changed into jeans and a sweatshirt, and had untied her hair, which now flowed over her shoulders.

"How about something to eat?" I suggested.

"Good idea," said Kate. "I'm famished."

"As long as we work while we eat," said Faraday.

I cooked bacon and eggs for the second time that day, and the bread was even staler than it had been the first time. But it was all I had in the house. I filled a jug with orange juice and brewed a large pot of coffee, and we ate around the island unit, whilst Dorian Slake watched us from a perch on the other side of the room.

As we ate, Faraday made me go through my story again, for Kate's benefit, and to ensure that he hadn't missed anything on the first telling.

He was particularly interested in anything I could tell him about Ernst von Draken. He seemed annoyed with himself for not having previously heard of this particular player in the British occult scene.

"I can't fathom how he hasn't crossed my radar before now," he said at one point. "When we spoke on the telephone this afternoon, my ignorance of him led me to believe that he was a person of no consequence. But that is clearly not the case. The association with Slake makes it all the more mystifying."

"Maybe he's been keeping a low profile," Michael suggested. "Waiting for his moment. Walpurgis Night next week, by all accounts, based on what Richard's told us."

"Possibly," said Faraday. "Tell me more about this woman who hangs around with him; the reputed witch called Catherine Falaise, assuming that's her real name."

"Well, compared to him, she's straight out of central casting," I said. "I mean, in the sense that he's this dapper, elderly gent, very old school, a little too oily and well-groomed for my taste, but there's nothing about him that screams devil worshipper. But she totally looks the part. She's got the whole gothic thing going on. Pale skin, long black hair, kind of scary looking, almost unnerving to be around, a real bad aura. She certainly looks like a witch."

"She's probably the one controlling the malevolent entity that appears in the house," said Faraday. "And whatever it was that terrified your friend so much that it killed him. A coven that was genuinely serious about the occult, as this one evidently is, would likely have at least one such adept in their number."

"She also has a real thing for this house, and the area around it," I said. "She spoke of it with a kind of reverence, like it was holy to her. Or unholy, I should say."

"You're not wrong there," said Faraday, grimly. "This is an unholy place."

"Anyway, she was definitely one of the ones there this evening," I said. "She's the one I had my camera pointed at when the flash went off. Minus her hood. No doubt at all that it was her."

"In that case, show me the photograph," said Faraday. "Just in case I recognise her."

I reached around me for the camera, which I had left on the counter by the sink, along with my torch and the other detritus from my excursion to Stokeley that night. I switched it on and brought up on the screen an image of the last photograph I had taken.

"Blimey," said Michael, looking over my shoulder. "We seem to have a picture of an old woman masturbating on a rock. Not one for the collection, perhaps."

"Sorry," I said to Faraday, as I passed him the camera. "Not very edifying."

"No," said Faraday with a raised eyebrow as he glanced at the image. "But suffice to say, I have no idea who that person is. Which serves to further underline the point that this coven remains very much an unknown quantity."

After I had cleared away the supper things, we went through into the cosier of the two sitting rooms, so that we could play the tape recording of the black mass. It was gone one o'clock by then, but I didn't feel tired. I'm not exactly sure what I felt. I felt anxious but somehow enervated; fearful but excited. I think, on some level, I believed that I was now part of something else, part of this group, part of its mission. I was part of something bigger than me.

We settled down by the unlit fire and listened to the tape, but the contents were just as indecipherable as the live performance had been. Von Draken had obviously been speaking in a foreign language – actually, reading from a script, as I noted to Faraday – but it wasn't one that any of us recognised.

"We're going to need a translator," Faraday muttered at one point, but he didn't elaborate on this.

After we had listened to the tape Faraday, as promised, talked more about his group.

"Please don't think that you're not owed some form of explanation from us," he said. "I completely understand that this is a highly unusual situation, with us descending on you like this. And yet, here we are.

"So, to answer your unasked question, who are we? Well, you could say we are a group of like-minded souls who happen to have come together to fight evil, and specifically the practice of satanism."

"How did you get started?" I said.

"I've been involved with this sort of thing ever since I was a young man," said Faraday. "You see, I had an experience once that had a profound effect upon me."

I looked at him enquiringly.

"I encountered true evil," he said, simply.

"How do you mean?" I said.

"I mean, I encountered evil in its purest, most unadulterated sense."

"Do you mean Dorian Slake?" I said.

"No. Slake and I crossed paths sometime later, and he was a mere amateur in comparison. This person, if indeed it was a person at all, was the living embodiment of everything most foul in our universe. I found it quite terrifying, just being in its presence.

"Anyway, the details are unimportant, but suffice to say, it convinced me beyond all doubt that there is true evil in this world; evil in its most primeval, unholy and existential sense. You could say that the experience changed me forever.

"And so, I decided that the best way to conquer my fear was to understand it. Hence, I embarked upon a complete study of the subject, becoming so expert that I ended up forging an academic career out of it. But it wasn't enough. I soon realised that I didn't just want to understand evil; I wanted to fight it, or at the very least aid and assist its victims.

"I began by counselling victims of satanism; those who had been lured into covens and then managed to extricate themselves, partly to help them, but also to help increase my own understanding. Some of their stories were horrific, and some of the poor souls were beyond help, I'm sorry to say, so addled were their brains by the things they had witnessed, and participated in. But I learned a great deal.

"I started to investigate specific covens and I began with Dorian Slake's. It wasn't here, incidentally. I knew that he lived somewhere around here, but until tonight I didn't know exactly where. This coven was based in London. Anyway, it was pure chance that I began with Slake. I was a lawyer then, and one of the coven members was a client of the firm I worked for. And that was how I came to have my one and only encounter with Dorian Slake."

"What happened?" I said.

Faraday looked at his watch and seemed to come to a decision.

"Very well," he said. "I haven't even told Kate and Michael about this – in fact, I've barely spoken of it to anyone, ever since it happened – but now that we're sitting here in Slake's house, and given all that's been going on, it feels somehow fitting."

He took a pipe from the pocket of his jacket and waved it in my direction.

"May I?" he asked.

"Absolutely. Please do."

Faraday lit his pipe and exhaled a long plume of smoke. He then settled himself into the armchair and began to tell his story.

"As I explained, when I was a young man, I was a lawyer, or at least, training to be one. I was not long out of university, and engaged as a junior clerk in one of the many venerable old law firms who occupied a certain part of London at one time. My father, you see, was very keen that I enter the law, as he had done before me, and at that time I was still acceding to his wishes.

"Slake was an obscure figure by then, and in as much as he was known about at all, it was almost entirely on account of his past association with Aleister Crowley. He was regarded as a spent force, and a very pale shadow of his former mentor, living alone in some remote part of the country – here, as it transpires – and going quietly mad.

"Well, we now know that he was engaged in something rather more substantive here than one might have imagined, building his temple to Satan beneath the long barrow. We also know that the reason he was losing his mind may have been on account of something he conjured here. Or else, perhaps something that has been haunting these grounds since Neolithic times, and has nothing whatsoever to do with satanism. But I didn't know any of that back then.

"What I did know was that Dorian Slake still headed a coven, one of the ones that Crowley had started, and that they met once a year, in a house in St John's Wood. On Walpurgis Night. I knew this because a former member of the coven told me about it. As I said, he was a client of the law firm I worked for, and I had recently assisted with the re-drawing of his will. A timely move, on his part, as it subsequently transpired. But during the course of my routine dealings with him, it became clear to me, if not to the senior partner in the firm for whom I was clerking, that our client was a very frightened man indeed, on account of some people he had become involved with. I strongly suspected that there was an occult angle to all of it, and I was proved right.

"When he left the office, I followed him, and managed to persuade him to talk to me. That might seem unduly serendipitous, but I think he was desperate to talk to someone. He told me that he had been a member of a satanic coven – Dorian Slake's coven – for many years, but that he left, and that he was now in hiding from them.

"There was no doubt that he was in a state of complete terror about this coven, and what they might do to him. I'm sorry to say that shortly after I spoke to him, the coven tracked him down and killed him. On this occasion, they didn't go to the sort of elaborate lengths they went to when they took the life of your friend, Richard. This was not an occult slaying. They simply cut his throat and dumped his body in an alleyway. Leaving a coven like that is simply not permitted, you see. Only death releases one.

"He had told me about the ceremonies performed by this group, every year on Walpurgis Night. These gatherings were depraved beyond belief. Various deviant sexual practices were involved, and their ritual always involved animal sacrifice, usually a goat or a lamb. The poor creature would have its throat cut, and then the members of the coven would smear themselves in its blood. Other things went on, too, things I don't even wish to speak of. And this man had participated in all of it, and so I can't quite summon much sympathy over his death, although I would certainly have tried to save him, if I could have done.

"Anyway, he told me that at the next Walpurgis ceremony, which was due to take place in a few days' time, Slake planned to kill a child. As a ritual sacrifice. The killing was to occur at midnight, at the culmination of the ceremony. It was believed that this would considerably enhance the potency of the coven's ritual; the spilling of fresh, innocent human blood. The child would be a mere infant, and was to be kidnapped from somewhere, although he didn't know where. He suspected an orphanage, or some other kind of institution.

"Needless to say, I knew that I had to stop it. Naturally, I went first to the police. I told them everything told to me by the former member of the coven, including the location of the house in St John's Wood where they held their ceremonies.

"Unsurprisingly, they found it all a little far-fetched, although they weren't ignorant of the fact that such occult practices took place. But they seemed to take the view that such activities were essentially harmless and amounted to little more than buffoonery. This, of course, was different. I had warned them that a human life was at stake, and so they were compelled to investigate. Up to a point, anyway. But their enquiries led nowhere. Slake was the only other member of the coven whose identity was known for sure, and he couldn't be located. They checked the address of the house where the sabbat was to be held, and it transpired that the property was empty, and virtually derelict, the previous occupants having departed some years previously. It was owned by a property company and scheduled for demolition to make way for flats. Those flats were subsequently built and stand there to this day. And so, they felt that there was nowhere else they could take things, and that was that.

"But I was a persistent sort of chap in those days, and I won't deny that the legal firm for whom I worked, and whose identity I had flagrantly – and entirely without their knowledge or permission, I might add – brought to the police's attention, carried a certain amount of clout. So, I eventually persuaded them to keep an eye on the place, and they further agreed to put a patrol outside on the night of the ceremony, just to be sure.

"But I couldn't quite let the matter lie, and so a few days later, on Walpurgis Night, I travelled over to St John's Wood. I soon found the property, although I hadn't been there before. It was a large mansion, of the sort one used to see quite a bit in London in those days, before they got carved up into smaller dwellings, or else knocked down entirely, as this place was scheduled to be.

"And there was not a policeman in sight. Not a patrol car, not a patrol, nothing. It was all subsequently explained away as a misunderstanding, but I suspect that somebody got to them. Somebody with a lot of power and influence. I'm sorry to say that some of these satanic groups have spread their tentacles into some of our most revered and trusted institutions, whether through association, indoctrination or blackmail. I have a feeling that might have been the case on this occasion.

"And so there I was, stood on a darkened and deserted pavement in the dead of night, with midnight less than an hour away, and simply at a loss as to what to do.

"In the end, you might say that instinct took over. And so I decided to go over there.

"I walked around to the back of the house, where there was a large garden. There was a gate at the back, which was locked, but I managed to climb over the fence quite easily, and it was all very overgrown, so I was well hidden from the house. I crept up through the garden until I got to a terrace that was raised off the ground, and with a stone parapet around it. Using this as cover, I peered through and saw light spilling beneath the shutters to some large doors opening out onto the terrace. So, I knew that the house was occupied, despite it being supposedly derelict and empty.

"I imagine that if those had been the days when one had a mobile telephone, that would have been the point at which I would have phoned the police, reported that an act of trespass and possible kidnapping was underway, and then withdrawn to await their arrival. But there simply wasn't time to run off and raise the alarm. I had to try and stop whatever it was that was going on in there.

"Trying to be as quiet as possible, I made my way across the terrace and around the house, and found a side door which led into a laundry room. Fortunately, it was unlocked. I stepped into the room and, as soon as I got a few steps in, I could hear them. There was chanting coming from somewhere, but for some reason I didn't think it was the lit room on the ground floor that I had just walked past. It sounded like it was coming from upstairs.

"I found the main staircase soon enough. It was a grand sort of affair that swept around a very large hallway and led up through an atrium to the floors above, with a minstrels' gallery on one side. There was still no sign of anyone, and it was very dark in there, with just a bit of light from the moon coming through the windows. But then I heard movement above me, up on the first floor.

"Making as little noise as possible, I went up the stairs. The place was a mess, and obviously hadn't been lived in for some time. There were hunks of plaster on the steps, amidst various other bits of debris, and the place had a sour, stale smell about it. But when I got to the first-floor landing, I could smell the incense coming from the coven's ceremony. I also saw light beneath a door at the end of a long corridor, and then I heard the sound of chanting again

"In something of a funk by then and having to resist the urge to simply run away, I made myself walk down the corridor towards the light. As I drew closer, I realised that the doorway led not to a room, but to another staircase, this time narrow and enclosed, and which dropped down a few steps, into a whole other wing of the house, or at least some sort of annex to it.

"I went down the steps into another corridor, which was very narrow, and with a bare timber floor. The sound of the chanting was quite loud by then, so I knew that Slake and his coven could only be a matter of yards away.

"I could see that the corridor opened out at the end to become a balcony, looking down over another room, which was clearly illuminated, and which was accessed from a spiral staircase. It was in this room that the ceremony was taking place.

"I crept along to the corner of the wall, and carefully looked down into the room. Below me, I could see the coven.

"The room had been decked out in satanic regalia, and there was an altar at one end, with a large upside down cross suspended from the ceiling above it. Thankfully, the coven – and there were thirteen of them; I counted – were all facing away from me. They were kneeling in a group before the altar, whilst one of their number – who I presumed to be Dorian Slake – stood with his back to them, and with his arms raised towards the altar, just like a priest at mass. And he was chanting something in a language I couldn't understand, and the others were repeating what he said, in much the same way that one might conduct a prayer.

"Apart from having their backs to me, they were all hooded, so I couldn't see any of their faces. In fact, the only face I saw that night was Slake's, and that was later on. But what I could see, crouching up there behind the balustrade to the gallery, made my heart shudder. Down in the room, behind where the group of satanists were kneeling to perform their devotions, wrapped in a blanket, and placed in a small box, was a baby. It appeared to be sleeping, although the poor thing had probably been drugged.

"It was a large room, and the coven was gathered at one end of it – the far end, thankfully, so there was a bit of distance between them and me – and by this time they were making quite a din, chanting manically at the man with his back to them before the altar. And then I noticed something else. The spiral staircase that led down into the room was fixed to the balustrade of the balcony by only a couple of steel brackets. In fact, it wasn't very sturdy at all, and was more of a ladder that was designed to be moved around. I subsequently learned that the room was inaccessible from below, because the connecting corridor had been blocked off by the developers who owned the building, and so the satanists had been using the lightweight staircase to get in and out of there. It was a massive stroke of good fortune, as far as I was concerned.

"I crept down the staircase as the group continued with their chanting, still with their backs to me. I went over and picked up the child. Thankfully, it made no sound. In fact, it was as docile as a newborn lamb. I then started to make my way out of there.

"When I was about halfway up the staircase, the chanting suddenly stopped, and as it did, Slake turned around to face his flock. And naturally saw me going up the stairs with the intended object of their sacrifice. Bedlam erupted, as you might imagine, and I raced up the stairs, put down the child and started to unhook the metal staircase from the balustrade. By this time, two of the satanists were coming up it, but I managed to get the thing detached and pushed it away from the balcony.

"That was when I saw Slake, or rather when I knew for sure that the person officiating over the ceremony was him. It was only the most fleeting of moments, but it remains stamped upon my memory.

"He had pushed back the hood on his cloak and I could see his face. It was as if time simply stopped, and we stared at each other, me up on the balcony, and him down by the altar, whilst his flock started to push the detached staircase back to the wall so they could swarm up it. He was as he appears in the portrait of him, but the look on his face was something I shall never forget. There was anger there, of course, but there was anguish, as well. It was as if the man was utterly bereft, almost in shock. He screamed something, but I don't think it was directed at me. It sounded like a scream of despair. That's always stayed with me, for some reason.

"I knew that they would get the staircase back in place again, but I had bought myself some valuable seconds. Carrying my tiny bundle, I ran back along the corridor and down the main set of stairs, and then went back through the house the way I had come. I considered finding the front door and bursting through it to the street outside, but I was worried that it might be locked, and I'd end up getting cornered. The coven must have re-attached the ladder by then because I could hear them thundering along the corridor above me towards the main staircase.

"I ran back out into the garden, scaled the same fence I had climbed over to get in, but one-handed, this time, and holding the child in my other arm. There was an alleyway running behind the house, and I bundled the child in its blanket into my coat and ran along it as fast as I could. It was a residential area, and I thought about knocking on one of the doors and summoning help, but I wasn't quite sure how I was going to explain myself, and I was very worried by then about the coven catching up with me, and so I decided that the best thing to do was to put as much distance between me and them as possible. I didn't stop running until I reached the nearest police station.

"That was my one and only encounter with Dorian Slake. My one fleeting glimpse of the man who used to own this house."

"What happened to the child?" said Kate. It was the first time that any of us had spoken, during the whole time Faraday had been telling his story.

"The child was perfectly fine, thank goodness. It was a little girl, and her name was Violet Elizabeth. She was only a few months old, and she was an orphan. She'd been snatched from an institution earlier in the day. Taken so that she could be killed in a foul and disgusting ritual, by evil, depraved people. But she was saved, thank goodness, and never knew anything about what happened to her that night."

"What about Slake?" said Kate. "Did you tell the police about him?"

"Of course. They followed up on it, and they interviewed him under caution, but they had no hard proof against him, and decided not to prosecute. It would have been my word against his, and I had only caught sight of him very briefly. And I couldn't identify anyone else in the coven, because they had all been hooded. So, Slake got away with it, and presumably came back here."

"Where he killed himself, less than a year later," I said.

"Yes. I heard about his death. Slake was just well known enough by then for it to make the papers. And so I assumed that was the end of the matter, not knowing that this epilogue to his life, as it were, would be playing out here some fifty years later.

"Anyway, over the years, I've continued to pursue covens right across the country, and even overseas on a couple of occasions, and done whatever I can to help close down their operations, generally by tipping off the police at an opportune moment, so that the participants could be arrested, or at the very least cautioned and warned off. Sometimes, by other, more direct means. I've had a few successes, and many more failures. I have good relations with some of the police forces in this country, and less good ones with others. I also work with mental health charities, the probation service, the church, anyone who can lend a hand, or who I can likewise assist. I've built up a reasonably good network of contacts, over the years.

"But I'm getting rather old for it all these days; a little long in the tooth, if you will, to be haring about the country in pursuit of devil worshippers. Hence my two excellent colleagues here."

He motioned towards Kate and Michael as he said this.

"Kate has told you a bit about the sort of things we do now," he said, "And you saw us in action tonight, although I have to say, the events of this evening were rather more action packed than I would have liked. We're a small group, and our resources are limited, but we go where we are wanted, and we help where we can help, and we do what we can."

"Thank you for explaining," I said. "And I couldn't be more pleased that you're here."

"And I couldn't be more pleased that you've agreed to stay on with us," said Faraday. "I could entirely understand your choosing to do otherwise, but this is your house after all, and I'm sure you'll be of great assistance to us. There's a lot that you'll be able to tell us about the lie of the land in all this, possibly more than you think. We shall certainly welcome your local knowledge. However, in spite of that, I'd like you to come away with me, tomorrow, just for the day."

"Okay," I said. "Where to?"

"We're going to Shropshire."

This seemed an incongruous destination, in the circumstances.

"Why are we going to Shropshire?" I said.

"There's someone there who should be able to translate whatever is on the recording we made this evening. And I'd like you to speak to this person, as well. I want you to tell him what you've told us. We'll need to leave early, to get there and back in a day. And we do need to be back here by nightfall. Given what you told us about von Draken's ultimatum, and what we know about the sort of dark power the coven is capable of manifesting, there's a strong probability that this house will come under attack by occult forces, perhaps as early as tomorrow night."

The matter-of-fact way in which he said this rather unnerved me, but I tried to push the thought out of my mind.

"Okay, so we'll leave early and go to Shropshire," I said. "And get back here before it gets dark. But who are we going to see?"

"A satanist," said Faraday. "We're going to see a satanist."

CHAPTER THIRTY-EIGHT

The Satanist, Part One

We set off after an early breakfast, with the rising sun still low in the sky.

Kate and Michael came downstairs as we were leaving.

"I left a spare front door key on the kitchen counter, along with my car keys" I said. "In case you need to go out. You're obviously not insured, so try not to have a prang on one of our narrow country lanes."

"Thanks," said Kate. "We'll be careful. We're going to go into Marlborough in a bit, and stock up on provisions. Doesn't seem right to eat you out of house and home while we're staying here."

"It wouldn't matter," I said. "But thank you, anyway. And needless to say, help yourself to anything you like in the meantime. And if you can find the entrance into the underground temple while you're at it, so much the better."

"If you haven't been able to find it, living here all this time, then I don't suppose we'll have any more luck. But we're certainly going to have a nose around for it. And we need to prepare for tonight. You know, in case this von Draken character follows up on his threat and mounts some kind of other worldly attack."

"Just another normal day, then," I said wryly.

"No, like I said last night, this is actually way out there, even for us," said Kate.

We smiled at each other. There was considerably more warmth in the way she spoke to me now, compared to our initial encounter, the previous night. Her hair was tousled, and there was still sleep in her eyes, but she was an attractive woman, I thought. And yet there was something about her, some reserve in her manner, a sadness perhaps, some hint of something in her past that weighed heavily upon her, which I couldn't quite read, and I didn't yet know her well enough to ask her about it. I wondered if I ever would.

Faraday looked remarkably fresh, considering that none of us had had more than a few hours' sleep, and also that he had a good thirty years me, and nearer fifty on Michael. He evidently had a formidable constitution, as well as a razor-sharp brain. Despite having known him for less than twelve hours, I wasn't even questioning the fact that he was in charge now. He had that sort of commanding presence and air of authority that I had used to find patronising and off-putting in others, but when projected by Faraday appeared utterly natural, drawing instant respect from me. It may also have had something to with the fact that I was both out of my depth on a gargantuan scale, and incredibly frightened.

But I realised in that moment that I actually wanted to follow him, even to the extent of driving with him to Shropshire to meet a satanist.

"Take great care, today," he said to Kate and Michael as we walked out into the driveway. "One presumes that von Draken will wait until nightfall before he attacks, as his medium will be able to wield considerably more power during the hours of darkness. But as she can evidently conjure the spectral old hag, or whatever it is, during daylight, an assault could come at any time. But my hunch is that they'll hold fire for an all-out attack tonight. Either way, be careful. I've left some notes regarding preparations in the kitchen. Read them, and make sure everything is in place by the time we're back.

"Michael, this is much more your area than Kate's, and we've talked about this sort of contingency before, so you'll need to take the lead on this.

"Kate, I need you to focus on more prosaic concerns. We're assuming that von Draken's mode of attack will be supernatural and demonic, but he could just turn up with his claque of devil worshippers and try to break in. Given the way his coven chased Richard through the woods last night, this must be a possibility, since they're clearly not averse to engaging in some rough tactics, even murderous ones. So, make sure that we're as physically protected as we can be. Check the perimeter of the property for entry points, particularly blind spots from where people could approach the house unobserved. Then do all the normal checks with regard to the house itself, and make sure all the doors and windows are secure. I want to get this place as locked down as we can possibly make it. When you're in Marlborough, buy some torches, and place them around the house at strategic points, in case von Draken cuts the power. And go to a builder's merchants and purchase some sheets of timber board, in case we need to barricade the windows."

"What is this, the Alamo?" I said.

"Let's hope not," said Faraday. "But I want to take every possible precaution. We have a long day ahead of us. Let's all try and use it well."

He looked at his watch.

"It's already half-past seven," he said, in a tone of mild displeasure, as if irritated that a certain part of the day had been lost.

"It will take us three to four hours to get where we're going, and the same back, so say eight hours of driving, and perhaps several hours up there, depending on how long it takes to translate the tape, so I would hope to be back here by seven o'clock at the latest, and it will be dark by about eight-thirty. That's a little tighter than I'd like, but we'll have to do the best we can. With luck, we may at least obtain some answers as to what's going on here."

As we drove away in Faraday's Range Rover, I looked back and saw Kate and Michael go up the steps into the house. A part of me wished that I could be staying there with them, instead of undertaking another trip into the unknown.

We had agreed that we would split the driving, in order to conserve our depleted resources of energy, or at least mine, with Faraday driving there, since he knew the way, and me driving us home.

We went into Marlborough and drove along the wide high street where we had rendezvoused during the excitement of the previous night. Once through the town, we headed towards the motorway over the great plains landscape, which looked as desolate and majestic as ever as we motored across it in the cool light of early morning.

We crossed the M4, and headed north in the direction of Cheltenham, with the countryside becoming flatter, and more Cotswoldian, a patchwork of fields broken by straight lines of stone wall. We had both been quiet on the journey thus far, Faraday doubtless as preoccupied with his own thoughts as I was with mine, although I felt myself drifting towards sleep, so much so that I had to shake myself to remain alert.

"Don't fight it," Faraday said, from the driver's seat beside me. "We have a long day, and night ahead of us. Try and get some sleep, and I shall do likewise on the return journey.

"Also, I need to think," he added. "I shall accomplish that more easily if it's quiet."

I gratefully accepted his advice, and let my mind go blank, my eyes fluttering closed as I allowed the steady thrum of the powerful engine lull me into sleep.

When I awoke, I discovered to my surprise that almost an hour had passed, and we were powering at some speed along the outside lane of a motorway.

"Where are we?" I asked, sleepily.

"Worcestershire," said Faraday. "The M5 in Worcestershire. But we shall be turning off shortly and travelling cross country the rest of the way."

Sure enough, a few miles later, we exited the motorway, and almost immediately found ourselves a veritable world away, in a setting that was deeply rural, and which became more striking still, the further we headed into it. Over to the north-west, we could see the range of hills that I knew to be the Malverns, looming over the patchwork plain, tantalisingly close to us.

Just after we crossed into Herefordshire, and without any explanation, Faraday turned off the road and onto a rough gravel track that led through thickly wooded heathland. Even though I knew it couldn't be so, it felt as if we had arrived at our destination, and I felt a sudden pang of anticipation blended with fear. But we pulled up outside a pleasant looking pub, which Faraday evidently knew from a previous visit, and where he had decided we would take a comfort break before continuing our journey northwards.

We ordered coffees at the bar, which were brought out to us in the garden, where we had gone to sit in order that Faraday could smoke his pipe. It was a lovely day by then, and still sufficiently early for us to have the garden to ourselves. It was a rather magical place, I thought, seemingly so cut off from any obvious sign of civilisation, nestling in its verdant cleft in the landscape, with commanding views across the treetops, and out towards the hills. I could almost have convinced myself that I was on holiday, and far from the cares of Badcombe Hollow, before Faraday predictably brought me back down to earth.

"I need to tell you something about the person we're going to meet today," he said, gently blowing steam from his cup of coffee.

"His name is Malachy Jones. I don't suppose that's his real name, but it's the name that he goes by, and by which I have known him over many years."

"And who is he?" I said. "What is he?"

"He's a satanist. And also, something of a magician. He is an adept with much experience in the practice of the dark arts, and with considerable power as a consequence."

"More powerful than von Draken's adept?"

"Unquestionably. If I thought we were going to be up against someone of half this person's power when we return to the house this evening, then I should be truly worried."

"So why aren't we? I mean, how come this person isn't helping von Draken? And how come he's going to be talking to the likes of us?"

"Because thankfully, satanism in this country, in all countries, everywhere, is extremely fragmented, and therefore a much weaker adversary than it might otherwise be. There is no coherent ideology, no single entity or even any sort of inter-connected network, merely a great many individual ones. Which isn't to say that there is no element at all of joined up thinking between the various covens, but that's the exception, rather than the norm. These groups generally operate completely separately of each other. That's when they're not actually at each other's throats."

I looked at him enquiringly.

"These people are like Marxists, or anarchists," he said. "Or the loonier fringes of the ecology movement. They're far happier fighting amongst themselves than confronting outsiders. Their real venom is nearly always directed towards other cultists. Hence there's no reason at all to suppose that Malachy and von Draken might be in cahoots. Indeed, all precedent would suggest otherwise. A high-level adept like Malachy would probably regard someone such as von Draken with complete contempt. That's if he's even come across him at all, although I'm rather hoping for our sake that he has. But if anyone can understand what we got on tape at that sabbat last night, he might just be able to.

"As to why he would be inclined to help us, well, let's just say that Malachy operates somewhat outside the mainstream. He doesn't run with the pack, and he has no loyalty or even connection to any particular occult group. He's a most un-clubbable kind of satanist, you might say, in large part, I suppose, because he regards his talents as being so superior to everyone else's. He occupies an extremely specialised, rather obscure and almost unique place in British occultism."

"How come you know him?" I asked.

"Because Malachy works both sides of the street. Just as he has no wish to have anything to do with any of the myriad groups and covens that seem to be proliferating at such a rate, he's not averse to shopping them to the likes of me from time to time. Occasionally, in the past, he's been a useful source of information."

"So, he's one of the good guys, then," I said.

"No," said Faraday, firmly. "He most emphatically is not. He is an untrustworthy and highly manipulative individual, who happens to be a skilled psychic, and who I wouldn't trust for a heartbeat, and neither should you. Believe me when I say that for every moment you are in his company, you are in grave danger, and you certainly do not want this person anywhere near the inside of your head."

"Understood."

"He can also be quite an unstable personality, not untypically so, for an addict."

"An addict? You mean, he's some kind of junkie?"

"Not in the way you're thinking. He's addicted to something far more potent than drugs."

"What?"

"Magic", said Faraday. "He's quite literally addicted to the practice of magic."

We resumed our journey, into countryside that became ever more rustic. It was a soft, gentle terrain, for the most part, a tableau of woods and rolling hills, farms and small holdings, punctuated with villages that were pretty and well kempt; neat lines of whitewashed terraced cottages beneath thatched roofs, and the occasional half-timbered mansion behind a high stone wall in expansive grounds; a scene that had likely changed little over several centuries.

Sometime after we left the pub, we turned off onto a minor road signposted to the Shropshire Hills. Here, the landscape became wilder still, and even more sparsely populated. The narrow lanes were overhung with foliage, making them dark. Every so often, the verges would part to reveal flashes of meadow and pastureland, bathed in sunshine, and then we would pass into deep shadow again.

The road started to climb, whereupon everything seemed to open out, and we were presented with a spectacular vista of hills and high escarpments, of rocky peaks and steep, grassy defiles.

On and on the road went, eventually levelling out at what must have been its highest elevation before plunging downwards again. We didn't see another car the whole way until, finally, we slowed at the junction to a gravel track that led into a forest.

"It's just along here," said Faraday, half under his breath. I detected a tension in him that I hadn't noticed earlier.

We entered the forest, leaving the light and space of the hill country behind us, and passing into a darker world. The rough, rutted road, presumably a logging trail, was long and straight and lined with tall fir trees, forming a canyon of thick greenery. Faraday steered the Range Rover along the precarious surface with seemingly fierce concentration, as he manoeuvred around large potholes filled with muddy rainwater, and at one point we slowed to drive carefully over a pile of fallen branches.

This Malachy person clearly didn't have many visitors, I thought.

After heading down into a steep valley, the scenery around us started to change. Here, the wood was much more ancient, the dense screen of conifers giving way to random clumps of oak and beech, with clearings of grass and ferns where the sun could penetrate, and which appeared as pools of light as a consequence. I opened my window, and let the sounds of the forest, a cacophony of birdsong, drift pleasantly into the car.

Passing beneath a canopy of gnarled, moss-covered branches that looked as if they had been crafted into an archway, Faraday turned onto a grass track that appeared to open out at its conclusion, a few hundred yards in front of us. I felt myself tense as I anticipated arriving at our destination.

The woods were thicker here, so much so that the area immediately beside the track was almost pitch black. Everything looked impenetrable and forbidding. It was as if we had entered a primeval territory, a place cut off from the world around it, and untouched by time. A lonely place. A dangerous place. My fears increased. I found myself not wanting to leave the sanctuary of the car and wishing we could turn around and drive out of there.

We emerged into the light of a clearing, and Faraday brought the car to a halt in front of a small stone cottage, with smoke rising from its chimney. Set in front of the house, and taking up much of this open area, was a haphazard arrangement of fruit and vegetable plots, corralled within enclosures of bean poles and string. A dilapidated old van stood off to one side of the garden, next to a scruffy looking timber outbuilding. The van had a roof rack, across which was stretched a tarpaulin, with what looked like logs and branches beneath it. There was a wide smear of rust across one of its back doors, and its bonnet was propped open.

I got out of the car and stretched and looked around. I noticed that there was no birdsong in this part of the woods. In fact, there was an almost deathly silence from behind the trees.

"Ready?" said Faraday, appearing beside me.

Just then, the door to the cottage opened with a loud creak and a man stepped out, appearing first as a dark silhouette before emerging from the shadow into the sunlight.

I can't say that he was what I expected, because I'm not entirely sure what I expected. He was a bit younger than Faraday, old but not elderly. He had long white hair, which he wore tied in a ponytail, and there was a wisp of beard on his chin. A small metal pentagram on a chain hung around his neck and rested at the top of the paunch of his stomach, over which was stretched a t-shirt stained with grease, marks which extended down to faded jeans that were frayed around the bottoms. He was wearing a ragged pair of plastic flip-fops over his bare feet, and I noticed that his toe nails were long and yellow, and caked with dirt.

He appeared neither surprised nor especially pleased to see us as he walked over.

"Well, well, well. Professor Faraday. I knew that someone was in the forest, but I had no idea it was you. To what do I owe this most unexpected of pleasures?"

He had the rasping voice of a heavy smoker, with just a hint of soft, west-country burr about it, and a tone that conveyed either mild disinterest or insouciant hostility.

"Good morning, Malachy," said Faraday. "You must forgive me for calling by unannounced like this, but I have a rather important matter to discuss with you, and time is very much of the essence. As you might have guessed, I am here because I'm in need of your assistance."

Faraday spoke in a manner that was measured, business-like, above all guarded. I got the sense that the two men were sizing each other up, and both were exhibiting a certain coiled tension. They were adversaries observing the conventions and surface pleasantries of a normal conversation, but each was ready to strike, should the occasion demand it. I felt my palms dampen and my pulse quicken as we stood out there, feet away from this strange magician of the forest, if that's what he really was.

"I thought we were all square on that front," said Malachy. "No longer in each other's debt, so to speak."

"We were never in each other's debt," Faraday said, in an even tone. "You provided me with information that proved to be rather useful, in return for which I used my influence to have your name removed from a certain police investigation."

"So, we're done then, Professor, is what I'm saying. All accounts settled. You off fighting the good fight, and me here, doing what I do, not troubling anyone, of no concern to anyone, of no interest to anyone, here in my enchanted wood."

"Yes, well I suppose that's one way of looking at it," said Faraday.

"Do what thou wilt, shall be the whole of the law. You know how it goes. I do no harm."

"Other than to yourself, and your immortal soul? Well, that's rather a matter of opinion, wouldn't you say? I take it that you're still a purveyor of spells and curses, and all manner of other trickeries, to the gullible and the desperate. The subject of that police investigation, as I recall."

"A man has to eat, doesn't he? Besides, you know I like to keep my hand in; stay on top of the game."

"I heard that the game might be getting on top of you."

"You heard wrong."

"I'm glad to hear it. Incidentally, the information you gave us did prove to be very useful indeed, so I should not want you to think that I am in any way ungrateful."

"The coven in Yorkshire?" said Malachy. "Genuinely glad to be of assistance with that one. I hear on the grapevine that the police have made some arrests."

"Then your information on the matter is more up to date than mine. But thanks to the names that you gave us, and our surveillance, we were able to put together a very strong case against the entire group, which we passed on to the police. It was likely only a matter of time before they took appropriate action."

"Well, for once, I'm on the side of our boys in blue. That was one very sick coven. Molesters and rapists posing as high priests of one of our most revered sects. It can only give us true believers a bad name, don't you agree?"

"A worse name, is how I might put it."

"Ouch. You're punchy today, Professor. And also, very worried about something. I can tell. It's literally seeping out of your aura. You're wearing it like a suit of clothes.

"Him, too," he added, nodding towards me, and acknowledging my presence for the first time. "And who is this, by the way? Your latest protégé?"

"Someone with rather an interesting tale to tell. I think you'll be sufficiently intrigued by what he has to say to spare the time for it.

"Not to mention the thing I've got in my bag," Faraday went on, motioning towards the canvas bag that was slung over his shoulder, and which I knew to contain the tape recording from the previous night's sabbat at Stokeley.

"What is it?" said Malachy, his eyes narrowing as he stared at the bag.

"Something I'd like you to listen to."

Malachy shrugged, as if resigned to his fate.

"In that case, welcome to my humble abode."

We followed him into the cottage, whereupon I was immediately hit by the strong smell of incense, blended with the equally pervasive odour of marijuana.

Malachy picked the remains of a spliff from a battered metal ashtray, put it to his mouth, lit it and took a long drag, blowing out a stream of smoke with evident satisfaction.

"I'm going to clean up, and change into something a little more respectable, if you don't mind," he said. "You caught me stripping the van carburettor, so I'm filthy. Make yourselves at home."

He left the room, taking the spliff with him, and I heard him go upstairs.

I looked around the little sitting room as Faraday settled himself into a surprisingly comfy looking sofa, covered in blankets. It was dark in there. The windows had no glass in them, just wooden shutters, which were half-open, allowing only a minimal amount of light inside. The only other illumination came from the smouldering flames of a wood-burning stove in the hearth, and a black candle flickering on the mantle shelf.

The room was overflowing with books and clutter. I walked over to a bookcase in the corner, its stuffed shelves almost palpably groaning beneath the weight of their contents, with books stacked flat on top of the rows of cracked, embossed leather. I perused some of the titles, which were mostly on an occult theme. On the wall next to the bookcase was a framed map of the night sky, covered in dense, ancient script, and beneath it a painting, the details of which were so dark that I could barely make them out in the gloom, but which I saw, on closer inspection, depicted a hillside cemetery at night. It reminded me of the paintings of a sabbat I had found with Megan at Badcombe Hollow, except here the details were even more phantasmagorical, with a sky that seemed to be on fire. It made me think of the end of the world.

Malachy came back into the room. He had changed into a long-sleeved shirt of a thick material, like hessian, and a pair of corduroy trousers, although he was still barefoot, save for his tatty flip-flops. He carried with him the faint smell of cloves and carbolic soap.

I went and sat beside Faraday on the sofa as Malachy lowered himself into a ratty armchair by the fireplace, watching us intently all the time. There was a glint in his eyes that I hadn't noticed before, and a slight smirk at the corners of his mouth.

"So, what's on the tape, then?" he said, nodding towards the canvas bag on the sofa next to Faraday.

"The proceedings of a sabbat," said Faraday. "It was recorded last night, in a ruined chapel, north of Marlborough, on the borders of Wiltshire and Oxfordshire."

Malachy gave a snort of derision.

"Nobody holds a sabbat on the twenty-fourth of April, less than a week before Walpurgis. Sounds like amateur night, to me. Can't believe you came all the way up here for that, Professor."

"That was also my initial reaction," said Faraday. "But I think there may be something more to this, and I'm hoping you might be able to explain what it is, or at least translate some of it for me."

"We'll see," said Malachy, non-committally. "Who was master of ceremonies, do you know?"

"A man called Ernst von Draken. Have you heard of him?"

Malachy threw back his head and laughed with a throaty rasp.

"In that case, we're definitely talking amateur night," he said.

"How so?"

"Because Ernst von Draken is a fucking amateur, that's how so."

"What do you know about him?"

"Only what I need to, which isn't much. Middle ranking follower of the left-hand path from way back; dropped off the scene years ago. Moneyed, but not particularly talented, and not as learned as he'd like you to believe, although he does have a formidable book collection. Inherited most of it from his father. He was the interesting member of the family. Erwin von Draken. Loyal disciple and key lieutenant of the infamous Dorian Slake, as it happens. Died a few years before his mentor, and sonny boy took up the mantle, but he was always a pale imitation of the father.”

Faraday furrowed his brow.

“That doesn’t make sense,” he said. “I investigated Slake’s coven in the 1960s, and I never came across that name.”

“You wouldn’t have. He changed it. Von Draken senior was Hungarian. He came over here after the war. He’d been a fairly high-level Nazi collaborator, so goodness knows how he pulled that off, but he was rich enough to grease a few wheels, I suppose. Maybe he had friends in the right places. The satanic brotherhood transcends borders, after all. When they’re not at each other’s throats, that is. Who knows? Anyway, having settled here, he wanted to anglicise his name, so Erwin von Draken became Edwin Jackson. And then his son took the family name back again, after Slake killed himself, and he assumed command of the coven. I suppose he thought it sounded more exotic; the cachet of a foreign name.”

“I think the coven is still operating today,” said Faraday.

“So? What of it? There are dozens of covens in existence, all across the country. There’s nothing special about von Draken’s, other than the fact that it used to be run by Dorian Slake. He may have been gamely keeping the tradition going, for all these years, but trust me when I say that he’s a very long way from the true centre of satanic power in this country, and he has no gift whatsoever for our craft. He’s actually a very poor magician, which is why he’s never really accomplished anything.”

“That may be about to change,” said Faraday. “We believe that he has engaged the services of a skilled adept. Her name is Catherine Falaise. Does that name mean anything to you?”

Malachy shook his head.

“So, this is really about Slake then, is it?” he said to Faraday. “I might have guessed.”

“I’m not sure that I follow you,” said Faraday.

“Dorian Slake. It still gets to you after all these years.”

Faraday scowled and said nothing.

“You know about all that, right?” said Malachy, addressing me for the first time since we had come into the house.

“Yes, he knows that I once had a run in with Slake,” said Faraday.

"He almost took him down for good," Malachy said to me, ignoring Faraday. "Close but no conviction, isn't that right, Professor? But you still managed to throw a major spanner in the works and disrupt his fiendish little plans. You must have really pissed off that coven. Lucky to escape with your life, I should think. But you could say that you won in the end. Slake never got over the disappointment and killed himself soon afterwards. One might say you drove him to it."

"I've no more idea than you have why Slake chose to take his own life," Faraday said, tightly. "I can't imagine that he was short of reasons. He was quite mad, as you know."

"History is written by the victors," Malachy said, with a shrug. "Anyway, all jocular badinage aside, Professor, let me sum up by saying that Ernst von Draken doesn't exactly measure up to his beloved mentor, or even his own dad. He's an amateur, like I said. He was an amateur when he took over the coven back in sixty-five, and nothing that he's done in the intervening period, including holding a sabbat on the fucking twenty-fourth of April, the stupid git, would suggest that he's any the wiser now."

"But you'll still listen to the tape," said Faraday.

"Sure. Why not? Not much else going on today. Merely a van carburettor to strip. Always time for some esoterica. Yes, I'll listen to it."

"Good. But before you do, I need you to listen to what my friend here has to tell you. I'd imagine that you'll find it rather interesting."

"That's hard to believe," said Malachy, his eyes flickering over to me with evident disdain.

"On the contrary," said Faraday, "I think you're going to be all ears. You see, Richard here has been living for the past few weeks in Dorian Slake's house on the Marlborough Downs. In fact, he now owns it."

Malachy raised his eyebrows in a theatrical manner.

"Well, I said this must all be about Slake, and yes, that is rather interesting," he said.

"And how's that working out then?" he said to me. "Come across anything that goes bump in the night?"

"You might say that," I said.

Malachy chuckled mirthlessly.

I looked over at Faraday and he nodded at me to begin my story.

We had discussed my doing this on the drive over, and I had it well prepared in my head by then. This would be the fourth time in twenty-four hours that I had told it.

I started at the beginning, with Alan's surprise visit to my flat, all those weeks ago, and I left nothing out, describing everything that had happened up to and including my escape from von Draken's coven the previous night.

Malachy listened quietly for the most part but made the odd interjection.

"Doreen Smithers was a highly accomplished witch," he said, when I got to the part of my story where I visited Stokeley for the first time. "Truly skilled. I never met her myself, but I know those who did. She had a real dark power and could put a curse on anything. It would have been her who put the curse on the house. She would have taught Slake a lot, I'd imagine. Far more than Crowley ever did. And they were lovers. I do know that much. I even heard he was the father of her daughter. She'd be a fairly old woman herself, by now."

"What became of her?" said Faraday.

"Mad as bat shit, so I understand. She's in an asylum, somewhere. Been there for years, apparently. But with parents like that, what do you expect? Not exactly a normal upbringing, is it?"

He gave a callous laugh. There was something cruel and pitiless about the man, I thought, a complete lack of human empathy that verged on the sociopathic. I couldn't wait to be away from this dark little house in the woods, and its even darker occupant.

"The significant thing about this temple that Slake supposedly built with the von Drakens," he said, when I got to the end of my story, "Isn't that you can't find the way into it – that's just a security measure – but the fact that it's never been used, and that it's intended to be used one time only, on this coming Walpurgis Night. And that they should wait so long. That they'd wait for decades. So, Slake would have known when he built the temple that he'd never get to use it. That does indicate a certain devotion, you might say, not to mention a high level of discipline."

"So, you are intrigued by that aspect to the affair?" said Faraday. "I thought you might be."

"I'm intrigued to the extent that one is moderately intrigued by the obsessive, fanatical hobbies of others. I'm not saying that the temple has any significance outside of the overactive imaginations of those who have been protecting it for all these years."

"What about the snake they sent me?" I said. "Does that have any special significance, do you think? I mean, symbolically speaking?"

"Yes, I did rather enjoy that part," said Malachy. "The old serpent in a box routine. Nice. Very old school. And yes, there is a certain significance to that, since you happen to ask. Aside from scaring you shitless, that is. Slake's coven was part of a serpent cult. Not so unusual, if you think about it. Goes all the way back to the Garden of Eden. But Slake's crew were definitely serpent worshippers. They used to play with live snakes in their ceremonies, and I presume that von Draken has continued that tradition."

"So, what do you think, overall?" said Faraday. "About all of this. What are your thoughts?"

Malachy said nothing for a moment, and looked down at his feet, as if deep in thought.

"I don't really have many," he said, finally. "The connection to Dorian Slake gives it all a certain historic interest, I concede, but apart from that, it sounds like a run of the mill satanic coven, if you ask me. A little more dedicated than most, perhaps, and from what you've told me about last night, certainly verging on the murderous, but essentially an irrelevance, in the great scheme of things."

"How can you say they're an irrelevance, when they had my friend killed?" I said, with anger creeping into in my voice.

"Maybe they did, maybe they didn't," Malachy said. "Sounds like your friend had been dabbling with some powerful forces, over the years. Who knows what demons he unleashed upon himself, real or imaginary."

"But if von Draken, or more likely his adept, did conjure something to kill Alan Mackay, how would they have done it?" said Faraday. "How would they have even located him?"

"He was a long-standing member of their coven, so they would have had a considerable psychic hold over him to start with. Not all that hard to establish telepathic communication with someone you've worshipped at a black mass with, assuming one knew what one was doing. I would imagine the final touch was obtaining an item of his clothing, or something else that he might have owned, and using that physical connection to find him and kill him."

"You mean like voodoo?" I said. "Like sticking needles in a doll?"

"Something like that."

"It's scarcely believable," I said, half to myself. "Even after everything that's happened these past few weeks, everything that I've learned, I still can't quite believe it."

"Can't quite believe what?" said Malachy.

"All of this," I said. "The supernatural, witches, magic."

He looked at me curiously for a moment, and then his eyes casually dropped down to the low table in front of me, and the battered old metal ashtray.

Suddenly, the ashtray moved; not much, but enough to make its base rattle slightly on the table.

And then, in one smooth, swift movement, the ashtray slid across the top of the table and over its edge, landing on the carpeted floor with a soft thud.

I gasped audibly and felt my whole body tense. Faraday remained silent, unmoved.

"Did you see that?" said Malachy.

"Yes," I said, my voice a whisper.

"Do you know how I did it?"

"No."

"Neither do I."

"No?"

"No. And yet, I know that I can do it."

He let out a deep breath and slumped back into his chair.

"Takes it out of me, though. There would have been a time when I could have flipped it back up onto the table and not even drawn breath. But not anymore. Don't have the stamina for it, these days. It's a young man's game, magic. Not that it stops me.

Sometimes I can't even help myself. It's like a nervous tic. But sometimes I do it for a reason. That time, I did it for a reason."

"What was the reason?" I said, still feeling shaken at what I'd just seen.

"To show you that nothing in this world is impossible."

There was silence in the room, broken only by the ticking of an unseen clock. Beside me, I sensed Faraday come to a decision.

"Will you listen to the tape?" he said, holding up the canvas bag.

Malachy nodded and Faraday reached into the bag and handed him a small tape recorder.

"It's in there," he said. "Just press play, and it will start from the beginning. It lasts for about ten minutes. We'll be outside, if you don't mind; enjoying some fresh air and your splendid garden."

"Be my guest," said Malachy absent-mindedly, evidently now more interested in the contents of the tape than in us.

We got up and left the room. As we exited through the front door I heard the amplified sounds of the previous night's satanic ceremony in the background, and I closed the door quicker than I might otherwise have done, so as not to have to hear any more of it.

"I hope you don't mind," said Faraday, as we stepped out into the sunlight. "I simply couldn't bear to be in that foul place, or in that infernal man's presence for another moment. I need to cleanse my mind while he listens to that tape."

"It's a relief to be out of there," I agreed.

I had supposed that Faraday might have wanted to talk to me about what we had just discussed with Malachy, but instead he wandered off into the maze of flower and vegetable beds, several of which he stopped to inspect, seemingly engrossed, as if visiting the garden of a stately home, and noting with approval the condition of the herbaceous borders. Perhaps this was his way of relaxing, I thought, as I followed aimlessly behind him.

After a tortuously slow circuit of the garden, we sat quietly on a wooden bench beside the door to the cottage, waiting for the magician to come out, or beckon us back in.

"It's killing him, you know," said Faraday, breaking the silence.

"What do you mean?" I said.

"The magic. It's killing him, slowly but surely. He's much weaker than when I last met him. It's why I described it as an addiction. It's why he as much as admitted that he can't stop himself. He can't live without it, and yet it's eating away at him from the inside."

A short time later, Malachy emerged from the cottage. He walked past us without saying anything and went and stood with his back to us at the end of the path, looking out into the forest.

"Well?" said Faraday, when he eventually turned round to face us. "What did you think of the tape? You understood it, I presume?"

"Yes, I understood it," said Malachy.

"So, what do you think?"

"What do I think?" Malachy repeated. "Well, I suppose I'd have to say, I think that Dorian Slake was one of the craziest bastards who ever lived. And I think Ernst von Draken may be even crazier. Crazy, and just possibly, incredibly dangerous with it. I owe you an apology, Professor. It was worth you driving all the way up here, after all."

He seemed to have lost some of his earlier bravado, as if listening to the tape had unnerved him somehow.

"What are you talking about?" Faraday said impatiently. "What's on the tape?"

"Some of the darkest magic I've ever heard."

"To what end?" said Faraday. "For what purpose?"

"It's a raising spell. Basically, that's what it is. It's a raising spell."

"A raising? You mean, the raising of a demon?"

"Yes. Von Draken's going to raise a demon. On Walpurgis Night. Five days from now. Except, it's not so much a raising. It's more of an opening. He's going to open something, you see. Or at least, he's going to try to. And he thinks that if he does, it'll let this demon in."

"What's he going to open?" I said.

Malachy grinned at me and then looked over at Faraday.

"Professor?" he said. "You want to take it from here?"

"The gates of hell," said Faraday. "He's going to try and open the gates of hell."

CHAPTER THIRTY-NINE

The Satanist, Part Two

"What?" I said, incredulously. "Okay, so that's a joke, I assume. You're kidding. You're obviously not serious. I mean, this basically proves that von Draken is a fraud. Case closed. Right?"

I looked over at Faraday, thinking that he might back me up, but he was staring thoughtfully down at his feet.

"For goodness sake, this is completely insane," I said. "Look, I accept that people worship the devil. I'll even accept that there are some strange phenomena in the world that I don't really get, like that bloody thing creeping around my house. But this? This is absolutely crazy. You can't expect me to believe it. Can you?"

"Von Draken would appear to believe it," Faraday said, softly.

"Which demon?" he asked Malachy.

"Astaroth," replied the satanist.

"The crown prince of hell. It would appear that von Draken is nothing if not ambitious. He'll need a human sacrifice, I presume, to enact the raising?"

"Not to enact it. I imagine that will be the usual chicken or goat. But the raising entails presenting the thing that's been raised with a human offering as it enters our realm, so in that sense, yes, it will require a human sacrifice."

"Oh, my God," I said. "We're taking this seriously?"

"A human sacrifice is always a serious business," said Malachy.

"Speaking from experience, are we?" I snapped at him.

"Never mind that," said Faraday. "Let's get back to the tape. What was the specific purpose of last night's ceremony? You said it was a raising spell."

"It was a raising incantation, to be absolutely precise."

"Whatever. Why do that five nights before Walpurgis?"

"Because, Professor, as you must surely appreciate, this isn't your everyday ritual cum magic show. This is an epic event they're planning. We're talking about unleashing the most powerful, elemental forces you can possibly imagine, the application of magic on a vast, apocalyptic scale.

"You don't go into something like that half-cocked. This is a once in a millennia opportunity to try and do something that's never been done before. This has been years, decades in the making. Started by Dorian Slake, to be finished by Ernst von Draken. And it has to happen on one particular night; this coming Walpurgis.

"No wonder they're so pissed off with you," he said, looking over at me. "You moving into that house has completely buggered things up for them."

"Why this particular Walpurgis Night?" said Faraday.

Malachy shrugged.

"Don't know. Some sort of planetary conjunction, I'd imagine," he said. "I haven't worked that part out yet. But I'd guess it has something to do with some unusual arrangement in the heavens, which happens to occur this year, the night before May Day. It's why they've had to wait for so long. Slake built a temple for the greatest satanic event of all time, knowing that he wouldn't get to go to it himself. Selfless of him, wouldn't you say? Handing it on to the next generation like that?

"Anyway, to get back to your question, Professor, in the weeks and months leading up to the event itself, the coven will have been very busy preparing for it. This has been a long time in the planning. They've been waiting decades for this, and they'll have been up to all kinds of stuff to get ready. Sabbats and special ceremonies, of the kind matey here witnessed last night. This will have required a lot of work. But last night's ceremony; that was the last but one; the last one before Walpurgis itself. Last night they were lighting the touch paper. So, stand back, boys and girls, because we're in for a very bumpy night."

"What do you mean, exactly?" said Faraday.

"I mean that if Walpurgis Night is the night of the raising; the opening of a portal into the satanic realm; then last night was the night of the summoning. You don't think that you just ask Astaroth to come on over into our world on a whim, do you? You need to get his attention, first; beckon him over, and let him know that you're laying out a pathway for him. It's a poor analogy, but imagine setting up an emergency airstrip in a remote location, and setting fires along the side of the runway, to guide the plane in. You might say that's what the coven were doing last night. They were rolling out the red carpet, and asking Astaroth to step onto it, five days hence."

"What's the significance of the temple being in that particular place?" I said. "Why is it beneath the burial mound? Why did Slake build it there?"

"That's obvious," said Malachy. "It's a highly sacred spot and Slake wasn't the first person to try and utilise that. The Neolithic people, or Bronze Age, or whatever they were, would have positioned that barrow very deliberately, as directed by the tribal shamans. There will be some powerful earth energies emanating from that spot. You have to remember, that whole plain around Avebury is a maze of ley lines, chakras, sacred springs, sacred hills, sacred bloody groves, you name it. My theory would be that the barrow outside your house is some form of nodal point that connects everything up, and Dorian Slake somehow found out, and that's why he built the temple there. Maybe the witch, Doreen Smithers, told him about it. Oh, and by the way, the reason the temple has never been used is because this type of ritual requires it to be done on virgin territory. The ceremony has to happen in a temple where nobody has ever worshipped before, and where nobody will ever worship again. That's why they had to build it from scratch, and that's why they've kept out of it, all these years."

"This is just too fantastic," I said.

"So you keep saying," said Malachy. "And yet here we all are. Standing in my garden. Talking about it."

He turned away from me and addressed Faraday.

"I need to listen to the tape again," he said. "And look some stuff up. Can you give me another hour?"

"We need to be back in Wiltshire by nightfall," Faraday said. "I'm expecting von Draken and his witch to launch an assault on the house tonight."

"You really do have your hands full at the moment, don't you? I only need an hour. You'll make it in time."

Faraday thought for a moment.

"Very well," he said. "One hour."

Without saying anything further, Malachy went back into the cottage.

"We might as well stretch our legs while we're waiting," said Faraday. "Let's go and explore the woods."

I stared at Faraday, in total disbelief at this statement.

"Let's go and explore the woods?" I repeated back to him. "That's really what we're going to do? We're going to go for a walk, in the *eff-ing bloody woods*. Well, that's brilliant. Great idea, Professor. Why don't we pack a picnic, while we're at it? And then all back to the gingerbread cottage for tea and scones, and more apocalypse chat. Tell you what, here's a better idea. Why don't we just get in the car and put as much distance between us and this weirdo as possible, head back to Wiltshire, and try and find out what's really going on at Badcombe Hollow?"

Faraday looked at me with a half-smile on his lips, and when he spoke, it was in the sort of patient but slightly weary tone I imagined him using to address a petulant student.

"My dear Richard," he said. "You evidently have a writer's gift for hyperbole and melodrama, but do please try to consider this in a calm and rational manner. This *is* what's really going on at Badcombe Hollow. At least in Ernst von Draken's mind, and that of his coven, or so Malachy seems to think. This is what this is about now, whether we like it or not, and however implausible it might seem. Hence, the only logical course open to us is to allow Malachy to put some further flesh on the bone, and see what more he can divine from that tape. And since I have no wish to sit in his company while he does this, I propose that we avail ourselves of more agreeable surroundings and stretch our legs for a while. You, of course, are free to do whatever you wish."

I tried to think of a smart rejoinder but couldn't.

"No, I'll stick with you," I said. "I definitely don't want to hang around here. Sorry. You know, about the outburst. It's just all a bit too Hansel and Gretel for me."

"Quite so," said Faraday, as he started to walk towards the trees.

"Aren't you worried about getting back in time?" I asked him, as I followed him out of the clearing and onto a narrow path that led through a dense thicket of trees.

"I am worried about it," said Faraday. "But any further information that we can glean from Malachy is too valuable to pass up. We need to find out as much as possible before we go back."

"Yes, well, I'm sorry to go over the same ground again but, to go back to my previous question, are you really taking this all completely seriously?"

He turned to face me, and we both came to a halt.

"What? The idea that von Draken's coven is going to raise a demon and bring about the end of days? Create a literal hell on earth? I confess that I find it very hard to believe. I'd even go so far as to say it's a lot of fantastical nonsense. It's one thing to accept that there are supernatural forces in this world that are without rational explanation, but I'd be inclined to say that this sort of thing is utterly beyond the realms of the possible."

"So why worry about it? That's what I was getting at before. Why bother about it, if it's all so completely fantastical? Why not let von Draken into the temple for an evening and have at it? He's going to be the one with egg on his face when it's all a damp squib."

"For two very good reasons. Firstly, von Draken does believe in this, and he's prepared to kill to make it happen. We're talking about the taking of a human life."

"Yes, but didn't Malachy say that would be right after the demon thing gets raised? So, if that doesn't happen, nobody gets killed, surely?"

"Don't count on it. Satanists like these with their blood up are liable to do anything. Even if the ceremony fails, they're as likely to kill the person they were going to sacrifice as leave them alive. So, that's as serious as it can get. Not to mention whatever other human depravity von Draken has planned for that night," he added.

"Okay, then. I get that part. What's the second reason?"

"The second reason is that I might be wrong. There is, I suppose, the infinitesimally small chance that the coven might somehow be able to pull this off. So why take the chance? You see the logic in that, I take it? However remote the possibility, the chance of this happening is still greater than zero. So, I say again – why take the chance? Do you see?"

"I guess so. The part about saving a human life was more persuasive."

"And that remains our top priority."

We spoke little after that, and for the most part kept our thoughts to ourselves as we followed the path through the forest. The lush greenery lulled me into a state of semi-somnolence, and I found myself following dumbly in Faraday's footsteps, mentally defeated, both by the absurdity of the situation, and by Faraday's seeming ability to win any argument, at least against me.

Eventually, we reached the top of a steep rise, whereupon we turned around and headed back in the direction of Malachy's cottage.

When we got there, the elderly magician was sat on a rough timber bench by one of his vegetable patches, a long spliff smouldering in his hand. The tape recorder was beside him.

"Yours, I believe," he said, as we approached, handing the device to Faraday.

"So, did you learn anything further?" Faraday asked him.

"Not as much as I might have hoped. But a bit."

He held out the spliff and raised an enquiring eyebrow. Faraday and I both shook our heads.

"Well, it's a planetary conjunction, just as I thought," said Malachy. "Mars and Venus, combined with a waning moon. It happens every few years, but not often on Walpurgis Night. The last time was in 1786, and it won't happen again for another hundred and seventy-five years. So, you can see why this coming April 30th is so important to von Draken."

"So, after this coming Walpurgis Night, von Draken can't try this again?" I said.

"Evidently not. There's something else. I missed it the first time. My understanding of colloquial Aramaic isn't what it used to be."

"That's what von Draken was speaking?" I said.

"Amongst other things. He was reading from a trionic text. Three ancient languages mixed together. Anyway, it's about the actual manifestation of the demon, subsequent to the ritual in the temple. It won't happen there. The demon won't manifest in the temple."

"What do you mean?" said Faraday. "Where will Astaroth appear?"

"Another location. But it won't be far away. It'll be somewhere nearby. Probably a couple of miles away. Maybe more. Maybe less. But not far. Von Draken and the coven will have to make their way over there after the ritual."

"And you've no idea where this is?" said Faraday.

"No. But this is Avebury we're talking about. There's not exactly a shortage of sacred sites for them to choose from. It could be on top of Silbury Hill, for all I know."

"But von Draken will know where it is?"

"One presumes so."

"Well, that's that then," said Faraday. "At least we now know what we're dealing with. Thank you, Malachy. You have been of very considerable help today."

"I'd say it's been a pleasure," said Malachy, "But I think we both know that would be stretching a point somewhat. But it's been interesting enough."

"I'll let you know how it turns out," said Faraday.

"Oh, I don't think that'll be necessary. I'll know how it turned out when I get up and look outside on May Day."

"I presume you're hoping that von Draken pulls this off?" I said.

There was an edge of hostility in the way I spoke to him. There was something about the man that I found irritating as well as distasteful, which made me want to needle him.

He looked at me for a long moment before speaking.

"You know something, sonny boy? You're about as relevant to me as a grain of dirt beneath my feet, so your opinion truly doesn't matter a damn. But I'll answer your question anyway, just for the hell of it. So, get ready for a surprise. I rather like this old world of ours, and I don't feel much inclined to see it change. Perhaps it was moving here that did it for me. I like this wood, you see. I like the trees. I like the peace and quiet. I like watching the sun break through the mist in the morning, and I like watching a full moon hang over the trees of an evening. Don't tell anyone, but I'm a very sad excuse for a devil worshipper, these days. I'm dug in, content, replete, high as a fucking kite, however you want to spin it, but believe you me, it's been a very long time since I wanted to see anyone end the world. So now that I've done a favour for you, perhaps you'll do one for me in return?"

"And what would that be?"

Malachy took a long drag from the spliff and gestured around him.

"Don't let Ernst von Draken fuck this all up," he said.

"You really think he could?"

"Yes. I know the Professor thinks this is all mostly smoke and mirrors, and most of the time, sorry to say, he's right. But this feels different. It really does. There was some truly dark magic on that tape. Some of the darkest I've ever heard, and coming from me, that's saying something. So do the best you can to put a stop to it, won't you? There's a good fellow."

I nodded at him and turned away.

As Faraday and I reached the car, Malachy called out to us.

"There's one more thing," he said. "Astaroth, the demon they're raising – he'll be close, by now. He's already here, you see, now that the coven has summoned him. He can't get in yet; not until the enactment of the ritual on Walpurgis Night; but he's here. He's sitting on the other side of the portal, in another time and space, waiting for his moment. But believe me when I say that he's very close to our world. You may yet come to feel his presence, before we even get to Walpurgis Night."

"What do you mean?" I said. "How will that happen?"

Malachy shrugged expansively, as if affecting a callous insouciance.

"Depends," he said. "There could be some atmospheric phenomenon. Or not. You might hear his voice. Or not. Or you might see him in your dreams. Hard to say. This has never been done before, so we have no precedent to guide us.

"But he's out there," he added, glancing skywards as he did so. "You see, he's been called, and now he's waiting to come in."

And with that, he turned and walked back to the house. For some reason, Faraday and I stood there and watched him until he got inside, closing the door on us with a soft thud.

"We need to get moving," said Faraday.

It was late in the afternoon by the time we exited the woods. The sun that had hung high above the trees as we had driven towards Malachy's lair was now sliding across the tops of the hills on the western horizon. We were cutting things a bit fine, if we wanted to be back at Badcombe Hollow before dark, but there was just enough time, provided we encountered no significant delays.

As we had agreed on the journey up, I drove so that Faraday could rest.

"I simply have to sleep for a while," he said, as we drove out of the woods. "I hope you understand, but it is absolutely imperative that I'm as alert as I can possibly can be, for whatever may happen tonight."

"So, you really think von Draken is going to attack the house tonight?" I said. "I mean, that he's going to unleash something … demonic … on us?"

"Yes," Faraday said, after a moment. "I don't think he has much choice in the matter. Timing is central to his plan. That's now clearer than ever. He needs to enact the opening on Walpurgis, which is only a few nights away. And he needs to do so from an underground temple. In the grounds of Badcombe Hollow. The entrance to which is so hidden that you haven't thus far been able to find it. Which implies that it will take some getting into. He needs time for that; time to get the thing opened up, and to get everything prepared for the ceremony. So, he needs you gone as soon as possible, and my guess is that he's going to use this Catherine Falaise woman, his adept, to summon up enough demonic energy to have you flying out of there, scared out of your wits, if not actually dead from the shock of it."

"Like they did to Alan," I said.

"I'm sure that would be their aspiration, but I doubt that they could achieve it," said Faraday. "The coven would have had a far greater hold on your friend. It's unlikely that they could manifest something quite so horrible for the uninitiated. But they will certainly try to produce something very unpleasant indeed. But we have the advantage over them. They don't yet know that we're there with you. There are countermeasures we can take, which they won't know about, and which should go a long way towards mitigating the effects of whatever the coven happens to conjure, under the direction of Ms Falaise."

"Countermeasures? What kind of countermeasures?" I asked.

"We'll get to that later, if you don't mind," said Faraday, sinking back into his seat, folding his arms and closing his eyes. "I really must sleep now."

I let it go, and moments later I looked over at Faraday, and saw that he already appeared to be in a deep sleep. I figured that he was one of those people who could just switch off mentally, on command, like flicking a switch. I imagined him disciplining his body to do this, training himself, over many years. Some eastern meditation thing, painstakingly learned, I thought to myself; further evidence of Faraday's strength of mind and erudite nature. It was reassuring, up to a point.

I wasn't in much of a mood to talk, anyway. As I steered the Range Rover through the twisting lanes that led away from the forest, my mind was assailed by myriad thoughts. Everything seemed so absurd, so crazy, and yet I knew what I knew, and here I was. I was as if I had plunged into an extraordinary journey that I was now compelled to follow through to the end. A small part of me felt exhilarated by this, but mostly I felt confused and afraid. I didn't relish returning to Badcombe Hollow at all, but at the same time, I felt incredibly anxious to get back there.

I tried to think about something else. I thought about Megan. I wondered what she was doing, now, at that precise moment. I wondered if she was thinking about me. I wondered if I might still have a chance with her, when all of this was over. But I was never able to keep this up for long. I always kept coming back to what the satanist had told us, and to the potential terrors that lay ahead that night.

We made better time than I had anticipated, and we sped southwards in a blur of fields and hedgerows, so much so that Faraday, who had awoken just after we exited the motorway, suggested that we stop for a short break.

"We don't want you nodding off and running us off the road," he remarked, as I pulled into the car park of a rather uninspiring looking roadside pub.

I was pleased to stop for a moment. I felt absolutely shattered, and it was barely dusk. I couldn't imagine how I was going to get through the night ahead.

I felt like a proper drink, but Faraday insisted that we have nothing stronger than mineral water.

"Because of what may come later," he said, by way of explanation.

We carried our drinks over to a table in the corner of the sparsely populated bar.

"Couldn't we just go to the police?" I said, as we sat down.

"And tell them what?" said Faraday, raising his glass to his lips with a soft tinkle of ice cubes. "That a reputed devil worshipper is going to try and bring about hell on earth on the night of 30th April? They'd laugh in our faces."

"There are other things we could tell them," I said. "We could tell them that they're planning a sacrifice. We could say that they're going to try and break into the house so they can get at their temple."

"I think we'd still get a fairly derisory reaction. Besides, no actual crime has been committed yet, not in the normal sense of the term. It would all be supposition on our part, as far as the police were concerned."

"But don't you have contacts in the police? You said that you've worked with them before; the thing that you and Malachy were talking about. Surely, they'd take this seriously if it came from you."

"I think you greatly over-estimate my powers of persuasion," said Faraday. "Besides, I've never had any dealings with the force that covers your particular county. And in terms of communicating this information at a suitably high level, I simply wouldn't know where to start. I don't believe I'd have much chance at all, in the very limited time we have available to us.

"I wouldn't know whom to trust, either," he added. "Satanic infiltration of the police and the judiciary is not by any means unknown. And even if we left out the occult angle entirely, and just focused on the potential physical threat to you and your property, then the most we could expect would be a police car at the end of the lane, putting its occupants in severe jeopardy. No. There may or may not come a time when we need to involve the police or other agencies in all of this, but we're not there yet. For now, this is a battle we must fight alone.

"Anyway," he said, draining his glass and setting it down neatly on a coaster, "Didn't you tell me last night that you also made a conscious decision not to involve the authorities, when the coven sent you a venomous snake in a box?"

"That's true," I said. "But things have moved on a bit. Back then, I was still looking at this like a journalist. I was protecting my story."

Faraday looked at me across the table.

"If you do ever write about this," he said, "Then I must insist that you make no reference to myself, Kate or Michael. Use pseudonyms, if you refer to us. That needs to be clearly understood, please.

"For our safety," he added.

"You have my word on it," I said. "*If* I choose to write about it. I must say, I'm surprised that you'd be happy about me writing about any of this, whether I used pseudonyms or not."

"On the contrary," said Faraday, "I am most keen that you should. It's the only way that the wider public will begin to understand this and realise what's going on under their very noses."

I finished my drink, and we walked back out to the car.

"You know, I think I'd struggle to make it all believable," I said, and we stepped into the car park and the din of traffic from the road.

"I'm sure you'll skill your way through the problem," Faraday said.

"I don't know if I believe it all myself, yet," I said. "Opening the gates of hell? That's a pretty far-fetched story, even for an old tabloid hack like me."

"Don't get too fixated on that part," Faraday said, as we got into the car. "We're a long way from that, even as an abstract consideration. One thing at a time. Get through tonight. Find the entrance to the temple. Stop von Draken getting into the temple on 30th April and carrying out some foul act. If we do that, then the metaphysical side of this is all moot anyway."

"Works for me," I said.

I steered the car out onto the road, and we resumed our journey back to Badcombe Hollow.

We continued to make good time, encountering only light traffic, but as we approached the point at which we would cross the M4, and head over the plain to Marlborough, everything suddenly slowed down, and before long we came to a complete halt behind a long line of stationary traffic.

"It's probably just a queue to get onto the motorway," I said, but as we remained sitting there, for five minutes, then ten, then twenty, it became clear that there was something seriously wrong ahead of us. Eventually, Faraday went off to investigate, and when he got back to the car, he was grim faced.

"There's been an accident," he said. "A caravan has tipped over, according to someone I spoke to. They're clearing the road now, but it could take a while.

"Damn it," he shouted, rapping his fist against the car door. It was the first time I had heard him raise his voice or display any sort of bad temper.

We continued to sit in the line of traffic, boxed in on all sides, and powerless to do anything about our predicament. I could sense the frustration and anxiety mounting in Faraday, as it grew dark around us.

"I must speak to Kate," he said, taking his phone from his coat pocket.

But moments later he was putting it away with a perturbed look on his face.

"I can't get through," he said.

"Maybe there's no signal here," I said.

"No, that's not it. I've got five bars."

"Well, perhaps she switched her phone off," I ventured.

"She wouldn't do that. My guess is that von Draken has jammed the signal. To prevent you from phoning out this evening and trying to summon outside assistance."

"He can do that?" I said.

"Oh, yes. He can easily do that. You can buy the jamming equipment on the internet. You, of all people, should know that. All it would take would be somebody stationed in the nearby woods with a signal transmitter, and he can effectively cut off all communication from the house to the outside world. I don't suppose you have a land line, do you?"

"No. Alan had it taken out, just before I moved in."

"It probably wouldn't have made any difference. Cutting a phone line is even easier than jamming a mobile phone signal."

Just as he said this, a gap appeared in front of us, and we started to inch forwards, a process that continued in painfully small increments, until we were eventually funnelled into a single lane to take us past the accident.

It was completely dark by then, and the moon was bathing the landscape around us in a pale blue light. I was starting to feel as concerned as Faraday, particularly now that our failure to contact Kate and Michael implied that something was afoot, back at the house.

Once we were past the debris and flashing lights of what appeared to have been a very bad road accident, we started to move a little more quickly, but the traffic was so dense that we never got to go faster than twenty miles per hour, which made our progress feel agonisingly slow.

It was only once we had crossed the motorway and got onto the road to Marlborough that we could get any sort of speed up.

I put my foot down and drove as fast as I dared across the moonlit plain, with Badcombe Hollow tantalisingly close by then.

Every so often, Faraday would try to phone the house, probably just for something to do, rather than in any real expectation of getting a reply, as he sat impotently in the passenger seat.

I slowed down when we reached Marlborough, albeit only marginally so – if we had encountered a police car, I would have been stopped, for sure – and as soon as we cleared the town, I accelerated as hard as I could in the direction of the house. I tore along the dark lanes, clinging to the line of the hedgerows, and screeching around corners. We were almost there.

I'm not quite sure what I expected to find when we got there. I had visions in my mind of demons wandering the grounds, and some sort of green soupy glow enveloping the house. Who the hell knew what we were going to find? All I cared about was getting there as quickly as we could. But my mind still boggled at the possibilities.

So, when we turned into the driveway in a great spray of gravel, I was relieved to see that everything appeared utterly normal. All was quiet, and lights shone in welcoming fashion from the windows.

I wondered if everything might be all right after all, and if our anxieties during the latter stages of our journey had been unfounded. But as Kate opened the front door, and I saw the fearful expression on her face, I knew that this wasn't the case.

"It's started," she said.

CHAPTER FORTY

The Attack on Badcombe Hollow

"What's happened so far?" said Faraday, brushing past me into the hallway.

"Can't you feel it?" said Kate.

I knew immediately what she meant. It was absolutely freezing in the house, so cold that our breath was fogging. And there was something else in the atmosphere; a foul, cloying smell that seemed to hang in the air, cloaking us in its putrid embrace.

Just then, Michael appeared from the kitchen.

"Evening all" he said with a wry smile. "Welcome to the house of horror."

"When did this start?" Faraday said.

"About half an hour ago," said Kate. "As soon as it started to get dark. Thank goodness, you're back. I tried to phone you, but I couldn't get any reception."

"I know," said Faraday. "We got delayed in traffic and I tried to call you, too. I think von Draken might have jammed the signal.

"Any other manifestations?" he said, looking from Kate to Michael.

"Not as yet," said Kate. "Just the cold and the horrible smell."

"Is this what you expected?" I said to Faraday.

"This is nothing," he said. "This is just a parlour trick. It's merely a prelude to what's to come. But they clearly wasted no time in getting started. They obviously want you out of this house very badly indeed."

"What the hell …?" said Kate suddenly, pointing out towards the driveway through the still open front door.

Creeping across the garden was the densest, most impenetrable wall of mist that I had ever seen. So thick was the cloud of fog that it looked more like a gigantic theatrical effect than anything produced by nature.

But realising that it had been conjured by von Draken's coven, and watching it roll up to the front door and start to climb up the house, I began to appreciate for the first time the sort of occult power we were up against. I didn't know it yet, but there would be far worse to come.

Faraday marched briskly over to the door and closed it.

"Another parlour trick," he said. "They can't hurt us with fog."

"Is everything ready?" he said, addressing Kate and Michael.

"Just like you wanted," said Michael.

"Good. We should get down there. Let's go."

"Get down where?" I said. "Where are we going?"

"The cellar," Faraday said.

"The cellar? Why are we going down there?"

But without answering, Faraday turned and started to make his way down the steps to the basement. Kate and Michael followed and, at a complete loss as to what was going on, I did too.

Once beneath the house, we followed Faraday into the room containing the rug covered pentagram. What I saw, when we got in there, made me gasp aloud.

The room had been transformed since I had shown it to Faraday less than twenty-four hours previously. The rug that had been used to cover the pentagram had been rolled up and taken away, and the tiled floor had been swept and washed, so that it appeared spotlessly clean. Large candles on stands had been put into the corners of the room, and smaller tea lights had been placed around the edges of the pentagram. They had all been lit, so that the room was softly illuminated in a tawny glow. In the centre of the giant geometric shape, now defined ever more clearly by its perimeter of flickering light, were several bottles of water, spare candles, some blankets, four crucifixes on long chains and the Bible I had seen Michael take from his luggage the night before.

"What on earth is going on?" I said, to no-one in particular.

"We're going to utilise Dorian Slake's pentagram for protection," said Faraday, stepping over the candles into the centre of the five-pointed star.

"I don't understand," I said. "I mean, surely, we can't be protected by that. It's evil, isn't it?"

"Nonsense," Faraday snorted. "It's nothing of the sort. The pentagram is one of the oldest symbols known to mankind. Its occult properties have been known about for centuries. It is neither good nor evil. That depends entirely upon how it is used. Dorian Slake used it for evil and depraved purposes. Tonight, we will use it for good and noble ones, as protection against von Draken and his coven."

"You've done this before?" I said, incredulously.

"Not exactly," said Faraday. "But believe me, this is our best possible defence against whatever foul evil the coven might conjure up this evening."

"That's actually quite hard to believe," I said.

"Then take it on trust," Faraday snapped, with obvious irritation in his voice. "There are only two alternatives to this course of action. Getting as far away from here as possible, and surrendering the house to von Draken, or going upstairs and being driven insane.

"The coven is going to throw everything it can at us tonight," he went on, his voice softening as he put a fatherly hand on my shoulder. "I have no way of knowing at this stage just how powerful von Draken's adept is, although on the evidence of the pyrotechnics thus far, it's clear that she has a gift for mischief, at the very least. The pentagram won't stop her, by any means, but it should go a considerable way towards blunting the effectiveness of the attack."

"If it's any consolation," Kate said, from behind me, "This is all very new to me, as well. But Julian and Michael know what they're doing. We need to do whatever they say, okay?"

I stepped into the pentagram, taking care not to knock over any of the candles.

"How long will it last?" I said to Faraday. "This attack? How long will it go on for?"

"Impossible to say. It all depends upon the capabilities of von Draken's adept. For all we know, the chill in the air and the mist out in the garden represent the summit of her abilities, although I doubt it, given the occult forces that were used to kill your friend. On the other hand, she may be able to keep it up all night. In all likelihood, it will be somewhere in between.

"She's in some danger herself, you know, as is the coven that will have assembled to help conduct her power. She's dabbling with some of the most elemental forces on the planet, and that's something that can easily backfire, and turn on the coven. Not that I suppose we shall get quite that lucky. But the process itself is completely exhausting. You saw the effect on Malachy this afternoon, when he moved the ashtray without touching it. Magnify that twenty-fold, and you have some idea of what this woman is going to put herself through tonight. If she takes it too far, she'll literally kill herself, and von Draken won't want to take that sort of chance with his most valuable asset. She's his trump card. She's his witch. He's going to need her on Walpurgis.

"In other words," he said, with what I imagined was supposed to be a reassuring smile, "This magical display that began when it got dark is most certainly finite in its duration. It can't continue indefinitely. It will end at some point tonight. We just need to get through it until it does.

"But we could still be here for quite some time," he said. "In which case, it would be wise to avail yourself of the facilities."

I looked at him blankly.

"The bathroom," he said.

"Oh, right. Got it. Wouldn't want to get caught short in here, that's for sure."

When I got back from the little cloakroom that a previous owner of the house had helpfully installed in the far corner of the cellar, Faraday and the others were arranging the blankets in the centre of the pentagram. When this was done, we sat down in a circle, facing each other.

"Do we link hands, or something?" I said, hoping that my question didn't sound facetious.

"Not yet," said Faraday. "For now, we just wait."

"How did it go with Malachy?" Kate said.

"Very interesting indeed," Faraday replied. "But we'll tell you about it later. After this. For now, we need to focus our energy on the thing that's going to try and get into the house."

His words, and the matter-of-fact way in which he spoke them, sent a chill through me.

"Here," said Michael, nudging me gently. "Take this and hang it around your neck."

He handed me one of the crucifixes.

"I'm not really a believer, you know," I said, taking it from him and putting the chain over my head.

"Nobody's perfect," he said, with a grin. "But it will help to protect you. And God doesn't care if you're a believer or not, contrary to what you may have heard. He just wants to keep you safe."

"Good to know," I said.

I looked around, and watched the others drape the crucifixes around their necks.

We sat there in silence for what felt like a long time, but which was probably less than half-an-hour. I was starting to wonder if anything was going to happen at all, and whether or not some cold air and mist really was all that von Draken's adept was capable of, and if this whole thing might be over, before it even got started. I was also beginning to feel rather sleepy.

And then the first attack started.

It began with footsteps above us; up in the hallway, approaching the staircase to the cellar.

"There's someone in the house," I hissed at Faraday, but he appeared to ignore me.

"How did they get through the locked front door?" I said, more loudly, causing Faraday to raise his hand to silence me.

"Because the thing that's up there isn't human," he said.

As he spoke these chilling words, I heard footsteps on the cellar stairs.

"Get ready, everyone," Faraday said.

Feeling more fearful than I could ever remember, I got to my feet and formed a tight group with the others, facing out of the pentagram. At the same time, the temperature in the cellar seemed to plummet. It suddenly felt freezing cold in there, just as it had earlier, upstairs, and I noticed our breath fogging.

The steps continued down the stairs with a heavy tread. The thing out there might not have been human, according to Faraday, but it was evidently big, whatever it was.

It approached the door and stopped. We had left the outer light on, and I could see its shadow beneath the door.

It knocked on the door; three sharp raps.

"Remain completely still," said Faraday.

For a long moment, nothing happened, and I started to pray that it had gone away, but then it knocked on the door again, much harder than the time before.

Again and again, it pounded on the door with seemingly inhuman force. The noise was deafening, and I could see the door straining against its frame, so much so that I almost expected it to burst off its hinges. Whatever it was that was out there, it was clearly intent upon getting in.

And then the pounding stopped, as abruptly as it had started.

We continued to stand there. It was now so quiet in the cellar that one could have heard a pin drop, had it not been for the tense and ragged breathing from the four of us. It didn't feel cold anymore, and our breath was no longer fogging. I wondered if von Draken's adept was only capable of producing a limited number of occult effects at any one time and was on the verge of asking Faraday about this, when I heard a voice on the other side of the door.

"Open the door and let me in," it said in a half-whisper. "Help. Let me in."

The voice was female, and it sounded very frightened. And I was almost certain that it belonged to Megan.

"For God's sake, let me in," it said. "There's something down here. Please help me. I know you're in there. Please, please open the door."

"I know who that is," I said. "It's Megan. The girl I told you about."

"It's no such thing," said Faraday. "It's a trick. It's a demon mimicking your friend's voice."

There was a loud scream from the other side of the door.

"Help me!" the voice shouted.

"It's Megan," I said. "I know it is. She must have come here looking for me, and then got caught up in whatever's going on out there. We have to let her in."

Just as I said this, there was another scream; the loudest and most piercing I had ever heard.

"I'm letting her in," I said, starting to step out of the pentagram.

Faraday grabbed me roughly by the arm.

"It's a trick, I tell you," he shouted.

"But I have to help her," I shouted back at him, struggling against his grip, and that of Michael, who was now holding my other arm.

"Don't be a fool," said Faraday. "This is a diabolical piece of trickery. The thing on the other side of that door is a demon. If you open it, you could kill us all."

"Damn you both," I cried, trying in vain to break free from them.

"Richard, wait," I heard Kate say. "Listen to Julian. He knows what's going on. You have to trust him, for all our sakes. Remember you told us that your friend was attacked by something in this house. Twice. And that she said she'd never come back here, ever again? So how likely is it that she's going to break in here, through a locked front door, in the middle of the night?"

I realised that what Kate was saying made considerable sense, even if I could have sworn that the voice outside the door belonged to Megan. I ceased in my struggle to exit the pentagram, and Faraday and Michael let go of my arms.

"I'm sorry," I said. "It's just that, it sounds exactly like her."

"That's perfectly alright," said Faraday. "We shall be severely tested tonight. This is merely one such test."

Everything was quiet for a while, and then came a faint sound that I struggled to detect at first, but when it grew in volume, there was no mistaking it.

It was the sound of sobbing. It was the sound of Megan sobbing.

I sat there listening to it, helpless to act, and praying that Faraday was correct about this all being a cruel demonic ruse.

A few moments later, I was in no doubt. The sobs were replaced by a low, snarling growl, like that of an animal, which grew to a horrific roar. It was the most terrible sound that I had ever heard. On and on it went, raging at the four of us, on the other side of the locked door, and within our protective circle. I ended up covering my ears and noticed the others doing the same.

And then it simply stopped, and everything was quiet once again.

But it was only a temporary reprieve. Kate suddenly let out a scream.

"Look," she shouted. "Up there!"

Above our heads, in the shadow of the ceiling, the faint outline of a shape had appeared.

It was a human face. It wasn't real; even I could tell that. It was more like a projected image, or a three-dimensional hologram. But that didn't make it any less terrible to look at. For a moment, I wondered if it was the demonic creature that haunted the house, but it was actually a far more horrible sight.

Great fangs hung from its mouth, from which came a foul smell, worse even than the stench that had clung to the house, earlier that evening. It touched the back of my throat and almost made me retch. Its face was covered in sores and lesions, and its hair was matted and filthy.

But for some reason, it was the creature's eyes that made the most vivid impression upon me. Hooded, like a serpent's, they were the cruellest, most piercing eyes that I had ever seen.

"Don't look at its eyes," Faraday shouted at me.

This should have been the simplest of tasks, but for some reason it took an enormous effort of will to drag my eyes away from it and look down at my feet.

Beside me, I heard Michael start to pray – first the Lord's Prayer, and then a prayer that I didn't recognise – subsequent to which he grabbed the Bible from the floor, flicked through it to a passage he had marked, and read from it.

The words meant little to me, but they were nevertheless comforting, and I allowed myself to be lulled by his soft Irish brogue as he enunciated the verses.

After what seemed like an age, but which was probably not very long at all, he stopped speaking, and I looked up to see that the awful, conjured visage had disappeared.

We sat down in the pentagram and shared some water.

"How much longer is this going to go on?" I said to Faraday.

"It can't go on for much longer," he replied. "This will be exceptionally debilitating for von Draken's adept. There's a limit to how long she can keep this sort of thing going."

But it was only a matter of moments before the next attack started, and it proved to be by far the worst thus far.

I first noticed it when something appeared to move on the floor in the corner of the room. It was just the faintest flicker of movement and I had no idea what it was, or if it was even anything at all, until it moved towards us, and into the glow of the candles.

"Bloody hell, there's a snake in here," I said, getting hastily to my feet.

"Keep calm," Faraday said, standing up beside me. "It's merely a conjuring. Stay in the pentagram, and it can't hurt you."

"I'm sorry, but that's a real snake," I said, as I watched it slither across the floor of the cellar. I recognised it as an adder, the same breed that had bitten me a few nights previously, the night before Ernst von Draken had come to this house, and threatened to drive me out of it.

The snake came to the edge of the pentagram, where it stopped, seemingly fixated upon us, its body coiled and ready to strike, and its tongue flicking menacingly.

"God, I fucking hate snakes," Kate said, with disgust as well as fear in her voice.

"I've got to say, Julian," Michael said, anxiously, "That snake does look very real to me, too."

"Yes, but not in the way you think," Faraday said, keeping his eyes fixed on the coiled serpent. "This is not the same as the thing that just appeared before us. That was mere illusion. This is real in the sense that the snake sees us, just as we see it. It is real in the sense that it consists of form and matter, flesh and bone, and if you stepped outside this circle and picked it up, it would bite you, and inject its venom into you. And yet it is not real, for all the physical danger it poses to us. It exists outside of our time and space, on another plane of reality. It has been summoned here from a parallel universe by a magician powerful enough to make a tiny rip in the fabric of time. That creature just crawled through that rip, but it cannot penetrate the protective power of this pentagram. If we step out of its defences, the snake will attack us. If we remain within them, it will not."

He spoke in a measured way; quiet, authoritative, exuding reassurance, and yet when another snake appeared, from a different corner of the room, I could feel myself start to panic.

It was similar to the adder by my feet, but brown, and with diamond shaped markings. It looked like a rattlesnake, and this was confirmed when a loud, urgent rattle sounded from its tail. It made its way over to the pentagram, and stopped next to the adder, both of them watching us intently.

The next snake to appear was easy to identify. It was a cobra, with gunmetal grey skin and a hood that spread open as it lifted the top of its body off the floor, just inches from the edge of the pentagram.

Two more snakes appeared, both cobras, and then another viper. And then they simply seemed to pour into the room so that, within moments, there must have been several dozen snakes in there, sliding over each other's bodies and surrounding the pentagram. It was like a scene from a nightmare.

"Remain completely still," Faraday instructed us. "We must stay within the pentagram."

As he said this, one of the cobras suddenly lunged at us with a rasping hiss, showing us its fangs. I screamed and then stumbled and fell backwards, almost knocking Michael to the ground.

"Stay still," Faraday shouted, as I clambered to my feet.

We continued to stand there, just as mesmerised by the snakes all around us as they evidently were by us. It was the most hellish experience of my life, but it was about to get even worse.

"One's got in," Kate suddenly shouted.

I looked over my shoulder to see one of the vipers crawling between two candles and into the pentagram.

I sensed something move by my feet. I looked down and, to my horror, saw one of the cobras. It was so close I could have sworn that its flickering tongue brushed the side of my shoe. I shrank further back into the pentagram, in a complete state of funk by then, and with rivers of sweat pouring down my back. The snake coiled back in a striking pose, its hood fully open.

"Damn it," said Faraday. "There are too many of them. The pentagram can't hold them."

I looked round and saw an adder strike at Michael, making contact with the underside of his shoe before retreating away from him. I was so terrified I could feel my whole body shaking violently. In spite of Faraday's strict instruction not to, I started to prepare myself for a run across the writhing mass of snakes to the cellar door. I no longer cared what might be on the other side of it. Anything was preferable to getting bitten to death by venomous snakes in here, I thought.

Then I felt Faraday pass me something. It was a small glass bottle with a cork stopper in the top.

"What is it?" I said.

"Holy water," Faraday said, thrusting bottles into the hands of Kate and Michael.

"What do we do with it?"

"Throw it at the snakes. It might be our best chance."

Our situation was so desperate, I was prepared to try anything. I pulled the cork out of the bottle and flicked a spray of water at the two snakes closest to my part of the pentagram. The effect was instantaneous. The droplets landed on their bodies with a hiss, as if I was throwing acid at them, and they instantly started to back away. I noticed a cobra near Kate do the same, and there was a shout of triumph from Michael as he evidently had similar success on his side of the pentagram.

"Thank the Lord, it's working," he cried.

The four of us continued to throw holy water at the retreating snakes, who seemed to vanish into the shadows at the edge of the room. Soon we could see patches of bare floor that had previously been covered in their bodies, and before long there was only one left. It was one of the adders, and it looked like the first one that had appeared in the cellar that night.

It coiled itself, and struck as us, one final, angry, defiant time. It was too far away by then to pose any danger, but we were still close enough to see the fangs inside its mouth. And then it slid over to the corner of the room and disappeared.

"How on earth did von Draken's adept ever get that to happen?" said Michael.

"By using some very dark magic indeed," Faraday said. "The most powerful I have ever witnessed. I'm sorry, everyone. I underestimated this coven. I underestimated what it might be capable of."

We sat down on the floor, exhausted by the tension.

For over an hour, nothing else happened, but we remained silent, scanning the darkened room for the slightest sign of movement.

"I think it might be over," Faraday said at last. "After that last display, I can't imagine that von Draken's adept has anything left to give."

And yet we remained there for another hour, just in case a further attack came. When we finally stepped out of the pentagram and returned upstairs, I saw from the tall clock in the hallway that it was just after midnight. Looking outside, I was pleased to see that the mist that had earlier swallowed the house in a dank embrace had disappeared, and it was a clear night.

I felt hugely relieved that it was over, and the others clearly did, too. As we went into the kitchen, there was an almost celebratory atmosphere amongst us.

"I think I'll put some coffee on," I said. "Unless anyone would prefer something stronger?"

"Something stronger," they all said in unison, and I went into the dining room and returned with a bottle of whisky and four glasses.

"Thanks for getting us through that, Julian," Kate said. "You too, Michael. I'm never going to look at the world in the same way again, after tonight."

"I'm sorry you had to go through it," Faraday said. "That you all had to. But at least we're still here to tell the tale. That was a very close-run thing."

He looked exhausted. His cheeks appeared sunken, and there were dark rings around his eyes. For the first time since I had met him, he was looking his age.

"God, why did it have to be snakes?" Kate said, as I poured a generous measure of scotch into everyone's glass. "I'm absolutely petrified of them. Always have been."

"As it happens," Faraday said, "We learned today that this coven is most partial to serpent worship. It probably also explains why they sent one to Richard the other day, concealed in a parcel. So, this may prove to be something of a recurring theme in the days ahead."

"Just my luck," said Kate.

"You should come and live in Ireland," Michael said. "We don't get them over there."

"Well, here's to Saint Patrick," I said, raising the whiskey to my lips. "I think he might have been with us tonight, in spirit at least."

Suddenly, there was a terrific crashing sound from the hallway. It was the sound of the front door being flung open.

We all rushed out there. What I saw, even given what had happened already that night, simply defied belief.

Hundreds upon hundreds of bats were flying into the house through the open doorway. Within seconds, they had filled the room, and yet still they continued to pour in from the outside. I felt them brush against my body, and the thrum of their wings was extraordinarily loud.

"Back down to the cellar," Faraday shouted. "Come on, quickly."

Pushing our way through the mass of tiny, flying bodies, we stumbled down the stairs to the cellar, which was also thick with bats, but when we got into the room containing the pentagram it was as empty as it had been when we had left it.

We shut ourselves in and resumed our places within the protective circle. From the other side of the door, I could hear the high-pitched chatter of the bats, who were clearly now in complete command of the rest of the house.

"You must all forgive me," Faraday said, still catching his breath. "That was very poor judgement, on my part. I had no idea that von Draken's adept was powerful enough to sustain an attack for this long. I'm afraid we might be in here all night, after all."

I sank to the floor, tired beyond description, and the others followed suit. Leaning our bodies against each other, we stared out of the pentagram, waiting for whatever was coming next.

After a while, the noise of the bats started to fade, and then ceased completely.

"At least they appear to have gone now," Faraday said. "That's some small mercy."

"Almost an anti-climax, after the snakes," Kate said.

"Yeah, but those things piss and shit, like constantly," said Michael. "This house is going to reek like a chicken coop."

"Great," I said. "Another plus when I come to sell it."

"There won't be any physical trace," Faraday said, seeming to take this seriously.

We continued to sit there in silence, and I started to wonder, again, if the attack to which we had been subjected that night was over. I was so shattered by then, I felt as if I was going to fall asleep, but I sank instead into a sort of waking trance.

"Did you hear that?" Kate said, jolting me out of my reverie.

I strained my ears to listen but could hear nothing.

"What?" I whispered.

"Something upstairs," she said.

And then I heard it. It was a low moan, human sounding, soon joined by another, from a different part of the house. Then came the sound of another voice, and then another, until eventually there was a cacophony of moaning and wailing all around us.

"What is this?" I said, looking at Faraday. But he merely shook his head. He looked as confused as I felt.

Soon, the despairing wails had reached fever pitch, and we all covered our ears.

When the noise finally stopped, we started to relax a bit, although we didn't talk much. I was lost in my own thoughts by then, reflecting on the circumstances that had brought me to Badcombe Hollow, and all that had happened to me there, culminating in this night of unique horror.

I tried to think positively about the future; about how I was going to sell the house, and what I was going to do with the money; about finishing my book; and about how I might possibly try and resume my relationship with Megan.

But for some reason I struggled to do this, and every positive thought I tried to summon up, instantly gave way to a negative one. A dark depression settled over me. Everything seemed completely hopeless, and this feeling grew and grew into a mood of total despair. I wondered if life was even worth living, and if I wouldn't be better off just ending it. I felt like getting up and walking out of the pentagram and into whatever dark embrace might await me on the other side. For the first time in my life, I wanted to kill myself, and I didn't understand why.

But I soon discovered that in this, I was not alone.

"Is anyone else feeling incredibly depressed?" Kate said, her voice quavering. "Like, massively so?"

"Yes, I feel it," said Faraday.

"Like you wouldn't believe," I said.

"I feel bloody suicidal," Michael said. "Quite something for a devout Christian."

"Von Draken's adept is doing this," said Faraday. "It's not you. It's not any of us. This is all part of the attack. She's drawing on the dark energy in this house. She's tapping into every foul deed and despicable act that's ever been carried out or contemplated here and transferring it directly into our heads. This is her last throw of the dice. Her last chance to beat us tonight."

Kate started to sob. It seemed incongruous, somehow, given the toughness she had displayed up until that point, but I could easily have cried myself. I had never felt so terrible. I felt like I wanted to die.

"We have to pray," said Faraday. "It's all we can do."

"I don't know how to," I said.

"Just listen to me, and then repeat what I say," said Michael.

We formed a tight circle, facing one another, and linked hands, and then we started to pray. Some of the prayers I recognised dimly from childhood, but most were unknown to me. I prayed as hard as I could, believing the words I was repeating for the first time in my life.

I'm not sure how long we prayed, but it might have been as long as an hour. Eventually, the feeling of depression started to lift and then, at last, everything felt normal again.

"I truly believe that it's over now," said Faraday.

"Are you sure?" I said.

"As sure as I can be. We made it through. We've beaten them. For tonight, at least."

But we continued to sit there for another two hours, just to be sure. By the time we extinguished the candles and left the cellar to climb up to our rooms for some much-needed sleep, the cold, grey light of dawn was breaking over Badcombe Hollow.

CHAPTER FORTY-ONE

The Next Day

Late the next morning, after we had all caught a few hours' sleep, Faraday gathered us together in the kitchen for a council of war.

"Last night proved to be a dreadful and quite horrifying experience," he said, standing as he addressed us from the head of the island unit, around which we were eating a late breakfast.

"I must apologise to you all," he went on. "I had no idea that von Draken's adept was anywhere near so powerful. It would appear that I have greatly underestimated this coven. But no longer. We know what we are up against, now.

"That said, I don't anticipate a repeat of last night's events. The application of occult power on that scale will have been extraordinarily debilitating to von Draken's witch, possibly even taking her to the point of death. You can rest assured that she will not be up and about as we are this morning. My guess is that von Draken will keep her under wraps from now until Walpurgis Night, when he'll need her services more than ever. But we must nevertheless remain in a state of high alert. We need to keep the pentagram in the cellar stocked with candles and other provisions, and ready to be used at a moment's notice. Michael, one of your jobs today, please, is to ensure that this gets done."

Michael nodded his assent over the rim of his coffee cup.

"Now," said Faraday, "It's time to tell you about the visit that Richard and I made to Malachy yesterday. It was rather interesting, to say the least."

Due to the excitement of the previous night, and our exhausted state afterwards, we had not yet had the chance to discuss what we had been told by the satanist. I let Faraday do the talking, and he spent the next ten minutes explaining Malachy's analysis of the tape of the sabbat, and its possible implications.

"Bloody hell," Kate breathed softly, when he had finished. "So, we're basically talking about the end of the world. The apocalypse. The end of days. That's really what we're talking about?"

"It would appear so," said Faraday, pouring himself another cup of coffee with a calmness that belied the enormity of this state of affairs. "A demon of that magnitude, unleashed upon the world, would create a literal hell on earth. Assuming, of course, that von Draken and his coven are capable of such a thing. Before last night, I would have said that they had virtually no chance of making this happen. Now, given what we know they can do, I'd say they have slightly more chance, although it's still a considerable long shot."

"I'm never going to look at the world in the same way again, after last night," I said. "Yesterday, I thought what Malachy told us was the biggest load of nonsense I'd ever heard. But now, after what we saw in the cellar last night, I'm prepared to believe anything."

"I feel the same way as Richard," said Kate. "Up until now, I've wanted to be involved in the fight against satanism because of the terrible damage it does to those who get involved in it, and even more because of the vile things that satanists themselves do to other people. But sitting here this morning, I realise that we're dealing with a whole different level of evil. I suppose you could say that I now believe there's a supernatural element to this, and I'm not sure that I did believe that before. I thought it was all trickery and sleight of hand. And people doing horrible things. Sick, disgusting, horrible things. But still just people doing bad stuff. But now I know it's different. Now I truly understand that there is a dark force out there, a demonic force. Julian, I honestly think this coven is capable of anything. I think we need to take this very seriously indeed."

"How do you feel about it?" Faraday said to Michael. "As a member of the church, you're the most devout of all of us. Do you think that such a thing can be done? Do you believe that an arch-demon like Astaroth can be raised?"

"It's never been done before," Michael said, thoughtfully. "But that doesn't mean it's not possible. Demons exist in another dimension to ours; a different time and space; a different reality, if you will. Therefore, on those relatively rare occasions when people have tried to commune directly with them – as Crowley famously did, for example – they've attempted to do so by stepping outside of our reality and entering the spirit world. So, the piece of ground they were standing on when they did their final spell may have looked the same, but it wasn't. It was part of another reality. You might say it was a case of going to meet the demon in their world, rather than bringing them here. Not that they would have necessarily appreciated the distinction themselves, but in effect, that's what they were doing."

"How did they do it?" I said.

"Painstaking preparation," said Michael. "Usually over many months, sometimes years. It would involve fasting, meditation, rituals – all designed to get one into a state whereby one can pass temporarily out of our realm, and into the realm of the demon. It involves leaving one's corporeal body behind and entering a different plane of reality. Some would call this the astral plane. Needless to say, it requires a lot of training and discipline to even attempt such a thing, not to mention the will to do so in the first place. Most of those who have tried it have either failed, given up or gone mad in the process.

"But this is somewhat different. What we're talking about here is von Draken's coven conjuring up an opening in the fabric of time and space. Like with the snakes last night, but on a far more gigantic scale It's about creating a portal and getting Astaroth to enter the world through it. It's about bringing the demon here, into our world. Bringing it here through a gateway that they're going to create."

He sighed heavily and shook his head.

"It's an understatement to say that this is very heavy stuff indeed. I must admit, I'm struggling to get my head around it. Even for a Catholic theologian, this is way out there. This is pure metaphysics. So, Julian, in answer to your question, I very much doubt that it's even remotely possible, but then again, why take the chance?"

"Yes, that's essentially my thinking on the matter," said Faraday. "I find it virtually inconceivable that what von Draken has planned can be made to work but given the cataclysmic consequences if he did pull it off, then if there's only the scintilla of a chance, we should do everything possible to try and prevent it."

"Such as what?" said Kate.

"We prevent the coven from getting into the temple on the evening of 30th April and performing their ritual. That would appear to be the essence of the matter."

"Well, that should be simple enough," I said. "They didn't get to frighten us out of here so, now all we have to do is sit tight, and keep the doors locked. Right?"

"Possibly," said Faraday. "But we're still grappling with some unknowns. We still don't know the way into the temple. If the entrance is somewhere outside the confines of the house, then the coven could theoretically sneak in there, and perform the ritual beneath our feet without us even knowing about it."

"Their desperation to force me out of the house would suggest otherwise," I said. "That must imply that the entrance to the temple is somewhere within the grounds of Badcombe Hollow."

"You're probably right about that," said Faraday. "But we still don't know for sure. We also don't know the lengths to which the coven might be prepared to go to take the house over by force. Would they be willing to countenance murdering us, for example?"

"Surely von Draken wouldn't go that far," said Kate. "I mean, it's one thing to try and scare us out of our wits, drive us mad, even, with an occult display like the one he put on last night, but actually killing us is a whole other ball game. There would be evidence, consequences. He'd go to prison for the rest of his life."

"He may not care about that," said Faraday. "If he wants to raise this demon badly enough, then he may not care about the consequences. And according to Malachy, the raising ritual will involve a human sacrifice. So, one may assume that he's already crossed the line when it comes to contemplating murder. Besides, if he's successful, then there won't be any repercussions. We'll be living in a whole new world; a satanic realm. What are four dead amongst thousands, millions of dead? I don't think we can take anything for granted, as far as this man is concerned. Who knows how far he may be prepared to go?"

"Not a comforting thought," I muttered.

We finished the rest of our breakfast in silence.

"What's the plan for today?" said Kate, as we were clearing things away.

"I'm going to have to leave you to your own devices," said Faraday. "I need to go to Oxford and pay a visit to my college. I need to do some research into this demon that von Draken is planning to raise. There are some rare volumes there that are kept under lock and key, away from the general public. Fortunately, the curator happens to be an old friend of mine. I'll be back before it gets dark.

"Save for checking that our various precautions are as they should be, I'd suggest that the rest of you have a light day and recover your strength after the excitement of last night."

"I know that I could do with going back to bed for a few hours," said Kate.

"Me too," said Michael. "I feel completely exhausted."

"I'm going to go into Marlborough for a bit," I said. "I need to run a few errands, and I'm also going to go to an estate agent and get them to put this place on the market. Once we get through Walpurgis Night, I want to get out of here as soon as possible."

"I can't say that I blame you on that score," said Faraday. "Very well, then. We'll rendezvous back here this evening."

"I'll cook dinner," I said.

With our plans for the day settled, Michael and Kate went upstairs, whilst Faraday went to gather his things before setting off, and I tidied up in the kitchen. Once I had everything squared away, I went through into the hallway, where I met Faraday coming down the stairs, carrying an attaché case in one hand, and with his coat folded neatly over his arm. I was about to wish him a good journey when we heard a piercing scream from above us.

Moments later, Kate appeared at the top of the staircase.

"I saw it," she gasped.

"Saw what?" I said, before Faraday could, although I was fairly sure I knew what it was that she had seen.

"That thing you told us about," she said, with disgust in her voice. "The mad old woman, dressed in animal skins."

She suddenly cast a fearful look at some sound behind her, but it was only Michael, coming to see what all the fuss was about.

"What's going on?" he said.

"I saw that thing," she said.

"What, the old hag?"

"I suppose so. I don't know what it was. I just know that it scared the shit out of me."

She came down the stairs, her arms wrapped tightly around her sides, as if exhibiting her revulsion at what she had just seen.

"Bloody hell, that was horrible," she said.

"Did it attack you?" I said.

"No. It just appeared in front of me."

"Tell us exactly what happened, Kate," said Faraday, speaking for the first time.

"Okay. Well, I got up to my room and I lay down on the bed and closed my eyes, and then when I opened them, she was standing there at the foot of the bed. Hence the screaming," she added.

"What happened then?" said Michael, joining us at the bottom of the staircase.

"Nothing," said Kate. "She just stood there for a few seconds while I screamed at her, and then she sort of faded away into nothing, and I got the hell out of there."

"I don't get it," I said to Faraday. "How can von Draken's adept be capable of conjuring up that thing this morning, after the sort of night she just had?"

"It really is most curious," said Faraday, shaking his head thoughtfully. "I must confess, I am at a loss as to how to explain it. I'd always assumed that the creature you had described so vividly was some kind of abhuman, created by the coven as a way of intimidating Alan Mackay, and then subsequently your good self. Now, I'm not so sure."

"But what could it be, if not the magical creation of the coven?" I said.

"I really don't know."

Faraday looked as puzzled as I had ever seen him during our short acquaintance.

"Michael, I'm going to be sleeping with you this morning," said Kate.

The young priest raised his eyebrows.

"I'm serious. I really need to get some sleep, and there's no way I'm going to be able to sleep by myself up there, after what just happened. We are platonically sharing a bed for the remainder of our stay here. Understood?"

"Understood," said Michael.

I looked over at Faraday, as if awaiting instructions, so used was I by now to accepting him as the leader of our group. He still appeared deep in thought.

"Well," he said at last, "I don't imagine we shall solve the mystery of this spectre, or whatever it is, by standing here. I suppose we might as well get on with our day. But take great care, everyone. There is real danger in this house."

"And I'll be sure to mention that to the estate agent," I said, as we all dispersed.

****

An hour later, I stepped out of the estate agent's office and onto Marlborough's bustling high street. Needless to say, I hadn't mentioned Badcombe Hollow's resident old hag, or the pentagram in the cellar, or the satanic temple beneath the long barrow, or the various occultists who had been drawn to the house by its dark energy, and its even darker reputation. But they had been suitably impressed by what I had chosen to tell them, and readily agreed to take the property on, confident that they would be able to facilitate a swift sale.

"There's a lot of demand for places on the west side of Marlborough," the agent had said. He was a callow young man, about half my age, to whom I had taken a mild dislike. "There are some lovely properties out that way. Very popular with the London set looking to move out into the sticks. They tend to be cash rich, after selling the pad in SW1 or wherever, so it usually all goes through quite quickly. I'd be very confident about selling this for you. Should be able to get at least a million and a half for it. At least. You might want to think of putting it on for one point seven-five. Anyway, we'll have a better idea of all that after I've been out to have a look. You looking to buy another place around here, by any chance?"

"No," I said. "I own a pad near SW1, as it happens. I'm going to move back there."

"Ah, right. Got it. Very nice. Well, let me know if you change your mind. I've got a very smart town house in Marlborough up for sale at the moment."

I had explained that the property wasn't yet legally mine but shortly would be, and we agreed that as soon as the formalities were completed, they would come and do a survey, and then put it on the market, with a view to it being marketed locally, online and in *Country Life*.

As I was walking back to the car, spending lots of money in my head, somebody called out my name. I looked around to see Megan standing a few feet away.

"Megan. What a surprise," I said. It was all I could think of to say.

She looked as lovely as ever. The sheen of her complexion, the glossy ponytail, the half-smile, the willowy figure – it was all as I had indelibly committed to memory. It was what I had longed for, these past several days since we had parted on such bad terms.

"Not really," she said. "I saw your car, so I've sort of been loitering around, hoping to see you. I was going to phone you, actually."

"Well, it's certainly good to see you," I said.

There was an awkward silence. We both seemed unsure as to how to proceed from this point.

"How about a drink?" we said at the same time, making us laugh, and breaking the tension.

We went into one of the high-street pubs. It was the same place where I had gone for a drink on my first evening in Marlborough, which now seemed a lifetime ago. As it was such a pleasant spring day, we carried our drinks out into a little courtyard, which was bathed in sunshine.

"Look," said Megan, as soon as we were seated, "I'm really sorry about the way things ended between us. I said some very harsh things, which I deeply regret now. I wasn't exactly thinking clearly at the time."

"I'm not surprised, given what happened," I said. "And it's me who should be sorry. It was bad enough you getting assaulted in my house once, let alone twice."

"It wasn't your fault. But it was a horrible experience, being grabbed like that, and practically throttled. Is she … it … still around?"

"Made an appearance earlier today, as it happens."

"Oh, my God. Was it … you know … violent?"

"No. Not this time, Thank goodness. It was just an appearance, and a fleeting one at that."

Megan shuddered.

"I presume that you coming out of that estate agent's just now means that you're putting the house on the market," she said.

"Yes. Once it's gone through probate. I naturally forgot to mention that it's haunted, or cursed, or whatever the hell is going on there. But yes, it'll go up for sale as soon as possible. I truly can't wait to get shot of the place."

An image of writhing snakes on the cellar floor flashed through my mind.

"And once we get through Walpurgis Night, of course."

"We?" said Megan.

"What do you mean?"

"You just said we. Once we get through Walpurgis Night."

"You'll be pleased to hear that I've enlisted some help. Well, not so much enlisted it as have it suddenly appear. Bit of a complicated story."

There was a long silence.

"I've missed you," said Megan.

"I've missed you, too," I said.

"I want to start over, Richard. I want things to be like they were. Or like they were getting to be, before that bitch creature intervened. I was having such a great time before."

"There's nothing I'd like more," I said. "Plus, I am selling that eff-ing house."

"Well, I think that's a wonderful idea, obviously. But I want more than that. More than just dating you."

"What do you mean?"

"I mean, I want to help again. Like I was trying to help before. Before that thing attacked me."

"Jeez, Megan, I don't know how I'd feel about that. I mean, I definitely want to see you again. But this thing at Badcombe Hollow; it's all gone a bit crazy. You can't imagine what's been going on, the past few days."

"So, tell me about it," said Megan. "Please. I've been so worried about you."

And so, I told her. I told her about visiting the spiritualist in Bath, the one whose business card we had found on the day we searched Alan's house. I told her about contacting Faraday, and how he had initially rebutted me, only to end up saving me, on the night I had spied on the sabbat. I told her about visiting Malachy, the satanist, and what he had told us about what the coven had planned for Walpurgis Night, and how this could bring about the end of the world, as fantastical as that sounded. I told her about Kate and Michael, Faraday's lieutenants, and how we had all pledged to see this thing through and ensure that Ernst von Draken did not have the opportunity to even attempt to enact his ghastly scheme. And finally, I told her about what had happened in the cellar the previous night.

"It's simply incredible," Megan said, when I had finished.

"I'm struggling to believe it all myself," I said "And yet, it's happening. I tell myself that I just have to get through the next few days and then, one way or the other, it will all be over."

"Well, at least you have people helping you, now. It must be quite a houseful over there."

"Faraday is certainly a character," I said. "He's like a man out of time; from another era entirely. But I must say, I'm glad he's around. Kate and Michael, too," I added.

"Safety in numbers," said Megan. "Actually, I'd feel a lot safer about going into that house, now that there's a group of you in there. I want to be part of your life, Richard, and that means helping you get through this. Besides, I can be of specific assistance, by the sounds of it."

"What do you mean?"

"You said that the coven is going to perform their ritual in the temple – assuming they ever manage to get into it – but that the manifestation of the demon will occur somewhere else, at another sacred site somewhere near Avebury. Well, I doubt that even your Professor Faraday knows more about the sacred sites of Avebury than I do."

"I'm sure you're right about that," I said. "And the more of us there are, fighting against von Draken, the better. Safety in numbers, like you say. But I can't tolerate the thought of putting you in danger. If anything happened to you, I'd never forgive myself."

"I'm not finished. There's something else. It's about that picture. The portrait of Dorian Slake. The one at the bottom of the stairs in the house that kept flying off the wall."

"What about it?"

"Actually, it's not the picture, so much as the numbers on the back of the picture. I had a thought about it. About what they might mean. It's just a theory, but I've been thinking about it, on and off, the past few days, and I think I might be onto something."

"What? Tell me."

"No. Not yet. I need to see the numbers again. It might just be a stupid idea. Let me come to the house and look at them. Then, if I'm right, I can explain it to you, and to this Professor Faraday."

"I don't know. I hate the idea of you getting into all of this. Last night was just so awful, and …"

"I'm in," said Megan. "It's settled. Look, I'm collecting my father from hospital this evening, but how about I come round to the house tomorrow morning, and we'll all put our heads together?"

I thought for a moment.

"Okay," I said. "You've convinced me. But you stay with us the whole time you're in there."

"No argument there."

"Thank you," I said.

I reached over the table and squeezed her hand gently. She squeezed back. Even this smallest of physical gestures was enough to make my heart skip a beat.

"I don't go to Devizes for another couple of hours," she said. "Will you come back to my house with me?"

"Your house?"

"Well, my rented room, to be more precise. But there's no one else there. The owners have gone off on another one of their trips. Will you come back there with me?"

"Sure. Why?"

"I think you know, darling. I think you know."

****

412

I lay back in the luxuriant comfort of Megan's bed, looking at the blue sky outside through a bay window above a dressing table. Birds were singing in the garden, and a light breeze was drifting through the window onto my face. Beside me, a half-sleeping Megan lay nestled in my arms.

I felt truly relaxed for the first time in weeks, and could easily have drifted off to sleep myself, but I didn't want to miss a second of my newfound contentment. Only the shadow of Walpurgis Night hung over me now, and with any luck that would be but a memory in a few days' time.

Beside me, I felt Megan stir.

"I could lie here forever," she breathed into my ear.

"I was just thinking the same thing myself," I murmured back. "Want to try?"

"Like you wouldn't believe," she said, sitting up in bed and rubbing her eyes. "But I've got things to do before I go and collect my father, and you need to get back to your little band of ghost hunters at Badcombe Hollow."

"Damn. I knew there was something."

"Until the next time?"

"Most definitely," I said, pulling her towards me and kissing her.

With some effort we pulled ourselves away from one another and got dressed, and then made our way downstairs through the rambling, empty house. I suddenly realised that it had been several hours since I had left Badcombe Hollow, and the others were probably wondering where I was.

I looked at my phone, which I had switched to silent back when Megan and I had gone into the pub and saw that I had received a message from Kate, which I opened.

"Where are you?!?" it read. "Are you OK?"

"Fine," I texted back. "Bumped into someone. Sorry. On the way home."

"All ready?" said Megan, appearing beside me.

Taking me by the hand, she led me out of the house and through the garden to the street, where my car was parked next to hers.

She folded herself into my arms, and we shared a long kiss.

"I'm going to miss you," I said.

"It's only until tomorrow."

"You're really sure about that? You know, coming to the house and everything?"

"More sure than ever. I'm falling in love with you, Richard. There's no way I'm just going to walk away from this. I'm in it till the end."

I kissed her again. I didn't want to let go of her.

"I'll be there by ten," she said, as she got into her car. "See you tomorrow."

She started the engine and blew me a kiss through the window.

I watched her drive away, feeling a curious mixture of euphoria and anxiety. In some ways, it felt like the happiest moment of my life, but I couldn't help but wonder if I was doing a very selfish thing by allowing Megan to involve herself once more in this whole gruesome business. Part of me knew that I was potentially putting her in grave danger.

And yet, I was missing her already, and the hours that were to pass before I would next see her seemed already to stretch interminably in front of me, just seconds after her departure.

Surely, she would be safe, with Faraday and the rest of us to protect her, I told myself.

Doing my best to put such fears out of my mind, I drove back to Badcombe Hollow.

CHAPTER FORTY-TWO

The Numbers on the Portrait

"I need to see the portrait of Dorian Slake," said Megan. "You see, I think it might hold a rather important clue."

It was the following morning – three days before Walpurgis Night – and Megan had just arrived at Badcombe Hollow.

There had been mixed feelings amongst the others when I had raised the subject of Megan helping us, over dinner the previous evening. Kate and Michael had been keen to augment our numbers in any way possible, given the evident power of the coven we were up against, and how stumped we all still were as to the location of the temple entrance. But Faraday was more reluctant.

"It could be incredibly dangerous for her," he had said, filling his pipe at the head of the dining table, as Kate and Michael cleared away the remains of our meal. "The events last night in the cellar, and those following the sabbat, have demonstrated two things. Firstly, the coven is quite prepared to deploy violence, and even to kill, in order to achieve their ends. Secondly, they are able to wield genuine occult power.

"And they'll be getting desperate by now," he added. "With Walpurgis Night so close, and with their temple so tantalisingly out of reach, who knows what lengths they may go to. We were woefully unprepared and, frankly, all over the blasted place at that wretched sabbat. You and Kate are lucky to be alive. And last night, as you well know, was a very close-run thing. I'm sorry to say, we've stayed one step ahead of them by a hair's breadth, up to now, and things could be about to get considerably worse. I'm not sure that I'd want to put someone else in this sort of danger."

"I understand," I said. "And it's troubling to me, too. In fact, if anything were to happen to Megan, then I'm not sure I'd be able to live with myself. But she knows about the risks. That thing upstairs has gone for her twice. So, she wouldn't be going into this with her eyes closed. And we need all the help we can get."

"No argument there," Faraday conceded, as I poured the remains of a bottle of red wine into our glasses. I had been down to the cellar before dinner and picked out two premium quality Burgundies from Alan's wine collection. Which was now my wine collection, I had reminded myself as I carried the bottles upstairs. I had been doing a lot of that recently, around the house. I was still finding it hard to adjust to my new situation, amidst everything else that was going on in my life at that moment.

"Plus, she does know an awful lot about the pre-history of this area," I said. "We've already speculated that there could be some connection there, given that the temple is sitting underneath a Neolithic burial mound."

As I said this, I found myself nodding in the direction of the doors onto the terrace, beyond which lay the long grass mound, invisible in the darkness.

"I agree that her input in that regard could be very useful indeed," Faraday said, as the others joined us at the table with a tray of coffee.

"Very well," he said at last. "We should take up your friend's offer of assistance. But for her own safety, we shall keep a very close eye on her, and she should not go anywhere in the house unaccompanied."

"Nobody should go anywhere in this house unaccompanied," said Kate.

"You're likely correct about that," said Faraday. "Although I am fervently hoping for a quiet night, tonight, following yesterday's various excitements."

He set down his coffee cup and sighed.

"And now, if you'll excuse me," he said, "I need to read through some of the material I collected from Oxford today. I suggest that the rest of you get some much-needed sleep."

Nobody demurred from this, and a short time after Faraday had left the room, the rest of us took ourselves off to bed.

The night which followed was as quiet as Faraday had hoped it would be, with no repeat of the previous night's occult attack, or sightings of the abhuman. Assembling in the kitchen for breakfast the next morning, it seemed that everyone was more refreshed than they had been for the past couple of days, although Faraday confessed that he had been up until the small hours, studying the two ancient, cracked leather tomes on the occult which he had brought back with him from Oxford the day before. However, he ruefully admitted that he had gleaned little of value from them, on the subject of the demon, Astaroth, and what might be involved when it came to summoning him to our earthly realm.

Megan arrived just as we were clearing up the breakfast things. She seemed pleased to see me, but I couldn't help but detect a certain trepidation on her part when she first stepped into the hallway.

"No sightings for the past twenty-four hours," I said, as I led her into the kitchen.

We assembled around the island unit and, after making the introductions, Megan got straight down to business, and asked if she could see the Slake portrait.

I fetched it from the cellar and laid it face up in its broken frame on the counter. The satanist stared up at us from his dark and gloomy milieu, empty save for skull and a solitary vase of white flowers. I thought how incongruous they seemed, and Megan must have read my mind, by pointing at them.

"You know," she said, "This isn't what this is about, but I do rather wonder about that vase of white flowers on the dresser, behind Slake."

"There's a skull, as well," said Kate.

"I know," said Megan. "That's probably more generic. But the flowers intrigue me. Why did he put them there?"

"You mean, why did she put them there," I said. "I don't think it's a self-portrait, any longer. I think the 'DS' in the bottom corner stands for Doreen Smithers, not Dorian Slake."

"Okay, sure, but same difference. Regardless of who did it, why put the flowers there?"

"To symbolise something, presumably," said Michael.

"Maybe," said Megan. "But they could have come from this garden. In fact, they probably did."

She turned to face me.

"Have you noticed a shrub with those sort of flowers?" she said.

"I can't say that I have," I said. "But it's been winter. Things are only just starting to come out."

"It was just a thought," Megan said. "Anyway, that wasn't why I wanted to come over today. This is the reason."

She lifted the painting off the counter and turned it over, so that we were looking at the back, and the curious set of numbers written there.

100685149763103699086715105677116668
189693112634099699152696118649047693
066647156656118681125708225668196629

We all looked expectantly at Megan.

"Look, it's just an idea," she said. "But I had a thought about these numbers. It's the main reason why I wanted to come over today. I had this idea, you see, except I obviously don't feel so confident about it now, with you all here."

"Please carry on, and don't worry about that," said Faraday. "None of us here claim to be omniscient, and we're all grateful for your help. Tell us your thoughts."

Megan looked down at the back of the portrait and ran her finger along the lines of numbers.

"Well," she said, slowly, "You see, the thing is, there's something about these numbers. They look completely random, and they all run together. But look how many numbers there are on each line."

"Thirty-six," I said. "I remember counting them, when I first wrote them down."

"Exactly," said Megan. "Thirty-six. There are thirty-six numbers on each of the three lines."

"So, one hundred and eight in total," said Michael.

"Yes, but I don't think that's what's significant. Thirty-six divided by six, is six. So, it's possible that we're looking at a series of six-digit numbers – six on each line, and eighteen in total."

"I see what you mean," said Faraday. "But why should it necessarily be six-digit numbers? Thirty-six is also divisible by three."

"Or eighteen," said Kate. "Or twelve, for that matter."

"Yes, but bear with me for a moment, and imagine that these are six-digit numbers," said Megan. "Because if they're eighteen six-digit numbers strung together, then it's possible that they could be …"

"Gridlines," Faraday finished for her. "Of course. Why didn't I think of that? These numbers could be gridlines on a map."

"I reckon so," said Megan. "In which case, the first two digits in each six-digit sequence identify the longitudinal grid lines on a typical Ordnance Survey map, and the third digit refers to the distance between that line, and the next line across. Same applies to the last three digits, to measure the latitude. Anyway, I'm sure I don't need to tell you how to read a map, but I'm almost certain that Dorian Slake wrote down these numbers as a reference to gridline markers on a map."

"And I'm almost certain that you're correct," said Faraday. "Well done, Megan. Well done, indeed."

Megan gave a little beam of pleasure, making me feel proud of her.

"The question now," said Faraday, "Is what they might mark."

"I'll get the map," I said.

I returned with the Ordnance Survey map of Avebury and the surrounding area. It was the one I had bought in London, before I first came here. Taking the map into the dining room, where there was more space, I unfolded it and spread it across the table.

Leaning over the map with a black felt tip pen, Megan asked one of us to call out the numbers in groups of six, which I did, and then she found each mark on the map, and marked it with a black cross. By the time we had finished, there were eighteen black crosses on the map.

"Okay," said Faraday. "They all appear on the map. So, what do they mark?"

"There are some fairly obvious places," said Megan. "Sacred places, you might say. Certainly, places of interest in the landscape. You've got Silbury Hill, Windmill Hill, the Devil's Dolmen, barrow locations, the middle of the main stone circle at Avebury."

She continued to run her hand lightly over the crosses on the map.

"Look," she said. "You've got the place where the Ridgeway crosses the Wansdyke. Places where trackways meet are sometimes thought to possess some mystical significance. And there are a few churches, maybe, it's hard to tell, but I reckon the cross in Avebury village is on St James' Church, and that makes sense, too, because churches were very often built upon old pagan places of worship. The new religion appropriates the sacred sites of the old, and all that."

"What about Badcombe Hollow?" I asked.

"No, that's not marked."

That seemed odd, I thought but didn't say.

"Let's make a proper list and see what we've got," said Megan.

I called out the numbers again, and this time Megan jotted them down on a pad, and then after studying the map, she made a neat annotation next to each number. She stood back when she had finished, and we all looked at the list.

100685	Silbury Hill
149763	Barbary Castle
103699	Avebury Stone Circle
086715	Windmill Hill
105677	West Kennet Long Barrow
116668	East Kennet Long Barrow
189693	St Mary's Church, Marlborough
112634	Adam's Grave Long Barrow
099699	St James' Church, Avebury
152696	Devil's Dolmen, Clatford Bottom
118649	Ridgeway and Wansdyke Path Intersection
047693	Cherhill Monument
066647	Kitchen Barrow Hill Long Barrow
156656	Barrow Copse Long Barrow
118681	The Sanctuary, Overton Hill
125708	Ridgeway and Herepath Intersection
225668	Multi-Trackway Junction, Savernake Forest
196629	St Andrew's Church, Wootton Rivers

"Well," said Michael, "They all seem to fit the bill of sacred site. Some more folkloric than others, perhaps, like the trackway crossings, but all of them with some kind of sacred or mystical association.”

“But no Badcombe Hollow,” I said. “That doesn’t make sense. And what’s the connection between the places?”

“I think the connection is on the map,” said Faraday. “And Badcombe Hollow is very much part of it. May I have the pen?”

Megan handed it to him.

“And I’m going to need a ruler,” he said.

I recalled seeing one on the desk in the study and went to fetch it.

Handing the ruler to Faraday, we all stepped back, and watched him as he stooped over the map. After studying it for a moment, he laid the ruler on the map, and started to draw a series of lines, connecting the crosses that Megan had made.

When he had finished, he tossed the pen down on the map and stood back, so that we could all see what he had drawn.

“Malachy said that this house and its long barrow likely stood at the source of a powerful mystical energy,” said Faraday. “He thought it might be some nodal point, connecting up various scared sites. It would appear that he was correct in his supposition.”

We continued to look down at the map, and the shape Faraday had drawn.

It was a giant pentagram, just like the one down in the cellar, and Badcombe Hollow was right in the middle of it.

CHAPTER FORTY-THREE

The Markers in the Landscape

Nobody said anything for a long moment, as we all stared down at the shape on the map.

"A pentagram," said Michael. "How very predictable."

Faraday ran his finger gently along the lines of the five-pointed star.

"This confirms why Badcombe Hollow is so very important to von Draken's coven," he said. "Or rather, why the temple they're so desperate to get into was built here in the first place. The burial mound out in the garden is at the centre of a sacred grid. No wonder it contains so much occult power. The ancient people who built it would have detected this power, or their shamans would have done, and so they chose to bury their dead here. And then, many centuries later, Dorian Slake arrives on the scene, and together with Doreen Smithers, they connect the dots and discover the hidden pentagram in the landscape. This is why Slake chose to build his temple to Satan here."

"Okay," said Kate. "But if that's the why, it still doesn't tell us the where. I mean, it doesn't tell us where the entrance to the temple is."

"No, that's true," said Faraday, tapping the map lightly with the ruler. "It's a highly intriguing development, and a good piece of deduction by Megan, but I'm not sure that it moves us any further forward, with regard to the matter at hand."

"It might tell us something else, though," I said.

Everyone turned to look at me.

"What I mean is," I went on, "It might not tell us where the entrance to the underground temple is, but it might still hold a clue to the ceremony on Walpurgis Night.

"Remember when we went to see Malachy?" I said, addressing Faraday. "Just as we were leaving, he said that the raising ceremony will be held in the temple, but the actual raising itself – the moment when the demon Astaroth steps through a portal and enters our world – will occur somewhere else; somewhere nearby. If that's the case, it would be logical that this place would also be located on one of the points of the pentagram, would it not?"

"Yes, I suppose it would," said Faraday.

"In which case," I said, "We're looking for a portal location in the landscape immediately surrounding Badcombe Hollow, marked by one of these crosses. I think I have an idea where it might be."

"Really?" said Faraday. I couldn't help but detect a trace of surprise in his voice.

"Yes, I reckon so," I went on, trying to sound more confident than I felt. "There is a place, you see, on one of those markers, which could be a highly suitable location for opening a portal to another dimension. Or at least, a place where someone might try to do so, if they believed such a thing was possible. It's also remote and discreet, and not too far away from this house. I think I know where the doorway is."

I looked over at Megan, and she smiled knowingly at me.

****

We ended up walking there. Or rather, four of us did. Michael stayed behind to keep watch over the house, just in case von Draken or one of his acolytes decided to put in an appearance. There had been talk of driving there, to save time, but given that the walk from the nearest parking place was not much further than walking there directly from Badcombe Hollow, we chose to walk. If the place Megan and I were thinking of was indeed the planned location of the demon raising, we were keen to measure in real time the distance from there to the house, and the temple beneath the burial mound. Besides, it was a pleasant, sunny day by then, and I think we all fancied the idea of some fresh air. In the event, it took about three quarters of an hour to walk there.

Faraday, predictably enough, was reasonably well schooled in the essentials of pre-history, but even he was somewhat taken aback by the sight of the Devil's Dolmen as we approached it.

"Goodness me, that really is most impressive," he said, as we stood beside the group of upright stones with a great boulder laid precariously across the top. Stones which had been put there some six thousand years previously by the tribes who had once inhabited this plain.

"And I assume that's the doorway, or portal," said Faraday, pointing towards the triangular shaped gap between the stones.

"It is," Megan said. "That's the doorway to the afterlife, for those who were buried here. Or so the ancients believed, at any rate. That's why this sort of stone structure is known as a portal tomb, and why it would have been situated here, next to a gigantic burial mound."

"Eh?" said Kate. "There's a burial mound here?"

"Yes. You're standing on it. The mound part has long been erased by centuries of ploughing, but we're basically standing on a megalithic cemetery. There's probably a lot of people down there."

"Whose souls would have passed through that portal, subsequent to burial," said Faraday.

"So people once believed," said Megan.

"And hence if something can leave our earthly realm via that doorway, presumably something else could use it as a way of getting here?"

"Presumably. I've never actually considered that as a realistic proposition. Until today, this was just folklore to me. But yes, I suppose so."

Faraday rubbed his chin thoughtfully, and then stepped forward to inspect the jumble of stones more closely.

"Tell us more about this place, Megan," he said.

And so Megan recounted what little was known about the Devil's Dolmen, just as she had for me, several weeks previously, on the first day I ever met her. As I listened to her expound upon the subject that she had such a passion for, I felt vindicated at having brought her into the group, and immensely pleased that she was there with us. But most of all, I was just glad that she was there with me, and that our relationship, which had appeared utterly doomed, just a day previously, was now stronger than ever. I was as keen as anyone to get to the bottom of the mystery of the temple, and to thwart Ernst von Draken's plans for Walpurgis Night, but more than anything, I wanted to get the next few days over and done with, so that I could begin building a future with Megan.

She came to the end of her peroration, finishing with the story she had told me about filling the depressions at the top of the capstone with water, late at night, and then returning in the morning to see if the water had been drunk by the devil himself.

"So, you see, there is an awful lot of folklore and legend about this monument," she said.

"And this could be the place where this whole situation reaches its conclusion," said Kate. "Which would mean that we're standing on the site of the apocalypse, brought about by whatever appears through that portal between the stones. The day after tomorrow."

"I suppose so," said Megan. "That part's not really my area."

We looked over towards Faraday, who had resumed his close inspection of the Devil's Dolmen and was peering through the presumed portal. Seeming to sense that he was being addressed, he turned around to face us.

"You mean," he said, "Will the end of the world take place in this valley, unless we stop it? I very much doubt it. But better not to take the chance, eh? Anyway, the more likely scenario is that von Draken and his demented coven kill an innocent person. That is most certainly something we must try and stop."

"And the sacrifice will happen here?" I said. "I mean, according to Malachy, this is where it all reaches its conclusion, right?"

Faraday stepped back from the dolmen and reached into his jacket pocket for his pipe.

"Almost certainly here," he said. "That would be my assumption. They'll conduct most of the ceremony in the temple, and then the whole coven will make their way over here, all thirteen of them, along with one helpless captive. Once they're here, they'll enact the final part of the ceremony, and get Astaroth, the demon, to step through the gap in the stones, and enter our world. They will then present the demon with his human sacrifice. And then, presumably, hell is unleashed here on earth."

He shrugged and rolled his eyes.

"That's my supposition, for what it's worth," he said. "Anyway, it's what the coven seems to believe. My main priority is to prevent von Draken from killing someone."

"Assuming this isn't all nonsense," I said, "What's the point of no return?"

"What do you mean?" said Faraday.

"I mean, let's say, the coven somehow gets into the temple, and does whatever it needs to do, and then de-camps over here, and does whatever it needs to do. At what point does it all become too late for them to be prevented from enacting their diabolical plan? Would it be here? Or would it be back at the temple?"

"Oh, I see what you're getting at," said Faraday. "Well, there is very little precedent for us to go on, as you can likely imagine, but theoretically, it should be possible to prevent the raising from here, right up until the point at which the demon manifests."

"And after that, it'll be too late to do anything about it?" I pressed.

"Presumably," he said. "It's really all speculation, you know."

"Isn't it possible to reverse a raising in the first few moments after it occurs?" said Kate. "I'm sure I've read that, somewhere. But it requires another sacrifice ... or something?"

She looked over at Faraday for guidance.

"Yes, that is apparently the case," he said. "Or, so people have theorised, at any rate. But yes, there is folklore on the subject that suggests that in the moments immediately following the raising of a demon, it should be possible to reverse the procedure – to send the demon back into its own dimension – by sacrificing a member of the coven who performed the raising. The demon can't return empty-handed, you see. An offering has to be made.

"This is all myth, by the way," he finished.

He nodded over towards the dolmen.

"Perhaps one would need to force a member of the coven through that opening in the stones," he said, causing us all to stare at the dolmen.

"You know," said Megan, "My archaeology professor would be throwing me off my Masters course, right about now, if he could hear any of this."

"And I have to say, he'd be right to," said Faraday. "Perhaps there's still time to transfer to Ancient Cultures and Folklore," he added, with a wry grin.

"Let's make sure it's all moot, anyway," I said, in an attempt to draw a line beneath this increasingly bizarre conversation. "Our job is to prevent the coven from getting into the temple. If we do that, then none of the rest of it matters, and we'll never know if Ernst von Draken would have been successful in raising a demon or not."

"Agreed," said Faraday. "Our chief priority is protecting the temple, and its elusive entrance. Let's hope we never get to the part that's supposed to happen here."

Shortly afterwards, we began the walk back to Badcombe Hollow. Faraday and Kate went on ahead, while I hung back with Megan, so that we could snatch a few moments alone together.

"So, what do you think?" I said to her.

"What? Of Professor van Helsing and his delightful assistant? Like you described them, I suppose. He's more charming than I imagined he'd be. Less fuddy-duddy. She seems a bit hostile and uptight."

"Really? You think?"

"That was my fleeting impression. Just a bad vibe. Maybe I'm really just jealous that she rescued you from a bunch of devil worshippers in some wood, somewhere."

"You really shouldn't be."

"I'm kidding. Well, sort of. And I'm very grateful that she did, of course. The other guy, Michael – you say he's training to be a priest?"

"Apparently so."

"And the three of them have banded together to fight the forces of darkness?"

"Yeah, something like that. No, when I said, 'What do you think', I meant more in terms of, well, what do you think about people battling against the forces of darkness, I suppose? What do you think about the whole thing? Everything we've been talking about this morning?"

"Like I've stepped out of the real world and into the pages of a horror novel," she said, slipping her hand into mine.

"I know the feeling," I said. "But after what I've seen, particularly over the last few days, I have to believe that this is all real. It's bizarre, but there it is. I just want to get through the next few days, sell that wretched house, pocket the money, and then move on."

"You won't be moving on too far, I hope."

"Until meeting up with you yesterday, I might have been, but now I'm thinking of doing some speculative house-hunting in and around Marlborough, the day after Walpurgis."

"Sounds like a very good plan," she said, squeezing my hand.

We continued the walk back to the house in companionable silence, as I thought wistfully about sharing a future with Megan without all the craziness of the past few weeks.

Perhaps the coven would just give up, I thought. It was hard to imagine that they would be able to force their way into the house, besides which, it would take them some time to open the entrance to the temple, wherever that was. And time was against them now, surely. It was just a matter of getting through the increasingly short period of time between now and Walpurgis. As we got closer to the house, I made a concerted effort to feel more optimistic about things.

As we turned into the driveway, I saw Kate and Faraday standing beside the front door. They were talking to Michael, who was holding a large book open in front of him and pointing at something inside. The three of them appeared highly animated for some reason, and as Megan and I crunched over the gravel towards them, Michael looked over at us, with a broad grin on his face.

"You look exceedingly cheerful about something," I said.

"You could say that," said Michael, snapping shut the book he was holding.

I looked at the cover. It was a plant encyclopaedia, published by the Royal Horticultural Society, which I recognised from one the shelves in the larger of the two sitting rooms.

"Well?" I said. "What is it?"

"I've found it," he said.

"Might have found it," Faraday interrupted.

"Okay, might have found what?" I said to Michael.

“The entrance to your underground temple, of course,” he
said. “In fact, it’s right behind you.”

CHAPTER FORTY-FOUR

The Entrance

I turned around and saw nothing but the large shrub bed in front of the clump of Scots Pines on their mound.

"What do you mean?" I said, turning back to face Michael. "I don't get it. What am I looking at?"

"I'll explain," said Michael. "We need to go back inside, first. Follow me."

We all trooped into the house and followed Michael into the kitchen, where I saw that he had laid the gloomy portrait of Dorian Slake in the centre of the island unit. He put the plant encyclopaedia next to it, open at a page showing a variety of evergreen shrubs.

"It was Megan here, who put the idea into my head," he said, causing Megan, who was standing beside me, to raise her eyebrows quizzically.

"It's the sprig of greenery, with little white flowers, in the vase behind Dorian Slake, you see," he said. "I thought I recognised the plant, which got me to wondering, and so while you were off investigating your dolmen, I tried to find it in this plant book I got from the sitting room. And I was right. I did recognise it.

"Choisya Ternata," he announced proudly, turning the book in our direction, and pointing to a photograph of a large shrub. "Better known as Mexican Orange Blossom. Evergreen. Glossy leaves. White flowers in spring and summer. Grows to about six feet, if you let it. Mildly sensitive to frost, and so it tends to prefer a sheltered spot. That's what's in the vase in the picture. So, then I went and had a little look around the garden. Come with me."

Michael led us back out into the garden. I sensed that he was enjoying his moment in the spotlight.

Outside the front door, he stepped onto the lawn, and pointed behind him, at the shrub bed beneath the Scots Pines.

"There it is," he said. "See the large shrub in the middle, by the edge of the lawn? That's the same plant that's in the picture."

I looked at the thick mass of green leaves he was pointing at. It had clearly grown considerably since the day Slake planted it, if indeed he had.

"I don't see any white flowers," said Kate.

"You won't," said Michael. "It's still a bit early. Another couple of weeks, maybe. But the leaves are very distinctive, if you know what you're looking for. That's a Mexican Orange Blossom. No doubt at all. There was one at the seminary in Dublin. I definitely recognise it."

"And you reckon the entrance to the temple is underneath that shrub?" I said.

"Could be," he said, with a shrug. "I mean, it's just an idea, but it would tie in with the Slake portrait."

Faraday was staring thoughtfully at the flower bed.

"Are there any other shrubs of that variety, anywhere in the garden?" he asked.

"Nope. I checked. That's the only one."

"Could it be that old?" said Kate. "Slake died fifty years ago, and the construction of the temple pre-dated his death by at least a decade. Would it still be here, after all this time?"

"No reason why not," said Michael. "It might have been cut back a few times in its life, and they top out at about six feet, which that is, but sure, Slake could have planted that there in the 1950s or 1960s."

"As the final act in concealing the entrance to the underground temple that he would never get to worship in," Faraday said softly, almost to himself, before turning to face us.

"Well done, Michael," he said. "And well done, Megan. It's a long shot, but the most plausible location for the entrance that we've found thus far."

For some reason I was sceptical. It seemed such an innocuous location.

"It's a fair way from the burial mound," I said. "Must be at least fifty feet away."

"More," said Faraday. "Seventy feet, at least. But the temple has to be accessible from somewhere, and that somewhere needed to be easily concealed. And relatively easily opened up again. People have to get into it, after all, on Walpurgis Night. That shrub bed is the closest practical spot to the burial mound. So Slake's Hungarian workers, or whoever they were, had to dig a seventy-foot tunnel from the entrance to the temple. So what? They were going to go to the monumental effort of excavating a temple beneath the mound. How much extra effort would a tunnel have taken? Given that Slake and his acolytes were planning to unleash an apocalypse upon the world, decades in the future, surely nothing would be too much trouble."

We stood there in silence for a few moments, and I knew what was coming next.

"Right, then," said Faraday. "Who's in the mood for a little light gardening?"

****

It took us most of the afternoon to get the gigantic shrub out of the ground. Because it was impractical for all five of us to get around the bush at once, we took it in turns to hack away at its myriad splays of foliage, while the rest of us sat in some deckchairs I found in the garage, chatting, or lost in our own thoughts, or even occasionally dozing. I can't pretend that we approached our task with any real sense of urgency, and I think we were probably glad to have the chance to take it easy for a bit. This wasn't so much the calm before the storm, as the calm between the storms. It was less than two days since von Draken's occult attack on the house, which had been preceded by the hair-raising events at the ruined chapel at Stokeley, and it was two days before Walpurgis. It was hardly surprising, therefore, that we all seemed to rather relish this odd little interlude in the garden, and the opportunity to apply ourselves to a purely practical task. It was actually quite an enjoyable afternoon.

The Dorian Slake shrub, as I had come to think of it, had grown and spread considerably since the time it was planted, so that by the time we had it cut down to its roots, an enormous swathe of the island bed had been reduced to a mess of cuttings and leaf litter. This we then raked back, and wheel barrowed over to a large pile we had created at one end of the garden. It looked like I was going to be having a bonfire, once this was all over.

As the shadows started to creep across the lawn Megan and I went into the house to make tea for everyone. Reaching for a large teapot I recalled seeing at the back of one of the kitchen cabinets, I felt Megan plant the softest of kisses on the back of my neck. She then hooked her arms around my chest and pulled me back towards her.

"Funny sort of day, isn't it?" I said, turning to face her.

"Certainly not the most conventional start to a relationship," she said. "But I'm glad I'm here, in spite of everything that's going on."

"I'm glad you're here, too," I said.

"Well, I kind of figured that. But I hope the rest of your little gang feels the same way."

"I've no doubt about it," I said. "In fact, I don't see how you could have made more of an impact. De-coding the numbers on the back of the portrait was a real breakthrough, and it was also you who put the idea about the bunch of white flowers into Michael's head. Pretty impressive for a morning's work."

"I think your Professor Faraday would have worked out the thing about the gridlines eventually. Or, one of you would. You have had rather a lot going on. As for Dorian Slake's posey of flowers, that was just a pure guess, and we still don't know if it's going to lead anywhere."

"Damn good effort, if you ask me," I said, kissing her forehead.

"We'll find out soon enough. If I was wrong, I owe you a new shrub."

"Forget it. The new owners can sort it out."

There was a long and pleasurable silence between us.

"Come on," she said. "That tea's not going to make itself."

A short time later, as Megan and I carried a tray of tea and cakes out into the garden, we found Faraday inspecting the cleared area, with a look of evident satisfaction upon his face.

"Time to start digging," he said. "But after tea, naturally."

We had our tea and then I went and fetched two spades from Alan's well-equipped workshop in the cellar – still very much a place of dread, for me, and hence somewhere I entered and exited with considerable alacrity – and Michael and I began digging into the area of earth we had stripped of its shrubbery.

Once we had gone down about a foot or so and revealed nothing other than more earth and a tangle of roots I started to wonder if this had all been a wild goose chase, and a waste of an afternoon which would have been better spent on other tasks, such as fortifying Badcombe Hollow against a forthcoming incursion by a coven of satanists. But we pressed on anyway.

When we got a couple of feet below the surface my spade hit something hard, making a harsh, metallic ring, and causing me to look round enquiringly at Faraday.

"Could just be a large stone," he said, puffing on his pipe.

"Or a brick," I said, brushing the earth off the spade and revealing a tinge of red dust on the tip.

"Pass me that trowel, would you?" I said to Kate.

Michael stepped back onto the lawn, and I knelt down with the trowel and started brushing away the earth at the base of the small hole we had made. Before long, I had revealed the top of what appeared to be a brickwork gully. The question now was what, if anything, this gully contained.

Michael crouched down beside me, and while I dug away carefully with the trowel, used his bare hands to move the loose earth to one side, and the square shape of the gully emerged before us.

"Maybe it's just a drain, or something," said Kate. "Or the entrance to an old well."

"Maybe," I said, non-committally, trying to keep the excitement from my voice, but deep down, I think I knew by then that we had located the entrance to Dorian Slake's temple.

Ten minutes later we stepped back and viewed the results of our labours. Standing a few brick courses proud of the earth bed which had once contained the glossy leaved shrub was a gully, a couple of metres square. And set into the gully was a door.

CHAPTER FORTY-FIVE

The Temple Built by Dorian Slake

It would be more accurately described as a hatch rather than a door; double-leafed and constructed of timber matchboard, set within a frame mounted to the brickwork gully. It looked like the sort of opening one would see to the cellar of a public house, down which a drayman would roll barrels of beer. Each leaf had a simple metal handle set beside its leading edge, through which a chain had been threaded, and secured with a padlock.

For a long moment none of us said anything. We simply stood there and stared at the result of our afternoon endeavours. I could hardly believe that we had actually found it.

"Well, well, well," said Faraday softly, almost to himself. "So, Dorian Slake really did build something here. And that's the entrance."

"There's a set of bolt croppers in the cellar," I said. "Shall I go and fetch them?"

"Yes, please do that," said Faraday, still staring transfixed at the hatchway.

I made my second visit of the day to the cellar, figuring that I was pushing my luck somewhat, but thankfully I managed to get in and out of there without incident. I carried the heavy bolt cutters outside, recalling the previous occasion on which I had utilised them, the day that Megan and I entered the locked room on the top floor of the house.

"Who's going to do the honours, then?" I said, hefting the cutters in both hands, and nodding down at the hatchway.

"Well, I suppose you should," said Faraday. "You do own whatever's down there, after all."

"Don't remind me."

"Wait," said Kate. "Are you sure about this, Julian?"

"What do you mean?" I said.

"I think what Kate is getting at," said Faraday, "And rightly so, I might add, is that by opening up this temple, if that is indeed what's down there, we are rather doing the coven's work for them, in advance of the raising ceremony they have planned for the day after tomorrow."

"Chopping up an old padlock isn't going to require much effort," said Michael.

"No, it won't," said Faraday. "I'm afraid we've already done the heavy lifting, so to speak, by clearing away all that shrubbery, and then digging out the entrance. That's several hours work we have saved the coven. I fear, in hindsight, that I may have been a little foolish in encouraging our efforts this afternoon. It may have been better to have left this flower bed exactly as it was."

"What's done is done," I said. "And it's not like we're going to re-plant all that shrubbery. I say we open the hatch and see what's on the other side. What does everyone else think? Kate?"

"I think I should have raised my reservations earlier," she said. "It's kind of moot, now, after all that digging about, and I must admit, I'm bloody curious to see what's on the other side of that door."

"I agree with Kate," said Michael. "We've come too far to turn back now. Besides, if there is a fully fitted out temple down there, we can always wreck the place, and maybe put a spanner in the works that way, as far as the coven is concerned. As long as that's okay with the owner of the property, that is," he added, looking over at me.

"No problem at all," I said. "How do you feel about it, Megan?"

"Oh, I'm all for going down there," she said, without hesitation. "But I do have a bit of a vested interest, you might say."

"I don't understand," I said.

"I'm an archaeologist, remember? And you've just opened up a tunnel leading into a Neolithic burial mound. This is the find of the bloody century. Obviously, I want to go in there."

"Fair point," I conceded.

"Your call, Professor," I said.

It was a moment before the older man spoke.

"On balance," he said, "I think the practical benefits of us seeing what's down there outweigh those of covering it all up again. We'll go down there. But we are going to exercise great caution as we do so.

"Michael, please go inside and fetch a crucifix, your rosary and a bible. And Richard, a couple of torches, if you will.

"Please don't think me overly melodramatic," he said to us. "But we've all seen enough by now to realise that there are some very dark forces at play here, quite apart from whatever human depravity Ernst von Draken and his coven may be planning to indulge in, down in that hole in the ground. It's not inconceivable that the temple has been booby trapped in some way, whether by physical means, or more otherworldly ones. So, we all need to tread very carefully. Understood?"

We nodded our assent, and then Michael and I went into the house; me to fetch two torches I knew to be in a drawer in the kitchen, and Michael to collect the accoutrements of his priestly vocation.

A short time later we were back in the garden, where we found Faraday pacing what was presumably the route of the tunnel from the hatchway to the burial mound.

"Quite a distance," he said, as we walked over to him. "One can only hope that the workers who built this shored it up properly. We wouldn't want anything collapsing on us."

Something else to worry about, I thought. Although it did make me think that if the tunnel had already collapsed in the intervening decades since Slake built it, then that was as good a way as any of preventing the coven from getting into their temple on Walpurgis Night.

"Let's get this thing open, then," I said, lifting the heavy bolt cutters.

I stepped over to the hatchway in the ground and felt a flutter of excitement in the pit of my stomach.

The bolt cutters went through the padlock like the proverbial knife through butter, but opening the doors proved to be rather more difficult. Michael thought the timber must have swollen in the frame, and it took both of us to pull up each leaf of the door, accompanied each time by a loud cracking sound.

We found ourselves looking at the top of a flight of steps, leading down into a pool of blackness.

"Wonder how far down it goes," said Kate, peering into the gloom.

I flicked on one of the torches and pointed it into the hole.

"Not too far," I said. "About ten or twelve steps, and then there looks to be a passage off to one side."

"Towards the long barrow, I assume," said Megan.

"Yes. It goes left. Towards the long barrow.

"Shall we?" I said to nobody in particular, whilst motioning towards the flight of steps. I wanted to go down there, but I really didn't want to go first.

"I'd better lead the way," said Faraday, much to my relief, and I handed him the torch.

He started to make his way down the steps, followed by Kate, and then Megan and I, with Michael bringing up the rear with the second torch. I noticed that he had hung his crucifix over his neck and wrapped the rosary around his wrist. The bible, he had given to Kate to carry.

When Faraday reached the bottom of the steps he stopped and waited for us until we were bunched together, watching as he shone his torch down the tunnel.

The walls were formed of grey blockwork, and the floor of bare, compacted earth. The tunnel was about a metre and a half wide, and perhaps a little over two metres high. The air was stale but breathable, and as far as one could tell, the passageway looked solidly intact, and not at risk of imminent collapse.

We started to advance slowly in a crocodile line, walking towards the long barrow, none of us saying anything. The sense of anticipation was almost tangible in the dead air.

After proceeding a little way into the gloom, however, Faraday suddenly stopped.

"That's odd," he said.

"What is?" Kate and I both said at the same time.

"Look," said Faraday, pointing his torch down the tunnel. "A little way ahead of us. Just before it gets to the vicinity of the long barrow, it veers off to the right, towards the road. I don't understand. Surely Slake would have had his people dig the most direct route and go towards the underside of the long barrow in a straight line."

"Maybe there was some sort of obstruction," said Michael. "You know, like tree roots, or something."

"They may have been trying to line up with the old entrance," said Megan. "That entrance would have been at one end of the barrow. The one facing the road. Don't forget, the Neolithic tribe who built this would have had to get into it, too. To bury their dead. I think Slake's diggers inadvertently broke into an existing passageway, and then utilised it for themselves."

"Let's press on, then," said Faraday. "But stay close together, everyone."

We followed the tunnel until we reached the bend, whereupon there was a change in our surroundings. Instead of modern blockwork, here the walls were flanked with sarsen stones. The tunnel was also narrower, although still wide enough for us to walk through.

"You were right, Megan," said Faraday, stopping again, and shining his torch over the upright stone slabs. "This part of the tunnel must be Neolithic in origin."

We continued on, knowing that by this stage we could only have been a matter of feet from the long barrow and, presumably, our final destination – Dorian Slake's satanic temple. But then we came across something else that made us stop in our tracks.

On the wall to our left, which would have been the wall closest to the barrow, were large holes, like viewing points, with rough stone copings. Faraday pointed his torch into one of the holes, revealing some sort of chamber on the other side.

"Catacombes," said Megan, the excitement in her voice unmistakeable. "A Neolithic burial chamber. Oh, my God. This is incredible. Forget about Dorian Slake's wretched temple, for a moment. This is one of the most amazing archaeological discoveries of all time."

"It is also a sacred place," said Faraday, "Defiled by those who put this tunnel here, to reach a temple venerating Satan himself. The ancient people buried here would not have interpreted it in such a way, of course. Their beliefs pre-dated Christianity by many hundreds of years. But they understood evil. They understood it because it has always existed. If they had known the purpose to which Dorian Slake intended to put their burial place, they would have been outraged. Of that you can be sure."

For some reason Faraday's words made me think of something, of some connection that was relevant to all of this, something important which we weren't seeing, but I couldn't quite get there. Something nagged at my brain about what he'd just said, but I couldn't work out what it was, like a *déjà vue*, or something half-remembered. It was annoying, and I knew it was going to bug me until I either deduced what it was or forgot about it, but right then there were more pressing matters at hand. By now, we couldn't have been more than an outstretched hand away from the entrance to the temple.

Sure enough, after advancing no more than a few steps further into the darkness, Faraday stopped again.

"It's here," he said. "We've found it."

We gathered around him, and saw a metal door, set into the sarsen rock. There was nothing in the slightest bit remarkable about this entrance to what was the lifetime ambition and grand scheme of a devil worshipper, I reflected, as Faraday moved the beam of his torch around the black painted metal. It was nothing more than a simple door, absent any surface adornment. But it was what lay on the other side that was making my pulse race. I felt suddenly frightened. I wanted to run back down that tunnel and out into the light. I wanted to be as far away from there as I could possibly be. I wondered if the others felt the same, even though we all knew that we were going in there.

"Is it locked?" I said.

"It doesn't appear to be," said Faraday, continuing to cast the light over the surface of the door. "Just a simple lever handle. But no sign of a lock. I suppose it would be deemed a little pointless, if someone was going to go to all the trouble of getting down here in the first place."

I ran my hand over the cold smooth metal.

"I can't believe we actually found it," I said softly. "And I really dread to think what might be in there."

"Perhaps something very foul indeed," said Faraday.

I depressed the lever handle and pushed gently at the door, which swung open with a gentle creak. It was pitch dark on the other side.

"Can I have the torch?" I said to Faraday.

He passed it to me. It felt heavy in my hand.

Taking a deep breath, I stepped through the doorway.

441

CHAPTER FORTY-SIX

Council of War

"I just can't believe the bloody thing was empty," I said, for what seemed like the umpteenth time. "I mean, it was almost an anti-climax. No, it was an anti-climax. Not that I wasn't scared half out of my wits, going in there. But it's just a big empty room. I don't get it."

It was later that evening, and we had just finished supper. Having returned to the house, more than a little perplexed, following our excursion below ground, we had spent a disarmingly normal evening together, cooking toad-in-the-hole and roast potatoes in the kitchen, which we ate crowded around the island unit, helping ourselves to more of Alan's vintage wine collection, and then repairing with coffee to the cosier of the two sitting rooms, where we were sitting now, chewing over the day's events.

"An empty room created at enormous effort and expense, don't let's forget", said Faraday, thoughtfully, filling his pipe.

"What did you really expect, anyway?" said Kate.

"I don't know, exactly," I said. "A pagan altar, I suppose. At the very least, that. And a pentagram on the floor, perhaps. Or the sort of satanic paintings Megan and I found upstairs, all over the walls. More than a bare concrete floor, bare concrete slabs on the walls and not a stick of furniture, that's for sure."

It had been a surreal experience, standing in that large room, at least the size of Badcombe Hollow's two sitting rooms combined, playing our torches across the blank, featureless walls. It was more like being in an air raid shelter, than being in a temple.

"Maybe the coven's going to bring everything like that with them," said Michael. "You know, set up camp, so to speak, when they get here. Von Draken's been at this a long time. He's probably not short of satanic bric-a-brac."

"I'm not sure," said Faraday. "That sort of thing is mainly decoration, like stained glass windows in a church. It's not an actual requirement for a satanic ceremony. For that, they merely need thirteen dedicated followers and the correct incantations. According to their own folklore, at any rate. Perhaps the empty temple is part of it, somehow. Maybe there's not meant to be any sort of adornment to the place, because it's supposed to be untouched. That might tie in with the notion of a temple designed to be used on just one specific occasion."

"Virgin territory," said Michael. "Previously untouched."

"Yes, something like that," said Faraday

"Anyway," said Michael, "The temple in the garden, or rather the ceremony that takes place within it, is about summoning the dark energy gathered in this nodal point of sacred sites. At its peak, supposedly, on this one particular Walpurgis Night. That's what's necessary to set this whole thing in motion. But it's a blood sacrifice at the portal site itself, at the dolmen, this devil's doorway, that brings the demon across the threshold, into our world. Does that sort of scenario make any kind of sense, Julian?"

"None of this makes any kind of sense," said Faraday, a note of tetchiness creeping into his voice. "We're dealing with people who are depraved at the very least, and probably half-mad. Who on earth knows what goes on in their minds? They could be planning to do anything. But as a working theory, it's as plausible as anything I can come up with."

"Which means, therefore," I said, "That even if by some chance the coven managed to perform their ceremony in the temple, we could still theoretically stop them at the dolmen."

"Theoretically," said Faraday. "But we shall be stopping them long before then. Our number one priority is the same as it always was. We prevent the ceremony from going ahead in the temple. That's all we have to do. And notwithstanding the fact that we've opened it up for them today, it is still standing on property for which you are legally responsible, and to which you have denied von Draken access. And if they resort to simple trespass, then all we need to do is contact the police. Let's keep things in perspective. We still have the advantage here."

"Except that we have no idea what they plan to do," said Kate.

"Yes, quite so. Except for that."

A short time later we decided it was time to call it a night. Faraday, Kate and Michael made their way upstairs while I walked Megan to her car. I had hoped she would stay the night, as I felt an almost desperate need to spend time alone with her, having been forced to share her with the others for most of the day. But she was going to Devizes that night, to stay with her parents, so that she could go with them to the hospital early the following morning, when her father was scheduled to have more tests.

"I have to go," she said. "Dad's feeling much better, thank goodness, and it looks as if everything is going to be okay, but Mum has been struggling to cope with it all, added to which she has an irrational dread of hospitals, and so I promised I'd go with her. Plus, there's bound to be stuff they need doing at home. But I'll be back here by the evening, and I can stay tomorrow night. And the next day. I can stay right through, if you want, until this is all over?"

"If it's what you want," I said.

We were standing beside the long barrow. It was a beautifully still, moonlit night, and the fields around the house had a silvery sheen about them.

"It is what I want," she said. "I want to be where you are."

We embraced, and as we did, I was plagued once again with feelings of guilt and foreboding, and with the thought that I was involving Megan in this for my own selfish reasons, and by doing so, leading her into grave danger.

I pushed the thought out of my mind.

"I'm glad your father is feeling better," I said, as she got into the car.

"You know, you're going to have to come and meet them soon," he said. "We'll have to do a lunch, or something."

"That sounds portentous," I said.

"Hardly, darling. Not considering the other thing you've got going on in your life at the moment. But I'd like you to meet them."

"I'd like to meet them, too," I said.

She smiled at me from the gloom of the car's interior.

"See you tomorrow," she said. "About suppertime?"

“Perfect. See you tomorrow.”

I watched her drive out of the gateway and down to the road, and then followed the beam of her car's lights across the plain until they disappeared from sight.

Just as I was turning to go back inside, I felt the phone in my pocket vibrate. I reached for it and looked at the screen.

Somewhat to my surprise, it was Darren Summers, my helpful private investigator.

Puzzled at why he should be calling me at this time of the evening, I hit the green button and put the phone to my ear.

“Sorry to call so late,” he said, once we had exchanged greetings. “It's about that case you put me on; your satanic cult down in the west country.”

“I thought you'd be done with that, by now,” I said. “It was being paid for out of rather limited funds, if you recall,” I added, a little nervously.

“Sure, no worries there. I haven't done anything on it since the last time we spoke. But you know how it is. You throw the net out far enough, and things take a while to come in. It's just a couple of loose ends, really, information that's come in today which I thought you'd want to have. I'm going away for a bit, tomorrow. New assignment. Going to be flying below the radar for a while. So, I thought I'd give you a call. If you're still interested, of course. How's it going down there, anyway?”

“In something of a holding pattern, you might say, waiting for the other side to make the next move, but I'm just about keeping on top of it all. I've enlisted some help. Anyway, yes, definitely still interested in anything you might have unearthed. What do you have?”

“Couple of things. Firstly, Doreen Smithers, the old witch you wanted me to look into. You said she had a daughter, who'd probably be about sixty now.”

“Yes. What about her?”

“I've found her.”

“Blimey. I didn't expect that. I mean, that was a real long shot. Are you sure it's her?”

“As sure as I can be. Abigail Smithers. Fifty-nine years old, and definitely not of sound mind.”

“Where is she?”

“In a priory.”

“In The Priory?”

“God, no. That would be something, wouldn’t it? I mean in an actual priory. In Hampshire. Run by the Catholic Church. Very discreet, out of the way place. I couldn’t find out much about it, but I did learn that they deal with cases of possession, people who’ve got involved in the occult, that sort of thing. Apparently, she’s a patient there.”

“That’s good work,” I said, as I started to walk slowly back towards the house.

I was intrigued by this development, but I doubted it was pertinent to the current business at hand, which was preventing the coven from getting into their temple, two nights hence. But it would be good background material, if I ever did decide to turn this whole experience into a book.

“It’s called the Priory of Saint Mary,” he said. “It’s a few miles outside Winchester. I’ll text you the address. But good luck trying to get anything out of them. They wouldn’t even speak to me, when I rang them.”

“How did you find out about it? About her?”

“Because she got sectioned, about ten years ago. Completely off her head, by all accounts. But the court records show that she was put into the care and responsibility of this religious institution.”

“Well, I’ll certainly check it out,” I said. “Thank you. What was the other thing you had?”

“It was about that Ernst von Draken character. I got a little bit more back on him. Nothing major, just some more stuff that came in on his finances, property, business dealings, etcetera. But there was one particular detail I thought you’d want to know about.”

“Tell me,” I said.

And so, he told me. And when he did, I felt the blood drain from my face.

CHAPTER FORTY-SEVEN

The Woman in the Priory

The Priory of Saint Mary stood veiled behind a thick screen of fir trees, and it looked as impregnable as it was imposing. It was situated at the end of a single-track lane, far from any other human settlement, and surrounded by large, empty fields.

Everywhere that day was shrouded in a dank drizzle, and my first sight of this gaunt institution made for a depressing scene.

The place had taken some finding, and it seemed that the proprietors liked it that way, for it was not marked on any map or signpost. Once I had reached the other side of Winchester and passed through the river valley that took me to the vicinity of the Priory, I had driven around for the best part of an hour until I found it.

I stopped the car in front of a pair of heavy metal gates, and got out to peer through the drizzle at this mysterious institution.

It may have been called a priory, but it was really more like a very large house, which looked as if it dated from the late Victorian era, and which appeared dark, gaunt, lifeless and faintly gothic, with a steeply gabled tower at one end. It was a bleak sort of place, especially on such a dreary day, marooned as it was within its little copse and encircled by a gently undulating, largely featureless landscape.

Somewhere behind those walls, I reflected, resided one Abigail Smithers, the only daughter of the late Doreen Smithers, the erstwhile witch of the Ridgeway, and the reputed offspring of the notorious occultist, Dorian Slake. She was in there, somewhere, locked away and apparently quite mad.

A weathered sign beside the gates announced that this was the "Strictly Private" property of the Priory of Saint Mary, with admittance by appointment only. Clearly, the Priory didn't care to either advertise its presence, or welcome passers-by or the merely curious. Fortunately, I had an invitation.

It had been Faraday who had insisted that I come here, after I recounted to him and the others the information unearthed by Darren.

"The Priory of Saint Mary is something of an anomaly, even for the Catholic Church," he had explained. "As I am quite sure the Roman Catholic member of our team would agree," he added, with a nod to Michael.

"No argument there," said the young priest. "In fact, I dare say that there would be those in the church hierarchy who would describe the priory as an aberration, although you don't hear much about them, these days. They were something of a big deal for a while, around the turn of the century – the last century, that is – but I would think their numbers have dwindled almost to nothing in recent years. There can't be too many of them left now, rattling around in that old mansion of theirs."

"That is also my understanding," said Faraday. "I've had some dealings with them, over the years. I've consulted with them occasionally. I recall a Father O'Rourke, being the head man down there, but he would be a considerable age, by now."

"So, who are they?" said Kate. "What do they do?"

"They're from the Jesuit Order," said Faraday. "And immensely devout. The Priory was established sometime around the early 1880s, with the specific aim of fighting satanism, and other occult practices."

"A little bit like us, then."

"Yes. One might say that. But for them, the emphasis is very much upon the spiritual fight against evil, as opposed to our more temporal concerns. Their main area of interest was exorcism, and that's always been a tricky subject within the Catholic Church. It's why they've tended to operate somewhat on the fringe of things. O'Rourke himself was certainly an exorcist of some repute, but that's always made him something of an outsider within his own organisation, hence his stewardship of an obscure priory. Anyway, from what I know, their focus, these days, is more about providing psychological and pastoral care for those impacted by satanism, than the actual exorcism of demons. I presume that's how the daughter of Doreen Smithers came to be put in their charge.

"It would be useful to speak to her," he added. "Goodness knows if the poor thing is capable of making any sense or not, but it would be worth a try, for any information about this forthcoming ceremony that she might be able to give us. If O'Rourke is still running things over there, I may be able to call in a favour, and get you in to see her, Richard. I'd go with you, but I must do more research into the raising on Walpurgis Night, and I want at least two other people here, in case von Draken tries anything. Now that we've opened the tunnel in to the temple, we can't afford to leave the property unattended at any time."

"I've got nothing else planned for tomorrow," I said. "See what you can do."

A telephone call later, it transpired that Father O'Rourke was still in charge of the Priory of Saint Mary and was prepared to meet me there at twelve o'clock the following day. However, he advised that I was unlikely to glean anything of value from Abigail Smithers, for reasons he would explain when I met him.

"You should go anyway," said Faraday. "Speak to O'Rourke and see if there's anything at all you can find out. She's been there for a number of years, so it's not inconceivable that she might have told him things."

"Okay, then," I said. "I'll go. Anything's worth a shot at this stage, I guess."

And so it was that I came to be standing outside the gates to the Priory of Saint Mary, a little later than planned, thanks to my having had so much difficulty locating it.

I looked for a bell to ring but couldn't see one. They probably didn't have many visitors, I reflected, but they must have had post, deliveries, tradesmen calling and that sort of thing. Save for throwing a stone at one of the windows, I wasn't sure how I was going to get their attention.

But they must have been waiting for me, because a moment later the front door creaked open, and a priest approached the gates.

"Father O'Rourke?" I asked, as he drew closer. He was an elderly man, in his late seventies at least and shrivelled with age. He walked slowly and with a pronounced stoop.

"Father Webber," he replied. "I'm Father O'Rourke's assistant. And you would be the gentleman from Marlborough, I take it?"

"Yes, that's me," I said.

"I'll open the gates for you," he said.

He took an improbably large key from his cassock and unlocked the gates.

"You can park around the side of the building, there," said Webber, dragging open the heavy metal leaves of the gates.

I got back in the car and drove through the entrance. As I turned to follow the gravel driveway around the building, I heard the gates clang shut behind me.

I found the mostly empty car park and after sending a quick text to Faraday, to confirm that I had arrived, made my way back round to the front.

The drizzle had intensified to steady rain, and the wind had picked up, so that it sounded like it was moaning as it rushed through the dark conifers that encircled the property. The priory walls loomed up before me as I walked around them, dark and forbidding, and without a sign of life from the inside. I felt a momentary, irrational shiver of fear at the thought of going in there.

Father Webber was waiting beneath the porch by the front door from where he had emerged, moments earlier. There was something crow-like about his appearance, hunched within his dark, priestly robes.

"Welcome to the Priory of Saint Mary," he said, as I approached, in a tone of voice that was far from welcoming. "I'll take you up to meet Father O'Rourke."

I followed him inside and he closed the tall, heavy door behind us, shutting out the sound of the wind and the rain.

We climbed a long, wide staircase through an atrium, at the top of which was a glazed roof-light, shaped like a dome, revealing a glimpse of grey sky above. As we neared the top of the stairs, I could hear the patter of rain on the glass, accompanied by another long moan of wind.

We reached the top floor, where I could see that the building split into two wings, either side of the atrium, with each served by a long fenestrated corridor. I followed the priest down the one to our right, along which there was a row of closed wooden doors containing, I presumed, accommodation for the residents. As we passed by one of the doors, I could hear the faint sound of a radio playing within, but aside from that, and a pervasive scent of disinfectant in the air, there was no other sign of life, or that the building was even occupied. It was a bleak place to be, on such a bleak day, I thought, as I walked slowly in step behind the elderly cleric, and I experienced a feeling of apprehension at the thought that I might soon be encountering the mad old witch called Abigail Smithers. I wondered if she resided behind one of the closed doors in this corridor and thinking this made me wish that I was anywhere other than this dreary old building. Even Badcombe Hollow seemed somehow preferable in that moment.

We had reached the end of the corridor, and a heavy oak door, which Father Webber knocked on softly and then opened. As he stood in the doorway with his back to me, I could feel the warmth of the room rush out into the draughty corridor. There was a short, muffled exchange between the priest and the person on the other side of the door, and then he turned and ushered me in.

"Father O'Rourke," he said, by way of explanation, and then, with a swish of his black cloak he brushed past me and headed back down the long corridor, leaving me free to enter. I walked in, and closed the door behind me.

Father O'Rourke's domain was a pleasant contrast to the remainder of the Priory; as seemingly inviting, one might say, as the rest of the building was somehow forbidding. It was a large corner room with windows on two sides and the walls were clad from floor to ceiling with bookshelves that seemed to groan beneath the weight of a thousand leather bound volumes. A fire crackled pleasingly in the corner of the room, and the air was thick with tobacco smoke. It felt more like standing in the cosy garret of an academic than the inner sanctum of a priest and reputed exorcist.

The priest in question rose from behind a large desk to greet me.

"I'm Father O'Rourke," he said. "Welcome to the Priory of Saint Mary."

His welcome was as warm and genuine in nature as his colleague's had appeared cold and forced, only moments earlier, added to which he had a pleasant demeanour, and I immediately felt more at ease. He was an elderly man who nevertheless radiated a certain youthful exuberance, with his ruddy, weather-beaten features, and his broad smile and his thick Irish accent. For some reason, I took an instant liking to him. Perhaps it was the extraordinary nature of everything I had experienced in the past few days, perhaps it was just some aura he manifested, but I felt oddly safe and protected in his presence.

"Thank you for allowing me to come and see you," I said, in a tone of voice more formal than I had intended.

"It was no trouble at all," said the priest. "Please, sit."

He motioned me to a high-backed chair that had been placed in front of the desk before sitting back down.

"Do you mind?" he asked, waving a packet of cigarettes in front of him.

"Not at all," I said.

He lit a cigarette from the smouldering butt of one he had plucked from a full ashtray, balanced somewhat precariously on the clutter of his desk. He took a long drag, exhaled with evident satisfaction and then squinted at me through the smoky cloud he had created between us.

"So then," he said. "I take it you're the gentleman from Marlborough who's been involved in a bit of a tussle with the forces of darkness."

"Well, I suppose you could put it like that," I said. "I understand that Professor Faraday has given you some of the background as to why I'm here, and what's going on. Or what we think is going on," I added.

"Yes," said O'Rourke. "I've spoken to the Professor, and he's furnished me with the bare bones of the case, and also explained the interest you have in one of our patients. But we'll get to that later, if we may. And I'll certainly give you all the help I can. But for now, I'd like to hear in detail about what's been going on over there, in that house of yours once lived in by a certain Dorian Slake."

"So, you've heard of Slake then?" I said.

"Oh, yes, to be sure, it's a name well known to me. I never had the displeasure of meeting the man, but I know as much about him as any decent person would care to."

"And what's your opinion of him, if you don't mind me asking?"

"I don't mind in the slightest, and I'm happy to tell you that, in my humble opinion, Dorian Slake was a sick and evil bastard, if you'll pardon my language, and a person the world is much better off without."

"Yes, well he removed himself from this mortal coil, so to speak, very close to what's now my house. Apparently, he was quite mad by then."

"Oh, I don't doubt that he was, Mr Weaver. Dabbling with the occult will do that to a person. But I feel not an ounce of sympathy for the man, only for the poor wretches whose lives he ruined; him and his infernal master and tutor, Aleister Crowley, another sick and evil bastard the world is well rid of. Still, one can only be grateful that in Slake's case he ended things when he did, before he could wreak further harm on the world."

"Isn't taking one's own life a mortal sin in your church?" I ventured.

"Aye, Mr Weaver, that it is. And I'm fairly sure you didn't come here to discuss theological doctrine with me. But in answer to your unasked question – If I had been there at the time, would I have stopped it? – Well then, let me tell you, if I had been there at the time, I would have put the noose around his neck myself, and kicked away the chair, and I would have done it with a song in my heart."

As he spoke the words, the priest's demeanour remained as warm and genial as it had when I entered the room, but I had no doubt that he meant what he said.

"Anyway, we appear to be veering a little off-topic," he said. "I'd like to hear your story, now, if you'd care to indulge me. I can assure you, I'm a good listener."

And so, I told my tale yet again. I really was becoming quite accomplished at doing so by then. True to his word, the priest was a good listener, and he spoke barely a word during my peroration, only interrupting it to pour me a cup of lukewarm coffee from a chipped jug, decorated with yellow flowers.

When I had finished, he got up slowly and walked over to one of the windows, where he stood with his back to me, surveying the gloomy scene outside.

"Well, that's really quite a tale you have to tell," he said, without looking around. "Scarcely believable, like something from the pages of a novel."

"But you believe me?" I said.

"Yes, I most certainly believe you. I believed you before you got here. Professor Faraday convinced me of that. But it was good of you to put some flesh on the bone, so to speak. It's really a most intriguing affair."

"So, what do you think?" I said, as he returned to his seat behind the large desk.

"Well, it's unquestionably a serious coven," he said. "This isn't your typical bunch of sad freaks screaming at the moon and having an orgy. Your experience within the pentagram demonstrates that. And given the way they pursued you after you interrupted their little sabbat, not to mention the venomous snake in a box, suggests that they have a propensity for inflicting violence, so they pose a considerable earthly risk, as well."

"This von Draken character certainly seems like a formidable adversary," I said.

"Maybe so," said the priest. "But it's the woman you should be more concerned about. This person who calls herself Catherine Falaise. The adept for the coven. The witch. She's the truly dangerous one. Ernst von Draken may be the ringmaster, but she's the power. Take her out of things and the coven would be massively diminished as a force.

"So, be very careful of her," he said. "She'll be by far the most powerful and the most dangerous of the thirteen."

"Duly noted," I said. "What about the rest of it? I mean, this bizarre scheme to raise a demon, tomorrow night. Do you think the coven could possibly accomplish such a thing?"

"Highly unlikely," said O'Rourke. "In fact, I'd say it's a virtual impossibility. But that doesn't mean they shouldn't be prevented from trying. They most certainly should be."

"Well, we'll do our best," I said.

"I've no doubt that you will, Mr Weaver. No doubt at all. And you couldn't have recruited a better comrade in arms for such a task as Professor Faraday."

"I think he recruited me," I said.

"Be that as it may, you'll make a formidable team, I'm sure. In any case, you do hold most of the cards."

"How do you mean?"

"I mean, you legally occupy the property your adversaries are so keen to get into. I very much doubt that a coven of thirteen satanists, some of them probably as elderly as me, are really going to be able to do anything about that, in a practical sense. And if they should try, then you can always appeal to a higher authority."

"A higher authority?" I said, looking at him quizzically. "Oh, you mean …"

I raised my eyebrows towards the ceiling.

"Actually, Mr Weaver, I meant the police. You could call the police. Trespassing is still a crime in this country, I presume. But if you should happen to have a direct line to the almighty, then by all means try that as well."

There was a twinkle in his eyes, as he said this, and I grinned sheepishly back at him.

"Sorry," I said. "No offence."

"None taken. You're not a religious man, I take it?"

"Well, not exactly … I mean, you know, C of E …"

"Yes, quite," he chuckled. "Well, don't be worrying about that for now. God is on your side in this venture you've embarked upon, even if you're not yet on his. Just remember that."

"I will."

He squinted at me through a haze of cigarette smoke.

"And now," he said, "We should get to the subject of Abigail Smithers."

"I understand that she's been with you for quite some time," I said.

"That she has. She's been with us for over ten years now, and I'm sorry to say that she'll never leave. She'll be here until the day she dies."

"That's a bleak prognosis," I said. "Would that be the case for most of your patients?"

"Thankfully not. We have eighteen people here at the present time. Eighteen patients, as you put it. We prefer to call them residents. We can accommodate up to twenty. At the moment we have eighteen. All of them were in a very bad way when they first arrived here. But then we are, you might say, something of a sanctuary of last resort. Their individual circumstances vary greatly, as you might imagine, but they all have one thing in common. They've all been involved, to some degree or another, in the practice of black magic, either as members of satanic groups or covens, or else through their own individual communion with the left-hand path. And they've all suffered great psychological trauma as a consequence. But most of them we can help. Perhaps not wholly cure, because some of the things these people have experienced, if only in their own minds, can never be erased from their consciousness. But we can help them to cope with it, and maybe even overcome it, and move on with their lives. At least in some form. It often takes years, but with the right blend of psychiatric therapy and spiritual enlightenment, it can be accomplished. But that won't be the case, I'm sorry to say, with Abigail Smithers.

"The damage is simply too profound," he said. "It's one of the worst cases I've ever seen in all my life. Satanic indoctrination and abuse of the foulest kind, resulting in acute dementia. The poor wretch was almost catatonic when she first came to us, and when she wasn't, she was terrified out of her wits. She's made some degree of progress, in the time that she's been here, and of course we avail her of whatever spiritual protection we can, from the many demons she's aroused. That's why she's here with us, and not in some other type of institution. We'll do everything that we can for her, including the saving of her soul from eternal damnation, but her mind will never recover."

"It's tragic," I said.

"No, Mr Weaver. Tragedy is when someone you love dies from a terrible disease. Or when a parent loses a child. This is pure evil. Exercised by others, upon others, and upon her. And by herself, of course. She bears much responsibility for her actions. But she was led there by some of the worst people on God's earth. You see, everyone here is a victim in that sense. These covens, like the one you're tangling with, they prey on the weak and the vulnerable, and they offer all the usual inducements. Well, there is no person more vulnerable than a child, and Abigail Smithers was inducted into that world as a mere babe in arms.

"She's the daughter of a witch. And a very powerful witch at that. And, what's more, a witch who consorted with one of the most evil men of the last century. Abigail's father. Dorian Slake. But it was the mother who fed her the poison. Slake had died by the time she reached infancy. It was all down to the mother, in poor Abigail's case, and a more wicked thing to do to a child could scarcely be conceived. One can only imagine the horror she must have witnessed."

I thought of the ruined cottage I had gone to at Stokeley, and imagined a young Abigail Smithers growing up there, watching her mother practice witchcraft and then practising it herself, and participating in all manner of depravity.

The priest's voice dragged me back to the present.

"So, I shall take you to see her, Mr Weaver, but I must warn you not to expect very much. The poor woman barely says a word, even on her more animated days, and I very much doubt that she has anything she can tell you that you or Professor Faraday don't know already. But the Professor said he wanted to leave no stone unturned, and I'm more than pleased to accommodate his wishes."

He got to his feet and motioned towards the door.

"Shall we?" he said.

I rose from my seat and stepped out into the corridor, where I waited for him to follow. When he emerged behind me, I noticed that he not only closed but also locked the door to his office, and then with a polite nod he motioned me down the corridor.

We returned to the atrium at the top of the staircase and continued across into the priory's other wing. The weather outside had cleared up a little, I noticed, and there seemed to be less of a chill in the building than there had been on my arrival.

When we reached the end of the corridor the priest took a bunch of keys from his pocket and unlocked a door that led to a narrow staircase.

"We have an attic floor at this end of the building," he explained, as he led me up the steep steps. "It's a more suitable location for those of our residents in the greatest distress, so as not to disturb the ones below."

At the top of the stairs there was a narrow landing with a slanted roof, where a priest who looked to be barely out of his twenties sat in a chair. He stood up as we approached and nodded respectfully at Father O'Rourke. He held a bible in his hand, which he had been reading from.

"This is young James," O'Rourke said to me.

"And this is Mr Weaver, from Marlborough," he said, addressing the young priest. "We're here to see Abigail. How is she today?"

"She's been quiet this morning," said the priest called James. "But she had another disturbed night. The night duty nurse said she got into a bit of a bad state and had to be given a sedative."

"More nightmares, I suppose," said O'Rourke.

"She calls them premonitions," said James.

"For some reason," O'Rourke said to me, "Abigail has been more agitated than normal, recently. Particularly at night."

James unlocked a door and opened it, and then stepped aside so that O'Rourke and I could enter. I followed the elderly priest into the room with something akin to a sense of dread, and the door closed behind us.

It was a plain sort of space, not quite a cell, but a bare, spartan room with whitewashed walls and little in the way of adornment, other than a simple set of furniture; a bed, a chipped and stained wardrobe and a couple of wooden chairs that looked as if they had come from a classroom. There was a toilet and wash basin in the corner of the room, partially screened by a curtain, and a large wooden crucifix hung on one of the walls.

A woman was sat on the bed, facing the window with her back to us. She made no move to look around, as if she was oblivious to our presence, and so we had to walk to the end of the room and then turn to face her.

Abigail Smithers may have only been a decade or so older than I was, but she had the gaunt and haggard appearance of someone much more elderly. She had long black hair that almost fell over her eyes and framed a face that was deathly pale. She wore a white night gown, and I noticed that her hands were clasped tightly together.

"Good afternoon, Abigail," said O'Rourke. "I'm sorry that you had a bad night, but I hope you're feeling better today. This is Mr Weaver, and he's come to visit you."

He spoke the words softly, in a voice imbued with gentle compassion, but there was no response at all from the woman on the bed, who continued to stare past us towards the window.

"Are you going to greet your visitor, Abigail?" said the priest.

There was still no response from the woman.

"It's as I feared, Mr Weaver," said O'Rourke, lowering his voice. "The poor soul is quite lost, you see, and so rarely communicates with any of us. Today is a typical day, like hundreds of others before it. I'm so very sorry."

I stared into the mad woman's face, hoping to discern some trace that she was even aware of our presence, but there was nothing.

"I'm sorry, too," I said. "But it was worth a try. I'm sorry to have disturbed you, Abigail."

O'Rourke laid his hand upon her shoulder and squeezed it gently, and then motioned for me to follow him out of the room.

Feeling partly disappointed at the lack of any response from Abigail Smithers, and partly relieved to be getting out of there, I walked behind the priest to the door. Just as we reached it, the woman spoke to us.

"He's coming," she said.

She still sat with her back to us, looking towards the window.

"What was that you said, Abigail?" said O'Rourke, walking back towards her.

I followed, so that we were once again stood before her, with our backs to the window. This time, she was looking up at us.

"He's coming," she repeated.

"Who's coming?" said O'Rourke.

"The desolate one. They've called him. I know they've called him. I felt it. And now he's coming."

She spoke in a low, cracked voice, with a hint of a west-country accent.

"When's he coming?" said O'Rourke. "This desolate one you speak of. When's he coming?"

A flicker of a smile crossed the woman's features and then she looked back down at her hands.

I felt the priest nudge my arm gently.

"You try," he whispered.

I knelt down so that my face was level with the woman sitting on the bed and she seemed to shrink within herself, as if she was afraid to look at me.

"Abigail," I said. "I think I know what you're speaking of. I know about them calling him. It's tomorrow, isn't it? They're going to try and bring him over tomorrow."

"Tomorrow," she repeated, without looking up.

"Abigail, I live in the house up on the plain. Your father's house. Do you remember it? You may have gone there when you were very little. The house with the big grass mound in the garden. Have you been there?"

For a moment I didn't think she was going to respond, but then she slowly looked up and spoke to me.

"Ma took me there," she said. "We went to the woods, and she showed me. She showed me the house in the hollow. She said it was the most important place in the world, and one day everyone would know about it."

"Good God Almighty," I heard O'Rourke exclaim softly behind me.

"I do know about it," I said. "I know about what your mother and father built there. I know about the temple under the ground. I've been inside it. I know what's supposed to happen there tomorrow night."

"You can't stop it," she said.

"Well, we're going to stop it," I said. "And the thing that they're trying to raise is not going to come here, and after tomorrow you won't have to be frightened of it anymore."

I wondered if I had overstepped my bounds somehow, by suggesting this, but there was no reaction from O'Rourke.

"I'm not frightened of him," said the woman. "He loves me. Ma said that he loves me. She said he'll protect me."

"Only God can protect you, Abigail," said O'Rourke. "Remember that."

"Maybe I don't want God to protect me, *Father*," she hissed, almost spitting the last word and with venom in her voice.

I was afraid of her then, and it was all I could do not to back away from her.

"Have you seen him yet?" she said to me, with a certain strength and confidence in her voice now. "Have you seen him in your dreams?"

"No," I said. "No, I haven't seen him. Have you seen him?"

"I've seen him. He comes to me when I sleep at night. I see him at night. I see him standing by the stones, waiting to come in. He's close, you see. He's so close I feel like I could reach out and touch him."

"What happens when he gets here, Abigail? What happens when they raise him? What happens then?"

She looked directly at me, through dead, black eyes.

"Then you all die," she said.

As she said this, it was as if the life went out of her, and her head dropped to her chest and she let out a long, ragged breath.

"You all die", she whispered, and then she drew her legs up onto the bed and lay down on her side.

"I think we should probably leave it there," said O'Rourke, as I got to my feet.

As we stood, the priest laid his hand on Abigail's shoulder and I heard him mutter a short prayer in Latin under his breath.

"The poor soul," he said to me, with a sad shake of his head. "All we can do is pray for her. And rest assured, we will do everything in our power to protect her from whatever it is that's to come, and from whatever monstrous evil that has been summoned to the edge of this earthly realm."

"Pray for us, too, Father," I said. "Pray for us."

"That I will, Mr Weaver. You can be quite sure of that."

He made as if to lead me out of the room.

"Wait," I said. "Just one more thing. There's one more thing I need to ask her."

CHAPTER FORTY-EIGHT

Things Change

By the time I got back to Badcombe Hollow the rain and murk of the day had been replaced by blue skies and warm sunshine. It was a truly glorious evening, and a reminder of how the days were getting longer, as spring started its transition to summer. Driving the last few miles to the house, past fields that were now abundant with crops, should have been a real pleasure, for this was the sort of evening on which to have not a care in the world.

Unfortunately, however, I had plenty, and all the bucolic splendour around me wasn't going to put them out of my mind.

But it was not the afternoon I had just spent at the Priory of Saint Mary that preoccupied my thoughts as I turned into the driveway and brought the car to a halt by the front door. It was something far worse. All I could think about by then was the second thing that Darren Summers had told me, when he had telephoned the evening before. It was this which had caused me such shock when I heard about it from the private investigator, and which I had discussed privately with Faraday, after the others had gone to bed, and which had weighed so heavily on me all the way to and from Hampshire.

I entered the house and after a quick check of the ground floor rooms, which were empty, as I had arranged for them to be, I went into the kitchen to wait.

A short time later I heard the sound of tyres on gravel, followed by an enquiring voice at the front door, which I had left open.

"Come on in," I called out.

Megan walked into the kitchen.

"Where is everyone?" she said.

"I think they've gone for a walk," I said, taking a long pull on the glass of scotch I had just poured myself.

She marched over and put her arms around me, and kissed the side of my head.

"I've missed you," she said.

"How are your parents?" I asked.

"They're okay. Dad's miles better, but unfortunately my mother was being even more high maintenance than normal, and that always gets a bit wearing. Plus, I've never been a great fan of Devizes, and we had to spend ages in town, doing shopping and stuff."

She disentangled herself, and I looked into her eyes for a long moment.

"Would you like a drink?" I asked.

"No. I don't need anything, thanks. What's going on, Richard? You don't seem yourself. What's happened?"

"I went to Hampshire. Been there most of the day. I just got back, as it happens."

"Oh, really? How come?"

"I went to see the daughter of Doreen Smithers."

She stared at me, wide-eyed.

"Oh, my God," she said. "How did you find her? What's she like?"

I got up and started to pace.

"Do you remember I told you that I'd hired a private investigator? Someone from my past, when I was a journalist. I hired him to look into all this stuff that's been happening; into von Draken and Slake and Doreen Smithers; all of it."

"Yes, of course I remember. But I thought that was over now. I thought you'd let him go, because you couldn't keep on paying him."

"Yes. I did do that. I did let him go. But he's a thorough sort of chap. He doesn't like to leave loose ends hanging. And so last night, just after you left, he rang me to tidy up a couple."

"And he found out about Doreen Smithers' daughter?"

"Yes. He tracked her down. She's in the care of some priests at an out of the way place in Hampshire. She's quite mad. Those rumours about her were correct. But she was just about lucid enough to speak about the demon raising tomorrow night."

"She knew about that?"

"Yes. She's known about it for years. She knew about the temple. She knew about this house. Anyway, Faraday thought I should go and see her. It turns out he's acquainted with the group of priests who run the institution she's in. No surprise there; kind of inconceivable that he wouldn't be, I suppose. But anyway, he fixed it all up for me. The man can certainly open doors. He thought it was important that we leave no stone unturned. While we wait for von Draken and his coven to make their move. So, I went over there. But it was a pretty ghastly experience, I have to say."

"I'm not surprised. No wonder you seem out of sorts. Did you learn anything? I mean, anything practical, that might help us?"

"Not really. Nothing we don't already know."

"What was she like?"

"Out of her mind. In a desperately sad state, you might say."

Neither of us spoke for a moment. I could hear the ticking of the grandfather clock in the hallway.

"There was something else," I said, at last. "There was something else that he found out. My private investigator friend."

"Well?" said Megan. "What is it? You're acting in a very strange way, Richard. And you're actually kind of scaring me. Tell me what's going on."

"It's about Ernst von Draken," I said.

"What about him?"

"My friend ran various checks on him, seeing what he could find out. There wasn't much. Ernst von Draken, it turns out, is very good at covering his tracks. But he found out a bit."

"And?"

"And it transpires that he owns a fair amount of property, and that included in his extensive portfolio is a house in Marlborough. As you can imagine, that got my attention."

"Yes, I can," said Megan. "It's not all that surprising, though, is it? I mean, it makes sense that he'd want to have a base somewhere close to his beloved temple. To keep an eye on things. Maybe to keep an eye on Alan, too."

"Or to keep an eye on you, perhaps?"

There was a moment of silence before she responded, and when she did, there was the faintest trace of a catch to her voice.

"I don't get what you mean," she said.

I turned away from her and walked over to the window. Long shadows lay across the lawn now, but it was still a perfect evening. Right then, I wished that I could be out there, and anywhere except in this kitchen with Megan.

"He gave me the address," I said, turning back to face her. "And it turns out that I know it. In fact, I've been there. With you. It's your house, Megan. The house where you supposedly rent a room. From some elderly couple, apparently, who are hardly ever there. Property of one Ernst von Draken."

"I don't believe it," she said, with the catch to her voice now more pronounced.

"Believe it. It happens to be the truth."

"Look, just because von Draken owns that house, it doesn't mean that I know anything about it. Maybe the people I'm renting the room from are renting the house from him. Or maybe he rents it through an agent. How should I know? All I know is that until you told me this, I didn't know anything about it. What do you take me for? I can't believe you'd accuse me like this. After all we've been through together. It's a disgusting thing to suggest that I might have known about this."

It was almost convincing, I thought. But I knew that it was all lies.

"Give it up, Megan. I've worked it all out, you see. You're one of them. You're part of the coven. One of the thirteen. You must have been one of the people chasing me through the woods at Stokeley. And I presume you must have helped summon up whatever the hell went on down in the cellar the other night. You've been playing me all this time. Playing me and spying on me."

"You fucking bastard," she hissed at me. "How dare you? I should walk out of here right now, for what you've just said."

"You should, but you won't. I think you want to know what I know. So that you can go back and deliver a full report to the coven."

"Fine. You've lost your mind, you know? But go ahead and share your little fantasy with me."

I knew by then that I was right about her; that any slight vestiges of doubt, or indeed hope that may have lingered in my mind were misplaced. Looking into her eyes now, I saw nothing but pure hatred.

"Well, this is what I've worked out so far," I said. "But feel free to jump in at any time and correct me."

"God, I don't know what I ever saw in you," she said.

"Right. Anyway, I suppose it goes back to your first visit. The day you turned up here, after von Draken had gone away empty handed. Back then, you didn't really know if Alan was still here or not. That's why you had Billy Matthews – one of your acolytes – keeping watch on the house. So, after von Draken breaks cover and comes over here, and I tell him that Alan has left the country, and I'm the new lord of the manor, he sends you in to make sure, and to see what else you can find out. You work your not inconsiderable feminine charms on me, and now von Draken has someone on the inside, reporting back on my every move."

Megan gave a snort of derision, but I ignored her and carried on.

"So, when I start investigating this whole business, you're there to help. I can't remember if it was me or you who suggested we search the house, looking for clues to Alan's whereabouts, but you certainly applied yourself to the task, even persuading me to break into that locked room on the top floor. I figure, by that stage, the coven must have been really starting to worry about where Alan had got to, so the more you could chivvy along my investigation, the better.

"And of course, following Alan's death, you were very keen that I accept von Draken's offer to buy this house. For my sanity and well-being, obviously. Truth be told, you almost persuaded me.

"And then, when Professor Faraday and his team got involved, up you pop again, helpfully inserting yourself into proceedings. Telling us about the numbers on the back of the picture. That was a nice move, in terms of proving your worth. It was a serious card for the coven to give up, but maybe you figured we'd get there in the end, or maybe you were just getting desperate by that stage, with the clock ticking down to Walpurgis Night, and you no closer to getting into your temple. Anyway, it established your bona fides as a valued member of the team.

"But planting the idea about the Mexican Orange Blossom in Michael's head was a real masterstroke. Although, I imagine that if he hadn't taken the bait, you would have led us to it some other way. The coven knew that the tunnel to the temple was going to take some getting into, time that was running out for them, thanks to my obdurate occupation of Badcombe Hollow, and now we've done all that hard work for them. Nicely played, Megan, very nicely played indeed."

"Thanks for the compliment," she said sarcastically. "You know that you can't prove any of this."

"I don't have to prove anything. We're not in court. I just have to believe it."

"Which you do, clearly."

"Yes. I do. But I haven't even gotten to the worst part yet."

"Which is?"

"I'm holding you responsible for Alan's death. You're directly implicated. Don't worry. I'll never be able to prove that in a court of law, either, but I still blame you for it.

"Remember the day we came back here from Windmill Hill to search the house? While we were upstairs, trying to get into that little attic room, a storm blew up, and it started to rain. When it was time for you to leave, you gave me some story about needing to run an errand in Marlborough, and you asked if you could borrow one of Alan's coats. Any of that coming back to you?"

"Not really. So what, anyway?"

"I now know that you were taking that coat for the coven. For them to use in the occult ritual that brought about Alan's death. All they required was an item of Alan's clothing, and you gave it to them. You helped them to kill him."

"Pure fantasy," said Megan, shaking her head. "You also seem to be forgetting one rather significant detail, which completely destroys your theory about all of this."

"Well, I certainly can't claim to know everything, Megan. Why don't you tell me what that is?"

"It's that bloody thing you've got in the house. The satanic entity, or whatever it is, that you think the coven conjured up to scare the shit out of Alan. It's attacked me twice, as you well know. In fact, it's made it incredibly hard for me to even come into this house, as you also well know. So how do you explain all that away? Or do you think that was all staged, in some way, just so I could establish my credentials?"

"No, I don't think it was staged," I said. "And it most certainly attacked you. And I've no doubt at all that you were genuinely terrified by it. But I understand the reason now. The answer came to me yesterday afternoon, when we were down in the temple. I just didn't realise it at the time. It was when Faraday was talking about the Neolithic people who once lived here, and how enraged they would have been, about Slake and his coven appropriating their burial site, for their own evil and depraved purposes.

"You see, I don't think von Draken did put that thing in here. In fact, when I mentioned to him once that he might have done, he seemed genuinely ignorant about it.

"So no, I don't think the coven conjured up that old woman. I think she's always been here. I think she belongs here. She's from the tribe who built the long barrow. And she's as mad as hell that your coven has defiled it by building a temple to Satan down there.

"Because the thing is, Megan, I've seen that thing a few times now, and every time it scares the hell out of me, just like it scared the hell out of Kate, the other morning. But here's the thing. Apart from the one time I tried to stop her attacking you, she's never lifted a finger against me or shown any sort of malice at all. And she didn't attack Kate, either. You, on the other hand, she seems to have a real problem with. She's gone for you twice, but she hasn't gone for anyone else. Just you. And I reckon, before you, Alan, and that's part of the reason he wanted to get away from here. And, who knows? Maybe she's what drove Dorian Slake to go and hang himself in those woods on the other side of the field. Seems like she has a real problem with devil worshippers. I have to say, I know how she feels."

"That's quite a convoluted theory you've put together for yourself," said Megan, icily. "Do you have anything else?"

"Just one thing."

I reached into my jacket pocket and retrieved the photograph I had put there that morning, before departing for the Priory of Saint Mary. I held it in front of Megan's face.

"You may remember this," I said. "It's a picture I took of you, the day we went to Windmill Hill together."

"What about it?"

"I showed it to Abigail Smithers, earlier today."

"Oh, I see. And I suppose you're going to tell me that she recognised me?"

"Yes, she did. But then, I'd expect a mother to recognise her own daughter. Abigail Smithers is your mother, Megan, which means that Dorian Slake was your grandfather. You're into this thing up to your neck, and you always have been, ever since you were born."

Saying nothing, Megan reached out for the photograph, and I gave it to her. She stared at it for a moment and then tossed it on the counter.

"Dear old mother," she said. "What a useless, pathetic wretch she is. How typically weak of her, hiding behind those priests. She's not half the woman my grandmother was."

"You need help, Megan," I said. "Maybe those priests could help you, too."

"Don't make me laugh," she said. "You don't have the first clue what this is all about. You don't know what's really at stake here. And don't presume to think you know anything about me, either. You don't know me at all. You're just someone I used. You're nothing. You're a worthless speck of humanity who's in way over his head. You all are."

"And you're a sad little girl who likes to worship the devil," I said. "On balance, I think I'd rather be me."

"So, what now? Are you going to throw me out of here?"

There was a defiance about her now, aside from the anger and contempt, as if she was challenging me.

"I don't think he'd do that," came a voice from the other side of the room, causing Megan to turn around sharply.

Faraday stood in the doorway, with Kate and Michael behind him.

"Richard is far too kindly a soul to throw you out on your ear," he said. "But we're not."

"Don't worry, Professor. I'm leaving."

Without looking back at me, she walked purposefully to the kitchen doorway, where Faraday, Kate and Michael stepped aside to allow her into the hall. Just before she reached the front door, she stopped and turned to face us.

"Don't get too carried away with your little victory this evening," she said. "If you had any sense, you'd get out of this house tonight and never come back. You really have no idea what you've got yourself into. And after tomorrow night, well, you'll all be dead, and that will be that."

She turned and walked out of the door. A short time later I heard the sound of her car starting, and then I heard her drive away from Badcombe Hollow in a noisy spray of gravel.

We went into the more formal of the two sitting rooms, where I slumped into an armchair, feeling emotionally exhausted and completely empty inside.

"Well, that's that, then," said Faraday, in a matter-of-fact sort of tone.

"Jesus, what a bitch," said Kate.

"I'm so sorry about all of this," I said, putting my head into my hands. "She's been playing me, all this time, and I fell for it; hook, line and sinker."

"Don't be too hard on yourself," said Faraday. "She deceived us all, but I'd say we've unmasked her just in time. Anyway, it's always better to know one's enemy, and she could have caused real havoc if she'd been able to maintain her cover here on Walpurgis Night. On balance, I'd say we're in better shape now than we were a day ago."

"What about her warning, before she left?" I said. "Her saying that we have no way of beating the coven and that we're … well, we're dead if we try? Does she – do they – really believe that? Or was that just a threat to try and get us to leave? Or was it just the bitter musings of a jealous ex-girlfriend?"

"Probably a bit of all three," said Faraday. "I wouldn't take it too much to heart."

"How can I not?" I said. "It brought home to me what a risk you're all taking, just by being here tomorrow. I really think that you should re-consider whether or not you actually want to stay here. We all should."

"Well, I'm definitely staying," said Kate. "We've come this far. We need to see this through."

"Me too," said Michael. "I may be the most devout one here, but I seriously doubt that this coven has the slightest chance of manifesting a demon. However, I equally have no doubt that the coven thinks that it can. And if they're planning to sacrifice someone as part of their attempt, then there's a human life at stake. That alone compels me to stay."

"That's pretty much how I feel about it," said Faraday. "So, I say we stick together, we remain resolute, and we shall get through this. What say you, Richard?"

"Okay," I said. "You're right. I'm sure you're right. But there's still fewer of us than there are of them, and they have been planning this for an awfully long time. I don't think we should underestimate them."

"And we won't," said Faraday. "But I have great confidence in all of you. And let's not forget the one piece of good news."

"Such as what?" I said. "I really don't remember any good news."

"Well, we now know for certain that the spirit haunting Badcombe Hollow has nothing whatsoever to do with von Draken and his coven."

"Doesn't that mean that we have another, completely random factor to throw into the mix?" I said. "Something we don't understand, can't control and whose actions we have no way of predicting. I'd say that arguably puts us in a worse situation."

"On the contrary," said Faraday. "As unnerving as its sporadic manifestations might be, its presence here has to count as an advantage. Just think about it. The spirit of what was probably once a Neolithic high priestess or shaman, enraged beyond measure at the satanic cult responsible for desecrating its sacred burial ground, is helping to guard this house."

"So what?" I said.

"So, if the forces ranged against us are anywhere near as powerful as the coven would have us believe, she may just turn out to be the best ally we've got."

CHAPTER FORTY-NINE

The Spiritualist Revisited

I saw the demon that night, in my dreams, and when I awoke, I could not help but remember what the woman in the priory had told me.

I had seen a figure, standing somewhere in the landscape of the plain, amidst a clutter of sarsen stones. It had its back to me, but I was walking towards it. I could hear screams around me, but I couldn't see from where or whom they emanated. It was like a cacophony of discordant shouting, bouncing off the stones. It was night-time, because everything was in darkness, but the sky above me was streaked with red, as if it was on fire. As I drew closer to the figure, I saw that it wore a long robe with a hood, and seemed impossibly tall, like a giant. Slowly, it began to turn its head towards me.

And then I woke up. It was 30th April. The morning before Walpurgis Night.

When I joined the others at breakfast, it became clear that I had not been alone in experiencing such a vivid and disturbing dream.

"We all saw it," said Faraday, filling his pipe at the end of the table, a grim look on his face.

"It was as Malachy warned us," he went on. "He said the demon was close, on the very edge of our world, waiting to enter. He said that we might see something like this, as the time drew near. It would appear that we have."

He seemed out of sorts that morning, I thought, sitting slightly hunched in his chair, and speaking with a tired voice. In all honesty, I couldn't help but think that he looked scared.

"So, what do we do now?" I said, to nobody in particular.

"We wait," said Faraday. "We wait until this evening, when we must presume that the coven will, somehow or other, endeavour to get into their temple, and when they do, we stop them."

"As simple as that, eh?" said Kate.

"One can but hope," said Faraday. "Look, if they cut up rough, we simply call the police and have them arrested for trespass or criminal damage or any of a dozen other infractions."

"What if they jam the phones again?" I said.

"Then one of us drives or perhaps runs far enough away from Badcombe Hollow to get a signal, or else goes directly to the police station in Marlborough. Anyway, I'm not so concerned about that. I'm more worried that they might invoke less worldly means to get in here, and having seen the sort of magic show put on by their adept the other night, another occult attack on Badcombe Hollow can't be out of the question.

"However, my other concern is that, given our occupation of the house, and our evident determination to prevent them from getting in here, they'll simply give up on the idea, and perform the ceremony elsewhere."

"In that case," said Michael, "It probably won't work, right?"

"Perhaps," said Faraday. "It probably won't work, anyway. But my worry is more that they will go elsewhere, and kill whatever poor, helpless wretch they've chosen for their sacrifice. So, they may not get into their temple, but a human life will still be lost."

"Where would they go, do you think?" said Kate.

"My best guess is that they would go to the Devil's Dolmen," said Faraday. "They'll go to the place where the ceremony is supposed to end, and where the human sacrifice is to be made."

"There are four of us," said Michael. "Perhaps two stay here, and the other two stake out the dolmen."

"I thought about that," said Faraday. "But it would mean splitting our forces, and we're thin enough on the ground as it is. Better we all stay here, I think, and perhaps have a rethink closer to midnight, and then head over there in force."

He got slowly to his feet and walked over to the window, where he stood with his back to us, looking out towards the long barrow.

"It really is a most curious business," I heard him say, almost beneath his breath. "A most curious business."

He turned around and addressed us from the head of the table.

"Well," he said, "We obviously have something of a wait ahead of us. I suggest we exert ourselves sparingly, for the remainder of the day, and conserve our energies for whatever it is that's to come."

"I'm going to check over the perimeter," said Kate. "And take a look up in the woods. It's a good place for an OP up there, and for all we know, the coven is keeping this place under a close watch as we speak."

"OP?" I said.

"Observation post," said Kate. "Old habits."

"Do that," said Faraday. "But be careful. If you should happen to encounter anyone from the coven, back off immediately. We're going to need you here, this evening, so remember that, in this situation, caution is the better part of valour. Observe and report back. I'm serious, Kate. No haring off and taking matters into your own hands, like you did the other night, notwithstanding the fact that you probably saved Richard's life by doing so."

"Don't worry," said Kate. "I'll be careful."

"I need to go into Marlborough," said Michael. "I'll get some more ecclesiastical supplies from the Catholic church there, so that we can keep the pentagram in the cellar well provisioned against all eventualities."

"You won't forget the other thing we spoke about?" said Faraday.

"No, I'll collect that as well. The priest is getting it ready for me."

"Collect what?" I said. "What are you talking about?"

"Something I discovered during my recent research, which we may or may not need to deploy, later tonight," said Faraday. "Not really worth discussing now," he added, somewhat enigmatically.

I looked over at Kate and she shrugged silently at me and raised her eyebrows.

"I'm going to pop over to Bath this morning," I said. "I thought I'd go and see Bethany Weyland again. She's the spiritualist who knew Alan, and who I went to visit on the same day I went to the sabbat in Stokeley.

"The day I spoke to you on the phone," I said to Faraday. "Anyway, I have quite a bit to update her on, since then, and she might have some useful input. So, in the interests of leaving no stone unturned, I thought I'd go over there and see her."

"Good idea," said Faraday. "Apart from anything else, it may be no bad thing to let someone else know exactly what's likely to be going on here tonight, just in case we don't happen to come through it."

"I hadn't thought of it like that," I said. "But I suppose that is a good idea."

"Right then," said Faraday. "We seem to have a plan. But do please ensure that you're all back here by lunchtime. We could well be up all night, tonight, so it would be wise to rest up this afternoon."

And with that, we dispersed from the dining room to go about our various tasks.

A short time later, I walked out of the house to my car, just as Michael was driving away in Faraday's Range Rover. I noticed Kate walking over from the paddock.

"All quiet on the perimeter?" I enquired.

"Seems to be," she said, coming to a halt in front of me and lighting a cigarette. "Nothing to report, at any rate, but I'll take a walk up to the woods in a minute. Not that I really expect to find anything up there, either, but I like to keep busy."

She leaned against my car and looked out across the fields. It was another beautiful sunny day, with more than a hint of summer in the air. As ever, the situation we found ourselves in felt utterly incongruous, in the midst of such bucolic prettiness.

"They'll wait until dark," she said, exhaling a long stream of smoke. "They'll wait until it's dark, and then they'll make their move.

"Assuming that they do," she added.

"Do you think they will?" I asked.

"Yes, I do. And so does Julian. In fact, I've never seen him so worried. You could tell this morning that he's not really himself. So, yes. After everything that's happened so far, and given what's at stake for the coven, and given what they believe then, yes, I think they'll come."

"And what then?"

"Well, then we'll see, won't we?"

"No, I meant more, do you think they can do the thing they think they're going to do? Raise this demon thing. Bring about hell on earth. Can they do that?"

"I seriously doubt it," she said, "Although the magic show they put on for us in the cellar the other night certainly makes me wonder a bit. But no, I don't believe they could do that.

"I don't really have that sort of faith, you see," she continued. "Not in the way that Michael does, or Julian, to a lesser extent. He once said to me that I don't yet know what I'm for, but I know what I'm against. I'm against the sort of sick bastards who dabble in black magic. Cults and covens. But I don't do all of this for spiritual reasons. I do it to help people. And that's what we generally do. We just help people. That's all I really want to do.

"You asked me the other day why I got into this, and I wasn't entirely straight with you. I'd like to be straight with you now, if I may?"

"Of course," I said.

She seemed to gather herself before speaking.

"I had a sister," she said at last. "She was my younger sister, and we were chalk and cheese, completely different. I was the sensible one who studied hard at school, captained all the sports teams, joined the army, got commissioned, etcetera. She was the pretty, flighty one, always being taken to parties when she wasn't getting into various kinds of trouble, and then dropping out of school halfway through the sixth form. In all honesty, we weren't really very close, plus there was a five-year age gap between us.

"Anyway, I went off and joined the army and started travelling the world, and she went and lived on a frigging commune, or something, with whatever shit for brains boyfriend she was shacked up with by then. I barely saw her for several years, just the occasional Christmas and that sort of thing.

"By then, she was more or less off the charts and into all sorts of weird stuff, you know, all very pagan. The last time I ever saw her – it was Christmas, and we were at our parents' house – she was wearing this giant pentagram on a chain around her neck. I didn't really know what it meant at the time, and I certainly wasn't interested. We barely spoke to one another, the whole time we were there. I should have tried harder. It's something I feel very bad about, now.

"I was out of the country when she died. In Afghanistan. Camp Bastion. It was my second tour. She killed herself, you see. She was in a coven, and she basically lost her mind, somehow, and took her own life.

"The army gave me compassionate leave and I came back to England, and that was when I first met Julian. He'd been brought in to advise the police on this coven she belonged to. It was a bad one. One of the worst. Real hardcore satanists. Julian didn't know too much about them, or how my sister got involved with them, but he told me what he could.

"Like I said, they were a bad bunch. Their leader had done time inside for child molestation. He was on the Sex Offenders Register, although why he was allowed out of prison to start with, I can't even imagine. But it seems he was a very charismatic sort of leader, so it was more cult than coven, according to Julian.

"Anyway, this group, or whatever you want to call them, they operated out of the Forest of Dean. They had some sort of camp there, like a commune, and they all lived together. They think they recruited my sister at a pagan festival she went to about six months before she died. That's the theory, at any rate. Easy pickings, I would imagine. As you know, these groups prey on the weak and my sister was certainly that. When they did the autopsy, they discovered that her system was riddled with heroin, so that was probably what gave the coven their hold over her. That, and whatever crazy shit they put in her head.

"The coven used to conduct its ceremonies in a ruined church, somewhere in the forest where they lived. Not unlike the sort of place where we saw the sabbat the other night. Anyway, as far as we know, they did some kind of ritual there one night, some sort of spirit raising, and whatever happened, it terrified my sister out of her wits. But at least she had the presence of mind to try and leave the group she'd been lured into joining.

"They found her in the toilets at Bristol Temple Meads railway station. She'd killed herself. She'd cut her wrists, and she bled to death. She had a train ticket for Cheltenham, which is where my parents lived, back then, so they think she was on the way there. And then, for some reason, she just couldn't take it anymore. And so she got off the train, and went into the toilets, and took her own life.

"Her name was Sarah, and she'd be thirty years' old, now."

I looked across at Kate and saw that her eyes were glistened with tears.

"I'm so sorry," I said.

"Needless to say, there's a part of me that blames myself," she said. "You know, for not being there for her more; for not being there when she needed me. And it wouldn't take much of a psychologist to work out that what happened to her is what motivates me to be here today, helping to guard a long barrow against exactly the same sort of people who drove my sister to her death.

"So, I buried my sister, I went back to Afghanistan to finish my tour, and then I came back to England and resigned my commission. As soon as I was free, I got on the first train to Oxford, tracked down Julian, and asked if I could work for him. Fortunately, he said that I could, and I've been with him ever since."

"Thank you for explaining," I said. "I do certainly understand your motivations."

She took a final drag of her cigarette and then bent down, ground out the butt on the gravel driveway and popped it in her pocket.

"Guess I better get up to the woods," she said.

"Wait," I said. "What happened to the leader of the coven? The one who got your sister into all of this. What happened to him?"

"Nothing," she said. "He was a tricky bastard, and the police didn't have anything to charge him with, just a lot of rumour and supposition. I mean, they knew he was guilty. Everyone knew. There just wasn't enough hard evidence to make a case that would hold up in court."

"So, he got away with it?"

"Not exactly," she said, pushing herself off the car. "He died about a year ago. Got himself blown up in his car, of all things. In the dead of night, on a country lane, in the middle of nowhere. Blasted to smithereens.

"By the way," she said over her shoulder, as she started to walk away, "I was in the Royal Engineers, just in case you wondered. And Julian doesn't know anything about it, okay?"

****

I made good time to Bath that morning and by just after ten o'clock I had found a parking space in Victoria Park and was making my way over to Bethany Weyland's house. The Royal Crescent was looking particularly regal on that sun drenched morning and despite everything that was going on, I found myself enjoying the walk.

I had telephoned ahead, to ask if I could pay this visit and, somewhat to my surprise, Bethany had sounded not just willing but eager.

"I really don't get many visitors, these days," she said, as she opened the door and I stepped into the grand entrance hall with its black and white tiled floor.

"Or clients, for that matter," she said, taking my coat and hanging it up, before motioning for me to follow her into the house. "Also, I have to confess, I was immensely intrigued by everything you told me the other day, not to mention rather concerned as well. I must say, it's something of a relief to see you.

"And a great pleasure, too," she added.

We had reached the sitting room and I sat down on the same sofa I had occupied on my previous visit, but this time, instead of taking her place opposite me, Bethany sat down beside me.

Coffee had been laid out on the low table before us and she poured us both a cup, and then she settled back into the corner of the sofa, and looked at me for a long moment before speaking.

"I was really quite worried about you," she said.

"That's kind of you," I said. "I mean, I'm sorry that you were worried. You shouldn't have been. We barely know one another."

She smiled, demurely, and crossed her long legs in front of her.

"Perhaps," she said. "But after everything you told me the other day, and as presumptuous as it might sound, I feel as if I know you rather well."

"I only wish that we had met under different circumstances," I said.

"Then it's unlikely that we would have met at all," she said.

We smiled at each other, and I wished that I could somehow close my eyes and fast-forward to the next day – the day after Walpurgis Night – and not have to experience whatever was to come in the hours ahead.

"I need to tell you about everything that's happened," I said.

"Of course."

"I mean, I need to tell you because someone else needs to know about this. In case … in case something happens to us tonight," I added.

"That's not something I wanted to hear," she said. "But I still think that you should tell me everything."

And so, I told her. I picked up the story from the moment I had left her house, just days previously, and I left nothing out. I told her of my attempts to make contact with Professor Faraday. I told her about going to the sabbat and how I was nearly caught, and how Faraday and his group had rescued me. I told her about the magician in the house in the woods, and his interpretation of the demon raising invocation at the ceremony. I recounted everything that had happened during that dreadful night in the cellar, when we had sheltered in the pentagram from all the foul and ungodly things that the coven's witch had thrown at us. I told her about the numbers on the back of the Dorian Slake portrait and how they had led us to the Devil's Dolmen, and then locating the entrance to the temple, and how there had been nothing inside. I told her about Megan, and her betrayal. And I told her about the woman in the priory and what she had told me.

Bethany listened in silence, never interrupting, and when I had finished speaking, she let out a long sigh and shook her head.

"It's far worse than I had imagined," she said. "It's scarcely believable."

"And yet you believe it?"

"Or course I believe it. I believe everything you've told me. I'm just rather relieved that I didn't know anything about this while it was happening."

"What about the demon raising, later tonight? Do you believe that? I mean, do you believe the coven could be capable of such a thing?"

She seemed to think about this for a moment.

"No," she said, at last. "No, I don't believe they would be capable of such a thing. These sorts of raisings have been tried before, of course – perhaps not quite on this scale, with decades of preparation and planning – but they've never worked. Often, the people trying it have lost their minds as a result. But that doesn't mean they shouldn't be prevented from trying, because you never quite know what might happen, if people attempt to manipulate dark forces in that way. There could be more than their mortal souls at stake.

"And your Professor Faraday is right," she continued. "This is a violent, probably murderous coven. There is likely a human life at stake here, at the very least."

"You mean the sacrifice at the stones?" I said. "The one that is meant to end the ceremony and enact the raising of the demon?"

"Yes, precisely. That is something you have to stop. But there are other dangers, as well, just by attempting something like this. By the sounds of it, the coven will be invoking some very powerful forces, elemental forces designed to rip through the fabric of time and space. They may not succeed in opening the gates of hell, but it's still highly dangerous."

"I wish I could understand this better," I said. "Although none of this seems anywhere near as outlandish as it did the first time that I came to see you, not now that I've seen what I've seen, but it's all so far from the world I understand."

"None of us understand it," said Bethany. "I've been studying this my whole life, and I feel like I've barely scratched the surface. That's why it's so dangerous, and it's one of the many reasons why people shouldn't seek to practice this sort of magic. It's like putting someone in a laboratory who isn't a nuclear physicist and giving them fissile material to play with. Same thing when you get thirteen people in a circle summoning the forces of darkness. You never quite know what might happen."

She put her hand on my knee and got to her feet.

"I'll fetch us some more coffee," she said.

I watched her walk out of the room and heard the click of her heels in the tiled hallway.

Despite the bizarre nature of our conversation, I felt relaxed and comfortable in this house, and in the presence of Bethany Weyland. I felt safe here. I settled back into the sofa and wished I could just fall asleep.

"You know, I'm really very sorry that I can't be there with you," she said, as she came back into the room, jerking me out of my temporary reverie.

She poured more coffee into our cups before sitting down again.

"It's just that place," she said. "I simply can't go there. I told you what happened to me the only time I did. The evil that resides in that house, the way it seems to seep out of it and create an aura over it like a shroud, and then infects everything around it – I've never experienced that before. I know that I'm attuned to pick up on that sort of thing, but it was nothing like I've ever confronted. I've never felt the presence of true evil, such horror and hatefulness, so strongly.

"But you don't sense it, I think?" she said.

"No," I said. "I don't. I guess I'm just not attuned that way."

"Don't take it as a criticism," she said, with a smile.

"Faraday feels it," I said. "Nowhere near as strongly as you, but he can still sense it. He said as much the first time he walked in there. He says that when this is all over, he'll arrange to have it cleansed, or something.

"I mean, spiritually,' I added. "Sorry, I didn't mean to sound flippant."

"Not at all," she said. "Cleansed would be exactly the right word. And that's something that can certainly be done, and something you should do, for your own peace of mind, once this is all over."

"Once this is all over, I intend to get shot of the place as soon as possible," I said. "But I think, in all good conscience, having the house exorcised of its evil spirits is the least I can do for the new owners.

"I do plan to stay on in this area, though," I added. "After the house is sold."

"I'm pleased to hear that," she said.

And I was pleased to hear her say that, I thought, although her words were disconcertingly similar to something Megan had said to me a few days previously. I winced inwardly, and for the umpteenth time since the previous day, at the thought of her betrayal, and still more at my own gullibility.

"Anyway," I said, "I'll do what I can to rid the place of whatever Alan and his cronies did to contaminate it, but with regard to the old woman guarding the long barrow, I think she probably comes with the deeds."

"Yes, I know," said Bethany, animatedly. "And isn't that just the most fascinating thing? I totally agree with your analysis, by the way, that she has nothing to do with the coven, and that she only attacks people associated with it. They didn't put her there. She's been there ever since the long barrow was constructed. She guards the barrow, like you said. I've no doubt that's what forced Alan out of there, and it may well have contributed to Dorian Slake's insanity and suicide. She's on your side in all of this."

"Not exactly the most reliable of allies," I said.

"No, of course not. It's a completely uncontrollable phenomenon. Her spirit exists on another plane entirely."

"Another plane?"

"The astral plane. She occupies a cosmic realm, the place between here and wherever we go when we die. She's always there, but you can't always see her. But she's always there, at Badcombe Hollow."

"Good to know," I said. "At least, I think it is."

"Well, I'm at least glad to know that someone from the spirit world is watching over you."

She smiled and seemed to come to a decision.

"There's something I'd like to give you," she said. "I wasn't sure if I would, before you came here today. I thought you might scoff at something like this. Well, not scoff, perhaps; you're too polite for that. But I thought you might not take it very seriously. Now, I think that you will."

She slid open a drawer set into the low wooden table in front of us and withdrew something wrapped in pale blue tissue paper. Placing the object on the table, she unwrapped the paper, and then handed it to me.

It was a piece of coloured glass, highly polished and with a similar size and heft to a large pebble, but with a slightly flattened top, into which was set the representation of an eye, formed by teardrop shaped bands of blue and white, with a black dot in the middle.

"It's an amulet," said Bethany. "Specifically, it's a Nazar amulet. It wards off the evil eye."

"Like a good luck charm," I said.

"Yes, exactly like that. It's a form of protection. Amulet means an object that protects a person from trouble. The Nazar amulet has been used since ancient times, and is a very universal symbol, these days, although it originated in the Middle East. Nazar derives from an Arabic word meaning sight, and the amulet relates to the notion of an eye for an eye. The eye depicted in this glass stone counters the evil eye. Hence it wards off evil. It's only a small thing, but I wanted you to have it."

"Thank you," I said. "I shall treasure it."

"Don't treasure it, use it. Keep it on your person."

She took the amulet from my hands.

"Here," she said, placing it in the pocket of my shirt. "Keep it here. Keep it with you, tonight."

"I will," I said.

I left shortly afterwards. I could have stayed there talking to her all day, but I knew that I had to get back to Badcombe Hollow.

"Thank you," I said, as we walked to the door. "It helps to have someone to talk to about all of this."

"Come and talk to me about it again, when it's all over," she said, handing me my coat.

"I shall do that," I said. "And I'll call you tomorrow, when hopefully it will all be over."

"I'd be grateful if you would," she said.

As I turned to walk out of the door, she reached out her arms, and drew me close to her in a tight hug.

"Be very careful," she said, her voice barely above a whisper. "I'll pray for you."

It echoed what she had said to me the last time I had left her house, but there was an intimacy in the way she spoke to me now, in contrast to the cool detachment she had displayed on my previous visit. As I walked away from her house that day, I knew that I wanted to see her again.

I just hoped I'd get the chance.

CHAPTER FIFTY

Walpurgis Night

It was early afternoon by the time I got back to Badcombe Hollow. I found the others in the kitchen, sitting around the island unit and picking at a plate of sandwiches.

"Any news?" I asked, taking a sandwich from the plate and perching at the unit.

"Nothing of any great import," said Faraday. "Other than the fact that the coven appears to be very much in the vicinity."

"I found the remains of a recent fire, up in the woods," said Kate, picking up a sandwich and then peeling back the corner to inspect the contents, wrinkling her nose with vague distaste, and putting it down again.

"Sorry," she said. "Fussy eater. But, yes, they were up there last night, for sure. The fire was still warm, and I can't imagine it would be anyone other than them up there."

"Was it by the clearing, in the middle of the woods?" I asked. "The place where Slake killed himself?"

"No. It was closer to here. By the edge, looking over at the house. Perfect spot for it. The fire was in a big dip in the ground, so we wouldn't have noticed it from here. But I reckon someone's been watching from up there, and they probably bugged out when they saw me walking across the field."

"Interesting," I said. "But hardly unexpected, given the imminence of the big night."

"And Michael saw von Draken in Marlborough," she added, having selected another sandwich and bitten into it with evident satisfaction.

"Oh, really?" I said. "Are you sure?"

"Pretty sure," said Michael. "I saw him walking along the high street, just as I was coming out of the church. Dapper elderly chap, white hair, camelhair coat?"

"That sounds like him," I said.

"Again," said Faraday, "Not entirely unexpected, and we know that he has a residence in town. Nevertheless, it would appear that the forces are gathering."

He looked better than he had that morning, I thought. The tiredness seemed to have gone from his eyes and he had a resolute air about him.

"So, what do we do now?" I said.

"We wait," said Faraday. "Absolutely nothing to do now except wait."

****

And so, we waited. I went up to my room, lay down on the bed and closed my eyes. I had imagined that I would find sleep impossible, but I soon drifted off. When I awoke, I read for a while, and then I fell asleep again.

When I woke up for the second time, it was late afternoon, and the sun was much lower in the sky. I had a quick shower and changed my clothes, remembering to transfer the amulet Bethany had given me into the pocket of my fresh shirt, and then I went downstairs, where I found Faraday with Kate in the sitting room, playing a game of chess.

I nodded a friendly greeting to them, but said nothing, as I made my way over to the armchair by the window with my book. It was curious, I reflected, how quickly we had become so comfortable and familiar in each other's company, these past few days.

Michael came in shortly afterwards and began to peruse the bookshelves.

"I put a chicken pie in the oven," he said.

"You made a chicken pie?" said Kate, looking over at him, whilst keeping her index finger poised atop a chess piece.

"No. I bought one in Marlborough this morning. Chicken and leek. It serves four."

He took a large hardback book from one of the shelves, sat down on a bean bag by the fireplace, and started to flick through it.

We remained like that for some time, sitting quietly in the cosy sitting room while the sun edged towards the horizon and the light seeped out of the day.

Michael went to fetch the pie from the kitchen, which we ate on our laps, since we couldn't be bothered to move to another room. I wondered about fetching a decent bottle of something from the cellar, but for some reason drinking alcohol seemed inappropriate, in the circumstances, and I doubted that Faraday would have approved. I went and fetched lemonade and glasses from the kitchen, and after we had eaten, I put on a pot of coffee. Faraday won the chess game.

"What time does it get dark?" I asked at one point.

"About half eight," said Kate. "Not long now."

As dusk reached the cusp of darkness, I went and checked over the whole house, and ensured that all the doors and windows were locked, and by the time I got back to the others, night had fallen.

We went into the kitchen to drink coffee, and then Faraday suggested that we repair back to the sitting room to continue our vigil.

"I'm going to take a look from upstairs," said Kate, who I noticed was toting a small pair of binoculars. "When they come, they'll probably come from the direction of the woods, and the bedroom on the west side has the best view."

"Good idea," said Faraday. "Do that, and we'll come and relieve you in a while."

For the next couple of hours, nothing happened. We continued to occupy the sitting room, for the most part, periodically wandering off to check around the house. I also went outside with Faraday to check the perimeter.

"It's a beautiful night," I said, as we stood on top of the long barrow, looking out across fields which were bathed in moonlight.

"It's a pity, in a way," he said. "A good rainstorm might have persuaded the coven to stay indoors, not that I imagine there would be much chance of stopping them, at this point."

"So, where are they?" I said.

"They're out there somewhere," he said, pointing over towards the woods. "Waiting. Just as we're waiting. But they'll make their move soon enough."

We went back inside and locked the door behind us.

"You know that von Draken has almost certainly got one of these," I said, as I turned the key in the lock.

"What? A key?" said Faraday. "I dare say that he probably has. If it comes to it, this will be more about you asserting your rights as a property holder, than von Draken somehow sneaking in here. Locking this door is almost moot, in a sense, with us here in the house. My guess is that he'll announce himself, somehow, and present us with some kind of threat or ultimatum. But I simply don't know."

I drew the chain across anyway and followed Faraday back into the house.

At about half-past ten there was a shout from upstairs, where Michael was taking his turn watching the field and the woods from the balcony outside Alan's bedroom.

We made our way hurriedly up the stairs, where we found Michael standing on the balcony with his back to us, looking out into the field.

"They're here," he said, as he heard us enter the room, and without looking around. "I guess it's started."

We joined him on the balcony, and as soon as I looked into the field, I felt a shudder of fear at what I saw there.

In the far distance, coming out of the woods and heading down the long slope of the field towards the house was a procession of people, moving in single file, with each of them carrying a burning torch. I counted the torches, and there were thirteen, just as there had been a few nights previously at Stokeley, except this time, I knew that Megan was one of their number.

After all the weeks of anticipation, after all the speculation, after all that had happened, the coven had finally arrived at Badcombe Hollow.

We watched in silence as they made their way towards the house. As they got to the bottom of the field and neared the edge of the property, they started to fan out and formed a line in front of the long barrow, where they stopped, just short of the fence.

For a minute or so they merely stood there, as silent as we were, so that the only sound was the faint crackling of their torches. And then, one of their number, the one at the end, who had led the procession down the hill, walked in front of the others, and took up a central position before them, whereupon he planted his torch in the ground and stepped back from it. Following his lead, the rest of the coven did the same.

"That must be von Draken," I said, in a whisper.

Whether they could see us or not, I couldn't be sure. We could most assuredly see them, although they were obscured by the darkness. But I wondered if the glare of their torches would prevent them from seeing us. Not that it really mattered, at that point. They must have known that we were waiting for them in the house.

A low chant erupted from the group. It started almost as a murmur and then increased in volume to a discordant moan in a language I didn't recognise.

"What are they doing?" said Kate.

"Getting ready for something," said Michael.

"This is just theatre," said Faraday. "I'm sure they know we're watching them. This is being staged for our benefit. It's what they do next that intrigues me."

The coven continued with their chant, and we continued to watch them. And then the sound reduced in volume to the sort of low pitch it had started with, and then it stopped entirely. At that point, and somewhat to my surprise, they all extinguished their torches.

It was harder to see them now, but they were still just about visible beneath the clear night sky, stood in a line, cloaked and hooded. For a moment, I wondered if they were simply going to charge at the house, and then their leader shouted what sounded like some sort of instruction, and the coven suddenly dispersed.

A few went off up the slope towards the steep bank at the back of the house, whilst another group including, I noticed, von Draken, went in the other direction, down the field towards the road, and the entrance to Badcombe Hollow. Meanwhile, three of the group, presumably from amongst the younger and fitter contingent, climbed over the fence, ran up and over the long barrow and headed across the driveway, and out of our sight, somewhere in the garden. I wondered if one of them was Megan.

"Guess we're surrounded," said Michael.

"What do we do now?" I said to Faraday.

"We go back downstairs," he said. "And Richard, please go and turn on all the external lights. If they're going to occupy the garden, we can at least deprive them of the benefit of darkness."

We rushed down the stairs and I peeled off to go and switch on the outside lights. When I re-joined the others, they had gathered in the hallway and I saw Kate tapping on her cell phone.

"No signal," she said. "They've jammed the phones again, just like the other night."

"No matter," said Faraday. "We anticipated that. We're not quite there yet, but should the time come, then you, Kate, must be the one to go and seek help. You're the fittest and best trained of all of us, but you'll need to evade whoever is outside and get at least a mile from here before you'll be able to obtain a signal again."

"I can do that," said Kate.

"Why not do it now, anyway?" I said, trying not to betray the fear in my voice. "They're trespassing, after all."

"Not unless we have to," said Faraday. "I don't want to split us up unless it becomes absolutely necessary. And whilst I have the greatest confidence in Kate, she might not make it, and then our numbers would have reduced to three, with the possibility of one of us being held hostage. We stand firm here, and refuse to let them in. I still can't see how they can force us to do otherwise, and in an hour or so's time it will be too late for them, anyway."

"Do you think they might try and burn down the house?" I said. "You know, smoke us out?"

"No," said Faraday. "Even out here, there's too much of a risk that someone would notice and alert the authorities. My guess is that they'll have one last go at negotiation, or at least intimidation, and then … well, what happens then, I'm not really sure."

There was a loud, pounding knock on the front door, startling us all.

"Don't open it," said Faraday. "If we don't open that door, then they can't get through it."

There was another loud knock on the door. I wondered how many of the satanists were standing on the other side.

Then there was a slight creaking sound, which I realised was the letterbox being pushed open. I saw a hand come through the aperture and then withdraw again before re-emerging, but this time the hand was clasped shut, forming a fist, and holding what appeared to be the end of a piece of rope. It pushed this through the door and into the hallway and then let go, so that it dropped onto the floor. By then I had realised that it wasn't a piece of rope. It was a long grey snake.

The serpent dropped gently to the floor and uncoiled itself by the door, lifting its head to look at us, which hooded as it did so.

"God help us, that's a black mamba," said Michael. "Those things are bloody lethal."

"Jesus," said Kate. "What is it with these people and snakes?"

"Stay completely still," said Faraday. "We need to try and manoeuvre it into something, some sort of container, and then we can move it out of the way and ..."

Before he could finish speaking, Kate suddenly stooped down, picked up a small scatter rug from the floor and threw it over the snake, whilst at the same time plucking a walking stick from the rack beside us and then launching herself at the writhing bundle.

She whacked the stick down on it about a dozen times while we stood watching her, somewhat aghast, and then she gingerly raised the corner of the rug with the stick before reaching down and pulling it off the snake, whereupon she bashed it over the head again and again until there was nothing left but a bloody pulp.

"I think it's definitely dead, now," she said, at last, and put the stick back in the rack.

"Sorry, Julian. Catching a venomous snake is really not something we have time for, right now."

"Not at all," he said. "Good initiative."

I used the rug to gather up the dead snake and then went and deposited the grisly bundle in the bin in the kitchen. And then as I went back into the hall, I heard the sound of smashing glass behind me.

We all charged into the kitchen and saw a large, jagged hole in the window above the sink, and broken glass littering the sideboard. On the other side of the window stood one of the coven, its face obscured by the hood of its cloak, and for a moment I wondered if whoever it was might be about to clamber through the window, but instead it raised back its arm and threw something into the house.

It was another snake, and I felt its body brush against me as it fell to the floor. It was different to the first one, smaller, like some kind of viper. I leapt back just as it struck out at my foot. Grabbing a saucepan from the draining board, I threw it at the snake, causing it to slither away, whereupon Michael appeared from around the corner of the island unit and stamped down with the heel of his boot on the snake's head.

"Another dead one," he said, picking it up by the tail and flicking it back out of the broken window. I noticed that the satanist who had been thrown it into the kitchen was no longer there.

"Are they just going to keep on doing this all night?" said Kate. "Do they really think that's going to be enough to drive us out of here?"

"I don't think this is entirely for us," said Faraday. "They're a serpent cult and I think this is somehow all part of the ritual. Whatever they've got in store for us is yet to come."

We didn't have long to wait. Just moments later there was another sound of smashing glass, this time coming from the front of the house.

It was in the eastward, more formal sitting room where we discovered the broken window. Lying on the floor, just by the foot of the chair into which I had once ushered Ernst von Draken, was a small, cloth wrapped bundle.

"Do you think it's another snake?" I said.

Faraday shook his head.

"No," he said. "I'm guessing it's some sort of message."

He knelt down and carefully picked up the cloth bundle and unwrapped it. There was a large, grey stone inside and it appeared to be covered in some kind of writing.

"What is that?" I said, squinting down at the mysterious script.

"Those are runes," said Faraday, pointing at the markings. "From an ancient, runic, pre-Germanic language. I think it's probably a curse."

"Do we get rid of it?" I started to say, but then Faraday suddenly gave a gasp of pain and dropped the stone as if scalded by it, and it landed on the carpet with a dull thud.

"Good God, no, surely not," I heard him say.

Smoke was rising from the stone. It was real smoke, not an illusion. I could even smell burning in the air. Somehow, inexplicably, the stone was dissolving into smoke before our eyes.

I wanted to ask Faraday something, although I'm not sure what, but in any event, before I could speak, there was a loud flash and bang, throwing us all to the floor. Feeling dazed, and trying to scramble to my feet, I realised that there was something in the room with us, something that had manifested itself out of the smoking rune stone.

It was a small, humanoid creature, like a goblin, with dark brown, leathery skin, black eyes and huge pointed teeth. It stared at us for a moment, and then started to flit about the room in a blur, flying from corner to corner, whilst emitting the most awful, ear-splitting noise, somewhere between a growl and a scream.

I saw it only fleetingly and, even in that moment, somehow had the presence of mind to question whether or not this thing was real, or merely some hideous manifestation summoned by the coven, because it flickered in and out of view, and seemed indistinct at its edges, like some sort of ephemeral hologram. Either way, it was enough to keep us rooted to the spot and distracted. And it proved to be enough of a diversion for the coven to get into the house.

As we cowered before the demonic creature, I heard a crashing sound from the kitchen. It sounded like someone bashing their way through the window the coven had broken when throwing the snake in there. A moment later, in the corner of my eye, I saw a black robed figure run through the hallway towards the front door.

"They're in the house," I shouted at Faraday, who was frantically trying to pull the vicious goblin away from Kate.

I made to run out into the hallway, to prevent whoever was out there from opening the front door, but then the goblin appeared right in front of my face, causing me to scream and fall backwards.

And then it simply vanished, and in the same moment three figures appeared in the doorway of the sitting room. It was Ernst von Draken and Catherine Falaise and, standing between them, Megan.

Von Draken and Megan were both holding automatic pistols, which were pointed at us, and the witch held a long, serrated knife loosely by her side.

"Good evening, Professor Faraday," said von Draken, with a cruel smile.

It was over. We had lost.

The coven was in control of Badcombe Hollow.

CHAPTER FIFTY-ONE

Prisoners

They made us kneel on the floor at one end of the room and put our hands on our heads. For an awful moment, I thought they were simply going to execute us. But it transpired that they had other plans.

While Megan and von Draken covered us with their pistols several other members of the coven came in and frisked us. One of them I recognised as the large, bearded man who had almost caught me in the woods at Stokeley on the night of the sabbat. A couple of the others, I noted, were relatively elderly – if not quite as old as von Draken or Faraday – and I wondered if this might possibly give us some small advantage if it came to a full-on fight between us. For the moment, however, such thoughts were entirely moot, given that we were being held at gunpoint.

It was a sickening feeling, for us to have succumbed so easily, and to have transferred the stewardship of Badcombe Hollow without a real fight. As I knelt there with a gun to my head, my mind was attempting to process all the myriad things we might have done to avoid such an outcome, and I figured that the others were likely doing the same. I was also aware that we were in a very bad situation indeed.

"Take them down to the cellar," said von Draken. "All except for him," he added.

As he said this, he pointed at Michael.

"You're staying with us," he said.

"Oh yes, and why would that be?" said Michael, defiantly.

"Surely you've worked it out by now," said von Draken. "I understand from Megan that you've all been very busy over the past few days, poking your noses into our business. In which case, you know full well what we're about to attempt tonight, and the key ingredient required in order to make our endeavour successful."

"No idea what you're talking about," said Michael, although I had a horrible feeling that we both did.

"An offering, of course. In a couple of hours' time, we shall be welcoming a most honoured visitor to our earthly realm and you, young man, will be our tribute."

It was just as I had feared. Michael was to be the human sacrifice whose death would conclude the ceremony at the Devil's Dolmen.

"I don't think so, you crazy bastard," said Michael.

As he said this, Megan suddenly stepped forward and smashed Michael in the face with the butt of her pistol. He screamed with pain and clasped his hands to his face. Blood was streaming from his nose, which looked as if it had been broken.

"Leave him alone, you fucking bitch," shouted Kate, at which point the bearded man stepped forward and kicked her in the stomach, making her clutch her ribs and gasp for breath.

"Take me instead," said Faraday.

It was the first time he had spoken since our capture, and his voice was calm and measured, in contrast to the violent chaos that was starting to erupt around him.

"Take me," he repeated. "I am the leader of this group. I'm sure that I would make a far more fitting tribute to your demon."

"On the contrary, Professor," said von Draken. "I understand that this man is in training to become a priest. Who could be better qualified for this task than a man of the cloth? What say you, holy man? Are you ready to serve your true master, tonight?"

He made a signal to the coven, whereupon several of them stepped forward and hauled us to our feet before forcing us roughly out of the room.

Once in the hallway, the two men restraining Michael by each arm handed him over to Catherine Falaise, who took hold of him from behind by the scruff of his collar and laid the serrated blade of her knife across his throat. His face was covered in blood by then and he looked as if he might faint.

"Don't try anything," she said to us. "Otherwise, I'll slash his throat and we'll use the girl for our sacrifice."

I looked out through the front door. Three of the coven were standing in the illuminated glow of the driveway, seemingly keeping watch on the front of the property. In the kitchen, I noticed, another two were boarding up the broken window, and I couldn't understand why they would think to do this. I wondered if it was to keep us contained in that house at all costs.

I think that Faraday, Kate and I had decided by then that there was no chance of over-powering the coven at that time, and that we would be better off re-grouping and waiting for a better chance. Although quite how we were going to get out of a locked cellar, I had absolutely no idea.

Von Draken joined us in the hallway and motioned for us to walk towards the door to the cellar. Megan stood beside him, and both of their guns were pointed us.

"You've made a real mess of that kitchen window," I said to him, for some reason.

"The least of your worries," he replied. "I gave you ample opportunity to leave this house and yet you chose to ignore me. This is entirely your own fault."

He opened the door to the cellar and instructed us to go down there, which we did in single file, with Faraday in the lead, followed by me, with Megan behind me, holding a gun to my head, and Kate at the back, followed by von Draken.

"Don't worry, Michael," Kate shouted, as we started down the steps. "This isn't over, not by a long shot. You stay alive, and we'll come and get you. This isn't over."

"Oh, but it really is, my dear," said von Draken. "It really, truly is."

When we reached the bottom of the stairs another member of the coven who had followed us down there pushed past us and opened the door to the room containing the pentagram. Von Draken turned on the light, the switch for which was located on the corridor side of the room. As on the night when we had been attacked in there, the room was set up to withstand an occult assault, with candles placed around the circled perimeter, and with bibles and vials of holy water in the centre. I reflected that this might well have provided ample protection against the spirit world but provided none whatsoever against people with guns and knives.

Megan drew me close to her as we stood there, waiting to go in.

"Having fun, darling?" she said.

I looked away, not wishing to engage with her, and sickened at the thought that the two of us had once been intimate.

Von Draken stepped into the room and looked around with evident satisfaction.

"Someone's obviously been busy," he said. "I recall painting this circle on the floor with Alan, just after he bought the house. I assume that you took shelter here the other night. It would appear that we're not the only ones prepared to adopt occult measures."

"The pentacle within the protected circle may be used for good, as well as evil," said Faraday. "As you well know," he added.

"This evening it will be used for neither," said von Draken. "Tonight, it is merely a gaol cell, to keep you contained until we return from the ceremony.

"Put them in there," he directed Megan and the other member of the coven, and they pushed us through the door and into the far corner of the room, before re-joining von Draken.

"Upstairs," he said to them. "Start taking the others over to the temple, including the priest. We still have a great deal to do."

They went up the stairs and out of sight. I wondered if it was the last time that I would ever see Megan.

Von Draken remained standing in the doorway, surveying his three prisoners in the corner of the room.

"I'm sorry to have to cut this short, Professor," he said. "As you can likely imagine, this is a very important night for us. And this time, rest assured that you shall not be saving the day as you did on that other night when our paths crossed, fifty long years ago. Yes, I was there. The night you took the child from us and thwarted the plans of my father, and my dear friend and mentor, Dorian Slake. I remember you, Professor. I saw you up there on the balcony, holding the child. I've waited many years to exact righteous vengeance for what you did.

"So, we shall return. And when we do, we shall have someone with us. I would imagine that he will be very keen to meet all of you. He will likely be in need of sustenance by then, and I simply can't think of a better offering."

With that, he slammed shut the door, locked it and switched off the light, plunging the room into almost total darkness, save for a couple of slivers of moonlight coming through the ventilation grates in the flower bed above us.

We heard him walk up the stairs and close the door to the cellar behind him.

For a long moment we simply stood there in the darkness, saying nothing.

"What did he mean?" I said, at last. "What did he mean about sustenance? About an offering? What did he mean?"

"He was referring to the demon they plan to bring through the portal tonight," said Faraday. "He's going to feed us to it."

CHAPTER FIFTY-TWO

Rescued

We lit the candles so that we had some light in there, and then we slumped to the floor, exhausted and defeated.

I could hear the coven milling about in the driveway outside, and a low murmur of voices. After a short time, all was quiet again, and I assumed they had entered the temple beneath the long barrow.

"So, what now?" said Kate. "We need to get out of here."

"Do you reckon we could break down the door?" I said

"It's a pretty solid looking door, so I doubt it. But there might be something else we could try."

She pulled off one of her boots and shook it, causing a small folding razor to drop to the floor.

"That coven needs some lessons in searching people properly," she muttered, as she put her boot back on.

I was gratified to see that we now at least had a weapon, but couldn't really see how that was going to shift the odds in our favour.

"What do we do with that?" I said to Kate, nodding at the blade.

"Two options," she said. "We could wait for them to come back, rush them at the doorway, try and slash von Draken's throat, at least, and then take it from there."

"I'm certainly prepared to try," I said. "But it sounds like a bit of a long shot. Besides which, they could well have a demon in tow by then. It's hard to see us overpowering that in the doorway."

"*If* they actually manage to raise a demon," she said. "We all know that's a highly unlikely outcome."

"In that case we'll just be facing a bunch of pissed off, murderous satanists," I said. "And Michael would probably be dead by then."

"Yes, I know. Better in that case that we try and break out of here."

"With a switchblade?" I said.

"We try and hack through one of the door panels," she said. "Then we could reach through to the other side and unlock it. I'm pretty sure they didn't take the key out."

"Or, we could try and take the hinges off," I said. I was dubious in the extreme that we would be able to cut through a timber door with a small knife.

"Yes, we could try that too."

"So, let's do it then," I said, getting to my feet.

"We should wait," she said. "For as long as the coven are here at Badcombe Hollow, they might hear us trying to get out. And they might well send someone to check on us before they decamp to the dolmen for the final part of the ceremony. I would, if I was in their situation. We wait until we hear them leave, and then we break out of here and follow them."

"If we can actually get out of here," I said.

"I know, but it's the best strategy I can come up with. What do you think, Julian?"

Faraday had not spoken a word during the whole time Kate and I had been talking. He sat with his knees drawn up before him and was staring fixedly at the ground. He looked like a broken man.

"What do I think?" he repeated. "I think that I've been a stubborn old fool, in my insistence that we tackle this coven alone, instead of alerting the authorities. Clearly, we were woefully underprepared tonight, a state of affairs that is entirely my responsibility, and because of that, not only have we failed to prevent this wretched ceremony from taking place, but I've very likely got us all killed, as well. So, I'm not sure that my advice is of any great value, any longer."

"Nonsense," said Kate. "The decision not to alert the police in advance was a joint one. We all agreed to it. What would we have told them, anyway? That a group of mostly elderly witchcraft practitioners were going to access a hidden temple underneath a long barrow, in order to bring about the end of the world? They would have laughed in our faces. Or else, at most, they might have put a patrol car at the end of the driveway, the occupants of which would now be either in here with us, or more likely sitting dead in their car with their throats cut. You've seen how determined this coven is, and the lengths to which they are prepared to go."

"And it's for precisely that reason that we should have been better prepared," said Faraday.

"I'm really not sure how we could have been," I said. "I think the only thing we got wrong was not sending someone off to raise the alarm when they first got into the garden. They were trespassing, after all. Maybe, in that brief window of opportunity, before they raised that creature thing in the sitting room, someone should have made a run for it. What the hell was that thing, anyway?"

"It was an absolute master stroke, that's what it was," said Faraday. "At least, it was from the coven's perspective. That, I never foresaw, even after what we witnessed in this room the other night."

"So, what was it?"

"The creature that we saw was the result of a runic invocation, a runic demon raising, if you will. I never anticipated that they might be capable of such a thing.

"That thing tonight, that sabre toothed goblin which came out of the stone, could easily have killed us. It would have done, in fact, had the coven not taken over, once we were all sprawling around helplessly on the floor."

"But it didn't look quite real," I said. "It was blurred at the edges, and looked transient, somehow, like it was just an image."

"I can assure you it was not," said Faraday. "If it looked indistinct, it was because it exists within a tiny rip in the fabric of time and space. It was emerging from the spirit world into our world. The coven could only risk bringing it here for the briefest of moments, because even they wouldn't have been able to control it, once it was fully loose. It would have been as much of a danger to them as it was to us. But they – or rather, their adept, Catherine Falaise – brought it over for just long enough to distract us and get into the house. It was a clever move, albeit a highly dangerous one."

"And they got it out of a stone?" I said, somewhat incredulously.

"Out of a rune stone," said Faraday. "That's what it was. There were runic markings on the stone. It was a casting of the runes, on an exceptionally ambitious scale. I never imagined that might happen. That was powerful, powerful magic, of the blackest kind. Quite incredible, really."

"Okay, well that's all fine and dandy," said Kate. "So, they did that, and they got the jump on us. Bully for them. But now it's up to us to take the initiative."

"I admire your pluck, Kate," said Faraday. "I always have. But at this precise moment, the coven seems to be holding all the cards."

"In that case," she said, "We need to try and turn the odds in our favour. Do you approve the plan?"

"My dear Kate, you've never needed my approval less, but yes, for what it's worth, I approve. We'll try and get through that door. But you're right; we should wait until the coven is off the property. It may be cutting things a bit fine, but it's the best plan."

"So, the ceremony in the temple goes ahead," I said.

"The ceremony in the temple goes ahead," said Faraday. "But we stop the raising and we save Michael at the dolmen. That's where the final enacting of the ritual takes place, so that's where we now have to stop them."

I knew that just getting through the door was going to be a long shot, at best, and that even if we did get through, we would have given the coven a considerable head start. And I also knew that even if we caught up with them in enough time to try and thwart their plans, it was now thirteen against three. But then, we all knew that, so there was no reason to labour the point. Better to conserve our energy.

I settled down in the pentagram to wait. Waiting, it seemed, had been very much the theme of that day.

We were mostly silent, and barely moved, other than to avail ourselves of the bottles of water that Michael had thoughtfully stashed down there, earlier in the day, along with the fresh candles.

Sometime later, we became aware of activity outside. There was a hubbub of voices from the driveway, which then faded, and was replaced by the faint sound of engines starting.

"They must have had vehicles out by the entrance," I said.

"They can't walk to the dolmen," said Faraday. "Not from here, anyway. It may be the middle of the night, but there would still be too much chance of attracting attention, given their number, and the way they're dressed. They have a prisoner, too. They'll get as close as they can by road, and then walk the rest of the way."

"Time to try and get through this door," said Kate.

She got out her knife and used its end to tap at the wood panelling to the door.

"So, what now?" I said, standing beside her.

"Now, I suppose I try and hack away at it," she said.

If this had seemed like a long shot before, it soon became evident that it wasn't going to work. Kate managed to get the knife into the door and started trying to cut into it, but it was a small blade and a thick door, and after a few moments the blade broke anyway, and that was that.

"Here, try this," said Faraday.

He had extinguished one of the candles and taken it from its large brass holder, which he was holding like a hammer.

For the next few minutes, we took it in turns to bash away at the door, focusing our efforts upon the panel immediately above the handle, thinking that if we could somehow make a hole in this, we might be able to reach through and unlock the door from the other side. We managed to put a dent in the wood, but it was clear that it was going to take a very long time to break through it, time that we simply didn't have. But we pressed on anyway. There simply wasn't anything else that we could do.

"Wait," said Faraday suddenly, just as I was drawing back my arm to whack the door for the umpteenth time. "There's someone outside."

I strained to listen through the flowerbed grating above us and to my horror realised that Faraday was correct. I could hear the crunch of gravel as someone walked across the driveway.

"The coven must have left someone behind to keep watch," Kate whispered.

"They can't have done," said Faraday. "They need all thirteen of them to be present at the dolmen, otherwise the raising has no chance of being successful."

"Well, there's someone out there," said Kate. "What do we do now?"

"There's nothing we can do but keep very quiet and play it by ear," said Faraday. "Whoever it is will have heard us, for sure, but if they are somehow associated with the coven, and they come down and open the door, then we might be able to rush them."

The sound of footsteps faded then and was replaced by the sound of someone knocking on the front door.

"That doesn't make any sense," I said.

We continued to wait and soon heard the footsteps in the drive again. They came to a halt right above us.

"Is anyone down there?" came a voice.

The voice was female, and I thought I recognised it.

"Is anyone down there?" the voice said again, and this time I knew who it was.

"Bethany!" I shouted up through the grate.

"Richard? Is that you?"

"Yes, we're trapped down here," I shouted. "We're locked in the cellar."

"It's Bethany Weyland," I explained to the others. "The person I went to see today. I can't think what she's doing here, but she may just have saved us."

"How do I get you out?" said Bethany, through the grate.

She must have climbed into the flowerbed, I thought, and pressed her face to the grate, for I could just make out a glimpse of her pale features.

"Easy," I shouted through the grate. "There's a spare set of front door keys under the shed."

"Okay," she said. "Where's the shed?"

"Round by the side of the house. Go back towards the front door, keep going and follow the house round towards the back. There's a shed there by the vegetable patch. It's raised slightly off the ground. Reach under the shed beside the door, on the side nearest the house, and you'll find a small tin, like a tobacco tin. The keys are inside it."

"Okay," she said. "I'll be right back."

We heard her move away across the drive.

"We may have been dealt our first piece of good fortune," said Faraday.

After what seemed like an inordinate period of time, but which in reality was no more than a few minutes, we heard the front door open above us. Then, moments later, the lock in the door before us turned, and Bethany was standing there in the doorway.

"Thank God," I said, stepping forward and embracing her instinctively.

She was dressed in a long, hooded parker coat, which reached almost to her knees, and I noticed that her face was as white as a sheet. I knew what a profound effect this place had upon her, and what a supreme effort of will it must have taken for her to come here tonight.

I made some hurried introductions and we all rushed out of the cellar and up the stairs into the hallway, and then out into the driveway. The garden was quiet and in darkness, the satanists having evidently decided to switch off all the external lights that I had switched on, earlier in the evening, although I could just about see the open hatchway to the temple, in the flowerbed by the Scots Pines.

"What now, Julian?" said Kate.

"We need to get after them," said Faraday. "Michael is in grave danger. I know that time is of the essence, but there is something in the house that I must go and fetch before we leave."

He turned to address Bethany.

"Miss Weyland," he said. "You have rendered an exceptional service to us, tonight, and I can never thank you enough. But I can't possibly ask you to remain with us any longer. These are some extremely dangerous people that we're dealing with, and they've kidnapped our friend. But I won't countenance putting you in any further danger. Besides which, I know, because Richard has told me, that you feel the evil in this place very strongly, and I know just what a supreme effort it must have taken for you to come here tonight. You should leave now."

"If you don't mind, Professor Faraday, I'd rather come with you. I feel like I'm a part of this now, and I can't just walk away. I know about the coven and the ceremony, and what they're planning to do. Richard told me this morning. And so, I can't walk away. I think you might understand what I mean by that. Besides, there are thirteen of them, and I think you need all the help you can get."

Faraday looked at her for a moment and then nodded.

"Very well," he said. "Thank you."

"Did you see the coven leave?" I asked.

"Yes. They were leaving just as I got here. I had driven past earlier and seen various vehicles parked outside. That's when I knew that something was probably going on. So, I parked my car quite a long way away and walked along the lanes to get here. As I approached the house, I heard voices in the driveway.

"I hid over by those trees," she said, pointing over at the stand of Scots Pines, "And I watched them leave. It was like they were coming out of the ground, but I now realise they were coming out of that hatchway that leads to their temple. They had someone with them. It must have been your colleague."

"How was he?" said Kate, urgently. "What were they doing to him?"

"He was blindfolded, and I think he had his hands tied behind his back. He was wearing a white cloak. They led him over to the cars – there were three cars; one of them was some sort of minibus or people carrier – and then they drove off."

"We should get going," said Faraday. "They have a considerable head start on us."

"Wait," I said. "Bethany, you said they drove away from here, but which way did they go?"

I pointed over towards the road.

"Did they go left, or did they go right?" I said

"They went right," she said. "They turned around in the road, and then they went right."

"What difference does it make?" said Kate. "We know where they're going."

"It might make some difference," I said. "It means they're going in from the Marlborough side. To the east of the dolmen. It's the way I went with Megan, the first time she took me there. You turn off the main road just before Marlborough and follow a long lane up onto the downs. There's a car park up there, and then a footpath that leads to the dolmen. But it's about a mile away from the car park. We can go the other way, from the south, the way we walked there the other day. We follow the lane, and cross the main road, and then we head down the grass bridle path that leads to the dolmen.

"In that," I said, pointing at Faraday's four-wheel drive Range Rover. "We might not get all the way to the dolmen but we can get pretty close. We may have a little bit more time than we thought."

"What about the gate by the main road?" said Kate. "We had to climb over a metal gate when we went there before."

"We did," I said, "But I'm pretty sure that it's secured by a padlock and a chain. We could cut through it with the bolt cutters we used to get into the temple."

"Good thinking," said Faraday. "We have a plan. But I must fetch something before we go."

He turned and walked briskly into the house.

"I'll go and get the bolt cutters," said Kate, following him in, and leaving Bethany and I alone in the driveway.

We looked at each other for a long moment.

"I really can't thank you enough," I said.

"I never could have lived with myself if I hadn't come here tonight," she said.

"How on earth did you manage it? Given what happened to you here before?"

"Because I thought long and hard about it all, after you left," she said.

"And because of what was at stake," she added. "If something is important enough, then you can put your mind to anything. At least I wasn't sick on the spot this time, but I've got to say, much as I don't relish chasing the coven over to the dolmen, I can't wait to get away from here."

She nodded over at the house.

"There is so much evil in there," she said. "It's like it's taken over the whole house. Every foul and terrible thing that has ever been contemplated within those walls, everything that has been enacted in there, it's seeped into the very fabric of the place. It lives there in that house, contaminating anyone who comes near it."

Kate and Faraday came marching back out of the house then, and we fell in step behind them and walked over to the Range

Rover, which was parked by the gateway. Kate had the bolt cutters slung over her shoulder, and I noticed that Faraday was carrying something wrapped in cloth.

"What's that?" I asked, as he stuffed the bundle into the side pocket of his jacket.

"You might say it's our weapon of last resort. It's a bottle. It's a bottle containing salt and mercury, mixed with holy water, blessed earlier today by a priest in Marlborough, and collected by Michael."

"What does it do?"

"On its own, nothing, but together with the right words …"

"The Incantation of Set," Bethany cut in.

"Correct, Miss Weyland," said Faraday. "The Incantation of Set. The Egyptian god of chaos. If it comes to it, invoking his power might create enough of a diversion for us to get Michael out of there."

"It could also be very dangerous," said Bethany. "For us, as well as for the coven."

"What are you talking about?" I said.

"I understand the danger," said Faraday, ignoring me and addressing Bethany. "I will use it only as a last resort. But we are four against thirteen, one of them a powerful witch. I would only consider deploying something like this in the deadliest of circumstances. Let's hope it doesn't get that far."

We had reached the car, and Faraday turned to face us, before climbing in.

"Right then," he said. "Now we stop it. We go to the dolmen, and we put a stop to this foul business once and for all."

CHAPTER FIFTY-THREE

The Devil's Doorway

Faraday drove, with Kate beside him in the front, and Bethany and I in the back. We tore along the darkened country lanes in the direction of the main road, and our confrontation with the coven.

"They must be nearly there by now," I said at one point, just for something to say. "The coven must be very close to the dolmen by now."

For some reason, Bethany gripped me by the hand. I didn't let go, and we continued to hold hands in the back of the car as we raced towards our destination.

When we reached the main road Faraday slowed down and turned off the headlights, and then, once at the junction, and with the lights of no other cars to be seen in either direction, he drove across the road and towards the bridle path opposite.

As we had anticipated, there was a metal gate across the path.

Kate picked up the bolt cutters and got out of the car. Although it wasn't going to take more than one of us to cut through the chain securing the gate, I was too anxious to sit still, and so I got out too and went with her.

In the event, it was harder to cut through the chain than we one might have imagined, due to it being so tightly wound around the gatepost. Hefting the heavy bolt cutters into position, Kate started to snip away at the coiled layers of chain link, but it was a laborious process. Every so often the cutters would slip in her hands, and she had to manoeuvre them into position again, usually accompanied by a torrent of curses.

Eventually she managed to cut through the final link, and then she unravelled the chain and tossed it into the hedgerow, while I swung the gate open.

We got back into the car, and Faraday gunned it forward.

I was immediately aware of the change of surface beneath us, as we exchanged flat tarmac for a rutted mud pathway.

We followed the track along its rather tortuous route before coming to a halt beside a dilapidated old barn, still several hundred yards short of the field containing the dolmen.

"We dare not go any closer," said Faraday, switching off the engine. "There's too much of a chance that the coven will hear us."

He let down his window with a quiet swish and the cool night air rushed into the car. I strained to listen, and at first, I couldn't hear any sound coming from the dark fields and hedgerows surrounding us, but then I detected a faint hum of noise. It was the sound of chanting. It meant that the coven had reached the dolmen and commenced their ceremony.

"We don't have much time," said Faraday, who had clearly heard the sound as well, and was making as if to get out of the car.

"Wait," said Kate. "We may not have much time, but we're only going to get one shot at this. Let me go and scope things out. Check the lie of the land. We don't want to go in there blind."

"We should all go," I said.

"No," said Kate. "The more of us who go, the more chance of one of us being spotted. I'll go. But I'll be as quick as I can. So, get ready to move as soon as I come back."

Faraday nodded his assent and Kate slipped out of the car and ran off down the track.

She was only gone for a few minutes, but the wait felt interminable. I sat there, hardly daring to breathe, and with my heart pounding in my chest. I wondered if I should have looked for some sort of weapon, before we left Badcombe Hollow, but couldn't think of anything more threatening back there than a garden spade. Even that would have been better than nothing, I thought.

Eventually, we saw Kate running back to the car, and we all got out to greet her.

"I saw them," she said. "They're in the field by the dolmen, and it looks like they're well into their ceremony. They've made a big circle of torches and they're standing there in a group next to the stones."

"How close did you get?" said Faraday.

"I got as close as the edge of the field. There's a hedgerow there that I hid behind. Any closer and they would have seen me."

"What about Michael? Did you see Michael?"

"I think so. One of them was wearing a white cloak. He was the only one who wasn't standing up. He was lying on the ground in the middle of the group, and one of the coven was standing over him, holding something."

"Damn it," said Faraday. "I was hoping we might be able to sneak in there, somehow, and get him out without them noticing. It's too late for that now. Any ideas, anyone?"

"We use the car," I said. "We drive in there and plough through them. They certainly won't be expecting that, and it might cause enough confusion for a couple of us to jump out and get Michael.

"Kate,' I said, turning to her. "What's the ground like, over there? Could we drive to the field?"

She thought for a moment.

"Yes, we could," she said. "They must get farm vehicles going over there, and so I'm sure we can."

"Is there a gate?" said Faraday.

"A metal one, and we won't be able to cut through that one; not without the coven seeing us. But the fence looked pretty knackered. I reckon that, with enough of a run-up, we could knock it down and drive through it."

"We'll have to try it," said Faraday.

"Wait," said Bethany, speaking for the first time since Kate had re-joined us. "Let me drive. I wouldn't be any good at the strong-arm stuff, but I can drive the car, and that leaves the three of you free to rescue your friend.

"I can do this," she added. "Trust me, I can do this."

"Very well," said Faraday. "But you're going to have to get us in there as quickly as possible, Bethany. Don't stop for anyone, or anything. These people have already shown that they are prepared to commit murder, so should you get the chance to run one of them down, take it."

"Julian, there's one more thing," said Kate, as we made our way hurriedly back to the car. "The chanting from the coven. They're shouting at the sky. They've got their arms stretched out and they're all shouting at the sky.

"And look over there," she added, pointing out towards the western horizon.

We looked in the direction she was pointing. Out on the horizon, odd looking red streaks, like trails from a jet, had appeared, and seemed to float above the earth. It might have marked the onset of sunrise, had it not been the middle of the night, and had we been facing east instead of west. It also resembled the sky I had seen in my dream the night before.

"It's close," said Faraday. "Astaroth, the demon is very close now. It's literally on the edge of our world. I can feel it. I can feel it in the air."

"I feel it too," said Bethany. "There's something profoundly evil being raised in that field. We don't have much time at all."

"My God," I heard Faraday say, under his breath. "They may just pull this off after all."

We got into the Range Rover, with Bethany in the driver's seat this time, and Faraday beside her, and me in the back. Instead of getting into the car with us, Kate stepped onto the running board on the passenger side and gripped hold of the door.

"Let's go," she shouted, and rapped on the roof with her fist.

Bethany started the engine and the car moved slowly forward, before picking up pace as we got further down the track. By the time we approached the field we were travelling at least twice as fast as we had before, making the car shake alarmingly as we bounced along the rutted track. I wondered how Kate was managing to hold on outside.

"Keep the lights off until we're right on top of them," Faraday said to Bethany. "And then put them on full beam. If we're behind the glow of the lights, it will make it more difficult for one of the coven to get a shot off at us."

His words were a reminder that at least two of the coven had firearms. I tried to prepare myself for whatever was to come and said a silent prayer beneath my breath.

As we turned the corner of the track, I saw the field, illuminated by the burning torches, and I could just make out the pile of rocks forming the Devil's Dolmen in the middle, as well as the ethereal shapes of the human figures beside it. It must have been at that point that they saw us, and the tight group of bodies, which had been gathered next to the dolmen, seemed to part and become more numerous as they turned to face us.

Just seconds later, Bethany made a sharp turn and the Range Rover lurched across the path and into the low barbed wire fence separating us and the field. I braced myself for the impact and it was a huge relief when we smashed straight through the fence, although we appeared to be dragging part of it with us as we careered through the field towards the coven, who by then had adopted a defensive formation in front of the dolmen.

As Faraday had instructed, Bethany hit the lights, illuminating the swarm of satanists. I saw Kate leap from the side of the car and pull a cloaked figure at the periphery to the ground.

"Head right for the middle of them," Faraday shouted, and Bethany pulled down hard on the steering wheel and we swerved towards the centre of the group.

Most of them jumped out of the way, but one of them defiantly stood their ground until the last possible moment and was clipped hard by the car, falling over with a scream of pain.

We screeched to a halt, right beside the prone body of Michael. To my relief, I saw that he was alive. He had his hands tied behind his back and was struggling to get up off the ground.

A shot suddenly rang out, and I heard something strike the window beside me, shattering the glass.

"Keep the engine running," Faraday shouted at Bethany, as he jumped out of the car.

I followed, and immediately found myself in a melee of cloaked figures. I plunged in and struck the first one in my path full in the face. I yelped with pain as my fist made contact but was gratified to see the person in the cloak drop to the ground.

However, this momentary victory was short-lived, as in the next instant I felt someone grab me from behind. As I struggled to get free, I looked around and saw Kate wrestling on the ground with two coven members. Faraday, meanwhile, was trying to get to Michael, but being held at bay by one of the satanists, who was waving a long blade at him. To my even greater alarm, I saw Megan a few yards away, un-hooded, and holding a pistol, which was pointed in my direction.

All of this took mere seconds to unfold, but I could tell by then that we were not going to overpower the coven. There were simply too many of them.

Faraday must have reached the same conclusion, because he suddenly turned away from the satanist with the knife and, with remarkable agility for someone of his age, climbed up onto the bonnet of the Range Rover and then hopped onto the roof. Even in the midst of that frenzied melee, I couldn't for the life of me think why he would do this.

By this time, I had wriggled free from whoever had been holding me from behind and was trying to get over to where Kate was still engaged in a vicious struggle with two of the coven members. As I did, I caught Megan's eye, and she fired her pistol at me. She could only have missed by inches, because I felt something fizz past my face.

I looked behind me and saw Faraday standing on the car roof, unwrapping the cloth package he had earlier fetched from the house. Then, in the same moment, someone else grabbed at me, and I spun around to find myself face to face with von Draken's adept, Catherine Falaise. She was holding the knife with the serrated edge that she had been wielding in Badcombe Hollow, earlier that evening, and she stabbed at my heart with it, her arm moving in a flash, and with incredible force.

I felt a painful impact in my chest, and went staggering back, convinced that I had been mortally wounded.

I dropped to the ground, clutching my chest, thinking that I was about to die in that field. But when I frantically stuck my hand in my shirt to locate the wound, I realised that I may have been winded but, for some reason, the knife had not penetrated.

It was a momentary reprieve, however, because then I saw Ernst von Draken marching towards me, pointing a gun at my head.

Suddenly, from behind me, I heard someone shouting, and I realised it was Faraday.

I could not understand what he was saying, because the words were in a foreign tongue, but it certainly got my attention, and even von Draken halted in his advance upon me to look over at Faraday, stood atop the Range Rover.

The Incantation of Set, I thought.

Seconds later, Faraday stopped shouting and for a moment there was complete silence in the field. And then he cocked back his arm and threw something at the Devil's Dolmen.

I heard the sound of glass shattering on the rocks and then saw a plume of blue smoke emerge from the place where the bottle had smashed.

What happened next, I really couldn't say, although Faraday tried to explain it to me later. Something seemed to come over the coven in that instant. Those who had been toting weapons suddenly dropped them, and all of the group that I could see clutched their hands to their faces. Several of them fell over, and there were cries of anguish all around.

By this time Faraday had leapt off the roof of the car and was pulling me to my feet.

"I've bought us some time," he said, "But we need to disarm them, and we need to do it fast."

The coven was still in a state of disarray, some of them coughing and spluttering, as if they had been tear gassed, although I knew that whatever had been in the bottle that Faraday had smashed against the rocks was something far more mysterious than mere gas. He had apparently enacted the Incantation of Set. This was a diversionary tactic by the god of chaos himself. What I couldn't understand was why it didn't seem to be affecting the five of us.

Kate extricated herself from the two satanists she had been grappling with, both of whom were kneeling on the ground, seemingly struggling to breathe, kicking one of them in the stomach and punching the other one in the face. She then raced over to Megan, who was trying to raise her gun and punched her straight in the jaw, causing her legs to collapse beneath her.

Faraday, Kate and I then moved quickly through the coven, punching and kicking them, or else just throwing them to the ground, and taking weapons from those who had them. Several of the group had knives, which we tossed out into the darkness, while Kate took Megan's pistol from her prostrate figure and stuffed it into her jacket. At the same time, Bethany had got out of the car, and was untying Michael. I didn't notice von Draken amidst the throng, and wondered if he had fled the scene.

Having been disarmed as well as discombobulated, the coven appeared to concede defeat, and they began to scatter. Still clearly reeling from the effects of whatever occult power Faraday had unleashed upon them, they staggered away from the dolmen. We watched them retreat across the field in the direction of the steep escarpment to the east. Some of them shouted back curses at us. One of the voices sounded female, and I wondered if it was Megan's. But in spite of their fury, none of them turned back towards us. The coven had departed from the Devil's Dolmen.

All except one of them. Catherine Falaise had made no move to leave and remained in place before us. She no longer had a knife in her hand, but she showed no intention of going anywhere. Perhaps, on account of her own esoteric powers, she was somehow immune to Faraday's incantation, or least less discombobulated than the others, and it was clear that the fight had not gone out of her.

She snarled at us, as Faraday and I circled warily around her, and what she said caused us to stop in our tracks.

"You're too late," she said. "You're pathetic failures, all of you, including those cowards who just ran away, our dear leader among them. They should have stayed, because you were too late. He's here. Can't you see? Astaroth has come to us. You were too late. And now, you will be the sacrifice, Professor. You're going to die in this field. You all are."

She pointed over towards the dolmen.

It was the first time in several moments that I had looked anywhere other than a few yards in front of me, and as I looked behind her at the dolmen, I saw that the red streaks in the sky, which we had earlier seen on the horizon, were now hovering over the field in which we stood. Even more alarmingly, I could see another reddish light, like fire, much closer to the ground, and shining through the triangular gap between the arrangement of the giant stones, the hole in the dolmen which Megan had once described to me as the portal to the afterlife; the place where the demon would emerge into our world.

"You're too late, you've failed," the old witch shouted at us. "He is here. Astaroth is here on our earthly realm. You have failed, all of you. Do you see? Do you see his light all around us?"

"Yes, I do see, Miss Falaise," said Faraday, sounding oddly calm. "But I'm sure that a practitioner of the dark arts as skilled as yourself knows that the summoning of a demon can be reversed with a reciprocal sacrifice. The sacrifice of one of the thirteen who enacted the ritual."

She continued to look at us, and then she must have realised what we were about to do, in the same moment that I did.

"No," she screamed.

"Grab hold of her," Faraday shouted at me, and in an instant, we were upon her, each of us taking hold of one of her arms, and we frogmarched her struggling figure over to the dolmen.

When we reached the stones, we braced ourselves for a moment and then, to the sound of her furious screams, we hurled her at the red light coming through the gap in the stones.

There was a huge bang all around us, like a gigantic crack of thunder, and Faraday and I were pushed back with great force to the ground. Scrambling to get back up on my feet, I looked over at the dolmen, and saw that there was no longer any light coming through the stones. I also saw that the skies above us were now completely clear, the streaks of red light having vanished in an instant. But of Catherine Falaise, there was no sight whatsoever.

I walked slowly over to the great pile of stones. Lying on the ground was the hooded cloak belonging to the witch, now a mere bundle of black cloth. I knelt down and lifted it, aware of the faint smell of burning, but there was nothing underneath.

"What happened to her?" I said to Faraday, who was now standing beside me. "Where is she?"

"In hell," said Faraday. "She's in hell."

CHAPTER FIFTY-FOUR

The Ghost of the Long Barrow

We didn't linger long by the dolmen after that. Much as we had seemingly averted something rather terrible from occurring, Faraday was keen that we get away, before anyone else happened to come into that field.

"I feel rather bad about knocking down that poor farmer's fence," he said to me, at one point. "And wrecking the chain to his gate. But there's nothing to be done about it now. I will, however, find out who owns this land, and send them some appropriate compensation.

"Anonymously," he added.

Bethany had got Michael untied by then.

"You're new," he said to her. "Don't think we've met before."

I made the necessary introductions, and gave Michael a brief re-cap on the events that had led us here, subsequent to his capture.

"What was it like?" I asked him. "I mean, what was the ceremony like? What happened?"

"I'm not too sure, really," he said. "There was a lot of chanting, and I think they killed a couple of chickens. I was blindfolded the whole time, so I wasn't really sure what was going on. I prayed all the way through it."

He got to his feet with a grimace.

"How's the nose?" I asked him.

"Bloody and painful," he said. "But I'm starting to think, possibly not broken. You guys saved my life tonight, you know?"

"I think we might have stopped something even worse than that," I said, nodding over at the Devil's Dolmen.

"What exactly happened, Julian?" said Kate, who had walked over and joined us. I noticed that she had an ugly bruise on the side of her face.

"I honestly don't know," said Faraday. "All we can be sure of is that the coven tried to raise something here tonight, and it looks as if they might have been successful."

"And we stopped it," I said.

"It would appear so. I suppose we'll never know what would have happened if we hadn't. But there was some very dark magic enacted in this field tonight."

"Not to mention by us," said Bethany. "The Incantation of Set. Congratulations, Professor. Not something I thought I'd ever see."

"It was a considerable risk," said Faraday. "But it was a risk we had to take, in the circumstances."

"Well, it certainly seemed to work," I said. "But there's something I don't understand. Why didn't it affect the five of us? Why didn't we experience the sort of chaotic reaction that the coven did?"

"You'd have to ask Set about that," said Faraday, enigmatically.

We gathered up whatever of the coven's weapons that we could find and put them in a bag, along with Megan's pistol, so that they could be disposed of in a suitably discreet manner. We then extinguished the torches around the dolmen, which made everything dark around us. In spite of all that had happened that night, it was still some time before dawn.

I managed to get a moment alone with Bethany, and we embraced tightly, which made me wince, due to the pain still throbbing in my chest where Catherine Falaise had tried to stab me.

"Are you okay?" she said, sensing my discomfort. "Were you injured?"

"Not exactly," I said, reaching into my shirt pocket and retrieving the Nazar amulet she had given me, earlier that day. There was a large chip on its glazed surface.

"She stabbed me," I said. "The witch stabbed me, just before Faraday did his incantation. And I'm pretty sure the knife hit this amulet, and that's why it didn't kill me, and just gave me a hell of a bruise."

I put the amulet back in my pocket.

"So, that's twice you've saved my life today," I said to her.

"I did say that it might protect you," she said.

"I know, but I suppose I wasn't expecting quite that sort of protection."

"The munificent gods work in mysterious ways," said Bethany.

"They certainly seem to," I said.

We were ready to leave by then.

"It's time we left the poor souls buried here in peace," said Faraday. "Their sacred place of burial has been defiled enough for one night."

We all got into the Range Rover, with Kate driving this time, and Faraday beside her, with Bethany, Michael and I squeezed into the back.

We drove carefully out of the field and onto the bridle path, and then made our way back to the road.

I felt completely exhausted, not to mention astonished and incredulous at what I had witnessed that night. I was also feeling mightily relieved, almost euphoric. We had won. After all the trials and tribulations of the previous few weeks, this was finally at an end. Dorian Slake's diabolical plan, decades in the making had been thwarted. The coven had been defeated. We had won, and it was over.

We dropped Bethany off at her car, which she had parked a mile or so away from Badcombe Hollow, back when she had commenced her rescue mission that had saved our lives, and possibly prevented something even more terrible from happening as well. I didn't want to see her go, but I understood the effect that the satanic curse placed upon Badcombe Hollow had upon her, and would continue to have, until it was thoroughly exorcised.

I walked with her to her car after the others had said their goodbyes, and waited while she got in.

"You know I can never thank you enough, for everything you did tonight," I said to her through the open window, as she was putting on her seatbelt.

"You don't have to," she said. "I just knew that it was the right thing to do, and I'm so glad that I did it."

"I'll see you again soon, I hope?" I said. "In somewhat less fraught circumstances."

"I'm looking forward to it already," she said. "Call me tomorrow, okay?"

She kissed her fingers, and then reached out of the car and pressed them lightly to my lips, before driving away into the night.

I got back into the Range Rover, and we continued on towards Badcombe Hollow.

"I'm looking forward to a bath and a stiff drink," Kate said, as we approached the house. "And not necessarily in that order."

"I'm just looking forward to going to sleep," said Faraday. "I'm getting a little long in the tooth for these sorts of operations."

"Personally, I just want to get out of this satanic fancy dress," said Michael.

However, as we turned into the driveway, we saw a car parked there. It was a black Jaguar.

"That's von Draken's car," I said, as we drew to a halt beside it.

We stepped anxiously out of the car, looking around us at the darkened garden.

"What do you think?" said Michael. "Do you reckon he's in the house?"

"Maybe the temple," Kate said. "Why would he come back? Do we go and look for him, or what?"

"That won't be necessary," came a voice from the darkness.

Ernst von Draken emerged from a behind a tree and stepped into the driveway. He had a gun in his hand, which was pointed at us.

"All of you stay right where you are," he said. "Anyone moves, and I'll shoot them."

"Give it up, von Draken," said Faraday. "It's over and you lost. So, give it up. You may have the gun, but there are four of us, and you can't kill us all that quickly. You won't get away with it, so give it up, leave and never come back."

As he said this, I felt Kate tense beside me, as if she was preparing to launch herself at the elderly satanist.

"I don't plan to get away with it," said von Draken. "But I promise you that I'm going to take the most immense pleasure in killing at least a couple of you. Starting with you, Professor."

He motioned with the gun towards the open entrance to the temple.

"Down there," he snapped. "Single file. And if anyone makes a move, they're dead."

In an echo from earlier that evening, when von Draken had marched Faraday, Kate and myself down to the cellar, the four of us did as instructed and entered the tunnel, with Faraday in the lead and me in the rear, and Kate and Michael between us. As I stood at the top of the steps, von Draken jabbed me sharply in the back with his pistol.

"Keep going," he said. "And no tricks."

I couldn't believe that this was happening. After all we had been through, and all we had survived, it was going to end like this, being murdered in a hole in the ground. My mind spun as I tried to figure how we might try and overpower and disarm von Draken, and I wondered if we might perhaps be at some small advantage, down there in a confined space, rather than out in the open.

The tunnel appeared very different to the first day we had come down here. The coven had strung up a series of battery powered lights, on poles, which illuminated the tunnel's entire length. We passed by the Neolithic catacombs and I saw that the metal door to the temple was propped open and light spilled out from within.

We entered the temple one by one, and when we were all inside, von Draken directed us into one of the corners and made us sit down on the floor. Then, without taking his eyes off us, he pulled a tall-backed chair, that looked like a timber throne, over towards him, and then he sat down, facing us. He let the gun drop down to his lap, while still pointed in our direction.

The throne-like chair aside, the squat, rectangular temple looked much the same as it had when we first came in here, although it was brightly lit now, with more strings of lights. There was one discernible difference, however. A giant pentagram, of similar dimensions to the one in Alan's cellar, had been chalked onto the floor. The four of us were sitting at the edge of one of the points, whereas von Draken had positioned himself, whether by accident or design, in the very centre of the pentacle.

"Why have you brought us here, von Draken?" said Faraday, speaking for the first time since we had entered the temple. "If you're going to do us in, why not have at it up in the garden? Why bring us down here, to your squalid temple to Satan?"

"Don't you understand, Professor?" said von Draken. "That is entirely the point. As I stated previously, I'm going to kill you, and care nothing whatsoever for the consequences of that. But believe me when I say that I shall take the most immense pleasure at the thought of you taking your last ever breath in this temple to our one true lord. A fitting end, I would say, after a lifetime of meddling in the affairs of others. I only wish that I could have enacted such an outcome sooner."

I felt Kate tense beside me, and thought for a moment that she was about to leap to her feet and rush von Draken, but Faraday seemingly sensed this too, and he put his hand on her arm to restrain her.

"Wait," I heard him whisper under his breath. "Not yet."

Von Draken continued to watch us from his throne, his eyes constantly flicking from one to the other of us.

"I suppose you all think you've been very clever," he said, sounding like a school master addressing a group of recalcitrant schoolchildren.

"And I suppose, in a way, you have been. Very clever and very lucky. Between you, you have managed to thwart something that was many years in the making. I suppose congratulations should be in order, but I thought I'd settle instead for good, old-fashioned revenge, now that I've got you all together.

"It was my father's idea," he went on, gesturing around him. "This temple. It was my father who had the idea to build it. When Dorian first bought the house, he had no idea of the power that was here. It was Megan's grandmother who told him about it; how all the various sacred sites up on the plain connected into this one central point that is the Badcombe Hollow long barrow. She told him how, if one could find a way of tapping into that, one might come to possess immense power. But it was my father who realised how this power could be used. So, you might say that he more than anyone else set these events in motion.

"My family is from Hungary, as you may know. My country was one of the Axis Powers during the Second World War, allied with Germany, and my father held a position of high responsibility, working for one of the regional governors. One of his duties was to supervise the removal from his area of the country certain, shall we say, undesirable elements."

"By undesirable, I assume you mean Jewish," said Michael.

"Perhaps," said von Draken. "Who's to say? They were complex times. I was not there. History is written by the victors. My father was a mere cog in the machine."

Michael gave a snort of derision.

"Anyway," said von Draken, "In the course of attending to his responsibilities, my father found himself, one day, overseeing the eviction and packing up of a large house on the shores of Lake Balaton. The house had a very impressive library, containing a number of valuable volumes, mostly dealing with the occult. Many priceless editions, one might say, although that is something of a misnomer in this case. My father obtained a very good price for many of the books in that library, as indeed have I, over the years.

"But there was one book that he kept. A codex from the early sixteenth century. A truly powerful book, believed to be the only one of its kind in existence. And it was in this book that my father found the raising incantation for Astaroth, and discovered that it could only be enacted at very precise points in the calendar, and only then by utilising the sort of earth energies which are rare in this world, but which exist in abundance up here on this plain, nowhere more so than in this particular spot.

"And so, my father suggested to Dorian that he build a temple beneath the long barrow. To enact the raising of Astaroth. The codex was very clear on that, you see. The raising incantation had to be performed in a temple built specifically for the purposes of raising this demon. It had to be a new temple, created solely for that reason, and it had to be built exactly like this, to these precise dimensions. And it had to be entirely plain, with no adornment whatsoever, not even a stick of furniture."

"You're sitting on a bloody throne," said Kate, caustically.

"This was brought here for the benefit of our guest," von Draken snapped back at her. "Had things gone differently this evening, it would be he who was sat here now, addressing my coven and instructing us.

"Having feasted upon you, beforehand," he added.

"The space had to be bare," he continued. "And the pentagram on the floor had to be marked out as part of the ceremony. And the temple could never be used, until tonight. It had to remain untouched.

"It took nearly two years, to build it. My father recruited Hungarian workers, to do the digging. Absolute secrecy was essential, you understand, so we only employed people from the old country, who couldn't speak English, and so couldn't be quizzed about what they were doing. It was quite a task, to get them over here, but my father was able to pull some strings.

"I was a young man, at the time, but my father entrusted me with supervising much of the construction. I lived here at the house, with Dorian, for much of that time, and he taught me a great deal, as did Megan's grandmother.

"We built the tunnel first. We knew we couldn't attract attention by digging down too close to the long barrow, because of its proximity to the road, hence we broke ground, so to speak, in the flower bed screened by the fir trees, some considerable way back. It took several months to construct the tunnel, although we had a slice of good fortune when we broke into the original Neolithic entrance to the barrow, which we naturally utilised for ourselves.

"It was well built. The tunnel and the temple. As you can see. Everything had to be properly supported, from above and to the sides, with walls made from concrete slabs. We knew that it would all be sealed up for decades before this night, and we couldn't risk it collapsing during the intervening period.

"Incidentally, it was Dorian's idea to plant the Mexican Orange Blossom on top of the entrance. It was well established by the time he died, and therefore concealed the opening from various subsequent owners of the property. A useful precaution, in the event that we were to lose control of the property, as we did for some time. I suppose I should thank you all for doing all that digging to get it out of the ground. We were running rather short of time by then, you see. So, I got Megan to point out the posey of flowers in the portrait of Dorian, and plant the seed in your heads. I understand that it was the priest here who made the final deduction. But if he hadn't, Megan would have led you to it some other way."

Von Draken gestured around him at the rectangular bunker.

"Digging the tunnel, however, was nothing compared to excavating this space around us. Twelve feet high, by forty-eight long, by thirty deep. A twenty thousand square foot cube, if you will, directly beneath the long barrow. An immense effort, you will doubtless agree, and one that created another, quite considerable challenge for us."

"Getting rid of all that soil," I cut in.

"That is correct," said von Draken. "In fact, it presented an even greater problem than you might imagine. The earth we walk upon is highly compacted. When you dig it up, it unspools, and creates a larger mass. You simply can't imagine how much earth was moved out of here, and every single ounce had to go out through that tunnel.

"Whereupon it had to be moved somewhere. We had already, by that stage, accumulated a huge amount of spoil from digging out the tunnel, which was lying in a great mound by the side of the house, where the vegetable garden now is. And so, we decided to move it to the top of the bank behind the house. There was really nowhere else for it to go. And then, the bank was built up as it is today and landscaped, creating the deep hollow that the house appears to sit in.

"It was an immense undertaking. All the more so when you consider that its three principle architects – my father, Dorian Slake and Doreen Smithers – all knew that they would never live to see the temple put to use. They would never witness the conjuring of Astaroth."

"So, when Slake killed himself, you lost control of the house", said Faraday. "That must have put a bit of a crimp in your plans."

"As you know, Professor, I very much hold you responsible for driving Dorian to his death. You are, however, correct. Losing control of the house was most regrettable. Back then, I did not possess sufficient means to purchase Badcombe Hollow myself and Dorian's executors sold it on the open market.

"But we knew that time was on our side. It was still fifty years until the ceremony, and we were confident that nobody would ever find the entrance to the temple. And you can be sure that we kept a good watch on the place, through its various ownerships, until …"

"Until," I finished for him, "You met a rich rock star, and got him to buy it for you."

"Something like that," said von Draken. "I first met Alan Mackay when he came into my bookshop in Bloomsbury, the one my father had established when he came to England after the war. It was a rather wet and miserable October afternoon, as I recall, and Alan was looking for an old book on the occult; nothing specific, just an old book with woodcuts. He said he wanted to use it on the cover of an album, or some such nonsense.

"I had no idea then who he was, and I was in the mood to dismiss him out of hand, but there was a spark of intelligence and curiosity about him which intrigued me. I took an old volume on witchcraft out of a locked cabinet behind the counter – a very valuable book, published in the nineteenth century, from the collection my father had obtained back in Hungary during the war, but written in English – and I said that I wasn't going to sell it to him, but I was going to lend it to him, and I wanted him to read it and then come back and talk to me about it.

"He took it away with him, and I wondered if I would ever see him again, but a week later he came back to the shop, having read the book and full of questions about it. In that moment, I knew that I had found a new recruit.

"And so, it all began from there. A year later, Alan was inducted into our coven, the same one started by Dorian Slake, and then run by my father before me. Then, sometime after that, Badcombe Hollow came up on the market, and I persuaded him to buy it."

"Did he know why?" I asked.

"No, not at first. Not for a very long time, in fact. There was simply no reason for him to know, so far in advance of the event. And it wasn't as if he was going to stumble upon it, accidentally. You know how difficult it is to find, and you were actually looking for it.

"Alan thought that we wanted the house because of its connection to Dorian Slake, so that the coven could worship here, but no more than that. And he certainly thrived in his new environment. Incidentally, you referred earlier to Alan's largesse in purchasing this house on behalf of the coven, but it might interest you to know that he became much wealthier in the years after he moved here. As did I. We performed much magic here; some memorable conjurings; much of it very much to the benefit of us both. Earthly pleasures, you see, have always been at the heart of our creed."

As he said this, he seemed to cast a lascivious glance in Kate's direction.

"When did Alan find out?" I asked. "When did you tell him about the temple, and about Walpurgis Night?"

For some reason, in that moment, I was more interested in von Draken's story, than I was in our predicament. Von Draken also seemed more interested in telling it.

"Less than a year ago," said the satanist. "Towards the end of last summer. It was Megan and I who told him."

He looked at me as he said this.

"She is my most devoted adherent," he said. "A real disciple to the cause, and a credit to the memory of her grandmother."

"Perhaps not to her mother, though," I said. "She doesn't seem to be doing so well."

"That is unfortunate," said von Draken. "Abigail, I am sorry to say, is of a much weaker disposition than her mother or daughter. I tried my very best with her, but to no avail. She was part of my flock for many years."

"She's part of someone else's flock now," I said, wondering how many other lives this man had ruined.

"Quite so. Megan, however, is my most trusted lieutenant, and she has known about the temple since childhood. Indeed, thanks to her archaeological training, it was she who deduced where the final part of the ceremony would occur. She knew that it would have to be the Devil's Dolmen. What could be more fitting than a literal doorway to the afterlife?

"And she was right," he added, with a trace of sadness in his voice.

"She and Alan were something of an item, by then, you might say," he said. "I had encouraged this liaison, since it helped me to keep Alan under reasonably close observation. He was guarding something rather important here, after all, even if he didn't yet know it."

"And so, Megan and I came to see him one day, to tell him. We sat out in the garden, under the pergola, facing the long barrow, and we told him. We told him all of it. About the temple, and the raising, and what we thought we could accomplish at the Devil's Dolmen on Walpurgis Night. The only thing we didn't tell him, was the location of the entrance and, to the best of my knowledge, he never discovered it. But aside from that, we laid it all out for him that afternoon, and his part in what was to come, not just as part of the coven, but as the guardian of the temple. We told him that he had been given a sacred duty, and that he should expect to be a big part of whatever followed the raising."

"How did he take it?" I asked.

"Not as I had anticipated, I am sorry to say. Alan was like a son to me, in many ways, and I thought I knew him as well as anyone can know another person, but it seemed that I had misjudged him, over those many years.

"Initially, I thought it might merely have been a case of pique; of annoyance that we had concealed the existence of the temple from him for so long. But it would appear there was more to it than that. He found the whole idea of the raising deeply alarming. He thought it was too dangerous, and that even if it wasn't successful, the application of magic on that scale could have unforeseen consequences.

"Sadly, I think he was just afraid, and simply lacking in sufficient mettle for the task before him. It would appear that he had grown too comfortable, living down here in his rural idyll, and he just wanted things to remain as they were.

"Megan and I persisted with him for the remainder of the summer, but as we got later into the year, it was clear that Alan was getting very cold feet about the whole thing."

Round about the time that he went to see Bethany Weyland, I thought, as I sat there listening to the old man talk.

"From then on, things became increasingly difficult between us," von Draken continued, seemingly engrossed in telling his story. There was a melancholy and reflective tone to his voice, as if he were conveying something which caused him great sadness. I wondered if we might exploit this potential weakness by getting the jump on him, somehow.

"At the beginning of the year we fell out very badly," he said. "He even forbade Megan and I access to the house. You see, I think, by then, it was about more than Walpurgis Night. His heart didn't seem to be in it, any more, and he was questioning the whole enterprise, and his part in it. A fit of conscience, perhaps. Or, I dare say that your priest over there would call it a crisis of faith.

"Really, most disappointing," he finished.

He said this last part in a weary, more in sorrow than anger tone, almost as if he was talking to himself, and unaware that we were there with him. I even wondered if he was in shock, after all that had gone on that evening. Again, I considered the possibility of us rushing him, but wasn't sure how to communicate this to the others.

But in that moment, von Draken seemed to snap out of his temporary reverie and levelled the gun in our direction. I could see the malice in his features, once again.

"He who has no stomach for the fight, let him depart. Isn't that how the saying goes?"

The bravado was back in his voice now, I noticed.

"Except, in Alan's case, you didn't let him depart," I said. "You tracked him down and had him killed."

"Yes, I did," said von Draken. "My erstwhile sorceress and concubine, Ms Falaise, accomplished that for me. After you so helpfully lent Megan an item of Alan's clothing, I might add, in order that we could enact the spell. There is no leaving a coven such as ours, you see. Only death releases one."

"At least Alan saw you for what you were, by then," I said. "You and Megan, and that hideous witch, and the whole sorry lot of you."

"I wouldn't be so quick to judge," said von Draken. "It would seem that my coven were not the only ones treading the left-hand path this evening, and practising dark magic."

He turned slightly in his chair to face Faraday.

"The Incantation of Set, Professor. Congratulations. I tip my hat to you. Very dangerous magic indeed, and quite a risk to all of you, wouldn't you say? To your mortal souls, as well as to your lives."

"Desperate situations call for desperate measures," said Faraday.

"Indeed, they do. And now, one can only speculate how different things might be, if you had just been a few minutes later, getting to that field."

"Hence my bringing you down here to execute you," he added.

"Really?" said Faraday. "I must say, I'm starting to wonder about that, von Draken. Oh, I don't doubt that you plan to fire that gun at me, but I think the real reason you brought us down here is to gloat. To show off your great subterranean construction, and tell us all about enacting your grand plan. But, you know, I'm starting to sense something else, sitting here and listening to you talk."

"And what might that be?" said von Draken. "Do please enlighten me."

"I think you're just a tiny bit relieved."

"Relieved?"

"Yes. Relieved that you're sat here with us, and not the infernal creature you tried to manifest, earlier this evening. I wonder if you even thought that the raising would be successful. I mean, you've had it pretty good here, these past few years, haven't you? Enjoying the hospitality of your wealthy acolyte, and running your coven, tantalising them for all this time with the promise of a great event on a far-off Walpurgis Night. It must have given you a lot of power, and the chance to indulge in those earthly pleasures you referred to earlier."

"You have no idea what you're talking about," von Draken snarled, with so much venom in his voice that I wondered if Faraday was trying to provoke him into losing control, so that we might try and overpower him.

"I'm not so sure," said Faraday. "I spoke to a satanist, the other day, who described you as being something of an amateur, and I think he may have been right. And your former companion, Miss Falaise, expressed a rather similar sentiment, you may be interested to hear, right before we despatched her. So, I wonder if you would really have relished sitting here at the feet of Astaroth, the crown prince of Hell. And I wonder what he would have thought of you."

"You may wonder whatever you want," said von Draken, getting to his feet.

He pointed the gun at Faraday, and then tensed, as if he was about to pull the trigger.

"I've waited a very long time for this, Professor Faraday," he said.

I started to push myself to my feet and, beside me, I saw Kate do the same.

It's now or never, I thought.

And then I spotted something in my peripheral vision.

There was someone crouching behind von Draken's chair, and in that moment, it raised itself up and stood behind him.

It was a woman. It was the spirit of the Neolithic shaman who guarded this place; the ghost of the long barrow. She wore animal skins which reached to her feet, and although her matted black hair covered much of her face, I could see the look of wild fury in her eyes.

For some reason, the spirit haunting Badcombe Hollow had chosen this precise moment at which to insert herself into proceedings. And I don't suppose that was any kind of coincidence. For the first time since becoming aware of her presence here, I didn't feel afraid of her.

I'm not sure if von Draken sensed that she was there, or if he detected something in my expression, but he suddenly swung around and found himself face to face with the enraged entity.

She grabbed him roughly by the throat and screamed into his face, causing him to let out a strangled cry of his own and drop the gun. I saw Kate swoop down and retrieve it, and when I looked up again, the spirit had vanished. It was the most fleeting appearance of the being that I had ever witnessed, but its impact was undeniable.

Von Draken had dropped to his knees, and was clutching his chest. He looked to be in agony, and I realised that he was having a heart attack. The ghost of the tomb had dealt him a fatal blow; a mortal shock to his body.

Something like this happened to Alan, I thought, as I watched the old man struggle on the floor in front of me. He was frightened to death, too, by the coven presided over by this man. The man who had boasted about this, only moments earlier.

"Do we call an ambulance?" I said to Faraday, as we stood and watched von Draken in his death throes.

"No, I don't think we do, do you?" he said, softly.

None of us dissented, and we stood and watched the elderly devil worshipper die, lying prone within the pentagram on the floor of his temple. When, a minute or so later, it became clear that he had breathed his last breath, Michael went and said a short prayer over his inert body.

"What do we do with him?" said Kate.

"We dump the body," said Faraday. "I don't think we really want the attention of the authorities at this stage, having avoided them up until now. We'll drive his car a few miles away and leave it by the side of the road. We'll put von Draken in the driver's seat. The police will assume he had a heart attack while driving."

Kate and I picked up von Draken, taking an arm each, and started to drag his body out of the temple. As we headed down the passageway, I heard the metal door clang shut behind us.

We manoeuvred his body up the steps and out into the garden, and then dragged it over to his car.

"I'll drive," Kate said, "And Michael can follow me in the Range Rover and bring me back."

Faraday nodded in agreement.

"So, that's that, then," he said, as we watched them drive back out into the night. "An epilogue to this affair we could have well done without, and another damn close-run thing. But at least it draws a line under the matter of von Draken."

"Were you trying to provoke him, back there?" I asked.

"Yes, as soon as I became aware of the presence of the spirit of this tomb," he said. "I told you she might turn out to be an invaluable ally."

"She was most certainly that," I said.

"We'll need to seal up the temple again," said Faraday. "But that can wait until the morning. In the meantime, once Kate and Michael are back, I suggest we all get some well-earned sleep."

"I think there's something I still need to do," I said.

It had been on my mind, ever since we left the dolmen, and in the last few moments I had made a decision.

"Megan," I said. "I need to try and find her. I want to see if I can help her. I mean, God knows, she doesn't deserve it, but for some reason, I feel like I need to try."

Faraday took his pipe from his pocket and started to fill it.

"Less than an hour ago," he said, "She tried to kill you by firing a gun at your head."

"I know," I said. "Not to mention planning to feed me to a demon."

"And yet you still wish to help her?"

"Perhaps I just want to draw another line," I said. "I want to offer to help her, at the very least. I want to look in her eyes and offer that. For some reason, I want to do that. Maybe it was the experience of meeting her mother the other day; seeing that poor demented wretch; sensing the torment she was in. I wouldn't wish that upon Megan. I wouldn't wish that upon anyone. So, I suppose I feel that I have to give it a try."

"She may be highly unresponsive to your efforts," said Faraday. "And she may still wish to do you harm. Have you considered that?"

"Yes, I've considered that," I said.

"In that case, it would appear that your mind is made up. Do you know where she might be?"

"I think I have an idea," I said.

CHAPTER FIFTY-FIVE

The Valley of Broken Stones

I knew that she would go to the old chapel at Stokeley. For some reason, I just knew it. There were all sorts of other places where she might have gone including, quite plausibly, the house in Marlborough belonging to the late Ernst von Draken. But I just knew that she would go to Stokeley.

So sure was I of her destination that I didn't rush to catch up with her. I drove carefully along the pitch-black country lanes, my mind still rattled by the events of that night. I could scarcely believe what I had witnessed by the Devil's Dolmen or indeed subsequently, but I knew that it had all happened. And now it was all over.

And yet, it wasn't really over. My pursuit of Megan through the deserted lanes off the Ridgeway was evidence of that. Quite why I should be so determined to find her was less easy to explain. Was I truly concerned for her welfare, as I had intimated to Faraday? Or was I trying to catch her in order to deal one final blow to the coven, and remind her of their utter defeat on that night? Or was I merely seeking some form of closure? It was hard to be sure, and I didn't care to dwell on it.

As I approached the village of Stokeley I wondered if I might shortly catch up with her; might glimpse the tail lights of her car somewhere in the near distance; but there was no sign of anyone or anything on the darkened plain. I felt completely alone up there, cocooned in the soft glow of the car's interior, but I never considered turning back.

When I reached the village, I slowed down to a crawl, just in case she should have stopped there, but the place was as seemingly devoid of life as ever. When I got to the other side of the tiny settlement I cast a quick look over in the direction of the old witch's cottage, and wondered if Megan might have gone there, but I didn't stop to check because I felt so strongly that it was the chapel to which she would be drawn in her hour of desperation; the defiled holy place which was so perversely sacred to the coven. What more appropriate sanctuary could there be for a satanist fleeing the wreckage of her twisted dreams?

I drove up the hill that I knew would lead me to the hidden valley, and as I did so I noticed a faint lightening in the sky and realised that morning was not far away. May Day was dawning. The day after Walpurgis Night.

I got to the top of the hill and turned into the trackway where I had parked on the night of the sabbat. And sure enough, there was Megan's car, just where I had thought it would be.

I switched off the engine and sat there for a moment, acutely aware of the quiet around me. It was still dark, but there was enough of the early light of dawn in the sky to be able see a fair way down the track. There was no sign of Megan. Imagining that she must have been at the chapel by then, I got out of the car and pulled on my coat.

Soon, I thought. In a short time, I will find her and I will confront her, and one way or the other, this will finally be over.

I began to walk along the track, feeling chilled by the cold, dawn air. Before long, I saw the woods that crowned the hilltop and from there I knew that it was only a short distance to the chapel in the steep combe, concealed within the folds of the earth in much the same way as Badcombe Hollow. A few short minutes later, I had reached my destination.

I stopped at the top of the escarpment and looked down at the grassy, rock-strewn floor of this mysterious upland valley. The valley of broken stones. A thick mist swirled below me, appearing quite white against the dark background, and shrouding the ruined chapel in its ghostly tentacles. I thought of Megan in there. I wondered if she was somehow anticipating my arrival.

I picked my way gingerly down the steep slope, anxious not to slip on the wet grass or trip over the sarsen rocks littering the landscape. When I reached the bottom, I gathered myself before walking over to the chapel. I was experiencing a real sense of fear by then, standing there in the rolling mist, with the walls of the chapel ruin looming up before me, and wondering what awaited me within. Some instinct deep within me made me want to turn and run from that place, but then I recalled the fate of my friend, terrified to death in a remote corner of the world, and at this woman's hand, at least obliquely, and I started to walk towards the chapel with grim determination.

The sky was getting ever lighter, and I knew that daybreak could only be moments away, but the fog on the ground now felt thicker, obscuring the break in the chapel walls that formed its entrance until I was almost upon it.

I stepped into the ruined shell of the building. It was empty. There was nothing there but broken ground and mist-soaked rocks. There was an ethereal, almost deathly quiet about the place and I could hear my ragged, fearful breathing. And there was no sign whatsoever of Megan. If she had been here earlier, then she was here no longer.

I made my way slowly around the interior of the wrecked building, much as I had done on the first day that I had come here, seemingly so long ago, but only a few weeks previously. Having brought myself here and having so acutely anticipated confronting Megan within these ruined walls, I was unsure what to do next.

My slow perambulation completed, I found myself back at the chapel entrance. The mist was starting to lift by then, but it still seemed to cling to the clusters of rocks, and it made for a gloomy scene. I felt exhausted and thought about giving up and making my way back to the car.

Suddenly, from out of the shadows, a face appeared, right next to mine and accompanied by a blood-curdling screech of pure hatred. It was Megan, and an instant later she was upon me, pushing me roughly to the ground and straddling me, with her hands around my throat. She was still wearing the black cloak she had worn at the ceremony and the make-up on her face was smeared, giving her a wild, garish appearance, and I could see a bruise on her cheek where Kate had punched her by the Devil's Dolmen. But it was the eyes that struck me the most, even as I lay there pinned beneath her weight, as she choked the life out of me. I had never before seen such venomous fury in a person's face.

She continued to grip me with almost superhuman strength, and at one point she lifted my head from above the ground and banged it down into the earth.

"You filthy bastard," she shouted at me. "Do you know what you've done? Do you know what you've ruined? What you've destroyed? I'm going to cut your fucking throat for what you've done."

I was struggling to breathe by then, and still in a state of shock at the sudden violence of Megan's ambush. I desperately tried to free my arms, so that I could get her hands off my neck and somehow throw her off me, but the more I struggled the harder she seemed to push down on me and the more helpless I became.

But in the end, it was her determination to kill me that saved my life. Taking one hand off my throat she reached into the folds of her cloak and produced a small, curved knife with a serrated blade and waved it above my head.

It was the brief window of opportunity that I needed. I used the relief of pressure on my throat and the rest of my body to free one of my arms, which I swung at her, catching her on the side of her neck. In the same instant, I pushed my hips off the ground with all the strength I could muster and rolled her off me, causing her to drop the knife.

As I struggled to my feet, she kicked out at me from her prone position, making contact with my knee and causing me to fall back to the ground. I tried to scramble away from her, but found my route blocked by a pile of stones and rubble.

By then she had recovered the knife and she leapt at me again, the point of the blade narrowly missing my face. Crouched above me, and with one hand gripping the collar of my shirt, she slashed at me with the knife and I twisted my face away, just missing the blade for a second time, but managing to grab her by the wrist. But still I was unable to push her body off of mine.

She may have thought she had me, by then, and that it was only a matter of time before she stabbed me to death and made me the latest blood sacrifice in that foul place of satanic worship. But I was fighting for my life, with the adrenaline screaming in my veins, and I felt possessed of far greater strength than I had the first time she pinned me to the floor. With both of my hands now pushing the knife away from my face, I drew back my knee and kicked her in the stomach will all my strength.

It was enough to push her off me, and by the time she had rallied and started to run at me again with the knife, I had got back to my feet and was ready for her. Rather than step back and brace myself for her attack I moved towards her, denying her the momentum of her charge, and whilst parrying her thrust of the knife with one hand, I used the other to punch her squarely in the face.

I hit her so hard there was a loud slapping sound as my fist made contact with her jaw. I felt a sharp pain across my knuckles, and I wondered if I had broken my hand, but it had been enough to immobilise Megan. She slumped to the ground as if stunned, dropping the knife by her side.

I quickly stooped down and retrieved it and then threw it away into the darkness where I heard it land with a faint clang in the rocks. I then looked back at Megan, who was slowly getting to her feet.

I wondered if she might spring at me again, but it seemed that the fight had gone out of her. The hatred was still there, but she was defeated. I don't think it was necessarily my punch to her face that did this. I think it was the cumulative effect of everything that had happened that night, and the dawning realisation that the coven had been thwarted, its members scattered, and their cherished plan to bring about hell on earth, decades in the making, utterly wrecked.

So, the hatred may still have been in her eyes, but there were now tears streaking her face. She was beaten, and she knew it. And in spite of everything, in spite of all her deceit and her treachery, and in spite of the fact that she had just tried to kill me, in that moment I felt only pity for her.

"It's over, Megan," I said, walking slowly towards her. "It's all over. Come with me. Let me get you away from here."

She may have known that she was beaten, but she had lost none of her defiance.

"Get away from me," she hissed, as the tears continued to roll down her cheeks.

"Megan, please," I said. "You need help. The things you've done, and the things you've witnessed, not just tonight, but all through your life … you need help. Your very soul is in peril. There are people who can help you. Please."

"I don't want your help," she said. "I don't want anything to do with you."

She almost spat the words.

It was staring to get light, by then, with streaks of orange in the sky, although the mist still clung to the sides of the valley, and for a moment we simply stood there, facing each other.

"Why, Megan?" I said. "Why did you do this? What was it all for?"

"You'd never understand," she said, her voice a whisper now, the screaming banshee of a moment ago now seeming like a little girl lost.

"You'd never understand," she repeated.

I took another tentative step towards her, and I saw the hatred and violence cross her face again.

"Get back," she snarled at me. "Get back, or I'll curse you to hell."

And with that, she turned her back on me for the last time, and walked away.

As I made to follow her, she seemed to sense this and started to run.

"Megan," I shouted after her. "Megan, come back."

If she heard me, then she gave no sign. I decided not to follow her. I stood and watched her clamber up the steep side of the valley. I could hear her sobbing.

As she neared the top the mist seemed to swallow her up, and then she simply disappeared from view, and I never saw her again.

I stayed there for a while, standing quietly amongst the broken stones. Sometime later, and with the sun now streaming across the plain, I left the ruined church and walked out of the valley.

EPILOGUE

From the *Marlborough and North Wilts Chronicle*

8th May 2015, p.9

BODY IN CAR IDENTIFIED

A man discovered dead in his car beside a country lane on the outskirts of Marlborough, on 1st May 2015, has been identified as Mr Ernst von Draken, 81, a rare book dealer from London.

The body was discovered by a man walking his dog, who immediately contacted police and ambulance services.

It is believed that the victim suffered a heart attack, and his death is not being treated as suspicious.

PC Mike Andrews, from Wiltshire Police, told the *Marlborough and North Wilts Chronicle* that the most likely explanation was that the deceased man had fallen ill while driving and pulled over to the side of the road, whereupon he suffered a fatal heart attack.

"It's very fortunate that, having become ill, the person concerned had the presence of mind to pull over," he said. "If this had happened while he was driving, it could have caused a very bad accident."

An inquest into the death was opened, and then adjourned.

From the *Marlborough and North Wilts Chronicle*

8th May 2015, p.17

STRANGE LIGHTS IN THE SKY

There is still no official explanation for what sounds like a curious light show in the sky, seen in the vicinity of Clatford and Manton, west of Marlborough, on the night of 30th April and 1st May 2015. However, in an area so steeped in ancient history, mythology and folklore, one shouldn't be surprised that this event has been the subject of a certain amount of speculation by conspiracy theorists.

According to witnesses, the west horizon of the Marlborough Downs was lit by a strange red glow in the early hours of 1st May. Others spoke of being awakened by a loud rumbling sound, like a thunderstorm, although the skies were clear, and the weather fine on that night.

Keith Pearson, a taxi driver from Marlborough, was returning home along the A4 in the early hours of the morning, when he noticed the light on the horizon.

"It was the oddest thing I've ever seen," he said, speaking exclusively to the *Marlborough and North Wilts Chronicle*. "I had taken a late fare over to Devizes, and was on my way back to Marlborough, when this strange, red glow appeared on the horizon, up over the downs. At first, I thought it was the dawn breaking, but it was way too early, of course, and in the wrong place, so it couldn't have been that. I can't think what it was, but it was like the whole sky was on fire. And then, a bit later, there was what sounded like a very loud clap of thunder, and then I noticed that the light had completely disappeared. It was very peculiar indeed."

Given the area's proximity to various military training areas and artillery ranges, one might imagine an army exercise of some kind to be the most likely explanation for the illuminations on the horizon. However, when approached for comment, the Ministry of Defence's public relations liaison for Wiltshire confirmed that no such military exercises had taken place that night anywhere in the vicinity of the Marlborough Downs. Naturally enough, this hasn't prevented some from speculating that some type of military experiment might have been responsible for the peculiar light show.

Speaking to the *Marlborough and North Wilts Chronicle* on condition of anonymity, a representative of The Wiltshire UFO Seekers Society claimed he was convinced that the military were conducting experiments with what he referred to as alien technology.

"We may have had a very lucky escape, that night, from what I've heard," he said. "When people tamper with forces they don't understand, it could lead to a very dangerous situation."

As outlandish as this explanation appears, it is unlikely to be the last, or even the most unusual theory for the events of last week, according to cabbie Keith Pearson.

"I've been driving a taxi in Marlborough for over thirty years," he said, "And it's fair to say you get all sorts of strange things going on around here, particularly near Avebury. They call this crop circle corridor, and for good reason, because we get loads of them in this area, plus all the so-called UFO sightings. The downs here seem to be a bit of a magnet for that sort of thing. I've even heard talk of witches' covens, and occult ceremonies going on, and people getting up to all sorts."

Whatever the real explanation for the lights over the downs that night, it would appear that, for some at least, this event was just the latest in a long list of strange phenomena believed to be associated with the area around Avebury. It is unlikely to be the last.

From the *Marlborough and North Wilts Chronicle*

8th May 2015, p.18

<u>KEEPER OF VENOMOUS SNAKES AND OTHER EXOTIC PETS ARRESTED</u>

A Devizes man has been arrested on suspicion of keeping venomous snakes and spiders in his house, in breach of the Dangerous Wild Animals Act (1976).

Acting on a tip off from a member of the public, police raided a property in Devizes on 5th May 2021, and arrested the owner, Billy Matthews, 38.

Inside the house, the police, who were accompanied by specialist snake wranglers and other animal welfare experts, found a number of venomous snakes, including an African black mamba, considered one of the most deadly snakes in the world, as well as cobras, rattlesnakes, kraits and adders. Several highly dangerous tarantula spiders were also discovered during the raid.

Speaking exclusively to the *Marlborough and North Wilts Chronicle*, David Eastland, a herpetologist from Bristol Zoo, who supervised the safe retrieval of the creatures, explained: "We get quite a few calls like this, but I've never before come across such a large collection of venomous snakes. There's a good reason why you need a special licence to keep these kinds of animals. They require expert handling, and they are exceptionally dangerous to humans. It's also not good for the welfare of the snakes. Anyone who has any suspicion that someone they know might be keeping snakes like these as pets should alert the authorities, otherwise there could be a terrible accident."

Matthews was bailed to appear before Devizes Magistrates Court on 14th June. The snakes and spiders retrieved from the property have been relocated to specialist facilities, including Bristol Zoo.

More details to follow.

From the *Marlborough and North Wilts Chronicle*

20th June 2015, p.62

<u>FOR SALE</u>

<u>A SUPERB VICTORIAN FARMHOUSE, SITUATED A FEW MILES FROM MARLBOROUGH</u>

Badcombe Hollow is set within a wonderfully peaceful and private situation in countryside to the west of Marlborough, and close to the Avebury World Heritage site. The house dates back to 1886 and was originally part of a working farm. Standing in extensive grounds, the house has been sympathetically refurbished, and looks out into spectacular countryside.

The house, on three floors, is constructed of limestone elevations under a tiled roof, and contains a number of original features, including open fireplaces, high skirtings, picture rails and sash windows. Complementing this traditional and elegant design is a modern, contemporary kitchen, and recently fitted out bathrooms.

Six bedrooms, two reception rooms, three bathrooms, kitchen, dining room, study and large cellar.

Set in 1.7 acres of mature grounds, including a garage and extensive kitchen garden, pergola covered terrace, and a paddock. The grounds also contain a Neolithic burial mound.

£1,750,000

Thursday 17th September 2015

It was a beautiful, sunny day, late summer on the cusp of early autumn. Faraday and I were sitting beneath the pergola in the garden of Badcombe Hollow, drinking coffee as we looked out towards the long barrow and the fields beyond, which were carpeted in post-harvest stubble, attesting to the gradual change of season. On the driveway behind us, the removal van from London had just arrived, although the movers had yet to commence work, and were drinking from water bottles by the tailgate, as they prepared themselves for the heavy lifting ahead.

Faraday had driven down from Oxford, earlier that morning, and I had taken him to a restaurant in Marlborough for lunch, before returning to Badcombe Hollow to await the arrival of the movers.

We had been in periodic touch, over the summer, but this was his first visit here since the events of Walpurgis Night and their immediate aftermath. We had talked little at lunch about what had happened on that night, and in the days leading up to it, but now, sitting just feet away from the long barrow, the conversation inevitably turned in that direction.

"And you say that Michael is back in Ireland," I said.

"Yes," said Faraday. "He's back at the seminary, completing his training. I would have liked to have kept him with Kate and I, but it appears that he has a genuine vocation to be a priest. But who knows? He may return to the group, some day.

"By which time," he went on, "He may well find Kate in charge. I think I'm getting a little too old to be chasing devil worshippers around the countryside. It's probably time for me to take more of a backseat, more of an emeritus position, if you will, and let the younger generation take the lead. Kate is highly capable, as you know, and very dedicated. And, of course, I shall still be around to help her, for as long as I can.

"We shall need more recruits to the cause, though," he added, looking at me enquiringly as he did so.

I smiled back at him. It wasn't the first time that he had floated this suggestion, in our conversations since Walpurgis Night.

"I'm flattered," I said. "And I have the highest regard for you and Kate, and for your mission. And it's not as if I have anything else to do. As I told you at lunch, I've had no success in getting my novel published, although I'm well along with writing the story about this place. But I really don't see what use I could be. Up until a few months ago, I didn't know the first thing about any of this."

"Oh, I don't know," said Faraday. "I would say you've learned a great deal, in a very short period of time. Besides, you have a good investigative brain, and you presumably now have the sort of independent means which would allow you the time for such an eclectic pursuit."

"You mean the pursuit of devil worshippers," I said, with a chuckle.

"Indeed. Anyway, think about it. And then talk to me again. Or talk to Kate. As I said earlier, she would have been here today; in fact, she very much wanted to be, but I've had to send her to north Wales, to assist the police in the investigation of a coven there. Under the radar, of course," he added.

"Another coven," I said.

"There's always another coven, and there always will be. Just as there will always be evil in the world. All we can do is fight it. One battle at a time.

"So, you'll at least think about it?" he said.

"I'll certainly do that," I replied.

I looked over at the long barrow. The temple was still down there, secreted beneath the ground, its location known only to a select few. I had long since covered up the entrance we had dug. I had even planted three Mexican Orange Blossom shrubs where the old one had come out. And the whole site, including Dorian Slake's diabolical temple, had been thoroughly, spiritually cleansed. Faraday had seen to that, enlisting the services of the Priory of Saint Mary, who at the end of that first week in May, had sent along an elderly exorcist, with two other priests to assist, with the express intention of ridding Badcombe Hollow and its immediate environs of all evil spirits.

I have no idea how they did this. They banished me from the property, politely but firmly, soon after they arrived, and I had spent the day in a café in Marlborough, mostly perusing the on-line listings of properties I might buy with some of the money I was going to get for Badcombe Hollow, waiting for them to call me to say that they were done. When I got back to the house, they had gone.

But it had worked. The exorcism, or whatever arcane ritual they had enacted there had worked. I knew that it had.

I knew this because a few days later I invited Bethany Weyland over to the house. I had been out with her several times, by then, and we had become more than close, and I wanted her to come to Badcombe Hollow. The spiritualist, who had so bravely and fortuitously come to our rescue on Walpurgis Night, was reluctant at first, but I eventually persuaded her.

I recalled how she had entered the house with great trepidation, and then how her countenance had perceptibly lightened as we moved from room to room, before finishing in the cellar, where I had re-covered the pentagram on the floor with a rug.

"No evil spirits here," she had said, brightly, as we walked back upstairs.

"But there may be the odd good one," she added.

I didn't say anything because I knew what she was referring to.

And I know this also – know that the house has been cleansed of the evil which once resided here – because, quite simply, I possess a faith now that I didn't possess before. And there it is. I have seen what I have seen. I cannot ever go back to being the person I was before. The events I witnessed at Badcombe Hollow, and at the Devil's Dolmen, have changed me forever.

"… have any regrets about that?" Faraday was saying.

I jerked my attention away from the long barrow.

"Sorry," I said. "I was miles away, for a moment. Do I have any regrets about what?"

"About deciding not to sell this house, after all. About selling your London flat instead and continuing to live here."

His words made me think of the van at the front of the house, loaded with my furniture and belongings from London. I thought of Bethany Weyland, as well, who would be arriving at Badcombe Hollow in a few short hours for dinner, and with whom I planned to spend much time here in the coming months.

"No," I said. "No regrets. I want to live here. And, you know, financially, it really didn't make all that much difference. I got enough from the sale of the flat in Chelsea to live on for the foreseeable future.”

“Do you worry that she might come back? If she knows that you’re here?”

“Who? Megan? No, I don’t worry about that. Maybe I should, but I don’t.”

“You must be careful,” said Faraday. “We defeated the coven on Walpurgis Night, but it’s not inconceivable that she, or one of the others, might try and take their revenge.”

“I’ll be careful,” I said.

I thought of the last time I saw Megan, running away from me into the dawn mist at the ruined chapel at Stokeley. I remembered her tears, her bitterness, her rage. I often thought of her; of where she had gone, what had become of her, and what state of mind she might be in.

“You know,” I said, “She is pretty spooked by this place, and its guardian spirit. I do have that in my favour, should she be minded to come back here.”

“Yes, I’ve been meaning to ask,” said Faraday. “Have you experienced any further sightings, since Walpurgis Night?”

“Bethany can definitely sense her presence. But I’ve only seen her once. It was two weeks ago. I came out here, early one morning, and there she was, standing on the long barrow. She had her back to me and was staring out across the fields. It gave me a bit of a fright, at first, and then I just stood and watched her for a while. And then I went inside, and when I came back out, she had gone.”

“In some respects,” said Faraday, “The existence of this otherworldly guardian of the long barrow was the most remarkable aspect of the whole affair. We’ll never know for sure what might have happened if we hadn’t got to the Devil’s Dolmen in time. But this spirit from the Neolithic world, and her presence here at Badcombe Hollow … well, it really is most extraordinary.”

“I suppose I should find it rather unnerving,” I said. “But for some reason, I don’t. It feels like she belongs here.”

In the corner of my eye, I saw that the movers had started to manoeuvre the first of my crates to the tailgate of the lorry, and Faraday must have noticed this, too, as he rose from the table.

"I should be getting on my way," he said, "And leave you to your unpacking."

We walked around to the front of the house, where Faraday stopped and shook me warmly by the hand, and then turned and stared over at the long barrow.

"It really was quite a business," he said.

"Yes, it really was," I said. "But we won in the end. This time, we won."

"Until the next time, then," said Faraday.

And with that, he climbed into his Range Rover, and drove away from Badcombe Hollow.

I knew that I couldn't delay directing the movers for much longer, but for some reason I felt compelled to go and stand by the long barrow. It looked so innocuous, on that warm and sunny September afternoon, like nothing more than a mound of earth and grass. But I knew that it was much more than that, and that aside from it being a burial chamber, there was something else down there, something hidden from the world, which could never be revealed. And I knew also that within that empty room beneath the ground, in that temple to evil constructed by the erstwhile owner of this house, there was real occult power; a nodal point connecting the sacred places in this most sacred of landscapes. Like the pentagram on the floor of the cellar, this power could be used for good, or it could be used for evil.

Dorian Slake had been its first protector. And then, sometime after him, Alan had taken on that role, before passing it on to me, even though I hadn't known it at the time. They had guarded it on behalf of those who wished to use it for evil. It was now my job to guard it against such people, to protect the secret, and to ensure that the temple was never again used as it had been on Walpurgis Night.

I am the guardian now.

THE END

Needless to say, *The Gates of Walpurgis* is a work of fiction, and not a very original one. It is not, most assuredly, a serious work about the occult or the supernatural, about which I know very little. It is simply a piece of bunkum.

It began life as the outline of a short story called *Notes from a Long Barrow*, set around a real, if obscure and little visited barrow on the outskirts of Winchester, in Hampshire. This story was never written, and morphed instead into what was intended to be a short-ish novel called *The Raising*, with the action moved to the Marlborough Downs, near Avebury. This then rather grew in scope during its early development, and having blithely cast a number of narrative balls up into the air in the opening chapters, I realised that it was going to take quite some time to negotiate them all back down to earth. Hence the rather long novel, subsequently re-titled as *The Gates of Walpurgis*, that you have just reached the end of. And a lesson to myself, perhaps, in the importance of having at least some idea of the course and conclusion of a work of fiction, before commencing on the writing of it. But there it is; a long and involved story. I had a lot of fun writing it, and I hope you had some fun reading it.

Most of the places referred to in the book are real places, including all of the ancient and historic sites in the vicinity of Avebury, including the Devil's Dolmen. However, Badcombe Hollow Long Barrow does not exist, and nor does the old farmhouse beside it, where much of the novel's action takes place. The location of Badcombe Hollow is more or less real, even if the immediate topography has been dressed with a little poetic license, and it lies, as described, in some empty country south-west of Marlborough.

The village of Stokeley, described as being in the lee of the Ridgeway, north of Avebury, and the ruined chapel nearby, were invented for the novel, and were not inspired by real places in any way whatsoever. The Priory of St Mary does not exist, and there is no such newspaper as the *Marlborough and North Wilts Chronicle*.

The markers in the landscape, as described in Chapters 42 and 43, are all real places and their locations do, very roughly, encircle the fictional locale of Badcombe Hollow. However, as you will not be surprised to learn, these markers do not form the shape of a pentagram. Or, at least, I assume that they don't. I've never actually checked.

Of all the various real places referred to in the book, it is the Devil's Dolmen, which comes to feature so prominently in the story, that I would recommend most one takes the time to visit. This truly remarkable megalithic construction, and its accompanying folklore, make for one of the most fascinating historic sites in England, which really should be more widely known about, and appreciated. The dolmen lies in a valley called Clatford Bottom, just west of Marlborough, and easily located on any Ordnance Survey map. The site is reached as described in the novel, although for a really satisfying excursion, I would suggest starting from Avebury and heading east, on foot, up and over the Ridgeway. When you reach the dolmen, you will more likely than not have it all to yourself.

All of the characters in the novel are fictitious. There never was a British satanist called Dorian Slake, and his association with the real-life Aleister Crowley has been invented. The bare bones biographical detail provided on Crowley, in Chapter 16, is correct and I simply inserted the fictional character of Slake into the later years of his life. For whatever it's worth, my own view of Crowley essentially accords with that expressed by various characters on the righteous side of the debate during the course of the novel, including the narrator, Professor Faraday and Father O'Rourke. I am most emphatically not a fan.

With regard to satanism, the supernatural and occult practices more generally, then I am more than happy to confess that I did no serious research whatsoever into these topics, nor do I have any personal experience of any of this. Again, for what little it's worth, I consider such activities as described in the book to be both risible and distasteful, and quite possibly dangerous, as well. Much better avoided, I would say.

This is a novel inspired wholly by popular culture, and a lifetime of consuming horror fiction and cinema. And that's as close to the subject as I ever wish to get. So, I understand if the satanic coven depicted in the novel appears rather cartoonish, because that was rather the point. They exist purely as the black hats of the story. Or black cloaks, if you prefer. They serve as the adversaries in the narrative; obstacles to be overcome, so that we can get to the end of the story.

Other aspects of the novel, about which I have little or no expertise, as may well appear evident to the reader, include, but are not necessarily restricted to, the music industry, the technicalities of phone hacking, tunnel and underground chamber construction, the legalities of putting property into trust and then gifting it, and how probate works. Of course, I could have taken steps to find out more about these matters, but I was anxious not to allow inconvenient facts get in the way of a good story.

Going back to influences, then there is one person who deserves special mention, and indeed thanks, and that person is the British author, Dennis Wheatley.

Wheatley, who lived from 1897 to 1977, was a hugely successful author, selling millions upon millions of books from the 1930s to the 1970s, but he was also much else besides. He served with distinction in both world wars, as a young infantry soldier at the front in WWI, and as an intelligence officer in Whitehall in WWII, where he crossed paths with a certain Ian Fleming. Indeed, it has been speculated that the recurring character Gregory Sallust, in Wheatley's espionage fiction, served as the inspiration for James Bond. He was also a great bibliophile, who at one time worked in the wine trade, and an acknowledged expert on the subject of brandy.

The volume of his literary output was simply remarkable and he enjoyed great commercial, if not always critical success. Along with Agatha Christie, he was one of the two most significant purveyors of British popular fiction of the twentieth century. In the years since his death, his work has come to be viewed ever more critically, doubtless due to the fact that his characters were typically drawn from the upper classes, and often express quite reactionary views, although this has never bothered me in the slightest. Dennis Wheatley was most emphatically not a man of our times. Thank goodness.

Was he a great writer? Not really. His books could be a little over-written and ponderous, with a tendency to go off at tangents and keep explaining the plot (much like my own book, I might add). But he was a great inventor of plots and teller of stories, with a particular gift for transplanting his readers into exotic and faraway locales, with his characters participating in contemporary events, whether that be in post-revolutionary Russia (*The Forbidden Territory*) or the Spanish Civil War (*The Golden Spaniard*). His prose may have been functional rather than elegant, but he had a gift for creating atmosphere, and you certainly learn things reading a Dennis Wheatley novel, with its many layers of detail. In the affectionate words of his biographer, Phil Baker, whose superbly researched book, *The Devil is a Gentleman*, is well worth reading, Dennis Wheatley was Britain's greatest ever bad writer. And there may well be something in that. Not a bad accolade anyway, in my view.

Wheatley's novels touched upon a great many genres, including much historical fiction, but he is best known for his books about black magic, even though they represented a relatively small proportion of his overall output. And it was these black magic novels to which I was initially drawn as a teenager, probably because of the luridly illustrated covers to his paperbacks, typically featuring a scantily clad young woman atop a satanic altar.

Notwithstanding the rather sensationalist material with which he was dealing, Wheatley took the subject seriously, undertaking a great deal of research and acquainting himself with some real-life practitioners of the dark arts. But he most certainly never participated in any of this himself, as he is at pains to point out in the Author's Note to *The Devil Rides Out*, and he always cautioned his readers against any attempt to tread the Left-Hand Path. The concluding paragraph to his note is worth repeating here.

> "Should any of my readers incline to a serious study of the subject [of the occult], and thus come into contact with a man or woman of Power, I feel that it is only right to urge them, most strongly, to refrain from being drawn into the practice of the Secret Art in any way. My own observations have led me to an absolute conviction that to do so would bring them into dangers of a very real and concrete nature."

Wise words, by someone who actually knew what he was writing about, unlike the author of this book.

Of all his black magic novels, none is more famous – or indeed, influential to the writing of my own novel – than his first work on this subject, *The Devil Rides Out*, which Wheatley wrote in 1934.

This book was an enormous influence upon *The Gates of Walpurgis*, most particularly in Chapter 40, when my characters take shelter from an occult attack on Badcombe Hollow by gathering within the outline of a pentagram on the cellar floor. Of course, my pentagram scene is nowhere near as good as Wheatley's, and is likely a rather pale shadow of it. But it was always going into the book. This is, after all, a black magic novel directly inspired by the works of Dennis Wheatley. I simply had to have a pentagram scene. And the so-called Incantation of Set, performed by Professor Faraday at the Devil's Dolmen in Chapter 53, was inspired, albeit only in quite a small way, by the Talisman of Set which features in *The Devil Rides Out*.

In addition to this, the house in St John's Wood described by Faraday as the setting of a black mass presided over by Dorian Slake in Chapter 37, was inspired by Simon Aaron's house in *The Devil Rides Out*. I might also add that any particularly sharp-eyed fan of Wheatley may discern a connection between the character of Bethany Weyland and Wheatley's 1948 black magic novel, *The Haunting of Toby Jugg*, but I'll leave you to work that one out for yourself.

However, the most significant influences of *The Devil Rides Out* upon my own book are in the form of two of the characters. Professor Julian Faraday, as it will come as absolutely no surprise to anyone with even a passing knowledge of Wheatley's books to learn, is very much inspired by the Duke de Richlieu. And Ernst von Draken was inspired by the character of Mocata, the head satanist in *The Devil Rides Out*.

Mocata comes to a sticky end, and therefore only featured in the one novel. But the Duke de Richlieu appeared in no less than eleven books, only three of which involve black magic. Urbane and erudite; a man of impeccable taste and impeccable breeding; the émigré Duke, or Old Grey Eyes, as he was sometimes referred to by his close companions, is my favourite literary character of all time.

I should also mention at this point, the excellent film version of *The Devil Rides Out*, made by Hammer Films in 1968, which has probably been as much of an influence upon me as the novel. Directed by Terence Fisher, with a screenplay by Richard Matheson, it stars Christopher Lee as de Richlieu and Charles Gray as Mocata. It is, I believe, one of the best films Hammer ever made, and a worthy adaptation of the source material.

Lee was a good friend of Wheatley's and was, I understand, quite influential in terms of persuading Hammer (for whom he made a great many films, most notably playing Dracula) to purchase the film rights to three of Wheatley's black magic stories. The other two were *To the Devil a Daughter*, made into a not particularly good film in 1976, bearing very little resemblance to the plot of what is, I happen to think, Wheatley's best book; and *The Satanist* – not a very good book, in my view, and which I'm guessing they bought so they could use the title, not that they ever did.

Christopher Lee was perfectly cast in the role of de Richlieu, even though he thought he was a little young at the time which, strictly speaking, he probably was. It is a great shame that the American director Joe Dante was never able to fulfill his ambition of remaking the film, and re-casting an older Lee into the role of the Duke. That said, Lee gives a commanding performance in the 1968 film, and certainly captures the sensibility of the Duke de Richlieu.

Charles Gray, a wonderful British character actor, is also superb in the role of Mocata and here, I have to confess, that in my creation of the character of Ernst von Draken, I have drawn far more upon the film version of Mocata than the literary one. The Mocata of the novel is a well-drawn but really rather grotesque character. Fleshy, rotund and with a lisping voice, he was a composite of two real-life occultists that Wheatley was acquainted with; the aforementioned Aleister Crowley, and the Reverend Montague Summers. Ernst von Draken, with his clipped upper class accent and condescending tone, is a direct facsimile of the Charles Gray character in *The Devil Rides Out*. They even dress the same way.

Of course, *The Gates of Walpurgis* contains a great many other influences, both literary and cinematic, which are too numerous to mention. But it is the works of Dennis Wheatley to which the greatest debt is owed. Without the inspiration gleaned from his books, this novel would never have been written.

I am very grateful to him, and dedicate this book to his memory. I like to think that he might have enjoyed it.

Richard Webster
Wiltshire, England
November 2025

www.ingramcontent.com/pod-product-compliance
Lightning Source LLC
Chambersburg PA
CBHW060753210726
48292CB00013B/62